She managed to say shakily, 'Now would be better. Go now.' Far better. This was dangerous, playing with explosive unknowns. She could get badly burned if she let herself drown in this trembling vulnerability. She might drown, never find herself again. She told her arm to pull away, but his fingers slid down and his thumb found her inner wrist. The caress shot right through her but she managed to turn her groan into words, to whispers. 'Scott, I—please, I want you to go away now.'

Why could he not let her play the harmless game of self-deception? She could say *go*, and he would touch her, kiss her, and somehow despite her protests he would make love to her before he walked away. She ached for his touch, but so much better if she said no even though she trembled for him, because she would have herself intact later. A night's passion, but not of her asking.

THE TOUCH OF LOVE

BY

VANESSA GRANT

MILLS & BOON LIMITED
ETON HOUSE   18-24 PARADISE ROAD
RICHMOND   SURREY   TW9 1SR

First published in Great Britain 1990 by Mills & Boon Limited

© Vanessa Grant 1990

Australian copyright 1990 Philippine copyright 1991 This edition 1991

ISBN 0 263 77017 6

Set in Times Roman 10 on 11½ pt. 01-9102-55497 C

Made and printed in Great Britain

This book is dedicated to
Jill and Nigel of *Magic Tern*,
companions on the voyage north

CHAPTER ONE

BY THE time he got to Queen Charlotte City, Scott thoroughly regretted his decision to take the ferry. He could have flown. He realised by now that he *should* have taken the jet from Vancouver to the Queen Charlotte Islands.

Instead, he had taken one ferry to Vancouver Island and another to Queen Charlotte, thinking that it would be better for the baby.

That was before he discovered that Robin Scott Alexander was subject to violent attacks of seasickness. Incredible that he and this baby could share blood, yet take to the sea so differently.

Sitting in the aft passenger lounge of the ferry, Scott crooned at the baby. Robin Scott howled back at him. Scott made rocking motions with his arms in hopes of enticing the unhappy infant into silence, perhaps even into sleep. During all his own years at sea, Scott had secretly believed that seasickness was psychological, a physical symptom of fear. Yet here he was, saddled with a two-month-old bundle of screaming, whimpering agonies, and a twenty-six-hour ferry trip. Psychological? He had always tried to be patient with his seasick crew members, but he vowed to be more sympathetic in future.

'Easy, kiddo,' he crooned, shifting the baby up to his shoulder.

Behind him, an irritable voice muttered, 'Shut that bloody kid up, for God's sake! I'm getting sick of this!'

7

So was he! Scott stood up with Robin in his arms and grimaced wryly at the amused stare of the matronly woman sitting opposite. Earlier, Scott had nursed the futile hope that she might offer to hold the baby, might silence Robin with some magical motherly touch. Unfortunately, his wishful thinking had been pure fantasy. The matron had smiled sympathetically, but had shown no sign of wanting to take over Scott's problem.

Walking, pacing between the rows of passenger seats on the *Queen of the North*, Scott finally soothed the infant into stillness. Silence, then the faint moaning, then the stiffening of the little body. He recognised the warning signs, knew he had only seconds to avert disaster. He dodged around two slow-moving, elderly men and dashed through the cafeteria, around three businessmen and a young mother with a toddler. He ran desperately for the men's room and—this time—got there before young Robin threw up all over yet another clean shirt!

A day and a night on the ferry and Scott had worked his way through three shirts and two pairs of trousers. And this was supposed to be simpler than taking the jet?

But it had seemed such a good idea. Robin Scott Alexander had been an angel back in Vancouver. Too young to realise he had lost his mother, to worry that his future was very uncertain, the baby had slept through the funeral, and had gurgled happily in his crib while Scott sorted through Donna's possessions, crating up the personal things that the baby might want some day, sending them on by courier to his own home on Cortes Island. Sorting, throwing out, saving, he had learned more about Donna than he had known during her short life.

While he sorted through the souvenirs of Donna's life, he had wrestled with the problem of this baby, Donna's child by a man she had never been willing to name. He did not want to leave the child to the whims of the social welfare system, orphaned and alone, and yet——

Then he had found the letters, just as Robin opened his throat and let out a mighty wail. A new nappy— thank the lord for the public health nurse who had come and shown Scott about nappies and formulas! Then a bottle, and, with Robin sucking contentedly on it, Scott had read the letters that gave him the answer to little Robin's future. One phone call and he was sure baby Robin's father would be flying to Vancouver to take charge of his son.

The Queen Charlotte Islands, those ancient bits of land in the cold Pacific waters of northern British Columbia. Scott had seen the hills and mountains from the decks of various ships over the years. Always passing by, he had never set foot on their shores. His memory held scraps of information gathered from magazine articles and film documentaries; an impression of ancient forests, of quiet, good-hearted people, a world apart from the rat race.

A good omen, he had thought. A home for young Robin amid the sounds of sea birds and the love of people close to nature.

Robin. Donna had named the baby after its father.

But there was no telephone number to match the name on Donna's letters. There could be any number of reasons for that. The man might have his number under a business listing. How the devil had Donna, a pure city girl, met a man from those remote islands? Scott had frowned down at the baby, staring into dark eyes that seemed black in most lights. A stranger, this baby, with dark hair and dark eyes, with none of the fair colouring of the Alexanders. Although young Robin Scott Alexander had never been exposed to the hot sun, his skin was darker than Scott's own weathered fair skin, and was certainly unlike Donna's smooth, pale flesh. Perhaps the father was Haida Indian, or part Haida. It was certainly a possibility, if he lived on the Charlottes.

Reading the letters Donna left behind, he had realised guiltily that he had been too busy with his own life, that Donna had needed him and he had not been there for her. And now little Robin needed someone. Scott frowned, realising he was planning to hand the infant over to a name on a piece of paper.

What other choice was there? Sylvia, Donna's foster-mother, was too frail to take on a child, and there was no one else. Caroline would be shocked if he suggested she look after this child, and rightly so. He shied away from the idea of asking Caroline to marry him and give Robin Scott a home and a family. Marriage had never had a place in Scott's plans for the future.

No. It was impossible for him to give the baby a home. A man could not look after a child by remote control from a ship in the Beaufort Sea, even if his year's work was usually completed in the eighteen weeks or so when those northern waters were navigable.

So the answer was in Queen Charlotte City, a mere hour by commercial jet from Vancouver. He had rejected the idea of the jet, not wanting to disembark at Sandspit airport with an infant, dependent on local transportation to get him across the harbour from Sandspit to Queen Charlotte, to find an address that was only a number on a piece of paper. He disliked the idea of being ejected from a taxi, complete with baby and nappy bag, to confront a stranger, yet knew he could not dump little Robin in a hotel room while he checked things out.

He might be able to rent a car at the airport, but he had been in enough small northern communities to know that he could easily end up stranded at the airport with a telephone number for a car-rental outfit, and no one answering at the other end. Far better to arrive with his own transport. After all, the *Queen of the North* made regular trips to the Queen Charlotte Islands. A big, modern roll-on roll-off ferry with state-rooms and dining-rooms. Better, travelling with a baby on the ferry, driving off in his own truck. Especially as Robin was such a placid little thing. The baby would sleep the voyage away.

In fact, Robin did sleep, all the way from Port Hardy across the Queen Charlotte Sound, to Bella Bella and across Milbanke Sound. Throughout the journey, Scott stayed at the baby's side, chained by his unaccustomed role as nursemaid.

Normally, Scott would have looked up acquaintances among the crew. He had caught a glimpse of the captain, had recognised him, and would have liked to make his way up to the bridge and share reminiscenses of their days as seamen on the coastguard's *Alexander MacKenzie*. Instead, he had stayed with Robin, appreciating for the first time how much a child could trap a young mother.

Then, in the middle of the night in Princess Royal Channel, the south-easterly winds had hit. Nothing dangerous, nothing he would have thought about twice, but enough to upset passengers with frail stomachs.

And Donna's baby.

When Scott went into the men's room to rinse out his first shirt, all he could see was the soles of shoes through the spaces below the cubicle doors. Sick passengers. Sick baby.

Robin alternated between screaming and throwing up all through the night, falling into a fitful sleep as the ship docked in Prince Rupert. Then, at noon, when they set sail again, Robin whimpered. They crossed Chatham Sound, windy but not terribly rough, and Robin writhed in Scott's arms. They cleared the islands into Hecate Strait, and the baby gave up any pretence of calm.

Queen of the North, big and sturdy though she was, shuddered as she crashed down on the steep waves of the Hecate Strait. A southeaster, with all the anger of the Pacific flooding into the big, shallow strait. The waves were steep and violent. Miserable going in the most seaworthy of vessels.

After changing out of his third shirt, even Scott couldn't face the thought of supper in the cafeteria, and in fact the kitchen had closed. Scott got himself hot chocolate from a dispenser, then took one of Robin's bottles down to have it warmed. Robin rejected the bottle in any case, and Scott didn't finish his chocolate.

They cleared the markers at Lawn Point and turned to make the run into Queen Charlotte harbour. Sheltered from the south wind by the mass of Moresby Island, the *Queen* settled into calm water.

Robin fell asleep just as the announcement came on the loud speakers. All passengers to the car decks.

The matronly woman from the passenger lounge stopped Scott as he started down the stairs to deck C. 'Next time,' she advised in husky, expert tones, 'give the poor thing a bit of Gravol before you take him on to a boat. He shouldn't have to be so sick. A bit of Gravol and he'd sleep the whole trip away.'

'Thanks,' he muttered, knowing there would be no next time. His custody of this child was purely temporary.

She bent to look at the baby, stroking his cheek with a gentle finger. Robin opened dark eyes and stared at her without expression and the woman looked from the baby to the man holding him. 'Takes after his mother, doesn't he?' she decided. 'He certainly doesn't look much like you.'

* * *

Melody tried the amateur radio on Sunday night, but conditions were bad. She could hardly hear the Vancouver net control, much less the Pacific ship stations. Nevertheless, she gave her call-sign.

'Go ahead, Mel,' net control replied. 'Call your station.'

She called Robin's high seas call-sign.

'He's answering you,' said net control. 'Do you copy him?'

'Nothing at all. I've got a lot of interference here.'

She heard net control informing Robin, 'She's got QRM. Try again.'

Robin called again, but she could hear only the distorted Spanish of a Mexican station riding in on sky wave. So she sent a brief, impersonal message to Robin via net control, and he passed back his position and his weather. Ten-knot winds. Clear skies. Everything's fine.

Amateur radio was too public for private messages, but she was glad to know that he was still out there, that if he had problems, they were too small for him to mention.

She signed off and threw the power switch on the noisy radio, then plotted the new longitude and latitude on her map of the Pacific Ocean. She stuck in one more pin, this one with a little red button on its head. If Robin wanted to get away from it all, he was surely succeeding. There was no land within six hundred miles of that pin.

She went for a moonlit walk, looking out over the harbour from her hillside vantage point. Earlier, she had seen the ferry coming in, had known that tomorrow there would be milk in the grocery store again. Thursday's ferry had not arrived due to bad weather, so the island residents hadn't had fresh milk in the stores for five days.

A cloud slid over the moon, throwing darkness around her. Below, lights streaked across the harbour. A gusty wind twisted down the hill where Melody stood. She shivered in her thick jacket. It was cold for April, fresh sea air on the wind.

She turned to go back home, clear-headed now, ready to work. She locked the front door as she closed it behind herself, discarded her shoes and went around locking up the rest of the house for the night. Then she went up-stairs to the sound-room Jeff had helped her build.

Tonight she closed the soundproof shutters on the dormer window. She was going to record and she needed to shut out the sounds of the wind and the night. And old Mr Edgley, who lived across the creek, complained when she polluted the air with music after nine at night.

She turned up the thermostat against the chill, although she would rather have lit a fire in the fireplace. She loved the warm crackling of flames licking on dried wood, but the noise would contaminate her recording.

For a moment she felt her own solitude, had an un-accustomed image of herself as a woman alone in an old wooden house on an empty hillside. Empty life filled with only the fantasies of music. It was an unpleasant image, not true, but it was the cruel vision Peter Hammond would have had if he could see her.

With the soundproofing shutting her away from the world, and the synthesiser turned on, she forgot time. She forgot Peter, who no longer had any rights over her mind. She forgot Robin in his little ship on the big ocean. She forgot everything but the music that possessed her.

CHAPTER TWO

MELODY woke on Monday morning at eight-thirty, later than usual, thick-headed and yearning to curl back up under the covers after her late night. She resisted the lazy impulse. Seven of the recordings were complete, ready for Robin and the band, but there were five more, ideas roughed out but not ready yet, and the recording studio was booked in Los Angeles for a date only six weeks away.

She got up and pulled on her housecoat, more for warmth than for modesty. She usually slept in an over-sized T-shirt. With the trees surrounding her house, the chances of anyone looking in on her were minimal. She was accustomed to wandering around the house in bare feet and the T-shirt most mornings until she had con-sumed at least three cups of coffee.

Not today, though. That wind was cold, and somehow the electric heating system was not keeping up with the cool wind. She went around turning up the thermostats in all the rooms, cursing Amanda and Charlie for their nineteen-year-old decision to pull out the oil furnace and install electric heating. It might have made sense back then, when electricity was so much cheaper, but now...

Of course, Amanda and Charlie had hardly ever been here to realise how much better the oil furnace would have been. There would have been something so much more *warm* about heated air blasting out of vents in the floor, but from their long-term hotel room in the Caribbean they could hardly be expected to think about

15

the virtues of cuddly warmth. It was just lucky that they had left the fireplaces intact!

She put on the coffee to drip, then took the recording she had made last night into the living-room and pushed it into the stereo.

The living-room was massive, a long room running from the front of the house to the back. It was divided into two parts, more by decor than by shape. The front, with windows looking out over the front lawn, through the trees to the water, was the public part, decorated with light, old-style wallpaper and big oak beams. There were two big over-stuffed sofas, the television set, book-shelves and coffee-tables, and a massive picture window.

The back was private, the walls dark walnut, the curtains a deep, rust-coloured brocade. Everything was warm and dark and private, even the two big easy chairs that faced away from the public part, looking out at shadowed moss under old, twisted trees, at the creek that murmured as it moved endlessly, dividing the Connacher property from the Edgley property.

The stereo system was at the back, positioned by Charlie for optimum listening from those two chairs. Typical Connacher priorities: music came first. Melody had installed the new ham radio transceiver there, too, mainly because it was close to the antenna tower she and Robin had put up years ago, when they had jointly gained their amateur radio certificates.

Her eyes fell on the radio transceiver and she smiled, thinking that Charlie would have a fit when he found out how she had contaminated his favourite room with the dits and dahs of Morse code, the howling and squealing of distorted radio signals. Certainly that had never been Charlie's intention when he and Amanda had bought this hideaway. But, possession being nine points of the law, Melody was the one in control here, no matter how the deed of title was worded. And Charlie might rant and rave, but in the end he would let her have her way. Years ago, after one disastrous attempt to put her on stage, Charlie had learned it was easier to give in to his daughter than to fight her.

Before turning the stereo on, she went to get a cup of freshly brewed coffee, then curled her feet up under her in the big chair nearest the window and reached one hand out to push the button that would start the music.

She listened with her dark eyes closed, her hands with their short, unpolished nails curled around the warmth of her coffee mug, her unbrushed brunette hair tumbled wildly around her head. The bass guitar took over the room, then the percussion instruments, then Melody's own voice, which was only a substitute to put the words in place over the music. It would be Robin singing the words in the studio, and in addition to this version she would give the band the written music and words, and a clean recording with only instrumentation, no voice. In fact, if Robin turned up in Queen Charlotte in time, she would get him to do the voice-over.

It was good, with the dreamy, poetic rhythm that she was best at. Her mind substituted Robin's deep, powerful voice for her own and she felt the excitement growing. This one was going to be winner. It might be the title song for the album.

The music faded to silence with a final, emotional chord from the bass guitar. All synthetic, the guitar and the percussion instruments, but Jeff had advised her well. The equipment upstairs could have lain in one of the best recording studios in North America, and no one listening could have told that this was not real musicians playing tunes to Melody's command.

She shut off the stereo and went for another cup of coffee, deciding against breakfast because she was out of yoghurt and had no milk to pour over her muesli. She would buy milk today, after her session upstairs and before she went to the radio station. She wrote herself a note—'milk'—and tacked it up on her bulletin board.

She washed up her supper dishes from last night as she drank the coffee, her mind already upstairs in the sound-room, then she poured another cup of coffee and carried it with her upstairs to her bedroom.

The doorbell rang just as she pulled the sweater out of its drawer. She hesitated, then started unzipping her robe. She would dress first. Nine o'clock on a Monday morning. Surely no one would be in such a massive hurry that they couldn't wait while she put on her clothes.

She shrugged out of the robe just as the buzzer went again. Damn! This was the islands and surely nothing was that urgent? It was probably the postman with the contracts from her agent. Peter always sent them by registered post, which she could never see the point of because it was no faster and they could easily be re-copied and sent again if they should go astray. Registered meant that she had to come to the door and sign for the envelope, inevitably meaning that she had to interrupt a session in the music-room, throwing everything out of sync and putting her back a half-hour by the time she got back to work and in the mood after listening to the postman's gossip. Melody knew her weaknesses. She was too easily distracted. Two or three small interruptions could throw her whole morning into a useless frustration. So she locked her door when she went to the music-room, turned the unlisted telephone off, and everyone knew that you didn't try to contact Melody Connacher before one in the afternoon.

She should be thankful that she was behind schedule this morning, that the postman would only interrupt her dressing, not her creative mood. She zipped the dressing-gown back up and went downstairs to the door, throwing it open.

'In a hurry this morning?' she asked mildly, her anger toned down to friendly criticism. Her temper flared quickly, but anger never lasted long for Melody.

The man in front of her was a total stranger.

Melody pushed her hair back in an unconscious attempt to tidy herself and look less like a sleepy slob. She said briskly, 'Yes. Can I help you?'

It was not the postman, not unless Canada Post had given up on blue uniforms and gone to immaculate grey trousers and leather, sheepskin-lined jackets. Not to mention the captain's hat that topped it all off, giving him the look of an inappropriately polished but tough man of the sea.

She started to smile, then the curve of her lips faded to a frown as she realised that his hazel eyes had no warm lights in them, his mouth no friendly curve to it. It was character in his face, she decided, not handsomeness. She felt a sensual jolt that surprised her, even while she decided thankfully that he was a stranger whose frown was not going to mean trouble for her.

'Is Robin Connacher here?' His voice was firm, pleasant, and he was accustomed to people jumping when he spoke. Behind him, she could see the black truck he must have driven up her twisted driveway. It was a four-wheel drive, shining and expensive. Like the man, it was obvious that the truck meant business.

'Sorry,' she said, smiling slightly, her mind putting musical notes to words about a sea-captain with a big truck and tired laughter-lines radiating from his eyes. He was obviously an islander, although she knew she had never seen him before. She would have remembered. He had the tough confidence that went with the wild north. A fisherman perhaps, maybe even a neighbour. The house down the hill had been for sale for six months now, and last week the estate agent's car had been there—he must have been showing someone around. There was no laughter in this man's voice or his eyes, though, so Melody snapped out of her whimsical daze and repeated more firmly, 'Sorry, he's not here.'

'He doesn't live here?' The voice seemed to lose something of its authority. 'This isn't Robin Connacher's house?'

'You've got the right place.' Did Robin live here? Did Robin actually *live* anywhere specific? She shrugged that question away and said, 'But you can't see him. Sorry. If you'll give me a message for him, I can see it gets delivered.'

'That won't do.' He was frowning.

She resisted an urge to salute and say, Aye, aye, Captain.

'I've got to talk to him.' He looked back at his truck and she followed his gaze, then stared at him when he grumbled, 'Did you ever think of getting someone in to fix up that driveway?'

'With four-wheel drive, I wouldn't think you'd have a problem,' she snapped back. 'My van does it all the time.'

He shrugged something away. Then the irritation was gone and he was smiling down at her. He wasn't a tall man, but then neither was she tall, and he had the big, heavy shoulders of a wrestler or a weight-lifter. She felt small and ridiculously feminine.

He said, 'I'm a bit over-tired. I took the ferry up from Port Hardy and didn't have a very good sleep in my hotel last night.'

She nodded and tried to pretend that she did not realise his eyes had fixed on the free swelling of her breasts under the soft housecoat. It was time he left, past time

she got to work. She could spend the morning on her
front veranda, feeling tousled and oddly vulnerable, or
she could work on the eighth song.

'Look, do you have a message for Robin, or——?'

He shook his head, pushing his hands into the pockets
of the leather jacket. 'No, I have to see him personally.
I take it he's at work? When will he be home? I could
come back this evening or——'

'He won't be here.' She heard a sound, muffled, like
a baby's cry, and he jerked around towards his truck.
She said, 'It's probably a raven. They're all over the
islands.' He must not be an islander, not when he talked
about staying in a hotel. She added, 'They're fantastic
mimics. The ravens, I mean. They can sound like a baby,
or a dune-buggy engine, or a rock dropping in water.'

His eyes flew from his truck back to her. The sound
came again before she realised that she was wrong, that
it was no raven. He looked uneasy, something she suspected did not happen all that often. 'It's a baby,' he
said.

She laughed. 'Your day to look after the baby?' He
was obviously not accustomed to the job.

The baby yelped again and he jerked, torn between
going to the truck and not going. 'No,' he said abruptly.
'I—oh, hell! Just wait a minute, would you?'

He ran to the truck just as the cries turned to wails.
He was back with the baby in his arms, holding it as if
he had done it a lot, but still with that uneasy look in
his eyes. The baby didn't stop crying, although he joggled
it gently and rubbed its back.

'Maybe it needs changing,' she suggested. 'Or
feeding?'

'Maybe,' he agreed. 'Listen, I really have to see Robin
Connacher. I'm Scott Alexander, and I've come up here
from the lower mainland specially to see him.'

She shook her head. 'I'm sorry, but you're out of luck. He's not here. As I said, I can get a message to him, but unless you want to sit around a few weeks waiting, you won't get to see him here.'

'Damn!' The baby's wailing gained power with the man's curse. He lowered his voice, pressing the baby against his shoulder and saying with a subdued anger, 'It's urgent that I see him. Wherever he is, I've got to get there and talk to him. I—— Who are you?'

She frowned, wondering just what Robin was involved in. Wild though he was, it really wasn't like her twin to get into the kind of trouble that brought tough-looking men to his door. If this tough stranger had come looking for Charlie, she could have believed it more easily. Her father was always in scrapes. But Robin?

'I'm Melody Connacher,' she said, suddenly wondering why he had a baby with him. A baby, and he was a stranger, staying in a hotel, so he had no family locally. Of course, he might have a wife with him, but in that case, why wasn't she in the truck, holding the baby? Where was the baby's mother? And what on earth was *he* doing here?

Realising that she should have been suspicious from the first, she demanded abruptly, 'What is it you want with Robin?'

'Where is he?' he countered, speaking softly so as not to disturb the baby's sudden silence.

'Away,' she snapped. She could feel her heart pounding. It would be hours after he left before she could get herself quieted and in a mood for working. Damn the man! 'Why do you want him?'

'It's personal.' The baby stirred. The man sighed in a way that made her remember that he had said he was tired. She almost invited him into the house, but she knew better than that. He could be anyone at all. An axe murderer. A baby kidnapper.

He demanded, 'Are you Connacher's wife?'

'Robin's not——' She broke off, knowing she should not give out personal details about Robin. Then, not realising she was going to tell him, she said abruptly, 'I'm his sister.'

'He's not married?'

She crossed her arms over her breasts and the man nodded, as if she had answered his question. 'You must have a phone number for him. Or an address, a hotel where he is at the moment. It's really very important.'

He was persuasive, his voice sending messages that said he was trustworthy and responsible and she could tell him anything. But her childhood and those two years in Los Angeles had given her a wariness that reminded her that Robin was famous enough to be fair game for all kinds of crazy schemes. 'No,' she said. 'I can give him a message if you like. Then if he wants to see you, he'll call you. I don't give out his phone number or his address.' She smothered a grin at that, thinking of city things like telephones, and Robin on his little ship in the middle of the Pacific Ocean.

The baby drowned out his answer with a powerful scream. Melody winced. The man holding the infant shouted to drown out the howling. 'Look, Ms Connacher, we've got to talk! But first of all this baby needs tending to!'

The wind twisted over the veranda and she hugged herself closer, aware of her bare feet as his eyes dropped to the hem of her housecoat. She snapped, 'It's not *my* baby.'

He scowled at her, the expression in his eyes as violent as his arms were tender on the child. The poor baby howled even more loudly. 'He needs changing, but it's bloody cold out here. Why don't you open that door and let us in. We can talk better inside.'

'No.' They glared at each other. A baby could be a novel gimmick to get into a strange house. It was not his house, but Melody felt nervous. Not that she thought he would physically force his way inside, but those eyes had changed from hazel to granite and he was the kind of man who got his way regardless of rules or opponents. She bit her lip and asked again, 'What is it you want Robin for?'

'Not me, it's the baby that wants him.'

'The baby?' she repeated, her voice sharp and startled.

'Yes. His baby.'

'His——' Her lips were open and nothing was coming out. Robin's baby? The baby *did* have Robin's glowing skin, his dark hair, a heritage from an unidentified Latin ancestor. Even the eyes. But—— 'You can't just burst in here and——'

'I'm not *in* anywhere,' he corrected wryly. She felt his presence like a physical blow as he shifted a few inches closer. 'I'm out in the cold.'

She shook her head, sending the curls tumbling as she finished in a rising voice '—and claim a strange baby is my brother's. You—you think just because he looks like Robin that you can——'

'Does he?' He looked down at the baby, his own eyes hazel again, assessing, as he said, 'I thought he must. He certainly doesn't look like Donna.'

Donna? She had never even *heard* Robin mention the name Donna! Surely Robin would have told her? Granted, they'd seen little of each other these last two years, but surely he would have told her if he'd fathered a child? This had to be a con, although this stranger looked far too blunt and direct for a con man. She bit her lip, unable to keep her eyes off the baby with Robin's eyes, her eyes. She said, 'I don't know anyone named Donna.'

'Can't we leave that until later?' His voice had lost the aggressiveness, but this firm, persuasive gentleness might be every bit as dangerous as the lord-high-captain voice. She started to tell him it was not her baby, that she had no reason to believe it was Robin's either, but before the words could come he seemed to read her mind.

He said, 'It's not *my* baby either, but it is crying, and shouldn't we look after its problems before we settle our own? A new nappy and a bottle of formula.'

'I don't have any nappies. You'll have to go down to the Shop Easy, or —' Suddenly she found herself with an armful of squalling baby. She clutched instinctively, afraid of dropping the infant. 'Listen, Mr Whoever-you-are, I don't know anything about looking after babies! You can't just dump it here and——'

'I'm getting the nappies,' he said, and he was gone, covering the ground between the veranda and his truck with quick strides. She stood in the doorway while the baby burped something up on her housecoat. She stared after the man, wondering if he really was getting nappies. It was more likely that he would get behind the wheel and drive away.

She shouted, 'If you drive off, I'm calling the police. They'll be here before you can back down to the road!'

He reached into the truck, then emerged with a bag that looked identical to those used by the young mothers around Queen Charlotte. It seemed very out of place in the hands of this muscular he-man type. He was grinning as he slammed the door of the truck and took the stairs up to the veranda towards her two at a time. 'Don't worry, I'm not deserting you. Nappies, as promised, and I believe you about the police. That driveway certainly wasn't made for quick getaways.'

He stopped, close enough that she could smell the soap he had showered with that morning. Fresh and tangy and masculine. She frowned. Her thoughts ran like a soap advertisement, and that should be a warning to her. If she didn't get to work soon, she would be doing advertising copy instead of songs.

He shifted the strap of the bag on to one shoulder and reached the other hand up. She jerked, thinking he was going to touch her, but his fingers brushed the baby's cheek, not Melody's. The infant turned his head towards the man's hand, opening his mouth and sucking noisily on a brown, callused finger. Watching, Melody saw the man's expression change to tenderness as he looked down at the suckling baby. She felt an impulse to reach up and trace the lines drawn on his weathered cheek by that half-smile.

'Are you going to let us in?' he asked, smiling widely enough for her to see laughter-lines crinkle around his eyes. He must have been psychic because he added, 'We're not dangerous.'

'Maybe not the baby,' she said, and his laughter sounded as she had imagined it would, full and real, not forced at all. She stepped back and he was inside before she had time to wonder if she was crazy.

He stopped inside the door, reaching back to close it behind her. She stopped too, waiting.

'Somewhere to change the baby?' he suggested.

She looked towards the living-room and he smiled, his eyes taking in its comfortable elegance. 'The kitchen table?' he suggested. 'That would be better. And we could start warming up a bottle.'

'We?' She looked down and found those eyes staring back at her. Her eyes. Robin's. The eyes they had inherited from their mother. The eyes this baby had inherited from his father? Perhaps. She knew she was not going to turn out the man and this baby, not just yet.

He said firmly, 'Yes, we. Until we get to this baby's father, you and I are the nearest thing it has to kin.'

'His mother? What about the mother?' Surely the mother had not pushed her child aside? 'Robin would never be interested in the kind of woman who——'

'She's dead.' He said it flatly, without emotion, but she stared at him. 'The kitchen,' he reminded her, and she wondered if he was as untouched as he appeared. What had the mother been to him? Kin? She stared at the baby and thought about the kind of odd, inter-twined relationships that seemed to belong in the madness that was LA and the world she had escaped.

The baby shifted and Melody could feel the dampness. First things first. She led the way, still holding the baby because he wasn't offering to. She stopped at the kitchen table and said firmly, 'You'll have to do this. I haven't a clue what to do.'

'You've never changed a baby?'

'Never,' she said firmly.

'Just my luck. I thought all girls baby-sat. Surely——?'

'I didn't have that kind of a childhood.' Now, why had she said that? As if she was inviting his interest! She saw the curiosity, the response that seemed to mean he was as aware of her as she was of him. She had never felt a response to a man's *smell* before. But her nostrils caught that after-shower scent again and she felt an answering quivering deep inside herself. 'Take it,' she said, holding the baby out, rejecting the crazy feelings.

His lips twitched, but he did not quite smile. He took the baby. 'Have you got a bath towel?' She went and got one and he nodded to the table. She spread it out, then watched as he efficiently stripped the lower half of the baby, put the nappy in a plastic bag and said, 'You'll have somewhere to dispose of that?'

'Yes,' she agreed, taking it. She was unable to resist adding, 'You, on the other hand, seem to be an expert in this baby business. Maybe you baby-sat for spending money when you were a kid?'

'No,' he said absently. 'I fished. Put a pot of water on the stove to heat up a bottle.'

A fisherman. She had been right. 'Aye, aye, Captain.' His head jerked around and she grinned. 'You're bossy, you know. You're used to giving orders.'

But she put the water on, although he was the one who fed the baby. 'Somewhere more comfortable?' she suggested, and he followed her into the living-room with baby and bottle. She wanted to sit across from him and watch, intrigued by the sight of the big man holding the tiny baby with such care, fascinated by the look on his face when he bent to watch the tiny person suckling on the rubber nipple.

Perhaps because she wanted so much to watch, and because the desire was uncomfortably stirring, she stood up and said abruptly, 'I have things to do. Make yourself comfortable. I'll be back in a few minutes.'

It was past time she got dressed. She ran up the stairs, leaving him behind.

Her sweater was lying on the bed, her jeans a jumble on the floor where she had dropped them when she picked up her dressing-gown to put it back on. She caught a glimpse of herself in the mirror as she shed the dressing-gown again.

She was tumbled, rumpled, as if she had just come from her bed. She had not yet brushed her hair into tame order this morning. Her lips, always red, looked fuller than usual, vulnerable. No wonder he had stared at her as she told him she was leaving him alone with the baby. She looked... sensual, she thought, not liking the word.

She dressed quickly, zipped her jeans up and pulled the sweater on. She brushed her hair briskly, taming her curls into waves. When she put the brush down, her hair had its daytime look, smooth and controlled as if she had just been to the salon. A pity, Amanda had always said, that Melody had the dramatic colouring, the full dark lips and the wonderfully wavy hair, when she was the one Connacher who hated to be up on the stage. Wasted.

She made her bed, pulling the blue pile spread smooth. She hung up her robe and put away her T-shirt. She pulled the bedroom door tight behind her and went down the corridor to the music-room, stopping at the head of the stairs and listening, hearing a faint murmur that might be her uninvited guest talking to a baby.

She moved from the synthesiser to the multi-track recorder in her sound-room, her hands hovering, but touching nothing. It was ridiculous to pretend she could work right now. She lifted the page of notes for a hauntingly sad song about a girl at the side of the sea, and her fisherman lover who went out on the herring fishery and lost everything in a cold, fierce winter storm. His life. His love.

She knew that when she went back to the song, the fisherman lover would have changed, taken on a reality that was beyond her usual fantasies. He was downstairs.

She was stalling and she knew it. Avoiding going back, avoiding the complication of this baby and the man. She had learned to protect herself from distractions, to shield herself from the rat race that destroyed what was creative in her, from the trivial tasks that sucked away her spontaneity. Not selfish so much as necessary, because she had almost lost herself before she learned to say no to the people who demanded parts of her.

'You're giving away your power,' Jeff had warned her three years ago. 'You're letting Peter and Robin and all the others have the energy you need, suck your talent dry. You think you owe them something, that you have to give because they ask, but you don't. You owe yourself something. Turn us off. Say no. Find yourself again.'

It had been difficult to say no to Peter. He was more than her agent. At first she had been flattered because he was good-looking and important and he seemed to admire her. She had wanted to be swept off her feet, in love, and he said he loved her. She supposed she had wanted to belong to someone who was actually *there* when she opened her eyes, not flying from Paris to Toronto to the Caribbean. She wanted love, and she had said *yes* when he'd asked her to marry him.

He had moulded her in the image he'd wanted, but she had almost lost herself in the process. She hated the publicity he had said was essential to her career, but when she had said so, his voice had turned from loving tolerance to a sharp weapon. So she had given in to him, but her songs had dried up and she had cried often without knowing why. She had wondered who she was and why she was and what it meant when Peter said he loved her, whether she really loved him.

That was when she had gone to Jeff, the sound man on Robin's band and a good friend. She had been desperate for advice, had known Jeff would see things more clearly than she could.

That horrible scene when she had walked out on Peter seemed unreal now, three years later. She thought it must be unreal to Peter as well. Peter was only her agent now, a good agent and a cool friend. Impossible to think that she had once believed she loved him.

Even Robin had been taking advantage of her in those days, holding her in the rat race of LA when she'd needed to be alone, insisting he needed her at his rehearsals. The day she had told him she was leaving, leaving Peter and LA and going to live in the house at Queen Charlotte, Robin had looked at her as if she had betrayed the bond they had shared from the moment of birth.

She had needed to put over a thousand miles between herself and the world of recording studios and high-pressure productivity, but she had her life the way she wanted it now. She had learned to say no. Most of the time, at least. But saying no to a baby? Robin's baby?

A part of her wanted to push the man back out of the door, to deny that this had anything to do with her. Another part remembered childhood, and backstage rooms, and Robin being there when Amanda and Charlie and everyone else forgot. Robin's child downstairs. If it was, it would be the closest thing to a child of her own that was ever likely to be.

CHAPTER THREE

THE baby was lying on its stomach on the sofa, a towel under it and a pillow placed to prevent its rolling off on to the floor. Melody stared down at the tiny form encased in a fuzzy garment.

The man was at the other end of the living-room, moving slowly along the rack of tapes and compact discs, perhaps assessing her, or Robin, by the music that he found there. He had taken his jacket off. Under it he wore a long-sleeved, off-white cotton shirt, the cuffs rolled back to his elbows. His arms matched his shoulders and chest, rock-hard and heavily muscled.

'What did you say your name was?' She moved towards him, wanting to pull him away from that part of the house, into the public part where he would be more easily controlled.

'Alexander,' he said, not looking up. 'Scott Alexander. You've got a lot of Robin Conners's music here, haven't you? I didn't know he'd done some of these albums.' He looked up then, smiling, thinking music instead of babies, it seemed. 'You're a Conners fan. So was Donna.'

His eyes rested on her change of appearance, the smoothly waving hair, the sweater that drowned out her figure. His expression became thoughtful, assessing, and she wondered what she had told him without knowing. She felt an uncomfortable excitement that left her slightly breathless.

She moved to take the compact disc case out of his hand. Incredible, but it seemed that he did not know. She frowned, but it was not her place to tell him. Not

32

yet, anyway. 'The long-playing records are a few years old. I don't think they're available any more. Done before Ro—Conners became popular. I've got all his——' She broke off and asked, 'Would you like a cup of coffee? Then, if you've got some kind of evidence that child is my brother's, perhaps it would be time to bring it out.'

He nodded abruptly and went to the sofa where he had left his jacket beside the baby. She followed him and took the bundle of letters that he held out. She wanted to take it away, to the kitchen or upstairs, somewhere private so that he would not be watching while she read.

She recognised Robin's handwriting. The first letter was dated June of last year, written from the house here.

Last June. Robin had turned up suddenly, storming into the house, taciturn and moody. It had been almost a year since he had spent any time in Queen Charlotte. According to Jeff, all winter Robin had been disappearing after every performance, although no one knew where. Melody had been too tied up in her own priorities to wonder much about either the disappearances or the moody visit in June. Robin's business, she had told herself. If he wanted her to know, he would tell her.

The answer was here, in a letter written by her twin to his love.

You have asked the one thing I can't give you, my darling. I hated the harsh words and anger of our parting, but now, with the anger gone, nothing is changed. Even for you, my love, I can't give up my career. I would not be the man you say you love if I killed that part of myself. I believe that we could make a loving home, a close family, without that sacrifice. If you decide to try, you know always how to reach me. If not,

there's no point in our seeing each other again,
is there? With love, and hope. Robin.

The other letters were older. Written in Robin's hand.
Love-letters. She did not read them.

'How old is the baby?' she asked, whispering.

'Two months.'

Conceived before they parted in anger. Already alive
in Donna's womb when Robin wrote that letter, although
Robin must not have known. Last June. She closed her
eyes and remembered Robin's visit. Two weeks of Robin
at his worst, difficult and moody, prowling the living-
room each morning. Watching for the postman?

She put the letters down, deliberately not handing them
back to him. 'By right those are Robin's.'

He nodded.

She said intensely, 'He didn't know. She must not have
told him about the baby. Robin wouldn't have taken off
if she had.'

'No,' he agreed. 'She didn't tell him. She didn't tell
me, either, who the father was. She said she loved him,
but she couldn't stand to be always like her foster—her
mother had been, always waiting for her husband to
come home.' Then, finally, he answered the question she
had not asked. 'She was my sister. She died ten days
ago.'

'Oh, God,' she whispered. 'Poor Robin.' The baby
shifted, grumbling, and Melody touched the little
shoulder, wondering how she was going to tell Robin.

'Now that you know why, will you tell me how to get
in touch with him?' His hands pushed deeply into his
pockets, his shoulders threatening to burst the seams of
his shirt.

She swallowed. 'You can't. Not now. He's in the
middle of the Pacific.'

'He's a seaman? On a ship?' He became briskly businesslike. 'Radio-telephone? All those big ships have radio communications these days.'

She prowled restlessly to the map of the world that was tacked up over the radio. 'Not a big ship. A little sail-boat. He's halfway to Hawaii on a sail-boat.' She swung back to the man and the baby. 'I can talk to him on amateur radio, but that's as public as shouting in the town square. I can't talk to him about something like this.'

He looked at his watch, frowning, then turned and stared at the sleeping baby. 'I could leave him with you. You're his aunt, after all. You can deliver him to the father.'

She could feel it closing in on her, could feel herself losing control again. How could she ever finish the songs in time if she had a baby to look after? What did she know about babies? She said desperately, 'And you're his uncle. And one hell of a lot more capable of looking after a baby than I am. At least you know how to change nappies, what to do about bottles and formulas. I don't know beans about any of that, and I can't——'

'Oh, for——' He prowled across the carpet, his voice angry but muted to avoid waking the baby. 'What I know about it you could write on a postage stamp. A half-hour with a public health nurse. What she told me, I'll tell you.'

'I——' Poor baby. Robin's baby. Of course, she would have to take care of it. Heaven knew how she would manage to finish the last five songs. She shrugged and said, 'I suppose you have to be back at work somewhere. What is your name again?'

'Alexander.' He looked down at the baby and something happened to the harshness in his face. He said, 'I'm due on board ship in three weeks. I had been planning a trip to Mexico with a friend in the meantime, but . . .'

She knew she was crazy to suggest it, but in six or seven days Robin would be in Hawaii, in reach of telephones and jet transport. Meanwhile, Melody simply had to work. She expected Mr Alexander to reject the whole idea, but surprisingly he agreed immediately, as if it were the most ordinary thing in the world, that two strangers should share care of one small baby.

She said bluntly, 'You've got to do your share. I'll help with getting him up, and evenings, and waking up in the night.' Her voice was brisk, and she wondered where her firmness was coming from. 'But from eight in the morning until one in the afternoon, I'm upstairs working, and little Robin is your problem. Then from two until four I'm gone.'

'Fair enough,' he agreed. 'As long as you tell your brother, get him to fly here as soon as he hits Hawaii?'

'Yes.' Robin's baby. Of course she would tell him.

'All right.' He looked around, taking in the rather formal furnishing. 'I'll get my things from the hotel, move in here. Do you think you could find a crib or something for the baby? One of your friends, or——'

'I don't know. I'll try. Mrs Winston might know of something.' His heavy brows lifted and she explained, 'She comes in once a week to clean. I'll call her and ask.'

He glanced at his watch and grinned. 'Later,' he suggested. 'It's eleven. According to our agreement, you should be upstairs working.'

She did not like leaving him alone downstairs. She could see his eyes watching, missing nothing, assessing. He would prowl through her books and her music, and somehow that seemed a violation of her private self. She knew she would not feel that way if Scott were one of the guests Charlie kept sending up to her. So she went upstairs, telling herself what a crazy fool she was, full of fantasies and foolishness. But upstairs she did not close off the dormer window with soundproofing, and knew it was because she wanted to hear what went on.

She heard his truck when he left. He must have taken the baby with him. She heard when he returned, too, and she left the synthesiser to go to the window. He carried the baby in first, then came back for the suitcase and a bag of groceries. He moved with a competent self-confidence. As if it were *his* home.

She opened the door to the sound-room, opening herself to his sounds. She could hear him walking downstairs. The kitchen. The refrigerator, she thought. The baby cried, but only briefly. He went to it. She heard him moving, and she went back to the synthesiser and stared at the paper, but his presence and the baby's were so strong that she could not get her mind on the words or the music.

One o'clock. She stayed in the music-room until the digital clock read exactly time. Then she went downstairs and he was in the kitchen, cooking.

'Soup,' he said, turning to the sound of her bare feet coming. 'Mushroom soup, and cheese sandwiches. And could you give Robin his bottle?'

'Robin?' She held him, thinking of an endless confusion of names. Donna must have wanted to remember the man she loved, but Melody decided she would call him Robbie. 'Robbie,' she said, aloud, as if christening him.

'Less confusing,' agreed Robbie's uncle as he handed her a warm bottle of milk. She put the nipple in the baby's mouth and the man said, 'No. Hold it like this or he'll get air bubbles.' His hand closed over hers to show her. She felt a jolt, as if he were high voltage.

She felt as if the man were watching her, although whenever she looked up she could see that the soup and the sandwiches were taking far more of his attention than the woman feeding his nephew.

It felt strange, this small life in her arms. How had she got to the age of thirty without ever holding a baby in her arms?

After lunch he settled Robbie on the sofa, then went to move his truck so that she could get her van out. He backed the truck out and stopped in the turn-around, smiling at her, lifting his hand as she reversed past him. As if it were a routine they went through often, his truck moving for her car.

As if they lived together always.

She drove to the radio station, too fast and too carelessly. If she did not get her mind on the important things, on her driving and her song-writing, she would have an accident. Or Robin would have no songs to sing when the recording sessions began.

Scott Alexander. Scott.

'It's ridiculous to call me Mister,' he had said, laughing when she did, the weathered lines around his eyes crinkling so that she had to smile back at him. 'Or for me to call you Ms. We're related, almost. I'm Scott, and you're Melody.'

He was at ease in her house, did not seem to mind turning his hand to any kind of work from chopping wood to changing nappies. He had started the washing-up as she finished eating. There was really nothing he did that she could object to. He was a helpful guest, and how many of those did she have? They were more likely to be careless and messy. Yet she wished he were not quite so comfortable in her home, as if it were *his* place. She could feel him taking over, could feel herself losing her peace and her solitude.

At the radio station John Wainright had everything ready for the two o'clock *Island Time* programme. John was easy to work with, relaxed and good-humoured. Melody always enjoyed listening to his pleasant baritone, as did the listeners. For her, co-hosting the daily session of *Island Time* was a part-time job, fun and good for keeping herself from getting house-bound. For John, radio was his career and he was a professional in his own laid-back fashion. He did the research, most of the interviews. Melody chose the music. On the air they were a smooth partnership, captivating their audience.

Today John introduced the show, then Melody read the news, followed by the marine weather forecast for the fishermen. She saw Laurie, the station manager, through the glass windows to Studio Two just as she finished the weather. She lifted her hand and Laurie smiled back at her. Everything was going smoothly.

John did a live interview with a Haida Indian chief about land claims, then Melody introduced an Anne Murray song. John threw the switch that brought the song on air and killed their microphones.

'Chief Hall always gives a good interview,' he said, smiling.

Melody glanced at her list of music. 'John, does your baby still use a crib?'

'No.' John chuckled. 'The little beggar kept climbing out and falling, so we put him in a cot. You'll have to come see him. He's not a baby any more, you know. They call them toddlers at this stage.'

'Could I borrow the crib?' She glanced up and saw his eyes dropping to her waist. She snapped, 'No! Don't be silly! A—a house guest.'

'Oh? Different from your usual theatre crowd?'

She shuffled papers, then spread them out in front of her. 'John, please don't ask a bunch of questions.'

He reached for the switch and his voice dropped as he spoke into the microphone. 'That was Anne Murray's latest. In a few minutes we'll be talking to the lighthouse keeper at Langara Island lightstation, where a dramatic rescue took place only yesterday. But first, Melody has more music for us.'

Melody introduced Robin's latest hit song. Few of the islanders knew that Robin Conners and their Robin Connacher were the same person, or that Melody wrote most of his songs. She introduced the song in the same way she would any other, and John brought it on air.

'We gave it away,' he told her as Robin's deep voice went out over the airwaves. 'Well, actually we loaned it, because Bev and I are planning to have another. But we could loan you a playpen. Bev used to use it for a crib when we went travelling.'

So Melody drove home with a collapsed playpen in the back of her van, and Bev's promise to come over the next day to look at the baby and give Melody a few tips on baby-care. Bev had not asked any questions. John must have told her that Melody did not want to talk. Not that it was a secret, exactly, but it seemed Robin's place to acknowledge the little baby as his child, not Melody's.

That night the radio interference was even worse than the night before. Melody could not hear anything but static. 'We'll have to try tomorrow,' she told Scott as she switched the transceiver off.

Scott was sitting in the chair across from her, his legs crossed, the fabric of his jeans pulled tightly over his muscular thighs. He had a history of the Queen Charlotte Islands in his hands. Laurie, the station manager, had given Melody the book last Christmas. Melody tried to think of her home back to normal, of the chair across from her empty and the man gone.

Soon. A few days and she would be able to move from room to room without seeing Scott Alexander. She shook her head slightly, trying to clear the images. As if he would always be there, the ghost of a man she hardly knew, haunting her with all the things that she was not born to be. She looked away from him, focusing on the transceiver she had switched off. The silence was full of whispers and murmurs and he could hear and understand all of them.

Nervously, she said, 'Ham radio's like that. The bands are good one day, bad the next. Sometimes it takes a few days, but I'll get through to Robin some time this week.'

Earlier, while she was at the station, Scott had chopped wood. The fireplace was crackling now, sending out a flow of warm air and the aroma of burning spruce. He had laid the fire while she was gone, and she had felt the warmth the instant she came through the door.

She wished he were not so helpful. In an odd way it threw her off balance. He set the book aside and moved along the shelves of records and tapes and compact discs. Her music, and Robin's, and their parents'. He took out a disc and she wanted to scream at him to get out, stop touching and looking and setting her nerves on edge.

The tension had been building inside her all evening. She could feel every movement he made as an abrasive scratch on the surface of her mind. He opened a plastic case and took a disc out, his callused fingers careful on the shining plastic. He put it into the player. Then the music filled the room and she forgot that she was irritated at the way he was taking over her home. It was Robin's voice, singing his first hit song, 'Girl on the Road'. The song touched Melody, as it always had, and she fell back in her seat, silent, listening.

He must have touched buttons on the stereo when the piece was over, because there was silence, the crackle of the fire and a small explosion of coloured flame, but not the opening notes of the second piece on the album.

'You should have told me,' he said quietly. His voice struck her with the sting of a subdued slap.

'Told you what?'

She twisted her hands together in her lap. He was a stranger, but he was slipping through the secrets and the barriers. She tensed as he walked over to her, but he only dropped a small leaflet into her lap, the insert from the album.

'That your brother is really Robin Conners.'

She had almost told him.

He bent over her, his fingers brushing hers as he opened the little leaflet. His voice was not soft now, but harsh and angry. 'There are the words to the songs, and the credits, or whatever you call them. "Girl on the Road" was written by Melody Connacher. That's your name. Your brother's name is Robin. It's a bit too much of a coincidence otherwise, isn't it? Conners. Connacher. A stage name.'

She stared at the paper, at his hand still holding it. There was a faint white scar on the side of his thumb. She said unsteadily, 'There was no reason to tell you. It wasn't your business.' She drew in a big breath, and added, 'You didn't ask.'

He had told her his sister was a fan of Robin Conners. That was the time for her to say, No wonder, because Robin and Robin are one and the same. The words were there between them, talk without sound, his accusation and her lack of defence.

Why should it matter? Somehow, it did. His eyes had turned to granite and her throat was dry and aching with something crazily like tears. She could feel the anger in him, could sense the instant when it burst, silently. She winced, from nothing more than feelings on the air, and he turned abruptly and walked out of the living-room.

She did not follow him, although her hands reached out as if to stop him. She heard the creak of the fourth step as he went upstairs. All right. Better that way, because now there was no need to feel she had to entertain him, to hover around when she would rather be alone.

Why did she feel as if she had done something hurtful? He was the one who was out of line, getting angry about nothing.

She turned off the lights and locked the doors, checked the windows. Not many people in Queen Charlotte worried about locking doors, but Melody was always aware of living alone, and with the doors and windows locked she felt more comfortable.

She went upstairs. The door to the bedroom she had given him was closed. She went into Robin's room where she had put the playpen. The baby was a soft, small, motionless form, lying on his stomach and breathing through his mouth. She stood staring down at little Robbie for a long time.

Tomorrow she would tell Scott Alexander that he could go. She would get Mrs Wilson in to help. There was no reason why she couldn't look after Robin's baby alone. She would far rather have that man out of her house, her world back to normal.

She bent down and touched the fine black hair on the baby's head. She thought of Amanda saying that it was silly to give children their parents' names, that it only led to confusion. Little Robin. Robbie. She wondered if Amanda would be a sucker for a baby, and discovered she had no idea how her mother felt about babies.

She wondered where it was that Scott Alexander had to be in three weeks' time. On board a ship, he had said.

It didn't sound much like a fishing boat, which had been her first guess. She wondered who the friend was, the one he had planned to go to Mexico with.

She went into her music-room and closed the door. She closed the shutters, too, and finally, in the quiet of the night, she was able to work.

She woke early, before the alarm rang. She lay still for a moment, listening to the whisper of wind in the trees outside. The house was silent except for the faint creaking that an old wooden building gave in the night. Even the wind outside was faint, rustlings through the spruce needles interspersed with magic silences.

She heard the baby then, a faint grumble that was closer than the wind. If he had woken earlier, she had not heard him. She slipped out of bed, her bare feet on the cool floor, and went to Robin's room.

The door to Scott's room was open slightly, as if to allow him to hear if Robbie cried. Melody slipped past the open door silently and went into the baby's room. She lifted the small, grumbling form up and cuddled him to her while she got a nappy out of the package. She changed him while he waved his chubby legs and arms aimlessly and made gurgling noises at her. She felt ridiculously pleased that she managed the small task without mishap.

She carried Robbie down to the kitchen, feeling more relaxed down there. She was less likely to wake Scott. There was an empty, dirty baby bottle in the sink, evidence that Scott had been up in the night with the baby.

She thought of his open door. She had left her own door open, too. Had Scott looked in on her in the middle of the night, staring at her sleeping form tangled in the covers? Was that why she had slept so restlessly? Why was she so aware of him? It was never like this with the strangers Charlie sent to visit. Even Jeff's visits hardly disturbed her work. She left him to his own devices when she wanted to work, sought him out when she felt like having a friend around.

She mixed the formula and heated a new bottle. Then she settled into her favourite chair by the stereo while Robbie curled against her and sucked noisily at his breakfast.

He fell asleep right afterwards, so she put him on the sofa as Scott had, with a pillow to stop him rolling off. She got herself breakfast then, a spoonful of honey over fresh yoghurt. Then she went back upstairs and dressed hurriedly, suddenly nervously certain that Scott would wake any moment, and aware of how little the T-shirt did to cover her.

Scott was still sleeping at eight; at least he had not come out of his room. Their deal said that it was his turn to look after the baby now while Melody worked. She grimaced at his door, but actually she preferred it this way, with him sleeping, out of her way.

She moved the playpen into the sound-room, careful not to bang it or make any noise. Then she brought Robbie up and closed the door, locking it because if the baby would be quiet she wanted to record this morning. She didn't want anyone walking in and throwing opening-door sounds over the six-string guitar.

Of course, he might knock loudly on the locked door, and that would ruin the recording, too. If he did interrupt, she would go up in flames and that would be the last time he would interfere with Melody Connacher when she was working!

She grinned at a vision of herself screaming at that muscular hulk of a he-man. Best done in fantasy, she decided.

'Time you got used to music,' she told the baby as she lowered him on his back into the play pen. He grinned and gurgled as she played back last night's work, and she warned him, 'Talk all you want now, but once the listening's done and I start laying the percussion track on, you behave and keep quiet.'

He squirmed and his mouth twisted, and Melody decided that it *was* a smile on his lips.

She had recorded the bass guitar last night, then layered the drums on top of the bass, using her multi-track recorder. Now she listened, and it was good. The rhythm was filling, the music gaining depth. She changed the disk in the synthesiser and played with the controls until she had the percussion sounds she wanted. She made notes on her paper while Robin groaned and grunted and whimpered.

She picked him up and raised him to her shoulder as she had seen Scott do the night before, remembering just in time to put a towel over her shoulder. Robin groaned, then burped sour milk on to her towel. She patted his back and congratulated him. Then his wide, dark eyes dropped and she put him down on his stomach. He twitched once, then promptly fell asleep.

The percussion layer went on like smooth butter on a sandwich. She worked, unaware of time passing, until it was finished. Then she played the recording back and knew that the words were not quite right. The second stanza would have to be changed to follow the rhythm and the mood. She played it again, humming the words. Then again, and suddenly the right phrase came to her.

It was almost eleven when Robin squirmed and grunted. Melody picked him up and rocked him with one arm while she finished her notes. Working with a baby in the house was going to be a breeze. She should have known, because Amanda and Charlie had sung their way around the world, dragging twin babies with them, and it had not visibly cramped their style. And as for the babies, she and Robin were healthy enough, normal enough. If Amanda could do it, Melody surely could.

Robin started to cry. Melody murmured, 'OK, I know. You want a new nappy.'

Scott was there in the hall when she came out of the sound-room with the baby. 'I'll take him,' he said coolly, and his eyes were granite again this morning.

'It's OK.' She shook her head and dodged his hands. 'I'll look after him.'

She walked past Scott, into Robin's room, the room that belonged now to both the small Robbie and her twin. She changed the nappy and Scott stood in the doorway, watching but not smiling at her this morning, just staring.

Finally he spoke, his voice cool and formal. 'I slept in.'

Robbie waved his legs and got the nappy snarled up before she could fasten the tapes. Without looking at Scott, she said neutrally, 'You said you were short of sleep yesterday.' She felt a tight band across her chest and wished he were smiling at her again. She felt as if she had lost something precious, and that was crazy.

'It's time for you to be working, I'll look after Robin now.'

'No need.' She managed the nappy the second time, and snapped up the legs of his all-in-one. She picked the baby up and held him in her arms like a shield as she faced Scott. 'He's not difficult.'

'He can be,' said Scott wryly.

The man was too big. He filled the doorway and made no move to let her past. She stopped, holding the baby tightly as she looked at him, wondering if she had imagined the warmth in those eyes yesterday.

She said, 'I've been thinking about it. You're right. There's no reason you can't leave Robbie with me. I can look after him.' She looked down at the tiny head. 'Consider him handed over. There's no need for you to stay.'

He didn't like it. She didn't know why. Yesterday he had wanted to push Robbie into her arms and walk away. Now he said, 'You go out every afternoon. You can't park Robbie in a playpen at the radio station.'

Amanda and Charlie had parked their babies in all sorts of places, many of them more chaotic than a modern radio station. She hugged Robbie closer and said, 'There's Mrs Winston. She can come in and look after Robbie while I'm out.'

'And the mornings? When you're in your music studio upstairs?'

She had not told him what was up there, in that room. Damn it, she had not told him much at all, but he seemed to know.

She snapped, 'Robbie's fine with me. Would you let me past? Please! I want to take him downstairs.'

At first she thought he would stop her, but he stepped back and she stumbled past, catching herself before she tripped. She got to the stairs before she realised that the playpen was in the music-room, that she had been working and had only stopped to change the baby. She turned and went back, and thankfully Scott was gone. The door to his room was closed.

She shut herself into the sound-room with the baby. Was he packing? She hoped so. He would go, and she would be alone with Robbie, and her life could return to normal. A new normal with her brother's child to care for. She supposed she should go back and ask Scott for his address, because she should send him word of his nephew from time to time. He would probably want to know how the child grew, although he had been quick enough to try to hand the baby over yesterday.

She had the sense not to try to lay the next track on to the new song. Not with her fingers trembling as if she and Scott had been screaming at each other out there. He had not even raised his voice, so why did she feel so shattered?

She played the recording back, then played it again. She made notes, but she would not touch the synthesiser until he was gone. 'You understand, don't you, Robbie?' she asked the baby as she took the soundproofing off the window. 'I'm not a stage type, like your dad or your grandparents. They can turn it on under pressure, but I need peace and quiet.'

Robbie gurgled and squirmed in agreement.

She picked him up and carried him downstairs in the end, because she really should be down there when Scott left, to get his address and say thanks and goodbye.

The door to Scott's room was still closed, or closed again. He was probably finished with it, had cleared it out, although she knew he had not started the truck outside. He must be downstairs. She could feel him in her house, knew he was not gone. He was like that, impossible to ignore, intruding without actually doing anything she could put her finger on.

He was in the living-room, prowling along the bookshelves. He had out a book and was standing, turning the pages. That was what bothered her, because he had not asked if he could read the books, had not asked before he played her music. She knew that Charlie's stray friends never asked, but somehow it was different with Scott. She put the baby down on the sofa again.

She said, 'I thought you would be gone by now.' She was shocked at the rudeness in her own voice.

His whole face was rigid, and his voice. 'I'm sticking around. I want to meet your brother before I entrust my nephew to his care.'

She gasped, then snapped, 'You weren't so fussy yesterday. You were in a hurry to hand over your problem and get the hell out of here.'

He swung away from her, going to the window. He sounded like the sea captain she had fancied he was, handing out decisions, orders. 'But I've had second thoughts. So, Ms Connacher, I'm afraid that I'm staying, whether you like it or not.' He turned and faced her. Arrogant, she thought. Bossy. She did not like him.

She glared at him and he stared back, and there was no way he was leaving. Short of her calling the police and having him thrown out, Scott Alexander was staying.

She said, 'I don't like it. I don't want you here.'

'I know.' Lines drawn between them. Battle lines, although what was there to fight about? He said, 'Don't worry, I'll survive it. It won't be the first time I've stuck around when I wasn't wanted.'

There was something ominous about the way he said the words, as if the man's will was as strong as his body. Easy to get along with yesterday when he seemed to approve of her. But since last night there had been coolness and anger instead of a friendship in its infancy. She was trying to send him away, and he was damned if he would go.

'Better,' he said softly, 'if you don't fight me. I'm staying.'

She could call John, ask him to come and throw out her unwanted guest. But John was too civilised for that kind of aggressive act, and he was her workmate, not a man to run to. There was Luke, Laurie's husband. Luke and Scott would probably be about a match for each other, both tough and hard and mostly hidden inside themselves.

Would they actually fight? Would Scott go that far, physically insisting on staying, even to the point of a fist fight?

Luke would want to know why, so would anyone she asked to help. She would sound like an idiot, because Scott would smile as he had yesterday and anyone would wonder just what her problem was. The baby's uncle, and she herself had invited him to stay only yesterday. She would never be able to voice the way this man made her feel, as if he could crush her will with one of those muscular hands.

'So I'll stay,' he said, conversationally but coolly. He turned the book in his hands. 'I'll enjoy your library. You've several books I've wanted to read.'

She wanted to hit him, but her small fists would make no more impression than her screaming voice.

'We have a deal, of course,' he said tonelessly. 'It's time for you to be upstairs writing Robin Connors' next hit song, isn't it? I'm the baby-minder, and I'll make lunch. How about a quiche?'

Her lips twitched and she felt the tension flowing away like a mysterious, wild river. He was smiling, saying, 'I know. "Real men don't eat quiche". I've heard that one. We'll call it egg pie, shall we?'

She realised then that he had won. He had turned her anger into laughter, and he was staying. She turned her smile to a frown and walked out of the room. There was nothing she could say that would not acknowledge his victory, so she would be silent.

CHAPTER FOUR

MELODY tried to pretend he was not there. Hopeless, but she managed a cool distance. Polite coexistence with Scott, while he chopped wood and devoured her music and her books, smiled coolly and made her uncomfortably aware that she was behaving badly.

He asked if he could use her telephone to make some long-distance calls, adding, 'I'll put them on my calling card, of course.'

'Why bother asking?' she snapped, wishing the words unsaid. He had been polite. She was the irrational one, telling him to stay, then turning surly and irritated at his presence in her home.

He called someone named Caroline. His wife, for all she knew. She heard him say the name and she walked away, not listening, or trying not to, but she felt relieved that his voice on the telephone sounded cool, not loving. He made other calls, but she made sure that she did not hear them.

Bev came on Wednesday morning and looked at the baby. Bev was a nurse and a mother herself, the nearest thing to an expert that Melody had available. Bev and Robbie gurgled at each other, then Bev asked Scott questions about formulas and nap times.

Scott and Bev seemed to like each other on sight. Melody felt uncomfortably tense listening to the easy conversation between her friend and Scott. He had hardly smiled in two days, and now he was laughing when Bev asked him how the baby had travelled, telling her about his disastrous trip north on the ferry.

He hadn't told Melody about the trip at all.

She felt like a child, left out, not knowing how to get in, telling herself she did not care. Bev was being friendly, and he was being the charming man he obviously could be without much trouble. No wonder he preferred to talk to Bev. Melody had frowned and snapped and, perhaps, even sulked. No wonder he had none of those smiles for her, with the laughter sparking in the crinkles around his eyes, breaking out in his low voice.

'What are you?' Bev asked, laughing at his account of trying to nurse a baby on a heaving ferry. 'You're a seaman, aren't you?'

He nodded. 'Master of an icebreaker in the Beaufort Sea.'

Melody supposed that he would have told her if she had asked.

Scott Alexander. Hard body and smiling eyes that could turn to stone. Dangerous. Bev obviously did not think so, but Melody had felt unsettled ever since she opened her door to him. Even when she was away at the radio station, just thinking about coming back, she could feel turmoil inside her.

Her instincts for self-preservation told her to deal with him as she had the other unsettling influences in her life. Shut him out. She tried.

On Wednesday night the net frequency was nothing but a mass of static. Melody had a noise level of twenty over nine, hopeless for talking to anyone. She wondered how long it would be before she could talk to Robin again.

Scott gave the baby his feed as Melody was trying the radio, then put him to bed. Melody disappeared into her music-room while Scott was in the bedroom with Robbie. She worked alone until eleven, then went silently to bed. Her new policy, she decided. She was avoiding Scott

Alexander. Much easier on her equilibrium if she did not see him. The light was shining up the stairs from the living-room, so she tiptoed silently past the stairwell to her own room and closed the door.

She lay for a long time in the dark, listening to the sounds of trees and wind and a fine rain outside. Scott was very quiet downstairs. She closed her eyes and tried to form shapes and colours, to drift on a dreamy tide of music to a place far away.

She jerked back to consciousness abruptly, lay awake listening to nothing, then the soft sound of a man's tread outside her door. A board creaked. A light switched on. She saw the crack of brightness under her bedroom door. She was very still, breathing very quietly, trying to catch at sleep again, not listening yet hearing every step he took.

He walked across the hallway to the baby's room. Silence, hushed. Back to the room he slept in. She had to stop thinking of it as *Scott's* room. It was not any-body's room. A spare bedroom. An assortment of people had used it. Robin's friends. Her parents' friends who turned up saying, 'Hello, Charlie said you might have a bed for me for a few nights. Just passing through, getting away from it all. Resting, you know.'

She had put up so many of them since she came back here. After all, Amanda and Charlie had sent a string of guests up here over the years. Most of them had been tended to by Mrs Winston who had lived in until Melody came back to take up residence.

Melody lay in her bed in the darkness, not listening, or trying not to listen, for Scott's sounds, trying to make sense of her own strange reaction to this one man. All those friends of her parents, friends of Robin's. She had invited them in and said, 'Here's the bed, and there's the kitchen. Help yourself. The beach is that way, four blocks downhill. Make yourself at home, just remember that if the door to the sound-room is closed, *don't knock on it and don't open it!'*

None of them had disturbed her peace, not since she had learned to stop feeling guilty about putting her work first. So what was different about this one man with his easy smile and his impenetrable eyes?

The crack of light under her door disappeared. The house groaned. She could hear a slow drip, water in the drainpipe. A very light rain, typical of the misty isles.

She must have slept. The sound of rain was gone when she opened her eyes again. There was soft light through her window from the rising moon. Her bedroom window looked out on the forest and she never closed her blinds.

There was no sound at all, not even the house making night groans. She got up and went silently barefoot to the baby. She had forgotten to open her door. He might have cried and she would not have heard. Scott would have heard, she supposed, because his door was open a crack.

Robbie was just starting to stir when she got there. She lifted him and changed him while he was still half asleep and had not found his voice yet. Then she carried him downstairs, because it was time for his night feed. Scott usually woke for this one. Melody seldom heard the baby until later in the morning.

She warmed the bottle, then went back upstairs, settling on her brother's bed with pillows behind her, holding the baby in her arms. Watching the little mouth sucking intently, she relaxed into a half-sleep herself. She had never really thought about having babies. It had not seemed to go with her life.

She tilted the bottle to stop little Robin from sucking air, drew her leg up to support the baby's little bottom.

He was so small, curled into the curve of her arm, his legs lying across her abdomen.

There was no sound, but she felt her heart stop, then smash into her ribs. She looked up and he was there. Scott. Standing in the doorway, looking at her. There was no light, but the moonlight was bathing her in a pale gleam.

She licked her lips without realising, staring at him. He was in shadow, a black form in the doorway. He moved and she could see the lines of him, the smoothness of his broad shoulders telling her that he wore no shirt. Then he came closer, and she could see him in sharp silhouette. He had put on his jeans, but she would swear he wore nothing else. He stood stiffly, watching her as if she held his attention against his will. Staring at her.

Her eyes flew down, to the baby in her arm, to the pale nakedness of her legs curled casually across the bed, the white edge of her T-shirt against her upper thigh. He moved and she jerked her gaze up, and now the moonlight showed his face, still and intent on her. She did not need to look down now, to know what he saw. Her free breasts, swelling under the thin cotton knit of the shirt. The baby pushed his fist into her breast and she heard Scott take in a shaken breath.

'Melody...'

It was just a whisper. She had never heard his voice like that, lower than ever, filled with tenderness and desire.

Somehow, she must move, must talk and break this spell. She swallowed and licked her dry lips, and his eyes were on her throat, her lips. She could see him clearly now, and his man's body did not try to hide that he wanted her. He had hardly touched her, not even casually, in the days he had been her guest, but right now his eyes were blazing through the moonlit room.

It was the moonlight. Her fault, not thinking to put on a robe. She shifted the baby and tried to arrange herself more modestly, but it was impossible because she was wearing next to nothing. The moonlight showed every curve she had in its sensuous, gentle glow.

'I——' Her voice sounded like his, low and seductive, like an invitation. She cleared her throat and said, 'It's all right. I'm feeding him.' He didn't move and she stumbled on, 'S—Scott...you can go back to bed. You don't need   '

Bed. She half choked, her arms on the baby. The bottle made a noise and she shifted it, but it was empty. How could she get up without that shirt shifting even higher on her hips?

Scott said, 'He's done that bottle. Give him to me and I'll put him back to bed.' His voice was normal now, but his eyes weren't normal. They were heated and filled with golden fire. She gulped as he reached down for the baby.

She scrambled to her feet. Scott turned to lay the baby in the playpen. Better, she thought in relief. The shirt hung halfway down her thighs now. She was uncomfortably aware that her breasts were two soft, sensuous swellings free under the soft knit, but when she started to cross her arms over them he stood up and she saw his smile growing, but it was more than a smile. It was a touch, a caress.

He said softly, 'That just makes it more obvious.'

She gasped softly and looked down, saw that she had pushed the swelling of her breasts up and dropped her arms abruptly. 'I—you—I'd better go back to... Goodnight!'

She moved, quickly. He moved, too. She stopped abruptly, but he was only half an arm's length away, between her and the door. She could see the bulge of his chest muscles, his heavy biceps pressing against his naked chest. She looked down, could not seem to stop herself, and his chest hair thickened as she followed it, then thinned as it trailed down to the waist of his jeans.

He had not taken time to put his belt on.

He was watching her, seeing everything. The way his naked chest affected her, her own awareness of his eyes on her. Her body, breasts swelling in some mysterious woman's reaction to this man's chemistry. There were no words, but so much said. He was closer, and in a second his lips would take hers. She felt it coming. Not his hands on her. She thought she would jump, run away, if his hands touched, but he held that back.

The softest brush of hard, full lips against hers. She shivered and the touch returned, brushing, caressing, light, not demanding. She tried to breathe and she could not. She tried to step back, but he had her trapped with only those teasing lips.

'Scott——' It was a gasp, air sucked in, his name distorted. His tongue slipped in, taking advantage of her whisper, a warm invasion along her inner lips. She tried to say his name, a protest, but the sound might have been anything. Her heart was panicked, thundering. Her chest felt like the frightened trembling of a sparrow.

He stepped back before the shivering could grow to push him away. Her eyes flew wide, staring at him, and he said softly, 'Stop looking at me like a trapped animal. You're free.'

She did not feel it. She was at the mercy of his touch, her breath falling into short, quick gulps as she saw his hands move and thought of his touch sliding along her screaming nerves.

He caught her wrists lightly and turned them, his thumbs stroking her inner wrist where the pulse throbbed, his eyes holding hers. She could not even seem to find the will to look away, although she could feel her pupils widening as his light touch caressed the soft flesh that led towards her inner elbow.

'Melody,' he said on a whisper. 'With a name like that, I should have known you'd be all softness and nerves.' He swallowed and she could feel his lips on hers, but he did not move. Just his fingers, sliding along her arms, sending her body trembling with heat.

She had to get away, wanted to get away, but it was she who moved closer as his callused fingers slid along her bare upper arms, fingertips sliding under the sleeves of her shirt, wrists brushing the fullness of her nearby breasts.

Then his lips were close and her breath turned to a gasp as he bent down to take her mouth. She shuddered, felt him tremble, and his hands closed on her arms, pulling her against his hard chest, trapping her hands which had somehow found their way into the curling hairs on his chest.

She tried to stare up at him, to say something that needed to be said, some protest perhaps, but his mouth took hers in a deep invasion that she could only return as her body sought the hard contours of his.

Moonlight. Starlight. The heavens spinning, something wild surging up inside her. His tongue explored the gift of her mouth and she learned that there were wild, shattering sensations that could curl along her nerves just from the touch of tongue and teeth, lips that made hers engorge and tremble with sensations of flame and a deep, shuddering urge to surrender more, to feel more, to drown in sensation.

His hands, sliding along her back, claiming her flesh, branding her with his hardness, the rough gentleness of his chest hair through the thin cotton, the gasping surrender that exploded in her when his hands slid to her hips and pulled her closely against his implacable need.

His groan, against her face, in her ear. 'Oh, God, Melody, how can you do this to a man?'

Her head fell back, somehow against his shoulder, her eyes opening slowly, unwillingly. His voice was hardly a whisper.

'Your lips always look like . . . as if they're waiting for a man's kiss. Full and red and sensuous.' He took them and she lost the reality her mind had started to grasp for.

Sensation. Warmth. The wonderful, deep trembling of heated need. Her hands found some freedom as he shifted to caress the curve of her back, the calluses on his fingers scratching slightly on the cotton of her T-shirt as they explored lightly the shape of her spine, the hint of her ribs, the full swellings that were her free breasts.

She gasped and suddenly she was heavy in his hands, his fingers forming her breasts, holding them up for the soft seeking of his lips. She groaned in the instant his lips touched. The cloth was not a barrier, but a teasing, sensuous tool, passing the warmth of his breath, the seeking firmness of his lips. She was trembling, her fingers clenching in the hair of his chest to try to keep some kind of sanity . . . her legs, weak and trembling, collapsing against his as he brought her hips close with one arm, holding her firm and safe from falling, but losing all feeling for up or down or . . .

She heard it, her voice but not hers, a moan that invited touching, kissing, possession. He heard it, felt it, and swept her up into his hard arms. Her head fell back against his arm, his shoulder, and she saw his face above her, a tenseness that was holding some kind of control. He swallowed, and she saw the spasm all along his throat, and the control, what there was of it, was going to end when he got her through that door, into that room.

On to his bed. She felt the softness as he lowered her and she scrambled, breathing shallowly through her mouth, coming off the bed on the other side and halfway to her feet, in a crouch like an animal facing a hunter.

'I...I...' She gulped in air, her hands out as if to ward him off although he was still, watching her, waiting for—for what? 'I—Scott, I—I didn't mean to—to—to do this.'

'This?' He rounded the end of the bed and when she jerked away, she found herself held by one hand, fingers around her wrist like a steel band. He said steadily, 'I didn't see you fighting me off.'

She shook her head, feeling the storm inside herself, the tension that she thought would be with her all through the night. God! She did not even know the man, and his touch, his kiss, had sent her wild. She would have done anything, given anything. Even now she was not sure that it would be different. If his fingers gentled to a caress, the shuddering need could overwhelm her and she would be at his mercy.

She realised from the way he was watching her that her breathing had turned into short gasps, as if he were caressing her. She whispered, 'Please, just—just let go of me and——'

His fingers tightened and she gasped. He released her abruptly and stepped back, but he was the other man, his eyes cold and his voice without the tenderness there had been only moments ago.

'You ask for it, wandering around in that bit of nothing.' His breathing was still heavy, but under control now. 'I see you go past every morning, walking past my door in your bare feet and bare legs, that shirt on as if it were clothing.' He reached his hands and traced the curves of her body, his hands neither gentle nor rough, his voice bringing heat to her cheeks. 'A man's only got to look at you moving to know what's underneath.' His hands found the swelling of her breasts and his fingers stilled, cupping, lifting to make the swelling more prominent. 'One message a man does not get, watching you walk past in that rig, is *no*.'

She gulped, feeling the hard response of her nipples to his touch, staring at the chill of his eyes, knowing they were cold although the moon was draining its light away from the room as it slid behind a cloud.

She whispered, 'I didn't—I just didn't think. I—I grew up in the theatre. Clothes, or the lack of them, didn't mean all that much.' She was talking fast, desperately, stumbling over her own words. 'Changing-rooms and people...people running in and out. I——'

His hands freed her. 'Melody, this is no theatre. Don't issue invitations unless you mean them. Not to me.'

She stared at him, nodded but could not get words out. He moved and there was room. She walked past him, out of his room, not looking back, but knowing, feeling, his eyes on her every step of the way.

Somehow, she got to her room and closed her door before she sagged against it and let the trembling of her body take over. So that was it. She had tried to call it distrust, discomfort with his easy way of settling into her home. She had never thought to call it sex. Physical attraction, the kind you read about, the sort of thing she had written songs about without knowing. The sort of emotion that knocked a girl off her moorings and left her trembling and aching for a man's touch.

She had never felt like this before. She shuddered, remembering how she had stepped into his arms. Maybe he was right. She had been teasing him, wandering around, past his open door, never really thinking that he might be awake and watching. Wanting her. Certainly there was no excuse for what she had done tonight. Lying with Robbie on the bed, hardly dressed herself. Had some part of her known he would wake and come? Had she wanted him to come?

He was more honest, reaching to take what she seemed to be advertising. Useless to pretend he had swept her away, carried her into his room against her will. What had he done? The lightest of kisses that shook her to her foundations, then a teasing caress of her bare arms with his fingers. She was the one who had flowed into his arms, who had given up her lips, had groaned his name and wanted, ached for, the touches, the caresses, the kisses.

And the loving.

He had only been about to take what she had seemed to offer. She hugged herself, wondering how she was going to face him in the morning, how she was ever going to get through the days from now until he left. Even now, that crazy part of her wanted to go back to his room, to accept what was in his eyes and his touch and his kiss, and to ask him to love her, to take away the ache that was consuming her.

She heard his step in the hall outside her door and her breathing stopped. Was he coming to her? If he did...

She felt herself trembling and knew that if he came to her now, she would not send him away. By morning, she thought, she might have the strength to know what was sanity and what foolishness, but tonight all she could feel was the echo of his touch. Sensation had drowned out thought.

* * *

He almost reached for her doorknob. His fingers were stretched out, curving to take possession of it. Would her door be locked against him?

Then he was past her doorway, going down the stairs, and the moment of insanity was behind him. He was not a randy teenager, unable to control his passions. He certainly did not need to reach out for a woman who swung wildly from giving to a virginal nervousness.

The night had turned clear and fresh after the earlier drizzle. He had intended to take his truck, to drive north along the narrow, winding highway that followed the east coast of Graham Island. But her van was parked behind his truck, and short of shoving the truck into four-wheel drive and putting big tyre tracks all over Melody's front lawn, he was stuck there until he could get her to move her van.

He walked down the hill to the intersection with the next street, then down a long curve to the highway, and finally to the water.

The shore here was barren, rocky and empty. The moon shone to show him his way. He walked until he found a lonely point of high rock, looking out over the water. He stopped then, staring out at the shadow of mountains to the south, across the harbour.

After a while he felt the peace of the night, could feel himself relaxing. He studied the sky, the oldest pastime of seamen. Polaris, of course, lying in the northern sky, higher than she would lie when he looked out from the deck of his ship. Orion there, lying low against the horizon.

What was it about the stars that brought calmness to him? The fact that the stars had not changed in their constellations? He grinned at that thought, but back there, with Melody warm and willing in his arms, the world and the heavens had shifted and he had almost gone spinning out of control.

Part moonlight, perhaps, although she had affected him from that first sight. She was part poet and part sorceress, he thought. Not the kind of woman he was accustomed to reaching for, not what he wanted when passion cleared his senses enough for him to see clearly.

Better by far for him to leave, to entrust little Robbie to her care and go back to a world where he knew the rules. Back to Caroline, who satisfed his needs without threatening the fabric of his life. Back to his half-built home on Cortes Island. Back to his work, piloting ships through the short northern summer.

That had been his intention when he came, to hand the child over as quickly as possible. Except that Robbie had become a person to him now, a small bundle of gurgles and helplessness that he could not abandon. And the father had become an unknown quantity. Robin Connacher, known only in his love-letters to Donna, had seemed a safe guardian for his young nephew. Robin Conners, emerging superstar singer, was another matter.

Scott picked up a stone and threw it into the water, watched the ripples move outwards, flowing along the moonlit, glassy ocean. He was fooling himself. Doubts about Melody's brother were only an excuse. He had commanded men long enough to know them with an unerring instinct. The man who had written those letters to Donna would not fail his own child. And Melody herself would certainly provide any warmth and love that might be lacking from the child's father. Hadn't he watched her holding the baby, her eyes wide and filled with tenderness and warmth as she looked down at Robbie in her arms? No, it was not Robbie's needs that kept him here. The baby would have the kind of stability and love that Donna had never had.

It was time he was honest with himself. From the moment he had stood on the steps of that old wooden house and stared at the tousled woman who opened the door to him with sleep-softened lips and wide, startled eyes, there had been a part of him, unacknowledged, that had known he had to have her. Despite Caroline, although to be honest he and Caroline had never exchanged promises of faithfulness. Despite anyone else who might stand in the way. Despite even Melody herself. Before he could walk away from this place, he must hold Melody Connacher in his arms, kiss those full red lips to swollen surrender, caress that seductive, soft-firm body to wild abandon, and possess her. Totally.

If it could be quick and clean and sudden, he thought, it would be over then. Tonight, if she had not drawn back, they would have been one in an explosion that would have shaken them both to the core, but in the morning it would have been over, and he would be able to walk away.

Now he was uneasy. He knew he was not going to do the sensible thing, was not going to leave, to run while he could. He was going to have her. His mind was already playing with ways to woo her, to seduce her into his bed—into her bed, actually.

He knew that the lovers' game of pursuit and seduction could turn to high explosives when the woman was Melody. He might win her surrender, then spend his nights forever staring up at the stars, remembering her soft heat in his arms, her eyes sliding through his walls.

Whatever peace Scott found staring at the stars over Queen Charlotte harbour, he lost it the next morning when the telephone rang. Melody was upstairs working in the music-room, so he answered.

'Is Melody there?' It was a man who was obviously startled to hear a strange voice.

'Sorry,' he said coolly, feeling an instant and inexplicable antagonism. 'She can't come to the phone right now. Can I give her a message?'

'Damn,' said the voice amiably. 'I thought I might get through early enough. She's working? She usually doesn't get in there until about nine in the morning.'

Scott snapped, 'Yes.' Whoever this was, he was evidently intimate with Melody's habits. 'Yes,' he repeated, his voice under control, and he tried to scorn his own possessive feelings. As if she were his. 'She usually comes out about one. If you——'

'OK. Ask her to call Jeff at home in LA, would you? I—no, damn it! That won't do. I'll be—look, who is this?'

'Scott Alexander,' he said abruptly.

A pause, then a half-laugh, and Scott felt like a stiff, awkward fool. 'All right, Scott. I'm Jeff.' The friendly voice ignored Scott's stiffness. 'Ask her to call me at Peter's between one and two, could you? If she doesn't, I'll try to catch her this evening.'

Scott delivered the message to Melody at lunch, his voice stiff. She had not met his eyes at breakfast, and did not now. He wondered why the hell he was staying around. Last night's explosive touching seemed like a far country now. There was only tension and, in Melody, no warmth at all.

No warmth, that was, until he said, 'Jeff called.'

'When?' Her lips parted and her eyes lit. He felt even more angry at the confident voice on the telephone. She asked quickly, 'Where is he? Is he coming up here?'

Scott shrugged angrily. 'He wants you to call him between one and two, at Peter's.' He walked away then, but he could hear her voice carrying through the house.

Everything was in her voice, her thoughts and her feelings. When she spoke, he always felt as if he had known her forever.

She was cool now, businesslike. 'Yes, it's Melody— no, I haven't, not yet. I keep telling you, registering it just slows it down. Registered goes through Toronto, and then Vancouver—I called for Jeff. Is he there?'

Then her words quickened, the warmth flowing through the telephone to the man who had called. He must have said something almost at once to make her laugh.

'Yes,' she said lightly, teasing. 'You told me to, and I'm doing my best. What's up?'

Scott shoved the plug into her sink and ran the water for dishes. It drowned out her voice, which was good, but he turned the tap off again abruptly.

'Super! When do you think? When? No, it's no problem. I'll shove you in Amanda's and Charlie's, or——' A pause, then a laugh. They had known each other a long time. Friends? Lovers? He pushed a small stack of plates down into the soapy water and the water surged up and sloshed over the edge of the sink. Melody said, 'I'll be waiting. Keep the pilot on course, and I'll be there to meet your plane.'

Listening to her telephone calls, wondering who meant what to her. Crazy behaviour for a grown man determined to keep control of his own life. This was beyond wanting, beyond infatuation. Too much, tentacles catching him in traps he did not want to spring.

Past time he got out of here. This afternoon he would phone and book a reservation on the next sailing of the *Queen of the North*.

CHAPTER FIVE

SHE really had to learn to keep her imagination where it belonged, in her work, Melody told herself. Crazy, but she had been feeling as if Scott had strings that would pull at her from a world away, that he was the man who could whisper her name and send her reeling, body and soul...today and tomorrow and forever.

Today and tomorrow and forever, words like a song. Perhaps that was it, the germ of a new song stirring in her. Not real feelings, not a frightening loss of control of mind and heart and life. Melody knew she sometimes went a little crazy when she was working. She always had. Her little bit of artistic temperament, she supposed, and no problem if she kept it inside her own head, or safely inside the soundproofed walls of the music-room. But to reach out her arms and whisper his name, to groan and feel the need to beg for his possession, surging and growing and turning wild and unchained within her——

That was madness.

Fantasy was her business, poetry. She had to learn to keep that part of her where it belonged, and Jeff's voice got her back on track. She hung up the telephone, then worked on reminding herself that Scott Alexander was a stranger, attractive and pleasant, but not touching even the surface of her life. For heaven's sake! What did she know about the man? He was Donna's brother, but she had never met Donna. He could feed a baby and change a nappy and he was a sea-captain who had to be in the Beaufort Sea in less than three weeks. Lord! She wasn't even sure where the Beaufort Sea *was*, except it was up north in the cold Arctic somewhere. And she damned well wasn't going to go running to her atlas to find out, either!

It did not matter. *He* did not matter. Not to her. He was a guest, like all the others, friends of Amanda and Charlie's, friends of Robin's. Here's your room and there's the kitchen and keep out of the music-room. Have fun, but don't bother the lady in residence.

She managed to believe it, almost, so long as she did not look too closely at Scott's eyes. Well, that was right. When had she ever watched those casual guests so closely?

She smiled at him and breezed out of the house before he could say whatever was in his eyes. She sailed through *Island Time* without thinking about him. Not much, anyway, and less all the time.

She was all right now. Unstable, but she knew that about herself. She was too easily vulnerable; needed to keep close to nature, a little isolated from the world. Here, in the space of a few days, a stranger from the wild Pacific Ocean had driven into her life with his big cross-country tyres and had turned her upside-down.

All right. So she was too easily thrown off balance, although she had not realised until the last few days that she had that kind of gasping passion buried inside her. Good for her song-writing, but best kept out of the rest of her life. She needed day following day with order, not with uncontrolled emotion. Look at the trouble she had been having with her work ever since Scott Alexander walked through her door!

She used the telephone at the radio station to call him. 'Scott? Look, I won't be able to get home for supper tonight. I've got to put in some overtime in the tape editing booth.' It was a lie. John did all the editing.

Scott's voice on the telephone told her he knew it was a lie, without words. Just undertones. Damn it! Imaginary undertones, as likely as not. Perhaps she was imagining it all, the messages in his eyes, the words unspoken and felt between them.

No matter. He was not important to her. Too dangerous.

She arrived home just before net time. She concentrated her hellos on baby Robbie, who was already drooping. She avoided talking to Scott, avoided looking at him. Then she brushed past them, the man and the baby, switching on the radio and muttering about the schedule.

She heard him going upstairs with the baby as she tuned up. It was not going to work. He was not one of the usual stream of strangers from the theatre world, invaders to be handled without actually touching them. Her people were the islanders, not the visitors, but although she had labelled him an islander at first, he was a stranger. Stranger from the sea. Stranger. Danger.

For the first time in days, the twenty-metre band was free of static. The Vancouver net control was loud and clear. She checked in, then net control called Robin's call sign. She heard her twin's voice, clear and close in her living-room. 'Melody, let's go up thirty. I'll call you.'

She shifted her frequency up thirty kilohertz and tuned in on Robin's powerful voice. His big voice was always a surprise to people who thought a slight form meant a light whisper of a voice.

'The trades are blowing twenty-five to thirty,' he told her, his voice excited. 'I've been making six knots all day.' She had been learning nautical terminology in the year since Robin dived head-first into sailing and yachting. Trade winds. A thirty-knots wind was about fifty kilometres an hour.

She felt Scott's presence behind her. She managed to keep her eyes from him, staring at the pencil in her hand, at the numbers on paper. Robin's latest position, longitude and latitude. 'Robin, when do you expect to be in Hawaii?'

She could hear the faint sound of Morse code from another amateur station, the quiet swish of Scott's shoes on her carpet, then Robin's voice saying, 'Four days, plus or minus the wind. You know how it is. No schedule out here.'

Robin had taken to the sea to escape the pressure of deadlines between appearances and recording sessions. Or had he been escaping his love for Donna, a woman who had wanted more than he could give?

What had Donna asked? That Robin give up his career, move into a house and stay in one place. That he give up his identity. Better, she thought, that Robin had resisted. Robin without music would be a pale shadow of himself.

She could feel Scott at her side. Did he expect her to tell about the baby? About Donna's death? On the radio? She keyed the microphone. 'Robin, be sure to telephone me the moment you get to shore.'

Her brother's voice snapped across the miles of ocean that separated them. 'Is Charlie's heart kicking up again?'

'No, nothing like that. It's—nothing like that. Just a snarl-up you'll have to deal with.'

Behind her, Scott moved restlessly. Angrily?

'OK,' Robin said with relief in his voice. She knew he would assume that the problem related to the upcoming recording sessions. It was forbidden to deal with business matters on amateur radio, so he said only, 'All right, Melody, if that's all, I'll sign off and go change my

Genny for the hundred per center. The wind's picking up. Eighty-eight, twin.'

Eighty-eight; love and kisses. Genny; Genoa jib sail. She smiled slightly and signed off, echoing his endearment. When Robin's voice had faded to memory, she threw the switch that brought silence flooding over the room and sat, staring at the radio, knowing she had to turn and meet Scott's eyes now. All day, she had been avoiding that.

'Why didn't you tell him?'

'On the air?' Her voice was rising as she stood up, defensive. Anger made it easier to stare at him coldly, with criticism. 'Do you know how many people are listening? Ham radio operators on several continents, not to mention the short-wave listeners! And you want me to tell him the woman he loved is dead? Flat, like that, while he's in the middle of the ocean? He'd be alone with it, out there, and I——' Her voice faltered to a gasp as she swung around to him, her hands settled on her hips and her head tossed back in preparation for battle.

The man who had fed the baby with tenderness in his eyes, that man was gone. Along with the man who had touched her, kissed her and lifted her into his arms as if his possession were total. Trapped by the harshness in his eyes, Melody felt her breath go short and her chest tighten.

Silence. Tension. 'What's wrong?' she whispered finally.

A spasm jerked across his face, then he relaxed as if he had forced the tension away. He said, 'I'm leaving on tomorrow's ferry,' and his voice held nothing more than the bare words.

'What about...?' She swallowed. 'You wanted to see my brother first. Robin. To be sure—to check him out.'

'I've a friend wating for me.' His jaw tensed. 'I'm supposed to be in Campbell River this week, then going on a trip with...'

To Mexico. With a friend. The woman he had telephoned? Caroline. Another sister? Girlfriend? Lover?

'Go, then,' she said, drawing all the old defences around her. Always, until Charlie and Amanda had dumped their children on the Queen Charlotte Islands, friends had been brief and transitory, here and gone; every warm contact formed had led to the pain of parting. Melody's childhood years were littered with half-memories of half-friendships, of people left behind and never seen again. As she had become older, friendships had taken longer to grow, and she had become the one on the outside. Robin had fused with the world of the stage, revelling in its excitement, but not his twin.

She had come to accept it, telling herself that it was a song-writer's lot, always being a misfit, that it was essential to the poet to view the world from the edge. Even here on her islands she was an oddity. A good place, though, for people who did not quite fit. Among the Haida, the fishermen and loggers, the island was scattered with intriguing misfits who had found a home on the misty isles where an individual was allowed to be different without penalty.

At ten years of age Melody and Robin had been thrown from their rambling backstage life into a housekeeper-supervised existence in Queen Charlotte. The islanders might have shunned the twins as outsiders, but instead they had given the newcomers the chance to prove themselves.

For Melody, the islands had become her refuge, her home, although Robin had always resented fiercely the fact that the authorities had caught up with Amanda and Charlie, insisting that two ten-year-old children could not spend their childhood without regular schooling. Robin had been singing regularly on stage that last year, while Melody had refused to join the act in front of an audience.

Now Scott nodded and said tonelessly, 'Yes, I will go. It's time. Do you need anything? Money?'

'Money?' she squeaked. 'Why should I ask for money from you? I——'

His hand caught her arm as it flung out in anger. His fingers burned her flesh through the loose knit of her sweater and he said angrily, 'For the baby. Is there anything you need for Robin Scott before I——'

'No.' The tight breathing was making her chest rise and fall visibly. Oh, lord! What had she thought he meant? He was staring at her, could see her face flaming. Her colour was always high, but now her cheeks were blazing, even her lips and her forehead, her throat. She gasped and the sound was echoed in his eyes.

She could feel the tension in him, explosive emotions boiling through her once peaceful home. It was in her, too, a violent something about to take her apart. She swallowed and jerked away, but his hand was still on her arm, burning although there was no skin contact.

'Let go of me.' The words were only a whisper. Her eyes got caught in his. The granite had changed to hazel and, as she stared into his gaze, his eyes turned dark and she forgot to breathe. She said, 'Tomorrow? You're going tomorrow?' and it was not her voice at all. Some part of her recognised the husky vulnerability that was a childhood memory of Amanda singing a love-song to Charlie on stage. She shook her head to reject the parallel and he nodded, understanding something that was not in words.

His thumb moved, calluses sliding along, catching the wool of her sweater, stirring the tender flesh at the inside of her upper arm as the heat of his moving fingers flowed through to her. He saw her swallow, saw her eyes widen and lose their focus. He was mesmerised, and his thumb stroked more gently, slipping over the barrier of her pushed-back sleeve, feeling out the softness of her fore-arm as his breathing paced hers. 'Tomorrow,' he echoed as her lips parted unconsciously. 'Or now,' he growled, and he was closer, his eyes on her lips, on the soft smoothness of her long neck, the trembling at the base of her throat.

She managed to say shakily, 'Now would be better. Go now.' Far better. This was dangerous, playing with explosive unknowns. She could get badly burned if she let herself drown in this trembling vulnerability. She might drown, never to find herself again. She told her arm to pull away, but his fingers slid down and his thumb found her inner wrist. The caress shot right through her but she managed to turn her groan into words, to whispers. 'Scott, I—please, I want you to go away now.'

His lips were closer. Her tongue slipped out to moisten her own swollen, dry lips and her teeth caught her lower lip.

He did not smile, just stared at her in the reddish glow that was the sun setting outside, draining light from the world. He lifted her hand and bent his mouth, not to her lips, but to her inner wrist.

She felt the trembling in her knees, the weakness, but she would not give in to the soft agony of his lips, his tongue playing along her pulse. Her fingers clenched on nothing. He felt the movement and whispered, 'If you want me to go, you'd better decide. Now.'

'Yes,' she gasped, but his tongue did not stop its erotic journey along the nerves of her inner arm, her wrist, the curve of her palm. As his lips moved, his eyes traced the motion of her breathing, finding the full swelling of her breasts under the oversized sweater. What if he touched there? His lips moved back to her wrist, towards her elbow, but his eyes were everywhere and she could feel the reaction in her body, tightening and aching. 'Go,' she gasped. 'Please go.'

He was not even holding her in his arms. What if he did? He was a foot or so away, the only contact his fingers on her wrist, his mouth along her forearm. And she could feel the hunger swelling inside herself. Her legs did not want to hold her. If she sagged closer he would touch and hold and take over what would happen. 'Go,' she whispered again, wanting him to pull her into his arms and end the tension.

He dropped her wrist. She stood motionless, vulnerable and exposed, because he could see and she could not seem to cover up what he was taking from her eyes. He raised one hand and slowly brought it to her. She could feel the movement of the air, herself shivering as his fingers slowly found the front of her sweater. She could feel herself tightening, and when his fingers stroked lightly over the peaks of her breasts through the wool, the hard buds of her nipples were so achingly sensitive with waiting, needing, knowing the touch would come, that she groaned aloud, choking the sound to a gulp and silence.

'Please,' she whispered.

He pulled his hand back, but his voice was seduction overlaid with a low anger. 'I don't ravish youngsters, music lady, and you're no child, so make up your mind.' His eyes found the thrust of her aroused breasts, telling her without words that he knew she wanted his touch.

'I don't understand what you mean,' she whispered, confused.

He shook his head. She felt the tension break when he turned away. She sagged down on to the carpet, staring at the fire as he moved around her room. She did not watch him, but the flames. He was moving, pacing. In a minute there would be his footsteps on the stairs. Why could he not let her play the harmless game of self-deception? She could say *go*, and he would touch her, kiss her, and somehow despite her protests he would make love to her before he walked away. Oh, God! She ached for his touch, but so much better if she said no even though she trembled for him, because she would have herself intact later. A night's passion, but not of her asking.

Love.

If she turned and looked at him, whispered a word of consent, it would happen. An affair, hot and quick and over. If it happened now, in the morning he would leave, or perhaps even earlier. He was a stranger, a sailor who had come and would go, and she knew almost nothing of him, except that he was tender with the baby, and that he was not a man for staying. And he would not take her and sweep her away on a tide of passion, not without making sure first that she was just as responsible as him.

Lover. A lover, for a night. Temporary. She tried to put the words into her mind, but although she knew he would walk away, his soul touched hers when their eyes met.

The music released her. Had he known it would? How much did he know? How far past her barriers could he see? She turned and the yellow flames from the fire were still in her eyes, but he was there, at the stereo, and the music was flowing over them both. Her own words, flowing over her mind, with meaning they had not had when she'd written them two years ago. 'Touch of a stranger, a lover's touch. Two souls meeting before they part.'

She did not look away, could not look away. He moved slowly, deliberately, crossing from the stereo to the fireplace where she sat on the thick carpet. Her hand moved and she saw it stretch towards him, but he passed her. He went to the fire and shifted a log, sending sparks blazing around. When he turned back to her he was all hardness and control.

She swallowed and her lips parted, but the words were somewhere else.

He said softly, 'Melody, do you want me to go away? Now?'

She shook her head, wordless. The door would close and the truck would drive down her tortured hill. She would have to go out and move her van to let him out, and she would be shivering, watching the red of his taillights as he drove away. Forever.

They would meet again. Around the baby. Over the years. But there would never be this, because whatever happened tonight would be isolated, a memory only. She did not dare let Scott be a part of her life; he could consume her.

He stroked the dark hair away from her cheek, his fingers curling around the full curve of her cheekbones. 'If I stay,' he said intently, his eyes on hers, 'you know what's going to happen.'

If he walked away now, she would never know what her own songs were about. Dreams, she had thought, writing them, but the dreams were here, now, in his eyes and her veins. She curled her fingers around his wrist and felt his pulse beating, strong and hard. And she said, 'Don't go. Not yet.'

It was like a song. The music. The magic. The slow dance of reality and anticipation. He sank down slowly beside her, not touching, only eyes, and she felt her lips curving in a smile as she turned towards him. The smile and the movement and the anticipation of his touch were all dreaming. His eyes followed the curves of her body and she realised that the sweater that covered everything, covered nothing.

She licked her lips and he touched them with his, pulling back to see her eyes. What did he want her to be? She saw his chest swell beneath the brown shirt he wore as he took in a deep, powerful breath. Her fingers curled, wanting to touch.

'Touch me. Touch my soul.' Words, a song, flowing over them. His fingers reached her shoulder and stroked her arm through the sweater, a teasing hint of later, of how his touch would be on her naked flesh. Her hand moved between them and she traced the contours of his hard chest.

He took her mouth. The music exploded.

She had needed this, had ached for him. His lips covered hers, and she opened to him, invited his invasion of her warm, moist mouth, shuddered and groaned soundlessly as her body flowed against his, his hands holding her arms, bringing her close, his arms surrounding her. A safe...warm...hot nest where there was only warmth and touch and feeling and the surging of the music felt in their veins.

Her breasts pushed hard against his chest. His hands spread out to span her back, fingers touching to make flames along her nerves. Her spine arched and he moulded her fine-boned torso to his hard muscles. She gasped as one hand slipped under her sweater and his fingers traced up her spine with sensuous, soft abrasion.

When he lifted his lips from hers, she found herself staring up at him, lying on her back on the soft plush carpet. Behind him, she could see the red brilliance of the sun's last glow, the sunset surrounding his head like a halo of fire. Longer days, she thought. Summer coming soon. Then she could think of nothing but him.

He said, 'I want to see you,' and she needed his eyes on her with the touch of a lover.

She stroked the crispness of his shirt, found the place between two buttons and slipped her fingers through, into the rough curls of his chest hair.

He growled, 'If you do that...' and she laughed, her voice husky and teasing and drowned out by the song. 'Touching. Loving. Your mind caressing mine.'

'Touch me,' she whispered, and his eyes turned to flames. His hands traced the shape of her, through the clothing, and she was naked while fully clothed, shuddering, feeling his caress everywhere. His hands settled under her breasts, curving to hold them, and she gasped, 'Please.'

'Don't be impatient.' He gave a low laugh, stroking her midriff, the sweater transmitting his message. Her eyes fell shut and there was only the soft teasing of his hands everywhere, and her fingers worrying at his buttons, her groan as he stroked her thigh through the jeans, her swollen breast through bra and sweater, her hip.

Then stillness. Her eyes dragged open. She had found her way through the buttons, or he had. His shirt was gaping open, her hands threading through the hair, finding the hard curve of his male breast, the arousal of his tiny nipples, the rigid tension of his upper abdomen. His fingers were resting on the naked flesh of her midriff, under the sweater, but motionless. In a second he would move, the sweater would be gone, then everything else, and she would go up in fire, consumed.

'Melody, are you prepared for this?'

She stared at him. His fingers moved, so slightly, and her flesh shuddered. Prepared? She was aching for him, needing him with a drugging, wild passion that had come from somewhere inside, from the place where the songs came, the secret, mysterious, all-consuming hidden part of her.

'Yes,' she whispered, because she had been waiting all her life for his touch on her soul. 'Please touch me.'

It was more than she had thought it could be, so much more. He pushed up the sweater, so slowly, and his eyes aroused her long before his hands and lips could touch. She writhed with impatience, with need, and the sweater was gone.

He cupped her breasts with love, and bent to the sweet curve that he had pushed up from her bra, his lips and his breath hot on her. Then he freed her of the scrap of lace with an abrupt motion and took his freedom of her warmth with his lips.

She would go mad with the sensations. Touching, fire, the song in her ears and her blood and the pounding of her wild heart. She twisted, writhed, told him with formless sounds how she needed the feel of his lips and his hands and his body on hers, while her own hands roamed over his chest and his shoulders with restless seduction.

'I've dreamed of you like this,' he groaned as he freed her of the last trace of clothing, as he bent to take the place of the flames playing light over her softly glowing flesh. The rough hair of his leg invaded the softness of her inner thighs and she moved to reach for his possession of her. 'Loving you,' he whispered, tracing fingers over the curve of her belly. 'Touching,' he breathed, and his lips moved to the places his hands had been. 'I dreamed of you needing me the way I burn for you,' he said harshly as she pulled him closer.

She rose to meet him and he filled her as the rain fills the river, the thunder invading the mountains with gasping rightness. His need was hers, and when she groaned, he shuddered with an echoing passion that grew to consume them both. Then the music was gone and the sun was gone, and there was only the explosion of the stars, the earth shifting, torn out of its orbit as she fell spinning into the place where there was no Melody, no Scott, only the soft, hot, wild, hard demand that was their shuddering fulfilment.

She lay very still, listening to the beating of his heart under her cheek. Slowly, the wild pounding calmed to a steady, strong thump. She wanted to lift her head and turn to see his face, but he was quiet, motionless, holding her, and she felt the words that he was not saying.

If she opened her eyes and looked into his, would he see how much he had taken from her? More than passion. She squeezed her eyelids tightly closed and held her body carefully relaxed. In her throat, words were welling up. Stay. Please. Don't leave me. Don't go away. Not today. Not tomorrow.

The music had stopped, but her mind played back the final song of the album, knowing those notes must have filled the dark room only moments ago, and that she had been too drowned in Scott to hear.

Instant replay, she thought, trying to feel cool and a little scornful of her own desire to reach and cling and whisper words of love and need. She opened her eyes without turning to see his face, keeping very still. His chest hairs, in front of her face, curled damply across his male breast. Behind him, the fire burned, low now, except for the occasional burst of blue flame as flames consumed sap on the wood.

She felt tension in his still body. He was waiting for her to sleep. She understood that, shared the unwillingness to speak or look. They had gone farther, come closer than either of them could handle. The knowledge hurt, and she knew that the dreams and the memories were going to hurt, too. The sight of him over the years to come was going to stir pain and longing inside her, because this could never happen again. She could not handle it without begging for more, for closeness and sharing and a relationship.

That kind of needing scared her silly. For three years she had been her own person, *needed* to be her own person. She must not let herself be swallowed up in emotion, passion, needing.

Not that she was at risk. Scott was going to run, too, just as soon as he thought she was asleep. All right. Better that way. The next time she saw him he would be a stranger again, the baby's uncle, and she would be safe back in her own world, insulated from the storm he had woken in her. She would dress very carefully, put on make-up and a cool smile, and he would never see anything but the well-groomed shell of her public self.

Scott looked in on Robbie after he had his things packed in the bag. The baby was just stirring, grumbling sleepily that it was time for his night feed. Best if he walked away and let Melody wake to tend the baby, but he picked Robbie up and took him into the kitchen. He forced himself not to look at Melody as he carried the baby past, but he saw her, lying nestled under the quilt he had brought down to cover her.

She was lying on her stomach, her face pillowed by her forearm. Her long, black eyelashes were fanned over her full cheeks. Even in sleep, with her normally sleek hair tumbled by the passion of their loving, she looked fresh and beautiful. None of her dramatic colouring was artifice.

He heated the bottle, fed Robbie, then burped him and changed him and put him back into the playpen upstairs. He stared down at the baby, feeling guilty in the knowledge that he was about to walk out on his young nephew. But he had to go. Self-preservation.

He had never met anyone like her before. The dreamy passion of her songs was there in her eyes, peeking through the barrier of her mask. He had sensed it from the first, had wanted her from the beginning.

She had been more than he expected, had touched him in places both moving and terrifying. Melody Connacher. Dangerous Melody. She looked so smooth and sophisticated, so carefully groomed, even in that sloppy sweater she wore. Controlled on the outside, with eyes exposing the emotional woman underneath. High colour in her cheeks. Eyes that went black with emotion. Body that curved to hold and comfort a small child. Lord! He had started dreaming about her! Then the dreams had burst the bounds of his sleeping fantasies.

Dreaming. And doing things for her. It had started out as the old, learned habit of his childhood, because he had known that she did not want him here, and he had felt a stubborn determination to stay.

Thrown into foster-homes when his parents died, Scott had learned quickly that while his two-year-old sister Donna was cute and cuddly, eight-year-old Scott was awkward and difficult. Donna could smile and gurgle and win anyone over. Scott had known, even at the age of eight, that he could not win his place in strange homes with a smile. Instead, he had worked quietly, looking for the jobs that needed doing, trying to make himself indispensable. The dishes. The rubbish. Chopping wood.

It had worked for three years, until their foster-mother had discovered she was pregnant and pushed away both Donna and Scott in favour of her natural child. When they were placed together again with a fisherman and his wife, Scott had vowed to make himself completely indispensable this time.

That was how it had started with Melody, he supposed. The old habit, quietly looking for tasks to do to compensate for his unwelcome presence. Then it had got out of hand, and he had fallen into the pattern of protecting her working time, sharing Robbie with her, sharing moments in the evening with her, lunches and cups of coffee, moments of listening to music.

Insane though it was, he had begun to think of this place as if it were his own home. Had begun to think of the woman as if she were his. That was the frightening part, because he had vowed years ago that he was never going to let anyone get close enough to tear his life apart by walking away. Never again. A child had little choice, but a man could choose his life.

Choose his women. Far better to have a woman like Caroline, cool and independent and more concerned with her own career than with their relationship. That was how he wanted it.

He stopped on his way out of the house, stood in the darkened living-room and stared down at Melody's dark curls. He caught himself before he actually reached down to touch her. If he touched, stroked, whispered her name, she would murmur and sigh and finally turn to him, open her arms to him and make him whole again.

Angrily, he broke away from her spell. Soft trap. How could a man possess her complexities? Song-writer. Semi-recluse. Hot, passionate lover. If he didn't get away quickly, she would have a stranglehold on his soul. She would have him begging for the moon, then she would drift out of his arms with a few words of poetry. He didn't need risks like that. A life of turning on the radio and hearing her words, dreaming of her with dreams he could not escape.

He managed to get the truck out without driving on the soft part of her lawn. He couldn't avoid leaving tracks on the edge of the grass, but he thought the grass would spring back if he raked it. He stopped the truck at the top of the twisting drop and pulled on the emergency brake. It would only take a minute to get her rake from the shed behind the house.

Get the hell out of here, before it's too late!

He had the door half-open, but he jerked it shut. The slam of metal on metal burst the quiet of the night. He clenched his jaw and forced his actions to slow. Then he let the brake off and eased his way down the hill.

Sneaking away, his heart pounding with turmoil. God! Here he was, thirty-six years old, and he felt the way he had when he was fifteen, after that big blow-up with Tom, his second foster-father. Scott had been kicked out of high school for continuous truancy, and Tom had laid the law down. School, or work, or get the hell out. Tom, accustomed to the harsh life of a fisherman, had enforced his anger with blows, and Scott had run when he'd caught himself about to strike back.

That night he'd been on foot, roaming Vancouver's streets, not driving a big, powerful truck along a winding island highway. Steamed up, angry, frightened and too foolish to admit it. He had moved from the respectable area into the wild, and somewhere in the angry night he had begun to see what was around him. Homeless people. Old men without families; girls pretending to be women, selling what should only be given with love.

Inside the houses, safe and secluded were the families. Scott had had no family except Donna, and his sister had been clinging to Tom and Sylvia so hard that she had hardly seemed to remember Scott was her brother.

He had felt cut off, isolated by the anger of the man he could not bring himself to call *father*. Then, somewhere between the drunk asleep in the alley, and the girl on the street who looked so much like Donna, he had lost the anger and realised that, no matter how alone he felt as a barely tolerated foster-child, it was nothing to the isolation of having no one.

In the morning, when Tom had arrived at the *Lady Sylvia*, Scott had been waiting. They had stared at each other. If Tom had said anything about the night before, Scott would have gone. Perhaps Tom realised that, because his face had worked silently, then he had nodded abruptly and said, 'Sandpaper in the wheelhouse. We're stripping down the gunwales to paint them.'

That stormy night had been over twenty years ago. Tom had never been his father, but after that night they had developed a restrained relationship that had worked. Perhaps by the time the old fisherman died they had become friends of a sort.

Turning back had been the right choice then, but tonight was different, the risks the other way, and safety was in getting away before he got in over his head. So he drove, instinctively putting miles between himself and Melody. He followed the only highway there was, the winding, narrow route north along the east coast of Graham Island. He had a lot of time to kill. The ferry that would take him away was not scheduled to leave until midnight. He had the dawn to wait for, then a full day.

He stopped at a stream beside the road, cupped his hands and filled them with cool mountain water. The water tasted of pine. There was a sign posted at the edge of the clearing where he had pulled off the road. He read the legend and learned that anyone who drank the waters of St Mary's Spring would always return to the Misty Isles.

He felt a sudden, irrational terror, as if the legend were another strand pulling him down into quicksand. He slammed into the truck and drove on and managed to talk sense to his crazy imagination. All right. Of course he would come back. For Robbie, his nephew. He would come back and visit, take his nephew out for fishing trips.

Would Robbie live here? Did Robin Conners actually live in the Queen Charlotte house, or was it merely a place he visited? Did Melody live alone with her music and her dreams? The music-room seemed to belong so totally to her that he had trouble imagining her sharing it with anyone else.

Were there men? Jeff, for instance? The man who had telephoned and seemed to know her habits so intimately. Would Scott come to visit Robbie, and find her with another man? Any man would want her, and this Jeff probably did. A woman like Melody, filled with warmth and dreams——

One day he would come back and she would be married. Another man's child would lie in her arms, nuzzling against her breast for comfort and food.

A car came at him, then swerved. Then the haze in front of Scott cleared and he saw the yellow line on his right. He was on the wrong side of the road! He jerked the wheel and the car flashed by, horn blasting in a wail of frightened protest.

He pulled off the road, still shaking from the close call. He could have killed the innocent driver of that car! He had to get control of himself, stop painting pictures of Melody on the telephone with a man named Jeff. Smiling and laughing. Excited.

Melody, her head thrown back, her mouth open on a gasp as Scott touched her throat with his lips. Melody, soft and wild under him, her skin glowing with firelight as he possessed her. His name, whispered on the night air. Melody's whisper.

CHAPTER SIX

MELODY wanted to go to Hawaii to meet Robin, but she hesitated to take the baby with her. Scott had had trouble with Robbie on the ferry. If the baby got seasick, he might well get airsick, too.

Scott. When would his name on her mind turn to something ordinary, instead of leaving her with this trembling emptiness?

Melody wanted to meet Robin in Hawaii, but could not accept the idea of leaving Robbie behind with Mrs Winston. The housekeeper had not been very much of a mother substitute for Melody and Robin. Maybe Robbie was too small to notice, but he had already lost his mother. He needed stability.

But to tell Robin about Donna's death on the telephone——

The baby started screaming just before noon the day after Scott left. Melody realised that her concept of time was changing, that life was organised into 'before Scott came', 'when Scott was here', and 'after Scott left'. He was the lover in her dreams, in her songs.

Jeff turned up just as Robbie started screaming.

'You drive,' she said as he walked through the door. 'To the hospital.'

He looked startled, but recovered quickly. 'Yes, ma'am,' he said and he got her there quickly.

The problem was diagnosed quickly. A night in the hospital and she had Robbie back, but with the caution, 'He's got a hernia in his groin. It's slipped back into place now, but watch him. It may have to be operated on, but we'd like to wait until he's at least a month older.'

Robin called the next night, the telephone ringing in the middle of the night. Melody stumbled downstairs to grab it before it woke the baby, Jeff, in the room that had been Scott's, slept through the noise.

Her twin's voice was vibrant over the miles. 'What is it? Don't tell me they've messed up on the dates for the recording studio.'

'You're in Hawaii?' Why had she not practised the words, ways to tell him. 'Do you know what time it is here? When did you get in?' Donna's dead. The woman you loved is gone.

'Just now.' He was laughing at her confusion, not repentant for interrupting her sleep. 'Just cleared Customs now and got my cruising permit. What's up, Melody?'

In the end she said it bluntly, because she knew no soft way. She blurted, 'Donna Alexander's dead.'

Nothing. He did not say a word. She gripped the receiver, wished she could touch him, see him. How could she have broken the news to him so brutally?

'Oh, God,' he whispered. 'No. Please, no.'

'Robin, there's a baby. Your baby.'

He did not hear. He whispered, 'Donna——'

She remembered when they had been twelve years old and he had tried to keep a trapped squirrel in captivity. It had died. She remembered Robin's face, his eyes just before he had stormed out of the house. He had been gone six days. Everyone had searched. Mrs Winston. The police. Even Amanda and Charlie, called home from a nightclub engagement in France.

She gripped the receiver tighter. 'Robin? I—look, what city are you in? Where in Hawaii? What marina? I'll come there. I——'

'No!' He sounded angry, but she knew it was not anger.

'Robin! Listen to me! Don't go off and—— The baby—the baby needs you. Your baby. Donna's——'

There was a choked sound, then nothing but the hollow sound of her own telephone.

She hung up quickly, hoping that he would call back, knowing he would not. He needed time. Why was it that they could never share their worst hurts with each other?

'Don't worry,' she told the baby softly as she fed him. 'He'll come. And...even if he doesn't, I'll look after you.'

Jeff knew nothing about babies and had no intention of learning, despite Melody's threat that she would tell his next girlfriend what a rotten baby-sitter he was. So Melody got Mrs Winston to baby-sit while she was away at the radio station. On Monday she went through *Island Time* in a fog, but on Tuesday she got hold of herself, and by Thursday she managed most of her time on the air without thinking about Scott.

Jeff made up for his inadequacy as a baby-sitter by overhauling her synthesiser while she was at the station, getting rid of an annoying buzz tht occurred whenever she tried to lay a percussion track over bass guitar. What he didn't know about synthesisers hadn't been discovered yet.

He was the kind of guest she had always liked. If he was hungry, he fed himself or went out to a restaurant. When he wasn't playing with her equipment he was reading, technical magazines and horror novels alternately. When she was restless and unable to work, he talked her into getting Mrs Winston for the evening and going out dancing at the hotel.

But Scott was haunting her daydreams, giving her nightmares. She was fighting a losing battle in trying to talk herself out of the infatuation. It had been too long since she had taken a romantic interest in a man. She had been too long in an emotional vacuum, with only the fantasies in her music-room. It hadn't been Scott, but her own needs exploding. It could have been any attractive man.

She did not believe her own arguments. There were attractive men all around her. Jeff was attractive, although she had never felt anything but comradeship with Jeff. There was a man in the advertising department at the radio station, too, tall and handsome and single, and he left her cold.

She was in limbo, unable to work or to think straight. She told herself it was Robin she was waiting for. He would call, or he would come, and until then she could not make any plans for her future. She wasn't sure why she had to plan, but she felt a desperate need for something to hang on to.

She stumbled through the days. Reality was the hours in the sound-room, letting her feelings loose on the music. Reality was holding Robbie in her arms. Everything else was a haze, but she had control. At the radio station, she made her voice light and warm and friendly. At home, she tended to Robbie's needs, fed him and changed him and sang to him. She listened to Jeff talking, nodded and murmured to keep his words flowing.

Would Robin never call, never come? Two weeks, now three? Three weeks, Scott had said. That was the day he brought Robbie to her. Three weeks and he had to be on board his ship. The days had passed and she had counted. Scott would be there now, on his ship, and she

had only a hazy picture of a formless ship in the midst
of the ice, Scott at the bridge.

She wished Jeff would go so that she could stop pretending to be cheerful. Then, suddenly, he did leave, and
it was worse, because she had no one now to distract her
from her thoughts.

Before Jeff left, he caught her chin with his long
fingers and tipped her face up, examining it carefully.
'Want to talk about it?' he asked.

She shook her head. She should have known Jeff
would see that she was disturbed, but talking about it
would only make it seem more real. Infatuation. Not
love. It would go away if she tried hard enough, waited
long enough.

He said simply, 'If you do, you know how to find me.'

'I know. Thanks,' she whispered.

He kissed her cheek and was gone, leaving her alone
with Robbie and her worries about Robin, her memories
of Scott.

Mrs Winston left for a holiday in Vancouver with her
husband, so Melody took the baby with her, playpen
and all, to the radio station. Scott would not like that.
She shrugged away that thought angrily, but the next
day she got Bev to look after Robbie. Robin Scott.
Donna had named her baby after the two most important men in her life, her lover and her brother. For
Melody, it meant that every time she said the baby's
name she would be haunted.

Once a week, everyone on board the *Jonathan Cartier*,
from the messman to the skipper, had a chance to make
a five-minute telephone call home.

Last year and the year before Scott had used the single
weekly call to phone Sylvia, his foster-mother, because
he had made himself responsible for her since Tom's

death. Sometimes last year Donna had been there, as if she needed that small symbol of family, talking to her brother, although at that time he'd had no idea she was expecting a lover's child. She'd been bright and independent, talking about her job at the medical clinic, her plans to redecorate her apartment.

This year Donna was gone, and Sylvia had confided that telephone calls flustered her, that she would rather have a short visit when he got his two weeks off. So Scott had left the company's number with a neighbour, eliciting a promise to send an emergency message if Sylvia seemed to need anything. Then he had made a quick trip back to the Gorge and checked that everything on his property was secure for his six-week absence.

He'd told himself that life would be simpler on the ship this year. No one to call, so he needn't bother with the hassle of riding the man-basket to the rig, of dressing up for the cold for just five minutes on the telephone.

He supposed he could call Caroline, but he had never called her from the ship before. She would be startled by a satellite telephone call, might wonder if he was trying to deepen their relationship. Relationship? That was a laugh after the fiasco of this last month.

He had fled Queen Charlotte, arriving in Campbell River in time to go on the promised holiday to Mexico with Caroline. Then, abruptly, he'd changed his mind at the last second. She'd shouted at him at the airport and he really did not blame her. If he was going to let her down, he could have done it earlier, in time for her to make other plans. As it was, she'd stormed through the security check-point, boarded the jet without him. And he had been glad to see her go.

He had taken the ferry to his property on Gorge harbour and spent two weeks of furious activity that put his construction schedule ahead by a month, but did nothing to erase Melody Connacher from his dreams.

He would not be surprised to go on his next leave and find that there was no Caroline in his life. He knew that it would be a relief if she dumped him. He had no business holding on to her in a cool, no-future relationship, especially not now that he could not think of touching a woman, even talking to one, without fantasies of a beautiful recluse on the misty isles.

And how the hell was he going to forget Melody when he had been stupid enough to have brought Donna's stereo walkman to the Beaufort with him, and all her Robin Conners tapes? Robin Conners, singing love-songs written by his sister. Love-songs making hot dreams in the cold Arctic.

The Beaufort. Secretly he'd always found it romantically remote. He had never before felt that he was flying off to nowhere. First the airline flight to Calgary, then the company jet to Tuktoyaktuk. Then the helicopter. Huddling in the shed at Tuk, taking off his boots and pulling on the survival suit for the helicopter trip. The suit had built-in boots, hood, mitts, and he'd always felt a sense of adventure, setting off into the ice fields, always enjoyed the cold air biting into his lungs as he ran out to the chopper, carrying his kit and his boots.

But this time the hour-long flight to the rig seemed like a journey to the end of the world, cut off from the warmth, from Melody.

He had resisted the urge to pick up a telephone and call her all through those two weeks at the Gorge. But as the chopper touched down on the rig he felt a desperate need to reassure himself that she was all right, that her voice still had its husky, warm tones.

Or was he fooling himself? She would be fine, of course she would. What he needed was to know that she was not in the arms of the man named Jeff. Scott angrily shoved the jealous thought aside.

He stumbled out on to the rig. It was colder, the ice biting into him as he breathed, wind driving the effective temperature down. He glanced at the ice-pack on the horizon as he dodged into another little shed, absently assessing it as one-tenth ice, perhaps two-tenths. Around the rig, of course, the ice had been cleared.

With the return to work, the details filled the place Melody had invaded. He absorbed the mood of the men around him, knew that there was no emergency, that today everything was going smoothly. He took off the helicopter survival suit, and handed it to Cal, the skipper he would be relieving.

'Bloody freezing today,' said Cal, as he always did.

'Not much warmer in Tuk,' said Scott.

'Don't know why I work in the Arctic,' muttered the older Master. 'I'm going to Acapulco, sit in the sun while you freeze your toes, and you'll be lucky if I'm here to relieve you next time.'

'I'll dream about you,' said Scott, grinning, but it was Melody who would fill his dreams. Cal put on the helicopter suit and Scott put on the anti-exposure coveralls that would float a man if he went overboard, and keep him alive if the water weren't quite so cold. Scott had no intention of falling in and trying it out, not in those waters.

Details took over. He shoved his pack into the net of the man-basket, caught hold of the net high up and stepped on to the wide ledge at the bottom. Then he nodded and the crane operator lifted him, swinging the basket out over the icebreaker alongside the rig. It was a routine task; the crane operator halted the swing and Scott gripped the net, leaning into the basket while it swung high over his ship. Then the operator released the brake and the basket slid downwards, settling on to the deck of the icebreaker *Jonathan Cartier*.

Details. Work. A problem with the starboard bow thrusters. Parts flown in by chopper. Ice maps studied each time they came in on the fax from Ice Central. This early in the season, the ice was still heavier than he liked. He watched the drift of the pack, the forecasts of the movement of ice. They all watched, the officers of the rig and the two supply ships. A change in the pack, ice drifting down on the rig, and the routine of their days could turn into a desperate race to get the rig out before the ice took over.

She was in his dreams, but he thought he had control of it. It was a complete surprise to him on the second Wednesday evening when he turned to the mate and said, 'I'll go across for my phone call first. Then you and the second mate can go while I man the bridge.'

Harry nodded, automatically accepting the Skipper's right to first go at the telephone. It was Scott who asked himself who the hell he was going to call, and knew the answer.

Jonathan Cartier was anchored off the starboard side of the rig, backed up on her anchor with lines on to the rig. An hour earlier the chopper had landed, bringing the relief second and third engineer and two seamen, and taking away four men for their weeks off. The chopper had brought supplies, too, groceries for the rig and the icebreaker, as well as the smaller supply ship. Harry, an avid movie-watcher, was excited because the chopper had brought new movies for the men to watch during quiet evenings.

Once the chopper was gone, and the supplies transferred, the icebreaker stayed in her position, half-moored against the rig. Scott rode across, his head tipped back and watching the cable, something he never did. The cables were tested regularly. A man was crazy to get up in the air clinging to an upside-down cone at the end of a wire, and then start thinking about the wire breaking, about things that would prevent him ever seeing a certain woman again.

He had never had a serious affair with a woman. Friends, yes. Romantic friendships, like his long-standing relationship with Caroline, but never a woman who had had the power to make him yearn for her when he was far away. It scared him, frightened him even more now that he was going to call her, and did not know what he would say when her voice came.

The radio operator on the rig was just about to put the call through when head office came on with a long message that sounded far too routine to take priority over Melody, but the personal phone calls always took second place to company business.

Then, too soon, the radio op nodded and Scott went into the little room where there was a chair and a telephone and nothing much else. Thank God he had privacy at least. If he sounded like an idiot, no one would hear but himself and Melody, and any enthusiastic short-wave listener who had a fetish for tuning in on satellite telephone conversations. He had no idea what he would say to her. He had never had any trouble talking to a woman before, probably because none of them had mattered very much. Now he felt as if every word he might say would be wrong, either too clumsy or too revealing.

What the hell did he want, anyway? Her face swam in front of his eyes and he tried to put his hunger into rational words to reassure himself. An affair? The kind of relationship he had enjoyed with Caroline?

Her voice sounded warm and clear. Very close.

'Scott?' He thought he heard her draw in a breath, like a gasp, but then it was gone and she said briskly, 'I thought you'd be in the far north by now.'

'I am.'

She gave a half-laugh, and he could see how her face would be, arrested, listening, a little startled. 'You have pay phones up there?' she asked, not believing it.

'No, it's a satellite system on the oil rig.' He caught himself on the verge of explaining the technical aspects of the system. He had five minutes, for God's sake! 'It—we get to make personal calls once a week.' He heard himself saying it that way, *calls*, knew he was not ready to tell her that she was the only person he wanted to talk to. He added quickly, 'How's Robbie?'

'Oh—of course, he's fine.' He heard a rustle and she said, 'He's here. I'm just burping him.'

He saw her, clearly, saw the tenderness on her face as she looked down at the baby. Then she spoke and he realised that he was sitting here, silent, saying nothing like a fool.

'What did you want?' she asked, then interrupted herself. 'Oh, Robbie, of course. You—you sound as if you're right next door. I—did you have fun in Mexico?'

'Change of plans,' he said abruptly. 'How are you? How's——?'

Her voice seemed brittle. A distortion from the satellite, or she was not comfortable talking to him. She said, 'Robbie's got a little hernia. The doctor says it might have to be operated on, but——'

That was why she sounded so odd. Not that she was remembering their last night with discomfort, wishing it had never happened. She was concerned about the baby. Scott breathed again and said, 'Where is he? In the hospital? I'll——'

'No. It's really not serious. The doctor says it's pretty common, and the baby's not in any pain. Just——'

'Do you want me to come?'

He was working out a radio message to the company for emergency leave when she finally answered, 'You can't, can you? Your ship needs you, and all that. And why should you? It's nothing serious.'

'He's my nephew, Melody. I'm not going to just fade away to nothing.'

She said tightly. 'You did. You disappeared in the— in the night, without a word.'

'It seemed the best thing. Melody——' If only he could see her, have some feeling for what she might be thinking. He felt uncomfortably aware that his time must be almost up. 'Melody, I can be there in less than twenty-four hours. If you need me, I——'

'I don't.'

All right. She didn't. He was the one having dreams, fantasies he didn't want, couldn't shake. He amended it to, 'If Robin needs me.' He told her how to get a message to him, then asked, 'What about your brother? Is he there?' What about Jeff? Who the hell was Jeff, anyway?

'Any day now. He called from Hawaii.'

Scott frowned. What was she not telling him? Her voice had tensed and he knew something was wrong. 'Isn't he behind schedule? He should be there by now, there in Queen Charlotte with you.'

'He's . . . delayed.'

He heard the knock on the door then. Five minutes gone. Melody gone, out of his reach for seven days, until he could call again.

She waited by the telephone the next Wednesday. He had not said he would call, but he had said phone calls once a week, and it was a Wednesday when he called before. She spent the whole week telling herself she didn't care if he called, except for when Robin came home and she really did manage to forget about Scott for a while.

At first Melody had thought Robin was reaching for his baby only because it was the child of the woman he had loved. If so, the infant soon wound its own spell over the man.

'I'm going to find a house,' he told Melody, young Robbie held against his shoulder for a burp. 'Come on, Robbie. One big burp for your dad. Not an elaborate house, though. Something that feels like home. Like this.'

'There's this house,' offered Melody. She watched the father and son, seeing Robin's dark eyes echoed in his child, his slight, fine-boned figure. She could share the work of bringing the baby up. 'It's as much yours as mine, and there's surely room. And jets to LA, you can make connection in Vancouver. You could——'

He shook his head, not smiling now. 'No, my dear twin. This is your haven, but it's not mine. I like these islands, but I probably wouldn't come back at all if it weren't that you were here, making this place feel like a home. If I lived here with Robbie, you know how it would be.'

He frowned at his son and said sombrely, 'She wouldn't marry me, you see, because she was certain that a performer couldn't make a home. That I'd be off and away all the time, always leaving her, and she'd be more lonely with me than without: I told her—I promised her that I wouldn't let it be like that. That we could make a home, a real home, even though I had to travel to perform. But she needed a home, you see. She'd lost her parents before she could remember, been a foster-child, had a foster-father who was always at sea.'

Melody did not know what to say. She thought she understood how poor Donna must have felt. Robin was so passionate, so effervescent, and so impulsive. A woman might worry that he would chain her, and then disappear.

Scott would have shared Donna's childhood. If it had made Donna insecure, it seemed to have made Scott strong. Had it also made him wary of loving and families?

Robin said, 'I promised her. She didn't believe me, that it could work, but—— Our child will have the home I would have given her if she'd lived.' He blinked, hard, and his jaw went rigid. Melody knew he did not want her sympathy to erode his self-control.

He said, 'Somewhere near Los Angeles, I think. Or at least somewhere close to a major airport where I can get to LA in a couple of hours. I'll find a housekeeper. Someone who's good with kids.' A wife was what he needed, she thought, but with the shadow of Donna in his eyes she could not say so.

He said, 'I'll be there every night I can.' He caught her eyes and held them. 'Melody, I'm not going to keep Robbie here. You know what would happen. I'd take advantage of you. You'd tie up the rest of your life with my child. It's time you reached out for your own life. I'm not going to give you excuses to hide away.'

What would he think if she told him that her life was growing its own complexities? People talked about twins' lives running in parallel, but this was ridiculous! Robin, with a child he had unknowingly fathered. And Melody——

'I've got two weeks,' he said, moving away with Robbie. 'I'm going to put Robbie to bed and——'

'For two weeks?' She had missed something here.

He smiled. 'No, idiot. For a nap. Then I'll get on the phone and organise things. Get estate agents looking, get something fixed up temporarily. I'll take Robbie to LA with me, to my apartment, and get someone to look after him while I'm working.'

She said, 'The studio's booked a week from now.'

'Practice sessions. Robbie can come to them.' He grinned and she laughed, thinking it a good thing that she had been taking the baby into her music-room, getting him used to the sounds. He added, 'Not to the recording sessions.'

The twins stared at each other silently across the room. He had always been so much a part of her life, but as adults they had both stood alone, going their separate ways. Robin into the heart of the music scene, and Melody staying on the fringes, needing quiet and order.

Finally she nodded. She was going to miss Robbie, but she could not cling to him now that Robin was here. 'Two weeks,' she echoed. 'I'll have the songs ready for you next week in LA.'

'You'd better,' he retorted, smiling. 'Are they good?'

'Wait and see.' They both knew she would not share them until the work was finished, even though there was little to do now but the final polishing. 'See you in LA in two weeks,' she whispered, and although he did not leave for two more days that was their real farewell.

She should have been in the music-room that evening, but the soundproofing would block out the telephone if it rang. Wednesday night. Scott.

She was right beside the telephone when it rang, sitting in one of Charlie's big chairs in the living-room.

'How's Robbie?' he asked.

'Fine.' She settled into the deep chair, her legs curled up. 'Robin's putting him to bed right now. The doctor says the hernia looks as if it won't need surgery.'

'And Robin?' He sounded as if he were close, perhaps only a block away.

'Good. He's sad about Donna. And he wants to meet you, to ask about her. He and Robbie are going to LA in a couple of days.' And she was going to miss them terribly. She would be following soon, but she knew that she would not feel this sense of family in the madhouse of the practice sessions for Robin's new album.

'I'll be back on the tenth of June, for two weeks. We'll get together then.'

We? Did he mean to come to her? Or just to see Robin and the baby? She stared at the library of music on the far wall and told herself that this was her life. Stable, her hideaway on the islands. She had no room for what he did to her. Hadn't she come here to find herself, to concentrate on writing songs?

'And the music?' he asked, as if he sensed the motion of her thoughts.

'Almost done.' Next Wednesday she would be in Los Angeles with the tapes. She almost said it, told him what hotel so he could call there. Then she stopped herself, afraid she was taking too much for granted, assuming he wanted to know her movements. In the end she changed her words to, 'What's up in the Arctic?'

'Ice.' His voice was wry. 'Lots of ice. We've spent the whole week fighting it.'

'How do you break ice? Do you just ram into it?'

He explained how the ship rode up on to the ice until the ice knife under the water broke through. Sometimes the knife under the bow wasn't enough. Yesterday *Jonathan Cartier* had jammed in the ice. Scott described how he had got clear by rocking the ship, pumping water from port to starboard tanks inside the ship.

'Actually,' he said, 'I pushed buttons and talked a lot. It was the engineers who did the work. Lots of noise,' he added with a laugh. 'I slammed the throttles from full ahead to full astern so many times, the chief engineer was ready to come up on the bridge and have my head.'

Five minutes. It was over so soon. Then she was alone with her thoughts and a clear image of Scott sitting across from her, as if they had talked for hours.

Why did he call? Once he had called someone named Caroline. Did he call her now, from the frozen north? Melody hugged herself, wishing she knew where this was going. It was one thing to write wild, emotional songs, but she liked to know where her life was heading. Maybe it was all the years of their childhood, of rambling from backstage room to backstage room, but when Charlie and Amanda had parked the twins in Queen Charlotte, Melody had vowed she was going to keep control of her own life after that. She'd slipped, getting caught up in the music scene when her own songs had started to sell, trying to keep up with the madhouse of the recording industry, of Peter with his demands that she fit the image of a popular song-writer and the fiancée of an upwardly mobile talent agent.

Upwardly mobile! God, she hated that phrase. It summarised all her agonies in Los Angeles. No matter how hard she had tried, it had never quite worked. Thank God for Jeff, who had shown her what she was doing with a few critical words.

She shivered, wishing Scott were there to light the fire for her. She was scared. Things were happening. She was losing control, and she knew that she could not hide from the changes. She was not sure what she wanted, but knew that, when Scott Alexander had walked into her home with a baby in his arms, her life had changed. It was never going to be the same again.

CHAPTER SEVEN

MELODY stayed to watch the recording sessions. Robin was surprised, but did not ask her why. Peter was less restrained.

'As your agent, I'm glad to see you're coming to your senses,' he told her as they stood together in the back of the control room. She was wearing jeans and a bulky sweater, and he had already told her that she should dress up more, you never knew when you might run into a news man. Now he said, 'You should be here until the recording's done. Friday I'm booking the Chapels for a party. You'll——'

'No.' She looked at him. He was tall and thin and nervy, his blond hair carefully waved across his forehead, his eyes watchful. 'No, Peter. I'm not doing any publicity stuff. Robin's the performer, not me.'

He was gearing up to argue. He was a good agent, and she knew she would be crazy to leave his agency, but he was not going to dominate her life. She cut off his words quickly. 'Peter, I'll do interviews, even a talk show while I'm here if you really think it's important, but I'm not going on display with rounds of parties and angling for gossip columns.' She shook off his frown and said firmly, 'I hate cocktail parties and I loathe publicity dinners and I won't do it.'

He opened his mouth to protest and she snapped, 'Accept it, Peter.' It was an old argument with them by now, but one she was determined never to lose again. 'Now stop talking and let me hear what's happening with this song.'

108

She turned away and forgot Peter as she watched Robin and his band turning her poetry into what had to be a hit song when it was released. Even the cynical sound man had a moody look in his eyes as he twirled the dials in the control room. As she listened, she could almost pretend that this was everything, that she would walk from here back to her island retreat and into her music-room where the world could not invade.

She left in the third week of recording, taking a jet from Los Angeles to Vancouver where she retrieved her van from the parking lot. It was time for her to deal with what was happening to her.

She could have telephoned. She had his number, the telephone that would ring at his house on Cortes Island. She had never been to the island, had never seen the little harbour where he had once told her he was building his home. But he would be back there by now. At least, he would have left the Beaufort Sea. She had looked on her map when he called, but even now she didn't know if the Beaufort was part of the Arctic Ocean or not. The map wasn't clear and she had not asked. She should know, she thought absently. He worked up there, and he had her life in turmoil.

She had no idea what she would do if he was not there. Leave a note, she told herself sharply, swinging her car on to the ferry at Campbell River. Lord, her life was one long sequence of ferry boats. Ferry from Vancouver to Vancouver Island. The drive up the island to Campbell River, then another ferry to Quadra Island. Scott had picked a spot that was almost as remote as her Queen Charlotte Islands. To get to Cortes, she had discovered, she had to go island hopping. From Quadra, she took another small ferry to Cortes Island. His island hideaway was definitely out of the rat race!

She had no address, just the telephone number and the knowledge that he had property on Gorge harbour. She should have telephoned from Campbell River, where she could get a hotel room if it turned out he wasn't at home. But what the hell would she say? What if he didn't want her here? What if a woman named Caroline answered? God! For all she knew, he might be married to Caroline. He had never said he was single. That was an assumption she had made. She knew so little about him. Incredible, because she felt as if she had known him forever.

'The Gorge?' The grizzled old man walking along the gravel road frowned at her. She had driven off the second ferry and stopped to ask the way. He was wearing old, patched overalls and a lumberjack's shirt, and he had not shaved in years. He frowned at her and gestured. 'Over there. Where else would it be?'

The Gorge. She knew it when she found it. She stopped the car and looked out over the small, enclosed bay, the rock bluff that gave narrow entry to the sea beyond. She could live here, walking out in the morning along the shore, looking up to the green trees, out over the cool, dark water. Neighbours, but not too close. A place for quiet of the heart, and poetry. Songs.

She shoved the van into gear, frightened by the way her thoughts kept doing that, weaving Scott and his world into her dreams as if he could be nowhere else. She heard the wheels crunch as she pulled back on to the road, and she tried to harden her thoughts.

Scott was not the only person who lived on the Gorge. She passed several driveways that led to little worlds on the water. Too many to go knocking on doors hoping for the right one. She remembered the telephone booth back at the ferry landing and wondered if she should go back, call him after all and hold her breath for the note of welcome—or rejection—in his voice.

She drove along the road, following the curve of the bay.

The name was carved on a beautiful, polished piece of cedar hanging at the end of the drive. Alexander. It wasn't an unusual name, but she turned into the drive and stopped when she could see the peak of the roof.

Cedar shakes, still glowing reddish in the sunlight. A new roof that had not had time to weather into the beautiful grey of the shake roofing that was so common in older houses in the north. She took her foot off the brake and let the van roll a few feet.

The house belonged among the trees, at the side of the ocean. All cedar, the style reminiscent of traditional log cabins, but with a modern crispness of line. A warm house, rambling along the curve of the hillside. She could see the edge of a big veranda where he must sit to look out over the water.

And Scott.

He had not seen her. He was at the far end of the house, standing in a clearing among the trees. He was facing away from her, but she saw him swing the axe up. She had not realised until that moment that she would know him anywhere, from any angle.

She had time to leave, to run. She could reverse and quietly crunch her tyres back out of his driveway. He would never know she had been here. She could go back to Queen Charlotte and——

Some things could not be hidden forever. She felt the nervous excitement of needing to know what would be in his eyes when he saw her; the fear that he would see what was in her heart. Love.

She looked down and saw that her hands were clenching the wheel. She released the steering wheel, but

...er fingers were trembling. She put the van back in gear and rolled down the short hill, coming to rest right behind the shiny black truck.

She stared at it, remembering Scott in her home, their two vehicles sharing a driveway. He had complained about her drive. His was straighter. Perhaps he did everything more logically, more rationally than she did. Cleaned out his driveways and took precautions against dangers and risks.

Risks.

He swung the axe again. On the block, a piece of wood split cleanly, the two parts dropping neatly to the ground. He bent to pick up a piece of wood from the ground and throw it neatly on to the pile. Then the other piece. Then he turned towards the driveway and she could see nothing in his face, certainly not welcome.

She scrambled out of the van, afraid that he would come to her window and tell her to go back. She told herself that there was no reason for him to send her away. Not when he had called her from the Arctic to talk about nothing much, as if he had wanted only to hear her voice.

He was wearing old jeans and a T-shirt from a hotel in Tuktoyaktuk. She stared at it, concentrating on the weird spelling of the Eskimo word as he came closer. Anything to avoid staring up at his face, his eyes.

'Do they wear T-shirts in Tuktoyaktuk?' she asked nervously. 'I thought it would be all fur parkas up there.'

He stopped walking, just out of her reach. 'Summer sun gets up to Tuk for a bit.' His voice was not smiling, nor his body, all muscles and hardness through the dusty jeans and the shirt.

She looked up and his eyes were hard, too, with none of the welcome she had hoped to see. So the telephone calls had been for Robbie, not for her. She swallowed. 'I wasn't sure if I could find this place. All I knew was

Gorge harbour, on Cortes Island.' She shifted from one foot to the other, the heels of her sandals sinking into soft soil. She looked down and saw she was standing on new grass.

He said, 'I don't imagine you had much trouble. At least I was home.'

'Did you call me again? I was in LA.' Had he? Or had he come, knocking on her locked door? She wished she had not come today, because this was not a man she could open up and talk to. Not the same man who had walked into her house with a baby, who had called and chatted about icebreakers over satellite telephone.

He pushed back a damp lock of sandy brown hair that had been clinging to his forehead. She bit her lip and wondered how to change this from a tense, uneasy staring match into something friendlier. 'It's a warm day for chopping wood, isn't it?'

He shrugged.

She caught herself before she gnawed on her lip. She pushed her hands into the deep pockets of her red cotton skirt and wondered if he thought she looked too garish in red, wondered if he thought she looked nice at all. She had put on fresh lipstick on the ferry, had brushed her hair although it was already smooth waves and healthy shine.

He pushed his hands into the pockets of his jeans, pulling the fabric tight. 'What do you want, Melody?'

Her eyes followed the stretch of the denim, then jerked back to his face. She knew her colour was high. Had he noticed her looking? If so, there was nothing in his face. No smile, no warm teasing light in his hazel eyes.

Where was the sense that she could read his thoughts, that they were talking without words? She looked away to the warm cedar of his home, the water beyond rippled by a late-afternoon breeze.

'Can I come in?' She hated the note of pleading that somehow seeped into her voice.

He shrugged and turned away towards the house.

She struggled over a lump in her throat and managed to make her own voice impatient. 'If you don't want me to be here, I'll go back.' She might as well. She was not going to be able to tell him.

He turned to look at her. 'How are you going to get back? Swim?'

'The ferry.' She had to look away. Lord, this was terrible! She said, 'I think I'd better go. Now.'

He didn't say anything to that at first, but she could not seem to move. Then, finally, he said gently, 'Melody, the last ferry left five minutes ago.' Then he turned and led the way up on to his front veranda.

'Go ahead,' he said, stopping to take his boots off on the veranda. 'Go on inside.'

She would have liked to stay on the veranda for a moment, to look out over his rocky beach and the small harbour, but his impatient voice made her nervous. She followed his gesture and found herself in a big, open room, hardly furnished except for an easy chair and a sofa. And two walls filled with books.

The room did not seem bare. Here, as outside, he had used the warm cedar that grew so plentifully on the coast. The floor was some kind of hardwood, she thought, glowing and beautiful. The fireplace was the most modern thing in the room, styled to look traditional, but with glass doors that allowed light and heat to flow into the room, while controlling the air flow for efficient heating.

'Do you like it?'

She swung around. He was just inside the doorway. He looked more approachable to her without shoes. 'Yes,' she said, not smiling because he wasn't. For a second she thought he was anxious for her answer, but decided it was just that he was not very happy to have her here. She turned away, moving to the picture framed over the fire. 'Ice fields?' she asked. 'Somehow, with the fire and this room, they don't seem all that cold.' He didn't answer and she moved to look at the titles on his shelves. 'I thought you said your house was only half finished.'

'This half,' he answered, moving to the fire. She felt a blast of heat and heard the crackling as he opened the glass doors and bent to feed in more wood. 'The living-room and the kitchen are mostly done, except I've got to go shopping for some furniture one of these days. If you want to see bare walls, framing and joists, there's the back half, and upstairs.'

'Oh.' She would have been happy to have a tour, but he had not spoken as if it were really an invitation.

He stood up and she jerked back to the books. It was not getting better. She wished painfully that she had not come. She watched as he pushed his hair back, releasing a small chip of wood that had been caught in the waves.

'Look, can you fend for yourself here while I get cleaned up?'

'Yes.' She made an abrupt gesture. 'Of course I can. Go ahead.'

He frowned and seemed about to say something, then nodded and walked out of the room towards the back of the house. The unfinished part, he had said, but she heard the sound of water running a moment later. A shower, she thought, so more than the kitchen must be finished.

She would have put on music, but there was no stereo. She went to the books instead, but they were almost as intimidating as the granite of his eyes. She took out a geology book and tried to absorb the words when she

ened it, then gave up and pulled out a book of tall
ships. She stood, turning pages, listening to the water
running somewhere close by. Scott's shower. She turned
another page and admired an old boat with an abun-
dance of white, square sails.

When the telephone rang, she almost dropped the
book. Then a door opened or closed somewhere and
Scott's voice called to her.

'Get that, will you? Take a message.'

She answered the telephone. It was a woman calling,
her voice sharp and startled. 'I must have the wrong
number.' The voice rattled off a number.

'No, you've dialled right,' said Melody, looking down
at the number on Scott's phone.

'Where's Scott?'

'He's ... busy. Can I take a message?'

'No, I—— Yes, all right.' The voice became brisk. 'Ask
him to bring my nightgown and my toilet things in to
Campbell River. The nightgown's in the drawer in his
dresser, and—— He'll know where to find it.'

The line went dead. Melody put down the receiver.
Well, that was plain enough. She pushed her hands into
her pockets and tried to tell herself that she was curious
about this room, about the scenery. Anything but the
woman.

When Scott came into the room, she was at the
window, looking out at the trees. She did not turn when
she spoke. That way she was able to keep her voice
casual.

'The bedroom must be done, too.' She heard the bite
in her own voice, but could not seem to stop it. 'Because
she said she left her nightgown in your dresser, and would
you bring it to her. And her toilet bag.' She turned and
Scott was in the doorway. She added, 'She didn't say
what her name was.'

'Caroline.' His hair was still damp, just starting
wave as it dried. He was wearing a pair of corduroy
trousers and a soft, bulky sweater and his face was
flushed uncomfortably. He said, 'She——'

Melody made a sharp gesture. 'Don't tell me!' She
had to be crazy, letting herself dream about him. 'I knew
there was a Caroline. You called her from Queen
Charlotte. I just thought—I don't know what I thought.'
She gulped and said, 'That she didn't matter, I guess.'

'Yeah,' he said uncomfortably. 'Look, I——'

She spun away from him, but where was there to go?
'You don't have to explain anything. It's not—you don't
owe me any explanations, or——'

He laughed harshly. 'You mean I can sleep with
anyone I like, and you don't give a damn?'

She smoothed her hands on her skirt. 'No,' she
whispered. 'I—I don't mean that. I—I just don't want
to hear about her.'

'Hell!' She jumped and he said, 'Damn it, Melody!
I'm sorry, but—I don't—— If there are rules for this
sort of thing, I don't know them. Caroline—we were
friends.' He grimaced and said, 'Not all my friends leave
their nightgowns in my drawers.'

Were, he had said. Past tense. She bit her lip. 'She's
not a friend any more?'

'Not that kind,' he said. 'Not since—— It was you I
called when I was up in the Beaufort, not Caroline. It
was you I went to see the minute I——'

And she had not been home. Her fingers curled into
her skirt and she whispered, 'I was going to tell you.
The last time you phoned me. I—I almost gave you the
number of the hotel in LA, where I would be. But I—
I don't know. I guess I wasn't sure why you were calling
me, if you would call again.'

She could feel the flush in her cheeks, but the ice was gone from his eyes. She could see the long breath that escaped his body, leaving it relaxed. He smiled and asked, 'Do we owe each other any more explanations?'

She shook her head, because she was not ready to tell him her secrets yet. He said, 'All right, then. Why don't you stop looking as if you want to run? I won't bite.'

'Won't you?'

He must have seen the nervousness in her smile, because he said, 'Melody, you may be stranded here until the morning ferry, but I won't expect you to share my bed, if that's what you're worried about.'

'Oh.' She felt deflated, confused.

'Shall we find something to eat?' he suggested. 'Have you had supper?' She shook her head and he said, 'Stop looking as if I'm the big bad wolf and we'll get some supper.'

She followed him through an unfinished hallway into a big kitchen. She was surprised at the modern brightness after the warm, glowing darkness of the living-room.

'No, Caroline did not design it,' he said sharply, reading her thoughts. 'I did. With the help of the cabinet-maker I hired.'

'I like it,' she said, and half smiled when she realised that her voice was placating. Then he laughed and somehow everything was all right.

'Omelettes?' he suggested.

'All right.'

She chopped the onions and he wiped her eyes when she cried from the fumes. Then he burned the omelette and insisted that he could do better.

It was going to be all right. She told herself that, watching him burn the omelette. 'Charlie always insisted he could cook,' she said, laughing, wrinkling her nose. 'You really burnt it, didn't you?'

'Yeah.' He opened a cupboard door and exposed a flip-top rubbish bin. 'Let's start from scratch. And this time I'll watch the stove instead of watching you.'

She gasped and he said, 'And who's Charlie?'

'My father. And he can't cook. When he threatens to, it means he's hungry and Amanda—my mother—better get in the kitchen or else he'll smoke up the whole house.' She smiled fondly. 'He's a real manipulator.'

'You love them?' He was keeping his eye on the pan this time, and the omelette came out of the pan light and aromatic.

'Yes. It wasn't a very conventional childhood, and their footloose lifestyle doesn't suit me, but Robin and I always knew they loved us.' He nodded and she remembered that his background had been foster-homes and probably not enough love.

'What about men?' he asked, and she did not turn the subject back to childhood. Sometime, he might want to share his with her. Maybe.

'Only one,' she said. 'We were engaged. That was when I thought being a song-writer meant I had to live in the madhouse with the musicians. He thought so, too.' She shrugged. 'He wanted me to be someone else.'

He was watching her. Somehow, she did not mind. He asked, 'And what did you want?'

She met his eyes. 'Not Peter.'

'Peter?' he repeated. 'Jeff called and asked you to call him back. At Peter's.'

She nodded. 'He's my talent agent. And Robin's. And Jeff's, for that matter. He's good, but I'm not in love with him. Sometimes I wonder if I ever was.'

He managed not to burn the second omelette. They sat together in the breakfast nook, eating slowly. 'It's good,' she said.

'What about Jeff?'

She looked at him. He was watching her, perhaps looking for a reaction. She wondered if she should resent the questions, but she wanted him to care. 'He's a good friend. When I was going nuts trying to be the fastest rat on the treadmill, he helped me see what I was doing to myself.' She stirred the omelette and said slowly, 'I've only been writing my songs in Queen Charlotte for a couple of years. Before that—— Jeff helped me find the equipment I needed, and he came visiting and brought me gossip and—— He's been with Robin's band from the beginning.' He was waiting for her to say something else and she said, 'We've never been lovers. He's more like another brother.'

'Caroline and I were lovers. You know that.' He stirred the omelette around on his plate without eating any. 'I think she appealed to me because she's all tied up in her career and didn't need me.' He shrugged. 'Maybe I appealed to her because I wasn't asking her to give up her independence or make any commitments that would interfere with her plans to become head of her department at the college.'

She frowned. It sounded cold-blooded.

He said, 'My parents died when I was eight years old. I started learning then that it's best not to tie your happiness to someone else's whim.' He said it flatly, as if it were a fact that had not changed.

'What about Donna?' He did not answer, but his sister was gone. Another lesson that might make it hard to trust in someone else. She dropped her fork on to the plate, and whispered, 'What about Robbie?' But in her heart, she was wondering, What about me?

He washed up their few dishes. She dried, opening cupboards to find the places for the plates and glasses.

'I thought of getting a dishwasher,' he told her as he rinsed out the sink.

'You could put it over there, couldn't you? There's room at the end of the counter. Actually, I don't use the dishwasher in my house all that much. Just when company descends.'

'Does that happen often?' He grinned.

'Men knocking on my door, handing me babies? All the time.' She fell abruptly silent then, thinking of what she had come to tell him, but she wanted very much to enjoy this evening first. 'Sometimes it's a madhouse. Charlie and Amanda send friends sometimes. Can we go for a walk? Would you show me the rest of your house?'

'Outside first,' he said. 'While there's still light.'

He loaned her a big, bulky sweater that hung halfway down her thighs, then he took her out walking along his rocky beach. He told her about the old man who lived around the curve of the bay, who remembered when the Gorge was wild territory accessible only by private boat. They speculated together on whether the pirates had ever discovered what a perfect pirates' den Gorge harbour would make, and he told her about his plans to have a wharf put in.

'I've got to straighten out the water rights first,' he said, and she memorised the lines that formed on his forehead as he concentrated on the prospect of getting through red tape.

'Would you have a boat?' She had never been out in the water in anything but a ferry.

'I don't think so, at least not a big one.' He stopped, looking back at his property, his house, as the setting sun bathed it in warm tones. 'I've got friends who have a sail-boat. It would be nice to have a place for them to tie up when they come cruising up here. I've got a run-about on the trailer in the garage. It's enough for what

I want, good for a run into Campbell River in an emergency or an afternoon salmon fishing.'

Later, she could not have said what else they talked about. Everything. Nothing. It was dark when he brought her back into his house. They went first to her van for her suitcase, which he insisted on carrying for her.

He did not kiss her. The moon was rising as the sun went down, but when he put her case into his bedroom, he said neutrally, 'You're tired. Get some sleep. The morning is soon enough for a tour of the house.'

Then he left her alone in the bedroom and she was crazy enough to open the drawers until she found one drawer which was empty except for a lacy black nightgown.

Melody had never looked good in black. She caught herself before she slammed the drawer shut, knowing that Caroline made no real difference. Caroline was history in Scott's life now. But what was Melody?

CHAPTER EIGHT

THE upstairs was a mess, sawdust and plaster dust everywhere. Scott told Melody to be careful not to trip over anything, and that it was going to be two more bedrooms with dormer windows and views of the ocean.

'And this part?' she asked, standing in the middle of the biggest, empty room.

He shrugged and saw her eyes crinkle with laughter. 'I don't know. I'll finish it, I guess, and wait for all my friends to descend on me, looking for a place to sleep.'

Looking at Melody as she stood at the newly framed window, he almost told her it would make a terrific music-room. That window could be shuttered easily. The walls could have soundproofing added. He had not yet put the plaster on them.

It scared him, thinking like that. He did not want to be aware of every move Melody made, every breath she took, but when she breathed he felt the pressure on his lungs. He liked the way she always went to the windows when she entered a room, as if the view meant as much to her as the walls. Caroline had walked around frowning at the exposed joists, the unfinished floors. Melody seemed to see through the construction to the dream he had of his finished home.

He did not want to compare her to Caroline. Because there was no comparison, and that frightened him most of all. Calling home from the Beaufort had suddenly come to mean talking to Melody.

He remembered the third time he had gone to the rig to call her, listening to the empty ringing. He had felt a sick fear that he would never talk to her again, never hold her in his arms again. He had waited for the next week, the next chance to call. Had waited for some message. Had finally flown out of Tuk to Calgary and gone to her island instead of to his own.

Her van had been gone. Her house had been dark. Empty houses and closed doors. He had managed to guess that she had gone to the recording sessions in Los Angeles. She had not said she was going, but he knew that was the deadline she had been working against in her song-writing.

It was not that she was gone, but that she had not bothered to tell him. As if it were not important enough. As if *he* were not important enough. That was when he realised that he had done exactly what he had vowed never to do.

An affair, he had told himself. After all, Melody was committed to her song-writing. She liked being a recluse between visits from friends and her brother. She was not looking for a deep relationship, for commitments or risks. Neither was he, damn it!

He had not expected to find that he was the one with his heart out. The discovery, standing on her dark doorstep, had sent him back here, panicked and determined to throw himself into construction, into reading about geology. Anything but thinking about her.

He had ploughed into the books. Every year he tried to learn something to fill the gaps in his education. He had never gone back to school, but he tried to make up for it by reading, studying, learning about the world he lived in. This year, he had decided, he would pursue books with a vengeance and to hell with the notion of getting a stereo to learn more about music so that he could share it with Melody.

As a child he had vowed never to give anyone the power to hurt him again by walking out on him or kicking him out So why was he up here, showing her his home and hoping she would like it? Why was he fighting the impulse to tell her how he could change it for her to share?

An affair, for God's sake. A friendship. Not a life.

'What's wrong?' she asked, turning to him as if she could see the turmoil inside him. She was wearing his sweater again, because the heating was not installed upstairs yet.

He pushed his hair back. 'Nothing. I've got to work on the fence at the back today. I want to put stain on before it rains.'

It would be better after she was gone. Then he would make himself remember that she was Robbie's aunt, too dangerous for touching.

'Oh?' She made it a question, asking, 'Do you want me to go?' She bit her lip.

He shoved his hands into his pockets to avoid touching her. 'You're likely to get paint-spattered if you don't.' He tried not to think about making love to her with the firelight playing on her glowing, naked flesh, with her eyes dark and passionate as he bent to kiss and possess.

'How's Robbie?' he asked desperately, pushing away his over-active imagination. She had been here since yesterday afternoon, yet somehow there had been no time to talk about his nephew.

He listened to her talking about Robbie, about her brother, and he knew it wasn't going to work. He was going to touch her, and if she did not run or scream, he was in trouble.

'You could stay a while,' he said, harshly cutting across her account of Robin's running into a reporter when he was out walking the baby in his new pram.

She fell silent, staring at him, her eyes wide and black and unfathomed. What the hell was he doing? Setting himself up to be slapped in the face? So she had made love with him. Once. It didn't mean—no, damn it! He didn't *want* it to mean more! He made certain nothing showed in his voice. He said, 'If you're taking a holiday, you could do some painting, some hammering if you like. You need a holiday.' She half smiled and he grinned, although inside he was afraid she would say yes and he knew he was in too deep. 'Or just sit around and read,' he added, and heard the hopefulness in his own voice.

Her hands moved to push into her pockets, but the sweater was in her way. He let his own hands free and possessed hers. Her fingers were cold, trembling. He rubbed them between his hands, to warm them.

She said, 'I'd better take the painting. You don't have a lot of light reading in those shelves.'

'We can go into Campbell River and raid the book stores,' he offered. Then he released her hands because he could feel the tension growing inside himself. He tried to tell himself it was nothing more than a shared holiday, an affair that would be a pleasant memory next year, but he kept remembering how he had felt standing on her doorstep, knowing she was gone and not knowing where.

Melody linked her hands together when he released them. In a second he would kiss her. She could see his eyes turning from hazel to a low fire, his firm lips parting just slightly. She knew that she had to stop him.

'No?' he said, and it was only half a question. He was picking up something from the tension in her, or did he simply read the thoughts right out of her mind? He stepped back and she saw relief in his eyes, as if he had not really wanted to want her.

'Not——' Not right now. Not yet. She licked her lips
and knew the words were not going to come. Practising
saying it was one thing, but this was impossible. She
wanted to stay, take the holiday he had offered. She
wanted to put on an old shirt of Scott's and stand beside
him, painting stain on to his fence. She wanted to read
his books, to watch him lighting the fire in the fireplace.
She wanted to talk and listen and share the silences . . . to
make love with him again.

She knew she could not possibly stay without telling
him first. She gulped and said, 'I guess I'd better go.'

'Why did you come?'

She could not read anything in his face. He was
waiting, watching, the ship's commander suspending
judgement. Crazily, that made it easier, because she could
harden her own voice too, and her mind. She turned
away from him so that he could not see into her eyes.
She stared through the window at the smooth, shining
water of the little bay, the narrow gorge that opened out
to the ocean. She said, 'I thought you should know, that
you had a right to know . . . I'm pregnant.'

She turned and he was staring at her. She wasn't sure
what it was in his eyes. He blinked and she thought
maybe it was shock. Of course it would be shock. She
had wanted it to be joy, but she should have known to
keep the fairy-tales in her music-room.

He said slowly, 'Say that again.'

She didn't. He had heard her the first time. She could
not keep staring at him, wondering what on earth he was
reading in her eyes. Was he reading her young dreams
of happy-ever-afters? Dreams that had been twisting their
way into her mind ever since that morning when he had
turned up on her front doorstep.

He pushed a rough hand through his hair, frowned
and asked, 'But how——'

'I wasn't on the Pill or anything.'

It was anger now, in his eyes, although his voice was as cold as the ocean where he piloted his ships. 'I asked you and you said——'

She remembered the warm fire, the heat that had flashed between them, undeniable as if they were two halves of one soul aching for unity. She gulped and admitted, 'You asked if I was prepared, and I—I didn't mean birth control. I just——'

He turned away from her. She did not realise he was going downstairs until she heard his boots on the stairs, steady and deliberate. She followed him, her sandals clattering down the stairs. She came to a stop in the living-room, out of breath, staring at him across the room. He was standing at the door and she wondered if he was intending to walk out on her, or to kick her out.

'Scott——'

He said flatly, 'I don't believe it. You can't be that naïve!'

Couldn't she? She had turned thirty last Christmas Day, but she had never really loved before, not in the way a woman loved a man. All her loving had been in songs, in fantasy. Perhaps she had hidden in her own fantasies, finding them safer than what she felt now.

She had been insane to come. She had thought——

He had a right to know, that's what she had thought. But under that, some crazy part of her had thought that he might feel what she did: a wild warm excitement, a rightness that the touch of a loving stranger had given birth to a life. Fate. Belonging.

She did not want to love anyone like this, so painfully. Not unless he could love her back. She pushed her hands into her pockets. She was cold in spite of the fire he had lit in his fireplace, despite the warm cedar. It was his eyes, and she knew there was never going to be anything for them.

Except the child they had created.

He was tensed up like a wire, his eyes almost glazed, his jaw clenched. Even his hands were clenched into fists at his side. What did he think she was going to do to him? Did he think she was trying to trap him into marriage?

She jerked her eyes away from him, but he was all around. The picture, the books, the fire, even the glimpses of water outside. She said raggedly, 'Look, I'm not interested in being lectured. I only came to tell you because——' she gulped '—because it's not the sort of thing you put in a letter. And I thought you had a right to know.'

She had thought he would welcome her, welcome her child. Secret fantasy, not acknowledged even to herself. Crazy woman. Fantasising song-writer. Poet.

He said flatly, 'What do you expect of me?'

He was staring at her and she could feel her eyes burning, her lids open too wide and her skin stretched too tightly over her face. If she didn't get out of here, she was going to cry. She must not let him see her cry, not when he was looking at her like that, his eyes harsh and his mouth a line of judgement.

She saw him swallow. His nostrils were flared, his voice bitterly angry. 'What did you expect, Melody? Did you think I would welcome your news? What was I supposed to say? Let's get married and have a happy-ever-after?'

She shook her head, although maybe that *was* what she had dreamed. He prowled angrily across his living-room and came back to confront her.

'What the devil do I know about families? About babies? Nothing!' His face was all harsh lines and angles. 'I can barely remember my own mother. All I know is from the outside, looking in. I haven't a damn clue in hell how to be on the inside, and you'd be crazy to think we could—we could...'

'Love each other?' It hurt to swallow, hurt more to whisper, 'Couldn't we try?'

'If that's what you thought——' He cleared his throat, turned to stare grimly at a tree outside. 'Why do you think I brought Robbie to you in the first place? I was desperate to get him off my hands. A baby needs a father who knows what the hell he's doing. All I know about families is what I learned as a kid. I learned how not to get thrown out. If I did enough chores, I got to stay. Maybe.'

Her hands reached out towards him, wanting to soothe the pain she could feel in him. 'Scott——'

He jerked away. 'A woman needs a man who can love both her and her baby without messing it up.' He started prowling again, came to rest in front of her, staring at her bleakly.

She said, 'You're afraid to try, afraid to take a chance. We could——'

'No, we *couldn't*!' He crammed his hands deeply into his pockets and turned to glare at the fire.

She stared at a place in the middle of the window and said tightly, 'The baby's not going to go away, Scott.'

His hands curled into fists inside his pockets. 'I'll—we'll make some kind of—some sort of financial arrangement.'

Oh, God! She could feel the tears coming. This was worse than she could have imagined. She walked past him. Then she was on the veranda, staring at nothing, and he was behind her. She made herself move, across the open expanse to the stairs, down to the grass.

She got to her van and the keys were still there. She had not even thought of keys, of her bag. She stared at the dashboard and knew she could not walk back into that house for her bag. It was in his bedroom, with her suitcase.

She turned the starter, but nothing happened except for the whine of the buzzer telling her to do up her seatbelt. She sat there, staring at the windscreen, and finally she realised that she had forgotten to put the car in parking gear when she stopped. The emergency brake was on, but the gear-shift was in gear.

If she sat here long enough, messing up the simple job of driving away, he would come through the door and she would have to look at his eyes again and know he was never going to care for her in the way she needed.

Never going to love her.

She must not cry. Whatever she did, she had to keep from letting the tears out until she was somewhere far away. The engine caught, finally, and she started reversing.

He was there, standing in the doorway, the back door, staring after her, blurry through the moisture in her eyes. She kept going, trying to go straight back and steady. He did nothing to stop her.

A giggle escaped her, but it was half a sob. What was he going to do about her suitcase? Would he send it to her? She might open her door to a knock and find a courier there, her suitcase returned. If this went on, his bedroom would be littered with mementoes of women who had once shared his touch but not his heart.

She was out of his driveway before she realised that she could not go on. She would willingly have risked driving forever without her driver's licence, just to avoid facing him again. But she could not even get off his island without her bag. No money for ferry fares, no credit cards for petrol. Not even a bank card to get cash from some strange, shiny bank.

* * *

There was no choice. She could sit here on a rock, looking out over the water forever, but the fact was that she could not get off Cortes Island without at least her purse, her money.

She had to go back and get it.

She hugged herself, realising that she still wore his sweater. She should have taken it off, put on her own jacket which was secure inside her suitcase. In his bedroom. It was one thing to say it, in her mind. I'll go back. Different to drive up and face him again. She could feel the nervousness quivering in her stomach, the adrenalin pumping, telling her to run, get the hell away from this whole mess. Hide somewhere. Plug herself in to some music and make the world go away.

She wrapped her arms tighter around herself. Around his baby. She wanted to think of it as hers, but she wanted it to be a boy with sandy brown hair that waved just a little. And hazel eyes that would look at her and smile. Oh, lord! This was terrible. She was turning into a stupid ball of jelly, tears coming every time she thought of his name, his eyes, his smile. Even his cold frown.

She would have nightmares of saying, 'I'm having your baby. When you touched my soul, we made a life of love.' Nightmares of her lips open and her eyes vulnerable, and his hard rejection, in his eyes and his jaw and the broad, hard back he turned on her.

He did not want her, did not want her child. She had read fantasies into the way he had held Robbie tenderly, the way he had moved into her life and her heart with crazy little actions like tending her fire and doing her dishes and cooking her breakfast.

Something moved out on the water. An otter? Or perhaps a dolphin? She was too far away, too high up to see clearly. She rubbed her eyes and it disappeared as the water came clear. She could not stay here forever.

The day would go, and she would be stuck here for another night. She had to get away, back to her own place where she could close doors against the world.

Cars kept driving by on the road behind her. She had pulled the van into a clearing, had walked to the rock on the water's edge. This didn't seem to be anyone's property, just a clearing on the Gorge. But sometimes the cars slowed and eventually someone might stop and try to talk to her.

Hi. Stranger around here?

Are you lost?

Or it might be Scott, come with her bag, helping her to be gone from his life.

She could not hide out on this rock forever. Could not face him either. Maybe on another day, after she got her defences up. She tried to turn what she was feeling into a song, but the aching would not turn into fantasy. Maybe it never would, and she would always feel it as a wound she could not erase with music.

Damn! Action. She needed action. She had always hated movies where the heroine agonised all over the screen, huddling in misery instead of getting up and doing something.

If he was outside, painting as he had said, then perhaps she could sneak into his house and get her purse out. He might never even know she had been there. Then she could get off his bloody island and back to her own.

She was not sure how far she had driven along the bay, knew only that she could see what she thought was the peak of his roof. If she drove back, he would see her van when it entered his drive. On the other hand, she could not safely park on the road by his drive. She might break into his house for her bag, then come back to find another driver had sideswiped her van because he'd parked on a blind curve. That was all she would need to turn this day into even more of a disaster!

She decided to walk back, but first she pulled the van further from the road, so that it was half hidden by an old maple tree. When she walked to the road and looked back, the brown van hardly showed from the road. Just in case Scott had driven after her, it was best if the van did not show.

Why fool herself? He was not going to come after her. She had walked away, had saved him the bother of sending her off. But why had he talked as if he cared last night, asking about the men in her life? And this morning, hadn't it been he who'd suggested she stick around?

But that was before she had told him about the baby. He might have been willing to love her a little, for a while, but there wasn't enough love in him for both her and a baby.

It was in the whole pattern of his life. There was no one in the centre of his life. He wanted it that way. She should have listened more closely, because last night, as they'd talked during his second try at cooking omelettes, he had told her that commitment wasn't in his dictionary. Until this morning, she hadn't realised that he meant he was afraid of trying.

It was a longer walk than she had thought, especially in the flimsy sandals that had been good for driving, good for standing around the studio in LA. Not good for walking the gravel shoulder of the road, but with the occasional car coming past fast and unexpectedly she dared not walk on the road itself.

There was a time, as a child, when her feet had been tough from the beaches of the Queen Charlotte islands. Then she would have thrown off her sandals and gone barefoot on the gravel, but now she gritted her teeth and tried to pretend she was not developing a blister where the strap rubbed across her big toe.

A car came from behind, slowing to a crawl. She kept moving, staring at the trees, hoping the driver would not stop. She did not want to talk to anyone, simply could not handle even the most basic social contact at this moment. After a moment of hesitation, the driver surged past and she was alone again.

How many more properties until she came to the board with his name on it? The next corner, perhaps. She looked down and plodded on. Then she put her foot down on a small rock and her ankle turned, jarring her whole body and leaving her with a sick feeling in her stomach. She closed her eyes and let the pain flow through her, and after a while it faded. She flexed the ankle and decided it was all right, and after a while the ache faded as she walked on.

His driveway. Where was Scott? She moved slowly, walking on the mossy growth at the side of the trees, hoping for silence and invisibility, wishing there were some other way to get off Cortes Island. Crawling back into the lion's den wasn't her first choice, but the only alternative was breaking into some stranger's home and stealing another person's purse.

Oh, lord! She should have used her fantasy time to weave stories of burglars slipping invisibly into log houses.

She heard him before she saw him. He was at the far end of the house. She could hear the slam of his axe hitting a block of wood, the thud of the splintered piece falling to the ground. Steady, regular, his axe smashing violently into the firewood. Taking out his anger, she decided. There was a violence to the rhythm that had not been there the day before.

She did not have to wonder why he was not painting, his chosen task for the day. Chopping wood was more satisfactory. He was probably fantasising that it was her head on the block as he swung. She shook that thought away. Foolish. She was the one with the fantasies. He kept his life under control, each event planned. His house was growing as he had planned. His nephew was firmly in his natural father's hands, as Scott had planned.

Her pregnancy had not been planned, because she had told him she was prepared and he had believed her. So he was rejecting it in a storm of wood-chips. Did that mean that he felt something other than simple rejection? If so, by the time he had finished piling the fresh wood, he would have worked out a plan to get even this event under control.

Some kind of financial arrangement, he had said. She did not want to be part of some cold plan for organising unwanted . . . unwanted lovers . . . unwanted babies.

She crossed the driveway to the far side, slipping into the trees. Thank goodness she had not put on the red skirt today, but a leaf-green one with a white blouse. And Scott's sweater covered the brilliance of her blouse pretty well. She thought that she might blend into the trees if he looked up.

He was wearing a checked shirt, so he had changed since she left. Maybe that was what had sent him out here in a fury of chopping: finding her bag and suitcase in his bedroom. She took a deep breath and stepped on a stick that snapped loudly.

She froze. From the water she could hear a faint whisper of water on rock. From the woodpile, nothing. She could not see him, either, but then the red checked shirt emerged as he stood up. Breathless, she waited for him to turn and seek her out of the trees with sharp eyes.

A bird cried overhead. Abruptly, Scott moved, then she saw the glint of the axe just before she heard the impact of metal on wood. He had not heard her, or had decided that the sound was nothing but the natural sounds of the forest.

She could not get her lungs working properly again until she had the bulk of his house between them. Then she stopped and sank to the ground, sitting on soft moss and breathing deep, ragged breaths until her heart stopped slamming into her ribs.

It was a good thing she had not set out on a life of crime. It was one thing to contemplate slipping into a house undetected, but the fact was that she was a bloody coward. The thought of Scott coming upon her, standing there with his shoulders squared and demanding harshly what the hell she thought she was doing——

The front door, through the veranda. That way she would not come in view of the woodpile again until she was slipping away. She took her sandals off at the bottom of his steps, remembering how they had clattered as she came downstairs only an hour ago. Or was it a lifetime ago?

She pushed the sandals into her big pockets, her fingers curling around the van keys in her right pocket, seeking reassurance that she hadn't lost her keys now, too. Then she went silently up the stairs and on to his veranda.

He had left the front door hanging open, the cool morning flowing into his home. She slipped inside, leaving it open, too. The fire was lower now, just glowing through the glass of the fireplace. He had not put any more wood on. She moved away from its beckoning warmth, away from the living-room, from his books and the picture of the Arctic ice. Into the hallway that was not panelled yet, with bare studs in the wall and the white of electrical wiring running along the studs.

His bedroom door was closed. She knew that she had left it open, but he would have slammed it closed after he changed his shirt. Trying to shut her away, because she had left her possessions behind. She opened it slowly, quietly. There were no creaking boards or doors in this house. No mistakes, because he was building it as it should be. She was the mistake, and she supposed he was out there regretting that he had ever looked at Melody Connacher, had ever touched her, had ever loved her. Because, damn it, he had loved her, whether he admitted it or not. It hadn't been just sex between them.

She thought of Robin's Donna, afraid to trust the man she loved, to share his life. Twins, she and Robin, living parallel lives. She shuddered, realising that if there had been a chance of a relationship with Scott she had blown it by dumping too much on him, too soon. Babies. Commitment. Forever. Love. It had felt like love, but he would not let love in. He had built walls to keep the loving out.

Her bag was on the dresser. She picked it up and pushed the strap up over her shoulder. Her suitcase was sitting open on the floor near the window. She wondered if she could close it and take it with her, and still be quiet enough.

Her heart was beating in rhythm with the swing of his axe. Here, inside, the sound was muffled, but impacting on her heart. She crossed to the case and pushed her things down, closed the lid and leaned on it to snap the locks. Then she froze.

The telephone was ringing. Her eyes flew to the bedroom door. He had closed it, but it was open now. If he came into the house to answer the telephone, he might realise she was here. As she heard the third ring, the axe bit into the wood again. Perhaps he could not hear it, or simply did not want to answer.

Was it Caroline? Would he go back to Caroline now? Had Melody read him entirely wrong? He had spoken as if she were the reason that Caroline was history, but that might have been her own desires interpreting his words.

A fourth ring. Five. Then six. If it was Caroline, then she was persistent, and she might win. Melody swallowed a lump and wondered if there was anything she could change by staying, by walking out there to the woodpile and telling him she was in love with him.

It stopped on the ninth ring. There was silence then, not even the sound of the axe biting into wood. The walls of the bedroom seemed to move in and out with each breath she took, the silence echoing and pounding in her ears. Then she heard the door.

Footsteps, not quiet or careful. He was in the kitchen, she thought. She heard the refrigerator open with a sucking sound, then close. A cupboard door. She had not upset the fabric of his life enough to affect his appetite.

She realised then that the room was starting to spin. She sat down on the edge of the bed, afraid she would fall and make a thud that would bring him in here. How long would it be before he went out again? Or might he come to his bedroom and pack her things to get them out of his sight?

She did not hear the door slam. Maybe he left it open again. Or perhaps he did close it, but she was caught in the memory of last night, sleeping in his bed, catching the scent of Scott on the sheets, falling asleep and dreaming that he held her in his arms, that he whispered how much he loved her, how she was the one woman who could turn his life to warmth and closeness.

The first she knew of his leaving the house was the sight of his red checked shirt through the window. She jumped and almost called out. She could not see his face. Only his back, walking away. She got up and went to the window, and there he was, walking towards the back corner of the house with a can of wood stain in his left hand.

Back to normal. He had planned to stain the cedar fence today. At least she had not prevented that.

She left the way she had come, carrying her suitcase and moving in stockinged feet, stopping to put on her sandals when she was on the grass. Out of his house. Out of his life.

CHAPTER NINE

PERCUSSION instruments drowned out the tempo of the bass guitar. Then nothing, just the echo of rhythm in the silence of the room.

Melody dropped her hands from the synthesiser. The multi-track recorder turned silently, recording nothing. She stared at the equipment, knowing it was useless. She had no idea if the song was good or bad. It felt dead, the words without meaning, the notes disconnected. She did not know if the lack was in her, or in the music she had written.

Last night she had reached for the telephone to call Robin, intending to play the music over the telephone and ask him if it was any good. He would have been astounded. She had never let anyone else listen to a song unless she was sure it was good. If she had no confidence in it, she was not willing to share any of her work.

She turned everything off and took the tape out of the recorder, placing it in its protective plastic case. Then she closed the door on the music-room and went out, locking the house.

She went to the radio station, although it was hours too early for *Island Time*. She wanted busy work, so she buried herself in the record library. She picked out other people's music, talked her way through *Island Time*, and felt a little better.

It was returning home that was difficult. It had never bothered her before when the house was empty. If she wanted to talk to the world, there was the ham radio.

And there was the music-room, always before filled with life and feeling. But now, three days living alone and she was ready to climb the walls.

She accepted Bev's invitation to dinner, spent an evening playing with Bev and John's two-year-old holy terror. The next day she went down to the college and picked up a copy of the new calendar; but none of the night-school courses would be starting until September, so that did her no good. She needed something to fill her hours now, to stop her from thinking.

Then she went back to the radio station, into Laurie's office, to ask the station manager about going to work full time.

Laurie was sorting through the results of a survey of listeners, turning endless pages of computer printout. She looked up at Melody, frowning, her lively dark eyes worried.

'Are you sure you want to, Melody? Full time, I wouldn't be able to release you for the recording sessions, you know.'

Melody wondered if she would ever be able to write another song. She could not say that to Laurie.

'Think about it,' said Laurie. 'And if you ever want to talk, I'm here, you know. About anything.'

Friends. She had more friends than she deserved. Jeff and Laurie and John and Bev. Yet she knew that she could not go to any of them for help. She had to be strong, to start planning for herself and the child. She had to find her own answer, not someone else's.

She went to her doctor and came home with a vitamin supplement and a book on looking after herself and the child inside. Queen Charlotte being the small town that it was, she suspected that within twenty-four hours everyone would know Melody Connacher was expecting a child. No one would be likely to say anything, not to her, but there were few secrets in a town this size. She did not think any of her friends would criticise her, but they would expect her eventually to confide in them.

Plans, she thought, and she went down to the basement to start cleaning out the storeroom. It had been waiting ten years or so to be organised, but now seemed a good time. Some of it was bits and pieces of Charlie and Amanda's theatre life. Some of it was from Robin and Melody's youth. She thought that if she cleaned the house, she might find her thoughts tidier, more purposeful.

At least there were the royalties coming in, and with Robin turning so many of her songs into hits Melody and the baby should not have to worry about how to pay the grocery bill for a while. Better if she could write more good songs, but if not she would go back and tell Laurie that she wanted to dedicate all her time to the radio station. She would tell her about the baby, and Laurie would understand.

Crouched on the floor amid the dusty memories, Melody picked up a bundle of paper with a garter holding them together. She slipped the garter off. A blue garter. Something blue for Amanda's wedding?

Love-letters, from Charlie to a younger Amanda. She thought of the letters Robin had written to Donna. Love-letters. Lovers.

She put Charlie's letters back where she had found them, without reading them. They were private, not hers to intrude on. She sat cross-legged on the basement floor, thinking about her parents as lovers for the first time. With a child's narrow view, she had never thought of their romance. She knew them as characters, as friends to each other and their children, as partners on the stage...but not as lovers.

What would they think when she told them she was going to have a child? They would accept it, but they would worry about her. From a distance, she thought wryly, because she and Robin had never been encouraged to lean on their parents. Perhaps that was the pattern they had learned, standing alone, because, despite the ways in which they were close, Robin had not told her of his love for Donna, and Melody was not reaching to tell her twin that she loved a man who did not want loving.

When the knock came, she knew that it would be Scott.

He had been in her mind, lying in the background through everything else, the doctor and the radio station and Charlie's love-letters to Amanda. In a few days, he would be back on his icebreaker in the Beaufort Sea. She had been counting the days. She thought she knew him well enough to know that he would want to settle his loose ends before he left.

She went up the stairs, dusting her hands off on the seat of her jeans. She felt that she was watching herself move, observing herself as she opened the door. Then he was there, in front of her, broad shoulders blocking out the light. His hazel eyes were serious, thoughtful. She wondered what he intended for them, for their child. Her eyes went past him, to the shiny black truck. She thought of the first time she had seen him, Robbie hidden in the truck.

He must have read her thought because he said, 'Nothing in the truck this time. Can I come in?'

She stepped back. He passed her and walked into the public part of her living-room. She closed the door and stood at the end of the sofa, watching him prowl the deep carpet. He stopped to stare at the fireplace. For a crazy moment, she thought he was going to kneel and start tending the fire. She wondered how she could think of this as the *public* area when they had made love just there, lying together on the deep carpet in front of the fire.

'I've been thinking.' His voice was strained. He swung around and they were staring at each other, like two people across a classroom. She had known he would be like this. Frozen. 'We'll get married,' he said coldly, deliberately.

She swallowed. 'Why?' There was no love in his eyes, his voice. She wondered what kind of a marriage it could be.

'Babies need families.' His face was expressionless.

She had to move. She gulped and walked past him, to the fire. She knew it was a warm June day, but she felt the trembling inside herself, like cold. Babies need families. Scott's family had been torn from him at a young age. He was still talking, his words falling into the quiet of her living-room. She tried to concentrate on what he was saying.

'... get married right away. I've got five days before I go back to the Beaufort. It's just long enough. We'll go down to the government agent this afternoon and apply for a licence.'

He dominated the room. He would dominate her life, but when she turned to face him his eyes were flat and lifeless. Not even angry. Whatever had been between them, the warmth and the sharing which had semed strong from the first day—— If she married him with his jaw set and his eyes determined, then it would be gone. He would have locked himself into a trap. A trap of his own choosing, but she would be the gaoler.

She moved her hand, a spasmodic movement. 'You make it sound like getting a fire permit.' Her voice was jerky, too.

Fire. There was no fire in him at all. Not now. He had it all under control. He started pacing, then stopped and stared at her, his hands clasped behind his back. He had worked all this out. What she thought, what she felt, did not matter. She was just a game piece he was moving. He wanted it that way, without feeling.

He said tonelessly, 'You can stay here for the summer. It would be better, until I'm finished my season in the Beaufort, if you were close to your friends. After that, you'll move to Cortes Island.'

'To your house?' It was a plan for strangers. 'Will you give me a room of my own?' He had built walls in his mind to keep her out. Walls. Rooms.

'If that's what you want.' He said the words as if he did not care.

She said abruptly, 'I'm going to make coffee.'

He did not follow her into the kitchen. She should have known he wouldn't. He had not come for intimacy, for sharing. He had come to look after his obligations. She poured water into the reservoir in the coffee-maker, spooned coffee grounds into the filter. She heard the music start. If she married him, it would be like this forever. Scott in the next room. Playing her music, touching her soul. She stared at the coffee-maker as it gurgled and hissed, and she thought of the letters in the basement. Charlie, hopelessly in love with Amanda. Her parents, together, walking through the life they had chosen.

She tried to shift her reality, to turn what she was feeling into a poem, words for a song. But it was too real. She could not remove herself from her own feelings by making them poetry.

She brought the coffee to him in the living-room. He was in the private part now, standing at the window, his shoulders broad through the warm brown of the knitted shirt he was wearing. She put the coffee down and felt the barriers in him. She could not reach, could not touch. She curled her fingers inwards, nails digging into her palms. Touching was important to her, she realised. Touching and loving. Better to live without him entirely than to walk through a life of walls and tension.

'Coffee,' she said, and he turned, as if he had not heard her until that instant.

The music was a soft background. Not her love songs, not Robin's deep emotional voice. He had picked a neutral, classical piece. Background, filling the silence. He did not reach for the cup she had set down on the end table for him. They stared at each other for an endless moment.

She clasped her hands together behind her back, licked her lips and whispered, 'Do you love me?'

His jaw flexed. Something in his eyes flared briefly and was gone. She felt tightness in her throat and swallowed.

'Scott, I want a marriage with love, with intimacy. I...I can't marry you if you're doing it just because...because you see it as your duty.' She saw his chest expand, felt the tightness in his breathing.

His words were stilted. 'I assume that it *is* my child?'

She felt as if he had struck with his closed fist. She gasped and his jaw became even more rigid. She blinked and managed to win a victory over the tears that wanted to flow. She whispered, 'I did not get pregnant to trap you. This is not a trap.' But it obviously felt like a trap to him.

Under his hardness must be some emotion, some caring. She had to believe that, had to trust her instincts. Loving Scott was not something that would go away, but if there was ever to be a chance for them, he must acknowledge their love, too.

'I didn't plan to have your baby,' she said, whispering. 'It just—that night...it was right. Loving, feeling love for you—— ' His jaw clenched in a spasm, but she remembered what had been in his eyes, in his voice as he whispered against her naked flesh. She said, 'You loved me, too, that night. We made a baby that night, and it will be a child of love. I don't regret it, and I *won't* regret it. I won't have him—I won't have our baby grow up in anything but a home of love.'

If she stayed, he would have to say something, to deny her truth, so she left the room as if she were running. She was afraid that if he denied what they had shared, the denial would become his truth forever.

She went to her music-room. Her haven, she thought uneasily, knowing she could not hide from her world, knowing she should face Scott and say something. But she could not handle it even one minute longer, her heart aching and her voice trembling, the tears so close—and his eyes so cold and closed.

She shut the door. He would not come into this room. If he did, he would be exposing himself to all the things he was afraid to acknowledge. Loving and risking. She did not close the shutters. She could hear the birds outside, and she would hear his truck when he started it. She wanted him to stay, but knew he would leave. He had come to offer marriage, but her price was far higher than he would pay.

Love.

Oh, God! Was she wrong? He had been dragged through homes that did not want him as a child. Maybe he could never reach for her. Maybe she was the one who had to take chances, accept his stilted proposal of marriage and hope he would learn to let himself love her.

She went to the window when she heard the sound of his truck. She watched him drive away, almost certain that she had just made a terrible mistake.

By eleven-thirty that night she knew that she had been mindless, asking a man who was afraid to love for words that would commit him. She dashed out and started her van, roaring down the hill and along the highway to the ferry terminal. If she was fast enough, there might be time. His car was probably aboard by now, but she could get a foot passenger ticket and run on just before they pulled out. She saw the lights of the ferry ahead, her hands trembling on the wheel because it wasn't too late yet. The ferry wasn't gone yet.

Then she saw the other lights behind her, red and blue lights flashing. Oh, God! Not *now*! The police. She jerked the wheel and stopped on the shoulder, hoping desperately that the police car would tear on past her, on its way to something more urgent than a mere speeding driver.

But the police car stopped too, pulling up behind her. She watched in her rear-view mirror as the officer got out and walked slowly forward to her car.

'In a hurry?' He looked very young, but his face had the stern authority to back up the uniform.

'I—I have to get to the ferry. It's——'

'Can I see your driver's licence and registration, please?' His voice was politely critical. 'If you'd gone slower, you'd have got there more quickly.'

It was no use. She rummaged in the glove compartment for the registration, in her bag for the driver's licence. He took the documents and went back to his car. She sat, watching the rear-view mirror, knowing it was going to take too long.

The officer came back eventually, after checking on the radio, she supposed, that she wasn't a wanted

criminal. He was writing out her speeding ticket as she
saw the lights of the ferry moving away from the dock.
Too late.

She called Scott's home two days later. There was no
answer. She called again the next day and wondered what
she would say if he answered. He did not answer and
she did not dial his number again.

She called the Caribbean two weeks later. Amananda
answered, her voice that magical, husky music that had
enchanted her audiences for decades.

'Darling,' she breathed, 'I was just going to call you.'

Melody laughed, knowing it was probably not true.
'How's the act?' she asked. 'Are you still throwing the
West Indies on their ears?'

'Of course, darling. What about you? Have you
written a gold for Robin yet?'

'Next week,' Melody said. She twisted the cord from
the telephone around her index finger. Amanda sounded
worried. 'I thought I might come down and catch your
act. I could use a holiday.'

'You'd be crazy,' said Amanda repressively. 'Come in
the winter. Right now it's a steam bath here. You'd be
dripping all over the hotel, and the audience is hell.
Honey, it's the off season.'

Melody frowned. 'I want to see you.' To tell them
about their coming grandchild, that had been her idea
when she picked up the telephone, but Amanda had
problems of her own.

Amanda said coolly, 'We're not at our best during the
hot season.'

'What's wrong?' Something was. 'Is Charlie OK?'

Amanda did not have a quick answer to that question.
Melody demanded urgently, 'He's not sick?' Three years
ago he had had a heart bypass. Ever since, he had insisted he was a young man again. Forty at least.

'No. Of course not.' Amanda took a noisy breath, then admitted, 'He's having trouble remembering his lines.'

Melody closed her eyes on a vivid picture of her parents. She did not know which town to attach the memory to. There had been so many. Just another memory, Charlie throwing back his words to Amanda on cue, and the audience laughing. Backstage, hidden in the shadows, Robin and Melody watching. After the laughter, came the hush. The music, and the Connachers had drifted from silence into a soft duet that caught the heart-strings.

'Mom——'

'We've been thinking of retiring,' said Amanda briskly, covering emotion now. Melody thought of Scott, covering emotion. Amanda said, 'I'm the business head, of course. I'm always the one counting pennies.'

'If you need a loan, you can always hit me up,' said Melody, careful to keep her voice light.

Amanda laughed and Melody relaxed. If her mother could still laugh, things would be all right. 'I'll hit Robin,' her mother said. 'I saw him on satellite TV yesterday. That concert in LA, and they mobbed him. They love him. And his new album's a winner. The title song——'

'Where did you hear that? It's not been released yet.'

Amanda laughed, a sound of happy victory. 'We've got our contacts, darling.'

It was the stuff of her childhood. Theatre talk. Melody let Amanda lead them away from the personal. They had never leaned on each other. Affection, yes, but all the Connachers knew how to stand alone. Even she and Robin, supporting each other as children because their parents were often away, but not sharing the secrets of their souls.

'I still thought I'd come down there,' said Melody.

'All right. If you must. Although I'd rather you waited a while.' Amanda paused, then said, 'And think about what you want to do with the house.'

'What?' Melody looked around her. The house. Her home. It had been hers and Robin's since they were teenagers. 'What do you mean?'

'Money,' said Amanda. 'I'm sorry, honey, but if Charlie and I are going to retire, we've got to liquidate some of our assets.'

'This house? You're going to sell *this* house?'

'Well, yes.' Amanda's voice was brisk again now that she had introduced the subject. 'So if you and Robin would get together and think about it. Whether you want it. Because, you see, we've had an offer. You remember Wendy and Ronald Saunderly? Last year, they were up for an autumn holiday. A good offer, and if we accept it, we can walk out on the club here.' She laughed, a sharp sound. 'Rather walk out before we get the axe, you know. Charlie would like to know we quit because *we* decided it was time.'

An offer for Melody's home, the house she and Robin had grown up in, the house she had naturally assumed she would have to bring her baby up in.

'The Saunderlys?' She remembered them. Talkative, too energetic, the woman raving about the peace and quiet as she bustled around the island. 'How long do you and Charlie have to make up your minds?'

'Fourteen days. Well, from the offer date. That was three days ago.'

Three days gone already. If Melody had not called her mother, would Amanda have called her? 'I'll talk to Robin. How much was the offer?'

Melody suppressed a gasp at the answer. From a purely practical point of view, her parents would be crazy to refuse an offer like that. Melody could not hope to match that price unless Robin wanted to share ownership of the house. A house that meant nothing to him, except that it was his sister's home.

Two weeks less three days, but she found herself doing the same thing Amanda had done, putting off calling Robin to talk about it. She hugged herself, wondering what there was in the world that was hers. Everything seemed to be slipping away. Robin's life and hers had been separate for years now, ever since she had left Los Angeles. Her parents would probably never come back to this country to live now. Amanda had said something about buying a place in Mexico. Melody was the only one clinging to the Connacher home on the islands.

She should not feel that a future without this house was a formless unkown. She still had the job at the radio station, and she could build a music-room anywhere, couldn't she?

She did not expect Scott to call. She knew his schedule as if it were her own. He had gone to the Beaufort on the twenty-fourth of June. She had deliberately set herself the task of re-organising her music library that week, and on the Wednesday night she had made sure she was very busy. She should be thinking about Amanda and Charlie, about how much money she could scrape up, and she was, in the back of her mind. In the front was the decision of how many categories to sort her music into, and whether Robin's albums came under the category of pop or easy listening.

She was playing the latest, analysing it, when the telephone rang. She picked it up without even thinking of Scott's name.

'What's been happening?' he asked, casually as if he were an old friend and not the lover she could never forget.

She sank into the big easy chair, cradling the telephone against her shoulder, breathing his name silently. Aloud, she said, 'Not a lot. I talked to Robin yesterday. He and Robbie are moving into the house he bought this week.' *Scott!* Her heart was pounding so hard she could hardly hear him talk.

'I know. I got a letter from him just before I left Cortes Island. He says that the little hernia is virtually gone. And Robbie's teething. And he has Donna's nose, which I wouldn't have guessed myself.'

She smiled, closing her eyes and knowing she could listen forever. They were friends, weren't they? Even if he could not admit to the love, he would not deny their friendship.

He asked, 'What's the music I hear in the background?'

With her eyes closed, she could pretend he was here, in the room with her. 'Robin's new album. It came by registered mail this morning.'

'I'd like to hear it.'

She wished he could be here with her. She could hold out her hand and he would take it, and they would share the music. 'I'll send it to you. How long does it take you to get mail up there?'

'Better save it,' he said. 'I don't have a disc player up here. Just a little tape player.'

'It's a tape,' she said, wanting him to be listening to the music. Several of the songs had been written with Scott in her mind. It was the only way she could say 'I love you'. 'I'll send it to you. Tomorrow.'

'All right. I'll probably have it in about a week.'

If he called next Wednesday, he might have the tape by then. When he listened, would he know it was love-songs for him? 'Where do you call from? Are you just closeted in there with the radio operator, or do they leave you alone?'

'It's a separate little room in the oil rig.' She heard him laugh, then he said, 'They don't broadcast us all over the rig. I guess the call is as private as any long-distance call that gets routed through a satellite. There's probably a few short-wave listeners around the world listening in, but—— Is everything all right? Have you been working?'

Not private enough for talking about the baby, but they could talk about almost anything else. She said, 'Working? A little. I—no, not really. I tried, but I guess I need a holiday from song-writing.'

Their five minutes were over before she could ask him anything about his day. A week. Seven days. She should be counting days until the deadline on the house offer, but instead she was waiting for Wednesday again, sitting beside the telephone for hours, then jerking the receiver up almost as it started ringing.

'Melody?'

She had to take a deep breath, to still her heart. 'Hi.' It sounded breathless and she tried again, 'Hi, Scott. Is it summer up there yet?'

'As close as it gets.' There was a smile in his voice. She closed her eyes and saw it. She pulled her legs up and said, 'Tell me what you did today.'

The ice flow had been heavier than they expected. Two of the big anchors that held the oil rig had become fouled and they had reset them. Routine, he said, and she wanted to know more.

'Five minutes isn't long to explain how we get those anchors down.' She loved his laugh. She was achingly happy that they were still friends. Time, she thought. If he wanted to talk to her, she could wait for years, and there might come the day when he would love her.

She gripped the receiver so tightly that the blood left her fingers, but she made sure her voice was easy and casual. He wanted it light, casual, so that was how it would be. She said, 'We could talk longer if you had a ham radio up there.'

He was smiling, saying, 'I'm not a ham.'

'You could learn,' she said. 'You're always studying new things.' Their time would be up soon. She bit her lip and said, 'I talked to Amanda.'

'Your mother?'

'Yes. She and Charlie are retiring.' She had not intended to tell him, had not wanted him to think she was loading her problems on him. 'She wants them to quit before Charlie gets fired. He's been forgetting his lines lately.'

He was silent for a few seconds, as if trying to tune in on her thoughts. 'Are you going down to see them?'

'I—maybe. Maybe after summer's over. It's deadly hot down there now, and Amanda doesn't really want me to come. I guess she doesn't want family out there, in the audience, seeing Charlie's bad moments.'

By the time summer was over, Melody would be quite obviously pregnant. Already, she could feel the thickening of her waist, the swelling of her breasts. 'Amanda wants to sell this house, so they can swing their retirement.'

'I thought it was your house. Will you buy it?'

'I don't know.' She shifted uneasily. 'For me, they'd put the price as low as they could. The offer they've got—I don't seem to be able to make up my mind.'

Why had she told him that? As if she wanted something from him. That was exactly what she *must* not do.

He said carefully, 'There's lots of room in my house,' and she closed her eyes painfully. Did he want her there? Really want her? 'That big room upstairs—your music equipment could go in there.'

She did not answer.

'Melody?'

In the Beaufort Sea, aboard the oil rig, Scott heard the signal that his time was up. 'Melody? I've got to go. I'll call next week.'

He wondered where she could be next Wednesday. He wondered what she would do, what decisions she would make while he was stuck in the ice fields, unable to reach her.

He should have told her that he loved her, but whenever he thought of saying the words something surged up and choked him. All the memories of other kinds of loving, and losing. All the years telling himself not to be an ass, never to risk himself again, not for anyone.

He tried not to think about it, tried to concentrate on work and make the days pass. Thursday. Friday. Saturday, and the ice maps were still showing a drift towards the rig. The captain of the rig held a conference with Scott and the captain of the smaller supply ship. They were all nervous.

She wanted love. He could not say those words, but he could build a music-room for her, and she might come even without the words. She would be close. When the child came—that scared him most of all. His child. A child needed love and stability. He didn't know if he could give love to anyone, but even in the midst of studying ice maps and worrying about the drift, Melody and her child haunted him.

On Sunday at five in the afternoon, the captain of the rig decided to pull out. Scott had a bad feeling about the whole operation, but the rig was not his ship and he said only, 'John, have you thought about waiting until morning?'

'I'm pulling out now.' John's voice was still sharp from a long argument with the drilling chief. Moving the rig meant capping the drill site and abandoning it. The chief believed intensely that they were about to hit oil, and hit it big.

The rig was anchored with eight Bruce anchors, four at each end. The supply ship and the icebreaker were responsible for slipping anchor for the rig. It was a task that nobody liked. Before they started, Scott checked the latest weatherfax pictures. There was no storm centre around them, but the wind had been brisk and freshening all afternoon. He didn't like the feel of it. If he had found a storm centre on the latest fax, or even a building depression, he would have gone back to John. As it was, he had nothing to base his feeling on.

The supply ship worked on one side of the rig, the icebreaker on the other. Scott was at the bridge of the icebreaker, watching the aft deck where his first mate, Harry, was working with two seamen.

On the deck, Harry, the mate, was pointing, ordering one of the seamen to pick up the buoy that marked the first anchor. Scott pushed the left throttle slightly forward and the right one back, jockeying the ship with the two prop washes. One of the seamen hooked on to the big cable that led from the rig to the anchor, then Harry limped across to control the winching. Scott saw the pennant come over the stern on to the deck. The second seaman hooked on to the pennant and Harry waved a signal to the bridge. Scott pushed both throttles astern, giving slack so the men could release the cable.

He spoke into the microphone hanging over his head. 'John, you can take number one. We've got the anchor here.'

'Roger, Scott. Anchor number one coming in now.'

On board the rig, a big winch started pulling in the anchor cable. The anchor itself was now below the ice-breaker, at the end of the hundred-foot section of pennant. The next step was to bring the seven-ton anchor on board the icebreaker.

From the bridge, Scott could see that Harry was moving clumsily. The mate had injured his leg last spring and refused to go back to the doctor when it kept pain-ing him. Scott watched as Harry stumbled and got in the way of one of the seamen. He had a vision of Harry crushed between seven tons of anchor and the crash rail.

He reached for the loud hailer microphone. 'Harry! Put the winch on hold and come up to the bridge for a minute.'

Harry came up, frowning and complaining. 'Look, Skipper, if we're gonna get those things up, let's get on with it. It's damned cold out there.'

'Ten minutes won't make any difference. You take the con. I'll do the deck work.'

It was unusual, but not outrageous. Harry had his British Home Trade Master's ticket. By this time next year Scott expected that his mate would have his own ship, and Scott knew that he would never be able to live with himself if Harry lost that aching leg in an accident Scott could have prevented.

As Harry had said, it was cold on deck. Scott worked steadily, directing the seamen. The first of the Bruce anchors came over the rollers and hit the deck with a resounding crash. No one flinched. They were all standing safely behind the crash rails, and the deck was made for blows like this. When the anchor came to rest, the men moved out to secure it.

Even with his thermal underwear, his woollen sweater and the big anti-exposure coveralls, Scott felt the cold everywhere as the wind picked up. He lifted his hand to signal Harry. On the bridge, Harry jockeyed the ship towards the second anchor's marker buoy.

Two anchors. Three. The fourth buoy, then the pennant secured to the winch. The last one. Scott signalled the seamen back as the shank of the big steel anchor slid out of the water. As the anchor hit the deck, the ship heaved on an angry wave. The anchor slid a noisy ten feet before the world stilled again. Behind the crash bars, all three men felt the shuddering blow of the anchor's impact.

'Get the lines on it before it moves again!' shouted Scott, and all three men went into action.

Scott was on his way to the winch when he felt the deck moving again. He spun around, knowing he was too late. The big anchor was sliding as if it were skating on an ice-rink. He could hear it, but it was coming incredibly fast for a seven-ton hunk of metal.

'Crash rails!' he screamed, pushing the seaman beside him towards the rails.

Then he dived, and he could feel it like a slow-motion play. Not enough time. The anchor. His own frail body. The crash rails with safety behind them. He knew he was not going to make it before the anchor hit.

He would never see Melody again, never touch her or feel the gasp in her throat, never hear her voice caressing his heart, never have the chance to build a room especially for her music, for her. He had dreamed of it, of leading her upstairs and seeing the pleasure in her eyes. He had dreamed of going outside, chopping wood and feeling her near, knowing she was upstairs, close by.

Little things. Trivial details of one day following another, with Melody close by, close enough to call, to touch, to feel her presence.

Their child. The idea of fatherhood had terrified him even more than the thought of commitment and loving. Now, too late, he realised that he wanted desperately to give it a try.

CHAPTER TEN

THE hospital corridor was cold and brilliant and completely immaculate. Melody had always hated hospitals, hated the thought of illness and waiting for bad news. She had no reason for it, just perhaps the fear of losing people she loved. She had never before spent a night waiting in a hospital waiting-room, not knowing what would come.

She was scared. More alone than she had been in all her life. There was nowhere to hide here, no music-room, no fantasies. Only the shining hospital that did not have the antiseptic smell she had thought was supposed to go with hospitals. And the man on the other side of the room, as silent as she was, waiting for news that did not come.

It was the personnel officer at the oil company who had telephoned Melody. Personnel had received a request to notify Scott Alexander's next-of-kin of an accident, but his recorded next-of-kin was a foster-mother in a home for the elderly. Scott, however, had visited the personnel office only a couple of weeks before.

'He made you beneficiary on everything,' said the brisk, friendly woman. 'His group insurance policy. His registered pension plan. So I thought you were the one to notify.'

'Where is he?' Scott. Seriously hurt. An accident on the icebreaker.

'They're airlifting him to Calgary.' The woman named the hospital and Melody had grabbed for paper and pen.

162

'They took him to Tuktoyaktuk by helicopter. A doctor met him at Tuk, and is accompanying him to Calgary.'

Tuktoyaktuk to Calgary. Three hours from the Northwest Territories port to the modern facilities of Calgary.

He was in Calgary long before Melody could get there. She had to wait for morning and the jet to Vancouver, then another two hours for a connection to Calgary. Then the hospital, and, it seemed, forever without news.

Scott had been taken directly to surgery, hours before Melody arrived. Then, about the time she landed at Calgary airport, he was rushed back into surgery a second time, haemorrhaging.

She had not seen him, would not be able to see him for hours. Critical, the nurse had said, and the doctor was too busy trying to save his life to talk to anyone.

Melody paced from the window that looked out on endless hospital buildings, to the corridor where eventually the surgeon must appear with news for her.

'Look, miss——'

She swung around. Her silent companion, the other man in the room. He stood, tall and lean and limping slightly as he came towards her. His voice was soft, with a precise accent. British, she decided, amazed that part of her mind could still function.

'Sit down,' he said gently, insistently, his voice taking on the faint burr of Scottish ancestors. 'You cannot pace the floor all day like that. Sit down and I'll bring a cup of tea for you.'

Tea. It sounded far better than the foul liquid she had coaxed from the coffee machine earlier. Even the bitter smell of it had made her feel nauseous.

He was gone for ten minutes or so, and came back with two steaming cups. Real cups, not plastic. She accepted the one he handed her, curling her fingers around it. He pulled a paper bag out of his jacket pocket and brought two doughnuts from it.

'Lunch,' he said. 'Of a sort.'

'Thank you.' Doughnuts, and Scott might be dying.

She breathed in warm fumes from the tea, sipped and felt the heat flow slowly down her throat. Soon she would make herself eat one of the doughnuts. She needed the strength. If Scott—*when* Scott got better, he would need someone. She shuddered, knowing that if he had not put her name on his personnel forms, no one would have called her. She might have been feeling uneasy, a sixth sense telling her something was wrong. She would not have known where or what.

The stranger held out the flattened paper bag. She took a doughnut from on top of it. It tasted sugary, too sweet. She chewed for a long time and finally swallowed without gagging and asked, 'Who are you?'

'Harry. The mate from *Jonathan Cartier*. You're the skipper's woman, aren't you?'

She wanted to be his woman, if he would ever let her that close. She said, 'I love him,' and it felt like a release to say it out loud.

He nodded. They fell silent, waiting together.

When Melody could sit no longer, she got up and prowled the little waiting-room. She walked to the window, then to the corridor. No one there. Back to the window again, then past Harry's feet to the corridor. Only a nurse hurrying somewhere else with a swish of rubber-soled shoes. Would they ever come to say Scott was going to be all right?

Soon, Harry would tell her to sit down. She looked at him, but he was staring at the floor between his feet. She sat down beside him, staring at the doorway to the corridor.

'It's my fault,' he said in a low, soft voice. 'I've got this bad leg, and the skipper's been after me to get to the doctors with it. I'm his mate.' She blinked and he said, 'First mate. Next in command after the Master.' She nodded and he explained, 'Yesterday we were bringing up the rig's anchors, and the skipper must have seen me trip on the deck. It's the cold, gets to the damned leg. I've been afraid to go to the doctors, afraid I'd find out it was—well, anyway, skipper put me on the bridge and took my place. That's why he was there when the Bruce cut loose, instead of safe on the bridge where he should have been.'

She hugged herself, trying to understand the strange terms. 'He's your captain, isn't he?' He nodded and she said, 'If he ordered you off the deck, you had to go. He wouldn't blame you, would he?' She wondered if she would ever feel warm again. 'Could you explain to me what happened? I don't know what the Bruce is, and I need to know what happened to him.'

'The Bruce is the kind of anchor we use on the oil rigs in the Beaufort. Here, have the last doughnut and I'll use this bag to show you.'

He drew the icebreaker for her and she found that asking questions and concentrating on the answers was easier than waiting.

A doctor came finally, trailing a mask and wearing tired lines around his eyes. He nodded to Harry and looked at Melody, saying, 'I'm Dr Walton. The nurse says you're waiting for word of Mr Alexander. Are you a relative?'

She licked her lips. She was the mother of his unborn child, the woman who loved him. Was that enough to entitle her to news? She said unsteadily, 'We're getting married,' because if he lived and if the offer was still open she was going to be his wife. She could not bear to spend the rest of her life knowing that if he needed her no one would call and she would not be there.

The doctor rubbed his forehead with his forearm. 'You can't see him yet,' he said flatly.

'Is he——?'

'In the recovery-room. The haemorrhaging has stopped. He'll have a couple of extra seams in the abdominal area, but he'll probably get through the next fifty years.' The doctor half smiled. 'That man of yours is one tough character. I think it's going to be all right. I—hey!'

She could feel the room spinning, then hard hands gripping her. The world steadied and he was glaring at her, frowning.

'I'm sorry. I just——'

'Get some rest,' he said sharply. Then his eyes became more intent and he said, 'You're gravid, aren't you?'

She blinked, pulling back from his steadying hold. 'What?'

He grimaced. 'Sorry. Medical term. Expecting. A child.' Her startled silence must have answered him because he said, 'Don't ask how I can tell. Something about the eyes. My wife says I should be a witch-doctor.' His voice shifted from indulgent to brisk. 'Look, you get out of this place. Check into a hotel, get some sleep. Have a long, relaxing soak in a tub. Then have a good dinner before you come back. Your man might be awake by then.'

She was breathing again, reassured by his matter-of-fact instructions. 'Can I leave the name of my hotel with the nurse?'

'Yes, and we'll call if you're needed. But don't worry. Your sea-captain's going to be fine. He'll be around to see his grandchildren born. You just make sure you get your rest. And regular meals.'

It was Harry who insisted on taking her to a nearby hotel, Harry who called back to the hospital with the telephone number of the hotel and room number, Harry who ordered room service for her and sat with her to make sure she ate it before he left her to sleep.

Amazingly, she did sleep.

He was asleep when she came into his hospital room. She stopped, seeing his face pale and still over the sheets, his arm outside the blanket, strapped to a board, a needle connecting by tube to an intravenous drip.

She could see nothing but his paleness and a frightening array of tubes leading everywhere. She moved closer, not breathing, reaching out to touch the ashen pallor that was his cheek. His eyes opened. She pulled her hand away. She wanted to say something, but no words would come.

He asked, 'Am I dreaming you?' It was hardly a whisper.

She shook her head mutely.

'Good,' he mumbled, and his eyes closed again.

There was a chair against the window. She carried it to the side of the bed, the other side from the tubes. His breathing was slow and steady.

A nurse came in and checked the bag on the intravenous drip, then left again only to return with a new bag of clear liquid. Melody watched the tubing swinging, her eyes tracing it to a needle in Scott's arm.

'What's in that?'

'Glucose,' said the nurse. 'It'll be a few days before he's ready to eat steak.'

She would wait as long as she had to for him to open his eyes again. And she wasn't going to ask for the moon this time. Just to be close by, to share whatever it was he was willing to share.

He groaned and shifted without rolling under the covers. The nurse said quietly to Melody, 'He's going to be uncomfortable for a while. Doctor says his signs are good, so don't worry.'

Eventually, another nurse came and told Melody to leave. Visiting hours were over. She went back to the hotel. She wondered where Harry was, then remembered that he had said something about going back to Tuk. She tried to shake the feeling of time suspended, but the only thing that really mattered was Scott back there in the hospital bed. She turned on the television and found herself watching the news, realising when the announcer said the date that tomorrow was the day Amanda and Charlie had to give their buyer an answer.

Past time for Melody to call Robin.

'Where the devil are you?' demanded her twin. 'Amanda's been burning up the phone lines. You were supposed to call her. About the house.'

The house. It had seemed so important. 'I'm in Calgary. I—quiet, Robin, and listen,' she added sharply as Robin made exasperated noises. 'Scott's been in an accident. He's—they operated and he's going to be all right. He—internal injuries. They were pulling anchor for the oil rig and the weather kicked up. One of the anchors got loose and caught Scott.'

'Are you all right?'

She said, without thinking, 'Yes, now that I know he's going to live.'

On the television, there was a picture of flames shooting up from an apartment building somewhere, then the announcer's mouth moving. Robin said, 'You're in love with him.'

'Yes.' She seemed to be telling that to everyone except Scott himself. She repeated, 'Yes.'

His voice was muted. 'Odd, isn't it? All these years and neither one of us got caught. Then Donna, and he's her brother'

'Robin——'

He said quietly, 'Don't, Melody.'

'But you haven't forgotten her. It still hurts. You haven't talked about it, but——'

He said intensely, 'I'll never forget her. But it doesn't hurt as much as it did. I've got Robbie, at least. Still, I'm not likely to forget that I'm the one who asked her for more than she could give.'

Melody closed her eyes and saw Scott in her own living-room. 'We'll get married,' he had said. 'Babies need families.' And she had known that he cared for her, even if he could not call it a name like love.

Not enough, she had told him.

It was years since she and Robin had shared the kind of closeness that enabled them to read each other's thoughts, but he said, 'Give him time. I didn't give Donna enough time, enough room. Don't make the mistake I made, Melody.'

She had, but maybe she would have another chance. She had sent Scott away, but he had called. Only one call a week, Harry had said while he was talking about the ship last night. One call a week, and Scott had chosen to call her. And he had put her name on his life insurance. For the child, of course, but it was a link that would grow between them. She remembered how he had cared for his nephew, little Robbie. He had said he didn't know how to be a father, but there had been love in his eyes and his voice as he'd held Robbie.

'I'll try not to,' she promised her twin. 'Will you call Amanda for me? Tell her I don't want the house. You don't want it, do you?'

'No. It's a nice house, but it's my past, not my future.'

Hers, too. Her future was with Scott, whether he was ready to accept it or not. 'Am I dreaming you,' he had asked. As if he expected her to be in his dreams. He had offered her his home, and she would go there. She would let him build her a new music-room, and she would make a home for him there. A family for him.

There was something else she had to do. For her family. 'Robin, Amanda said Charlie's flubbing his lines.'

'Damn! Poor old beggar. So that's why they're talking retirement.'

'Yes. I wanted to go down there, to—well, in case they needed anything from us. And just to go. But Amanda was pretty determined I shouldn't.'

Her twin said, 'I don't doubt it. Charlie would hate to blow his lines with his only daughter there to see him perform.' He thought for a second, then said, 'Look, I'll go down. They haven't met Robbie, and I've got a couple of weeks before the screen test thing Peter's got me lined up for. I'll take the grandchild down, and Charlie will never know he's being watched over.'

'Perfect. And if they ask for me——'

'You're tending the fevered brow of their future son-in-law. Same to be introduced at a later date, and, no, you don't want the theatrical family descending and frightening the poor lad off.'

She choked on a laugh that was half sob. Robin was assuming a lot, and so was she. If Melody looked like moving in on him, Scott might just run hard and fast the other way.

Meanwhile, Scott was getting better, and being far too irritable for Melody to feel tempted to tell him how much she loved him, how her world was moving again because she hadn't lost him to a big anchor and the angry sea. She visited him every day, but daily he seemed more restless and bad-tempered.

The doctor took her aside as she was arriving at the hospital one afternoon, saying, 'Listen, you're the one who's going to have to keep him in line. The fool is determined to ignore the fact that he's not a hundred per cent.'

'He's not worse?' She panicked.

The doctor sighed explosively. 'No. Healing too quickly for his own good. He's getting restless, and I can't stop him from going home. But I've managed to get a pretty good picture of his plans. He expects to be chopping wood next week, and working on some damned building he's got to get done upstairs.' He frowned and said sternly, 'He's got to lay off it for at least six weeks.'

She was not at all sure that she could influence Scott's actions, especially as he grew more impatient and moody with each day of hospital convalescence. Dr Walton was adamant that he must not leave hospital for at least eight days after the surgery.

'And you absolutely have to have someone there to look after you,' he added on the seventh day.

Scott frowned mutinously at that. Melody was standing at the window, looking out and listening. She turned around and said to Dr Walton, 'I'll be there to look after him. I'm going home with him.'

'And no wood-chopping,' went on the doctor. 'No swinging hammers or axes or lifting weights, or whatever nonsense you've got in mind. Not until I've had you back here in four weeks' time to check that incision.'

Scott nodded curtly, his eyes avoiding Melody's.

'All right, then,' said the doctor. 'Tomorrow you're free.' And he walked out.

Melody could hear his shoes squeaking as he went down the corridor outside. A buzzer rang in the corridor. Scott said curtly, 'Who decided that you're coming home with me?'

She crossed her arms and cupped her elbows with her hands. 'I decided. You need someone, and—and——' And she loved him. She flung her hands out and said in an exasperated voice, 'Stop being so difficult. You know you need someone.' She swallowed, gulped and added steadily, 'If you don't want it to be me, then I'll get a nurse.'

'God forbid! I've had it up to here with nurses!'

'Then you're stuck with me, aren't you?'

They stared at each other, both breathing a little heavier than normal. Then Scott made a gesture of impatience. 'Go and get some rest. I'm tired.'

She tried to tell herself that he hated being sick, that so many men were poor patients. Look at Charlie the Christmas she and Robin had turned nine. And Robin with chicken pox. She giggled and thought of her twin at seventeen, laid low by a messy, itchy child's disease. Scott, with his recent foul temper, was in good company.

Theoretically she understood, but she had trouble coping with his bad temper.

He hated being an invalid, so she tried not to be obvious about watching over him the day they went to the airport, but just getting dressed and sitting in the taxi seemed to have exhausted him. He growled at her all the way to the airport, but the first real explosion occurred as they got out of the taxi at the terminal.

'Dr Walton arranged a wheelchair,' she told him. 'Just wait here and I'll collect it.'

He blocked her way, his face pale and his eyes angry. 'I am not going through this terminal in a damned wheelchair like an invalid!'

A porter, rolling past with a cart of luggage, craned his neck to stare.

'You're crazy,' she said, wishing she hadn't chosen exactly those words when she saw the irritation in his face. 'Scott, who do you think they have wheelchairs for in an airport? Be sensible and——'

'I don't need it.' He reached for her bag and she jerked it back.

'No. You're not to lift anything heavy.'

He cursed and walked into the terminal. They walked to the gate in an angry silence. She could see the muscle in Scott's jaw twitching from tension as he stood waiting for his boarding-pass to be accepted by the security agent. Then he moved stiffly into the waiting-room and took a chair.

She sank down beside him and heaved a sigh of relief. He was sitting with his eyes closed, head back against the wall. He opened his eyes as she watched. They stared at each other.

'I suppose I'm being totally unbearable?'

Her lips twitched. 'You're not your usual charming self.'

'Sorry.' He grimaced. 'The wheelchair might have been an idea. See if you can organise one in Vancouver.'

Then he picked up a magazine from the table beside him and concentrated on reading it until the pre-boarding call came. To her relief, Scott made no objection to their boarding ahead of the others.

He stood back so that she could have the window seat, then seemed to fall asleep as soon as he sat down. She wished that she had asked Dr Walton to keep Scott an extra day or two in hospital, but knew Scott would never have stood for it.

The plane began to turn slowly, moving away from the gate. Melody flexed her fingers, tensing for what was coming. The stewardess moved to the front of the cabin and the routine instructions began. Melody craned her head to be sure she had located the emergency doors.

'You're nervous about flying?'

She jumped at Scott's voice. 'I thought you were asleep. I'm not exactly afraid, but I drive when I can.'

Outside, the world started to spin past them in a blur, the jet roaring down the runway in preparation for takeoff. Melody felt Scott's hand cover hers. His felt cool and dry.

'It's all right,' he said quietly.

She realised then that she was pressed back into the seat, her fingers curled into the arms. He turned her hand over and threaded his own fingers through hers. When she looked at him, his eyes were closed again, but he still held her hand.

The jet left the ground with a sickening lurch. A moment later Melody closed her eyes against a glimpse of the wing pointing down at Calgary. She did not open them again until she heard the sound of the engine changing as they levelled off above the clouds.

The first thing she saw was Scott's hand, and her own fingers clenched tightly through his. She relaxed her grip, looked up and found his eyes on her.

'OK now?'

She nodded.

'I'll be here for the landing, too, just in case you want to hang on.' She stared at him and he said seriously, 'I haven't had much practice soothing fears, but I'll do my best.'

She stumbled with an apology. 'I don't mind landings so much. I just tell myself it's almost over, we're almost down, and it's easier. With the take-off—— You know, I always take the ferry when I'm going to LA, with my van. That way I can drive as far as Vancouver, leave it there and fly to LA.'

The stewardess came to Scott's side and he ordered milk for both of them. 'Milk?' Melody echoed. 'I'd have liked a——'

'Milk,' he said firmly, sending the stewardess away with a nod. Then he said quietly, 'You're feeling a bit nauseous, aren't you? The milk might help. I noticed you've gone off coffee lately.'

She had learned that she could avoid most of the morning sickness if she did not drink coffee. She was not comfortable with telling him that, or for that matter with his noticing her discomfort. The baby was a subject she found very difficult to talk about with him, perhaps because she did not really know how he felt about it...or about her.

She was relieved that he slept most of the way to Vancouver. She saw the stewardess about a wheelchair for Scott in Vancouver, and was promised one would be waiting for them when they disembarked.

To her relief, Scott did not object when the time came, although he refused to consider her suggestion that they break their trip in Vancouver and stay overnight in a hotel so he could get some rest.

'I'm not a bloody invalid,' he snapped when she made the suggestion.

'Do you want to get better or not?'

It was a good thing she had not gone in for nursing. She seemed to have no patience at all. They hardly spoke through the rest of the journey. Just one word from Scott. 'No!' he said, when she suggested another wheelchair at Campbell River.

They came off the plane, into the last terminal. Soon, she thought, she would have him home and then, surely, he would go to bed and get some rest. She did not like the colour of his skin, the deepening lines on his forehead, and she was exhausted herself.

He sank into a seat at the Campbell River terminal and she said briskly, 'If you'll just give me your keys,

I'll bring your truck around. It's in the parking lot, isn't it?'

He uttered one short, tired expletive and she snapped back, 'Scott, there's no reason I can't drive your truck!'

He closed his eyes and muttered, 'They're back on the *Jonathan Cartier*. My keys. My wallet.'

It was too much. She had dealt with his temper all day, and now this when she was so close to exhaustion.

'What?' she asked, hearing the echo of his voice.

'Rent a car,' he said, and it was the measure of his own exhaustion that he did not insist on going with her to the car-rental counter.

CHAPTER ELEVEN

MELODY sat on a rock at the water's edge, her legs crossed, her chin in her hand, staring at a place where a loon had disappeared a moment ago. Two weeks, and neither she nor Scott had mentioned the future.

Magical weeks, if she did not think ahead. They had gone for long, slow walks through the lightly populated island. Scott had taught her the names of the trees, the nesting patterns of a multitude of strange seabirds. In return, she had started to teach him Morse code.

From his telephone, while he slept, she had called Laurie at the radio station, apologising for leaving her high and dry.

'I can't tell you when I'll be back. Or if,' she'd admitted. 'You'd better find someone else.'

'Let's leave it in the air,' said Laurie. 'I'll fill in a bit myself. I always miss the hands-on stuff. Let me know.'

The next day Scott took her to a deserted cliff-side where he showed her the bald eagles nesting. She told him about her one disastrous appearance on stage when she was seven years old. She had frozen and Charlie had ad-libbed all around her, and she'd refused ever to go on again.

She made quiche and he ate it, and they laughed about his calling it egg pie, but he refused to eat yoghurt when she bought it. He made a fire in a pit outside and they had a barbecue because he said he'd never been to a barbecue when he was a child.

She wanted to tell him that she loved him, but was afraid to say the words in case he would not want to hear.

He told her about Tom, the foster-father who had taken Scott on his fishing boat and taught him to love the sea. About Sylvia, Tom's widow, who hated being left alone and lived in a home now.

Another day, while he slept, she called Amanda and Charlie and learned that the papers had been signed. The house was sold. She called Mrs Winston and warned her the buyers were coming to look.

'You're moving, then?' said the woman who had been housekeeper to the Connacher twins since their childhood.

'Yes,' said Melody, because that much was certain. Mrs Winston deserved to be told more, but Melody could only say, 'I'll call you when I know something definite.'

Soon, she would have to go home and pack. She put off the decision, put off worrying about where she would be moving. Once, Scott had told her that she could move into his home, that he would make room for her music upstairs. Once, he had said they should marry. But since his accident he had not referred to either the marriage or the unfinished room upstairs.

He talked freely about his other plans for the property on the Gorge. He was going to build a small bathhouse and sauna at the base of the hill behind the house. He wanted to turn the unfinished downstairs room where she was sleeping into a library some day. He drew sketches of his plans and asked for her ideas, but he never said one word that referred to her staying.

She did not have the courage to ask him.

Behind her, she heard the door of the veranda as it swung shut. A few minutes ago the telephone had rung.

Something to do with the machine Scott was hiring to dig out the foundation for the bathhouse. Although he was not allowed to do any work himself, he was managing to organise quite a bit of action by telephone. Soon, she knew, it would be impossible to keep him from working.

Without turning to look, she knew when he was behind her, knew he would be leaning against the big rock with his arms crossed and his eyes narrowed against the power of the sun.

'Did you get them for Monday?' she asked. Everyday questions. She savoured the sweetness of his nearness.

'No. It wasn't the contractor.'

'Oh.' She twisted and found him watching her. Something in his eyes started her heart keeping time in a slow thud. 'What--who was it?'

'Your mother.'

Oh, lord! What on earth had Amanda said? 'Did—did she want me to call her?'

He shrugged. Yes? Or no? She heard the loon calling from the water behind her, but could not turn to look. He said, 'She said to tell you the possession date is the end of August, and can you organise clearing out the house by then?'

She nodded mutely.

'You didn't tell me the house was sold.'

'No.' Because that would bring up the question of where she was going to move, and she was afraid to break the bubble. She pushed her hair back, wished it were long hair and could drop over her face to hide her confusion. He was not pleased to know that she was homeless. 'I—did you tell her I'd call?'

'I didn't get the chance. She said she wanted to meet me, she and Charlie.'

Oh, lord! She knew what was coming. He unfolded his arms and crossed them again. She bit her lip, very much the same as she had at the age of seven, on stage with everyone watching, messing it up and unable to escape.

'She referred to me as your young man.'

'Robin,' she whispered. 'Robin must have said something.' She wished she could flee, but there was nowhere else she would want to be. She loved him. God, she loved him so much that she knew even her songs would dry up if she could not share her life with him.

'Where would Robin get that idea?' he asked.

She shook her head. From her. Because she had told Robin she loved Scott. She saw a glimpse of colour behind Scott's shoulder and she grasped at the distraction. 'There's a car...or a truck. Coming here, I think.'

'Going past,' he said. He did not turn to look.

The sound of the engine faded. She got up from the rock, wondering what came next. Was he trying to find the words to send her away? If he started talking about support payments and medical coverage, she thought she would scream.

She said helplessly, 'It's time for lunch, isn't it?' Lord, why wouldn't he stop looking like that? She was scared.

He did not answer and she could not stand here just waiting. She said uneasily, 'I feel like I'm on display. As if—I'll make some soup, shall I?'

He followed her to the kitchen. She tried to act as if he was not there, to move around with some kind of purpose. She got out a tin of soup and a saucepan. She went into the odds and ends drawer for the tin opener, stood staring at bits of string and a roll of electrical tape, trying to remember what she was looking for.

Tin opener, that was it. She pushed the drawer in and got the right one open. Scott was looming, saying nothing, and she felt as if everything was going to explode.

'You look as scared as I am,' he said quietly.

She dropped the opener. It clattered to the floor. She bent to get it and he said, 'Leave it.'

She whispered, 'What do you want?' Her throat was dry and tight.

A muscle twitched in his jaw. He said, 'You.'

The ring of the telephone broke the silence. They stood locked in silence as the rings continued. His eyes were almost black with some kind of emotion. She licked her lips and caught her bottom lip between her teeth. The telephone gave one last ring and then stopped.

He said, 'I want you to stay here.' There was no feeling in his voice, although his eyes were black and filled with tension. She swallowed and no sound came. He must know that she wanted above everything to stay with him.

His hands were hanging at his sides, fingers hanging down. His face was haggard. 'When I was a kid, when my parents died, Donna and I went to our first foster-home——' He shrugged, showing no emotion although she knew it was there. 'Donna was just a baby, didn't really know what had happened. I didn't settle in very well. They made it plain—lord, I don't even know what their last name was now, I was supposed to call them Mom and Dad, but they made it plain that if it weren't for Donna, they'd send me back where I came from. Wherever that was.' He shrugged uncomfortably. 'I don't like talking about this. The house was—anyway, after a couple of years we were both moved again. The foster-mother was expecting a child of her own, couldn't handle us.'

She wanted to go to him, to put her arms around him, but something in his voice forbade touching. He said, 'I made sure I worked hard enough to be able to stay at the next place, but I was only working for one thing. To have total control of my own life. I didn't want my happiness in anyone else's hands.'

She had not known the details, but she had known it would take time. She would be patient, would not ask for anything he was not willing to share. She would love him, but she would be quiet about it.

He said, 'I went to sea because the sea doesn't ask a man to be anything but what he is. Because I could——' He shrugged away emotions he could not put in words, and said, 'I bought this place for myself, a place no one could kick me out of.' He added flatly, 'I did not build this house to share with anyone else.' He grimaced at his own words and said, 'This was the place where I was safe.'

Was. Until now. She must have made some sound, because his eyes changed. She whispered, 'Then why are you asking me to stay? You don't have to.' Every word hurt as it passed her throat.

She saw his fingers curl in on themselves. He said harshly, 'When that anchor was coming at me, I knew it was the end. A man doesn't lose in a battle with seven tons of steel and survive it. I jumped for the crash rail, trying to get behind it, and I knew I wasn't fast enough. And the only thing I could think of was you.'

She formed the words, 'I love you,' but the words would not come out.

'I wanted to hold you in my arms, to go to sleep feeling you. I wanted to see you when I woke up in the morning.' His eyes closed and his voice deepened. 'I wanted to see our child, to hold it, to watch you holding the baby we made.'

She moved then and her hand found his chest. She could feel his heart hammering against her palm. He said, 'When we made love, I thought you were too dangerous, that I couldn't afford to feel what I was feeling for you, but I couldn't seem to keep away from you. I had to phone you from the rig, and when you didn't answer——'

'I love you.' It was only a whisper, but this time she managed to get the words out, although he did not seem to hear.

His chest was hard, the muscles rigid under her hand. 'When you came here, the first time, I was just beginning to admit to myself that I needed more than one night with you. I wanted you closer, sharing...the whole idea terrified me, but I couldn't seem to push you away in my mind. Upstairs, that morning, when I asked you to stay for a holiday—I was really starting to ask you to move in, to live with me, but I got scared. I'd never had a relationship that mattered with any woman, wasn't sure I could do it, not with the load of hang-ups I'd carried out of my childhood.'

She told him, 'I wanted to say yes. For a holiday, or forever; but I had to tell you about the baby first.' She felt the shudder go through his chest. 'Scott, I wasn't trying to trap you. I—we can take time. We can——'

His hands possessed her arms, his fingers digging in. 'I know I was terrible...brutal to you when you told me you were pregnant, I...I don't know if—— Can you understand, Melody? I just couldn't cope with it. You were putting all these images in my mind, loving and families and babies, and they were the kinds of dreams

I just couldn't believe in, I'd never—I wanted . . . wanted it all so much that it terrified me, so much that I——'

She slid her arms up, around his neck. He was so tight, so tense. She wanted to tell him that it was all right, but did not know how to reassure him.

His hands moved to her back, bringing her close against him. 'There's just never been anybody that mattered in my life who didn't disappear on me—either by dying or by kicking me out.'

'So you had to push me away?' In a crazy way, she understood.

He nodded, staring down at her bleakly. 'When you told me—I—at first I couldn't believe it. I hadn't even considered it might happen. You. And a child. And love. All in my reach. It would have been heaven, except I knew I was afraid to try. Afraid I'd blow it, I guess.' He shook his head, admitted, 'I'm still scared witless. I want you. I want our baby. But I don't know if I can love either of you, or both of you, the way you deserve. I'm not sure I know how.'

'I love you.' He heard her this time. Her voice was strong and her arms were tight around his neck.

'I need you loving me.' He groaned, 'Melody, without you at my side, my world is all black and white. There's no colour.'

He was still frowning and she covered his lips with hers. 'If I can't love you, I'll never be able to write another song, another poem.'

'Oh, God!' He shuddered, then his lips possessed hers, hard, and his arms held her close and tenderly. 'I dreamed of you loving me. What did I do to deserve you?'

He had loved her. She did not say the words because he was not ready, but she knew that words were unnecessary. His arms were holding her and his eyes were loving her. She shivered and felt his body respond and knew that she was home.

She whispered, 'All my life, I wanted a home that was really mine. Moving around all the time, and the crazy scene that was the music world. I tried to pretend I was at home when I went to Queen Charlotte, but——' She swallowed and said raggedly, 'When you came to my door, that was the first time I believed there was something more to loving than the fantasies I spun in my music-room.'

His hands slid under the loose cotton of her blouse, fingers shaping the satiny flesh underneath. She was losing the slender curves that he had once made love to, but his touch was trembling and his voice intense as he murmured, 'I want to pick you up and carry you into my bedroom.'

He felt her body's response to his suggestion and laughed huskily. She warned, 'You'd better not. The doctor would have my head.' His lips possessed hers and she managed only to gasp, 'What about lunch?'

'Loving first,' he growled, and something seemed to catch in his throat.

She pressed her lips against his throat and said softly, 'You don't need to say it.'

He silenced her with a kiss.

She had thought her body would be awkward, but his touch was magic, and when she trembled she could see his eyes flash in response. Then he took her hand, and they were in his room, moving to the big bed. He lay down with her, touched her, and it was more than it had been before. Deeper and more shattering, filled with a long tenderness that brought tears to her eyes.

'Don't cry,' he said, holding her, slowly exploring her lovely softness with his fingertips. 'Please don't cry.'

She moved closer, into his arms, her flesh merging with his, telling him without words that the tears were for feeling, for fullness. For love, not sadness.

'I love you,' he said, and the world went still.

'Was it hard to say?'

He bent over her. 'I've loved you for so long. The words have been inside, trying to get out.'

'I've watched you with Robbie,' she whispered. 'You're going to make a wonderful father.'

'If you're there to help me. You will be, won't you? You're going to marry me?' She saw his face go harsh and cold, but she understood now that it was only a mask.

'Yes.' She returned his kiss, giving herself up to her lover. 'I love you...I've always loved you. Forever.' She would tell him so often, make sure he did not ever forget.

Then he touched her intimately and she gasped and moved closer, returning his caress. He groaned and moved over her and there were no more barriers. They were together, beyond walls or restraints, pleasuring each other almost beyond bearing. She held him close when she felt the powerful build-up to his release, felt the answering pressure inside herself, heard her voice making formless sounds of needing and loving.

He groaned her name, and his love, as he took them both beyond the stars. Then he held her in his arms, closely against his heart, and when their pulses quieted, they slept. Together.

Outside, on the water, the loon bobbed up from the glassy bay, craned his long neck and looked towards the silent house. Overhead, an eagle swooped down from a cloudless sky. In the kitchen, the can opener lay open on the floor, forgotten.

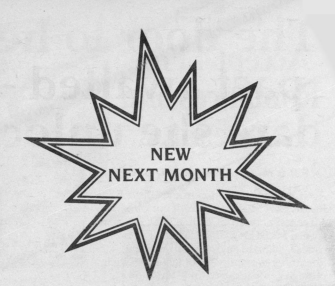

**NEW
NEXT MONTH**

Follow the fortunes of love in our new zodiac romances.
Every month we will be featuring a new hero and
heroine with different star signs as they embark upon
the romance of a lifetime.

Discover whether they will find a match made in heaven
or are destined to be star-crossed lovers!

Watch out for this new title amongst your Mills & Boon
Romances from March.

Mills & Boon

Accept 4 Free Romances and 2 Free gifts

• FROM MILLS & BOON •

An irresistible invitation from Mills & Boon Reader Service. Please accept our offer of 4 free romances, a CUDDLY TEDDY and a special MYSTERY GIFT... Then, if you choose, go on to enjoy 6 more exciting Romances every month for just £1.45 each postage and packaging free. Plus our FREE newsletter with author news, competitions and much more.

**Send the coupon below at once to:
Reader Service, FREEPOST, P.O. Box 236, Croydon, Surrey CR9 9EL**

✄ — — — — — ┤ **NO STAMP NEEDED** ├ — —

YES! Please rush me my 4 Free Romances and 2 FREE Gifts! Please also reserve me a Reader Service Subscription so I can look forward to receiving 6 Brand New Romances each month for just £8.70, post and packing free. If I choose not to subscribe I shall write to you within 10 days. I understand I can keep the free books and gifts whatever I decide. I can cancel or suspend my subscription at any time. I am over 18 years of age.

Name Mr/Mrs/Miss ———————————————— EP86R

Address ————————————————————————

————————————————————————————————

———————————————— Postcode ——————————

Signature ——————————————————————————

mps MAILING PREFERENCE SERVICE

A SPECIAL GIFT FOR MOTHER'S DAY

Four new Romances by some of your favourite authors have been selected as a special treat for Mother's Day.

A CIVILISED ARRANGEMENT
Catherine George
THE GEMINI BRIDE
Sally Heywood
AN IMPOSSIBLE SITUATION
Margaret Mayo
LIGHTNING'S LADY
Valerie Parv

Four charming love stories for only £5.80, the perfect gift for Mother's Day . . . or you can even treat yourself.

Look out for the special pack from January 1991.

Next month's Romances

Each month, you can choose from a world of variety in romance with Mills & Boon. These are the new titles to look out for next month.

DOUBLY DELICIOUS Emma Goldrick

MEMORIES OF THE PAST Carole Mortimer

DEAL OF A LIFETIME Susan Napier

THE GIFT OF LOVING Patricia Wilson

TROUBLE ON TOUR Kay Thorpe

GIVE AND TAKE Kate Walker

THE DIRECTOR'S WIFE Lindsay Armstrong

ROMANTIC JOURNEY Stephanie Howard

A LOVE THAT ENDURES Clau.dia Jameson

LOST IN A DREAM Sandra Marton

PRIVATE PROPERTY Rosalie Ash

DISASTROUS ENCOUNTER Kerry Allyne

IMPOSSIBLE INHERITANCE Annabel Murray

KEPT WOMAN Karen van der Zee

STARSIGN

THE DEVIL HIS DUE Diana Hamilton

UNFAIR ASSUMPTIONS Emma Richmond

Available from Boots, Martins, John Menzies, W.H. Smith, Woolworths and other paperback stockists.

Also available from Mills and Boon Reader Service, P.O. Box 236, Thornton Road, Croydon, Surrey CR9 3RU.

LEFT YOU DEAD

Pet⟶ ⟶amⁿ ⟶ ⟶ ⟶ ⟶ bestselling author, best known ⟶ ⟶e and thriller novels, and the creator of the much-⟶ved Detective Superintendent Roy Grace. Globally, his books have been translated into thirty-seven languages.

Synonymous with plot-twisting page-turners, Peter has garnered an army of loyal fans throughout his storytelling career – which also included stints writing for TV and producing films. He has won over forty awards for his work, including the WHSmith Best Crime Author of All Time Award, the Crime Writers' Association Diamond Dagger and a BAFTA nomination for *The Merchant of Venice* starring Al Pacino and Jeremy Irons for which he was an executive producer. Many of Peter's novels have been adapted for film, TV and stage.

www.peterjames.com
🐦 @peterjamesuk
f peterjames.roygrace
📷 @peterjamesuk
You[Tube] Peter James TV

The Detective Superintendent Roy Grace books in order:

DEAD SIMPLE

In the first Roy Grace novel, a harmless
stag-do prank leads to deadly consequences.

LOOKING GOOD DEAD

It started with an act of kindness
and ended in murder.

NOT DEAD ENOUGH

Can a killer be in two places at once?
Roy Grace must solve a case of stolen identity.

DEAD MAN'S FOOTSTEPS

The discovery of skeletal remains in Brighton
sparks a global investigation.

DEAD TOMORROW

In an evil world, everything's for sale.

DEAD LIKE YOU

After thirteen years, has the notorious
'Shoe Man' killer returned?

DEAD MAN'S GRIP

A trail of death follows a devastating
traffic accident.

NOT DEAD YET

Terror on the silver screen;
an obsessive stalker on the loose.

DEAD MAN'S TIME

A priceless watch is stolen and the powerful
Daly family will do *anything* to get it back.

WANT YOU DEAD

Who knew online dating could be so deadly?

YOU ARE DEAD

Brighton falls victim to its first serial killer in eighty years.

LOVE YOU DEAD

A deadly black widow is on the hunt for
her next husband.

NEED YOU DEAD

Every killer makes a mistake somewhere.
You just have to find it.

DEAD IF YOU DON'T

A kidnapping triggers a parent's worst nightmare
and a race against time for Roy Grace.

DEAD AT FIRST SIGHT

Roy Grace exposes the lethal side
of online identity fraud.

FIND THEM DEAD

A ruthless Brighton gangster is on trial and will
do anything to walk free.

LEFT YOU DEAD

When a woman in Brighton vanishes without a trace,
Roy Grace is called in to investigate.

Also by Peter James

DEAD LETTER DROP   ATOM BOMB ANGEL
BILLIONAIRE   POSSESSION   DREAMER
SWEET HEART   TWILIGHT   PROPHECY
ALCHEMIST   HOST   THE TRUTH
DENIAL   FAITH   PERFECT PEOPLE
THE HOUSE ON COLD HILL   ABSOLUTE PROOF
THE SECRET OF COLD HILL   I FOLLOW YOU

Short Story Collection
A TWIST OF THE KNIFE

Children's Novel
GETTING WIRED!

Novella
THE PERFECT MURDER
WISH YOU WERE DEAD (*A Roy Grace Quick Read*)

Non-Fiction
DEATH COMES KNOCKING: POLICING ROY GRACE'S
BRIGHTON (*with Graham Bartlett*)
BABES IN THE WOOD (*with Graham Bartlett*)

LEFT YOU DEAD

PETER JAMES

PAN BOOKS

First published 2021 by Macmillan

This edition first published 2021 by Pan Books
an imprint of Pan Macmillan
The Smithson, 6 Briset Street, London EC1M 5NR
EU representative: Macmillan Publishers Ireland Ltd, 1st Floor,
The Liffey Trust Centre, 117–126 Sheriff Street Upper,
Dublin 1, D01 YC43
Associated companies throughout the world
www.panmacmillan.com

ISBN   978-1-5290-0426-7

1 3 5 7 9 8 6 4 2

A CIP catalogue record for this book is available from the British Library.

Map artwork by ML Design
Typeset by Palimpsest Book Production Ltd, Falkirk, Stirlingshire
Printed and bound by CPI Group (UK) Ltd, Croydon, CR0 4YY

MIX
Paper from
responsible sources
FSC® C116313

Visit **www.panmacmillan.com** to read more about all our books
and to buy them. You will also find features, author interviews and
news of any author events, and you can sign up for e-newsletters
so that you're always first to hear about our new releases.

In memory of our beloved Oscar, and to all pets everywhere, thank you for the unconditional love you bring your humans. And a special shout-out to Spooky, Wally, Willy and Woo, and all the rest of our furry and feathered gang!

SUSSEX

A/M23 to Croydon

Ashdown Forest

Haywards Heath

Burgess Hill

CID HQ Malling House

Lewes

Newhaven

Seaford

Peacehaven

Beachy Head

A27

All Saints, Patcham

Henfield

Tesco Holmbush

BRIGHTON

HOVE

Brighton Marina

Shoreham Airport

WORTHING

Isle of Wight

4 miles

6 kilometres

1

Most Sundays, at some point, they bickered over something. Mostly about nothing important. And mostly it blew over quickly when they just looked at each other and laughed it off. And this Sunday afternoon, coming up to their fourth wedding anniversary in just a few weeks' time, was no exception. Today's bickering had been about cat litter.

Niall's driving scared Eden at the best of times, although he'd only had the one accident. A few years ago, he was driving them home from a date and had rolled their car. He had been showing off, stupidly, he confessed. They'd just bought a new – well, second-hand – Golf GTI and he was demonstrating how quick it was when, in the murmured words of one of the traffic cops to colleagues attending the scene, he'd run out of talent.

Today they'd been arguing for the past half-hour as they headed home. And, as ever when Niall was annoyed, he drove their BMW faster than normal. They'd already had one near miss as he'd passed a car towing a caravan, pulling in just feet in front of an oncoming Land Rover.

Great, Eden thought, *I'm going to die any minute and my last words on earth will have been 'cat litter'.*

'Look, do we really need to get it now, darling?' Niall said, calming a little. 'I want to try to catch the end of the Grand Prix.'

'You can watch it on catch-up.'

'Not the same.' He wound down his window and chucked a

tired piece of gum out, fished in his pocket and chewed on a fresh tab.

'I wish you wouldn't do that – wrap it up and put it in a bin,' she tutted. 'We do need to get it now, you were going to pick it up on Friday and you forgot,' she reminded him. 'And you were going to pick it up yesterday and you forgot again.'

'I know, but I was busy – trying to earn money. Three airport runs and only one stingy tip.'

'You should think about working for Uber. You can rate your passengers, give them one star if they don't tip.'

'The day I work for Uber,' he replied, 'will be the day I own it.'

She let that go, Niall and his big dreams, not wanting their row to flare up again. 'It'll take me just five minutes to dash in and get it.'

He grunted.

She leaned forward and picked his iPhone up. 'Just going to look at the photos you took today.'

'Can't believe you let your phone battery run so low, it has a much better camera.'

'I would have charged it in the car if you'd remember to get a new cable that actually works. I've turned it off to conserve what's left,' she said, flicking through the maze of apps.

'You should have charged it last night.'

She shook her head. 'Well I didn't.'

He grunted again.

'Christ,' she said, continuing to look through his apps. 'How many apps do you have on here? You must have over a hundred! Bet you don't even remember what half of them are. You said you were going to get rid of the ones you never use.'

'I will when I have time.'

She shook her head, grinning. 'If it makes you happy to have them . . .'

He grinned back. 'Actually, it makes me 'appy.'

'That's terrible!' She found a folder labelled Photography, which contained the camera and albums, and tapped on Photos. There were several, taken earlier this afternoon, of the beautiful exterior of a grand Elizabethan mansion and its magnificently kept grounds looking their best in the late summer sun. The lake. The views across the South Downs. Then several of her, in tight white shorts and a pink top, leaning against a wooden railed fence, with the lake behind.

'Wow! You've taken some great ones of me!' she said. 'Love them. Well, some of them.'

'They'd have been even better on your phone.'

Surreptitiously, she deleted the ones she liked the least, leaving just one that she was really happy with, the one of her standing with the lake in the background. Then she went back to going through the apps. 'What's this one – MindNode?'

'No idea.'

'I'll delete it for you, shall I?'

'Go ahead,' he said, with faint irritation in his voice.

She continued through, deleting a couple more after questioning him on them.

As they entered the 40 mph limit on the Upper Shoreham Road, he pointed through the windscreen at the thickening clouds. 'Rain's forecast in two hours. I've got to do a Heathrow pickup tonight and I really want to do a bike ride after the Grand Prix, get in some cardio before I have to go. Can it wait until tomorrow?'

'The cat won't know to cross its legs, darling,' she said. 'Just pull up outside, I can run into the store, grab some and be straight out again. I'll be five minutes.'

'Promise? I know what you're like when you get into a store – you just start buying everything else you think you need.'

She grinned at him and touched his thigh suggestively. 'You're all I need.'

'Yeah yeah!'

She leaned over and kissed him on the cheek. And immediately saw that strange, unsettling look in his eyes. So different to when they had first got together, when she saw only deep love. 'I promise,' she said.

Niall's mother was Spanish. He had a shock of dark-brown curls and a face that had reminded her, the first time she saw him, of a younger version of the actor Dominic West. When he smiled, he was the handsomest man on earth. When he was angry, he looked almost Neanderthal.

Their regular Sunday pastime was visiting National Trust properties whenever possible, which were free on their membership card. But this afternoon they'd been to Parham House, owned by a different trust, wandering around its glorious deer park.

Niall drove into the car park of the huge Tesco superstore, three miles to the west of their home in Brighton. And was immediately annoyed by the queue of cars in front of them. 'Look at this – shit, baby – this is going to take ages.'

'Just stop the car and I'll jump out and run in while you park. Then I'll come and find you.'

'That stuff's heavy – are you sure?'

She gave him a sideways look. 'When did you last actually get any?'

'Um – I don't remember.'

'So how do you think it appears in the house? By magic? Does the Tooth Fairy bring it?'

'OK, OK, muscle woman – look, I'll pull in over there.' He swung into an empty bay, some distance from the store.

Grabbing her handbag, Eden jumped out, blew him a kiss, slammed the door and hurried off through the maze of vehicles.

Niall turned up the volume on the radio and listened to Laura Palumbo singing 'Life Goes On'.

It was followed by another song. He was tempted to light a

4

cigarette, but Eden didn't like him smoking in the car. She didn't actually like him smoking at all. So he just sat, listening to the music, looking anxiously at his watch then at the car clock. Van Morrison's 'Brown Eyed Girl'. Then another song, Johnny Cash, 'You Are My Sunshine'. They both loved country and western. Maybe she'd be back before the song ended – this was one of her faves.

But she wasn't.

Another song played. Then another.

Twenty minutes had passed, he realized. *What's going on?* he wondered. *She's probably shopping for more stuff, despite her promise.* The sky was darkening further. His chances of catching the final stages of the Grand Prix were fading. He had recorded it and could watch it later or tomorrow, but that really wasn't the same. Now his concern was to get home before it started raining and to head out on his bike.

He looked at the car clock, then his watch yet again. Another song. Twenty-five minutes. Then half an hour. *What the hell are you doing in there?* In a flash of temper, he punched the steering wheel boss – and winced in pain.

He would give it another five minutes, he decided.

How long does it take to get a bag of cat litter?

It was coming up to 3.50 p.m.

Finally, losing his patience, he decided to go and find her.

2

Sunday 1 September

A tall, ginger-haired employee, with a badge that read *Tim*, blocked his path.

'I'm afraid we're closing in ten minutes, sir,' he said courteously.

'I'm just going to help my wife with a bag of cat litter,' Niall said.

'Oh, of course, that's fine, sir,' he said, stepping aside. 'The cat litter's down aisle two.'

Niall entered the vast interior, which was thinning out. There were lines of customers at each till, and more at the self-checkout area to his right. But Eden wasn't among them.

He saw another member of staff, a woman with long brown hair. 'Excuse me, where do I find aisle two?' he asked.

She offered to take him, but he asked her to just direct him.

He hurried down an aisle of dairy products, with books and DVDs to his right, towards the rear of the store, barging past a woman with a small child who shouted something at him. Waving an apology, he turned right at the deli counter, as directed. He made his way past several aisles, glancing down each one, and finally came to the one marked *Pet and Animal Supplies*.

It was empty, like all the others.

He strode down it to the fast-diminishing queues at the checkout tills. No sign of Eden – what on earth was she doing?

6

Increasingly irked now, he strode up and down the deserted aisles of the store. Stopping in front of *Cereals,* he pulled out his phone and called her.

'This number is currently unavailable, please try later.'

Turn your bloody phone on.

A big, tubby security guy swaggered towards him, radio clipped to his chest, a bunch of keys hanging from his belt, like a gaoler's. An amiable but no-nonsense face. 'I'm sorry, sir, we're closed now. If I could ask you to make for the exit.'

'I'm trying to find my wife,' Niall replied. 'She came in over half an hour ago and I can't find her anywhere.'

'She's not at the checkout?'

He shook his head.

'Want me to put a request out on the tannoy?'

'If you wouldn't mind. Maybe someone could check the toilets in case she's sick or something?'

'Your wife's name is, sir?'

'Eden – Eden Paternoster.'

'Eden, as in garden of?'

Niall nodded.

The guard spoke into his radio.

Moments later, Niall heard, through the tannoy, 'Would Mrs Eden Paster-Noster please go to the customer service desk at the front of the store, where her husband is waiting.'

Niall didn't bother asking him to correct the announcement.

The guard indicated for him to follow. 'I'll have someone check out the toilets, sir. Can you give me a description of the lady?'

'She's thirty-one, five seven, shoulder-length brown hair, wearing a pink-coloured top and white shorts.'

Deadpan, the guard led Niall through to the front, stopped near an employee who was stacking tins of beans on a shelf and spoke into his radio. Then they walked on, bypassing the checkout counters and the news stand, and stopped at the customer service desk over to the right of them. There was a small blue-and-white podium a short distance away with two large computer monitors. Both showed empty aisles.

'We'll take a look at the whole store, sir,' the guard said. He worked a toggle on a control panel to the side of the desk. Aisle after aisle appeared, with just a few members of staff who were restocking shelves. No Eden.

The last customers were now going through the checkout desks. Niall could see the self-checkout tills were empty.

The security guard's radio crackled. He listened briefly, then turned to Niall. 'There's no one in the toilets, sir. You are sure she came into this store?'

'Yes, absolutely.'

The guard asked an employee at the customer service desk to put out a Code Six call. Moments later, her voice rang through the tannoy.

'This is a colleague announcement for all managers – Code Six in progress.'

Several employees materialized over the next couple of minutes. Seven, Niall counted.

The guard spoke to them. 'This gentleman's wife is missing. Age thirty-one, shoulder-length brown hair. She's wearing a pink top and white shorts. Name of Mrs Eden Paster-Noster. Please do a sweep of the aisles.'

'*Paternoster!*' Niall corrected him this time.

'Apologies. Mrs Eden *Paternoster*,' the guard told them.

As they all hurried off, the guard turned to Niall. 'She couldn't have left the store?'

'Well, she knew where I was parked.'

'She didn't go to Marks and Spencer, maybe, or McDonald's?'

'Not unless either of them sells cat litter.'

Again, no smile.

'She didn't leave just as you came in, and you missed her, sir?'

Niall shrugged. That was possible. Maybe he was making a huge fuss over nothing. He tugged his phone out of his pocket, checked just in case there was a text or WhatsApp from Eden, then dialled her again.

And, again, it was unavailable.

'They both shut at four too?' Niall asked.

'M and S, yes. Not McDonald's.'

Five minutes later, all the employees doing the sweep of the store had returned. Eden wasn't on the premises.

Niall thanked them and had a sudden feeling that he was being a total idiot. What if the guard was right and he had missed her somehow, Eden coming out as he'd gone in?

He walked swiftly back through the emptying car park towards the dusty, black BMW convertible. Even though he'd put the roof up and was sure he'd locked it, he peered through the window when he reached it.

She wasn't in the car.

3

Roy Grace pulled his Alfa Romeo coupé into the largely empty car park across the rural road from Ford prison, in West Sussex, shortly after 4 p.m. The Detective Superintendent was dressed in weekend casuals, jeans, T-shirt and a light jacket. He'd deliberately chosen to come at the weekend to make this a private visit, and had pulled a favour from the Governor, whom he was friendly with, to ensure this wasn't recorded as official business. Grace suspected there was going to be a very good reason why he wouldn't want his boss, Assistant Chief Constable Cassian Pewe, to know about this visit and quiz him on his purpose, as he surely would have done if it had been during work time.

Police officers rarely felt comfortable doing prison visits, knowing that if they were unlucky enough to be there when a riot happened to kick off, they'd be the first target for the inmates. It didn't matter how you dressed, you could be as casual as you liked, your job was ingrained in your skin as potently as cheap aftershave. Most cons could smell you a mile away. Copper. Scum. Pigs. Filth.

He had come out of curiosity, after receiving a handwritten letter a while ago from his disgraced former colleague Detective Sergeant Guy Batchelor.

Roy,

Hope this finds you well. Not much to report here, other than waiting for the appeal hearing against the length of my sentence. Other prisoners haven't been as nasty to me as I feared – so far, anyway.

I'm writing because I may have something of interest about our mutual friend. No names mentioned because all these letters are read, but I know you were interested in doing something with that church bench. I may be able to help you. Perhaps you could come over – I can promise you it won't be a wasted journey.

All my best to you and all the team – hey, I miss you all.

Guy

The letter contained a cryptic clue which his wife, Cleo, had solved for him. *Church bench* equalled *Pew*, she'd suggested, brilliantly.

For almost two years, Assistant Chief Constable Cassian Pewe, his direct boss, had been the bane of his life, to the point where Grace had been seriously considering leaving Sussex Police and taking up a Commander role he'd been offered in London's Metropolitan Police, just to get away from the vile and odious man.

He opened the driver's door with some misgivings and stepped out into the vast empty space and silence beneath a mackerel sky which seemed to share these misgivings, and which, from his limited experience of sailing, he knew heralded rain in a few hours. But it was still a warm afternoon. As he walked through the car park and then crossed the road towards the compound of single-storey buildings, he thought that if it wasn't for the high mesh fencing, the place could have been mistaken for a holiday camp.

Men's prisons in Britain were categorized from A to D. Cat A were high security, housing violent and dangerous convicts such as serial killers and terrorists who posed the greatest threat to the public, police or national security. Cat B were also high security, but for those who were deemed less of a threat, as well as for prisoners in the local area and those who were being held long-term. Cat C were training and resettlement prisons, enabling prisoners to develop skills to use on their release. Cat D, like this one, were open prisons, for those regarded to be a minimal risk, mostly white-collar criminals, but also for inmates from higher category prisons who were nearing the end of their sentences and were considered safe and suitable to soon re-enter the community.

All the same, he slipped his warrant card under the glass shield of the security desk with the same unease he always felt arriving at any prison. He waited while the serious-looking woman on the other side, who was neither pleasant nor unpleasant, studied his identity, before shoving the small grey tray containing his warrant card back at him. 'Please put your phone and any valuables in one of the lockers behind you, Detective Superintendent.' She gave him only the very faintest nod of acknowledgement that they were both on the same side here.

Roy complied, immediately feeling naked as he parted with his ID and phone – his lifeline to the outside world – set the combination and stepped through the electric door, which immediately closed behind him like an airlock.

Tabloid newspapers regularly ran shouty headlines about how cushy life inside British prisons was. But he bet none of their editors had ever sampled even just one night at Her Majesty's Pleasure.

He hadn't either, but he'd talked to plenty of people who had. And no one, ever, had told him it had been a party. In many prisons, such as Sussex's Category B, HMP Lewes, on some wings the inmates were forced to share a cell with two bunks and a toilet with no seat behind a plastic shower curtain, just three feet from the face of the unfortunate on the lower bunk. And had to try to sleep on pillows harder than breeze blocks.

At least here, in Ford, he knew each prisoner had his own decent, if cramped, cell.

After a couple of minutes, a second door opened and an officer, with keys hanging from his belt, greeted him with a friendly smile and an outstretched hand. 'Detective Superintendent Grace, don't know if you remember me from Lewes prison, a couple of years ago?'

Roy Grace, who had a near-photographic memory for names and faces, looked at him. Short grey hair and rounded shoulders. 'Andrew Kempson?'

'Well, I am impressed!'

Roy shrugged.

'Very good to see you again, sir. The Governor thought it best you came after general visiting hours were over, and he's arranged for you to meet former Detective Sergeant Batchelor in a private interview room, cameras off, and the Governor knows you are going to be handed some evidence.'

Unlike some prison officers, Kempson at least seemed refreshingly respectful to his charges. Roy Grace followed him across a wide, open courtyard, past a row of prefab single-storey buildings. Several men were mooching around, some stooped, with that air of total defeat he'd observed on previous prison visits, others looking more determined and purposeful. One, with a rake and bin bag, looked like he was actually happy to be doing something useful.

They entered a large room that felt like an impoverished, denuded public library. Several prisoners were seated at bare tables, either reading newspapers or books, in front of racks of shelves containing, almost exclusively, crime novels. Among them he noticed several by Martina Cole, Kimberley Chambers and Ian Rankin. Following Kempson, Roy was ushered by the officer into a room at the far end.

And was greeted by the sheepish smile of his former colleague and, until recently, one of the most capable detectives on his team.

Guy Batchelor, with his burly physique, rose from a chair.

Some while ago, the Detective Sergeant had totally lost the plot when a woman he'd been having an affair with, and to whom he had apparently made all kinds of promises about a future together, had trapped him in a web of lies. It had resulted, if Batchelor was telling the truth, in a furious row, in which, through an escalating chain of events, she'd ended up dead in a bathtub, and he'd panicked. In the ensuing downward spiral, the DS had attempted to commit suicide and Roy had risked his own life trying to stop him.

Throughout his life – and career – Grace had always been prepared to see the best in people. He believed, with some exceptions, that most human beings were fundamentally decent, and that it was stuff beyond their control, whether abusive parents in their childhood or something that happened later in their lives, that skewed them onto the wrong path.

So when Guy had made contact saying he wanted to see him because he had something that might be of value to him, Roy had decided he would see him, both because he was intrigued by what Guy might have to say, but also just to talk to him. And because maybe, in some small way, he could help this man who had ruined his own life and the lives of others in a period of madness.

All the same, he was here with some reservations.

It was just like any other interview room. A metal table, hard chairs, wide-angle CCTV camera up near the ceiling. A red note-book sitting on the table.

'I'll be outside,' Andrew Kempson said. 'I'll be back in an hour but shout if you need me.'

'I doubt that will be necessary,' Grace said.

Kempson gave him a 'you never know' shrug, and shut the door, more softly than some officers might have.

4

Roy Grace shook Batchelor's hand, trying to mask his surprise at his appearance. The former DS had aged a decade since he'd last seen him in court. And one of the things that was different about him was that he no longer reeked of cigarette smoke.

'So, how are you, Guy?' Grace felt so many conflicting emotions, actually seeing him. Batchelor had once been a family man and a highly respected detective. Grace knew that for the rest of Guy's life, the knowledge of what had happened and the guilt would haunt his dreams and his every waking thought. It would never leave him. And what future lay ahead for him, once he walked out of the prison gates, he couldn't even begin to guess at.

'Yeah, all right actually. A lot better since I was moved here. Lewes was a real shithole. Five days confined to my room because there weren't enough officers. No shower or change of clothes. It's OK here, I can cope.'

Grace nodded. He'd always hated corrupt police officers and was intrigued to know more as to why Guy Batchelor had become corrupt himself. He was now paying a terrible price. Life gave you second chances for most screw-ups you made. But killing a fellow human being was crossing the Rubicon.

Then an old saying he had once read came to his mind: *Before you judge a man, walk a mile in his shoes.*

Pulling up a chair opposite Guy, he sat down.

'Honestly, boss, I'm gobsmacked you actually came.'

Grace shrugged. 'Guy, I'm not condoning anything you've done, by this visit. But I do know shit can happen to any of us, at any time. Who was it who said that we are all just one pay cheque away from being homeless? Anyway, it took a while to organize but I'm here now.'

It was good to see Guy smile, he thought. And that smile momentarily dropped the decade from his face.

Batchelor raised his arms expansively. 'Sorry I can't offer you a drink, boss. Sort of got limited facilities here.'

It was Grace's turn to smile. Then, serious, he said, 'So, tell me? Good cryptic clue by the way.'

'Figured you would get it.'

'Actually, Cleo did.'

Batchelor tilted his head and said wryly, 'Not losing your touch, are you?'

'Want to end up in a Cat A prison or do you want to tell me about my good friend, Mr Church Bench?' Grace said, with mock severity.

'I'll go for the second option.'

'Thought you might.'

'OK – when I was in Lewes prison, in a tastefully furnished double room with en-suite bog, last redecorated circa 1890, I had a cellmate who, like myself, had never been *inside* before. He was a very charming Indian man, a stockbroker with a small London City firm. As you can imagine, we had many hours, especially because of staff shortages, in which we were locked in the cell with nothing to do except read, watch television or chinwag.'

Grace nodded.

'He liked to talk. When I went in, I'd tried to keep it quiet that I'd been in the police, obviously, but it was common knowledge before I'd even arrived. My cell buddy – I won't give you his full name, let's just call him Raj – told me he'd become friendly with a senior copper in the Met a few years back. At the time this officer had been with the Serious Fraud Office and they were investigating a wealthy client of Raj's firm who had alleged links with organized crime. Anyhow, those links turned out to be unprovable and the investigation was dropped. But, in the interim, Raj had struck up a friendship with the Met detective.'

'Whose name I might possibly know?'

'Quite possibly.' Guy gave a thin smile. 'Raj slipped a few insider-trading tips to said officer, enabling him to amass considerable personal wealth. Quite illegally. Raj's firm, a relative minnow by City standards, had outperformed the stock market for their clients for several years – through this insider trading practice.'

'Then the crunch came?' Roy Grace suggested.

'Exactly. Raj's company had hit the Financial Regulator's radar. Raj's buddy in the Met made a phone call to tell him to get his house in order, PDQ. It was a deliberate breach of the Data Protection Act, providing information that should not have been disclosed. He may well have also perverted the course of justice.'

'And?' Grace quizzed.

'As a result of this call, Raj was able to take preventative action to reduce the evidence that would be recovered by the Met when they raided his home and business premises. That tip-off, Raj told me, probably halved his prison sentence. He's expecting a future visit from the Met Financial Crimes Team to find out what more he can say about his former clients – he wants to use his information as a bargaining chip to try to get moved from Lewes to an open prison in the Birmingham area to be closer to his family.'

'So, do you want to confirm this Met detective's name?' Grace said.

Guy Batchelor grinned again. 'It's as you deduced, Sherlock – or rather, Cleo did. Her maiden name's not Watson by any chance?' He opened the notebook on the table and began to read, stumbling at times as he tried to decipher his own handwriting – a problem Roy Grace had often encountered himself, as a junior officer, taking statements in the days before they had become mostly electronic.

When Batchelor had finished, Roy had to restrain himself from punching the air with elation.

Stockbrokers routinely recorded all phone conversations with clients, as proof of any instructions should the client dispute one. Guy Batchelor had just read out the details of a digital recording of Cassian Pewe, pleading with Raj to wipe all records of him making stock purchases and sales over the previous three years before the investigation. Apparently Raj left the evidence with a family member before being imprisoned.

If the real recording was anything close to what Raj had apparently recited to Guy, this was dynamite.

Roy Grace said nothing for a short while, thinking it through. Then he said, 'There's one thing I don't understand, Guy – which is why you're telling me this?'

Batchelor shrugged. 'Two reasons, boss. One's personal, the other isn't. Personal first. I sent a request to ACC Pewe, asking if he would appear as a character witness at my trial, and he never responded. I sent the request three times.' He shrugged again. 'Second reason is I know how much he fucked you around. You always stood by me. I remember your words in court, despite all I'd put you through. I didn't deserve it, but I'll respect you forever for it.'

'Can you do me a favour, Guy? Keep this information confidential for the moment. I'd like to take it directly to Alison Vosper – she's now a Deputy Assistant Commissioner in the Met. At the time Pewe appears to have committed these crimes he was a serving Metropolitan Police officer. Will you do that?'

'Of course.'

'I really appreciate you coming forward with this information, whatever your reasons for doing so.' Grace sat for a moment, thinking. 'So, if I need what you have in that notebook, can I use it? You can expect a visit from the Met's Anti-Corruption Team, and probably sooner rather than later.'

Batchelor shoved it across the table towards him. 'It's yours, take it. I kind of feel I owe you one.'

Roy Grace had been asked a number of times over the years if he had ever felt his life had been on the line during his work as a police officer. And his answer was, yes, on several occasions. The most recent of which had been, despite his fear of heights, scaling the vertical, interior ladder of Brighton's 531-foot-high i360 tower in an attempt to stop a panicked Guy Batchelor from jumping off the top. What had been far worse than climbing up it, when he had been fuelled by adrenaline, was having to climb back down, knowing that if his grip slipped for just one moment he would have plunged to certain death.

'You could say that,' he replied. Then he held up the notebook. 'Consider the debt paid, with interest.'

5

Back in the prison car park, Roy Grace sat in his Alfa, window cracked to let in some breeze, and opened the red notebook. His hands were shaking as he began to read Batchelor's notes – or rather, began the slow work of deciphering them.

Half an hour had passed, he realized with a start, by the time he had finished. And his hands were now shaking even more. Shit, if this was true, he would have ACC Cassian Pewe bang to rights!

He started the car and headed back towards home, his mind in turmoil. He felt conflicted. If what Guy had given him was genuine – and he little doubted it was – and if this Raj, whoever he was, would hand over the recording of Pewe and testify – and he had a good motive for doing so – then Cassian Pewe's career was toast. And he might well face a prison sentence.

But Grace wasn't smiling as he drove. Sure, Pewe was a pain in the arse, but he churned over in his mind for some minutes the morality of destroying a fellow officer's career – however much he loathed the man. Could he do this? Deep down he knew that, having this information, it was now his duty to do so, and immediately.

He pulled into a lay-by on the A27 and switched the engine off. He picked up his phone, found Alison Vosper's mobile number in the address book and dialled it.

Expecting it to go to voicemail, he was both pleasantly surprised – and somewhat nervous – when she answered on the third ring.

'Roy! Nice to hear from you. So have you changed your mind and decided to take my offer of a Commander role in the Met? I presume that's why you're calling?'

'Well, ma'am, not exactly – though this is connected to your offer, albeit in an oblique way.'

'Oblique? Should we be doing our heads in with words like "oblique" on a Sunday evening?'

In all the time he'd known the former ACC of Sussex, he'd found it hard to tell when she was being nice, indeed humorous, or just plain sarcastic.

'I'll skip the *oblique* and come straight to the point, ma'am.'

He summarized what Guy Batchelor had told him earlier, much of it seemingly confirmed by the notes in the red book.

She was silent for so long after he had finished that he began to wonder if they'd been cut off. Then, the tone of her voice very different, serious and to the point, she said, 'Roy, how certain are you this former officer has told you the truth?'

'One hundred per cent,' he said, without hesitation.

'Even though he's serving time in prison?'

'He's not looking to get anything out of this personally, ma'am.'

'So why has he given this to you?'

'Because he hates corrupt coppers, even though he is one – perhaps he doesn't see that – and he wanted to repay me for standing up for him at his trial with a character reference.'

'Always loyal to your team, aren't you?'

'It wasn't loyalty, ma'am – his appalling behaviour was out of character and the court needed to hear that.'

That seemed to satisfy her. 'OK, Roy. Don't discuss this with any of your colleagues in Sussex. Can you scan and send me the contents of the notebook as soon as possible?'

'I can do it when I get home – half an hour.'

'Good. What I'll do is place this in the hands of the Met Anti-Corruption Unit.' She paused. 'Roy, I don't need to tell you this is a very delicate scenario – it needs to be handled both carefully and highly confidentially.'

'Absolutely.'

'I will also personally brief the Chief Constable of Sussex and the Police and Crime Commissioner – they need to be made aware. I don't need you to do anything else at this stage.'

'Understood, ma'am.'

Ending the call, Roy sat for some minutes feeling an almost overwhelming sense of calm. As if the monkey that had been on his back for longer than he could remember had suddenly been prised away. He looked forward to getting home and, hopefully with the rain some hours away, firing up the barbecue before it got too dark.

6

Niall Paternoster pocketed his phone and stood by their car, looking all around, puzzled. Just where on earth was she? No way would Eden have gone to McDonald's, she loathed it. He often had a Big Mac when he was out on the road, and had long stopped telling her except when he deliberately wanted to hack her off, because he would always get a lecture. And she couldn't accept their vegetarian stuff was any good.

Had she gone to M&S? She liked their food halls and still bought stuff there even though, with his reduced income, he felt they couldn't afford their prices any more – not until they were back on their feet, at least. OK, fine, she was still earning decent money, thank God. But much of it went to paying the mortgage and the rest of the bills.

He was well aware she had more income from a portfolio of rental properties she'd built up before they'd met, from savvy investments she'd made from her savings. But they'd always agreed she shouldn't dig into them, and he had no involvement in how she ran that part of her finances, or any of their finances in truth. He told her he wanted their basic food and limited treats – including booze – to come from whatever pittance he got from journeyman cabbing. It was another serious bone of contention, with Eden telling him that his idea of the man being the family breadwinner was just ridiculously old-fashioned – and insulting.

Ever since his printing business had gone under, earlier this

24

year, he'd been driving his mate Mark Tuckwell's Skoda taxi on a casual basis, in the hours Mark didn't want to work. Which was mostly nights through into early morning. Picking up drunks, with the ever-present risk of them projectile vomiting and costing him a £350 clean-up. As well as the occasional fare doing a runner.

He made his way over towards the huge M&S store, but even from a hundred yards away he could see it was closed. No sign of Eden anywhere. He phoned her again. Unavailable. He texted her and WhatsApped her, with the same message. She had said there was some charge on her phone. She must have switched it on by now if she was OK?

Eden, this is not funny, where the hell are you? I'm worried.

He returned to the BMW and waited. Another ten minutes. Fifteen. The car park was emptying. *Shit*, it was now 4.25 p.m.

He sat in the car and tried to think through the possibilities of where she could be.

Kidnapped on her way to the store, or in the store?

Ridiculous.

Came out of the store lugging a heavy sack of cat litter and couldn't find him?

She'd have called or texted him, surely?

Suddenly taken ill?

Passed out somewhere?

They'd searched the store.

Babes, come on, where are you?

He stopped to think. Eden, with her Irish ancestry, had a fiery temper. There had been a few times in the past when they'd had full-blown rows over seemingly nothing, driving somewhere, when she'd told him to stop, got out of the car and taken a taxi home.

He paused for a moment. But they hadn't rowed today, not really, surely? For God's sake, cat litter? But he knew she was independent and spontaneous. Could she have bumped into a friend in the store and asked for a lift home?

She'd done that, also, once before after they'd had an argument. But today it hadn't been like that.

Maybe if he drove home, he'd find her there, and she'd have a perfectly rational explanation – one he'd overlooked? Although, right now, he couldn't think what.

He started the engine and drove an entire circuit of the car park, including checking the service areas behind the stores.

No Eden.

Debating which route to take, he decided on travelling east along the busy Old Shoreham Road, checking his phone for a message at every traffic light he stopped at. All the time thinking. Wondering where, just where she could be.

Nevill Road was almost a mile long, on the outskirts of the City of Brighton and Hove, running north from the Old Shoreham Road, passing the Greyhound Stadium, skirting the border of Hove Park, up to the edge of the city near the South Downs National Park.

Niall turned left at the lights, drove up past the school, then turned left again onto the driveway of their red-brick semi opposite the stadium. He pulled up a couple of yards in front of the motorcycle storage container which housed his Honda Fireblade – which Eden refused to ride on – and his equally cool Trek road bike. Checking his phone yet again – still no word – he climbed out and walked up to the brilliant-white front door, which he'd repainted, along with all the outside woodwork, during the plentiful free time he had these days. He went inside and called out, 'Baby! I'm home!'

He was greeted by a pitiful miaow.

'Eden?' he called again, louder.

Another miaow. Even more pitiful. Reggie peered accusingly at him from the kitchen doorway. They'd named the platinum

Burmese cat after the gangster Reggie Kray because the cat was, in their view, a vain bully but with huge charm and an insatiable greed. He also had a damned annoying miaow. Didn't seem to matter how much or how often they fed the increasingly plump creature, he always wanted more. Some while back, Eden suggested they should have called him Oliver Twist. But that was lost on Niall.

As were the cat's cries now.

But not the stench that greeted him.

Weren't cats supposed to get the hang of peeing and pooping outside? Another thing he had blamed Eden for. She'd refused to let Reggie out for months after he'd had his jabs and his nuts removed, because they lived on a main road. When she'd finally allowed him out, it was strictly just in the back garden which they'd had cat-proofed as much as possible. As a result, Reggie now went out for hours on end, then hurried back indoors, through his flap, whenever he needed to do his business.

Hence the need, still, for cat litter.

Ignoring the creature's cries, he checked out the living room, which was separated from the dining area by an archway. The chess game they were in the middle of sat on the coffee table, a white sofa either side. Suspiciously, he glanced at it, just in case she'd sneaked home to cheat and had removed another piece. He was already a rook down. But it was pretty much as he remembered. She was winning, as usual.

Calling out again, he hurried upstairs and into their bedroom, with its tented ceiling. Eden's idea, when they had first moved in. She'd seen it in some designer magazine and thought it would be romantic to sleep in what she thought felt, sort of, like a Bedouin tent. Except you could now see dozens of dead flies through the fabric when the lights were on.

'Eden!' he shouted and went through into the en-suite bathroom.

It was empty.

He looked at his watch again. Then was tempted to check the result of the Grand Prix, but didn't want to waste any precious time. Sod Eden, whatever her stupid game was, he thought, stripping off his sweaty top and shorts, going through into the bathroom and dumping them in the laundry basket. He washed his face, slapped cold water on his chest, slathered himself in his favourite aftershave, then put on a fresh T-shirt and shorts and his cycling socks and shoes.

Next, he bunged his phone, a shirt, slacks and shoes into a rucksack – he would change into them later before his airport pickup – and wriggled it onto his back, hurrying downstairs as he did so. Grabbing his front-door keys, he went out to the storage container, checked the bike's tyres were hard enough – thank God, they were – and clipped on his helmet.

Moments later, after locking up, he stood on the driveway, looking up and down the pavement for any sign of Eden. The sky was darkening, but he didn't care if he got wet. He pushed off, mounted and pedalled hard. If she wanted to play games, that was fine by him. No doubt she would be home by the time he'd done his airport pickup and got back to Brighton.

7

'God,' Cleo said. 'The poor man – he gave up the throne for the woman he loved and the Royal Family back then really treated him like shit, didn't they? Do you think he deserved that?'

'Darling, I don't think you can trust a single word on that show – I'm sorry, but it makes me angry. If you're going to make a historical drama, you've a duty to your audience to make it accurate, don't you think?' Roy Grace said.

Stuffed from their barbecue, which they'd just finished before the rain started, they were snuggled up on the sofa with an equally stuffed Humphrey between them, who seemed as absorbed in the television programme as they were. After months of showing signs of pain, he had managed to jump up on the sofa for the first time in ages, so the massage treatment he'd been having was seemingly getting him back to normal and helping his condition. Roy had a small glass of rosé and Cleo, pregnant, a glass of water and a bowl of spicy nuts – her latest craving – beside her. The boys were up in their rooms, Noah fast asleep and Bruno no doubt gaming.

Hugging Humphrey, Cleo said, 'I hate to say it, but you were right, Roy. Humphrey wasn't really getting angry with the kids – he was actually in pain. Now look at him after his massages. It's amazing, he's back to soppy Humphrey.'

'Yep.' Roy stroked him. 'Good boy, very, very good boy!'

They'd finally got round to watching *The Crown*. It was 1953.

The Duke of Windsor, having refused to attend the coronation of his niece, Queen Elizabeth II, without his wife, Wallis, the Duchess of Windsor – who had pointedly not been invited – was watching the coronation on a tiny television at their French chateau, with Wallis and a group of their friends. He was standing, cigarette in hand, giving a running commentary on the proceedings, clearly wistful at all that might have been for him. And very bitter at how he had been treated.

'At least the Duke and Duchess had the good fortune to be in a decent chateau – unlike our holiday-from-hell one that I booked us!' Cleo said.

'Hey,' he said. 'We chose it together.'

'Well, next time, let's try to make a better choice, eh?'

Cleo smiled thinly, then looked back at the screen. 'You're right about this show. I was rubbish at History at school,' she said. 'I didn't like my History teacher, so I hardly learned a thing. Now I'm fascinated by it, I want to learn as much as I can, but how can we tell in this series what is the truth and what isn't? I read an interview with the writer, talking about a scene he made up. So how do we know just how much he's invented?'

'I totally agree,' Grace replied. 'If I watch something historical, I want to believe it's accurate, otherwise what's the point? Whatever distortions in this or any other period drama, you'll have millions of people forever believing mistakenly that that was the truth – and that's very dangerous. And not just this show, but countless other so-called historical dramas.'

'Also,' Cleo said, 'it's hard to judge anything that happened in the past by the standards we have today, isn't it?'

'Sure. Attitudes in general were different then. Divorce is part of life today – back then it was pretty much a cardinal sin.'

She looked at him quizzically. 'Would you have given up the throne for me?'

'Without a second's thought.'

She thumped him playfully. 'Liar!'

'I totally would have!'

The dog responded by farting. Both batted away the toxic smell with their hands. 'Humphrey, no, that's disgusting!' Grace chided.

The dog gave him a baleful but unapologetic eye.

'And very disrespectful in front of Her Majesty, Humphrey!' Cleo complained, picking up the remote and freezing the video. 'I can't stop thinking about what you told me earlier, your visit to Guy.'

Batchelor's notebook lay on the table in front of them.

'It could end Cassian Pewe's career,' she said. 'But what if it backfired?'

He nodded. 'I know.'

'They'd be relying on the evidence of a convicted, bent stock-broker and a police officer convicted of manslaughter. How well do you think that would play?'

'In the right hands, it would be goodbye Cassian Pewe.'

She nodded at the television. 'When he was King Edward VIII, he made a massive miscalculation, and lived out the rest of his life a sad and lost man, who had given up the trappings of royal life.'

'And your point is?'

'Swap Wallis Simpson for Cassian Pewe for a moment. You are risking everything that you have over him? You know the Chinese proverb, don't you?'

'Which is?'

'Before you seek revenge, first dig two graves.'

He smiled. 'I will. One for Cassian Pewe and one for his ego.'

8

Mr and Mrs Sutherland, account customers of Mark Tuckwell, were a sweet, wealthy couple in their eighties. They divided their year between their house in Naples, Florida, their flat in Marbella and their penthouse on Hove seafront.

Niall had helped them patiently as they made their way at a painfully slow pace from the airport to the taxi and then from the taxi to their flat. He lugged in Mr Sutherland's Zimmer frame, Mrs Sutherland's folding wheelchair and an incredible amount of luggage which he had only just been able to fit into the taxi, and then carried each of the almost unbelievably heavy suitcases into the rooms they directed.

'You are so kind,' Joan Sutherland had said. 'There's really no need.'

'It's no problem,' he said, sweating profusely.

And bless Mr Sutherland. Tipping Niall, he'd pressed a banknote into his palm, thanking him for his help, and told him to go and buy himself a few drinks. Niall, imagining it to be a tenner or maybe a twenty – or perhaps even a fifty – thanked him profusely. But when he checked it as he got into the lift, he saw it was just a solitary five-pound note. Either the sweet man wasn't quite up to speed with the times or his eyesight was failing. Or maybe he was just a tight-fisted old bastard.

Due to a French air-traffic controllers' go-slow, which had impacted much of Europe, the flight had been over an hour late.

As a result, Niall – cycling the mile back home uphill from the Tuckwell house after returning the taxi – didn't get home until just after 11.45 p.m. By the time he took off the fuel cost and Mark deducted his cut, he'd be left with about fifty quid for over five hours' work. Well, fifty-five quid, actually, including the tip.

Throughout the evening he'd repeatedly called Eden, but her mobile remained unavailable. It was the same with the house landline, no reply. Even so, he had little doubt, as he entered the house, that he would find her either in the lounge in front of the telly or upstairs in bed watching some crime series on Netflix or Amazon Prime.

The lounge was in darkness. He could hear no sound upstairs. Maybe she was asleep. If she was cross with him, hopefully she'd sleep it off and be in a better mood in the morning. He climbed the carpeted treads softly, not wanting to wake her, walked the few steps along the landing towards the bedroom door, which was ajar, and pushed it open further. Despite the heavy curtains, thanks to a street light right outside, their bedroom was tinged at night with a faint orange glow.

He saw their bed, neat and tidy, duvet on top, plumped pillows and an array of cushions, just as Eden had left it this morning.

OK, he thought. *What game are you playing, babes?*

Despite his tiredness, definitely needing a drink now, he went down to their sleek, modern, charcoal-and-white kitchen, took a beer from the fridge and searched around in the drawer for the bottle opener, where it normally lived, cursing when he couldn't find it. *Why couldn't Eden ever put things away properly?* He tried another drawer full of graters and other cookery gubbins, rummaged about, then cried out as he felt a sharp pain.

'Oww, shit!' He'd sliced his index finger open on a razor-sharp potato peeler. 'Shit!' he said again.

Blood dripped onto the white marble work surface. He sucked

his finger, slammed shut the self-close drawer and looked around the worktops. And noticed a large knife missing from the rack. *Why the hell couldn't she ever put anything back where it belonged?* Not that he was obsessive, but he enjoyed cooking when he had the time and was always careful to keep everything in order.

More blood dripped onto the floor. He sucked his finger again, then gripped the bottle, placed the cap against the edge of the worktop and banged it hard with his left fist. The cap flew off and froth rose out of the neck of the bottle. He swigged it, then pulled out his cigarettes, lit one with the lighter from his pocket, grabbed a saucer from the drying rack for an ashtray and sat on a high stool at the island breakfast bar unit.

Eden didn't like him smoking indoors, but to hell with that right now. If she didn't like it, she could walk into the room and tell him.

He sucked his finger again, tasting the coppery blood and wracking his brain. Stood up and went over to the pine Welsh dresser, the one antique in this room, where their best crockery was stored behind the glass doors, and glanced down at a framed photograph of the two of them on their honeymoon in the Maldives, in better financial times. They'd paid the resort's photographer to take a series of photos of them and this one had been their favourite. Eden in a pink sundress and himself in a navy-blue T-shirt and shorts, holding hands and running along the sand at the water's edge. She looked pretty damn gorgeous and he looked bloody handsome. The perfect couple.

Once upon a time.

Next to it sat the leather-bound address book with their initials embossed on the front in gold, a wedding present from someone – he had forgotten who. Despite Eden's expertise in computer technology, she'd always insisted on keeping the names and addresses of all their friends and relatives – and tradespeople – In this book. Glad about that now, he picked it up, carried it back over to the breakfast bar, sat, took a drag on his cigarette, another swig of his beer, and began thumbing through the book. Thinking.

She had four really close friends. Close as hell. In the last couple of years, since their disagreements had become more and more frequent, he was sure she'd started turning all of them against him – he could tell, he wasn't an idiot. Always a slight frostiness when he met any of them.

In the morning, if she still hadn't turned up, he would call them. And her mother. Her sister. And anyone else he could think of. But he was pretty sure she'd be home sometime soon. Totally trolleyed and apologetic, like the last time she'd done this to him.

He finished the drink and the cigarette, then had another of each.

Quarter past midnight.

No Eden.

Where are you?

He went to bed.

9

Niall Paternoster was woken with a start by the clatter of the letter box. The orange glow of the street lighting had been replaced by daylight. From the brightness around the edges of the curtains it looked like a fine day. He glanced at the clock radio by his bed: 7.03 a.m. The morning paper delivery, he realized.

Then he realized something else as he became more awake. The right-hand side of the bed was empty. Undisturbed.

Hauling himself up against the headboard, he reached over to the table, grabbed his phone and peered at it. No texts. There were a couple of emails, which he opened. One was from a newsfeed he subscribed to, the other was spam his filter hadn't picked up. No word from Eden.

He slipped out of bed, padded out onto the landing and checked the spare room, where she sometimes slept on the few occasions when they'd had a really bad row. But the bed was clearly unused. 'Eden!' he called out in the forlorn hope she was somewhere else in the house. But the only reply was a plaintive miaow from Reggie downstairs. No doubt hungry, as ever.

'I'll be down soon, Reggie!' he called out.

The cat responded with a noise that sounded like he was being tortured to death.

Niall went back into their bedroom, sat on the edge of the bed and ran his fingers through his hair. Thinking hard. He rang Eden's mobile, but nothing. Was its battery completely dead? He had to keep trying. Who to call next? Her four best friends, Georgie, Dem, Helen and Sharon? Her sister? Her mother? The local hospitals, Worthing and the Royal Sussex, in case she'd been in an accident or taken ill?

He went downstairs, threw a handful of dry pellets into Reggie's bowl to shut him up, made himself a strong coffee, then began phoning each of Eden's girlfriends in turn, telling them what had happened. What he got back from each of them was concern for Eden, but not much sympathy, nor surprise. No, they hadn't seen her. Would he please let them know when she turned up?

Of course.

He rang the hospitals. No patient by the name of Eden Paternoster had been admitted during the past twenty-four hours.

Next, he rang her elder sister, Evelyn. She and Eden were close, too. Evelyn hadn't seen her either. Nor had her brother, Adam – her parents sure had referenced the Bible for their children's names. He rang her mum, who had never liked him, and was interrogated by her for a full ten minutes.

Ending the call, Niall continued thumbing through the book. Who the hell else might she have contacted?

He made more calls. Finally, all out of ideas, he looked at the ridiculously modern and stupid clock on the wall. The one she had chosen, which had no numbers on it, so you had to look at your watch anyway to be sure of the time.

8.55 a.m.

The house phone rang. Hardly anyone rang that these days. He dived over to the dresser, where it sat, and snatched the receiver off the cradle. Eden?

It was her mother, wondering if she had turned up.

'No, Margaret,' he said. 'Not yet.'

'Will you tell me when she does? I'm really worried about her.'

'Of course I will, Mags,' he assured her in his warmest, most wonderful and caring son-in-law voice. 'You'll be the first.'

'Have you called the police?'

'No, but I'm thinking about it if she doesn't turn up soon, as I just told you.'

Ending the call, promising again to let her know the moment he heard anything, he stared at the address book. There was no one else he could think of. He'd exhausted all the possibilities. Hadn't he?

Who hadn't he thought of? What hadn't he thought of?

Through the window on to their small rear garden, he could see a bird drinking from the ornamental birdbath that Eden topped up with water every day. Then Reggie began whinging. 'Way past breakfast time, eh?' Niall said. Reluctantly slipping off his stool, he walked over to the cupboard where Eden kept the pouches of cat food, took one out and opened it. Reggie leaped onto the draining board and carried on whining and trying to eat while he emptied the contents into the red bowl.

He put the bowl on the floor, went back to his bar stool and sipped his coffee. Then he noticed that the finger he'd cut last night was bleeding again – he must have done it opening the cat food. Sucking it, he decided maybe it *was* time to call the police. On the other hand, perhaps he should give her a little longer. See if she turned up to work today, first?

He decided to get some exercise, go for a bike ride down to the seafront, and give her time to make contact. If not, when he came back he'd call her work number. If she hadn't gone into work – she'd told him she had a really busy day with a new computer system being installed – then he would really start to worry.

10

An hour later, shortly after 10.15 a.m., with still no sign of Eden, he ate a few mouthfuls of cereal, called her mobile once more – no dice – and then her direct work line. It went to voicemail. Next, he called the main switchboard of the Mutual Occidental Insurance Company and, when it was answered, asked if the operator could locate his wife, telling her he'd already tried her direct line.

After putting him on hold while she tried several different departments where Eden might be, the woman told him that no one had seen her yet, although, she added helpfully, she had been expected in for an 8.30 a.m. meeting.

Niall thanked her and ended the call. *Shit.* He tried to think back clearly to yesterday afternoon. But his mind was in turmoil. Cat litter. Was he going crazy? They'd been squabbling in the car, hadn't they, just petty stuff? He'd dropped her off at Tesco to buy cat litter. Hadn't he?

His nerves were in tatters. He took an energy drink from the fridge and downed it. Just as he finished, a text pinged in on his phone. Eden? He looked at it and saw to his dismay it was from her mother.

Any news?

Time to call the police, he decided. But on what number? Two weeks ago, a drunk shitbag he'd picked up in his cab in the centre of Brighton, who he'd driven to north of Gatwick Airport, had done a runner on him in a Redhill housing estate, leaving him with forty quid on the meter. He'd called the police 101 non-emergency number the following morning to report it. It had been seventeen minutes before it was answered. He'd been assured by the operator to whom he gave the details that some-one would be in touch. But no one had.

To hell with that.

He dialled 999.

It was answered on the third ring. 'Emergency, which service, caller?'

'Police, please.'

There was a brief wait, then he heard a polite, assured voice.

'Sussex Police, how may I help you?'

'Hi,' he said. 'I'm worried that something's happened to my wife. She's disappeared.'

'May I have your name and address, please, sir?'

He gave the details to her.

The call handler asked him for his wife's name, age, date of birth and address, which he gave her, struggling for a moment to remember whether Eden had been born on 2 or 3 March 1988. He settled on 3 March.

'Can you please give me a full description of your wife and the clothes she was wearing when you last saw her?'

He repeated the description he'd given to the security guy at the store the day before, adding in a few extra details. 'She's thirty-one, five seven, shoulder-length, straight brown hair, wearing a pink T-shirt and white shorts.' Then, remembering, he suddenly realized he'd given the security man a wrong description. She'd been wearing her hair up yesterday, pulled back and clipped into a kind of bun, the way she wore it when she couldn't be bothered to wash it. He corrected the description to the call handler.

Continuing, sounding as if she might be reading from a script, she asked Niall what he thought might have happened, and if he could describe in as much detail as possible the circumstances of her disappearance.

He told her all he knew.

Next, sounding even more like she was working off a script, she asked him for information about her family, friends and work colleagues.

He answered in as much detail as he could.

When he had exhausted the list, she asked him, 'Does your wife have any previous history of disappearing?'

'No, never.'

'She's never gone missing before?'

'No – OK, she did do something about a year ago, when we'd had a row. She went into a supermarket and bumped into a friend, and asked her to give her a lift home, leaving me waiting in the car. She did that just to get back at me.'

There was a pause, during which he heard the tapping of keys. Then she asked, 'Was that just a one-off situation?'

'Yes.'

'Do you and your wife argue often?'

'No – no more than any other couple.'

More tapping of keys, then, 'Does your wife have any history of mental health problems?'

'No, none.'

'Has she ever self-harmed?'

'Self-harmed? Like cutting herself, do you mean?'

'Any instance where she might have deliberately injured herself?'

'Absolutely not,' he said.

There was a brief silence, punctuated with more key tapping, then she asked, 'Has your wife, Eden, ever talked about suicide with you? Have you ever considered her a suicide risk?'

'No, no way.'

'So you wouldn't consider it a possibility?'

Niall nearly shouted at the woman. 'Not remotely. I cannot in a million years believe she would do that. And all we'd been bloody arguing about was cat litter. You think she'd go and kill herself over cat litter?'

There was no response for a moment. Just the sound of a keyboard again. Then the woman said, 'If you can remain where you are, sir, I'll dispatch a unit to you as soon as possible.'

'Sure,' Niall said. 'I'm not going anywhere. How long do you think that will be?'

'I'll do my best to get a car to you within the next hour. If anything changes in the meanwhile, please call us back.'

Niall said he would.

11

'Tell me I didn't hear you right,' Glenn Branson said. He had barged into Roy Grace's office, as usual without knocking, and perched himself in front of the Detective Superintendent's desk, chair the wrong way round, so that he was leaning, arms folded, across the back as if he was in some Wild West saloon – the position he regularly favoured.

Just when he thought that Glenn Branson's ties could not get any brighter or more lurid, the thing knotted to the DI's pink shirt this morning, now flipped back over his shoulder, looked like an angry, striking cobra.

Grace sipped his coffee, both irritated and pleased at the same time by his colleague's uninvited appearance in his office. Irritated because he was trying to concentrate on writing an update report on his experiences in the Met with the Violent Crime Task Force, which the Chief Constable had asked for in order to see what Sussex Police could learn to help them with the surge in knife crime in the county. And pleased because he always liked Branson's company, and he could do with a distraction from two hours of fierce concentration.

'You heard me right.'

'Chicken *husbandry*? Excuse me, just what is that? You're not getting weird on hens? I mean, there are some pretty kinky websites out there – but chickens?'

'Matey, I can't help your warped mind. But this isn't going to

43

feed it. Cleo and I are doing a course in chicken husbandry at Plumpton Agricultural College tomorrow. A one-day course. Bruno's taken a big interest in our hens, he really seems to love them – two in particular, the ones with the fluffy feet. Bruno's named them Fraulein Andrea and Fraulein Julia. We want to encourage his interest.'

Branson leaned forward, frowning quizzically. '*Fraulein Andrea* and *Fraulein Julia*? What kind of names are those for hens?'

'You have a problem with them?'

He grinned. 'Whatever floats Bruno's boat, I suppose. His U-boat.'

Grace shook his head at the comment about his German-born son. 'Not funny.'

Branson raised his arms apologetically. 'Yeah, sorry. So, this chicken husbandry thing, does it have a forensic application?'

Grace grinned. 'I'm taking a day's leave – OK? I'm owed a ton of leave. What is your problem?'

The DI shook his head. 'Detective Superintendent Grace, Head of Homicide for Surrey and Sussex Police, takes day off to learn how to look after chickens.'

'And your issue is, exactly?'

Branson laughed. 'Farmer Grace.' He shook his head, smiling. 'I can just see you rocking up to the next murder investigation in green wellies, chewing on a piece of straw.'

'And what if I do?! Which do you think came first – the chicken or the egg?' Grace asked.

'The rooster, obviously. Typical male.'

It was Grace's turn to smile. Then his phone rang.

It was Alison Vosper.

'Ma'am,' he said respectfully. 'Can you hold for just one moment, I've got a weird-looking creature in my office.'

He waved a dismissing hand at Branson.

Branson took the hint and headed to the door.

'OK, I'm with you now, ma'am.'

'Nothing too nasty, I hope, Roy?'

'Just one of those bitey insects you get this time of year, but it's gone now.'

When Alison Vosper had been an ACC at Sussex, one of Grace's colleagues had nicknamed her No. 27, after a sweet and sour dish on the local Chinese takeaway menu that they frequently used on long shifts. You never knew quite what you were going to get with her. Sweet or sour. But something in her tone indicated *sweet* right now.

'I'm calling you with an update,' she said. 'I've already spoken to your Chief Constable to put her in the picture. I've also raised this with the Commander in charge of Anti-Corruption in the Met and he's picking this up straight away as a matter of urgency.'

'Thank you, ma'am,' Grace said. But the news didn't fill him with elation, rather the reverse – it made him feel flat. However much he despised Pewe, and all corrupt police officers, the knowledge that what he had told her would destroy Pewe's career – and probably the rest of his life – was still a tough one on his conscience. As well as Cleo's warning words from last night.

First dig two graves.

And the knowledge that all he had told her was on the word of Guy Batchelor, a disgraced former police officer in prison, and the contents of his notebook.

But despite all Batchelor had done wrong, he trusted him on this.

Enough to gamble his career on, should this backfire?

He just hoped, as Guy had assured him, that the genie was already out of the bottle, and Pewe was on borrowed time.

'Just remember, Roy, this stays strictly confidential.'

'Of course, ma'am, absolutely. Thank you for the update.'

The moment he put the phone down, it rang again. It was

Norman Potting, sounding worried. 'Chief, I've just had a call from the quack – I rang the surgery about some symptoms I've been having for over a month now.'

'Your prostate?'

'No, touch wood, that's all tickety-boo now. No, it's something else. He wants me to come in this morning, which I guess is not good news.'

'Norman, I'm sorry to hear that. Let's hope it's just something minor. Will you call me as soon as you've finished with the doctor? And, of course, if you need to take any time off, that goes without saying.'

'Thanks, but it won't come to that, chief, I'm a tough old bugger!'

Roy put the phone down and sat back in his chair. With the DS's age and his previous health issues – plus the knowledge he didn't really look after himself – he was worried about just how serious this might be. The old warhorse was not a man to wear his heart on his sleeve.

He was fond of the sometimes curmudgeonly detective and, if his news was bad, he and Cleo would support Norman all they could, both as a friend and as a long-time colleague.

Shit, he thought. What was it about bad news coming in threes?

12

One of their colleagues on B-Section of the Brighton and Hove Response, who was a bit of a comedian, had once named them Little and Large, and the moniker had stuck. It wasn't an entirely unjust description. PC Holly Little, who was known to her colleagues as the Pocket Rocket because of her short stature but feisty nature, was always the first to dive head first into a brawl or any other kind of dangerous situation. Her much older colleague, PC John Alldridge, with whom she was regularly partnered, was a six-foot-four, eighteen-stone former rugby forward, known as the Gentle Giant. He had recently transferred back to Uniform from CID because he missed the adrenaline rush of response work and wanted to spend his last couple of years before retirement back where he had started his police career, on Response.

The shift was getting tedious as they cruised the quiet Monday-morning streets of Brighton and Hove in the marked car. At the best of times, this shift was usually uneventful – criminals tended to get up late, even on fine days like this one.

So far, there had only been one shout – a Grade One – responding to an anxious call by a neighbour reporting that the people in the flat next door were killing each other. When they got there, on blues and twos, it had turned out to be a false alarm. The young couple had been happily watching an old Paul Newman and Elizabeth Taylor film, *Cat on a Hot Tin Roof*, which was about marital strife and involved a lot of shouting.

Little and Large had both shaken their heads. It was a sad indictment of modern society that a seemingly healthy and fit young couple could be at home watching movies on a glorious Monday morning. But hey, maybe they were night workers or on holiday, they weren't to judge.

'Did you hear what Jonno said the other day?' Alldridge asked.

Little shook her head. Jonathan – Jonno – Mackie was popular in the force. A plain-clothes cop, six foot two tall and solid with it, not many people wanted to mess with him, and he loved nothing better than to prowl, in the shadows, the city's crime hot spots.

'He nicked an Eastern European pickpocket in West Street the other night.'

Holly grinned. 'Seriously?'

'Apparently this good, honest citizen was just trying to warn the man that his wallet was sticking out of his back pocket.'

'Almost as good as my bag-snatcher.'

Alldridge remembered that. Holly had been off duty, drinking with friends in a pub, when she'd seen a man acting shiftily. Minutes later, he had ducked under a table, grabbed a handbag and legged it. She'd chased him for a mile before bringing him to the ground with a rugby tackle. His excuse was, he swore blind that he thought he saw the owner leaving without it, and was running after her to try to catch her up and give it back. Yadda, yadda, yadda.

Alldridge was in his twenty-eighth year in the force and, apart from his spell as a detective, always as a uniform PC. Like a number of his colleagues, he'd never wanted promotion, always turning down every opportunity he'd been given – and as a popular and respected officer, he'd been offered plenty. He was happy to be back in uniform again after his time as a DC with Roy Grace's Major Crime Team, which he had enjoyed. But he loved even more being a front-line copper, where he could sometimes make a real difference to people's lives.

Over the years he'd seen so many of his mates go up the promotion ladder, getting more and more pay but less and less bang out of the job as they became increasingly desk-bound. His wife worked for a bank on a good salary and, like himself, had a sizeable pension coming, so it wasn't the higher pay and bigger pension promotion offered that drove him.

They were financially comfortable and he was happy with the career decisions he'd made; the only cloud now looming over the horizon was retirement. Plenty of his mates in the force couldn't wait for their day and would announce gleefully, 'Only sixty-two more shifts to go!', 'Only seventeen more shifts to go!' But he wasn't counting. At the time he'd joined, when you hit thirty years' service you took your pension and went, making room for younger, supposedly brighter people to fill your shoes. But at forty-eight, he hardly felt like a dinosaur, he relished his experience and still felt fit enough. He was considering whether maybe he would stay on a few more years.

Holly Little drove west along the seafront, while John Alldridge, doing his best as ever to make his massive frame comfortable in the small car, enjoyed the glorious view out over a flat ocean to his left. It was 10.30 a.m. The tide was way out and a few people were on the expanse of mudflats, some walking dogs, along with a couple of lone detectorists sweeping away. A few holidaymakers and local beachgoers were already staking out their claims on the pebbles with their towels, rugs, baskets and folding chairs. Hunkering down for what promised to be a fine day. In Alldridge's view, September could often be a glorious month, summer's last throw.

The pair had been on shift since 6 a.m. 'I'm feeling peckish,' Alldridge said. Living out of town in Horsham, just over thirty minutes away, he'd been up since 4 a.m., and he guessed his colleague, who lived in Brighton and a lot closer to the police station, must have been up since around 4.30. 'You?'

She nodded. 'Did you bring anything in?'

He shook his head.

'Me neither. What do you fancy? A fry-up?'

'Shall we try that new place along Church Road?' he suggested, mindful of his ever-expanding waistband. 'They do a great veggie one.'

She screwed up her face. 'Not what I fancy right now.'

He patted his belly. 'Yeah, nor me. They do proper stuff, too. So, how's the bambino? How long?'

'Five,' she said.

'Five months to go?'

She nodded – did she look a tad wistful? he wondered.

Alldridge knew that she and her partner had been trying for a baby for over four years, if not longer. 'How are you two feeling about it?' he asked as she indicated right and halted at the traffic lights at the bottom of Grand Avenue, beneath the stern statue of Queen Victoria.

'Pretty excited! Do you remember how you felt when your wife was expecting your first baby, John?'

He nodded. 'I do. Terrified.'

'Really?'

'All the things that could go wrong. The responsibility of bringing a kid into the world – not like something we'd bought from Amazon and could send back if we didn't like it.'

Holly grinned. 'But you did like it – her?'

'Totally, utterly, without reservation. One of the most beautiful moments of my life. I remember thinking as I held Rachel in my arms, her umbilical cord still attached, that I would take a bullet for her. I still feel that – and for both my children. You'll feel it, too.'

She smiled. 'I guess – whatever strange world he's born into.'

'He? You know the sex?'

The controller's voice came through their radios, interrupting them. 'Charlie Romeo Zero Five?'

Alldridge answered. 'Charlie Romeo Zero Five.'

'Charlie Romeo Zero Five, we've a concerned gentleman whose wife went into Tesco Holmbush at around 3.15 p.m. yesterday and has not been seen since. Normally I'd give this to West Sussex, but they have no units available and the gentleman lives in Hove. Can you attend, Grade Two?'

'Yes, yes,' Alldridge answered, and caught the 'sad face' grimace of his colleague. She would have preferred a Grade One, when she could have put on the blue lights and siren – one of the big bangs all response officers got from the job.

He punched the address the controller gave him into the satnav, then they both listened to the details she had for them as they headed towards Nevill Road.

Seventeen minutes later, Alldridge radioed the controller to confirm they were at the address. Was there any update? he asked.

There wasn't. That was the end of the controller's role in this incident and they now held the baton.

13

Niall Paternoster heard the doorbell chime. He hadn't been expecting the police to arrive so quickly. The call handler had said an hour, which he'd taken to mean two hours, or three, or whenever we can be bothered to send someone. This was around half an hour. He hastily downed the rest of his second Red Bull and dumped both cans in the kitchen bin, dug a mint gum from his shorts pocket and popped it in his mouth.

Chewing hard, he hurried through into the lounge and peered out of the window. He saw a police car, the blue-and-yellow Battenberg paintwork gleaming in the bright sunlight. Two figures, partly obscured by a rose bush, stood on the doorstep. He heard a faint staccato, crackly burst of voices.

Opening the front door, he was greeted by a short, black female uniformed officer in her early thirties with spiky black hair and a chubby, impish face, and a tall, burly uniformed white male, in his late forties, with a genial, slightly apologetic expression. Both of them were bulked out by their stab vests and batteries of kit.

'Mr Niall Paternoster?' the woman officer asked.

'Yes.'

The tall officer fiddled with the radio clipped to his chest and the voices of his radio chatter quietened.

'I'm PC Little and this is PC Alldridge. We understand you've reported your wife missing?'

'Yes, since yesterday afternoon.'

'May we come in, sir?'

'Please,' he said, stepping aside and ushering them forward. 'Thank you for—' He finished the sentence by windmilling his hands.

Closing the door, walking with a confident swagger, Niall led the way into the modern, minimalist lounge at the front of the house. Directing the officers to a sofa, he sat in the identical one facing them, across the glass coffee table with the chessboard. 'Can I get you anything to drink? Tea, coffee, water?'

Holly glanced at her colleague, who shook his head. 'We're fine, thank you,' she said. She could smell the residue of cigarette smoke and had noticed Niall was looking wired as he opened the front door. She studied the man for a moment, who was chewing mint gum – to mask alcohol? In his thirties, she guessed, he was good-looking in a slightly rough way, with short but unruly brown curls, the shape of someone who worked out, and muscular tattooed arms.

Glancing around routinely, she took in the elegant, tidy room and saw that one wall was entirely book-lined. Mostly crime novels and true crime books, apart from some shelves that were filled with DVDs, almost exclusively again crime dramas and true crime documentaries. There were framed photographs of Niall Paternoster and, presumably, his wife above the ornamental modern fireplace, and more sun-faded photographs in the bay window at the front, one in a large silver frame obviously taken in a studio. There were several well-tended plants in modern pots and the inevitable huge, flat-screen television on the wall.

She noticed Niall Paternoster kept sucking on the index finger of his right hand. When he removed it from his mouth, a thin ribbon of blood formed.

'Are you all right, sir?' she asked.

He smiled sheepishly. 'Yes – I cut my finger on a damned potato peeler.'

'Vicious things, potato peelers,' John Alldridge said.

Niall stared at him, unsure if he was making a joke. Alldridge's deadpan expression gave him nothing.

'Mr Paternoster, can you give us some details about your wife, please, and the reasons why you are concerned about her?' Holly Little asked.

Over the next five minutes, Niall repeated the information he'd already given to the call handler as the officers went through their questions, the tall male one tapping away ploddingly with two fingers on a tablet.

When Niall had finished, the woman officer asked him, 'Have you checked if your wife's passport is here? Or has she taken it?'

He looked dumbfounded for a moment. 'Well – I – I didn't think to look. Hang on a sec, we keep them in a drawer in my office.' He jumped up. 'I'll just check.'

He hurried out of the room then returned a couple of minutes later, looking shocked. 'It's not there,' he said. 'Mine's in the usual place but hers isn't there.'

'Can you think of any reason why it isn't there?' Alldridge asked.

He shook his head. 'No – none – it doesn't make sense. We always keep them together.'

'What access does your wife have to a mobile phone, an iPad, laptop or any other mobile electronic device?' Little asked.

'She has a phone, of course, and an iPad and laptop; she's forever posting stuff on social media,' Niall said.

'Are any of them here?'

'Her iPad and laptop are. She has her phone with her – she never goes anywhere without it – but it was very low on battery, which is unusual. I couldn't get through to her when I tried to ring her. She told me she'd switched it off to save juice, but I kept trying in case she switched it back on.'

'What about her car?' Little asked.

'It's outside – the BMW Three Series convertible.'

'And your own car?' Alldridge asked.

'I don't have one at the moment. I lost my business – it went under – we share hers. I drive a mate's taxi and occasionally use it if I'm stuck for transport.'

Alldridge nodded, then peered at the chessboard for some moments before looking up. 'So, the last time you saw your wife was in the Tesco car park?'

'Yes, as I said, she was going to run in and grab a bag of cat litter. She insisted on going to the Holmbush store because she said it's the only place where the one she wants is always in stock.'

There was a brief silence, broken by Holly Little. 'How would you describe your relationship with your wife, Niall?'

He shrugged. 'It is – you know – OK. We have our ups and downs – don't any couple?'

'What kind of downs?' Alldridge asked.

Again, Niall shrugged. 'Normal stuff. Stupid arguments – you know – bickering over nothing.'

'Such as?' Alldridge pushed.

'Well.' Niall pinched his chin. 'Yesterday it was about the cat litter.'

'Cat litter?' Little prompted.

'Yes. We'd been out for the day – lunch and a walk around the grounds of Parham House, near Pulborough – it's the sort of place we'd like to live one day.'

'Beautiful place – that's a big ambition,' Alldridge said.

Niall's eyes narrowed. 'Yep, well I'm planning to launch an internet venture that's going to be big, too.'

'You'd been out for the day, what then happened?' Little prompted, ignoring his hubris.

'I was in a hurry to get back to catch the end of the Belgian

Grand Prix and Eden wanted to pick up some cat litter on the way home.' He raised his hands. 'We had a bit of a to-do about it.' Blushing, he said, 'It probably sounds stupid.'

'Most rows are over small things,' Holly Little said with a forced smile. 'Did you row often?'

'Often enough. But not really *rows*. As I said, just silly stuff.'

'Enough for your wife to leave you, do you think?' She came back at him a lot more sharply now.

'No way.' He sucked the blood away from his finger again.

'You said she took her handbag with her when she left the car,' Alldridge said. 'What did she keep in it?'

'Honestly? I've no idea. The usual stuff, I suppose – wallet, credit cards, phone, some make-up – oh and some mints – she had a thing about not wanting bad breath.'

Masking something on her breath, like you? Holly Little was tempted to reply. Instead, she said, 'Do you think she left because of something you said?'

He reacted like he'd been stung by a wasp. 'What – what are you implying?'

'I'm not *implying* anything, sir.'

'Presumably you and your wife do online banking?' Alldridge asked, jumping in to calm him down.

'Yes.'

'Have you checked your bank and her debit and credit cards to see if she's spent anything since you saw her? For instance, did she buy any cat litter?' he asked.

'Good point,' Niall said. 'She only ever uses her debit card – she doesn't like running up interest. Give me a moment, I'll check our online banking.' He lifted up his phone, tapped the screen and waited. 'No transactions on her regular card,' he announced. 'I'll just check the other card.' He tapped the screen again, then after a short while shook his head. 'Nope. She's not bought anything or with-drawn any cash since I saw her, not from the accounts I can see.'

Alldridge looked again at the chessboard, studying it more closely now. He frowned, thoughtfully. 'You're in the middle of a game?'

'Yes, Eden and I play regularly – she taught me how to play a few months ago. We used to play Scrabble, but she has a much better vocabulary than me – she's better educated – and always thrashed me. She thought if I learned chess, we might be able to play something that's more of a level playing field for us.'

Alldridge nodded. 'Who's white?'

'Eden.'

'And whose move?'

'Mine.'

The officer leaned forward, studying the pieces more intently now.

'Do you play?' Niall asked.

'Yes, whenever I can – I'm a member of a chess club.' Alldridge nodded thoughtfully. 'Interesting situation you're in.'

'Not great, a rook down, eh?' Niall said. 'I think I'm struggling.'

'Looks like she used Botvinnik's classic English Opening and you've countered with his French Defence,' Alldridge said approvingly.

'I'm not too up on all the Grand Master moves,' Niall said. 'I tend to play survival chess.'

Smiling, Alldridge studied the game for a few more moments then switched his attention back to the job he was here to do. 'It may be a silly question,' he said, 'but have you checked the house thoroughly? The outside? Do you have a garden shed?'

Niall looked, for an instant, as if the thought had not occurred. 'Yes, well, yes, there's not exactly much to check.' Then, defensively, he added, 'Like . . .' He windmilled his arms again. 'This place is not exactly a stately home set in rolling acres, is it?'

'Like Parham House?' PC Little interjected.

'Is a huge mansion like Parham House the kind of place you feel you should be living in?' Alldridge said a little sarcastically.

'Yes, and as I said, one day I – we – will.'

The two officers shot a glance at each other. 'I think it might be a good idea if we check the house and your garden with you, sir,' Holly Little said.

'Be my guests, but I can tell you, she's not here.'

'Let's make sure, shall we?' she said.

14

Monday 2 September

Niall stood up, clearly rattled. 'Right, this is the lounge – front parlour – *drawing room*—' He assumed an exaggeratedly posh accent. 'And this,' he pointed through the archway at a smoked-glass dining table with four white suede chairs, 'is the *formal* dining room.'

Next, they went into the kitchen. 'Wow, this is nice – I'd love a kitchen like this!' Little said.

'It's very nice but it sure wasn't cheap,' Niall said.

Alldridge eyed him with growing discomfort. Holly stopped and stared at the island unit, and then at the floor. 'Blood?' she asked, noticing the red blotches.

'From the damn potato peeler,' Niall replied. 'You're thinking I murdered her, aren't you? I saw you looking at all the crime books and DVDs in the living room. If I'd murdered Eden, do you really think I'd leave bloodstains everywhere?' He shook his head. 'I'm not a complete idiot.'

Both police officers smiled. But there was no humour in their expressions. 'Can we see upstairs?' Holly Little asked.

'Sure. Then after that I'll give you a tour of the garden – sorry, the *grounds* – to see if you can find evidence of a freshly dug grave, eh?' He half smiled.

They carried out their check of the house, then went out into the well-tended garden. The immaculately mowed lawn was lined on either side with a riot of colour. Flowers and shrubs, all weed-free. There was a potting shed and a little wooden summerhouse, both in good condition, sited attractively between two mature fir trees at the far end.

As they walked along, Holly Little observed, a little enviously, 'Someone has green fingers, what a beautiful garden – all we have in our flat are window boxes.'

'That's me,' Niall said proudly. 'My hobby – passion. I do all the beds and Eden looks after the lawn.'

Little stopped to admire one dense plant that was chest-high, full of bright-red flowers that were in the shape of long, narrow brushes. Part of one side of it was missing – it looked like it had been broken away. 'This is stunning!'

'*Callistemon citrinus*,' Niall said. 'Or in English, a bottlebrush plant. One of my babies. Unfortunately, Eden got rather distracted the other evening when she was mowing the lawn – she said our new mower ran away with her – and she took a chunk out of it.'

'Will it grow back?' Alldridge asked.

'If disease doesn't set in.'

Both officers noticed the slight anger in his voice as he said it.

He led them out to the front to the bike storage unit and unlocked it. Alldridge and Little scanned inside. Other than a dark pool of dried oil on the floor, it was spotless, a Honda motorbike, a posh road bike and two paddleboards propped against one another.

They went back indoors and sat in the lounge again.

'Can you think of any reason at all why your wife might not have come back to you in the car park of Tesco yesterday, sir?' Holly Little asked.

'No, none. None at all, it makes no sense.'

'Do you or she have any enemies that you are aware of?'

'Enemies?' Niall looked genuinely surprised. 'No, none – other than her mother.' Then he quickly added, 'Joke!'

'Your mother-in-law?' Alldridge probed. 'Is there some animosity between you?'

'Oh, plenty,' Niall said with a tinge of bitterness. 'She always felt her daughter could have done better.'

'You're sure your wife isn't with her now?' PC Little asked.

'I told you, I've checked with everyone, including all the local hospitals. I've had three texts from her mother this morning asking if I have any news of her – want to see them?'

'If you don't mind.'

He showed the officers each of them, in turn.

'Has your wife ever experienced any mental health issues?' Alldridge asked.

'Other than she must have been mad to marry me?' Niall said with a grin that fell from his face as fast as his comment fell flat. 'No.'

'All right,' Little said. 'I'm afraid this is a bit of a difficult question: is there any possibility Eden could have a lover – someone she might have run off with, perhaps even abroad?'

There was a long silence before he answered. Both officers watched him intently. 'I don't think so, no. To be honest, she's never been like that. Mind games are more her thing.'

'What do you mean by *mind games*?' Alldridge asked.

Niall pointed at the chessboard, then, after a moment's thought, raised an arm towards the bookshelves. 'She loves puzzling things out. That's why she likes detective novels and crime dramas. She's always trying to get ahead of the detectives in them – and mostly does.'

'OK,' Holly Little said, and gave her partner a subtle nod for confirmation. 'I think we've covered everything for now, sir.' She gave Niall Paternoster her card, on which she had written her mobile number. 'I'd appreciate your calling me, any time, if you hear from Eden or if there are any other developments. What we would like to take with us is a recent photograph of her that we can circulate.'

'Sure,' he said. 'I'll find something.' He jumped up again and went out of the room. The two officers exchanged a glance. But Little signalled her colleague not to say anything and walked through into the kitchen, followed by Alldridge. She pointed down at the skirting board and he nodded, picking up on it, also. It looked a good deal cleaner than the ones elsewhere in the house, and there was a faint whiff of bleach. The floor around it looked very freshly cleaned, too.

Paternoster returned with a photograph of Eden standing in front of a Christmas tree, champagne glass in her hand. 'This is a really good one,' he said, handing it to Little. Then, his voice slightly choked, he pleaded, 'Please find her.'

'Nice-looking lady,' she said.

Eden was wearing a short emerald dress, her centre-parted brown hair, elegantly cut, fell just short of her shoulders, and, like Niall, she had perfect teeth.

'She is,' Niall said. 'She's beautiful, she's the love of my life.'

'But this was taken at Christmas?' Alldridge questioned. 'Don't you have anything more recent?'

'Well, yes, but I particularly like this one.'

'It would be helpful to have something more up to date, sir,' Alldridge pressed.

'OK, right.' Niall tapped his phone and studied it for some moments, flicking his finger. Then he looked up with a broad smile. 'Stupid me! I took a great one of her yesterday at Parham House.' He handed the phone to the PC.

Both officers studied the photograph of the attractive woman, brown hair pinned up, in a pink top and white shorts, with a lake in soft focus behind her.

'If we could take the one of your wife in front of the Christmas tree and if you could email us this one – to the address on the card I gave you – right away—'

'Yes, yes, of course. Please, please find her for me,' he repeated plaintively.

As he walked them to the front door, Holly Little said very formally, 'We'll do everything we can. And be sure to call me if she comes home or if you hear from her.'

'Of course.'

Suddenly, Alldridge bent down and said to him, almost conspiratorially, 'Black Queen's Knight to King's Pawn three.' He tapped the side of his nose. 'Don't let on I told you.'

As soon as he had closed the door on the officers, Niall hurried back into the lounge before he forgot what the tall copper had said.

Queen's Knight to King's Pawn three.

He feigned the move. Shit, it was one he had not spotted! The copper was right. Eden had totally missed it! If he made the move, she'd be in check. The only choices she'd be left with would be losing her King – game over – or her Queen – pretty much game over, too.

He looked forward to seeing her face when she came home and finally, for the first time in countless games, he would win.

Checkmate!

15

On their way out to the car, Alldridge stopped by the bin and raised the lid. Among the smelly detritus lying inside he clocked an empty bleach bottle, but said nothing until they were back in the car.

'Nice man – not,' Little said quietly, after making sure the car windows were closed. 'Cat litter?' She shook her head.

'Bleach bottle in the bin,' Alldridge murmured.

'Who's the house-proud one, then?' she quizzed with a wry smile.

He nodded.

A rust-bucket of an old Vauxhall Viva with no apparent silencer shot up the road at high speed, two youths in it, baseball caps the wrong way round. Ordinarily they would have pulled out and stopped it, but not now.

'It's usually the small things people have the biggest arguments about, isn't it?' Holly said.

'Tell me about it! Barbara whacked me over the head with a pillow the other night because I was snoring! And last week I was trying to sleep in on Saturday morning after being on nights and she decided to hoover the bedroom!'

'Hannah and I had a row a couple of weeks ago because I'd put half a tin of baked beans in the fridge instead of pouring them into a bowl and covering them. Apparently, the tin reacts with them, so she said.'

He scratched the back of his head. 'I was scene guard on a house, some years back, where a guy had bludgeoned his wife to death with a cricket bat because she'd rearranged his sock drawer without his permission.'

They sat in silence for some moments. 'What do you think's really going on here?' she asked.

'Clean skirtings, smell of bleach and empty bottle? Has his wife disappeared – done a runner – or did he kill her, is that what you're thinking?' Alldridge asked.

'Aren't you?'

He nodded.

'Her passport missing might be significant, don't you think?'

He didn't reply straight away, then he said, 'Yes, but perhaps not in the obvious way.'

'Meaning, John?'

'That he wants us to think she's gone away, perhaps?'

She nodded. 'Good point. Your time as a detective wasn't entirely wasted!'

'It did open my eyes.'

'And anyhow,' she said, 'I've never been able to trust a bloke who appears to resent his wife's wealth.'

Alldridge concurred. 'Let's move away from the house.'

'Food?' she asked. 'Try for breakfast again?'

'Good plan.'

Half an hour later, with the residual reek of curry from the last crew out in this vehicle replaced by the much more appetizing aroma of egg and bacon sarnies, they were both feeling better. Parked on Church Road, in front of the cafe, they ate hungrily in silence. Alldridge finished ahead of Little, wiped his mouth with a paper napkin and suggested they inform Golf 99 – the duty Inspector at Brighton nick – of their concerns.

Little agreed.

Alldridge radioed the Control Room and was told, to his

dismay, the day's duty Golf 99 was Andy – 'Panicking' – Anakin. In his long experience, Anakin was the last person you'd want to involve in a crisis, but all the same, he had no option. The Inspector wasn't always totally useless, just mostly.

Moments later, they heard his voice, a little too high-pitched and highly strung, through their radios. 'Inspector Anakin.'

'It's PC Alldridge and PC Little, sir.'

'What is it? I'm in the middle of a situation.'

From the hysteria in his voice, it sounded like he was the man, at this moment, single-handedly responsible for keeping Planet Earth on its axis and preventing it from spiralling off and sending all its inhabitants into oblivion.

Alldridge was long enough in the tooth to not take any crap from his superiors. 'We have a situation, too, which we need to discuss with you, sir,' he responded calmly and firmly, giving him a brief outline. From Anakin's response, it didn't sound like he'd absorbed much of what he'd been told.

'I'm at the cell block doing a vital custody review, I can't do anything at the moment – I'm dealing with a matter of national security.' Then, turning more antsy, he said, 'Surely you know normal process for a misper is not to do anything until a twenty-four-hour review, John, unless there are other factors?'

'I do, sir,' he replied, trying to be as respectful as possible to someone he considered a total moron. 'But neither PC Little nor I think this is a matter for *normal process*. We need to step it up now proportionate to the risk.'

Anakin's voice increased in pitch again – the human race was clearly in severe and imminent peril. 'If that's your assessment and you need to action now, call the duty DI – it's Bryce Robinson today. I've got to go.'

The radio went dead.

The two PCs looked at each other, shaking their heads. 'Know about the Peter Principle?' Alldridge asked her with a grin.

She frowned. 'The *what*?'

'Some guy back in the 1960s or 70s came up with a theory that sooner or later in any hierarchy people get promoted to the level of their incompetence.'

Holly laughed. 'Oh my God, so true about him!'

'Just a shame that *Anakin* doesn't rhyme with *wanker*.'

'That doesn't stop him from being one, though, does it?'

'Nope.'

16

It was just gone midday when John Alldridge decided to contact the duty Detective Inspector at Brighton police station.

In contrast to Andy Anakin, who'd made them feel almost idiots for troubling him, DI Bryce Robinson was calm and sounded immediately concerned by what they told him. With his background as a former school teacher before joining the force, he was a good listener.

'You've done the right thing,' Robinson said. 'Do you have any hypothesis about what we're dealing with?'

'We do, sir,' Alldridge said. 'We have a few.'

As he spoke, Alldridge could hear the tapping of keys, which indicated the DI was taking notes. 'Our first is that, following their argument, Eden Paternoster met someone she knew in the store and left with them, scared to remain with her husband. Or simply, afraid to go back to the car, she went off on her own accord to seek refuge with a friend or member of her family. Her husband claims to have called everyone he can think of who she might have gone to, but if he has any history of violence, they might be shielding her and denying she's with them.'

'Very possible,' Robinson said. 'But I've just checked the name and address you've given me, and there's no record of police having ever attended. No complaint or apparent history of domestic abuse. What's your next hypothesis?'

'That Mrs Paternoster has a lover. Her passport is missing. Could they have gone abroad together?'

'You've got a recent photograph of her?'

'Yes, sir, a couple – one taken yesterday. I have it digitally.'

'Good, send it over to me as soon as we're done and I'll have it circulated.'

'Our next hypothesis is that the lady might have tried to make her own way home and something happened – perhaps she was involved in an accident and is unable to make contact. But her husband says he's called all hospitals in the area, so this seems unlikely. Our next is that she's had some form of mental health episode and is now disorientated and lost.'

'From the information you have,' the DI asked, 'how do you rate that on a scale of one to ten?'

Alldridge and Little looked at each other. He held out his hand, holding up his forefinger. His colleague nodded.

'One,' he said.

'And your next?'

'She's been taken against her will.'

'Is he wealthy?'

'No, sir. He told us his business went bust and he's now driving a friend's cab.'

'So, we can rule out kidnap for monetary gain?'

'I think so, sir, quite safely.'

Robinson was silent for a short while. 'Beyond these hypotheses, do you and PC Little have any views on what may be going on here?'

'We both noticed a very cleaned-up kitchen skirting board and floor area, and the smell of bleach,' Alldridge responded.

'Sir,' Holly Little added. 'Neither of us were comfortable with Mrs Paternoster's husband. It seemed to us he might be hiding something.'

'Such as?'

'Well, we'd like someone to look at the Tesco store's CCTV footage to see if she did actually get out of their car, as he claims, or ever went into the store at all.'

Robinson was silent for some moments. Then he said, 'She's been missing since shortly after 3.15 p.m. yesterday. According to her husband, she's not with any of their known contacts, and she failed to show up for work today, despite an important meeting?'

'Correct,' Alldridge confirmed.

'And while the missing passport might indicate she has left the country, or is planning to leave, you feel it could be a double-blind?'

'We do, sir,' confirmed Little.

'OK, I'm not at all happy about this situation, from all you've told me,' the DI said. 'You are right to be concerned. I'd like to run this by Major Crime and see what they think. You've done good work, both of you.'

17

Just gone midday, Roy Grace was reading through his completed draft report for the Chief Constable and was starting to think about lunch when he was interrupted by his job phone ringing. He answered it.

'Sir, it's Bryce Robinson. I have you down as the on-call SIO?'

Grace had been so absorbed in the report, and his thoughts about Guy Batchelor and Cassian Pewe, that he'd forgotten he'd assumed the role, from 7 p.m. last night until the same time next Sunday, as the duty Senior Investigating Officer for the Surrey and Sussex Major Crime Team.

'Yes, that's right, Bryce,' he said to the DI, trying not to sound too thrown. 'Tell me?'

Robinson talked him through the disappearance of Eden Paternoster and his concerns.

When the DI had finished, Grace asked him, 'Who were the officers who attended at the Paternosters' house?'

When he heard one of them was John Alldridge, he immediately took what he had heard even more seriously. 'Alldridge was on my team for a while, Bryce – he's sound, a very good copper.'

'I agree with you, sir.'

'It's good to raise this,' Grace said. He asked the DI to recap on a few points on which he wasn't clear, then he sat thinking for some moments. 'I wouldn't ordinarily be worried after someone was missing for such a short time, but there's something about this that feels wrong. You've done the right thing, calling me.'

Robinson was one of the diminishing number of senior officers in the force who remembered that Roy Grace's own wife, Sandy, had disappeared, well over a decade ago now. And he was glad it was Grace who was the on-call SIO – some might have been dismissive, but from his own past experience, he clearly wasn't.

'Leave it with me, Bryce, I'll have it looked into right away. You've circulated her photograph?'

'I have, sir.'

'Good work.'

Ending the call, Roy Grace thought for a short while. Ordinarily, he would have delegated a routine suspicious misper enquiry to one of his team, but something about this one intrigued him. And besides, he'd been deskbound for several weeks. One thing he'd always promised himself, each time he had been promoted further up the ranks, was that he would never end up as a desk jockey, as so many of his colleagues had, and that he would always try to remain hands-on whenever he could.

But there was something else here that resonated powerfully. The memory of that day, on his thirtieth birthday, when he'd come home, looking forward to a romantic celebratory dinner with Sandy, only to discover she had vanished off the face of the earth. And the years of hell that had followed, during which, while continuing to function as a homicide detective, he'd spent every spare second of his life searching for her and wondering what might have happened to her. If Eden Paternoster had done a 'Sandy' on her husband, Niall, then he really felt for the poor bastard.

He called Glenn Branson.

'Boss?' the DI answered.

'I'm just calling to see if you need any groceries?'

'What? You've taken up moonlighting for Ocado to supplement your income?'

'Haha.'

Grace brought him up to speed on the Paternoster situation and the DI immediately became serious. 'Doesn't sound good, boss, but one thing doesn't make sense.'

'Tell me?'

'Well, if I'd *disappeared* my wife why would I call the police and get them crawling all over me – rather than give it a few days?'

'Who's to say he hasn't already given it a few days?'

'I'm not with you.'

'What if he's planned it all carefully?' Grace posited. 'He's murdered and disposed of his wife already and now he's faking her vanishing, by way of an explanation?'

'I guess that's a possibility,' Branson replied.

'Speed is of the essence, I think we're going to need to get on this one straight away, it really doesn't feel right. Meet me in the car park. We're going to Tesco Holmbush.'

'Great! I'll bring my shopping list with me.'

18

As Roy Grace and Glenn Branson walked across the busy Tesco car park, the DI cast an eye up and down his boss – something he did frequently, to Grace's irritation – before nodding approvingly. 'Nice whistle,' he said. 'New?'

'Cleo took me shopping – it's nothing special. I picked up a couple of lightweight work suits in the sales.'

Branson reached out a hand and felt his jacket lapel. 'Quality threads? Bespoke tailor?'

'On my salary?'

Then Branson frowned disapprovingly at his tie. 'Too conservative. You should go bolder.'

Grace gave him a sideways look. 'Are we done on the sartorial inspection?'

The DI shook his head. 'Nah, you need me to take you shopping again.'

'I remember the last time you did. It took three months for my credit card to stop smouldering.'

'Yeah? And look what you pulled from wearing that gear – Cleo! And did I get any credit? Nope, just you whinging on about the cost! So, anyhow, Niall Paternoster – strange name.'

'Strange name?'

Branson nodded.

Grace looked at him quizzically. 'So that makes him a suspect?'

74

'Just saying – Paternosters are a kind of lift, with no doors. You jump into them, onto a moving platform.'

'They have one at Munich Police HQ, I've been in it,' Grace said. 'A bit weird.'

'They sound bloody dangerous.'

'And your point is?'

'The name – it's odd.'

They walked through the automatic doors of Tesco into the cool, air-conditioned interior.

A red-haired employee, with the name *Tim* on his badge, was adjusting a display advertising a special offer for wines. Grace approached him and showed him his warrant card. 'Detective Superintendent Grace and my colleague, Detective Inspector Branson, of Surrey and Sussex Major Crime Team. We'd like to speak to your Head of Security, please.'

'Yes, yes, of course, sir. May I tell her what it's about?'

'A lady has been reported missing by her husband. He believes she came into this store yesterday afternoon, but he has not seen her since. We'd like to view the CCTV footage from between 3 p.m. and 4.30 p.m. yesterday, and we would like to talk to any members of staff who were present then who might have seen her.' He showed him, on his tablet, the photograph of Eden Paternoster that Robinson had emailed.

The man frowned. 'Ah, yes, this rings a bell. I think her husband came in just before we closed yesterday. I spoke to him at one point and we searched the store thoroughly.'

'And you didn't find her?'

'No, we didn't. She certainly wasn't in here.' He hesitated. 'If you'll just wait here a moment, officers?'

'Sure.'

He hurried off.

'With the amount of security in this place we must be able to find something to help with this,' Branson said, looking around, trying to spot the cameras. Following his gaze, Grace nodded, then out of the corner of his eye saw Tim hurrying back towards them, alongside a woman he was surprised to recognize.

In her late fifties, with a mane of side-parted silver hair, she wore a chalk-striped trouser suit and high-heeled shoes that made her taller than he remembered. As she approached with an outstretched hand, she gave him a broad grin of recognition. 'My God, Roy! I keep reading about you all the time in the *Argus* – so happy to see you got promoted to where you deserve! I understand you wanted to see the Head of Security – that's me!'

He shook former Detective Inspector Corinne Edgerton's hand warmly. Corinne had been one of his team when he was first promoted to Major Crime. He could not believe – and was so happy to see – that she had landed here, in this role.

He introduced Glenn Branson, who had been a uniformed PC at the time when she'd retired, then briefly outlined the situation. 'What I would like to see is video confirmation of Eden Paternoster leaving her husband's car at the time he has stated.'

Corinne Edgerton nodded, a little dubiously. 'We can take a look at the car park CCTV, but we don't have a lot of coverage there. Our main cameras are above the aisles, looking down for shoplifters – and monitoring our staff, too.' She smiled. 'Let's go up to the CCTV room and see what we have from yesterday, both outside and inside. We should certainly pick up this lady inside the store, if not outside also.'

For the next thirty minutes, Grace and Branson sat with Edgerton in front of the bank of monitors, in the small room one floor up from the public area of the store. They watched all recordings from each camera, firstly those covering outside, and then those covering the aisles, from fifteen minutes before the time that Niall Paternoster had claimed he'd driven into the car park and his wife had jumped out of the car to dash into the store, until half an hour after the store had closed.

The exterior cameras scanning a limited area of the car park had recorded no sign of the Paternosters' black BMW entering. But that did not mean it hadn't – it was a vast area and with only limited CCTV coverage. Grace had been hoping to see footage of Eden Paternoster getting out of the car, which would have established that her husband had been telling the truth.

The cameras covering the front entrance of the store had not shown her either, neither entering nor leaving. And she had not appeared on any of the cameras that were strategically sited to monitor the aisles in the store. There were a dozen cameras covering the vast interior space. With Edgerton operating the control sticks, they forwarded slowly through each of them in turn, occasionally zooming in on anyone who remotely fitted Eden's description and freezing the image while they checked against her photograph. But finally they were satisfied, supported by the fact that no one working in the store had seen her, that there was no evidence she had been here at the time her husband had said.

'Would it be possible, Corinne,' Grace asked, 'for her to have entered the store any other way?'

She thought for a moment. 'The lady could have come in via the staff entrance at the rear, but she'd have had to have known the key code.'

'How often do you change that?' Branson asked.

'God, probably not often enough. I've been here five years and we've only changed it a handful of times.'

Grace gave her a reproachful look.

She smiled. 'I know, *mea culpa!*'

'So that is a possibility?' Grace asked.

She shook her head adamantly. 'If she was in this store, she would have been picked up on one of the cameras. No question. And you've seen the one almost directly above the cat litter – animal products – section.'

Either, Roy Grace thought, Eden Paternoster had never entered the store at the time her husband claimed, or—

Her husband had the time wrong?

Or he was lying?

A-B-C.

That mantra from the Murder Manual replayed in his head as it did so often when confronting a potential crime scene. *Assume nothing. Believe no one. Check everything.*

Grace's phone rang. He saw on the display it was Norman Potting.

'Need to take this,' he said and stepped outside the office.

The DS sounded upset. 'It's bad news, Roy,' he said, his voice low, almost a growl.

'I'll come now. Meet you in Bill's in Lewes in thirty minutes.'

'No, please don't worry, I just thought you should know – in case I have to take any time out.'

'I'm meeting you at Bill's in thirty minutes. That's an order!'

Roy put his head back through the door. 'I'm sorry, mate, something's come up. Can you deal with this and I'll see you back at HQ.'

After Grace apologized to Edgerton and left, Branson asked her to replay all the digital recordings from 3 p.m. to 3.30 p.m. yesterday, just for belt and braces.

Half an hour later, they were still in the same place. Nothing.

Branson then asked her to play again all the footage up to 4.30 p.m. They saw a man with tousled hair, dressed in a faded T-shirt – an old Pink Floyd one – and cut-off jeans approach the front entrance and speak to Tim outside, then go in.

'That's the husband,' Corinne said. 'He came in and questioned members of staff, after which they did a thorough search for her.'

'Could you print me off an image of him?' Branson asked.

'Sure, though it won't be great quality, I'm afraid.'

'That's fine,' he said.

Next, they went to her office. Branson was conscious it was Monday lunchtime and the store was busy. But Corinne was anxious to help him. Over the following hour she had the entire staff of the store come in one by one and look at the photograph of Eden Paternoster.

Each of them shook their head in turn. No one had seen this woman yesterday.

19

Bill's was a cafe-restaurant, occupying a corner site on cobbled Cliffe High Street in Lewes, the county town of East Sussex. It had a green-and-white frontage, flanked by outside tables beneath its awnings. As Roy Grace arrived there at 1.45, with the lunchtime rush tailing off, he was pleased to see several tables free. He chose an end one, well spaced from the next table, which was also unoccupied, and sat down.

He pulled out his phone to check his messages, but before he had a chance, he saw the bulky figure of Norman Potting lumbering towards him. He stood to shake his colleague's hand. Usually irrepressibly cheerful, Potting looked gloomy. 'Thanks, chief,' he said, pulling up the chair opposite and lowering his frame onto it.

A waitress appeared. Potting ordered an Americano with hot milk and Grace a tuna sandwich and sparkling water. Potting didn't want any food.

'Tell me?' Grace said.

'Can you keep it confidential, chief?'

'Of course.' Grace noticed Potting's voice was sounding more gruff than usual.

The DS looked at him with baleful eyes, and for the first time in a long while Grace noticed he was looking his age – and more. 'I might have the big C back,' he said flatly.

'Shit, I'm sorry, Norman. It's not your prostate, you said?'

He shook his head. 'For some while my voice has been a bit – you know – hoarse, and I've been coughing a lot.' He touched his throat. 'And I've felt a lump on my neck. I ignored it for a while, but thought I'd better let the quack know so I rang the medical centre on Friday and told them. I had a call first thing this morning that he wanted to see me right away.'

'What did he say?'

'Well – he's usually a pretty positive chap but he looked worried. He knows I smoked a pipe for years and that I'm overweight, drink a bit – don't we all?'

Grace smiled sympathetically. 'Drink? In this job, yes.'

'He ticked me off for not coming to see him sooner. Told me that with my lifestyle I'm high risk.'

'What is he worried you might have, Norman?' Grace probed gently.

'Well, he wants to eliminate the possibility I might have laryngeal cancer.' He put a hand to his throat again and stroked it absently.

'So he thinks it's only a possibility?' Grace said, trying to reassure him.

Potting nodded. 'Apparently, from what he said, there are lots of symptoms that can mimic this. But he did point out at least twice that those at high risk from it are smokers, drinkers and those who live an unhealthy lifestyle.' Potting gave him a shrug and an almost childish grin. 'Guess I tick all those boxes. But if my number's up, at least I can say I've had a bit of a life, eh?'

Grace smiled and wagged a finger at him. 'Stop it! You are only in your fifties, that's no age, OK? He said you're presenting symptoms, but he wants to *eliminate* cancer, not *confirm* it, right?'

Potting nodded, a little sheepishly.

'So, don't talk yourself into an early grave.' Grace tapped the side of his head. 'I'm sure mental attitude has so much to do with fighting anything that's wrong with us. Be positive, yes?'

Potting nodded again.

'What's your doctor's plan?'

'He's referring me to an ENT surgeon, who'll do a biopsy, CT scans, chest X-ray, ultrasound and a laryngoscopy, I think it was, he said. But it'll be about two weeks before I get the appointment.'

Their drinks arrived and they waited until the waitress had moved away.

'Two weeks?' Grace said.

'Two weeks in which I'm going to be, frankly, worried as hell.'

'Listen, he said he wanted to eliminate the possibility of cancer. Take that as a positive. Even if the news is bad, cancer treatment is getting better all the time.'

Potting looked back at him bleakly. 'I googled laryngeal cancer after I left the surgery. It has one of the worst survival rates of any cancer.'

'Then stop googling it, OK? That's an order. Think positive. That's another order.' Grace stared hard at him, their eyes meeting. 'I know it's easy for me to say, Norman, but really, please keep thinking positive.'

'Understood, chief. I'd rather you didn't – you know, tell anyone just yet.'

'Of course.'

20

Grace and Branson sat opposite each other at the small round meeting table in the Detective Superintendent's office. They had mugs of coffee and Grace's fast-emptying packet of chocolate digestives in front of them, as Branson, complaining he hadn't had lunch, worked through them. Two photographic prints of Eden Paternoster, from the digital images they'd been emailed, also lay there, one with the background of the Parham House lake and the other in front of a Christmas tree.

'Any more thoughts, Glenn – other than how many crumbs you can drop on my table?'

'Sorry, boss!' Branson swept them dismissively onto the floor with his hand and grabbed yet another biscuit. 'The Amazing Disappearing Eden Paternoster!' Then he looked apologetic. 'I'm sorry, that was a bit insensitive.'

Grace shook his head. 'I'm over it – long over it.'

'Doesn't something like this bring it back?'

He nodded, wistful for a moment. 'Always. And if Eden has genuinely disappeared, then I'd feel something of the husband's pain, yes. But this doesn't smell at all right to me. The husband says she went into the store to get cat litter and disappeared. But his car isn't picked up by any camera out in the car park, his wife isn't picked up going into the store and she's not been caught on any camera inside the store. We know from the staff that he was there, but no one can recall seeing her, although they must see hundreds of people every day. And in any case, my sense – hunch – is this is more than just a routine misper situation, especially with what John Alldridge noticed.'

Branson studied the photographs for a moment. 'Nice-looking lady. I agree, but maybe we should have a chat with Mr Paternoster – don't you think?' He reached over and rummaged in the now almost empty packet. 'No passport smacks to me of someone doing a runner – with a lover – possibly?'

Grace looked thoughtful. 'Possibly. How about we drop in on him, unannounced, and have a friendly, sympathetic chat?'

Holding up half a biscuit, with a cartoon-like bite shape missing, Branson replied, 'Good plan, boss.' The rest of the biscuit disappeared.

'I do have a hypothesis.'

'Yes?' Branson asked.

'Maybe she got too close to your chomping jaws and you mistook her for a chocolate digestive.'

'That's not even slightly funny.'

As Glenn pulled out onto the main road a few minutes later and accelerated ferociously, Grace said, subtly trying to make him slow down, 'Um, you know how you often see flowers attached to trees at the scene of a fatal?'

'Uh-huh.'

'Biggsy in Traffic told me it's because people always drive at what they're looking at. You lose control on a bend and you see you're skidding straight towards a tree, so you stare at the tree – and whoomph! You drive straight at it and hit it. If you'd stared past it instead, you'd have missed it.'

'That so?'

Grace nodded. 'Another thing a trauma specialist once told me is that the worst thing you can hit is a tree.'

'Why's that?' Branson said, taking a sharp bend at a speed that nearly defied the laws of physics, as Grace warily eyed a very large beech ahead.

'He said, always hit a wall, because that'll collapse. But hit a tree and what that does is absorb the impact and then give it all straight back to you.'

'You'd rather I hit a wall than a tree?'

'Mate, can you just slow down, for Christ's sake? I'd prefer neither.'

Fifteen minutes later, at a quarter to four, Glenn Branson pulled up the silver, unmarked Ford in Nevill Road, in front of the Paternosters' house. Nodding at the Greyhound Stadium opposite, he asked, 'Ever been to the dogs?'

Grace nodded. 'Yep, last year Cleo and I went – I was asked to present the prizes for an evening that was fundraising for the Sussex Police Charitable Trust.'

'Did you have a punt?'

'I thought it would be polite – and it was for a good cause.'

'How did you do?'

'We were put at a table with a CSI who breeds racing greyhounds as a hobby. He gave me a tip – always bet on one you see having a dump before the race.'

'Did you?'

'Yep,' Grace said.

'Yeah? And?'

'Lost every sodding race.'

Branson laughed. 'Shit happens.'

'Or maybe it didn't.'

21

Monday 2 September

Roy Grace and Glenn Branson got out of the car and walked up to the Paternosters' front door. The top half was frosted glass. Grace pressed the bell and heard musical chimes. Followed by the miaow of a cat.

They waited.

After several seconds, Grace rang again. A shadow appeared behind the glass, then the door opened, just a few inches. A male voice commanded, 'Back! Back, Reggie!'

The door opened wider and they saw an unshaven, tired-looking man in his thirties with muscular arms, wearing denim shorts, a T-shirt and flip-flops. He was stooping, holding a grey Burmese cat. On one wrist, Grace noticed, he wore an Apple Watch and on the other a Fitbit.

Looking up at them, he said, 'Sorry, can't let him out the front – the last one got run over and I was to blame.'

'Mr Niall Paternoster?' Grace asked.

'Yes.'

Grace held up his warrant card and introduced himself and Branson.

Niall gave a smile. 'Detective Superintendent? Major Crime Team? So, you've not palmed some junior lackey off on this?' Then he hesitated as a thought seemed to strike him, and his face fell. 'Oh my God – have you found her? Is that what—?'

'May we come in, sir?' Grace asked politely, ignoring the comment.

They entered the small hallway as the man shut the door behind them. Grace glanced around; the interior was modern, fresh-feeling, minimalistic, but there was a faint smell of fried food and cigarette smoke. The smell seemed incongruous – the floral scents of expensive diffusers would have gone more appropriately with the decor, he thought.

'Have you found my wife?' Niall asked again with a nervous edge.

'No, sir, I'm afraid not,' Grace said. 'We'd just like to have a chat with you.'

Niall expanded his arms. 'Absolutely! And thank you for coming. Would you like something to drink? Tea, coffee?'

'We're good, thank you,' Grace said firmly.

They followed the man through into the modern-looking lounge and sat down on the white sofa he indicated. Niall Paternoster sat opposite. Grace noticed an ashtray on the coffee table that was crammed with butts.

'Mr Paternoster, could you talk us through the circumstances of your wife's disappearance? Starting with the last time you saw her?' Grace asked.

'What, again? Don't you people talk to each other? This isn't the first time I've gone over this.'

Grace didn't tell him that one reason they liked people to recount events multiple times was that if they were lying, they would often start making mistakes or inconsistencies. All he said was an apologetic, 'I'm sorry, sir, but it is important we understand exactly what happened and the timeline.'

Paternoster sighed. Then, as if suddenly realizing he was behaving strangely, his demeanour changed completely, all eager to help now. 'The last time I saw Eden was yesterday afternoon. We were heading home after a nice day out. We're members of

87

the National Trust and we like visiting their houses – a regular thing we do on Sundays. But yesterday, actually, we went to Parham House.'

'And everything was fine between you?' Branson interjected.

There was a moment's hesitation. 'Well, we'd had a bit of a stupid argument – over cat litter.' He recounted the circumstances, leading to Eden jumping out of the car in the store's car park to go and grab a bag of the stuff.

'That was the last time you saw her?' Grace asked.

'Correct.'

So much of this was resonating with Roy Grace. That nightmare, twelve years ago, on the evening of his thirtieth birthday.

'Do you have any way of knowing if she actually went into the store?' Branson quizzed.

Paternoster glared for a moment as a flash fire of irritation ignited, but he kept his calm. 'No, I wasn't following her, but that was my assumption – it's the only reason she got out of the car.'

Paternoster went on to tell the officers what had happened subsequently, after she had failed to reappear. That he'd gone into the Tesco store shortly before closing time, and the staff had searched the place but not found her. How he had called her phone repeatedly, even though he knew it had very little battery left, then her friends and family, as well as checking with all the local hospitals. When he had arrived back home, he'd searched the house for her but there had been no sign. Everything he said, so far, tallied with the briefing Grace had been given from Detective Inspector Bryce Robinson.

Niall told them he had called her again today, checked online again for any activity on her credit cards and bank statement, as well as her social media – she was always active on Twitter, Facebook and Instagram, but there had been no posts. And that he had already relayed all this to the two police officers who'd attended earlier.

When he had finished, Grace, watching him intently, asked him a question which momentarily threw him. 'What did you have for breakfast today, Mr Paternoster?'

'What does that have to do with anything?'

'Could you tell me?' he coaxed gently, watching the man's body language intently.

He looked nervous. 'If you must know, I had brunch – two fried eggs, bacon, pork sausage and baked beans – oh, and fried bread.' Then he gave a sly grin. 'But don't tell Eden because she's been trying to wean me on to birdseed and fruit.'

Still watching him intently, Grace asked, 'She's concerned about your health? What else has she tried to get you to do?'

Paternoster brushed his brow. 'Oh God, she's always trying to push me on to some new fad or something. Recently it's been to exercise more, although I'm always out on my bike anyway, stuff like that, to get through my depression after losing my business.'

Grace processed this. 'Was the car park at Tesco Holmbush busy when you arrived there yesterday?'

To Grace's disappointment, the man seemed confident in his reply, which indicated he was telling the truth. 'Yes, it was – that's why she got out, to avoid us being stuck in the traffic there.' He paused. 'Why did you ask me about breakfast – what does that have to do with anything?'

'The house smells of something being fried.'

'So?'

Grace raised his hand appeasingly. 'Just a copper's curiosity.'

Niall frowned, then challenged, a little aggressively, 'How does this have anything to do with my wife disappearing, exactly?'

Grace was glad to have the man rattled. He caught Branson's eye. The DI knew exactly what he was doing. People made mistakes when they were angry. Niall Paternoster had now given him one reason for getting rid of his wife, albeit a small one – their constant arguments. But was there more to it? Did he actually despise her? Did he hate her enough to kill her?

People had murdered their partners for smaller reasons than this. Again, watching his reaction carefully, Grace said, 'Mr Paternoster, we have watched the Tesco Holmbush CCTV covering the period you were there yesterday. We've studied footage of the car park, the entrances to the store, and footage covering all the aisles. We've also talked to staff members present yesterday. There is no sign of your wife in any of the footage, and no staff member can recall seeing anyone resembling your wife. Are you sure you're telling us the truth?'

To Grace's disappointment, Niall again answered confidently.

'I'm absolutely sure. And why wouldn't I be telling you the truth?'

Grace stared at him, levelly. 'You really are certain you're telling the truth?'

Niall Paternoster stood up suddenly, his eyes blazing now. 'This is outrageous,' he said with real fury. 'You come into my house and accuse me of lying? I took my wife to the store to get cat litter. She got out of the car, headed off and then just literally vanished. I'm sick with worry, I don't know what's happened. You don't believe me, do you? You think I'm lying, don't you?'

'We're not saying that, sir,' Grace replied calmly. 'I asked you a question. You're telling us your wife has disappeared, but there is no evidence she was ever at the place you said.'

'Meaning what, exactly?'

'Meaning that we, as the police, have a duty of care.'

Niall Paternoster glared at him in silence for some moments. 'I don't think I should say anything more without my solicitor present.' He twisted his hands together; a sign of anxiety, Grace recognized.

'You are not under caution or arrest, Mr Paternoster,' he said.

'We are simply here to have a chat with you to see if we can help find your wife.'

'Do I look stupid or something?' Paternoster replied. 'I phoned the police because I'm concerned about my wife going missing, and I get a Detective Superintendent and Detective Inspector from Major Crime arriving at my front door. I didn't ride into town on the back of a truck – I can tell I'm under suspicion. I'm sorry, gentlemen, I'm not saying anything more without a solicitor.'

Grace stood up and, unprompted, Branson did the same. He pulled out his card and put it down on the table. 'My numbers are on that – I'd be grateful if you would either call the landline or my mobile if you hear anything from your wife.'

Niall Paternoster glared at him again.

Nodding at the man's phone on the sofa, beside him, Grace asked, 'Do you like your iPhone?'

'What's it to you?'

'I'm thinking of upgrading to one, as my private phone. I'm told the camera is great. But I've heard that some phone providers work better on it than others.'

'Eden has one too,' he responded warily.

'And you have no reception issues?' Grace asked, all friendly now.

He shook his head. 'Not on O2, no.'

'Could you let me have your wife's number, please?'

'I thought you coppers would already have all that important stuff.' He looked momentarily flustered. 'It's – erm – 07771 . . .' He hesitated and grinned inanely. 'You know, I can't bloody remember it – I have her in my contacts and never actually dial the number itself.'

Grace nodded sympathetically. 'I'm the same – not sure I know my wife's number either.'

The man studied his phone for some moments, pressing keys,

then, looking at the display, read out the number, which Grace noted on his tablet.

They walked to the front door. As they reached it, Grace turned to him. 'If you could also let me have your number, I'll call you if we have any information about your wife.'

Niall Paternoster gave it to him.

'Please let me know if you hear from Eden,' Grace asked. 'We may need you to come to Brighton police station to give a statement – and, of course, you'd be welcome to bring your solicitor. But I can assure you our priority at this stage is to find your wife safe and well.'

'At *this stage*?' Niall Paternoster said with a frown.

'Thank you for your time, Mr Paternoster.'

22

'Nice try,' said Glenn Branson, as they drove away.

Roy Grace, head down, had the Photos app on his phone open. He tapped out a message and Branson heard the *woosh* of an email going.

Without responding, his radio on loudspeaker, Grace called Aiden Gilbert in the Sussex Police Digital Forensics Unit.

After a brief while, he heard Gilbert's ever-enthusiastic voice. 'Hello, boss, how can I help you?'

'We have a potentially urgent situation, Aiden, regarding a misper. I've just emailed you a photograph of a woman taken early afternoon yesterday. Could you have someone take a look at it and verify the time and date, please?'

'Sure, boss, we're pretty inundated but I'll get someone on it as quickly as I can.'

Grace then rang DC Velvet Wilde, who he'd asked to join his newly formed Outside Enquiry Team.

'I've got two O2 phone numbers – I need a plot of both their movements yesterday, between the hours of 9 a.m. and 6 p.m. How quickly do you think you could get that?'

'O2 are pretty good – should be able to let you have that within a couple of hours if I let them know it's an urgent authority.'

'They'll need it confirmed in writing.'

'I'll sort that, boss.'

Grace thanked her and ended the call.

Glenn Branson turned to him. 'My, are you the sly one!'

'Sly?'

'The way you teased the information about his phone out of Paternoster.'

Grace gave him a knowing glance. 'I'm a detective, and your tutor. How many chocolate digestives does it take to activate your brain cells – or have they put it into a digesting slumber?'

'Yeah, yeah, funny! So what else did you pick up from him, Sherlock?'

'Possible tension between him and his wife. His comment about the fried breakfast?'

'I got that, too.'

'Could he be playing away? Or she?' Grace posited.

'Possible.'

'Let's get the Outside Enquiry Team speaking to the neighbours and friends and see what we can find out about their relationship.'

Branson nodded. 'Sounded like money could be an issue.'

'And the cat.'

'Blaming him for their last one being run over?'

'So you *were* awake.'

23

Twenty-five minutes later, having picked up a wrap and a banana and a couple of chocolate bars, Glenn Branson manoeuvred the car into Roy Grace's parking slot on the Sussex Police HQ campus. It was a privilege reserved for SIOs; most detectives and other staff who drove to work had to take their chances on the streets beyond. Climbing out, he and Grace headed towards the bland, low-rise building that now housed the Major Crime Team after its second move in the short while they had been here.

Back in Grace's office, Branson devoured his food, sharing one of the chocolate bars with Grace, then went to pick up a couple of coffees, leaving Roy thinking back to his earlier meeting with Norman.

He had been keeping positive in front of Norman, but he was concerned about what he'd heard. Despite his bravado about being a tough bugger, Roy knew that, underneath, Norman was a vulnerable man who still hadn't got over the death of his fiancée – if indeed he ever would. To cope with this new ordeal, he was going to need all the support he could get, particularly from himself, Cleo and all the team. He'd already spoken to Cleo on the phone and she was researching the condition and treatment so they could talk about it later. She was going to speak to her sister, who had experienced the same type of cancer and had been clear of it for over five years.

Glenn Branson came back in with two steaming coffees and dug his hand into the digestive packet, still there from earlier. He pulled out the last biscuit, proffering half to Roy, who shook his head, and polished that one off, too, in a shower of crumbs. Seeing his boss's look of disapproval, he swept those onto the floor, as before. 'So?' he said.

Grace was pensive for a moment. 'I'm even less happy having met him,' he said. 'The more I think about it, the less I like it.'

'Even though he answered all your questions truthfully? I was watching his non-verbals, too.'

'It's not a foolproof test. Especially if someone knows they're being observed – then it's easy to manipulate. I just don't like the man. You?'

'I agree, boss.'

'So, let's recap on what we have. Niall Paternoster calls the police this morning. His story is that his wife, Eden, went into the Tesco Holmbush superstore to buy a bag of cat litter at around 3.15 p.m. yesterday. And he claims he's not seen or heard from her since. You and I interviewed him, and his attitude was aggressive and defensive. Ordinarily with a misper, dependent on the risk assessment, we'd wait twenty-four hours after they were last seen before the enquiry could be elevated. Again, all dependent on the risk assessment.' He glanced at his watch, then looked at his colleague. 'Are you comfortable waiting, knowing what we have?'

Branson shook his head. 'Not really, no.'

'Nor me.'

Grace's job phone rang. He answered, and almost immediately switched it to loudspeaker.

Branson recognized the voice of Velvet Wilde.

'Boss, O2 have come back to me,' the DC said. 'I've got a plot of the two mobile phone numbers.' She read out first Niall Paternoster's. 'Between the hours of 9 a.m. yesterday and 11 a.m.

it was at one of a few possible addresses in Nevill Road, Hove. It then moved west to the vicinity of Parham House, near Pulborough, in West Sussex. It remained in that area until 2.45 p.m. when it headed east, stopping at around 3.15 p.m. in the vicinity of the Tesco Holmbush superstore just north of Shoreham. It remained in that area until approximately 4.20 p.m., when it returned to Nevill Road, where it seems to have remained until around 5 p.m. The phone then moved its position, via a road in Portslade and then Devil's Dyke, towards Heathrow Airport and later that evening returned back to Nevill Road. Since that time it has been static in Nevill Road.'

Grace jotted down the details. 'And the second number?'

'Well, we had to go back a bit further than the time you gave us because it seems either to have been switched off or its battery went flat Thursday evening. At 6 a.m. Thursday, it moved south, down Nevill Road, across the Old Shoreham Road and down to the seafront, where it turned east and continued to the start of Brighton Marina. It then turned back, west, retracing its path to the Nevill Road address. The distance covered was approximately 8.4 miles and the timings indicate the pace to have been a run.' She paused for a moment. 'I know it wasn't in my brief, but I thought it was worth checking the run against a few apps and we discovered that it had been recorded on a Strava app, belonging to Eden Paternoster – the owner of the phone.'

'Nice work, Velvet!' Grace said.

'Thank you. At 7.50 a.m. the phone then moved north to Croydon to an area we've identified as the Mutual Occidental Insurance Company. It remained there until 5.45 p.m. when it then headed south, reaching the Nevill Road address at 6.35 p.m. It remained static there until 10.10 p.m. on Thursday, which was the last signal from the phone.'

'Nothing since then?' Grace asked.

'Nothing,' Wilde confirmed.

He looked at Glenn Branson, who frowned, *What?*

He nodded back. Then he said, 'That's very helpful, Velvet.'

'Do you need me to plot it further back?'

'Not at the moment. I'll let you know.'

'Sure. Anything else I can help you with?'

'Not for now – but if you can email me a summary of all this, please.'

'I'll ping it across in a few minutes.'

Grace thanked her and ended the call. Frowning, he turned to Branson. 'What do you make of that?'

'Eden goes for an early morning run on Thursday – like you often do yourself. Then she drives to work. She drives home that evening. Then her phone goes dead around 10.10 p.m. And stays off. She has a responsible job in IT at a major insurance company, and she clearly uses her phone not just for work but for recreation – like recording her running on Strava. So, let's say it did die from a flat battery at 10.10 p.m., why would she not charge it all Friday, Saturday and Sunday? Does that make any sense?'

Grace shook his head pensively.

'Let's hypothesize for a moment,' Glenn Branson said. 'He murders his wife on Thursday night and then plays a charade of a day out at Parham House, ending up with her disappearing at a Tesco store on the way home, apparently going in to buy cat litter. Would he be dumb enough to think we wouldn't check her phone activity?'

'You've met him,' Grace replied with a sideways glance. 'I'm not the world's leading authority on tattoos, but did you see the one on his arm of the grim reaper?'

Branson grinned. 'Yeah, let's hope he's not acted that out.'

'I agree,' Grace said. 'For one of my birthdays, Sandy got me a voucher from a tattoo parlour as a present.'

'Yeah?'

'I was never brave enough to have it done. She wanted me to have my name and her name with a heart between on my arm.'

'Lucky you didn't. Cleo would have been mightily impressed – not!'

Grace grinned. 'You could say that.' Then, serious again, he said, 'It seems that Eden is a successful woman, hard-working, in the prime of her life, with a close circle of friends and work colleagues. It doesn't make sense that she has just disappeared and we have found no social media activity since her disappearance. Do you agree?'

Glenn Branson nodded his head.

At that moment, Grace's phone rang again. It was Aiden Gilbert and he sounded puzzled. 'Can I clarify something, Roy?' he asked, the phone on loudspeaker.

'Tell me?'

'That photograph of the woman in front of the lake you sent me? You said it was taken yesterday, early afternoon?'

'Yes, correct – from what I was told.'

'Not according to the digital date stamp, Roy. On first examination, it wasn't taken yesterday, it was taken at 1.50 p.m. on Saturday August the twenty-fourth. Over a week before.'

'You are certain, Aiden?'

'Completely, Roy.'

Ending the call, Grace called Cleo to tell her that they were going to have to postpone the hen husbandry course tomorrow.

24

'It is 6.30 p.m., Monday September the second,' Roy Grace announced to his freshly assembled team. 'This is the first briefing meeting of Operation Lagoon, the investigation into the disappearance of Mrs Eden Paternoster, last seen according to the questionable information given by her husband, Niall, shortly after 3.15 p.m. yesterday, Sunday September the first, in the car park of the Tesco Holmbush superstore, pictured behind me. I'm sure some of you are already familiar with that store and use it?'

He noted a few nods.

On one whiteboard behind Grace was pinned the two photographs of Eden Paternoster, the one in front of a Christmas tree and the one in front of the Parham House lake. They were accompanied by several more photographs of her, sent in by her husband.

One was of Eden with Niall, their arms around each other, a couple who seemingly could not be more in love, in front of the beautiful ruins of moated Bodiam Castle. Another was in front of Hangleton church, Niall in a suit, sporting a red carnation and beaming, and Eden in a long wedding dress, holding a bouquet, smiling radiantly.

On the second whiteboard was a sequence of photographs of the interior and exterior of the Tesco superstore, taken by Crime Scene Photographer James Gartrell. Each was labelled. Various angles of the car park, the public front entrance, the staff entrance and the goods receiving bay. The ones of the interior of the store showed the manned and unmanned checkout tills, several aisles and each of the CCTV camera locations. Beneath them was the poor-resolution image of Niall Paternoster in denim shorts and T-shirt, taken from the CCTV, in the entrance to the store at 3.50 p.m. yesterday.

On the third whiteboard were two association charts, one showing Eden Paternoster's family tree, the other her and her husband's friends and colleagues. These were a work-in-progress, with more names and details yet to be filled in.

'All routine procedures regarding a misper have been followed, with photographs of the missing lady circulated,' Roy Grace said, addressing his team seated around the long, oval table in the Major Crime suite conference room. 'However, we have reason to suspect we may be looking at something more than a standard missing person enquiry. The purpose of this briefing is to update you on our enquiries so far, and to establish lines of command and duties, together with roles and responsibilities. I will be acting as Senior Investigating Officer, with Glenn Branson as my Deputy.' He nodded at the DI, to his left, who held his pen poised above his Policy Book. 'Jack Alexander will run the enquiry as Action Manager and Allocator, linking into the HOLMES team, and will also manage the Outside Enquiry teams.' HOLMES – or correctly HOLMES 2 – was the acronym for the Home Office Large Major Enquiry System.

The tall young DS beside Glenn Branson acknowledged this. 'Yes, sir.'

'The Intelligence Analyst will be Luke Stanstead.' Grace smiled at the young man, who was in a wheelchair pulled up to the table, sitting lower down than the rest of the team. The popular officer had been paralysed in a swimming pool accident a few years earlier. Grace admired the man for his resilience. Away from work, Stanstead had become a front runner and leading light in wheelchair rugby. The HOLMES Supervisor would be joining the team tomorrow, back from her day off. The other HOLMES roles would also be filled during the next few hours.

Grace went on to name his Exhibits and Disclosure Officers, his go-to Financial Investigations Officer, Emily Denyer, the almost impossibly young-looking Crime Scene Manager, Chris Gee, and Sergeant Lorna Dennison-Wilkins as POLSA – Police Search Adviser – as and when needed, to manage any searches.

Checking his notes, he continued. 'Our Outside Enquiry Team will consist of DS Potting and DC Wilde, DCs Soper and Hall, and the third pair of DS Exton and Polly.' Investigating Officer Pauline Sweeney, known to everyone as Polly, had just retired as a police officer but immediately rejoined the team as a civilian in an identical role. 'I've appointed Emma-Jane Boutwood as FLO – she has attended at the Paternosters' home but Eden's husband told her, at present, he wants to be alone. I will keep this situation under review.'

FLOs – Family Liaison Officers – were allocated to the immediate family members of any Major Crime victim. Their role was twofold, the first being to provide a dedicated officer to act as a conduit between the family and the investigation, obtaining any information and evidence from them and also passing information from the SIO back to the family. A secondary role was to provide a presence and emotional support, from conversation to preparing meals and doing essential shopping. Emma-Jane's rejection by Niall Paternoster might be further grounds for suspicion, Grace felt.

Detective Sergeant Martyn Stratford would run the Enquiry Intelligence Cell as the Intel Manager supported by their own staff.

Grace went on to detail the situation leading to the purported disappearance of Eden Paternoster, his and Branson's subsequent visit to the Tesco store earlier, followed by their interview with her husband at the family home on Nevill Road. And then the bombshell, from Aiden Gilbert, about the time and date on the photograph Niall Paternoster had claimed had been taken yesterday afternoon, but which in fact had been taken over a week earlier on Saturday 24 August.

'As a result of this,' Grace continued, 'I asked Velvet Wilde to extend the plotting of both of their phones back to that day, and Aiden's findings verify this. Both their phones travelled together from their house in Nevill Road to Parham House on the afternoon of Saturday August the twenty-fourth, spending about three hours there before returning to Nevill Road.'

He held up the printouts from the plots of Niall and Eden Paternosters' mobile phones that Wilde had sent him. 'I'll pass these round so you can see for yourselves.'

He allowed the team some moments to absorb all of this and to circulate the printouts. Several of them scribbled details in their investigators' notebooks.

DS Alexander raised his hand. 'Sir, what car or cars do the Paternosters own?'

'They share use of a BMW Three Series convertible,' Grace replied.

'A recent model?'

'I took a note of the registration,' Branson interjected. 'It's a two-year-old model.'

Alexander nodded. 'I'm pretty sure these have in-built satnav. Perhaps worth having the Collision Investigation Unit take a look at it and interrogate the satnav – and the car's computer system. They'd almost certainly be able to establish its movements over the past couple of weeks.'

'Good point, Jack,' Grace said, making a note. He looked around his team and settled on DC Soper. 'Louise, your husband knows a thing or two about BMWs, doesn't he?'

She smiled. 'A little.'

'Done a bit of racing in them, right? I'm sure some of it's rubbed off on you – I'll give you the action of getting the satnav checked out by the Collison Investigation Unit, as Jack suggests.'

'Of course, boss,' she said.

'I'm sure some of you are thinking "overkill", Roy Grace said. 'Surely this is just a case of a wife who has, for whatever reason, legged it, perhaps with a lover, like a thousand partners, of all genders, before her? But I think this is something more and very serious for a number of reasons. Firstly, Niall Paternoster told us his wife seldom went anywhere without her phone charged and she was always using social media. And yet on the day he tells us she disappeared, he claims her phone had either died or was switched off. In my view, that's a little too convenient. Especially when put together with his lie about when the photograph was taken. I'd like to hear any of your opinions.'

Emily Denyer raised her arm. 'Sir, regarding the phone, could it simply be that she'd forgotten to charge it? We've all had that happen. And did he actually see the phone in the car?'

'Good point, Emily, but it doesn't explain the photograph. And two things make me doubt what he said about the phone. The first is that he told us he had repeatedly dialled her number. If she'd left it charging at home, he'd surely have seen it when he got back to their house. The second is that I peered in the window of their car as we left and I saw a phone charger in there, plugged into the socket. When we met Niall Paternoster, Glenn and I established that both he and his wife have the same make and model of iPhone. If it had been me in that situation, and I never went anywhere without my phone, I would have taken it and charged it in the car during the journey. Wouldn't you?'

She nodded. 'If it had been me, yes, assuming the charger was working – they can be temperamental.'

'Her husband claims he looked everywhere for her phone

when he got home, without success, so he is certain she has it with her,' Grace said. 'So where is it?'

'He's lying, chief,' Norman Potting said. 'Sounds to me like he's disposed of it.'

'OK, Norman, let's go with that for a moment. For what reason would he have disposed of it?' Grace asked.

Potting scratched his head. 'Because there was something on it that he didn't want us to find?'

'Any idea what, Norman?' Glenn Branson asked.

'He didn't want anyone tracking his communication to her, perhaps,' Potting ventured.

'A phone with a dead battery doesn't give off any signal,' Chris Gee said.

Grace jotted down in his notebook that the missing phone should be a line of enquiry. His job phone rang.

Raising an excusing finger, he answered.

It was ACC Pewe. 'What the hell's going on, Roy?'

'One moment, sir.'

Had the shit already hit the fan? he wondered. Had Alison Vosper already started the investigation? Surely this was too soon?

Excusing himself, he stepped out of the room into the corridor and closed the door behind him. 'OK, sir, I'm back with you.'

'Back with me or out with the fairies?' Pewe said in his normal, angry whine.

'Beg pardon, sir?'

'How long have you been a police officer, Roy?'

'About twenty-four years, sir.' Saying *sir* increasingly stuck in his craw.

'And how many of those as a detective?'

'Twenty-two, approximately.'

'And how many missing person enquiries have you dealt with during this time?'

Now he knew that Pewe had no idea what was coming his way. Despite his cockiness, Grace maintained his veneer of respect. 'I haven't counted – *sir*.'

'Have you counted how many officers and support staff you have on this one, Roy?'

'I haven't, exactly, no.'

'Well, let me tell you something, you've got more people working on this case than you have brain cells.'

Roy Grace said nothing. Sometimes silence was the best reply, especially when dealing with a total asshole like Cassian Pewe.

After several moments, the ACC said, 'Roy?'

'Sir?'

'Did you not hear what I said?'

'Yes, I heard.'

'And?'

'And what?'

Pewe's voice was becoming increasingly high-pitched, as it always did the angrier he got. 'A married woman goes missing, which happens all the time. But you, in your infinite wisdom, take it upon yourself to deploy half the resources of the Major Crime Team on one woman who's been gone barely twenty-four hours?'

Calmly and quietly, Grace replied, 'As I'm the Head of Major Crime you either have to accept my judgement when I decide to elevate, based on the evidence I have, what might seem to be a routine enquiry into a crime-in-action, or else replace me if you have no confidence in me. Personally, I'm fine either way – *sir*.'

Roy Grace knew Cassian Pewe was well aware that he had an open offer to move to the London Metropolitan Police in a Temporary Commander role, which would put him on equal status to Pewe. He was confident the idiot would back off. He was right.

'If you have good reason for what seems to me to be complete overkill, perhaps you might have had the courtesy to brief me first,' Pewe said sullenly.

'I've been a little busy today,' Grace replied, a tad facetiously. 'Forgive me for putting the police ethic, to serve and protect, above informing you what was happening. But with a possible crime-in-action and, in my view, a life at stake, I thought you would be big enough to park your ego and let me get on with my job.'

He could hear the barely restrained fury in Pewe's voice. 'Don't push me, Roy.'

Push you? Grace thought, mindful of Guy Batchelor's notebook sitting on the desk in his little office at home. *I'll push you. All the way over the cliff edge, like I should have done when I had the chance but instead I hung on to you to save your sodding life and risked mine doing it.*

'I'm not *pushing* you, sir, I'm merely trying to do my job. I appreciate that, under some circumstances, we would wait longer after someone was reported missing by their partner before elevating it to a misper enquiry. But in my judgement and after my risk assessment, we're not looking for a misper.'

'Really, Roy? So what are you looking for exactly?' Pewe whined.

'Proof of life – *sir.*'

25

There was a long silence. Finally it was broken by the ACC's voice.

'You'd better be right,' Pewe retorted lamely.

Roy then ran through the lines of enquiry his team were following and gave Pewe an update. 'So actually, *sir*, I hope I'm wrong,' Grace said.

'Meaning what exactly, Roy? You're a homicide investigator through and through. Don't pretend otherwise. I know you, and what you and all homicide investigators like more than anything is a good murder – what do you call it – a *Gucci* murder? You're not hoping she's alive at all, are you?' he said snidely.

'I am, for your reputation, sir. We need to keep the crime stats down, don't we? To make you look good, right?'

'I told you not to push me, Roy.'

'Is that because you know just how far you might fall?' Grace responded facetiously, killing the call with a broad smile.

Oh yes, he was enjoying this. He felt the way he did in the weekly Thursday-night poker games he used to attend whenever he could, with a bunch of police colleagues. The rare, incredibly exciting moments during those games when he held a pretty much invincible hand. A full house, Aces on Kings, four Aces or – something which had happened to him only once in all the years he had been playing – an unassailable Royal Flush. Ace, King, Queen, Jack, Ten of the same suit.

It was that Royal Flush he held now. And he was loving it.

As he re-entered the room, still smiling, his phone rang again. Certain it was Pewe, Grace rejected it and muted the phone.

He addressed the team. 'We are finalizing the strategies for forensics, search and arrests, and establishing the key lines of enquiry which will be circulated. A crucial line of enquiry at this stage is the victimology. Speaking to Eden's friends, work colleagues and family will be a critical part of this.'

He turned to Branson. 'Glenn, we've heard Niall Paternoster's account of dropping his wife off in the car park of Tesco Holmbush and her apparent vanishing. Despite all his supposed endeavours to contact her, as he told the officers who attended at his house this morning, and you and me subsequently, so far we have nothing to confirm that his missing wife is OK. He made a couple of comments, which I relayed to you, that gave me cause to believe all was not good between them.'

DS Exton raised a hand. 'Boss, given the photograph's analysis from Digital Forensics, do you think Eden Paternoster was even in the car at all yesterday afternoon?'

'It's a good question, Jon. My hypothesis at this point is no, his wife was never in the car. This is a cover story her husband's made up and it all sounds very plausible – at least to him, in his mind. I think it is very possible Niall Paternoster murdered his wife sometime before Sunday afternoon. One urgent task for the Outside Enquiry Team will be contacting her employers again, Mutual Occidental in Croydon, for more information. Apparently, she has not been to work since Thursday of last week.'

He looked at Luke Stanstead. 'Can you continue to develop the sequence of events and timeline and share it with the team?'

'Yes, sir.'

'Perhaps Paternoster hasn't taken into account the CCTV coverage that the Tesco store has. There is clearly no evidence, from the footage or the staff interviews, that his wife was either in the car park or the store at the time he claims. All we know for certain, from the plotting of his phone, is that he drove to Parham House at the approximate times he told us, wandered around the grounds for three hours and then drove to the Tesco store before going home. There is nothing to support his assertion that his wife was with him during this time. And the evidence from Aiden Gilbert's Digital Forensics Team indicates this. It's my view that he is trying to mislead or misdirect us.'

There was a brief silence, broken after a short while by DC Hall. 'The CCTV only covers limited areas, doesn't it, boss?'

Grace nodded. 'Yes, correct, Kevin.'

'So she could have gone into the store without being detected?'

'It's possible but extremely unlikely. One of the photographs of the interior shows a camera in the aisle where the cat litter is kept.' Grace turned and pointed at the specific photograph on the whiteboard. 'If she'd gone in to buy cat litter, as he claims, she would have been picked up on CCTV in that aisle.'

Hall nodded.

Grace continued. 'Another action I want is a check of the index of the Paternosters' BMW with all ANPR cameras in Sussex, all speed and traffic light cameras, and with the Highways Authority cameras measuring traffic flow. We'll see if there is any tally with a cell-site analysis of both of their phones.' He made a brief note, then looked up again.

'OK, everyone, from the evidence to date, I'm elevating Operation Lagoon from a missing person enquiry to a "no body" murder enquiry. My Policy Book will reflect my decision.' He glanced at his watch. 'DI Branson and I established earlier that Niall Paternoster drives a mate's taxi mainly during unsociable hours – usually starting at midnight at weekends and 10 p.m. during the week. Let's get that vehicle checked on the cameras, too. Velvet, team up with Polly.' He turned to DS Potting and DS Exton. 'Norman and Jon, I want you to go straight from this meeting and arrest Niall Paternoster on suspicion of murdering his wife. I will policy this decision and my reasons for making it, most important of which is the recovery of evidence that might be in the house. I don't think we'll require support from the Public Order Team – but if you meet resistance, we will deploy them. So I think we should have them standing by.'

Both officers nodded.

'We'll then see if we get anywhere interviewing him lawyered up.' He turned to Gee. 'Chris, I'd like you to attend as Crime Scene Manager.'

'Yes, sir.'

'I want you to draw up the forensic strategy. I need your team to look for any signs of bloodstains and cleaned-up blood. Have them look through all Niall Paternoster's clothes.' He turned and pointed at the photograph of him in Tesco yesterday. 'Especially look for the clothing he was wearing yesterday, on the day he claimed she disappeared. Take anything you can find of hers – toothbrush, hairbrush, diary, the usual stuff – anything that might have her prints or DNA, for lab analysis. As we are treating the entire property as a crime scene, we all know the drill. It's possible he might have killed Eden some days earlier, so organize a sidescan sonar search of anywhere that looks recently screeded, particularly the garden. Lorna, can you pick that up?'

'Yes, boss,' she said. 'My POLSA colleague, Sergeant Barbara Onoufriou, can start work in the house, garden and any searches arising from our presence there.'

Grace turned back to Gee. 'Chris, one thing in particular I want you to look for is evidence of any missing bedding, in particular a duvet or duvet cover.'

Gee nodded, making another note.

'Worried Mrs Paternoster might be out of her comfort zone, chief?' Potting quipped.

It brought a few grins. Grace smiled at the DS. 'Norman, I know you've tended to favour divorce in the past, but just supposing you decided to murder your wife, what would you have in your house that you'd utilize to carry her body out of your home and into your car, to take her to a deposition site?'

Potting thought for a moment. 'I don't know, boss – maybe a tarpaulin or a roll of spare carpet – or perhaps plastic sheeting?'

'OK,' Grace said. 'Do you have any of those things in your home, Norman?'

He shook his head. 'No.'

'Exactly. What you do probably have is a duvet. Right?'

'Yes,' he replied hesitantly.

'Duvet covers or curtains are the favoured items for a person who murders their partner to wrap the body in. They don't like to see their dead lover's face looking at them.'

Kevin Hall chipped in. 'You've got to remember, boss, Norman's a farmer's son – he's used to sleeping on straw.'

Grace grinned, then said, 'Chris, look at the beds for any missing duvets, and the closets and airing cupboard for anything like a pillowslip with no duvet cover – they tend to come in sets. And check the curtains.'

Gee nodded.

'Jack, can you contact the duty Inspector to set in motion a rota of scene guards?'

'I have that on my list,' replied Alexander, who was noting down all the actions.

'Good stuff.' Grace went on, turning back to Gee. 'I noticed when DI Branson and I interviewed Paternoster that he was wearing an Apple Watch and a Fitbit. Arrange for those to be taken off him and sent to Digital Forensics when he's booked in to the custody block.'

'Absolutely, sir.'

Turning to DC Soper, he said, 'As I requested, Louise, seize the BMW and have Collision Investigations examine its satnav and computer, and collate that with what the ANPRs show –

they should reveal where it has been during the past two weeks. We may be looking for possible deposition sites for Eden's body.'

'Will do, boss.'

He turned to Emily Denyer. 'I need you to find out everything about the couple's finances. Any insurance policies on her life, anything that might indicate her husband having something to gain from her death.'

Then he briefed his Outside Enquiry Teams. 'Go and talk to all the Paternosters' immediate neighbours. See what they know about the couple – and, crucially, when any of them might have seen Eden. Maybe some of them had security cameras outside their houses. We need to establish the last confirmed sighting of her. We also need to check the CCTV in and around the stores at the Holmbush Centre. With the new information we have received regarding their phones, I want checks to be made at Parham House for both last Saturday and yesterday to see if there is any record of the Paternosters being there on either or both days. They are closed now but it needs to be done first thing in the morning.'

They all nodded.

He then dealt with the intelligence requirement, including database checks, family history and social networking activity, and asked DS Stratford to draw up the strategy, before turning to DS Alexander.

'Jack, also get the team, when checking Parham House for both weekends, to look for any evidence they may have such as CCTV, ticket registration, visitor books, credit card receipts – see what that throws up.'

He finally addressed Stanstead again. 'Luke, collate what the Intelligence Cell finds on both Niall Paternoster and Eden – any past criminal activity by either of them and as much background as you can get.'

'Yes, sir.'

Grace made some notes, then looked up. 'Any questions?'

Norman Potting raised a hand. 'Chief, one thing we haven't covered is the possibility of Eden Paternoster having an affair.'

'Good point, Norman,' Grace said. And nearly added, *Especially coming from a man with your track record.* 'If that is the case, hopefully we'll learn something from the interviews with her family and friends from our Outside Enquiry Teams.' He looked around. 'Any more questions?'

There were none.

'OK, I will attend for the arrest. We'll all meet back here at 8.30 a.m. tomorrow for reports on initial findings. Good luck, everyone.'

As the team filed out, several of them making space for Luke Stanstead to propel his wheelchair, Grace made further entries in his Policy Book. Then he checked his phone. There was a text from Cassian Pewe.

My office. 9 a.m. tomorrow.

He hesitated before replying. Just a small – tiny – victory that he knew would piss the ACC off even more.

No can do. Have to drop my son at school then have a briefing, after which I need to watch interview of murder suspect of Eden Paternoster. Might be able to make later.

To Grace's slight disappointment, Cassian Pewe didn't rise to the bait. Almost instantly, the ACC texted back a lame,

Understood. Let me know when you are free.

He didn't bother to reply, turning his focus to the evening ahead. An arrest and a raid. He hated to admit Pewe was right in what he had said about homicide investigators liking nothing more than a Gucci murder case. This sure felt like one, and he was on fire.

26

Nevill Road had a suburban feel about it, Roy Grace always thought, slightly marred by it being a main thoroughfare in and out of the city. There were a few blocks of low-rise flats and a large school, but most of the houses were attractive, red-brick semis. The kind of affluent, middle-class neighbourhood where it was hard to believe anything bad could happen.

On this fine, late-summer evening, there was the smell of back-garden barbecues in the air. The tantalizing aroma came through the car's open windows. They were parked several houses back from the Paternosters' and Grace thought ruefully that he would have loved to be home right now, firing up their barbecue and enjoying an outdoors meal with Cleo and the family.

Glenn Branson gave an exaggerated sniff and nodded approvingly. 'It's making me hungry, boss,' he said.

'Everything makes you hungry!' Grace grinned.

'Yeah, well, I'm a growing lad!' he said.

Grace reached across and patted the DI's belly. 'You sure are.'

'Yeah, yeah. It's actually my six-pack. You're lucky to share your life with someone who cares about nutrition.'

'Cleo's actually made me care about it more, too, but I admit I still love the occasional steak even though we eat mostly veggie or fish.'

'And bangers? And lamb chops?'

'Uh-huh.'

'You need to be careful with fish – all that mercury.'

'Seems to me it doesn't matter what you eat, vegan, vegetarian, pescatarian or carnivore, you're going to ingest chemicals that are crap for you,' Grace said.

'I wouldn't worry about it, you're long gone.'

'Thanks, buddy.'

They watched in their mirrors as a white van pulled up behind them. On their radio they heard the voice of Inspector Julia Ford. 'Public Order Team in situ, sir.'

'Roger that, Public Order Team,' Grace responded.

The heavies, in their body armour and visors, looking like Stormtroopers, were now here and ready if Niall Paternoster put up any resistance. But Grace doubted he would.

The rest of his team was in place in unmarked vehicles, parked up ahead of them, a short distance beyond the Paternosters' house.

Adrenaline coursed through him. Raids like this were a big high. This was one of the reasons he'd never gone for further promotion – and he was already at a higher grade than an officer attending an operation like this should strictly be. But he didn't care. The chance to seize a villain red-handed was the ultimate buzz for him – and always would be.

He radioed Barbara Onoufriou, confirming that she was ready with her Search Team the moment Potting and Exton came out with Niall Paternoster. And confirmed with Chris Gee that he was ready to take command of the property as Crime Scene Manager.

Next he called up Potting on his radio. 'Ready, Norman?'

'Roger that, boss! Yes, yes.'

'Good! Go, go, go!'

A few cars ahead, he saw the tall, lean, suited figure of Jon Exton emerge from the passenger door and stand on the pavement. He was joined moments later by the robust frame of

Norman Potting. He watched as they conferred briefly, then walked down the pavement and stopped for a moment outside the front of the Paternosters' house before striding up the steps to the front door. Potting pressed what looked like the doorbell and followed with a rap on the door.

Grace held his radio up in front of his face, his heart in his mouth. This was always the moment where something could go horribly wrong, such as the occupant opening the door with a gun in his hand. But he didn't think so, not right now – they'd given Niall Paternoster no reason to expect what was about to happen.

He held his breath.

The door was opening.

27

'If you're trying to sell me something, I'm not interested. OK?'

Norman Potting stared back calmly at the angry man with untidy hair standing in the doorway, dressed in a crumpled T-shirt, shorts and flip-flops. 'Must be your lucky night, sir,' he said. 'We're not.' He held up his warrant card. 'Detective Sergeant Potting and Detective Sergeant Exton from the Surrey and Sussex Major Crime Team.'

Niall Paternoster's demeanour changed instantly. Anxiously, he blurted, 'Have you any news of my wife? Eden? Has she turned up somewhere? Has she been found?'

'Afraid not. Can we step into the house and have a word with you, sir?' Potting replied.

Paternoster stepped aside to allow them in.

'Niall Paternoster, I'm arresting you on suspicion of murdering your wife, Mrs Eden Paternoster. You do not have to say anything, but it may harm your defence if you do not mention, when questioned, something which you later rely on in court. Anything you do say may be given in evidence.'

The man looked in total shock, Norman Potting thought. He was so stunned that he barely even noticed DS Exton stepping past him, seizing his wrists and cuffing his hands behind him.

'I'm sorry,' Niall said, looking genuinely bewildered. 'This isn't making any sense. I called you guys this morning because my wife had disappeared – and now you're arresting me? On what grounds?'

'Did you not hear what I just said?' Potting asked.

He shook his head. 'No – I—'

'Would you like me to repeat it?'

'Please,' he said lamely. 'Oh my God, is she dead? Please not, please tell me she isn't. What's happened? Have you found her body?'

He was crying. Potting thought, *Crocodile tears?*

'We've not found your wife's body, Mr Paternoster,' he said. 'We're hoping you can help us with that.'

Niall shook his head, sobbing and sniffing. 'I'm sorry, this is insane – completely ridiculous. Why would I murder her? Murder the woman I love?'

Ignoring his protestations, Potting said, 'You will be entitled to legal representation if you don't have your own solicitor, but I'm afraid I can't say any more at this stage. We will now take you to the Brighton custody centre.'

'What about the cat?' Niall asked.

'Cat?' Potting queried.

'Reggie. He's about somewhere, probably asleep upstairs.'

'Officers will be here and will take care of him, if you tell us what he needs.'

Niall Paternoster looked on, in even more bewilderment, as several men and women in oversuits, protective shoes, rubber gloves and face masks stood waiting on the pavement, while a uniformed officer stretched a line of blue-and-white crime scene tape across the front garden wall, pausing to let him and the two detectives leave, each officer holding an arm.

One of the men in oversuits approached, glanced at Paternoster's wrists, and spoke to the two detectives.

'When you book him in to custody can you have them bag the Fitbit and Apple Watch separately, and get them across to Digital Forensics ASAP?'

'I'll make sure of it, Chris,' Exton replied.

As he was led away, up the pavement, hoping to hell none of their neighbours was watching, Niall Paternoster noticed the two officers who had come to his house that morning. He shouted out at them. 'Hey, Detective Superintendent, can you tell me what's going on? You've got no right to do this to me. I know my rights.'

A moment later, a firm hand pushed his head down, propelling him into the rear of a small Ford, behind the front passenger seat.

'You've got this all wrong!' Paternoster said as the door closed on him and one of the arresting officers climbed in beside him in the rear. 'Can't you people get anything right? You're meant to be trying to find my wife! What the hell is all this about?'

Jon Exton turned to face him. 'Perhaps it's because we don't believe you, Mr Paternoster.'

'Don't believe me? What do you mean? Don't believe what? My wife has vanished and I'm going out of my mind with worry. What the hell don't you believe? Haven't you checked out the CCTV footage at Tesco Holmbush?'

Exton continued staring at him. 'That has been done. The footage has been studied. Outside and inside the store. You were there, but your wife wasn't.'

28

After Potting and Exton had driven off with their prisoner, Roy Grace didn't strictly have a further role to play tonight, other than as the SIO to make his own initial assessment of the crime scene. The fewer people who entered a potential crime scene the better, to limit contamination. He watched Gee sign the scene guard log and go into the house, and Barbara Onoufriou and four Search Team officers walk round to the rear garden. But he was too curious to leave. All his instincts were telling him something was very definitely wrong here.

Turning to Branson, he said, 'You can go home, mate, I want to hang around a bit.'

'I'll stay with you, boss.'

'Honestly, you don't have to. Go and cherish your family.'

The DI shook his head. 'The kids are at their grandparents and Siobhan's taken a day off – she's been out with her sister at the final wedding dress fitting. She said they were going to dinner together – which is shorthand for getting trolleyed.'

Grace grinned. 'Think I would too – at the thought of getting married to you!'

'Your humour doesn't improve with age.'

'Nah, just my wisdom.'

After worming into fresh forensic suits, overshoes and gloves, and pulling on masks, they approached the Paternosters' house. The young, uniformed PC scene guard standing behind the tape was in for a long night, until the poor sod was relieved around 6 or 7 a.m. tomorrow, depending on how they worked their shifts these days, Grace thought. Both of them signed his log and ducked under the cordon.

The guard contacted the Crime Scene Manager, who came out into the tiny front garden to join them.

'All OK, Chris?' Grace asked.

'We've found two laptops and two iPads – I'm having them bagged and sent over to Digital Forensics. Any chance Mr Paternoster would oblige us with the passwords, do you think?'

'That will be a good test of whether he's going to cooperate. If he won't give them, it might indicate he has something to hide – I'll make a call. And we'd like to take a look around if you're happy, Chris? I want to get more of a feel for the place, but if you'd prefer us to stay outside, I'd understand.'

Gee smiled. 'You'd both be welcome, sir. You came here earlier today, so I don't think we have to be worried about contamination from either of you. I've already had a quick look round and there's no obvious sign that any section of the carpets have been cleaned recently. There are two tiled areas, the kitchen and en-suite bathroom floors – if you could avoid walking on those for the moment, sir. We're taking a close look at the kitchen where the attending officers earlier noticed recent cleaning and saw fresh blood – which Mr Paternoster blamed on cutting his finger on a potato peeler.'

'Of course,' Grace said.

The bathroom, in particular, was where a lot of domestic murders happened, because the killers thought they were easy places to rinse away and wipe clean any bloodstains. But, Grace well knew, what many murderers did not realize was that most bathroom tiles were very slightly porous. You could wipe the surfaces completely clean of bloodstains, but if the tiles were lifted, there was a high probability of finding that some small amounts of blood had seeped through them. Which was why he always encouraged his Forensics Team to dig up floor tiles and check their reverse.

The plugs, drainage and U-bends were also often areas of rich evidence retrieval. The other key place to check for blood was the outer surface of the sinks – offenders would often carefully clean the inside, but forget the outside area.

At least the press and media hadn't yet picked up on what was happening, he thought, relieved – although it wouldn't be long, for sure. The press and blowflies – both could smell a dead body from miles away.

Trailed by Branson, he followed Gee's footsteps across into the hall, along the track that had been laid down to the kitchen door. A Forensic Officer in full protective clothing was kneeling by the sink next to an open cupboard door, pulling out the contents of the rubbish bin one item at a time with gloved hands, examining each carefully before placing it in a bin bag on the floor beside her.

'Checking the bins,' Gee said. 'After that we'll work on the surface of the floor tiles then dig them up and look at the flip sides. Is there anything in particular you'd like to see while you're here?'

'I'd like to take a good look around the living room and the master bedroom,' Grace said.

'No problem at all. Go ahead.'

Leaving the Crime Scene Manager in the kitchen, Grace led the way through into the open-plan living-dining area. He called Norman Potting and asked if Niall Paternoster would give up the passwords for both computers and iPads, assuming he knew his wife's.

'We're just arriving at the custody centre, chief, I'll ask him and bell you back.'

'Tell him any cooperation would count a lot in his favour.'

'Yeah, well, he's not being very cooperative at the moment.'

Grace began looking again, in more detail than he had on his previous visit, at the elegant, minimalistic decor. The two white velour sofas. The smoked-glass bookshelves stacked with crime novels and true crime non-fiction. The fancy, ultra-modern electric fireplace and the row of framed photographs of the couple on the mantelpiece above it. Copies of most of them they'd already seen, pinned to the whiteboard in the Major Crime suite conference room. 'Does anything strike you as odd, Glenn?'

Branson frowned. '*Odd* as in what?'

'As in not fitting?'

'Not with you, boss – not sure what you mean?'

'This is quite an elegant house. Classily decorated and furnished by someone with taste. Did Niall Paternoster strike you as a man with delicate artistic flair?'

'Not exactly. No. So how did he strike you?'

'A typical hunk, with more muscles than sense. This must be the work of his wife.'

Branson nodded. 'You mean, decorated by someone with flair?'

'Exactly.'

The DI shrugged. 'But that's not unusual in relationships, to have one partner the artistic or brainy one and the other the muscle. That can work.'

'But maybe Eden became fed up when his business failed, the physical attraction at the beginning has gone and the relationship has broken down?' Grace suggested.

'Yeah, and as they've got older they've changed, one more than the other? Perhaps this is what has happened here?'

'But if Eden is the brains, and the original passion has gone, wouldn't she be the one who'd want to leave?'

They were interrupted by Grace's phone ringing. It was Norman Potting.

'Chief, I've got all the codes.'

'Nice work,' he said, and jotted them down in his notebook as Potting read them out.

Turning back to Branson, he said, 'Interesting he gave up the codes.'

'He must be thinking he's got nothing on his computer or iPad or on hers that could be incriminating, boss?'

'Maybe. Or just knows we'd break the codes anyway so he's trying to be a good boy, to give us the impression he genuinely wants to cooperate in finding his wife.'

'Taking a risk, isn't he?'

Grace frowned, thinking through what it actually might mean. 'If he has killed her, he might be thinking that by giving us the codes, we'll look less thoroughly. If he hasn't topped her, then he's nothing to hide anyway.'

'And what do you make of it?'

Grace shook his head. 'Early doors. I'm staying with my hunch that he's murdered her and disposed of the body. But I question, from his attitude and demeanour, whether he's *disappeared* the body effectively. My guess is he's dumped her in water or dug a shallow grave – hopefully the BMW's satnav might tell us where. If I'm wrong and he's put her in the sea or in Shoreham Harbour, we have to hope she'll float ashore.'

'And if not, wise man?'

Grace smirked. 'Then we really will have a "no body" murder investigation on our hands. Challenging but not impossible to get a conviction – if we can get the Crown Prosecution Service onside and then a half-decent jury.'

They stayed in the living room for some while, assimilating their surroundings, then made their way upstairs, keeping to the narrow metal stepping plates the CSIs had laid down. Another Forensics Officer was on the landing at the top, on his hands and knees, painstakingly fingertip-searching the carpet.

'Where's the master bedroom?' Grace asked him.

The officer indicated with his hand. 'First door on the right, sir.'

Grace led along the track, followed by Branson, into a bedroom that was entirely neutral. A deep-pile off-white carpet, white bedding, pillows, cushions, white furniture and a white fabric ceiling that made them feel like they were in a tent.

Marie Desmond, another Forensic Officer, was on her knees pulling stuff out of a deep drawer beneath the bed. Books, an assortment of lacy black underwear.

'Opening a brothel are you, Marie?' Grace said.

'Want me to put this on the Sussex Police eBay site?' she retorted with cheeky glee, pointing at a delicate camisole.

He nodded towards Branson. 'Yep, Glenn here will be putting in bids!'

She held up something black, with a strap, that looked like a dildo.

'What's that?' Branson asked, his face a picture of horror.

'A torch – I know what you were thinking!' she replied matter-of-factly, smiling. 'We've not found any signs of a missing duvet or duvet cover, sir,' she went on. 'Just these and a load of old junk so far.'

Then she reached deep into the rear of the drawer and came out with one final item under more lingerie. She frowned at it. 'Well, well, well, what's this?'

The two detectives peered at the iPhone in a sparkly case. Grace shot Branson a glance and was about to say something, when another officer emerged from the en-suite bathroom, holding up a large plastic bag that was securely closed with tape. As he came into the room Grace immediately saw that the bag contained an item of clothing.

'I noticed a small screw on the floor in the bathroom,' the officer said. 'I checked and saw it had come from a wall access panel, so I removed the other screws and found this hidden in the cavity.'

'Oh God,' Grace said. 'If that's—'

The officer looked at Grace and pointed to the bag. 'I think that's blood, sir, and do you see the tear there in the material?'

29

Joseph Rattigan had a poker face beneath spiky grey hair, a gut straining the buttons of his pale-blue shirt and a sloppily knotted tie. He was dressed in a chalk-striped suit that might have been made-to-measure, but not for him.

There had been a time when this Legal Aid solicitor, younger and fresher-faced, had been the bane of any officer with a newly arrested suspect, but now in his late fifties, the lousy pay and tough hours had worn him down, blunted his passion. The fire that had once raged in his belly had been doused by too much beer and junk food. His voice these days was bland and flat, as if he didn't care, was ready to accept defeat because, sod it, no client was worth dying in a ditch for.

Just before 10.30 p.m. Niall Paternoster and Joseph Rattigan had completed their private conference ahead of his initial police interview at Brighton custody centre.

This would be the first of several interviews to be carried out over the next couple of days, following a strategy Norman Potting and Jon Exton had agreed with a tier five interview adviser, DC Alec Butler. The adviser's role was to agree the strategy with the SIO and deal with not only the questioning of the suspect but also those that required special consideration or were deemed to be significant witnesses – sigwits.

Potting and Exton led Paternoster and his solicitor into the interview room. For the next forty-five minutes, they first went over in detail Paternoster's initial account of his version of what had happened the previous day. Then they covered the couple's background, relationship, financial status and current domestic situation.

The interview concluded with Potting leaning across the table towards the suspect. 'Mr Paternoster, we've taken note of all you've said. The purpose of this initial interview has been to enable you to give a full account and your version of events prior to your wife's disappearance. But you need to know that police officers have checked the CCTV at the Tesco Holmbush store, both inside and out, as well as showing your wife's photograph to every staff member who was working there. There is no sign on any CCTV footage of your wife being in the store and no member of staff recalls seeing her.'

Paternoster turned, bewildered, to his solicitor. 'This is crazy! It just can't be – it doesn't make any sense.'

Rattigan nodded, eyes wide open and vacant, like a zombie that wasn't home.

'We will continue with our second interview at 9.45 a.m. tomorrow,' Potting said. Then, speaking to the mic, he added, 'First interview with Niall Paternoster terminated at 11.22 p.m.' He stopped the recording.

30

Roy Grace arrived home just before midnight, but despite being tired, his brain was buzzing. He now had more than enough to put a sock – or rather a blood-spotted T-shirt – in Cassian Pewe's mouth tomorrow. And he dearly wished he'd have the opportunity to shove that torch right up his jacksie.

Humphrey greeted him at the front door with a chewed-up pink unicorn in his mouth, stuffing tumbling from its ripped-open midriff all over the floor. He let him out into the balmy, warm air and the light of a near-full moon, and took him for a short walk along the cart track that was their drive. As he walked and the dog ran off after a scent, Grace breathed in the delicious, sweet smells of freshly mown grass and of the surrounding countryside that he loved so much. Strange to think, as he did this time each year, that the nights were starting to draw in and autumn was on its way.

A bat flitted overhead. He could hear the distant baa-ing and bleating of sheep. He really fancied a drink and suddenly a cigarette, too – which he hadn't had for ages – but decided against both. He needed to get some sleep, as tomorrow, with all they'd found tonight at the Paternosters' house, promised to be a long day. But he hoped the brief walk might be enough to settle both Humphrey and himself.

Ten minutes later, he opened the front door, knelt and scooped up the bits of the unicorn's white fluffy innards, then led the dog through into the kitchen, and opened the treats tin. He took a bone-shaped one out and held it up. Obediently, Humphrey jumped into his basket and Grace gave him his biscuit. 'Night, boy!' Then he turned the light out and headed upstairs as quietly as he could.

As he switched the landing light off outside their bedroom, he turned on his phone torch at the same time in the hope of not waking Cleo. But he could see she was awake.

'Hi, darling!' she said as he crept into the room, her voice only very slightly sleepy. An instant later her bedside light came on and she peered at him, blinking.

'Sorry to wake you, darling,' he said.

'You didn't, don't worry, I've only just come to bed.'

'You stayed up late. Everything OK?'

'Not really. Some issues with Bruno – tell you tomorrow.'

He sat down on the bed and kissed her. 'You can tell me now, if you want?'

Looking down ruefully at her swollen midriff, she said, 'What I really want is a glass of wine. Or two. Or three.'

Alarmed, he said, 'Why, what's happened?'

'Your sweet little boy.'

Grace had noticed over the past months that whenever Bruno was well-behaved, Cleo referred to him as *our son*. But when he'd behaved like a little shit, he suddenly became *your boy*.

'Tell me?'

'I had a crazy day in the mortuary, didn't get home until nearly 7 p.m. Kaitlynn collected him from school much earlier. You'll never guess what he did?'

'Try me?'

'He'd let out all the hens.'

'He always does that.'

'Yes, in the garden. But this evening he'd let them out into the field – he said he'd decided it was cruel to keep them cooped up in such a small garden as ours. It must have been that fox, the one we've seen in the garden, right? It got Bella while they were out there.'

'Bella?'

She nodded.

'No, not poor Bella.' He felt really upset.

Bella was their favourite hen, named after one of Roy's team, Bella Moy, Norman's fiancée, who had sadly lost her life two years ago. She was the smallest and the most affectionate of all the hens they had, always coming running towards them and the only one that would let them pick her up and cuddle her.

Cleo had tears in her eyes. Grace kissed her again. 'How bloody stupid of him. What did he say?'

She shook her head, signalling disbelief. 'That it would be wrong to blame the fox. That it was probably hungry.'

'He didn't accept any blame himself?'

'I don't think he knows the concept of blame.'

Before he could respond, she went on. 'That's not all. I had Mr Hartwell on the phone for half an hour.'

Hartwell was the headmaster.

'What did he say?'

'He's a nice man and he really wants to help, but he said they're at their wits' end with Bruno. Apparently his behaviour hasn't improved over the summer: he still won't engage with any of his fellow pupils and has already been rude to all his teachers, and it's only the first day back. Mr Hartwell says that unless Bruno's attitude improves before the end of this term, he is very sorry but he won't be able to return next year.'

Grace said nothing for some moments, reflecting. Bruno was the son he never knew he had. He had learned, only on her deathbed, that his long-missing wife, Sandy, had left him soon after discovering she was pregnant with this boy. He'd subsequently found out that, in those years after she'd left, she'd led a wayward life, joining first the Scientologists, then another cult in Germany. She got bigamously married to a rich guy, then they separated after just two years. Unbelievably, at some point she'd become a heroin addict, before getting clean and working to help addicts, first in Frankfurt and then Munich.

Grace wasn't sure at what point it had all gone wrong for her, but from what Sandy had told him, she had drifted into a hedonistic lifestyle while in the company of the persuasive, charismatic cult leader, and she'd found it nearly impossible to pull herself out of it. He'd tried to get Bruno to talk about this time without much success, and he could only guess at what impact this peripatetic life with an unstable, erratic single parent had had on him.

And he was well aware that uprooting Bruno from his roots in Germany and bringing him to England at the age of ten was again disruptive for him. But he'd hoped that introducing him into a stable, loving and welcoming family environment might have helped him settle down. So far, it seemed not. Whatever Sandy – the woman he had once considered his soulmate – had instilled in their son, she'd left him with strange values and a seriously skewed moral compass.

'I'd be happy to go and speak to Ted Hartwell. Maybe we've never explained Bruno's background fully enough to him. What do you think?'

'It's worth a try. I'll come with you. I'm sure there is good inside Bruno – maybe we just have to dig deeper to mine it out.'

'I've got it in my diary that I'm taking him to school tomorrow, is that right?'

'Please. I've got eight postmortems. I've got to be in at 7 a.m.'

'No probs, I'll take him and have a chat with him in the car.'

'Good luck with that.'

He cocked his head. 'Meaning?'

Cleo gave him a sleepy smile. 'I do think he responds to you better than he does to me. But . . .'

He kissed her on the forehead, undressed, hanging up his suit and his tie, then went through into the bathroom and dumped his underwear and shirt in the laundry basket. He picked up the tube of toothpaste and, as the electric brush whirred, tried to focus back on the Paternoster case, but it was Bruno at the forefront of his mind.

And it was Bruno that kept him awake for much of the night. When he did lapse into brief sleep, he repeatedly dreamed of the boy and woke each time with a feeling of dread.

31

Tuesday 3 September

'Success is all about being ahead of the curve.'

An appropriate metaphor for a dealer in performance cars that his bank manager had used, 'Lanky' Larry Olson rued.

'But sometimes,' his bank manager told him, turning him down for a further business loan, 'you can be too far ahead of the curve. Ever heard the saying, "It's the second mouse that gets the cheese?"'

Larry had come in early this morning to open up his small showroom with its big name, Sussex Sporting E-Cars. The location, in a mews off Church Road, wasn't helping, because there was hardly any through traffic. He should have been bolder and gone for a prime site when he'd opened, but he had worried that the rent would have stretched him too much.

The gangly fifty-five-year-old was dressed as he was every day of his working life, in a sharp suit, shirt and sober tie. He had a mop of thinning fair hair turning to grey, big blue eyes, a winning smile, and was charm personified. His first wife had told him he could sell fridges to Eskimos. His second that he could sell guano to bats. His future third wife had told him, three years ago, that he was nuts to give up his lucrative job as the top salesman for Jim Spatchcock Honda.

But hey, when he'd hit fifty he'd seen Jim Spatchcock in the *Sunday Times* Rich List with a fortune of over £200 million from his chain of car dealerships around the UK. Sure, Larry knew he earned good money himself, but it was peanuts compared to that. With retirement looming too close for comfort, it was now or never if he was going to strike out and make his fortune.

The way forward, for sure, was in electric cars. He used his savings, remortgage money from his house and a decent bank loan to start this specialist business, trading in second-hand electric performance cars.

Except the business, which had started two years ago, wasn't as of yet booming the way he had anticipated, and he was fast running out of cash – and credit.

As he stared around the shiny, brand-new-looking stock of cars in his showroom, he was reflecting on just how poor business had been during these past months. The words from a record made by his favourite-ever comedians, the late Peter Cook and Dudley Moore, came to mind.

Moore was interviewing Cook in his persona of the world's most unsuccessful entrepreneur, Sir Arthur Streeb-Greebling, about his latest catastrophic venture, a restaurant serving only frogs and peaches, situated in a bog in the middle of the Yorkshire Moors. In response to the question about how business had been, Cook replied, 'Business hasn't been and there hasn't been any business.'

Which was pretty much how he felt, Larry reflected.

So far he was surviving, just. But with the further loan he'd been hoping for now turned down, he needed to make some good sales – and quickly. And he had one very big prospect coming in this morning to test drive the most expensive car in the showroom. A top spec, two-year-old BMW i8 hybrid. New, it had cost close to £130,000. He'd managed to buy it at an auction of cars seized back by finance companies for a knock-down £37,000 and had it advertised at £89,500. If he got that price it would hand him a profit of more than £50,000, which would see him through for a good few months.

The potential customers, a young couple, Christopher Goodman and his fiancée, Sophia, had come in on Saturday and made a beeline for the car, both clambering in and sitting there, admiring it.

If there were two things, above all, Larry had learned in thirty-seven years as a car salesman, the first was that customers did not always end up buying the first car they sat in – mostly because they couldn't afford it. And second, that it was usually the woman who made the decision on what car to buy.

He had left them alone for some while, then casually sauntered over, copy of the *Argus* in his hand, and knelt beside the passenger door so as not to intimidate them by looking down at them. 'Hi!' he said breezily. 'I'm Larry. Are you Albion fans?'

Another of the things he'd learned was never to open a conversation talking about cars.

'Not really,' the young woman said, 'but my fiancé is.'

'What do you think of the latest signing?' Olson asked, raising the paper, with the news being the headline item.

'£14 million. A lot of money – let's hope he does the magic, right?' the guy said.

'Oh yes. I'm right with you!' Larry paused a moment. 'If there's anything in here you'd like to take a look at, just shout.'

'We actually like this,' the guy replied. 'We're getting married next month and we're planning a motoring honeymoon through Europe – so we're looking for something suitable.'

'Congratulations!' he said. 'I'm Larry Olson, by the way.'

'Chris Goodman, and this is my fiancée, Sophia.'

'A delight to meet you, Chris and Sophia!'

This was definitely hopeful, he decided. 'Are you looking to exchange anything?' he asked, as the next step to drawing someone in.

'We have a Lotus Elise, but we're happy to sell that privately.' Goodman held the wheel and fondled the gear shift, the smile on his face spreading. Then they both got out of the car and walked around it.

'She's a beauty, isn't she?' Larry encouraged. 'You know what, we're only here for a short while. Live the dream! If you can afford it, why not?'

It was that phrase, 'If you can afford it', that hooked them, he had learned. Oh yes!

And he could see that the words had struck home.

'Imagine gliding away from your wedding reception in this beauty! And there are very good finance deals at the moment,' Olson said, pushing at temptation. 'Might even be able to get you zero interest for the first twelve months.'

It was the generous terms he had to offer from finance companies, enabling customers to buy something they thought would be beyond their reach, that usually clinched it. And who would dare to admit they couldn't afford it?

'You're asking for £89,500?' Sophia said, looking at the price displayed on the windscreen. 'What would be your best price, if we were interested?'

'Let me talk to my boss and see if we can do anything.' Larry winked. 'Give me a couple of minutes.'

'Sure.'

He walked to the rear of the showroom and through the door into the empty double garage at the rear, closing it behind him. There was a kitchenette in there. He sat on a stool at the table for a carefully timed five minutes, reading the paper, then he went back into the showroom and approached the couple with a beam.

'My boss says he would take £88,000 and throw in a year's tax and warranty.'

'What about servicing charges?' Goodman asked.

'I'm sure we could do something on that, too.'

Sophia knelt and studied the tyres.

'All replaced three months ago, I understand,' Larry said.

She stood back up and looked at her fiancé. He was nodding enthusiastically. She turned to Larry. 'OK, we'll think about it.'

Quoting one of his favourites, from Robert Browning, Larry Olson's parting words to the couple had been, 'Ah, but a man's reach should exceed his grasp, or what's a heaven for?'

It had been no surprise to him when Christopher Goodman called, later that afternoon, asking first if the car was still available, and then, sounding very relieved it was, to book a test drive. Could Larry hold the car until Tuesday morning?

He'd given him the usual patter that he had someone else who was interested coming back on Monday, but for a £5,000 deposit, fully refundable, he'd hold it until midday, Tuesday. And he would need to see on Tuesday either a bank statement showing he was good for the finance or a reference from his bank manager, along with his driving licence.

Goodman had replied that he would bring both. And the deposit had been paid minutes later.

Larry walked across the showroom floor shortly after 7.30 a.m. with a spring in his step. He already had a selection of financial options printed out to show the punter just how incredibly affordable it was.

He only had one slight concern, and that was the weather. It was dry at the moment, but rain was forecast for a little later. Electric cars, especially this BMW, had phenomenal acceleration, and even this BMW with its sure-footed handling could easily catch out the inexperienced driver on a slippery, wet road. But hey, hopefully it would still be dry for the test drive.

And he was confident that, once he had driven it, Goodman would be smitten.

Suddenly he felt a tightening in his chest and a pain, like indigestion. The pain shot acutely down both his arms. It was another angina attack coming on. His heart specialist had been trying to fix a date to book him in for a triple bypass, but Olson didn't have time for that, not at the moment, when he had to focus on keeping his business afloat. Maybe if he got this sale he could then afford the time.

He dug his hand into his jacket pocket, pulled out the vial of tiny white nitroglycerine tablets and popped one under his tongue. Within half a minute or so the pain began to subside. Shit, the symptoms were coming on increasingly frequently now.

You'd better buy this car, Christopher Goodman. You won't just be saving my business, you might be saving my life.

And with his lovely, caring Irish girlfriend, Shauna, life was really good for him again, after the trauma of his health scares. He would have the op and afterwards he would do his damnedest to get fit again. He had promised her that.

Manoeuvring some of his other stock out of the way, he slid open the showroom doors, grabbed the BMW's keys off the hook on his office wall and decided to take it for a quick spin round the block to check everything was working fine, after a few weeks of it sitting idle in the showroom. Unplugging the charging cable, he then, mindful of his bad back, eased himself gently into the driver's seat with a pained grunt, glided the car silently out of the showroom, drove north up to Church Road, Hove, and turned left. It was 7.45 a.m.

32

Roy Grace turned his Alfa Romeo right into New Church Road. Bruno, hair neatly brushed as ever, dressed in his red school blazer, white shirt and striped tie, grey trousers and black shoes, sat beside him, silent and stroppy. It was 7.45 a.m.

Bruno was in a particularly strange mood this morning, barely saying a word during the half-hour drive in the early rush-hour traffic. In response to his father's question about what he had on at school today, he just tut-tutted loudly, intently studying his phone. From the sounds coming out of it, Grace guessed he was looking at TikTok.

Attempting again to engage, he asked if he was playing any sport this afternoon, but all he got in response was Bruno sighing loudly in an irritable 'leave me alone' fashion.

For a while, Grace turned up the volume on the radio, tuned to Radio Sussex, listening to the news and traffic reports. He'd been hoping to have a good chat in the car with Bruno, but so far that hadn't happened. He'd learned that ignoring the boy was sometimes the best tactic to get him to speak. The tactic worked now.

'Why do you think school is so important?' Bruno asked suddenly.

Roy turned down the radio. 'You don't think it is?'

'Most teachers I have are useless. I know more than them,' he said.

'You do?'

'Yeah.'

'What makes you think that?'

'I don't *think*, I *know*.'

'You do?' The small boy's confidence – and arrogance – at times was breathtaking, he thought.

'Yeah, I tested my Geography teacher yesterday. I asked him what the capital of Kazakhstan was. He didn't know.'

'I don't know either,' Grace said.

'You're just a police officer, you're not paid to know the capital of countries. Mr Maitland is.'

'So what is it?'

'Nur-Sultan.'

'Nur-Sultan?'

'Yes. I know the capital of every country in the world. Mr Maitland doesn't even know how many countries there are. I asked him, he said there were one hundred and eighty-seven.'

'How many are there?'

'One hundred and ninety-five.'

A sleek BMW i8, a car Grace had always quite fancied, travelled past in the opposite direction at what seemed to be over the speed limit. 'There are one hundred and ninety three that are member states of the United Nations and just two, the Holy See and the state of Palestine, which are not. Taiwan, the Cook Islands and Niue should also be on the list, really, in my opinion.'

They were approaching the school. 'You know what I think, Bruno, you should go on *Mastermind* with your specialist subject as Geography,' he said, trying to lighten his son's intense seriousness.

'Why would I want to waste my knowledge on a quiz show?' Bruno retorted calmly, but with underlying anger in his voice.

It wasn't the first time Roy Grace had thought it, as he shot a glance at him. The boy seemed so much older than his years.

Were he and Cleo badly underestimating Bruno's intelligence? Had they put him in the wrong school? Should he be in some hot-house academy?

'So, you know more facts than your Geography teacher – do you have other teachers where you know more than they do?'

'Of course, all of them.'

'Would you prefer to be in a different school?'

Bruno wasn't yet aware of the headmaster's threat to expel him.

'I don't need to be in this school, it's a waste of my time and talents. I need to be in a school that will challenge me.' Bruno glanced disdainfully out of the window. St Christopher's was coming up on their right. 'Did you know that the ancient Egyptians, when they died and were mummified, had their favourite pets killed and mummified, to go in the tomb with them?'

Grace looked at him. 'I wasn't aware of that, no.'

'Do you think they did that because they wanted company in their tombs or because they worried their pets would miss them too much – or that no one would take the same care of the animals they did?'

Frowning, Grace slowed, turned into the side street, drove up a short distance before making a U-turn, and pulled up some yards short of the school gate. 'I honestly don't know, Bruno. Their whole culture and views on death were very different to ours.'

'Why don't our teachers tell us important things like that?'

Grace thought for a moment before replying to his son's question. 'Perhaps they don't believe things like that are important or relevant in our modern world, Bruno.'

'Education's a joke, don't you think? I can learn more from Google than any teacher can tell me.'

It took Grace a few seconds to process this. He'd not particularly enjoyed his own school days, and his performance in class had been disappointing to his parents, only just scraping through essential exams at pretty much the lowest pass grade. The reality was, he knew, that with his academic record he wouldn't have stood a cat-in-hell's chance of getting into the police today.

And with similar cockiness to Bruno, he thought, with a grin, *That would have been their big loss!*

A boy also in a red jacket, about Bruno's age, jumped down from a Defender that had pulled up in front of them. A young girl, similarly dressed, was disgorged from a Mini. Both entered the gates.

Turning to Bruno, who was unclipping his seat belt, Grace said, 'Go for it, speak your mind. Tell them what you think they should be teaching you!'

The boy hesitated, frowning. 'Really? You think so?'

'Sure. Be brave. Remember, fear kills more dreams than failure ever can.'

Bruno looked puzzled. 'Dreams? Is there any point in dreaming anything? Look at my mother.' He shook his head. 'The teachers aren't worth it. But is anything in life worth it?'

'What do you mean by that?'

'My mother had so many dreams, but they were all shattered and there was no way to put the pieces back together. Life sucks. School sucks.'

Before Grace could respond, Bruno opened the door, climbed out and slammed it behind him. Without looking back, he strode towards the school gates, ignoring two other pupils who were also approaching them.

Grace sat still, watching him until he had disappeared. *Life sucks. School sucks.* He wondered again, as he had constantly ever since discovering that he had a ten-year-old son, what kind of bizarre upbringing Sandy had given him to jade him and make him so cynical.

He was clearly bright, bright as hell.

Dangerously bright.

Heartbreakingly bright.

But Bruno's unpredictability worried him. The child psychiatrist, Dr Orlando Trujillo, who they'd taken him to see, told them he thought it was just a phase Bruno was going through. Still adjusting to the loss of his mother, to relocating to a new country, that it was his way of putting a defensive shield around himself.

Grace hoped Trujillo was right. He wasn't sure what else he and Cleo could do, other than looking for a different school for advanced children. But would even that be the right thing? This school here had a terrific reputation.

It was ironic, he thought, as he drove off, rain starting to fall, his focus starting to return to Eden Paternoster and the briefing meeting in half an hour, that he'd always held the view that well over ninety per cent of crimes were committed by people who had suffered terrible childhoods – alcoholic or abusive parents, broken homes. That was exactly Bruno's upbringing, too. A drug addict, single-parent mother.

They needed more advice, and quickly, if they were to avoid Bruno not being allowed back to the school again after the end of this term. He resolved to get home early from work and talk it through with Cleo. Maybe try to have a heart-to-heart with Bruno – if the boy would be willing to open up even a fraction.

33

At 8.45 a.m. Roy Grace sat with his assembled team in the conference room, for the second briefing of Operation Lagoon, having just completed a brief management team meeting.

'I have some significant developments to report,' Grace announced. 'The first is that Niall Paternoster, Eden's husband, was arrested yesterday evening on suspicion of her murder and detained overnight in custody. He will be formally interviewed again this morning by Jon Exton and Norman Potting in line with the interview strategy. DC Alec Butler, our tier five interview adviser, will update us later about what was said last night. This was only his first account and, to date, he has not been challenged on anything he has said.'

He glanced at his notes. 'During the search of the Paternosters' home in Nevill Road, last night, some substantial evidence came to light. The first of which was a mobile phone which we have established belonged to Eden Paternoster. Her husband claimed she had brought it with her on their Sunday outing to Parham House, but the battery was low. The Forensics Team, however, found the phone in a drawer in her bed, concealed beneath a pile of her lingerie.'

'Totally pants!' Potting said, grinning and looking around.

Grace looked at him a little more sympathetically than normal. 'But we do have something else that may be significant, which was found wrapped in plastic concealed behind a wall-inspection

147

plate. A torn ladies' T-shirt, presumably belonging to Eden, on which there are some small blood spots. It has been sent for fast-track processing at the DNA lab.'

He looked at his team, letting that sink in before continuing. 'They also found evidence of blood on the kitchen worktop and the floor tiling beneath, samples from which have been sent for testing, too. Further of note,' he added, 'there's a wooden knife rack with a knife missing – and from the position and size of the slot, it would appear to be the largest of the knives.'

He paused for a moment. 'Two perhaps even more significant items were discovered during the search. Both of these were secreted under a loose floorboard in a spare bedroom. The first was Eden Paternoster's passport, which her husband indicated to the officers who attended yesterday morning, PCs Alldridge and Little, was missing from its usual place.

'The second was a white gold wedding ring and another diamond ring – possibly an engagement ring. The wedding ring was engraved on the inside with the initials EP-NP, 19.09.15. The initials of Eden and Niall Paternoster and the date of their wedding. When Niall was booked into custody last night, a wedding band was removed from his finger. It had the same initials, reversed, and the same date. This would indicate to me that either she had removed it – together with her engagement ring – before her disappearance, or perhaps more likely if he did murder her, that he removed both to hamper identification.'

There was a brief silence. Several of the team made notes.

Grace continued. 'At this stage, I'm challenging anything that Niall Paternoster has told us and going solely with the facts we have.' He turned to DS Alexander. 'Jack, is there any update from your house-to-house enquiry team from the neighbours?'

'Not yet, sir. It's a priority action this morning.'

Sergeant Dennison-Wilkins turned to Grace. 'Boss, as the missing knife may be important evidence, we have taken a photograph of the matching knives. I'll have all the gardens bordering the Paternosters' house searched and all bins in the neighbourhood by Barbara Onoufriou and her team.'

'Do you know when rubbish collection day is?' Grace asked.

'Tomorrow, sir, so we'll be getting it done today.'

'If you need more resources to search the immediate area, let me know.'

'I will need more,' she said.

'Fine, draft in some extra staff. Norman, Jon, you'd better leave for the custody centre to carry on with the interviews, keep me posted.'

He was interrupted by his phone. Raising an apologetic hand, he answered. It was Aiden Gilbert, from Digital Forensics.

'Roy, I've got the data from the phone we were sent over last night – registered to Mrs Eden Paternoster.'

'Hang on, Aiden, I'm in a team briefing – I'll put you on speaker. Can you update the team?'

A moment later, everyone in the room could hear Gilbert's voice. 'Hi, everyone. I can confirm, on examining the phone we were sent last night, according to the phone records and plot from O2, that the last time this phone was active was Thursday of last week, August twenty-ninth, until 10.10 p.m. It had left its previous location in Croydon, Surrey, at 5.45 p.m. and travelled south to Brighton, to Nevill Road, Hove. We've identified the Croydon location as the premises of the Mutual Occidental Insurance Company, which I understand to be Mrs Paternoster's workplace. No calls were made before it was switched off.'

'Hi, Aiden, Glenn Branson here,' Branson called out.

'Yes, Glenn?' Aiden responded.

'Was the phone's battery flat when you received it?'

'No, it wasn't, but it didn't have much charge and was switched off.'

'Thanks.'

Grace thought for a moment. 'Aiden, your team has Eden Paternoster's iPad as well as her laptop and phone. Have you had time to check out her social media activity again?'

'There's been no more activity, at the moment. So far we've identified she has Twitter, Instagram, Facebook, LinkedIn, TikTok and Strava on these devices.'

'I'd appreciate it if you can let me know, soonest, if there is any activity on any of these.'

'We'll be straight on it.' There was a brief pause. 'Also, Roy, we've been working through the night on her husband's phone. We may have some potential information for you shortly.'

Grace thanked Gilbert, ended the call and turned to DS Alexander. 'Jack, I need you to prioritize the action with Mutual Occidental and find out who last saw Eden at work.'

'I'll do that straight after this, sir.'

Grace thought briefly through the possibilities, trying to make some sense of the convoluted information. Niall Paternoster claimed the photograph of Eden in front of the lake at Parham House had been taken on Sunday, yet Aiden Gilbert said it was date stamped over a week previously. Did the husband really think they would believe him? One of his favourite quotes – from Einstein – suddenly sprang into his mind: *Two things are infinite: the universe and human stupidity; and I'm not sure about the universe.*

He turned to Stanstead. 'Luke, have anything for us?'

He nodded. 'I do, boss. The information we have received from the Intelligence Team and the victimology enquiries. Eden Paternoster's maiden name is Townsend. If I have the correct family history, which I'm pretty certain I do, she has a previous record as a victim of DV. When she was sixteen, back in 2004, her mother stabbed her father fatally. For that, her mother got two years, suspended, for manslaughter. Eden was in the room when it happened.'

'A suspended sentence, which means,' Branson said, 'the court and judge and jury trying her pretty much felt she was justified, right?'

'Self-defence?' Grace questioned rhetorically.

Grace made a note in his Policy Book, that when obtaining the medical records for Eden they would need detailed information on the likely impact on the victim through medical consultation, and how that might present and play out in later life. Next to it, he wrote, 'Significant factor?'

Under the thirty-six-hour rule they had until around 9 a.m. tomorrow to make the decision whether to charge Niall Paternoster, release him or apply for a warrant of further detention, if necessary. For that, they would need sufficient grounds to convince a magistrate to grant it.

'EJ,' Grace said, 'there's a very bright child psychologist I know, Orlando Trujillo. Try to get hold of him and when we have Eden's medical records run the history by him and ask for his views on how that might have shaped her personality. I'm particularly interested in how she might have subsequently reacted to domestic abuse or violence – I'm speculating here based on what I and DI Branson felt after talking to her husband, that he might be an angry and controlling man. I've got Trujillo's contact details on file and I'll give them to you straight after this meeting – and I'll sanction his fee.'

'Yes, sir.'

Addressing the civilian Financial Investigator, Emily Denyer, he asked, 'Anything to report?'

'I'm preparing the necessary paperwork and I've already made a number of requests to the financial institutions to gather the details for the background checks, sir,' Denyer said.

'Anything that comes to light, tell me immediately – don't wait for this evening's briefing.'

'No, guv,' Emily said.

Each team member then provided an update on their own investigations. Grace thanked them all and ended the meeting, remaining seated to write up notes in his Policy Book.

While he worked on it, he reflected with a tinge of sadness that when he'd first started as a Senior Investigating Officer, the main purpose of the Policy Book was to help inform other detectives who carried out regular reviews of a Major Crime investigation in progress, looking to advise on anything the SIO and his team might not have thought of. But these days its prime purpose was to protect the SIOs from any accusations of wrongdoing and also to justify his decision-making process. Just one more example of how he and his colleagues spent more time these days protecting their backs than doing the job they were paid to do. Which was to save lives, serve and protect.

But he did look forward to seeing Cassian Pewe's face when he met with him later this morning and presented him with the latest evidence.

Although not as much as he looked forward to hearing what it looked like when Pewe was confronted with a photocopy of Guy Batchelor's notebook.

His train of thought was disturbed by his job phone ringing.

'Roy Grace,' he answered, and heard Gee's voice at the other end.

'We have an interesting development, boss,' said the Crime Scene Manager. 'You'll never guess what we found in a cupboard in the utility room.'

'I'm all ears, what did you find?'

34

Ducking his head against the cloying, misty drizzle, Larry Olson gently eased his tall frame into the passenger seat of the low, squat BMW. He winced twice from the shooting pains of his prolapsed disc as he did so, then pulled the gull-wing door shut with a reassuring *clunk*.

Turning to his customer, he said with a beam, 'That sound, Mr Goodman, that's the build quality of German cars. Other manufacturers around the world have strived for decades to achieve it, but the Germans still do it best.'

Christopher Goodman was chewing gum, barely listening. He was looking around the interior, sinking his head back against the rest. He opened his door and pulled it down, closing it again. *Clunk*. He nodded.

Olson knew that after a long spell of dry weather, what you needed was a prolonged heavy downpour to clear the road surface of rubber and oil residue. The worst thing you could have was this kind of drizzle, which would turn the road into a skating rink.

With an output of 368 brake horsepower when both petrol and electric motors kicked in, this car was a phenomenal machine, with experienced hands on the wheel. But on a slippery surface, with someone unused to the power it unleashed, even with its four-wheel drive it could very quickly turn into a pendulum attached to a rocket.

'Be very gentle on the throttle in these conditions, Mr Goodman,' he urged, trying to sound calm. 'She can really bite back!'

Goodman kept his foot on the brake and tapped the start button, and the dash instantly came alive, but he looked momentarily puzzled by the lack of engine noise. He sat for some moments, holding the wheel.

'In D the petrol engine will kick in when you press the accelerator.'

'Got it!' Goodman released the brake and put the car in Drive, and it glided slowly forward into the quiet street.

Gently does it, Olson thought. Prayed. He pointed out the wipers as the screen was fast blurring over, and Goodman compliantly switched them on. He pressed the accelerator and a split-second later there was a roar as the petrol engine fired, the back twitched and the car very nearly swapped ends.

'Whoahhhhh!' Goodman said, swinging the leather-rimmed wheel wildly, just catching the twitching car one way, then the next. Getting it under control, more by luck than talent, he said, 'Bit of a tank slapper, eh?'

With his voice trapped somewhere down the bottom of his gullet, all Olson could do was nod.

They stopped at the T-junction with the wide, smart residential street of Westbourne Villas, then, very gingerly on the pedal now, Goodman turned right and drove slowly (*Thank you, God!* Olson thought) up to the next junction, with the wide and relatively busy New Church Road.

'OK if we head out into some open countryside to exercise her legs?' Goodman asked.

No, not OK, not at all OK, a voice cautioned inside Larry Olson's head. *But you need the sodding money badly, very badly!* another voice in there shouted more loudly.

35

Alec Butler sat in the tiny, sound-proofed observation room adjoining the interview room in the Brighton custody centre. The DC was watching the proceedings on the monitor, relayed from the single overhead CCTV camera next door.

Having agreed their interview strategy with Grace, Norman Potting and Jon Exton sat on one side of the modern rectangular table, opposite Niall Paternoster, who looked haggard and unshaven, his hair dishevelled, and his solicitor, who had a notebook in a tired leather folder in front of him.

The first interview, last night, had been to establish Niall's accounts that he had already given to the police. This second interview would continue obtaining Niall's account, and covering points that had been raised during the investigation to date. A mixture of garnering information and gently probing aspects of the suspect's story.

Niall was dressed in the regulation police tracksuit which appeared at least one size too big for him. His solicitor looked like he'd slept in his clothes, as he always did.

Alec Butler's personal opinion of Legal Aid on-call solicitors, already starting from a low base, had descended to even lower depths after the recent discovery that one of Brighton's most prominent ones had secretly been a major county lines drug dealer.

Touching the screen in front of him to start the interview, Potting glanced up at the clock on the wall. 'It is 9.43 a.m. Detective Sergeant Norman Potting and Detective Sergeant Jon

Exton interviewing Niall Paternoster, under caution, in the presence of his solicitor, Joseph Rattigan.'

They each introduced themselves for the benefit of the recording.

'Niall,' Exton began, 'last night we went through in some detail your account of the movements of you and your wife over the last weekend, leading up to her disappearance at Tesco on Sunday afternoon. This interview will continue dealing with those details and we also need to ask you some additional questions. Can you tell us about where you and Eden were on the weekend of Saturday the twenty-fourth of August?'

Paternoster cleared his throat to compose himself. 'I'd had an overnight taxi fare from Manchester and didn't get home until about 10.30 a.m. so I showered and went to bed. I stayed in bed until about 4.30 p.m. Eden had been out to lunch with a work colleague. We stayed in for the rest of the day. On Sunday we spent the day in the garden, I moved some plants, Eden mowed the lawn. I think I washed the car in the afternoon.' He hesitated. 'In the evening I listened to some music and Eden was watching episodes of *Criminal Minds*, some FBI profiler thing she liked.'

After a brief silence, Potting asked, 'Niall, during the search of your house following your arrest last night, blood was discovered on your kitchen worktop and on the floor area beneath. How do you account for that?'

'I already explained that to the two officers who came to see me yesterday morning, after I called the police to report my wife missing,' he replied. 'I told them I'd cut my hand on a potato peeler when I was rummaging in a kitchen drawer for the bottle opener. I was frustrated because my wife never puts anything back in the right place.'

Potting continued. 'Was your wife with you when you cut your finger – as you mentioned – on the potato peeler?'

Ignoring a cautionary look from his solicitor, he responded,

'No, she wasn't with me. How clear do you need me to make it? Eden got out of my car in the Tesco car park at around 3.15 p.m. on Sunday and vanished off the face of the earth. I tried to open a bottle when I got home, you know, to calm my nerves – I was sort of angry and worried about her at the same time – and I cut my finger. I did not squirt blood over my wife as she wasn't there.'

Potting waited patiently for him to calm down. Then he asked, 'Can you run through the account that you gave to the police regarding Eden's passport?'

Paternoster recounted his explanation about the passport to the officers. He also confirmed that he did not know the whereabouts of her mobile phone.

The two detectives then asked him a number of questions about his and his wife's friends and relatives and their community ties. He told the officers about Eden's work and office colleagues. Once that part of the interview had concluded, Potting turned to him. 'Niall, during the initial search last night at the house, forensic officers found a T-shirt hidden behind a bathroom inspection plate in your en-suite. Early examination of the T-shirt revealed what appeared to be some blood spots and a tear.'

Paternoster gave a convincing performance of looking mystified. 'I'm sorry, I've absolutely no idea what you are talking about.'

'You weren't wearing one of your wife's T-shirts when you cut your finger, by any chance, or used it to wipe the blood away?' Exton asked.

Niall looked at him quizzically. 'Why would I have done? She's about four sizes smaller than me. No, no way. Maybe she fell over running and cut herself.' He frowned. 'Look, if you think I killed her you're completely mistaken. I loved her, for God's sake. I've been in financial shit since my business went bust – she's kept us afloat. Do you people seriously think I would have killed the gravy train when I was down on my luck?'

Both detectives stared at him levelly. Then Exton said, 'Is it correct that when the two officers attended yesterday morning, they asked you about your wife's passport? You went to get it, then told them it had gone from its usual place?'

Ignoring another warning glance from his solicitor, he said, 'Yes, correct.'

'Giving the officers the impression that she had taken it with her, wherever she had gone?' Exton continued.

'Yes – well – that was my conclusion. Why else would she have taken it?' Paternoster replied.

'We're not here to speculate,' Exton said, giving Rattigan an exaggerated smile. 'We are trying to establish facts. You have repeatedly maintained that your wife has disappeared. Certainly, it would be logical if she had disappeared that she would take her passport with her. Would you agree?'

Rattigan looked like he was going to object to that, but then leaned back in his chair and let it go.

Exton went on. 'Niall, do you have any explanation for why your wife's wedding ring, engagement ring and passport were discovered by our Forensics Team last night? They were concealed underneath a bedroom floorboard.'

He shook his head, looking numb. Neither Potting nor Exton could read his expression. Then, anger rising, he said, 'I – you – you found – you found WHAT? Her wedding ring and passport?'

Rattigan leaned across to his client and spoke quietly. There was an exchange of nods.

'Can you explain these items, Niall, and the hidden T-shirt?' Exton pressed.

Niall looked at both detectives. 'No comment.'

Rattigan made some notes, looking relieved. 'I have advised my client not to answer any more of your questions until I have spoken to him again. I suggest we reconvene this afternoon,' he said.

Norman Potting leaned forward and placed a finger on the control panel to terminate the second interview.

36

Despite the bad start to the test drive, Larry Olson had to admit his customer knew what he was doing. Goodman had done a lot of track days, he'd reassured Olson, as well as an ice-racing course in Sweden a couple of winters ago. Once he'd got the feel of the BMW, he'd handled it well through the fast, wet, twisty two-lane road over Devil's Dyke and onto the A23.

On the return journey there had been a couple of moments when he'd overtaken a little sharply, but they'd made it without Olson needing to reach into his pocket for the vial of white pills.

Now they were inside the city limits, heading downhill in the relative calm of a 40 mph limit. Goodman duly braked as they approached the 30 mph roundel, muttering that he'd been caught in a sneaky radar trap just past this sign a couple of years ago.

Olson could relax again now and resumed his sales patter, not that he really needed to. He was pushing at an open door. He could see from the broad smile of his customer's face that he was all but ready to sign any piece of paper he shoved under his nose, once they were back in his showroom.

They turned left at traffic lights onto the Old Shoreham Road, in electric mode now.

'She's so incredibly smooth!' he said, beaming. 'And silent – a different experience. And does she go, wow!'

'She does. And economical, too! Around town you'll get up to ninety-one miles per gallon!'

'Awesome!'

Olson directed him to make a right shortly after the next set of lights. A left, then another right down a short, winding road until they reached a T-junction back at the wide New Church Road, lined on both side with large, detached houses and some blocks of flats. He kept the spiel going as Goodman, clearly concerned about his licence, kept the speed to a rigid 31 mph. They were approaching, to their left, a school for posh kids which had a good reputation. Olson had educated all three of his own there up to public school level. Back in the days, he rued, when he was earning proper money.

But were his kids, all grown up now, grateful? Hell no, they'd sided with their mother after he'd traded her in for a younger model. *Embarrassingly young*, his daughter had said, the last time they'd spoken, more years ago than he could recall.

The rain, which had eased earlier, was now coming down heavily again and the windscreen was misting. Just as he leaned forward to switch the demister on, Goodman shouted out a petrified, 'NO!'

Olson was thrown forward against his shoulder strap as the car braked hard. He just saw a flash of red, then heard a sickening thump. Someone small, arms splayed wide out, eyes frozen, hurtled over the front of the car, thudded against the windscreen, then vanished. There was a heavy bang on the roof.

The car slewed to a halt.

There was a moment of absolute silence.

Then Goodman shrieked, 'OH SHIT, OH GOD, OH SHIT.'

37

The navy, white and turquoise helicopter of the Kent, Surrey and Sussex Air Ambulance was flying eastwards just below the 500-foot cloud ceiling. A few minutes earlier the MD902 had lifted off from Worthing Hospital in West Sussex and was now on a heading back to the Rochester City Airport base to refuel. And also to give the crew, who had been up early, a much-needed comfort break and a caffeine hit.

They had just dropped off a seriously injured farmworker. The unfortunate thirty-three-year-old had fallen into a threshing machine, which had severed his right leg below the knee and ripped off his right arm below the shoulder. He'd said to them apologetically, before they'd put him into an induced coma, that it had been his own damned stupid fault – he'd removed the safety mechanism, which was there to prevent just such an accident from happening. He'd done that, he said, because the machine had kept jamming and it gave him quicker access.

Luckily for the man, they'd reached him less than four minutes after receiving the call – the accident scene was almost directly in their flight path after returning from attending a motor scooter accident near Arundel. The rider there had suffered nothing worse than a broken leg and she'd been taken by road to hospital. If they'd been much longer before reaching the farmworker, he would have bled out and died, for certain.

The pilot, Andrew Delaney, and the paramedic, Kirsten

Dunwoody, sat up front, and the trauma doctor, Julian Turner, sat behind them, writing up his notes. All three had their helmets on. It was 10.15 a.m. and they were just over two hours into their eight-hour shift.

Turner looked up from his tablet and peered out of the window to his right, which was beaded with tiny drops of rainwater. He took in the familiar lush landscape below. The views from the helicopter still excited him after four years of doing this job, and he joked to friends that he had the best office in the world. Swathes of green Downland slid past, patchworks of fields, isolated houses, occasional swimming pools and tennis courts, lakes, reservoirs, the dark, straight stretches and winding ribbons of road, and, far over to the right, the English Channel, the sea a flat grey today. The only thing he struggled with was the topography. From up in the air, the hills below were flattened out and although he knew the key landmarks, he got confused at times, trying to figure out exactly where they were.

Delaney, a highly experienced pilot, ex-Fleet Air Arm and then ten years ferrying workers to and from North Sea oil rigs, had an ability Turner really admired. He was able to land the machine in often seemingly impossible places and pretty much regardless of the weather, inspiring confidence in everyone who flew with him. One advantage this helicopter had over many other makes was its tail design, which made landing in confined spaces with people around much safer.

'Tell me, guys,' the pilot's posh voice came through their speakers, above the roar of the twin engines. 'I don't get it.'

'Get what, Andrew?' Turner queried. 'You're still the best-looking man in this chopper, in case you're worried?'

'Never forget it! I'm talking about that last shout. I mean, bloody hell? The manufacturers of that threshing machine do all they can to make it safe and the guy takes it upon himself to undo all that. I mean, hello?'

'I agree, incredibly stupid?' Kirsten Dunwoody said in her Aussie accent which always, Turner thought, made everything she said sound like a question, as it did now. 'Poor man. Let's hope he makes it?'

'Andrew, you know the problem with making anything idiot-proof?' Turner said. He provided the answer without waiting for a reply. 'It's that idiots have a great deal of ingenuity!'

At that moment the alert on the comms panel in front of the doctor flashed, signalling a new incident. He leaned forward and answered. The despatcher's voice, sounding crystal clear, said, 'Helimed Six Zero?'

'Helimed Six Zero,' Turner answered.

'I have you approaching Brighton, correct?'

'Correct,' the doctor confirmed.

'RTC in New Church Road, Hove,' the despatcher said. 'Car versus a schoolboy. We've had lots of 999s coming in. It sounds bad. It's a wide road, Andrew, do you think you can land there? Alternatively there's a park nearby.'

'I know it,' the pilot replied. 'I can get us down there fine.'

'RPU will clear an area for you. What is your ETA?'

'I have visual on Shoreham Power Station chimney. I'm two minutes west of it.'

'Two minutes, A-Firm.'

Instantly Julian Turner focused his mind. A car versus any human being was never going to be good news, let alone a child. It was sheer luck for the boy that they were so close – if anything could be done for him, this Air Ambulance, which was to all intents and purposes a fully equipped mobile Emergency Department, would give him the best chance.

It was against the regulations to unclip his harness before landing but, as they flew over the city limits and started to descend, Turner placed his hand on the buckle, at the ready, so as not to waste a split-second when they were down. Immediately following a major trauma, there were two critical time frames for the victim: the Platinum Ten Minutes and the Golden Hour.

The Golden Hour was that crucial first hour during which a severe trauma patient arrived in a hospital, when the team threw every resource they had at them to understand the extent of their injuries and do all they could to keep them alive. Because if they could get them through that hour then they had an increased chance of saving them.

The Platinum Ten Minutes was all down to him and the paramedic – so long as the victim wasn't trapped. If he assessed they needed urgent hospitalization, their task would be to stabilize them and to ensure they moved them safely, then get them off the scene and into the helicopter within ten minutes – to give the victim as much of the Golden Hour as possible in hospital.

Boy versus car.

Blunt force versus a robust but fragile human.

Turner had done a PhD on the subject of trauma as well as having written a series of articles for *The Lancet*, the widely respected medical journal, on the subject of blunt trauma. He was now writing a medical textbook on the treatment of trauma victims.

The subject that interested him greatly was the amount of impact a human being could sustain and live. He had an opportunity to study it through the victims of accidents he came across in his current work with the Air Ambulance, as well as through forums of trauma doctors and collision investigators around the world.

A straight fall of fifty feet onto a hard surface was the maximum the majority of normal, healthy adults could survive, and that was if they landed feet first with bent legs. Falling from significantly higher than that, the odds reduced to ten per cent. Beyond seven storeys, any fall onto hard ground would be fatal. Lighter, more supple children had a slightly better chance.

He had a particular interest in road traffic accident injuries. Wearing a tightly fitting seat belt, without allowances for crumple zones, the maximum sudden stop an adult human could survive, in theory, was a 60 mph impact – two cars head-on at 30 mph each. Any higher speed and there would be massive rupture damage to the internal organs. The spleen, kidneys, liver and heart would all tear their restraining tendons, and the brain would ricochet around inside the skull, causing severe internal damage.

The pilot's calm voice crackled through their speakers. 'Shoreham, Helimed Six Zero, five hundred foot Portslade, inbound Hove, major road accident.'

The crisp reply from Shoreham Air Traffic Control came back. 'Acknowledged. Surface wind at Shoreham two four zero at ten knots. We have IFR traffic, a King Air inbound 1,500 feet Devil's Dyke.'

'Thanks Shoreham, will call again lifting.'

For tight landings like this, both medics acted as crew, peering out of the windows for hazards and, in particular here, cables. As their speed of descent slowed, he could see flashing blue lights on the roofs of several police vehicles, each marked with their call signs. A white-and-blue BMW i8 had slewed at an angle. A short distance behind it several people stood or knelt around a crumpled figure lying on the road. A police officer in a fluorescent jacket was acting as batman, signalling them in.

Turner knew this long and very wide road well – as a child he had lived in one of the quiet, tree-lined streets that ran south from it down to the seafront. With its mix of detached houses, many now occupied by medical practices, elegant Victorian semis and terraces and low-rise flats, this whole area, being so close to the beaches, was a popular and much sought-after residential neighbourhood.

The pilot manoeuvred the helicopter by hover-taxiing just a couple of hundred yards in front of the BMW, a little to the right, then left, before it touched down almost imperceptibly and settled on its skids. The pilot, keeping the engine running, said, 'Go!'

Turner pulled off his helmet, grabbed his bag, pushed open the door and jumped down, followed a few seconds later by the paramedic. She stopped when she was clear of the rotor blades to turn back and give the pilot a thumbs-up.

38

Turner ran up to the BMW and stopped for a brief moment to assess it. Damage to a vehicle would tell him a great deal about the likely injuries sustained by the pedestrian.

Also, with older and cheaper vehicles, skid marks would be a good indicator of speed, but not on a wet road, and in any case this modern BMW's braking system eliminated those. The Collision Investigation Unit would calculate the car's speed later, using the BMW's onboard computer and any local CCTV, by creating a computer-aided mock-up of the accident.

Looking at the front of the car, he saw that part of the number plate was broken off and there was a severe dent in the bumper, indicating it had struck the boy in the legs, likely breaking both of them but hopefully not shattering his knees, which could impact on his future mobility, if he survived.

In any frontal collision between a motor vehicle and a pedestrian, there were three possibilities. The first was that the victim had gone underneath the vehicle. The second was that they'd been thrown sideways. The third was that they'd gone over the top, which looked to be the case here.

The round bullseye break in the centre of the windscreen indicated that the boy had struck it with some force. The only part of the boy's body hard enough to have created that, in toughened glass, would have been his skull. He looked at the spiderweb crack more closely to see if he could spot any strands of hair, which he could, and fragments of skin and blood from the scalp, which he saw were also present.

Next he looked at the roof and saw the marks where the boy must have struck it before bouncing off and into the road.

Not good.

He and Dunwoody ran past the car. A woman, a member of the public, was supporting the boy's neck, and looked like she knew what she was doing. First-aid trained, he thought. Good. Two police officers were also kneeling beside him.

Dunwoody whispered into Turner's ear. The classic gallows humour that helped keep them sane at times, when dealing with situations that might otherwise make them weep. 'Is it a *stay-and-play* or *scoop-and-run*?'

'The latter,' he whispered back.

The colour of the boy's bloodstained face was alabaster. Turner knelt beside him and immediately felt for his pulse.

It was alarmingly weak.

39

An hour and a half after the morning briefing meeting had ended, Roy Grace stood outside Cassian Pewe's office. He'd long got used to this game the ACC played of making him wait, often for up to an hour, for no other reason Grace knew than he could. Power play. Childish, but he'd enjoyed keeping him waiting in turn. It had just gone 10.30 a.m. when he'd eventually arrived at his office, and now he'd been waiting close to half an hour.

Finally, just as Pewe's staff officer came out of his own office and said, 'The ACC says to go in,' Grace's job phone rang. He ignored it. Moments later, as he entered, his personal phone rang. Barely glancing at it, he hit the decline button.

Mr Immaculate sat behind his desk, studying something on his screen. There was no welcoming smile. Just, without looking up, a sharp, 'So? You'd better have something good for me, Roy.'

'I have – *sir*.'

And more than you bloody know. Clearly, the nuke hadn't hit him yet. But it would be any day soon.

Closing the door behind him, he walked over and stood in front of Pewe. As he had anticipated, he was not invited to sit at either of the chairs in front of the large, shiny desk, but he sat down anyway.

'Perhaps you'd care to update me?' Pewe said, still apparently focused on his screen on something more important than his visitor.

To his joy, Pewe's aggressive – and dismissive – demeanour faded fast as he recounted the events of the past twenty-four hours, and the evidence that had come to light. Saving the best to last.

Grace's job phone rang again, and once more he rejected it.

'I hope you're not just virtue signalling, Roy,' Pewe said when he had finished, using the corporate newspeak that constantly left Roy baffled – and wondering if Pewe had any idea what it meant, either. 'This does change the optics.'

'I had my eyes tested a couple of months ago,' Roy retorted facetiously. His phone pinged with the voicemail tone.

Pewe stared at him for some moments. 'I suppose you think that's funny? You seem to be quite the comedian recently.'

'I don't find anything funny about murder – *sir.*'

'Which is what you think we have here?'

Keeping his patience, Grace answered, 'That's how the evidence is pointing. Unless you have a better theory – something you feel I've missed, perhaps?'

Pewe, riled by Grace's attitude and perhaps, Grace thought, by his own misjudgement of the situation, waved a dismissive hand. 'Go, get on with it.' The ACC tapped his keyboard and leaned forward dismissively, absorbed once more in whatever was on his screen.

Interview over.

As Roy Grace left the room, closing the door behind him and stepping onto the landing, he was anxious to check his phones and see who had been trying to contact him so persistently. With the offices of the Chief Constable, the Deputy CC and the two other ACCs around him, as well as those of Pewe's shared staff officer and his PA, he was conscious of his total lack of privacy. Pulling out his job phone, he was about to press the voicemail button when he heard footsteps coming up the stairs.

Two uniformed officers, wearing the white caps of the Road

Policing Unit, appeared with grave expressions. He recognized both of them. PCs Trundle and Edwards.

'Sir,' Trundle said. 'We were told we'd find you here.'

Always friendly and respectful on the previous occasions they'd met, their demeanour now made his stomach churn with anxiety as if a barrel of icy water had been tipped over inside him. It was an old police saw that two officers in white caps, knocking on your door in the middle of the night, was never going to be good news. Nor in the middle of the morning.

'Richard,' he said, his voice trembling uncharacteristically. 'Hi.'

Oh God, had something happened to Cleo on her way to work?

'Pip - what - what brings you guys to these hallowed halls?'

'We need to speak to you, sir,' Trundle said. 'Can we go somewhere private - downstairs perhaps?'

'Yes - yes. Of course.'

He followed them back down the stairs and they stopped in the hallway. Closed doors lined the corridor along it.

Something was badly wrong.

Please God let Cleo be all right.

'Sir,' Trundle said. 'I'm sorry to tell you - your son, Bruno, has been involved in a road traffic collision.'

It took some moments for the words to sink in.

'What? I dropped him off at school. I saw him go in. You must be mistaken - I mean - there's no way - he's in class all day.'

'He was identified at the scene, sir. We asked one of the teachers - we knew he was from the school because of his uniform.'

Roy leaned against a wall, feeling hollowed out. 'Identified? At the scene? Teacher? What - is - I - what do you mean?'

'It's all very sketchy at the moment, sir.'

Grace choked on his words. 'How - how - how is he?'

'He was unconscious, sir, and has been taken to the Royal Sussex County Hospital.'

'How the hell did he get out of school?'

'I'm sorry – we don't know. Inspector Biggs has been trying to contact you urgently. We've been trying to find you and your staff said you were at a meeting here.'

'Bruno? You're sure it's him?' Grace said, his voice barely a whisper, knowing the futility of that question.

'Yes, I'm afraid he's not good, sir, it looks very serious,' Trundle said gently.

'You said he was unconscious?'

Trundle and Edwards nodded. 'That's right,' Trundle said. 'The Air Ambulance attended and flew him to the hospital – that would have been just under an hour ago. We don't know the extent of injuries, but we have been told it's a life-threatening situation and we should take you to him urgently.'

Roy Grace felt like a drain plug had been pulled inside him. 'What – what happened?'

'All we know is that the driver was breathalysed and was negative. He is currently being interviewed by the RPU. Inspector Biggs has authorized us to blue-light you to the hospital. And your wife, if she is able to come, too?'

All his usual composure gone, Grace was shaking. He nodded. 'Thank you,' he said weakly.

'We have a car outside.'

He followed them numbly along the corridor and out into the light drizzle. Edwards opened the rear door of the car and Grace climbed in. The officer helped him with his belt, then they drove down the ramp to the barrier. As it lifted, with Trundle driving, Edwards switched on the blue lights and siren.

'Do you have any more info on what happened, guys?' Grace asked.

Pip Edwards turned to face him. A highly intelligent officer who had been an engineer before joining the police, he said, 'It's too early, sir. Apparently, one witness said he'd seen him looking at his mobile phone and stepping into the road. But eye-witness reports at RTCs are often unreliable, as I'm sure you know.'

Grace nodded, feeling his eyes welling up. He called Cleo, hoping to hell it wouldn't go to voicemail as it normally did when she was busy. But, to his relief, she answered on the second ring.

As he ended the call, he asked Trundle to swing by the mortuary to collect her.

40

'You're not serious?' Larry Olson asked, standing shocked and bewildered among the mass of emergency service vehicles. His customer, having thrown up on the road, was now sitting in the back of a police car. Nearby, a shocked-looking woman was talking to an officer with a body-worn camera. She looked like she was giving an account of some kind.

It was a single vehicle accident with one pedestrian casualty. The Forensic Collision Unit Team were busy measuring and taking photographs to secure evidence, including a drone to obtain a perspective of the scene. The prime objective was to collect the evidence quickly and efficiently because, with the location being right outside the school, they wanted to clear the area before parents and children started to gather, mid-afternoon.

There were police cars and motorbikes everywhere, a fire engine, a Collision Investigation Unit van and a cordon of blue-and-white tape all around, with a large bunch of rubber-necking public outside it, phone cameras held aloft. It felt like being in the VIP area of an event he really did not want to be attending. Olson noticed a local news reporter talking to bystanders and taking photographs of the police activity.

The Road Policing Unit officer, who had introduced himself as Inspector James Biggs, said, 'I'm afraid it's standard procedure, sir.'

'You're impounding my car?'

'We are, sir. It's what happens to any vehicle involved in a potentially fatal accident.'

'I – I need it – I need it for my business to survive. When – when do I get it back?'

'I can't tell you that at the moment. It will be a month or so at best – maybe two – until we have completed our enquiries.'

'Two months?' Olson's voice rose several octaves in desperation. 'Two months? My customer wasn't to blame, two witnesses said he was driving within the limit – the little boy just stepped out in front of us – he was looking at his damn phone. I was in the car. My customer was driving sensibly, keeping strictly to the 30 mph limit. There wasn't anything he could do.'

'I'm sorry, sir,' Inspector Biggs said. 'I can't comment on any witness accounts.'

'Why on earth would you need the car for that long?'

'We may have to release it to the insurance company. There's quite a bit of damage on the vehicle. They will probably make a decision on whether to repair it or write it off.'

'Write it off?' Olson calculated the poor value he would get from an insurance company. No way. 'I can get that fixed at a local body shop.'

'That will have to be a discussion with you and the insurers, sir.'

Olson stared around, bewildered. A police officer with a broom was sweeping broken glass into a dustpan. Two other officers were taking measurements with a laser device.

'We will do what we can to get the car released as quickly as possible, sir, but I'm afraid we're going to need to establish whether there was anything defective such as the vehicle's brakes or steering,' Biggs said.

Olson shook his head. 'This is ridiculous. The car was in perfect condition – all my cars are fully checked out before we put them on the forecourt. I can't afford for you to have this car for two months.'

'That's not really the issue here, sir,' the Inspector said patiently. 'There's a human life involved. A child. At this moment, he's my primary concern.'

'Yes, I understand that, but I still have to keep my business alive.'

'Frankly, sir,' James Biggs said, 'right now all I care about is doing my best to establish what happened. A small boy has been airlifted to hospital on life support. Forgive me for borrowing your terminology, sir, but we are concentrating very hard on keeping him alive.'

41

On the journey to the mortuary to collect Cleo, Roy Grace sat tense in the rear seat of the speeding police car, desperately worried for Bruno. His phone rang and he answered instantly.

'Boss,' said Branson, 'I've heard the news and we're all gutted – and hoping he'll be OK. Kids are resilient, you know.'

'Yep,' Grace replied bleakly. 'Let's hope so.'

'Don't worry about anything here, I'll take care of it all – do whatever you want to, take whatever time you need, and just know that we're all here for you.'

'Thanks, I appreciate it. Let's quickly run through the actions for today so that you can deal with anything that comes up.'

'You sure you want to?'

'We have to, Glenn. Let's just talk over everything so you have all you need.' Grace just managed to keep his focus despite the enormity of what he might now be facing with his son. 'That last piece of information that came in this morning from Chris Gee at the Paternosters' house – what do you make of it?'

Gee had delivered an interesting development. The forensic team had discovered two sacks of cat litter behind a large bag of barbecue charcoal in the cupboard in the utility room.

'Would you forget you had two sacks of cat litter in your house, boss?'

'I don't think so – if I had a cat.'

'Yeah. Don't think I would either. I guess it could happen but maybe Niall Paternoster thought we wouldn't find it?'

'We've already figured Niall Paternoster's not the brightest flame in the bonfire. He told us that he and his wife' – it took Grace, with his distracted mind, a moment to recall her name – 'Eden, had argued because they needed cat litter, which is what he claims she went into the store to get. On the face of it, Gee's discovery certainly casts some doubt on that story, don't you think?'

'Just a little, in my humble opinion.'

'We have just under twenty-four hours left to keep Paternoster in custody. When Exton and Potting lob the cat litter in, see how he reacts. I'm unlikely to be back in the office for a while, but please ring me with an update and leave a voicemail if I don't pick up.'

'Will do, boss.'

They were just driving in through the mortuary entrance. 'OK, thanks, just about to collect Cleo, then on to the hospital. I'll call you later when I get a chance.'

'I hope you have some positive news about Bruno – we're all thinking of you.'

As Grace ended the call, a tear from one eye trickled down his cheek. Then his phone rang.

It was Cassian Pewe.

'Roy?' His voice was all charm and sympathy. But there was something else underlying his tone that unsettled Grace. 'I've just heard the terrible news about Bruno. God, I'm so sorry. Please take whatever time out you need. There are moments in life when family has to come first. I'll speak to your team and tell them to give you whatever space you need.'

'Very good of you, sir.'

'Keep me updated on Bruno's progress, will you?'

'Yes, sir, thank you, of course. I'm on my way to see him now.'

'We're all praying for you – for him.'

Cleo was already standing outside the front door, head bowed against the drizzle. Trundle jumped out and held the rear door open for her. She climbed in, her face white, gripped Grace's hand and hugged him tightly. 'Darling, this is so dreadful, any news?'

He shook his head, then they both sat in silence as the car headed out through the mortuary gates.

'Bruno is young,' she said. 'Kids are more supple than adults, they have a far higher chance of surviving impacts.'

But he was barely listening to her. He was thinking about something Pip Edwards had told him on the way here, that a witness had told the police at the scene that she'd seen the boy on his phone at the side of the road moments before the collision.

He was trying to think back to the last conversation he'd had with Bruno, in his car just a few hours ago, before he'd dropped him at school.

Education's a joke, don't you think? I can learn more from Google than any teacher can tell me.

Is there any point in dreaming anything? Look at my mother. The teachers aren't worth it. But is anything in life worth it?

Some while later, after Grace had dropped his son off and seen him enter the gates, Bruno had left school during break time and stepped out into the road in the path of a car.

So many bad memories returned. Sandy, Bruno's mother, had died after being hit by a taxi in Munich.

Surely this couldn't be happening again?

Bruno had to survive this, he had to.

He was still deep in troubled thought when they arrived at the Emergency Department entrance to the hospital, pulling up beside a row of ambulances.

42

Tuesday 3 September

A staff nurse with a yellow plastic tag reading *Hello my name is Nadine*, who had been waiting for Roy and Cleo, escorted them through the normal mayhem of the Emergency Department receiving area. Roy felt in a daze being here as he numbly followed, past the hectic reception counter, screened-off beds, patients on trolleys in the corridor waiting to be processed, and into the quiet, bland calm of a Relatives' Room, spritzing their hands at a sanitizer dispenser before entering.

The nurse gave them a form for Bruno's medical history and a consent form, told them the A&E consultant would be along to see them in a short while and offered to get them drinks. Grace gratefully asked for a strong black coffee and Cleo a glass of water.

As she left, they sat down in front of a coffee table sprinkled with a bunch of magazines and children's books. Cleo read the consent form while Roy read through the medical history form, feeling utterly helpless. Bruno had been with them for such a short time, during which his health had been fine, apart from a cold in February, and he knew very little about his son's previous medical history. All Sandy had said in her suicide note that she had written him was that she was worried about him. But no more.

Had he had appendicitis? Tonsillitis? Any operations? He had no idea at all. He looked up at a row of information posters on the walls, but took none of them in. Memories of the surreal time he'd visited Sandy in hospital in Munich, when she was in a coma, were flooding back. Bruno surely couldn't go in a similar way to his mother.

This nightmare was unfolding before his eyes. He felt bleak and close to tears. That poor, troubled little boy. Sure, he was strange, but wouldn't any child be, after his upbringing with his erratic mother? Roy had really hoped that giving him a stable, loving family life would eventually change him. And it would, dammit. Bruno was going to survive this and if – no, *when* – he came out of hospital they would make even more of an effort with him, do whatever it took. Maybe, he wondered silently, he should quit his job and properly be around for him?

The door opened, interrupting his thoughts, and the nurse came back in with their drinks. She set the coffee down in front of him and said apologetically, 'I'm afraid it's from a machine – I added an extra shot of espresso to try to make it stronger.'

He thanked her, signed the consent form and explained about his lack of knowledge of Bruno's medical history. She was sympathetic and told them not to worry. Just as she departed with the forms, a stocky, balding man in his early fifties, dressed in green scrubs, came in. He had a kindly face and a professional aura that instantly inspired confidence.

'Mr and Mrs Grace?' he asked with a trace of a Brummie accent.

'Yes,' Roy Grace replied. He recognized the man, they'd met before on a couple of occasions: once when his officer EJ Boutwood had been crushed by a van and badly injured, and the other time when the American hitman, Tooth, had been brought in here after being hit at high speed by a bicycle. Adrian Burton, Senior Intensive Care Consultant. 'Good to see you again,' Grace said.

'I'm sorry it's under these circumstances. I just wanted to let you know that your son is in the hands of four consultants here: a paediatrician, an intensive care specialist, an A&E consultant and an orthopaedic consultant. We've got Neurosurgery and Radiology waiting to review him.'

'How is Bruno? What can you tell us about him, so far?' Grace asked.

Burton wrung his hands together absently, which Grace, from all his knowledge of body language, did not interpret as a good sign. 'Well, at the moment he is being assessed by the radiologist, who is carrying out a trauma CT. Your lad has head injuries and a possible fractured skull, but we don't know enough at this stage. We need to see the extent of his internal injuries before I can give you a real indication of his condition.'

'Can we go and see him?' Cleo asked.

'Not just at the moment. I'll let you know as soon as you can, and I'll take you to him.'

'Dr – Mr Burton,' Cleo said. 'Please be honest with us. Is Bruno going to survive?'

There was an uncomfortable moment in which the assurance seemed to drain from the consultant's demeanour. 'Ordinarily I would do my best to give a positive prognosis. But I know from your lines of work you are both strong people, so I'm not going to dress this up – I assume that's what you want from me? Honesty?'

'It is,' Grace said.

Cleo nodded in agreement.

'OK. Bruno's been admitted with a very weak pulse. Our initial assessment is that he has massive internal bleeding – probably from a ruptured spleen, which can be dealt with if that's the case. More of a concern is the potential brain damage, along with other internal damage, and we won't know that until the CT scan is done. But what I will say, to give you something positive, is that youngsters like Bruno are able to absorb remarkably high levels of impact, compared to adults.'

'As I keep hearing,' Grace said, more harshly than he intended.

His reassuring smile returning, Adrian Burton said, 'I'll be back with an update as soon as I have it but it's likely to be at least an hour or so. Meanwhile, please do be assured your son is in the very best hands. We're fortunate in having all our senior consultants on duty today.'

43

For the next twenty minutes, Roy paced up and down the room like a caged, distressed animal, barely saying a word, consumed by his own thoughts.

His phone rang. He was about to silence it when Cleo said, 'Take it, darling.'

After a moment's hesitation, he answered.

It was Glenn Branson. 'What news, boss?'

'Nothing so far, just waiting. I'll let you know when we find out anything.'

'We're all here for you. As I said, don't worry about anything at work, we're taking care of it.'

'Thanks, mate.' He fought hard to hold back tears. 'What's happening at the coalface?' He glanced at his watch. It was just gone 1 p.m.

Cleo remained seated, staring into space. She was finding it impossible to concentrate on anything.

'Norman and Jon have headed back over to the custody centre, and Paternoster's solicitor is on his way, too. We'll see his reaction to the cat litter surprise – not.'

'Yes. You'll call me?'

'If you want? Are you sure?'

'I am,' he said emphatically.

'There's another development – look, I don't want to be bothering you at this time, boss.'

'Don't worry, I'll tell you when to leave me alone. I'm sure Bruno will be just fine, he's in the best hands.' He caught Cleo's eye and she nodded encouragement back.

'Louise Soper spoke to the Collision Investigation Unit at Shoreham and they suggested it would be best if she took the Paternosters' car, along with someone from Digital Forensics, over to the main BMW dealership, where they have all the diagnostic kit to interrogate the onboard satnav. She's now done this and reported back. There's something very interesting and possibly significant. Several things actually.'

'Yeah?'

'Well, the first is the timing of that photograph of Eden Paternoster in front of the lake at Parham House. Her husband claimed it had been taken this past Sunday afternoon, the first of September. But Aiden Gilbert has already established from the digital date stamp that he was lying, and it was actually taken over a week earlier, at 1.50 on Saturday August twenty-fourth. You know that already, right?'

'Yes.'

'Well, EJ, who has been working with me, now has corroboration from the diagnostics team at Chandlers. The BMW's satnav log, which records all journeys whether it is activated or not, shows it travelled to Parham House that afternoon, and was there, stationary, during the exact time this photograph was taken. This is further corroborated by Aiden Gilbert's analysis of Niall Paternoster's phone. The plot of its movements matches exactly that of the BMW. As does the plot of Eden Paternoster's phone. Which indicates that the couple actually drove there together, in this vehicle, eight days before he maintains he took the photo of her. And this is doubly confirmed by Louise's interrogation of the ANPR cameras. These corroborate all the BMW's movements, with further evidence from two Highways Authority traffic-flow cameras. The examination also confirms the journey to Parham House from Niall's account of what happened this past Sunday.'

Grace thought for a moment about the ramifications of this. Was Paternoster thinking his lie about the photograph date wouldn't be found out?

Branson continued, 'We've heard back from our enquiries at Parham House and there's no CCTV or records to confirm either Niall or Eden were there on either weekend. And there's more. This is where it gets even more significant.'

Grace took a sip of the coffee. It was hot and very slightly fizzed the tip of his tongue.

'The Outside Enquiry Team spoke to the Paternosters' immediate neighbour, to the north of their house. An elderly, retired woman who they described as something of a busybody – but with all her marbles. She said that around 6.30 p.m. last Thursday, August twenty-ninth, she was out weeding her lawn and could smell – and hear – the Paternosters were having a barbecue in their back garden. Some while later, she can't remember exactly when, she heard them having a terrible row. She said that wasn't unusual, she'd often hear them arguing about something or other, but she said this one was particularly bad. They were screaming at each other and at some point it sounded like one of them had hit the other. She'd been so worried that she'd seriously contemplated calling the police, but she didn't want the Paternosters to think of her as the nosy, interfering neighbour, so she'd left it and went indoors – there was something she wanted to catch on television.'

'Did she hear anything more?' Grace asked.

'Not of the row, no. But what she did hear, she said, because she's a light sleeper, was the Paternosters' car starting up at 2.10 a.m. She was precise about the time, she said, because it woke her and she looked at her alarm clock. She heard it drive off. She was surprised because it was unusual, although she hadn't thought too much of it, as she knew from her occasional chats over the garden fence with the Paternosters that Niall often worked night shifts driving a taxi.'

He paused before continuing, sounding increasingly excited. 'Now get this. The plot of the BMW's satnav and of Niall Paternoster's phone indicate he departed from their Nevill Road home at 2.11 a.m. and headed north-east towards Ashdown Forest – also confirmed by two ANPR cameras. He arrived at a location we've identified as a car park on the edge of dense woodlands at 2.48 a.m. and remained static in that vicinity for just over an hour. From there he travelled to Shoreham Harbour, arriving at 4.35 a.m., heading to a point that we've identified as the east mole of the harbour breakwater. Niall Paternoster's phone was then shown as leaving the BMW and heading down to the end of that mole, returning to the BMW minutes later.'

'Taking in the early morning sea air?' Grace ventured.

Cleo looked up at him, puzzled, then got up, walked around the room and sat back down again.

'A normal thing to do in the middle of the night, wouldn't you say, boss?'

'Doesn't everyone?' Grace replied flippantly.

'The BMW and Niall Paternoster's phone returned to the locale of the Paternoster home at 5.02 a.m.'

Grace thought this information through carefully before replying again. 'The couple had a row. It ended with what the neighbour thought might be a blow. Then in the middle of the night Niall Paternoster drives to a forest. Are you thinking what I'm thinking?'

'Deposition site?'

'Unless he has a particular interest in forest wildlife,' Grace replied. 'Then he drives to the harbour. A second deposition site?' He frowned. 'I'm trying to make sense of the timeline here. The previous Saturday they drive to Parham House and take photographs. The following Thursday they have a row, which a neighbour hears, and suppose he kills her. Did he dismember her, which might account for the blood at the house? He then drives out into the forest and buries part of her body. The rest he dumps out to sea at the end of the harbour, where there are strong currents. Four days later he reports her missing, giving the explanation that she went into a Tesco store to buy cat litter and vanished off the face of the earth. Am I missing anything?'

'I think we're on the same bus,' Branson replied.

'We need an underwater search team to check out the area around the harbour mouth. But it's strongly tidal.'

'It was an ebb tide at that time, boss, which means that anything he dumped in the sea would be carried some way out.'

Grace was pensive for some moments. 'Ashdown Forest?' He knew, from experience, that some parts of Sussex were more conducive to burying a body, or body parts, than others. Much of the county was on chalk, which made digging a grave deep enough to conceal a body a challenging task, even more so during the summer months when the soil was dry and hard.

Thirty miles south of London, located in the north of Sussex, Ashdown Forest had originally been created as a medieval hunting forest soon after the Norman Conquest. More recently it was the home of Winnie-the-Pooh. And with its sandy soil, it was a very easy place to dig a grave.

Few domestic murders were ever planned meticulously in advance and from what he had seen of Niall himself, a man with a clearly volatile temper, and from what the neighbour had reported, this had all the hallmarks of a classic and tragic argument gone too far. If he had murdered his wife, Ashdown Forest would have been geographically perfect for Niall Paternoster. The internal police statistics on deposition sites showed that normally killers would drive their victim's bodies a maximum of thirty miles from the crime scene, wanting as short a journey as possible for fear of either being stopped and searched or having a crash.

Ashdown Forest, with its mix of open heathland and dense woods, spread over a wide area, made it tricky to search, and Grace wanted this done quickly. With the current warm weather, a body would decompose rapidly, making the task of forensic examination increasingly hard. There was also the risk, in woodlands, of foraging animals carrying off body parts for food and clothing items for nests and lairs. If the killer was fortunate, a body in a shallow woodland grave could be completely gone in just a few weeks. And if the body was already dismembered, which is what this sounded like, that could happen much faster – in just days.

Grace went through a mental checklist, rattling off items to Branson. 'After the POLSA has made the assessment, get the team to search the immediate area of the forest car park. Get the handlers to bring cadaver dogs. At the same time, put a drone up to do a wider sweep.'

Human bodies were heavy to carry, so if Eden had been buried intact, her body was likely to be close to the car park. But if it was only body parts he was carrying, Niall could have ventured much further away. 'Deploy the volunteer search team – see if you can get them out today. And one other thing: we may well need the help of the pollen lady, depending on what's found in the forest. If it's what we expect, pollen evidence on the foot pedals of his car and on his shoes might help put him at the scene.'

'All noted, boss. I don't think your good buddy, the ACC, will be happy sanctioning the cost of the dive team and all this as well.'

Ever since Sussex Police's own dive team, the Specialist Search Unit, had been dismantled, they now used the services of a private firm. They were highly effective but didn't come cheaply.

'No,' Grace replied with a smile, so absorbed back in his work that he had momentarily forgotten the nightmare this day had become. 'He won't.'

44

It was over an hour after he had ended the call with Glenn Branson before the A&E consultant returned to give Roy and Cleo an update on Bruno. Adrian Burton looked more gravely serious than he had previously. Roy and Cleo were sitting together holding hands and comforting each other.

'The report I have from the orthopaedic consultant who's viewed the trauma CT scans is that Bruno has multiple fractures to his lower legs, rib cage, right hip and left shoulder. These are relatively easy fixes. He does also have, as we suspected, a ruptured spleen, and he is currently in theatre having an emergency splenectomy. That is a very straightforward process and people can make a full recovery with that, although they may be dependent on some medication on a permanent basis.'

Grace looked at him, sensing something more was to come. He could see it in Cleo's face, too. 'But?' he asked, pushing the question out there.

Adrian Burton nodded solemnly. 'I'm afraid there is a but, yes. Bruno's head has suffered a massive trauma, and possibly a secondary one, consistent with hitting two hard surfaces – in my experience of such collision victims his head would have come into contact first with the vehicle's windscreen and then with the road. He doesn't have a fractured skull, which is a positive, but he's not waking up, which is a concern. We'll be doing an MRI scan after twenty-four hours.'

'What is his potential brain injury, in layman's language?' Grace asked.

Cleo interjected. 'Swelling.'

Burton nodded. 'Because of his ruptured spleen and his dropped blood pressure, there's been a further insult to his brain – which we call a secondary brain injury – hypoxia. The team are doing all they can to try to get Bruno's numbers right and to extubate and stabilize him – and hopefully limit the hypoxia. He's been given three sets of drugs – ketamine to sedate him, rocuronium, a paralysing agent, and alfentanil, an analgesic.'

'So, in your opinion, doctor, what is his prognosis?' Grace asked.

'I'd be lying if I told you both it was good. It isn't – but he's got a strong heart and for the moment we've just got to hope for the best.'

'And pray?' Cleo asked.

Burton smiled thinly. His eyes signalled, *Why not?*

'I know you're giving him the best care you can,' Grace said. 'But is there anywhere – a neurological unit in some other hospital – London, perhaps – that has any facilities you don't have here? I don't mind what it costs – we'll pay for a helicopter, or anything.'

At this moment, Grace thought, he would pay every penny he had in the world to save this boy. Even if it meant selling their house.

Burton shook his head. 'We're a regional major trauma centre, we've got a neuro ICU, and in this acute episode he's better off here. If you were talking about rehab in the future, then we could look at that, but we are a long way off from that at the moment. Even if there was a better facility somewhere, he is so unstable at the moment that I honestly don't think he would survive the journey.'

His words slammed into Roy's stomach like a massive punch. Dimly, he was aware of Cleo taking his hand.

'Bruno's being moved to the ICU – I'll come back soon and take you up to see him,' Burton said and left the room.

45

At 3 p.m., Jon Exton and Norman Potting returned to the Brighton custody centre to carry out their third interview with Niall Paternoster, in the presence of his solicitor.

Seated across the table in the interview room, after completing the formalities, Exton asked, 'Can you tell us about your movements each day last week, Niall?'

Niall ran his tongue around the inside of his mouth, thinking. 'Yeah, Eden was at work all week and I did some taxi-driving. Early in the week I had a few airport runs from Heathrow and Gatwick, and in between those I tried to get out on my bike as much as possible and enjoy the weather. The second part of the week was quieter for me, mostly local pick-ups off the ranks.'

Exton continued, 'Did you work every evening?'

'Yes, except Thursday – such a glorious evening, we had a barbecue in the garden.'

Exton said, 'Was the barbecue a success?'

Niall glanced at his solicitor, who frowned back. Then replied, 'I'm not sure what you mean by a *success*?'

'Simple,' Exton replied. 'Did you both enjoy it, have a nice, happy evening?'

'Is this relevant?' Rattigan asked.

'It is, yes,' Exton responded.

Niall replied, 'Yes, it was a success, I think, we both enjoyed it – although we did have a minor disagreement over the smoke that was coming from the meat.'

'A minor disagreement? Can you tell us about that?' Exton asked.

Niall smiled, a little nervously. 'Eden is a perfectionist and was giving me tips on how to cook the steaks. She was moaning that there was too much smoke. Although we had a few words it was good-natured, nothing nasty.'

'OK,' Exton said. 'So the barbecue went well. How much had you both had to drink?'

'Eden was pretty sober, she doesn't drink much – she thinks I drink enough for the both of us. I certainly had a few and when we went to bed I was out like a light. I didn't wake up until the next morning when she'd already left for work. A colleague was picking her up.'

'So what did you do Friday?' Exton asked.

'Cleared up the barbecue and hung around the house most of the day. I biked down to the beach and had a swim, then I went to the gym. Eden got back at the usual time from work and we had a quiet evening. The rest of the weekend is what I have told you we did already, a number of times – nothing changes.'

Norman Potting took over. 'Thanks for that, Niall. Let's go back to your finances, shall we?'

Paternoster gave him a sardonic smile. 'That's easy. I've got no money, my business went bust. Eden is the one with the cash. She's paying the mortgage and, so far, the bank haven't come calling. I know she has her own bank account with money in that she had before we met. I've never asked too much about that, but I know she's not short of a bob or two.'

'So if anything happened to her, what would happen to her money?' Potting continued.

'I imagine it would come to me. We did make wills after we married and left things to each other. And I—'

Suddenly he faltered, his voice cracking. Tears trickled down his face. 'You don't want to believe me, do you? You think I've done something to Eden and I'm covering it up. I'm telling you the truth. I don't know what's happened or where she is. You must believe me. I'm completely lost.'

He buried his face in his hands.

Potting and Exton sat still. Then Exton asked the solicitor, 'Would your client like a short break?'

Paternoster shook his head. 'No, I'm fine, let's get this over with.'

Potting, his tone a little gentler, said, 'Niall, we want to find out what has happened to Eden as well, that's why we are asking all these questions. You're telling us that apart from the occasional husband-and-wife disagreement your relationship was good. We have a number of detectives working on trying to find Eden and it's important you tell us the truth and hold nothing back. Everything you've told us about what the two of you were doing last week is correct?'

'Yes, it is.'

After several more minutes of questioning, during which Niall Paternoster continued to maintain that he was completely baffled by Eden's disappearance, Potting fell silent for a moment. 'All right, Niall, we will be speaking to our colleagues to ascertain what they have found out from their enquiries and we will then conduct a further interview with you later today.'

'Third interview with Niall Paternoster terminated at 3.37 p.m.,' Exton announced.

As Niall Paternoster was returned to his cell, Potting and Exton joined DC Butler for a debrief. All three of them agreed they believed strongly Paternoster was lying to them, and he was hiding the truth of what had really happened.

46

The line of twenty-odd volunteers of the Sussex Community Search Team, wearing orange-and-yellow high-viz tabards over their summer rambling gear, were stretched out to the right and left of Rodney Allbright. The majority, like himself, were well past retirement age, which gave them the freedom to be called out at a moment's notice. Each had a whistle hung from a cord around their neck.

Oh yes, such fun, and with such valuable purpose, Allbright thought, as he strode in his trusty hiking boots through the wet undergrowth. He loved these callouts, which happened every few weeks.

Ever since his retirement, over ten years ago now, from the Brighton firm of chartered accountants, Hartley Fowler, where he had spent his entire working life, he now had a new purpose as a member of the Sussex Community Search Team. A purpose he had badly needed after his wife, Maureen, with whom he'd planned so many things to enjoy in his retirement, had suddenly passed away from a massive stroke five years ago.

Along with his fellow volunteers, supervised by two Sussex police officers, he had great satisfaction in being part of a team that was readily willing to do anything, from trying to find a runaway child or a sufferer from dementia who had wandered from his or her home and not been seen by a distraught spouse for several days, to – like now – searching for the remains of a woman who was, according to the briefing, missing, presumed murdered.

So far, in four years of being a member of this team, he himself had not found anything. It had always been another member, somewhere along the long line that stretched out either side of him, who had stumbled across an item of clothing or a rucksack concealed in the undergrowth or what looked like a shallow grave or, on one occasion, a frightened missing child halfway up a tree.

He glanced at his watch: 4.32 p.m. Sunset today was around 7.30 p.m. They had about three hours before the light failed sufficiently for the search to be abandoned for the night, to be resumed in the morning. Somewhere in the distance he heard the sound of two dogs barking.

He strode on, maintaining the prescribed gap between himself and his colleagues on either side, passing a variety of trees on this damp September afternoon. Beneath the peak of his golfing cap, his eyes were focused on the dense undergrowth of mostly heather and bracken, looking for any sign at all of something other than the natural flora and fauna of the forest.

He had always loved trees and there were numerous fine specimens here of sweet chestnut, hazel, alder, silver birch and Scots pine. Trees had always been of particular interest to him and to Maureen. Their longevity had fascinated both of them. He was passing some now that had been around a century and more before he had been born, and would, unless they were coppiced, doubtless be around for further centuries long after he'd gone.

He and Maureen had planned several of their rambling holidays around sites of ancient yew trees. The year before she died, they had visited the fabled Fortingall Yew in Perthshire, Scotland. It was estimated to be over 2,000 years old and some people reckoned it might be as old as 3,000 years, way preceding the birth of Christ. A couple of years earlier, they had visited an even more ancient specimen in Defynnog in Wales, which some experts dated at over 5,000 years old.

Yews held a particular fascination for him. Historically, in the past millennium, they tended to be planted in churchyards, because their leaves were poisonous to cattle and churches were the only gardens protected by walls or rails. And they were planted for a reason – they were the best wood for making longbows, the standard weapon for British soldiers in the centuries before firearms had made them redundant.

Maureen had often urged him to apply for the quiz show *Who Wants To Be A Millionaire?* because, she ribbed him, he was a mine of useless information, much of it involving trees.

But there was something else about these majestic structures. He wasn't a fanciful person, but like all humans with enquiring minds, he was puzzled by aspects of life. The same questions so many asked. *What happened before we were born? What will happen after we die? Why are we here?*

Rodney Allbright wasn't a man with a whimsical imagination, yet sometimes, when he walked past a particularly magnificent specimen, like the massively thick and tall chestnut he was passing now, he did wonder whether trees had an intelligence which we humans were oblivious to. Trees just *existed*. They didn't need education, they didn't need to cover their surroundings in tarmac so they could move around, they didn't need to build structures to live in or burn fossil fuels to stay warm. They didn't need electricity or to buy stuff wrapped in layers of packaging or a million other pollutants that messed with the ecology of the planet. Trees just – *were*. Tall, serene, smart? Giving back to Mother Nature nothing more and nothing less than they took from her.

One of the last things his beloved Maureen had said to him before her stroke was, 'You know, my love, sometimes I wish I'd just been born as a tree.'

A flash of colour snapped him out of his reveries.

He stopped in his tracks. Had he imagined it?

The rest of the search line team carried on. He turned back and probed the bracken with his stick. *Bloody hell*. No, he hadn't imagined it.

A woman's blue-and-white trainer lay on its side at the edge of what looked like a recently dug area.

He reached for his whistle and blew it.

And as he did so, something else caught his eye. A glint of light in some brambles a short distance away. A shard of broken glass?

47

Roy and Cleo sat beside Bruno in the ICU of the Royal Sussex County Hospital. The boy was dwarfed by the mass of technology all around him. He lay, eyes closed, breathing through a clear plastic endotracheal tube connected to a high-tech ventilator. Much of his marble-coloured face that was visible was covered in abrasions. His right cheek had a dressing on it. His normally neat blond hair was tousled and greasy. His bruised left hand had two cannulas taped to it, with lines leading up to pumps, regulating the flow from the bags above. An arterial line came out of his wrist. ECG circles were stuck around his chest, with red, yellow and green wires running from them to another monitor that beeped steadily.

Two nurses and a registrar were all busy checking tubes and lines. The Intensive Care consultant talked Roy and Cleo through what was happening and all the monitoring equipment.

Grace's eyes went up to the bank of monitors on shelving above him, one with a zigzagging line on a small green screen and a row of others giving digital readouts on red screens. He raised his arm over the boy's head and gently tidied some of his hair. 'Hi, Bruno, it's your dad, I'm with you. Can you hear me?'

They were screened off from the rest of the ward by green curtains. There were constant, intermittent beeps, and the occasional whine of an alarm somewhere near. All the initial tests on

Bruno had been completed, and he now lay in an induced coma. He would remain in this, Roy and Cleo had been informed, while monitoring continued.

He looked so vulnerable, Grace thought. All his previous concerns about his son were forgotten – he was now desperately anxious for the poor little chap. Wishing there was something, anything, he could do. Wishing he could wind the clock back and, instead of dropping him at school this morning, have done something different. Maybe carried on talking with him?

A couple of hours ago, Cleo had rung home to see if their nanny could stay late tonight with Noah. She reported that Kaitlynn said she was willing to do anything that could help. She and Jack were due to go out to dinner. But, of course, she would cancel it and stay as long as was needed – all night if that helped.

When Roy wasn't fretting about Bruno, he spent much of the time pacing up and down, still thinking about Operation Lagoon. Thinking through Niall Paternoster's comments and body language when he and Branson had interviewed him yesterday. Thinking about what did and did not fit with the evidence his team was uncovering. Evidence that was increasingly damning.

A swish of curtains made both of them turn round, and they saw Mel, a staff nurse, enter the confined area, closing the curtain behind her. She gave them a breezy but sympathetic smile. 'I'm going off shift shortly. I know how concerned you are to be at your son's bedside, but we're going to be keeping him in this coma for the time being. You are, of course, very welcome to stay here, but I think you'd both be much better off going home and getting a good night's rest.'

Cleo looked up at the displays on all the monitors to which Bruno was attached. There'd been no apparent change in his condition, so far as she could see.

'If there's any deterioration in Bruno's condition to worry about, you'll be called immediately,' Mel said. 'But, honestly, there isn't anything for you to do here for now. I would go home and get some rest. Perhaps we'll have better news tomorrow.'

'Is that likely, do you think?' Grace asked in a quiet voice.

She hesitated awkwardly. 'Are either of you familiar with the Glasgow Coma Scale?'

Cleo nodded.

Mel indicated with her finger for them to follow her, and they stepped out through the curtains into the ward.

Her voice dropping to a whisper, Mel said, 'We never know how much patients in a coma can hear. Bruno had a score of seven, which isn't good. But,' she added, her face brightening just a fraction, 'we never know for sure. I've seen people make a complete recovery from a far worse prognosis than Bruno's.'

As she left, Roy turned to Cleo. 'Remind me, what does a score of seven mean?'

'It's not great, darling,' she said. 'The scale relates to responsiveness to stimuli – to pain, verbalization and eye-opening. Below eight means possible severe brain damage. The highest a patient can have is fifteen.'

'And the lowest?'

'Three – which often indicates brainstem death.'

'So, seven is some hope?'

She nodded bleakly and replied in a whisper. 'Yes. Some hope for sure.'

He nodded.

'Listen, Roy, we'll stay here tonight so we can be close to Bruno in case anything happens. Leave the arrangements at home to Kaitlynn and me.'

They returned to Bruno's bedside. Grace looked down at his vulnerable young son and held his hand. 'Don't worry, Bruno, we're both here for you, we're not going home.'

They were interrupted by Bruno's personal nurse, who said she needed to carry out some checks and asked them to return to the Relatives' Room. Cleo took Roy's arm and they walked down the corridor, sobbing.

48

'You're not coming in?' It was a bad reception area and Glenn Branson's voice crackled fuzzily through Roy Grace's phone.

'No, Cleo and I need to be with Bruno, it's not looking good. Can you run things for me?'

'Of course, Roy, seriously, leave it all with me.'

'Do me a favour. When I do come in, probably tomorrow, will you ask everyone not to ask me how I am, because—' He took a moment, choking on his words.

Sounding deeply and genuinely sympathetic, the Deputy SIO said, 'Absolutely. But make sure you're certain about coming in.'

'I will,' he said heavy-heartedly.

'How is Bruno?' Branson asked.

'Not good – not at all good. He's in an induced coma, which they're hoping will reduce the swellings on his brain, but he has multiple head injuries.'

'God, it's awful, you both need to be with him. I'll run the briefing and give you an update afterwards.'

'Thanks. I appreciate it. You're a good friend.'

'You helped me when I was splitting up with Ari, when I went through all that shit of the separation and she tried to stop me seeing my kids. I'm here for you and always will be.'

Grace barely managed to utter his thanks. His eyes stung with tears.

49

Twenty minutes later, Glenn Branson sat at the head of the crowded conference room table, with his briefing notes and Policy Book in front of him.

'This is the third briefing of Operation Lagoon,' he said, then coughed and sipped some water, clearing a frog in his throat. 'The investigation into the disappearance of Mrs Eden Paternoster. As we know, she was last seen by her husband in the car park of the Tesco Holmbush superstore two days ago, just after 3.15 p.m. on Sunday the first of September – *if her husband is to be believed.*' He said the last few words with cynical emphasis. 'There have subsequently been a number of developments giving us grave concern for Mrs Paternoster.'

He looked down at his notes. 'I'm going to summarize the information – and evidence – we have so far. First is that Niall Paternoster claimed he dropped his wife at the store to buy cat litter, saying they had run out of it. When he met with uniform officers at his home yesterday, he told us that his wife, Eden, was annoyed with him because he'd forgotten to buy any cat litter himself, the day before. But this story has been thrown into doubt by Chris Gee's team – they discovered two large sacks of cat litter clumsily hidden at the back of a cupboard in the utility room. Would anyone forget they had two sacks of the stuff? From what we know so far, Eden Paternoster was a clever, intelligent and efficient lady – I'd say it was pretty unlikely she'd have forgotten she had two whole sacks of the stuff in the house.'

He looked around at his team and saw nods of concurrence. Several of them were making notes.

'Next,' he said. 'Despite the Tesco store having CCTV coverage both of the exterior and interior, there was no image of Eden Paternoster at all. But there is footage of Niall inside the store shortly before closing. There is also no footage of her from the CCTV cameras of the immediately neighbouring Marks and Spencer store or the McDonald's. To add substantial weight to this, there is the photograph on Niall Paternoster's phone of his wife in front of the lake at Parham House. He claims he took this earlier that afternoon. But according to the analysis done by Aiden Gilbert's Digital Forensics Team, this photograph was date stamped over a week earlier, on Saturday August twenty-fourth. This is corroborated by the plot of Paternoster's mobile phone, showing he was there at exactly that date and time.' He looked at Louise Soper. 'I believe you have further information on this, Lou?'

'I do, boss. On the advice of the Collision Investigation Unit, I had the Paternosters' BMW Three Series transported to the local main dealer in Portslade. They carried out an analysis of the data from the car's onboard computer system. Its movements tally exactly with the plot of Niall Paternoster's phone and the journeys we know about. It was stationary at Parham House, West Sussex, during the exact time the photograph of Mrs Paternoster was taken, at 1.50 p.m. on Saturday August twenty-fourth. This tallies with the three ANPR cameras that picked up the BMW on both its outward and inbound journeys. In addition, we have the plot of the car's journey first to Ashdown Forest early last Friday morning and then to Shoreham Harbour, with corroborating evidence from four ANPR cameras.'

Branson thanked her. 'We'll come on to the findings, so far, at Ashdown Forest in a few minutes. But before we do that, something I feel is very significant are two rings found underneath bedroom floorboards by the Forensic Team. One is almost certainly Eden's wedding band and the other would seem likely to be her engagement ring. Removed and concealed. The first question this begs is why someone would remove their wedding and engagement rings? And, secondly, why they would hide them?'

'Fear of being burgled?' Norman Potting ventured.

'Fair point, Norman,' Branson replied. 'But it makes you wonder why she removed them – if indeed she did. Could it have been her husband, thinking that would make identifying her body harder?'

'What do we know about the state of their marriage, boss?' Jon Exton queried.

Branson turned and looked at the association chart behind him. 'Have any of our Outside Enquiry Teams talked to her friends yet?'

'Her immediate family – including mother and sister – have been contacted. Her mother didn't have a good word to say about her son-in-law,' EJ Boutwood answered.

'You should talk to my ex-mother-in-law!' Norman Potting said.

'All four of them?' EJ quizzed.

Potting blushed. 'Yes, well – don't think they'd have many good words to say about me.'

'Any good reason for that?' EJ asked cheekily. 'And by the way, how did that Swedish detective you were sweet on work out?'

'Don't ask.'

'OK, you two,' Branson admonished. 'You haven't contacted any of her friends yet, EJ?'

'I have the names of four of her best friends, sir. I'm planning to speak to them tonight.'

Branson turned to the Intelligence Cell and asked for an update.

Martyn Stratford replied, 'Sir, I've been doing some background on Niall Paternoster. I've found two things that might be of significance. First, he started his career as a butcher's assistant – working for a firm up near Fiveways in Brighton. The second and possibly more significant thing is that he emigrated to Perth, Western Australia, when he was twenty-two. His business partner, an Aussie called Karen Dale, wasn't wealthy but had a bit of money. They worked, at the time, as sailing instructors. They were with a client in a small yacht off the coast of Perth and according to him they were caught out at sea one night in a storm and she went overboard. Her remains were never found.'

'And he inherited the business?' Branson asked.

'Well, he sold the business off soon afterwards for about thirty thousand pounds. He returned to the UK and a couple of years later he received a caution from Brighton and Hove Police, for a minor assault that occurred in a late-night taxi queue altercation, so we have his DNA on record. But, other than that, he's clean.'

Branson stared at him. 'That's very interesting indeed, Martyn. And it could well be extremely significant. Well done.' He made a note. 'OK, the next thing I have from the Digital Forensics Team is Eden's lack of activity on social media. She normally posted daily on Facebook, Twitter and Instagram. But there's been no activity on any of her accounts since 7.17 p.m. last Thursday August twenty-ninth. This coincides with the very concerning report from the Outside Enquiry Team about the row a neighbour heard the Paternosters having on Thursday evening. And, subsequently, the sound of the Paternosters' BMW being driven in the early hours of Friday morning, on a journey which has been plotted by the car's onboard computer, tallying with the plot of Niall Paternoster's phone from Digital Forensics and from a number of ANPR cameras that clocked the vehicle's journey first to Ashdown Forest, then to Shoreham Harbour and then back to their home in Nevill Road, Hove.'

He paused to let this sink in before continuing. 'Under Chris Gee's direction, Forensics Teams have been deployed at Ashdown Forest, and the dive team, Specialist Services International, in the area around the harbour mole.'

'Would that be at a mole-ecular level, boss?' Norman Potting quipped, and chortled, looking around a sea of blank faces for an audience.

With everyone aware of the gravity of the situation with Grace's son, even though Grace himself wasn't present, no one was in the mood for Potting's humour.

Branson gave him a withering glance. 'Thank you, Norman. Chris will be giving us a significant update shortly.' He looked down at his notes, then at DS Alexander again. 'Jack, it says here that Eden Paternoster didn't go into work at the insurance company, Mutual Occidental, last Friday morning.'

The Detective Sergeant nodded. 'Correct, sir. She was expected at a staff meeting, at 8.30 on Friday morning, but she never appeared, nor did she phone in sick. I've got Polly going back to the company tomorrow to speak to her work colleagues.'

Branson turned to the Crime Scene Manager. 'Chris, what can you tell us about the blood found in the Paternosters' house?'

'Quite a bit, sir. The Forensics Team found some recent bloodstains at the house. Some was in the kitchen, which Niall Paternoster claimed came from his cutting his finger on a potato peeler that was in a kitchen drawer while rummaging for a bottle opener. But that doesn't explain a bloodstained T-shirt found hidden behind the panel in the en-suite – blood which the forensic lab has confirmed has Eden Paternoster's DNA. As well as the blood found around the kitchen unit, which is a mix of both hers and Niall Paternoster's.'

'The kitchen knife is still missing?' Branson asked.

'Well,' Gee said, and hesitated. 'Maybe, but possibly not.'

'Meaning what, Chris?' Branson prompted.

Looking expansively at the team, Gee said, 'It's early doors, but as the boss told you, we have a major search of an area in Ashdown Forest currently under way. Just over an hour ago a woman's blue-and-white trainer, with a matching shoe size to Eden Paternoster, was found alongside what looks like a shallow grave with no body in, which we have declared a crime scene and is currently being excavated. Close to that we've recovered a kitchen knife with bloodstains. I've not had a chance to examine it myself, but from the photographs that have been sent to me, it looks a pretty close match to the one missing from the knife rack in the Paternosters' house. It's being sent to the DNA lab for priority analysis.'

'This knife,' Branson said. 'It was the largest in the rack?'

'Yes,' Gee confirmed.

Branson shot a glance at DS Stratford, then back at Gee. 'The kind a butcher might use to cut up an animal?'

'Quite possibly, yes.'

'Are you excavating through the night?'

'We are, until midnight.'

'If you find any human remains, please call me, and I'll come over.'

'I will do, sir,' Gee said.

Branson thought about the knife. He knew that in any stabbing where a knife without a hilt, such as a kitchen knife, was used, when plunged into a human body it would very likely strike bone, causing the assailant's hand to slide forward from the handle onto the blade and create a deep cut. In the majority of stabbings the offender's blood would be mingled with the victim's. If this knife which had been found had any trace of Niall's DNA, it would be a major step forward.

He made a note then looked up at the Crime Scene Manager

again. 'Did your team have any luck locating a will in the house, Chris?'

'Not so far, sir, no. But they are still going through the contents of filing cabinets in a spare room being used as an office, and two more cabinets we found up in the loft.'

Branson nodded, then turned to Emily Denyer. 'Emily, you've been investigating the Paternosters' finances. How's that going?'

'Well, quite interesting, sir – particularly in light of what we're hearing and from the interview with her husband. Mrs Paternoster seems to be a wealthy woman – in relative terms. She is very much the breadwinner in the relationship, earning substantially more than her husband. The house is in her name, probably because she is the one who put down the original deposit when they bought it. That lump sum came from a combination of her savings and an inheritance from her grandmother, who died five years ago. The mortgage appears to be paid off, possibly unknown to Niall, and at the present time, Eden Paternoster has just over £10,000 in cash savings, invested through her personal account at the HSBC bank in Ditchling Road, Brighton. I'm awaiting replies on her rental properties and there are still a couple of organizations I need to hear back from, too. I'm also trying to track down any life insurance that may exist.'

Glenn Branson thanked her and made some more notes, giving time for this significant information to sink in to everyone. 'Nice work, Emily,' he said.

Exton and Potting updated the team on the interview that had taken place earlier, and then Glenn addressed them all. 'We've heard the evidence so far, which points to Eden Paternoster being murdered by her husband. We also now have a motive – in fact, possibly two motives. The first is financial. Would Niall Paternoster stand to gain from his wife's death? Clearly yes. In the event of her body not being found, he would have to wait seven years for her to be declared legally dead. He could sell the marital home – which would, subject to the provisions in any will, of course – net him a considerable sum. The house is worth, at current values, around £600,000.'

He paused to look at his notes. 'Of potential interest to us is a discovery from text messages on his phone, as well as the O2 data, that he had a liaison at 5.30 p.m. on Sunday with a person – or persons – unknown. The number appears to be for an unregistered pay-as-you-go, and there was no answer when we tried calling. It is my hypothesis that this as yet unknown person could be his girlfriend. From all the evidence I've heard so far – and from having met the man myself, along with the boss – this enquiry has the hallmarks of a marital breakdown due to infidelity.' He paused again for a moment to make another note, before continuing.

'From my reading of Niall Paternoster, we have a man with an inferiority complex. This is not helped by his wife earning far more than him. And her owning the marital home. Let's consider for a moment that his assignation last Sunday might have been with a lover. What does that leave us with?'

Potting raised a hand, but Branson, seeing from his expression that another fatuous remark was coming, ignored it, instead continuing himself. 'A very real and compelling motive to murder his wife. Her money, his lover, or both.'

He looked around the table. No one stirred.

Then he looked at his watch. 'We can hold Niall Paternoster in custody until 9.45 a.m. tomorrow, after which we either have to charge him or go for a further court extension or release him on police bail. I am speaking to CPS but, from all I'm hearing, we may have sufficient evidence to charge him with his wife's murder, if we want to go that route. Does anyone disagree?'

No one did.

50

Ending the meeting, Branson asked Norman Potting and Jon Exton to come to his office. When the door was closed and they were seated he said, 'OK, let's consider our options. As I said, I'm pretty confident with what we have that the CPS would sanction us charging Niall Paternoster with his wife's murder, despite there being no body – so far. But I'm not sure that would be our best tactical move and, of course, we don't know the full results from the searches in the forest.'

'Tactics? Why do you say that, sir?' Exton asked.

'If her body, or part of it, is found, that's one thing. But I'm puzzled by the trainer and the knife being discovered outside this shallow grave. If Niall Paternoster went to the trouble of taking her body out to the forest and burying it, why not bury the trainer and the knife with it?'

'Perhaps he did, boss,' Potting suggested. 'And forest wildlife predators disturbed it – we've enough past experience of that happening.'

Branson nodded. 'Yes, very much a possibility, Norman, animals might remove body parts and items of clothing, but I don't know any animal that would take a kitchen knife. We'll see what Lorna's team find from their excavations but my sense is that it will only be items of clothing, and that her body might well have been dismembered and disposed of in bits – especially now we

213

know that Niall was once a butcher – most likely in Shoreham Harbour. If that happened last week, most, if not all, would have been picked clean by crustaceans and fish by now. Either of you having shellfish for supper tonight?'

Both Potting and Exton grinned. Exton looked queasy. 'Actually, Dawn is cooking me a prawn curry.'

'Better check where she got the prawns,' Branson said with a dark grin.

'I bloody well will!'

'If Lorna's team doesn't find any human remains tonight,' Branson continued, 'then I think our other two options might be better. We could go for a further extension to give us ninety-six hours of detention, and see what else comes out of the wood-work. But the option I personally favour is releasing him on police bail tomorrow morning before the 9.45 a.m. deadline, and seeing if I can get approval to put surveillance on him. Before we do that, I'd like you to continue to interview him, make the challenges and see how he reacts to the discovery of the two sacks of cat litter in his house – but leave out our activity in the forest. He'll probably pick it up in the media but if we tell him we're looking there, he definitely won't return.'

Norman Potting frowned, then made a strange, rapid movement of his lips, which he often did when he was thinking. It looked as if he was swilling mouthwash. 'What about all the other evidence?'

'Let's keep some of it in our back pocket for now, Norman. Niall Paternoster's hung his whole story on his wife needing cat litter. Focus on that, and challenge him over the other evidence found in the house to see how he reacts, prior to his release before the deadline. Then what I'm thinking is a press confer-ence, where I will make an appeal for any sightings of Eden or any information that will assist the investigation.'

Both detectives looked at him for some moments. 'That could

be a smart move,' DS Exton said. 'You're thinking about a possible girlfriend – the assignation on Sunday evening?'

Branson said, 'I'll be running my thoughts past the boss later to make sure he's up to speed and on board. I want to nail this. If Paternoster has somehow managed to disappear his wife's body, we'll need to establish a motive for murder that's a bit stronger than an argument over cat litter. An affair would be a pretty good one.'

'I've never had to murder any of my exes,' Potting said.

'Really, Norman?' Branson said. 'How come?'

'Because,' he said with a wry smile, 'they always dumped me first.'

51

As soon as Exton and Potting had left his office, Branson called Roy Grace and updated him. He told him interviews with Paternoster would continue that evening and again in the morning, and they would be challenging him on the evidence they had established. Then he told him of the plan to release Niall Paternoster in the morning, assuming no remains of his wife were found before then, and to make a public appeal via a press conference for information on Eden.

'I'd like you to stand in for me and take that conference, Glenn.'

'Of course, boss.'

'You'll have to update ACC Pewe – with his ego he'll probably want to muscle in and get his mugshot in the *Argus* and the *Brighton and Hove Independent*, and on Latest TV and all the other news.'

'I can handle him.'

'I know you can.'

There was a brief moment of silence, then Branson said, 'Just know we're all here for you. Especially me. If you want to bell me any time, day or night, that's fine, yeah?'

Grace was too emotional to reply.

Cleo had gone home to pack an overnight bag for them both to sleep here in the hospital. As he sat alone in the Relatives' Room, along with everything else he was dealing with right now, he was thinking of that hapless expression on poor Norman Potting's face yesterday. For much of the time that he'd known him, with his portly figure and terrible comb-over – before he'd gone for a more modern shaven head – Norman had to have been one of the world's most unlikely – and most unsuccessful – philanderers. And yet the man, who was still one of the best detectives Grace had ever encountered, had somehow charmed one of the brightest members of his team, and had been on the verge of marrying her before her tragic death trying to save a little girl from a fire.

He felt the tugging in his heart for Bruno. The terrible anxiety eating away at his insides like acid. With his brain roiling with fear for the boy, he was on autopilot, barely able to concentrate.

In need of some air, he left the hospital, grateful for the fresh evening breeze, even if it was laced with traffic fumes. He took a short stroll and sat for a while on a low wall. When he went back inside, he paused to squirt sanitizer on his hands, then followed behind a doctor in scrubs towards the Intensive Care Unit.

As he reached it, he glanced through the window of the secured doors towards Bruno's bed.

It was empty. All the machines had been switched off and were silent, the displays blank.

Christ.

For an instant he stood, feeling like his blood had turned to ice.

'Can I help you, sir?'

Grace turned and saw the doctor again, a handsome-looking Asian man in his late twenties. His badge gave his name, Amil, and underneath the words *ICU Registrar*.

Bewildered and terrified, he stuttered, 'My – my son – I just came back to see how he was.'

'Bruno?' the man asked, calm and with a reassuring air.

Grace nodded. 'Where – where is he?' Terrified of the answer.

'He's been taken for an MRI scan, he should be back shortly, sir. Perhaps you'd like to wait in the Relatives' Room and someone will be along to let you know when your son is back. I'll take you there.'

'Don't worry, I know where it is, my wife and I are staying in there.'

Numbly, he walked back out of the ward, into the same windowless room, and sat back down. A few minutes later the door opened and the stocky ICU consultant he and Cleo had spoken with earlier, Adrian Burton, came in. He had a strange, unsettling look on his face.

'You're working a long shift today,' Grace said, trying to sound jovial and not succeeding.

Burton smiled thinly and said, in his warm Brummie accent, 'I felt I owed it to you and your wife to stay on and make sure we're all doing the very best for your lad that we can.'

Standing up, Grace thanked him, then asked, 'How is he? Can I see him?'

'I'll take you in to see him in a minute, but I'd like to talk to you first, please?'

Grace felt another cold flush deep inside him. 'Sure,' he said flatly.

'Roy, normally we'd wait twenty-four hours before doing an MRI scan on a trauma victim, but Bruno hasn't been maintaining his blood pressure or pulse, so the team needed to see what was going on. If I can explain in layman's terms, as the brain swells from a trauma it *cones*. Basically, it gets pushed down into the base of the skull – the technical term is *foramen magnum*. Bruno doesn't have any skull fracture, which, ironically, is unhelpful in this situation, because a fractured skull could absorb some of this increasing pressure.'

'Clearly a tough nut, like his dad,' Grace said, attempting a smile.

Burton gave a kindly smile back. 'Clearly.' Then his face clouded. 'But the pressure has caused a real problem for him.'

'How – how serious a problem?' Grace asked, aware his voice was faltering.

'I'm afraid it is extremely serious,' Adrian Burton said. 'The next step tonight is for Bruno to be taken into theatre again – the leading neurosurgeon in Sussex is on his way, and he'll insert an intracranial bolt to monitor the pressure.'

'What will that do?'

'Shall we sit?' the consultant said.

Reluctantly, he sat back down and Burton joined him. 'Basically, as I just said, as the pressure rises, the brain gets pushed down, further out of the skull, putting increasing pressure on the brainstem, which is essentially the basic life support. As the pressure on the brainstem continues to increase, it causes the loss of ability to maintain the brainstem's functions. This in turn causes loss of pulse, blood pressure and temperature regulation, which are the very basic functions of the brainstem. So even though your lad's had the bleeding treated, at this moment the team still can't get his blood pressure and everything related stable.'

'I think I follow,' Grace said. 'What – what does that mean for his prognosis?'

Burton looked at him, their faces just inches apart now. Grace could feel the warmth of the consultant's breath with a faint, not unpleasant, tinge of garlic. 'How honest and explicit do you want me to be?'

'I'd prefer you to be totally honest and not dress anything up.' He stared back at the consultant levelly, with an inkling of what might be coming, however much he dreaded what he was about to hear.

Burton gave an uncomfortable smile. 'I know you coppers cope with some of your worst horrors through gallows humour.

So do us medics. Some of us call the MRI scanner the "doughnut of death". Apologies if that's offensive.'

Grace shook his head. 'I get it.'

'What it showed with Bruno is a tight brain with widespread contusions – both bruising and ischaemia – where his low blood pressure has further impaired his brain functions. And now a brain that's swelling and pushing down, out of the skull. I wish I could give you better news but I can't.'

They were interrupted at that moment by Cleo returning, with a small holdall. She sat down and Burton quickly recapped for her. Then he said, 'I don't want to mislead you or give you false hope. I'm afraid to say we're rapidly approaching the point at which there will be nothing more we can do for him.'

Grace stared back at the consultant. 'Nothing? What do you mean, *nothing*? There's always something, surely? There must be some doctor – neurologist – neurosurgeon – somewhere in the world – who could help him? I don't care what it costs. I'll do anything. Anything at all.'

Burton sat in silence for some moments, his eyes fixed on the couple. Then he said, 'Believe me, if there was anything we could do, anything that would give a chance, however small, that Bruno could be saved – other than by a miracle – I would suggest it. But he wouldn't survive a move from here to any hospital, anywhere – and we really do have top consultants, please believe me on that. I know from some of our staff that you've been critical of this hospital in the past, but we've made huge strides. The neurosurgeon who's on his way is world class.'

Grace looked back at him through misted eyes. Memories of being at his father's bedside as he lay dying, then his mother's, came flooding back, overwhelming him. 'Isn't there anyone – don't they have brilliant neurosurgeons in America at some of their teaching hospitals? Germany? Russia? Is there anyone at all?'

'If there was even a one per cent chance, I would suggest it.'

'What about this intracranial bolt – can't that possibly help?'

'It won't treat the injury, it will just monitor the pressure inside the brain,' Burton replied.

'So what's the point in doing that?' Grace said, his anxiety rising even further.

'I'm afraid its main purpose, normally, is to confirm brain-stem death. If Bruno has avoided that and does, by a miracle, pull through, it is very likely he will have permanent brain damage.'

'How serious? I mean – how impaired would he be? Would he be able to function normally? Go back to school?' Cleo was strug gling to keep her voice down.

Burton stared at her levelly. 'We'll know more later, after the neurosurgeon, Mr Hoyle-Gilchrist, has seen him.'

Grace folded his body, resting his head in his arms, as he fought off tears. He lost track of the time as he sat, before finally straightening up again and gratefully accepting a tissue the con-sultant passed him from a box.

'You both need to remain strong,' Burton said gently. 'We'll keep you informed every step of the way, but I would urge you to prepare yourself for the worst.'

52

Two hours later, finally and reluctantly dragging himself from Bruno's bedside after talking to him incessantly, with no response, before he had been taken off to theatre, Roy Grace left the ward and peered into the Relatives' Room. Cleo was dozing in a chair and looked up as he entered.

'A guy – a porter, I think – has gone to get us two camp beds.'

He smiled. 'Good. If I can sleep. Be back in a few minutes.' He closed the door quietly and walked a short distance along the deserted corridor, checking his phone in case there was any message from Lorna. But there was nothing. Then he hunted for the mobile phone number of the Road Policing Unit Inspector, James Biggs, unsure if he had it. To his relief, he did. It rang several times, and just when he was convinced it was going to voicemail, he answered with a curt, 'Inspector Biggs.'

'James?'

The tone of the Inspector's voice changed instantly. 'Sir?'

'I apologize for calling so late.'

'Call me any time, sir, twenty-four-seven. I'm so very sorry about your son. How is he?'

'I'm at the hospital now and it's not looking good, I'm afraid. Bruno—' Grace had to stop for a moment to compose himself. 'He has serious brain damage. At the moment his prognosis is pretty poor, to be honest.'

'I'm extremely sorry to hear that, sir. I'm afraid it looked to me, from the damage to the vehicle, that his head had taken quite an impact. We've made enquiries at the school and it happened during break time, when all the kids were outside. Bruno somehow managed to find his way out of the grounds.'

There was a brief awkward pause. Then James Biggs said, 'Is there any information I can help you with, sir?'

'Yes, there is, please. I'm struggling to understand what exactly happened – I mean – what was he doing crossing the road? I dropped him off at school this morning myself. He was in a strange mood, but that wasn't unusual for him. He should have been in class all morning – I'm curious about what he was doing out of school and crossing the road.'

'We're still gathering information – seeing what CCTV from the surrounding properties will give us, if anything. I've also put out an appeal for any motorists with dashcams who might have been in the area at the time, as well as to any cyclists with GoPros or similar. At this stage we're talking to independent witnesses. Our best so far is an elderly lady who my officer Tom Van der Wee spoke to at the scene. He said she was out doing her morning constitutional with her dog – a Westie – and noticed a St Christopher's boy looking down at his phone as he walked along the pavement.'

'What was he doing out of school?' Grace quizzed again.

'We don't know that yet. She'd spotted him from some distance by his red jacket. According to her account, she saw him walk out straight into the path of a sports car. She described him being struck by the car and landing on the road. Tom said the lady was pretty shaken by the experience but managed to give him a fairly clear account.'

Grace absorbed this before replying. 'Is she saying that he hadn't seen the car?'

'Yes, I'm sorry, sir. It was a BMW i8 sports car that was up for sale. It was being driven by an interested potential customer, with the owner of the company, Sussex Sporting E-Cars, beside him. From the measurements my team have taken so far, all the indications are that the car was being driven at a speed right on the legal limit. But we have, of course, impounded it.'

Grace took some moments to process this. 'What do you think actually happened?'

'Too early to say, Roy. I need input from the Collision Investigation Unit, which will take some days. But at the moment, it looks like Bruno was distracted by his phone when he stepped off the pavement. We will carry out cognitive witness interviews with this lady and any others who come forward and see if we can learn more. I'll keep you updated on any information that comes in from our public appeal.'

'Thanks, James, I'd really appreciate that.'

'I'll keep everything crossed for your lad making a full recovery.'

Grace thanked him and hung up, blinking away tears.

53

Feeling completely hollowed out, Roy and Cleo sat in the Relatives' Room eating some kind of pasta with plastic forks. Macaroni, linguine, fettuccine, penne, whatever. Although they'd not eaten for hours, neither of them had any appetite.

'I just can't believe it. He's that bad . . . this is awful, darling.' Cleo's voice was breaking up and she started crying again.

He hugged her tight.

She bowed her head for some moments, then looked up at him, sniffing and wiping her tears. 'Look, I wasn't going to tell you this, not tonight anyway, but maybe you should hear it before you see it for yourself.' She fell silent.

'See what?'

She shook her head. 'Forget it, I shouldn't tell you. Now isn't the time.'

He looked hard at her. 'You can't leave me dangling. What is it? Tell me?'

She shook her head. 'I shouldn't have raised it, not tonight.'

'Well you have,' he said, his anxiety rising again. 'So what is it? Tell me, please?'

'Bruno's two favourite hens, Fraulein Andrea and Fraulein Julia.' She looked at him flatly.

'Yes, what about them?'

Hesitating again, she said, 'I went out this morning to let them out. But I couldn't find them anywhere. So I looked inside the hen house thinking they might be broody and sitting in nesting boxes. They were in there.' She looked at him with a strange expression.

After some moments, Roy Grace said, 'Broody, as you thought?'

She shook her head. 'No, Roy. They were dead.'

'Dead?'

She nodded.

'Poor things. It said in that book you got that sometimes they die suddenly and young – often when an egg gets stuck. Is that what happened – they got egg-bound?'

She gave him a resigned look. 'I wish I could say it was.' She shook her head again. 'But I don't think getting an egg stuck would do that to Andrea and Julia.'

'What is it? What aren't you telling me?'

'Both had their necks wrung, their heads twisted round the wrong way.'

54

'The time is 7.39 p.m., Tuesday,' Norman Potting said for the benefit of the recording. 'DS Potting and DS Exton interviewing Niall Paternoster, under caution in the presence of his solicitor. This is the fourth interview.'

'Niall,' Exton began, 'can we go back to your wife's engagement and wedding rings and her passport. Why were they apparently hidden under a floorboard? How did they get there?'

Looking increasingly ragged and short-tempered, Niall replied, 'I haven't a clue.'

Exton looked him in the eye. 'Did you put them there?'

'No bloody way. I can only think Eden put them there.'

'Why would your wife do that?'

'I haven't a clue. You're the detectives, not me.'

Ignoring the remark, Exton glanced at his notes.

'Your wife is normally active on a number of social media platforms, but there's been no activity by her on any since Thursday night. Can you explain that?'

'I was with her through until Sunday afternoon, so I don't know why she didn't post. She's always on it, bloody lives on it.'

Exton nodded politely. 'You told us you didn't know why Eden wasn't answering her phone and that it appeared to be switched off. Can you explain how it came to be underneath your bed in the house? How did it get there? Were you responsible for hiding it there? Is there something you're not telling us?' He stared hard at Paternoster, but the man just gave a 'couldn't care less' shrug.

'I don't know. I didn't put it there, I have no idea.'

Norman Potting took over. 'Niall, when we interviewed you earlier, you told us you had a nice evening last Thursday, you and Eden having a barbecue at home. You mentioned having a minor disagreement over smoking meat, but no more than that, correct?'

'Yes.'

'Officers have spoken to your neighbours. Your next-door neighbour told us something different. She said she heard raised voices, a violent-sounding argument and what seemed to be some sort of blow delivered. She was so concerned she thought about ringing the police.'

'That's rubbish,' he replied angrily. 'I told you we had an argument but it's nothing like she's describing.'

'Why would she make it up?' Potting asked.

'She's a nosy old bat and she doesn't like me for some reason. Probably wants to get me into trouble.'

'Other neighbours have corroborated what she said. They heard the row, too,' Potting said calmly. 'Can you explain that?'

Paternoster looked at Rattigan, who gave him a signal. He turned back to the detectives. 'No comment.'

Potting continued. 'When you gave your account about what the two of you did last week you told us your wife had gone to work on Friday. We've checked with her company and they tell us she never turned up and it surprised them as she missed an important meeting. Can you explain that?'

Paternoster's brow furrowed. 'What? This is complete nonsense, she went to work and then came home, she'd have told me if she hadn't gone into work – and no way would she have missed an important meeting – she's very conscientious.'

Norman Potting paused for a moment. 'Niall, could you tell us again about your journey home from visiting Parham House, last Sunday afternoon, the first of September. You made a stop on your way?'

'Yes,' he replied sullenly. 'As I've told you and your colleagues repeatedly, I stopped at the Tesco Holmbush superstore at approximately 3.15 p.m.'

'What was the reason for that?' Potting asked disingenuously.

'God, how many times do I have to repeat this? People talk about wasting police time, what about you wasting our time?'

Rattigan looked at his client with a nonplussed expression.

'Please could you answer my question,' Potting persisted.

'I – we – stopped at the store because my wife needed to buy a sack of cat litter.'

'Why did she want to buy a sack of cat litter?'

'Because we'd run out of the stuff – I'd forgotten to buy some the day before.'

'You'd run out of cat litter?' Potting asked.

'Yes,' he replied tetchily. 'Is there some part of that you don't understand?'

Potting did not respond for some moments, while he made a note, then he looked back at him. 'I'd like to ask you a question about your wife, Niall. Is she good at running your house?'

'What does that have to do with anything?' his solicitor jumped in.

'If you'll allow me to continue,' Potting said, with consummate politeness, 'I think it will become clear.' He turned to Paternoster. 'If I could repeat my question, was your wife good at running your house – your home, Niall?'

'She doesn't run the home, we run it together,' he said reluctantly.

'Would you say she would have known when you were critically low of household items – such as cat litter?'

'Yes, absolutely.'

'In your opinion, is it likely she could have forgotten that she had any cat litter in your home last Sunday, when she asked you to stop on your way back to buy some?'

Niall took some moments before answering. 'No, no way.'

'You are certain?' Potting said. Playing him as if he were a well-hooked fish.

'Yes.'

Potting nodded calmly. 'During the search of your house last night, two large sacks of cat litter were found at the rear of a cupboard, in the utility room off your kitchen. Do you have any explanation for that?'

Paternoster stared back in numb silence for some moments, then he said, 'I'm sorry, I don't believe you.'

'Really?' Potting said in a commanding performance that brought a faint smile to Exton's face. 'So how do you explain that? Do you have any explanation for how they got there or are you saying the police planted two sacks of cat litter in your house?'

Paternoster looked dumbfounded. He stared at his solicitor, then up at the ceiling and around at the walls. 'Two sacks of litter?'

'Correct,' Potting said. 'Two large sacks of Tesco Lightweight ten-litre cat litter – several weeks' supply for a normal household cat.'

Paternoster ran his hands through his hair, looking genuinely confused. Then he said, 'All I can think of is that Eden must have bought the stuff in Tesco after I dropped her off and someone she met in the store drove her home. Or it was there all along but neither of us realized. That can happen, right? You forget you have something in the cupboard – it's not the strangest thing in the world, is it?'

Jon Exton looked down at a wad of notes in front of him, and leafed through a couple of pages. 'Niall, I have a copy of a print-out of all sacks of cat litter sold in the Tesco Holmbush store between midday, Sunday the first of September, and 4 p.m., when the store closed. There was just one sack purchased, at 1.34 p.m., a time you say you were at Parham House. There were no other sacks purchased that afternoon.'

'Their computer must be wrong,' he said flatly.

'Are you suggesting that the store may have had technical issues on last Sunday afternoon?' Potting asked. 'Their CCTV down, perhaps, and their inventory computer system also?'

Paternoster looked down at the floor. 'If there are two sacks of cat litter in our house, either my wife had a major memory lapse or, yes, the Tesco inventory system must be wrong.'

'Let's hypothesize for a moment,' Potting said. 'In the event that the Tesco inventory system was working fine, and your wife did not buy any there, are there any other stores where, between 3.15 p.m. and 4 p.m. when all stores close on a Sunday, your wife could have bought two sacks of cat litter? Of the particular brand that Tesco sell? Tesco Lightweight ten-litre sacks?'

'There are other stores in and around Brighton, yes,' he replied.

'Is any of this relevant?' Joseph Rattigan asked.

'Very,' Potting said. 'If you'll allow me to explain. Your client has told us he dropped his wife outside the Tesco Holmbush store at 3.15 p.m. on Sunday afternoon. That left her with a forty-five-minute window to find a means of transport and another Tesco store that stocked the same product. Our Outside Enquiry Team have established two other stores within a forty-five-minute radius that do. Neither of them sold any during that window of time.' He sat back.

'My wife must have got distracted, in that case,' Paternoster said lamely.

Exton said, 'I now want to speak to you about your visit to Parham House. You produced to the police a photograph that you said was taken on Sunday when you visited there with Eden. This would indicate that the two of you were together at Parham

House on Sunday the first of September. We have had the photograph analysed and we know it was taken a week earlier on Saturday the twenty-fourth of August, around the same time. What do you know about that?'

Paternoster replied angrily. 'I don't know what you're talking about, the photo was taken on Sunday, not the week before. I've already told you I was asleep in bed last Saturday afternoon, nowhere near Parham House. You've got all this wrong.'

Exton continued. 'If that photograph was taken a week before, that means there is nothing to suggest Eden was still alive on Sunday, particularly when no one has seen her, she didn't go to work and there's been no social media activity.'

'This is ludicrous, I didn't kill her. How do we know she's even dead?'

'There is a large kitchen knife missing from the set in your kitchen, Niall,' Exton said. 'Do you know where it is?'

'No, I don't, and you can't have looked properly – it must be in the house somewhere. If you're thinking I used it on Eden, you're mad.'

'Is that what you believe?' Exton asked. 'You've told us about the financial background to your marriage and your understanding that if something happened to your wife you would be the main beneficiary.'

'Like I said, we both made wills, leaving stuff to each other – isn't that normal?'

'Niall,' Potting said, 'as part of our investigation we've looked into your time in Australia – tell us about Karen Dale, your business partner there.'

'Oh God, you think I murdered her? Seriously? We went into business together and it was going really well until the accident – it was a well-documented and witnessed accident. I was devastated because she was a good friend. I decided to come home, partly to get away from the memory.'

'Came home with the money, then?' Potting pressed.

Niall shook his head in exasperation. 'Yet again you think I'm lying. Nothing I say is going to convince you I'm innocent, is it?'

'From the evidence we have so far, you were in a failing marriage and in a financial mess. We've found bloodstains in the house, a knife is missing and there were two bags of cat litter in the utility room. In addition, your wife's passport and rings were recovered and her mobile phone was found hidden under your bed. You seem to have lied about the photograph and your movements last week, and you have also lied about the barbecue. What else have you lied about?'

'This is just so much rubbish. I haven't done any of these things, you're just twisting it all around to suit your story.'

Ignoring him, Exton said, 'There is also evidence that the car was used in the early hours of Friday morning when Eden didn't turn up at work. We think you've killed her and have tried to cover your ground but have made mistakes.'

Niall jumped to his feet aggressively. 'I'm just not—'

'Please sit down,' Exton said. 'Please tell us calmly what you have to say about the evidence we've highlighted to you.'

He remained on his feet. 'I'm not talking to any of you lot any more, there's no point, you've made your minds up.'

'Please sit down,' Potting said. 'Otherwise we'll have you taken back to your cell until you've calmed down. We still want to talk about the hidden T-shirt and your kitchen that has been recently bleach cleaned.'

Paternoster sat back down reluctantly. For the rest of the interview he replied 'no comment' to every question.

Potting and Exton terminated the interview at 9.45 p.m.

55

Roy Grace lay awake for a long while, unable to sleep. Partly because of the uncomfortable camp beds they had been given, but also the nightmare unfolding in the hospital. Bruno was almost certainly brain dead.

His thoughts went back to the last conversation he'd had with his son as he'd dropped him off at school in the morning.

Did you know that the ancient Egyptians, when they died and were mummified, had their favourite pets killed and mummified, to go in the tomb with them?

Do you think they did that because they wanted company in their tombs or because they worried their pets would miss them too much – or that no one would take the same care of the animals they did?

It was 3 a.m. Somewhere out in the darkness of the city he heard a pitiful squealing sound. A creature in utter terror. It went on and on. An urban fox taking its prey. He'd heard that sound several times before and it always distressed him, but tonight he thought bitterly, *Well, at least there's two of our hens you won't be taking.*

He thought back to the conversation he'd had earlier, with Inspector James Biggs of the Road Policing Unit, and the statement he'd related from the witness who saw Bruno's accident.

What if he had done it deliberately to end all this? Did he kill the hens? Because in his confused mind he was worried they would miss him too much?

234

Trying to turn his thoughts back to the Paternosters, he eventually lapsed into sleep, awaking sometime later from a nightmare in which Cassian Pewe was holding two dead hens up from lengths of string and shouting at Grace that it was all his fault.

Finally, shortly before 5.30 a.m., after lying for ages, tossing from side to side, wide awake, he crept out of the bed and along to the bathroom where he was able to shower and clean his teeth. When he returned, Cleo was still asleep.

He kept thinking about Bruno's obsession, ever since he'd come to live with them, with serial killers. But what the hell did strangling his two favourite hens have to do with anything? Anticipating his death? Or what? Was it definitely Bruno or was it someone else who had killed the hens?

A dark thought struck him. Was that just practice, before something on a larger scale? Something human?

Just before 6 a.m., Cleo stirred and reached for her phone.

'I'm messaging Darren,' she said. 'Telling him I won't be in today. I'll stay with you here.'

'Are you sure?'

She kissed him. 'I'm sure.'

'Thanks,' he said. 'I think we're going to need each other.'

56

'You know what this is?' Niall Paternoster said, tired and ragged after a sleepless night on his narrow bunk and brutal pillow. 'It's a stitch-up.' He was alone with his solicitor in a small interview room at the custody centre.

'Stitch-up? By who? What do you mean, exactly?' Joseph Rattigan asked. 'Are you suggesting the police are fabricating evidence against you?'

Paternoster raised his hands in despair. 'I don't know what to think. It's just crazy – I mean – just *crazy.*'

'The evidence against you is not looking good, you'll have to admit,' Rattigan said, tapping his bundle of papers. 'I'm afraid.'

'Not looking good? You're my brief! I thought you were meant to be on my side?' He pointed at the door. 'If I've got that wrong then I need to find someone else.'

'Please calm down.'

'Oh, you don't want to lose your fee, is that it?'

'Would you like to know what my fee is?' the solicitor asked.

Paternoster shook his head. 'All you lawyers, you're fat cats, that's what I do know.'

'My Legal Aid fee is less than £150. That's for consulting with you yesterday, being present during the interviews with the detectives, meeting with you again today and meeting with you however many more times you need.'

'Are you serious?'

Rattigan nodded solemnly. 'That's the value the Legal Aid Agency place on us.'

Niall did a brief mental calculation. 'I would have earned more than you driving my cab.'

'You would, yes. Do you still want me to leave?'

Niall shrugged.

'So, you dropped your wife off in the car park of the Tesco Holmbush store at around 3.15 p.m. last Sunday and you've not seen her since?'

'Correct. Do you believe me?'

'If what you're telling me is the truth, then I believe you.'

Niall looked at him, face on. 'But you don't believe me, not really, do you?'

Rattigan sat up straight. 'I'm not permitted to tell lies, either to police officers or in court. If I act for a client who tells me they are guilty, then my job is to try to reduce their sentence to the best of my ability. If my client tells me they are innocent, then I have to do all I can to prevent them from being convicted. Does that help?'

Niall shrugged again. 'Am I right that they have to release me this morning or charge me?'

Rattigan shook his head. 'They can apply for a further exten-sion and, with the evidence they have, they would almost certainly get it.'

Niall Paternoster looked bleakly down at the table in front of him. 'You don't believe me, do you? I love Eden, why would I harm her?'

'If I had a pound for every client who'd said that, I would be a lot wealthier than I am, Mr Paternoster, believe me.'

'What do I have to do to convince you – and the police?'

'At this stage, we need proof that Eden is alive and well.'

'And how do you suggest I find that while I'm locked up in here?'

Rattigan nodded. 'As I said, the evidence against you isn't looking good, so far, from what I've heard. It seems to be both clear-cut and damning. But you're saying it's a stitch-up. I'd very much like to hear your reasons why you feel that in light of all we've heard.'

Niall Paternoster told him.

57

'Hello my name is Nadine' greeted Roy and Cleo Grace in the Intensive Care reception and led them straight back into the Relatives' Room. She deflected their questions on how Bruno had fared overnight with a pleasant but non-committal, 'Dr Williams, the Intensive Care consultant, will be briefing you on Bruno's condition. I can tell you that he had a comfortable night after surgery, with no dramatic changes.'

She offered, as before, to get them drinks and – as if it was Groundhog Day, Roy thought – returned a short while later with a glass of water for Cleo and a coffee with an extra shot of espresso for him, then left them alone.

Cleo squeezed his hand. 'Maybe he's improved overnight,' she said.

'Then he can go home and murder more hens?' Immediately, Grace, who was feeling tired and fractious, regretted saying that. 'I'm sorry, darling, that was insensitive. I didn't mean it that way, we don't even know for sure it was him.'

She gave him a look, a gentle, knowing smile that said, *Yes, sadly, we do.*

Five minutes later, as they entered the curtained-off area, Roy Grace reeled with shock at the sight of Bruno. He looked even smaller and even more dwarfed by all the technology around him than before. But it wasn't this which gripped his gullet and twisted his gut. It was the sight of the bolt sticking out of the top of the small boy's head. He had to pinch his mouth with his hand to stop himself from crying out.

From the corner of his eye, he could see that Cleo, who was used to the most terrible sights daily in her work, was shocked too.

The intracranial bolt the consultant had talked about was just exactly that. Somehow he'd been expecting something else – although he didn't know what. Just something tiny taped to his skull, perhaps. But not this.

It was a proper shiny bolt, with a nut, and a cable coming off it to a black box with a digital display. It was the kind of nut and bolt you might see on a radiator or a bicycle wheel.

The display was giving a reading of fifty-seven.

'Hi, Bruno,' he said, trying to sound cheerful. 'It's your dad and Cleo here.' He knelt and kissed his son's cold, clammy cheek, stroked his forehead and then held his right hand, which was limp and tiny. 'How are you doing, soldier?'

He studied Bruno's face intently, but there was no flicker of reaction, his eyes firmly closed. Just a faint motion of his chest as he breathed.

Glancing around, he saw that the doctor had quietly retreated, leaving them alone.

'Hello, darling,' Cleo said. She kissed Bruno too, and took his other hand and held it tightly. 'Your dad and I are here. Can you hear us?'

There was still no reaction.

They sat down in the two chairs beside the bed and talked to him for ten minutes, about school, about Humphrey, about how he was getting on with his computer games, and about the app TikTok.

After a while, the consultant returned. In a quiet voice he invited them to come out for a chat. They returned to the Relatives' Room and sat back down.

'This induced coma, he's still in it?' Grace asked.

Williams shook his head. 'No, we ended that early last night. We've removed all of his sedation and drugs that would keep him asleep. This is how he is. Did you feel he responded to you at all?'

Grace looked at Cleo. She shook her head.

'No, he didn't give any indication,' he said.

'I'm afraid, honestly, you're not going to get any reaction from him.' Williams paused. 'You obviously saw the intracranial bolt.'

'It's not a good look,' Grace said, attempting the merest trace of humour. 'Something out of *Frankenstein*.'

The consultant continued his sympathetic expression, nodding. 'It performs an essential task of telling us the pressure inside his skull. I know it was explained to you earlier, but the higher the pressure from the swelling brain, the more it crushes the vital brainstem. In a normal, healthy brain, a reading of five to fifteen millimetres of mercury is normal. We consider badly raised pressure to be above twenty-five.' He hesitated a moment, then said, 'As you may have seen, Bruno's current reading is fifty-seven, and it is rising steadily.'

Cleo was about to reply when the door opened and they were joined by two women in regular clothes. One was in her fifties with an earnest expression and reminded Roy of the actress Helena Bonham-Carter; the other, twenty years her junior, had a slim figure, a tangled frizz of bleached hair and striking features.

'Mr and Mrs Grace,' Williams said, a little stiffly, 'if I could introduce Imelda Bray, our resident counsellor, and Charlotte Elizabeth, who is our transplant coordinator.'

'Excuse me, who?' Grace said, looking confused.

'Ladies, I wasn't expecting you just yet,' Williams said testily, as if frustrated by the interruption.

They stood there looking a little embarrassed.

Williams turned back to Roy and Cleo. 'I'm afraid there has

been no improvement in your son's condition – in fact, it's got quite a lot worse.'

'Jesus, what? Does that mean he has any chance at all of pulling through?' Cleo asked desperately.

Williams looked as though his shoulders had suddenly become heavy. 'I'm so sorry.'

'What do you mean worse? I didn't think it could get any worse.' Roy choked out the words and looked at the two women. 'I'm sorry, who are you again? What are you doing here?'

'Can we go back to Bruno now?' Cleo pleaded.

'Just a moment, please. I need you both to focus on what I'm saying. I'm afraid we are not going to see any improvement in your son's condition. He is stable at this moment, but he is, sadly, brain dead and is not going to get better – there is no chance of recovery. I've had his diagnosis verified independently by one of my colleagues – a neurosurgeon – who has not been involved with your son's care. He has examined Bruno and has confirmed that your son is brain dead. We have run the tests and studied his CT and MRI. He has rising intracranial pressure and a Glasgow Coma Score of three, with no sedation.'

'Oh God, will you just let us see him?' Cleo asked, crying.

'Of course. But I just need to take a couple of minutes to explain who these two people are and what they can do for you.'

'Are there any other possible outcomes, Dr Williams?' Cleo asked through her tears.

'I'm afraid not. I can always get a third opinion, and arrange for further tests to be carried out as soon as possible, so you can have another professional diagnosis. I'd be quite happy to do that. But I don't feel it will give you the answers you are hoping for. I am sorry but I am certain that your son will not recover.' He smiled apologetically, gesturing helplessly with his arms. 'I wish so much that I could give you more positive news.'

'We do appreciate your honesty, it's just so hard to take this all in,' Roy said, his voice trembling. 'I can't believe that's it. Nothing anyone can do. Yesterday morning I dropped him at school alive and well, and now, nothing at all anyone can do.' He paused and wiped his eyes with the back of his hand, then looked at Cleo before turning back to the consultant. 'But I do trust your advice, we don't need another opinion and more tests. We know we're in a hopeless situation.'

Williams gestured to the two women still waiting near the door, and stood.

'I thought it would be helpful for you to meet Imelda and Charlotte at this stage, because we may have to move quite quickly.'

'Meaning what, exactly?' Grace asked.

Looking genuinely like he felt their agony, Williams said, 'If you were to consider organ donation, we would have to carry that out soon after a diagnosis of brain death.'

Neither Roy nor Cleo replied. They both just looked at him.

'If you decide it is something you might consider, Imelda is here to help you deal emotionally with that decision. Charlotte will be able to discuss with you the options regarding organ donation – and I want to stress on her behalf that you absolutely do not have to go down that route if you don't want to. But, I'm sorry to say, the reality is that our technology can only support Bruno for so long.'

Grace stared up at him, then at the faces of the two women. Then back at Williams. 'I thought you could keep someone on life support indefinitely?' Grace said, his voice sounding very small suddenly.

'Yes . . .' Cleo added, clinging on to any flicker of hope. 'You do hear stories of people in a persistent vegetative state, who make a recovery, sometimes months on, don't you? Sometimes years on? Mel, the nurse, said yesterday that she'd seen people make a complete recovery.'

'It does happen, yes,' the consultant said. 'But not in this case. We can keep his body technically alive for a while, but Bruno has zero brain activity. If we turn off his life support, he will quietly slip away as his vital organs fail and then we could not use his organs for donation.'

Grace looked up at all three of them and then at Cleo. She squeezed his hand again. 'So, Doctor – and Imelda and Charlotte – if this was your child, what would any of you do?'

They looked at each other. Then Charlotte Elizabeth said, 'Three people die in the UK every day waiting for a liver transplant, many of them children and teenagers. The figures are similar for heart and lung transplants. I've seen just how much parents of children in Bruno's situation are comforted by knowing their organs have been given to help other people live. But I would never morally blackmail anyone into agreeing to this. It is an immensely personal decision that you have to make.'

'It's really my husband's decision as Bruno is his son by his previous marriage,' Cleo said. 'But what organs would you want to take – harvest?'

'That would be entirely up to you,' Elizabeth said, looking at Grace. 'You could give a part donation, such as heart, lungs, liver and kidneys, or a more full donation, which would include his eyes to help blind people see again, skin, bones, bone marrow.'

'If,' Roy Grace said, 'and only *if* I agreed, would there be any difference to Bruno whether it was a partial or total donation?'

She gave him a deeply sympathetic and understanding smile. 'The only difference would be in the number of people he could help.'

'Is there the remotest danger Bruno would feel anything? Like, pain?'

Charlotte Elizabeth shook her head. 'It's a good question and let me assure you that Bruno would absolutely not feel any pain at all. I could explain the process, if you would like?'

Both of them nodded.

'The first thing to do is perform tests to confirm the brainstem is dead, which we have done. Then the transplant team would want to harvest the organs as soon as possible, after testing they are in good condition. It's a difficult job but they are really skilled at it. At the same time, the team would be starting to look for suitable recipients, who could be anywhere in Europe. Once they've been identified, whether within the UK or on the continent, teams would motorbike or fly in for the relevant parts and rush them to hospitals where the recipients would already be anaesthetized in anticipation of receiving the transplants.' She paused for a moment. 'It would be impossible to overstate just how grateful recipients – and their families – are.'

Grace looked at Cleo and saw the quiet encouragement in her eyes. Then he looked up at the coordinator. 'If I – we – consented, would we ever find out the names – identities – of the people – who received Bruno's organs?'

She nodded. 'We can't initially tell you any names – that depends on whether they or their families agree. But for sure you would be able to know just how many people – and where – were helped.'

Roy Grace nodded, trying to think clearly through his muzzy brain. 'I'm sorry if I'm being forgetful, but can we go through the situation again as I understand it?'

'We all understand how difficult this is for you. For anyone,' Elizabeth said.

'Thank you.' His eyes were misting. 'So, you need to keep Bruno on life support?'

'That's correct, yes,' Dr Williams said. 'We could maintain him on that for a short while.'

'But the moment you took him off the support mechanisms, he would pass away fairly quickly?'

'Correct, yes.'

'So all of you agree that Bruno is brain dead?' Cleo asked, partly resigned, partly disbelievingly, and partly just for it to sink in.

'I'm afraid so,' Williams said.

Grace sat in silence for some while, squeezing Cleo's hand and feeling the pressure back. Thinking.

Sandy had vanished twelve years ago. He'd never even known she was pregnant. The last time he had seen her, she was lying in a High Dependency Unit in hospital in Munich, severely injured after being struck by a taxi, plumbed into a forest of life support and monitoring equipment.

Then she had died and left him with his challenging son, who, until that point, he had never known existed.

And now Bruno was lying, similarly, in England, after being struck by a car.

How had it come to this?

He looked up at Dr Williams, at Imelda Bray, at Charlotte Elizabeth. Like himself, he knew, these people were professionals who dealt with situations like this on a daily business. Just as he himself regularly talked to the loved ones of people who had been brutally murdered, for these three, this was just routine, however much they dressed it up with sympathy and understanding. They could have been door-to-door salespeople, he thought darkly for a moment, trying to flog him a vacuum cleaner or an insurance policy or double glazing. They were trying to sell him the idea of transplants. His son's organs and other body parts.

Feeling a surge of sadness, which he swallowed back, he asked the consultant, 'Is it going to make any difference if we agree to it now or in a few hours' time – or tomorrow?'

'There is some time pressure for you to consent, Mr Grace. With every hour, as Bruno becomes increasingly unstable, the blood supply to his heart and kidneys, in particular, will lessen and the quality of the organs will suffer. Those organs only remain viable for transplant for a short while, so we always try to arrange transplants for as soon as possible.'

Williams looked at his two colleagues. They both nodded.

'So,' Grace said, 'if we were going to consent to organ dona-tion, the sooner we did it, the more valuable it would be?'

'That is correct,' the consultant said.

'Can we go back and see my son?' Grace asked.

'We'll take you to him now.'

'May I suggest one thing,' Grace said solemnly. 'Out of respect, we don't talk about Bruno's condition, or anything to do with possible transplants, in his presence.'

'Understood,' said Williams quietly.

58

They remained at Bruno's bedside for twenty minutes before returning to the Relatives' Room with Williams and the two women.

After some moments, Grace asked, 'If – if we did agree to donating some – or all – of Bruno's organs, what would the process be?'

The counsellor, Imelda Bray, then said, 'We would give you all the time you need to sit with him. What we could do is dress him in his favourite clothes: does he have a cap or a T-shirt, or something like that, which he loves to wear?'

Grace nodded. 'Yes, he does.'

'Perhaps you could bring them. We could play his favourite music. If he's into computer games, bring one in, something like his iPad, if he has one?'

'He does, yes,' Cleo said.

'Then the best thing for you,' the counsellor said, 'is to say goodbye to Bruno on the ward before we take him down to the operating theatre.'

'If we agreed to donate everything that could be helpful,' Grace asked, 'what would be left? What I – I mean – is that his mother is buried here in Brighton and I'd like to bury him near her grave. Will there be something to bury?'

'Of course, plenty, darling,' Cleo interjected.

Imelda Bray gave her a knowing smile. 'You're the expert on this.'

'But not on my stepson – I – couldn't . . .'

'Please don't worry, we wouldn't dream of that,' Charlotte Elizabeth said. 'Our own team are very experienced in this. You would be able to give him a proper funeral.'

Roy and Cleo sat in silence for a long while. Finally, Roy stood up and held out his hand to Cleo. Addressing the three hospital staff, he said, 'You've been incredibly helpful, I'm very grateful. If you could give my wife and I some time to go away and discuss this . . . who should I call when we've come to a decision later today?'

Imelda Bray gave him her card. 'It has my mobile number – you can reach me any time.'

He glanced at the card then pocketed it. 'Thank you, all of you, for being so helpful. I'll try to get back to you as quickly as I can.'

He turned away, so they couldn't see his tears, opened the door for Cleo and followed her out. As he did, his job phone rang.

59

'I'm just in the hospital,' Roy Grace answered. He looked at his watch: 6.45 a.m. 'I'll call you back, Glenn? And will you take the morning briefing?'

'Sure, but just call me whatever I'm doing and I'll answer.'

He turned to Cleo. 'Let's go get some air – find a cafe and get away from the hospital for an hour or so – there's nothing we can do here at the moment.'

She nodded. 'Yes, good idea. But call Glenn back if you need to, it might be urgent.'

'Nothing's as urgent as this. I'm thinking I'll go in once we've had some breakfast, to see the team, if you're OK with that. I'll make sure I'm back at the hospital with you straight afterwards,' he replied.

'Makes sense. I'll go back and stay with Bruno.'

They left the front entrance of the hospital and walked out into the early morning light. 'There's a decent place, I seem to remember, if we go down to St James's Street,' she said. 'Not far away.'

They walked in silence. All he wanted to focus on was the dilemma facing them over Bruno and what decision to make.

A few minutes later they entered a large modern-feeling cafe. Johnny Nash's 'I Can See Clearly Now' was playing quietly. Grace wished he could see clearly himself. Several people were seated having breakfast, but they spotted an empty sofa with a coffee table in a far corner, which looked out of earshot to anyone else. They ordered a double espresso for him and a peppermint tea for Cleo, then sat down next to each other on the squishy leather.

Cleo looked pale and very distressed. 'God, my darling,' she said quietly. 'I can't believe we are in this situation.'

'Yep.' He looked down at the oak table and said nothing more for some moments.

'What are your thoughts?' she asked.

'I – I guess I'm still trying to take it all in. This time yesterday I was dropping him at school. Now I—' He stopped and closed his eyes tightly, trying to hold it together.

'One double espresso and one mint tea,' a voice said brightly.

Grace heard Cleo thank the server. He opened his eyes again. 'Shit, there's a lot of stuff in life you don't have a clue about until it hits you, isn't there?'

She smiled back.

They sat for some while without speaking. Grace sipped his coffee, grateful for its strength.

'What I think,' Cleo said, 'is that you shouldn't rush a decision.'

'What about the organs deteriorating, or is that just their sales spiel?'

'I don't think a few hours will make any difference.'

'Is there anything we're missing? Is there something we could do? Some surgeon, somewhere in the world, who could save Bruno?' he asked.

'You know, darling, we're hoping for a miracle that isn't going to happen. If we lose the transplant window, no one gets helped by his death.'

'You're right.' He sipped some more coffee in silence.

'What I'm going to suggest, my love, is that because you've been thinking of nothing else throughout the night, you need some time away to think clearly. I've found so often in life that when we're in a difficult place, the right decision finds us. Make time to go for a walk on your own, and I'll do the same. Then let's speak around lunchtime and see where we're at.'

They hugged, with tears rolling down their cheeks.

As they left the cafe, Roy noticed a text had come in from Glenn Branson.

Bell me urgently, if you can, boss.

He hit the DI's speed-dial button.

'What's up, Glenn, what's urgent?'

'I thought you would want to know right away. There's been a credible sighting of Eden Paternoster.'

60

Roy Grace, curious about the reported sighting of Eden Paternoster, and highly dubious, was tempted to call back Glenn Branson as he drove to the Sussex Police HQ. But he wanted to use the twenty minutes or so the journey would take to keep his focus on Bruno.

His mind kept admonishing him shoutily. *Miracles happen – wait for one, Bruno will suddenly start speaking. He'll defy those bloody doctors.* Another voice in his head was telling him not to be stupid, that he needed to start grieving.

Somehow, when he arrived back at work, he managed to avoid bumping into anyone, entered the sanctuary of his office and shut the door. As soon as he sat at his desk, he called Glenn Branson.

A couple of minutes later, the DI was seated opposite him, in his favoured position with the chair the wrong way round. 'How is he?' he asked.

'I'll come to it, but I want to hear first about this credible sighting of Eden Paternoster.'

'You don't need to be here, Roy – you look terrible – I mean it in the nicest way.'

Grace nodded. 'I need to be, my mind is all over the place, I need something else to focus on, to keep sane, OK?'

Branson smiled. 'Understood,' he said gently. 'I've actually got quite a bit more to report. But yeah, this sighting: a prison officer, who works at Parkhurst in the Isle of Wight, saw the article and Eden Paternoster's photo in the *West Sussex Gazette*. She is positive she saw Eden Paternoster on the Isle of Wight Hovercraft ferry on the evening of Sunday September the first.'

Grace frowned. 'The same day Eden's husband claimed he'd dropped her at the Tesco store and she'd vanished? Which Aiden Gilbert has discredited?'

'The same day, boss, yes. But what makes this sighting particularly interesting is that Eden Paternoster has Isle of Wight family connections – her grandfather worked in a hotel in Seaview and she has a number of cousins there.'

Grace had spent several childhood holidays on the Isle of Wight. A few miles south of the coast of Hampshire, it was the second smallest county in England, with a population of around 140,000. One of its claims to fame was that it housed Parkhurst prison, once one of the country's highest-security jails, which had hosted, at various times, the Yorkshire Ripper Peter Sutcliffe, the Kray Twins and Moors Murderer Ian Brady among many of the nation's most notorious and repellent criminals. But in recent years, he recalled, following a number of high-profile escapes, it had been downgraded from a Category A to a B.

'OK,' Grace said. 'What information can you get from the Isle of Wight Hovertravel company? Do we have a name the ticket was booked under?'

Branson shook his head. 'They don't take names – it's only an eight-minute ride. I've spoken to the boss, Neil Chapman, a very helpful man. You can buy tickets for cash at the terminal or online or by card. I've sent DC Hall down there to have a trawl through the online name and credit-card bookings for Sunday afternoon and evening, then he's going over to the island to talk to the prison officer.'

'Tell him to bring back a tube of Alum Bay sand,' Grace said.

Branson frowned. 'Alan Bay?'

'*Alum* Bay. Used to love it as a kid – it's famous for its cliffs of multicoloured sand. You can buy tubes of it, all different colours.'

Branson gave Grace a strange look. 'How many tubes do you want, boss?'

'Just reminiscing, I always wanted to take Bruno there—' He tailed off.

'Ah, right. OK.'

'Get all the names of Eden Paternoster's relatives on the Isle of Wight. And there must be CCTV?' Grace said, snapping back into professional mode.

'There is, yes. They have it at the hovercraft terminal in Southsea and at Ryde on the Isle of Wight. There are also onboard cameras.'

'Have you got the footage?'

Branson shook his head. 'Not yet, thanks to GDPR.'

General Data Protection Regulation was one of the banes of modern life that even the police, regardless of the urgency of an enquiry, had to abide by.

'I've done the application for the DP2 form to the Hovertravel GDPR officer. I'm hoping to hear back from them shortly. The good news is that they keep all CCTV for thirty days. So long as we don't get a jobsworth, they'll burn off a copy to a USB stick, which Kevin Hall can bring back.'

Grace thought for some moments, absorbing this. 'As soon as you get it, I'd like to see it.'

'And maybe Haydn Kelly?' Branson said.

Kelly was the pioneer of Forensic Gait Analysis, who Grace used regularly when he was available to help confirm or deny a suspect from the way they walked.

'Yes, if the facial images aren't clear enough and if there's any footage of her walking,' Grace said. 'Before then, are we going to review the footage of Niall Paternoster's interviews with Jon and Norman?'

'Yes.' Branson glanced at his watch. 'We've another starting shortly, we can see that first.'

'What are the other developments? You said you had quite a bit more to report?'

'I do, and this is where it gets more complex. The Dive Team have only started this morning. But the Search Team have been in Ashdown Forest since yesterday evening. They've found a number of items of bloodstained clothing in what looks like a hastily dug grave close to where the trainer and the kitchen knife – a match to the set in the Paternosters' kitchen – were found. But no body parts.'

'You've sent all the items for DNA analysis?'

'They're at the lab now.'

Grace considered this. 'Just clothing. No body parts?'

'No, but there's something else I don't think I've updated you on, boss, from last night's briefing, which might be very significant. Especially regarding the knife. Niall Paternoster started out in life, after school, as a butcher's assistant.'

Grace stared at him, thinking hard. 'That *might* be very significant.'

'Indeed.'

'In woodlands, in particular, dismembered body parts can be carried off by predators within a very short time. Foxes, badgers, birds of prey – and all the rodents. That could explain why the team hasn't found anything yet, potentially five days after it was left there.'

'But what about the head, boss?'

'I'll put good money on that being in the harbour,' Grace said. 'Unless it's in the Isle of Wight and walking around, still attached to her body. We need to get that footage from the hovercraft.'

'Sometime today, hopefully.'

'Good.'

Branson glanced at his watch. 'We should go over to the custody centre and watch this morning's interview with Paternoster. Are you OK to meet up?'

'Sure.'

61

As they walked along the corridor, Branson asked, 'So, what news on Bruno? How's he doing?'

Grace was silent for a moment, then said quietly, 'Not great, Glenn, not great at all.'

A young DC walking past the other way greeted them with a 'Good morning, sir, good morning, boss.'

They both acknowledged her politely. Then Grace said, still quietly, 'He's brain dead, there's nothing they can do. It absolutely breaks me.'

Branson stopped. Grace stopped too. 'What?'

Grace nodded.

'That's terrible.' Branson shook his head and looked at him balefully. 'What – what's the prognosis – what do the medics say?'

'They're asking Cleo and me if we would consider organ donation.'

Branson's eyes widened. 'Isn't there a chance he could recover?'

'No. I mean – from what they say – there's no way he will.'

'You don't have to make any decisions immediately, do you, boss? People can stay in that state for a long time. Wasn't there a case in the papers recently of a teenage girl who'd been in a coma for three years after a car accident and then recovered completely?'

'It's different with Bruno. We've had it all explained to us –

258

about how his brain is swelling – *coning*, they call it – and crushing his brainstem. His chances of recovery are zero, and if we don't make a decision quickly, his most valuable organs for transplant will atrophy.'

Glenn put his huge hand around Roy's shoulder and squeezed. 'Just know I'm here for you any time you want to talk. If you'd rather go back to the hospital now, to be with him, please do that.'

'I appreciate it, thanks, but I'm coming with you to see this interview. It's helpful for me to be away from the hospital at the moment . . . we all cope differently.'

As they walked on, around a corner, they saw Norman Potting and Jon Exton standing, conferring, outside the interview room. The door was closed.

'Sir, chief,' Potting said, acknowledging them. Exton turned and saw them, too.

'All set?' Grace asked quietly.

Exton jerked his head towards the door. 'Paternoster's in there with his brief, boss,' he replied, equally quietly.

Somehow mustering a smile, Grace said, 'Remember, confirm the lie then hit with the truth.'

'Absolutely, chief,' Potting said. He gave a thin smile back.

Two minutes later, Grace and Branson sat next to each other in the windowless cubicle adjoining the interview room, watching the CCTV monitor on the wall.

Inside the room they saw Niall Paternoster and his solicitor on one side of the table, and Exton and Potting on the opposite side. Paternoster, with two days' growth of stubble, looked pallid from lack of sleep.

'The time is 8.17, Wednesday, September the fourth,' Exton announced. 'DS Exton and DS Potting interviewing Niall Paternoster in the presence of his solicitor, Joseph Rattigan. This interview is being recorded onto a secure digital network.'

They all introduced themselves. Exton recapped on the interview from the previous evening and then he sat back. The two detectives looked at Niall for a few seconds. 'Is there anything you'd like to add to last night?' Potting asked.

'I've got no comment to make.'

'According to your phone, on Sunday the first at 5.30 p.m. you met up with someone. Who was that person? Your girlfriend?' Potting asked.

Niall: 'No comment.'

'Your phone and recent phone records have been examined by our investigation team,' Potting continued. 'At 3.23 p.m. on Sunday afternoon a text was sent from your phone, the hard copy of which I have here.'

Joseph Rattigan indicated he wanted to see it, and Potting passed it across to him. Immediately an increasingly agitated Niall, his face flushed, leaned over to look at it. Then he whispered to his solicitor, who nodded back.

'On the advice of my solicitor I have no comment to make.' He shifted uncomfortably in his seat; his face was pale and he was looking extremely anxious.

'Niall, could the reason you did not see your wife perhaps be because you were preoccupied with your mobile phone, sending a text?' Potting quizzed.

Paternoster jerked as if he'd had a small electric shock.

The solicitor frowned. This was clearly news to him. 'Does this have anything to do with Mrs Paternoster's disappearance?' He looked at each detective in turn.

Potting replied, 'Of course it does, we are trying to establish what your client was doing on Sunday afternoon when he alleges his wife went missing.' He turned to address Niall. 'It appears to me that you were communicating by text on at least two occasions on Sunday afternoon and chose, when you gave your account, not to tell us. Who is that person you were communicating with?'

'No comment.'

Exton continued to press Paternoster. 'Niall, the sent text message at 3.23 p.m. that you have a copy of reads, "See you 5.30 XXXX". It was sent to an unregistered pay-as-you-go phone, approximately five minutes after you claim your wife left the car to go into the Tesco store. Can you tell us who the intended recipient was?'

Niall Paternoster turned to his solicitor, who shook his head.

'No comment,' Paternoster said.

Exton held up another sheet of printout, which he passed across the table. 'This contains triangulation plots obtained from the two phone companies to which your phone and the anonymous phone were registered. When you sent that text, the location of the anonymous phone was in one of a number of houses in Barrowfield Drive, Hove. At 5.30 p.m. your phone and the anonymous phone had both moved to a point where they came together at a location three miles to the west of Brighton. This location has been identified as the vicinity of the car park of the Devil's Dyke beauty spot. It indicates you had a rendezvous with the owner of the anonymous phone at this location. Can you tell us anything about this?'

Paternoster, looking very concerned now, again turned to his solicitor, who shook his head once more.

'No, look, I've told you I loved Eden. That's all I'm saying.'

Potting interjected. 'Niall, I'd like to remind you that you are under caution. That means, as I'm sure your solicitor has explained to you, that anything you say may be admissible in court. "No comment" does not go down well with juries and we are inviting you to provide information to confirm what you are telling us about your wife's disappearance.'

* * *

In the observation cubicle, Grace glanced at Branson. Clearly, the surprise phone evidence had rattled the solicitor.

Whispering, although he didn't need to, Branson said, 'Did you pick up on that, boss? I *loved* Eden.'

Grace nodded tersely. 'Freudian slip?'

'Quite a slip, wouldn't you say?' Branson added, then was silent for a moment. 'But people get het up in interviews – they can be pretty intimidating. Can't always take everything at face value. Yet there's something else he said in a previous interview that's significant and which maybe backs up this slip. He said, *Do you people seriously think I would have killed the gravy train when I was down on my luck?* Gravy train. That's a pretty strange remark, don't you think?'

'Very,' said Grace. 'Like implying, *I love my wife because she brings in the money.* Not because she's anything else. Not because he loves her to bits. She's just his cash cow – for want of a better expression. And now we see he had a get-together up on Devil's Dyke later that Sunday. What kind of person are you going to meet at a local beauty spot late afternoon? Your accountant?'

Branson grinned.

'There's definitely something going on here. Speak to Chris Gee and get his team to search through all the paperwork in the house and see if he can find Eden Paternoster's will – Niall said they'd both made one. That might be revealing. I've already given Emily Denyer the action of getting us a full report on their finances. I'd like to know what he might have to gain by Eden's death.'

In the interview room, Exton said, 'Last night we told you about the evidence we have discovered that suggests you may have harmed your wife. A central part of your explanation was your visit to Tesco for cat litter, but we now know you didn't need any cat litter. Further, and perhaps more significantly, nobody in

Tesco saw your wife there to corroborate your story. We have now made you aware that we know about your contact that same afternoon with an unknown person. Why don't you tell us the truth?'

'No comment,' Niall said flatly. 'I'm not answering any more of your questions.'

Rattigan said to the detectives, 'Gentlemen, it is now 8.40 a.m. You have until 9.45 a.m. to either charge or release my client.'

'Thank you,' Norman Potting replied politely. 'We have until 9.47 a.m., actually, but let's not split hairs. Interview terminated at 8.40 a.m.' He reached forward.

The monitor went blank and silent.

62

In the observation cubicle, Glenn Branson asked, 'How are you reading Paternoster's body language?'

'Extremely uncomfortable,' Roy Grace replied. 'You?'

'Copy, boss.'

Grace smiled. 'You've been watching too much American TV.'

'Would you rather I said "well dodgy"?'

Grace smiled thinly, then fell silent.

After some moments, Branson said, 'So, what do we think?'

There was no reply.

He glanced round. Grace was crying.

Branson waited patiently in silence.

After a couple of minutes, Grace sniffed, wiped his eyes with his handkerchief and apologized.

'You don't have to apologize for anything. I wish I could do something, say something. I can't begin to think what you're going through – I can feel some of your pain, but not the enormity of what you're facing.'

'What would you do?'

'Me?'

'Yes, in my situation. Hang on for a miracle, which isn't going to happen, if the medics are right? Give him the dignity of keeping his body intact for his funeral? Or—' He fell silent again.

'Or donate his organs?' Branson prompted.

'Yes.'

Branson took a few moments before replying. 'If we're dismissing the possibility of his ever recovering?'

'We are.'

He nodded. 'You've already said that the longer you leave it to make a decision, the more likely it is that some of the major organs won't be viable for donation, if I understood it?'

'Yes, correct.'

'OK, well, once someone's dead, their soul – if we have one – departs elsewhere, leaving behind an empty shell. That's how I see it. The shell just rots away. If you could have the knowledge that his death has helped some others to live, and some others to have a better quality of life, wouldn't that at least make some small sense of what's happened – and give you and Cleo the knowledge that you've done a good thing?'

Grace gave a slight smile which was layered with sadness. 'I appreciate it, you're pretty much echoing what Cleo said to me earlier. Yes, you're right.'

'But, ultimately, it's only you and Cleo who can make the decision, and it has to feel right.'

'Thanks, it is feeling right.'

'Why don't you go now and deal with it – that's far more important than what's going on here, I can handle this.'

'I will, but another fifteen or twenty minutes isn't going to make a difference. So let's just review the footage from last night, OK?' He spoke firmly, as if he'd now made up his mind and his decision had freed him.

'OK.'

'Norman and Jon did a good job, but—' He hesitated.

After some moments, Branson prompted, 'But?'

'Let's look at it now.'

Branson pressed the control buttons and the interview from the evening before began to replay. Both of them watched it,

Grace particularly intently. Suddenly, he called out, 'Stop!'

Obediently, the DI hit the pause button.

'Replay that and watch Paternoster's reaction,' Grace said.

Moments later, the segment played again.

Norman Potting was speaking. 'During the search of your house last night, two large sacks of cat litter were found at the rear of a cupboard, in the utility room off your kitchen. Do you have any explanation for that?'

Niall Paternoster stared back in silence for some seconds, then he said, 'I'm sorry, I don't believe you.'

'Pause it again!' Grace said.

The image froze.

'He's either a damned good actor,' Grace said, 'or he's telling the truth.'

'And we know he's not telling the truth.'

Grace looked pensive. 'Roll it on.'

Norman Potting was speaking again. 'Do you have any explanation for how they got there, or are you saying the police planted two sacks of cat litter in your house?'

Paternoster looked at his solicitor, then up at the ceiling and around at the walls. 'Two sacks of litter?'

'Correct,' Potting said. 'Two large sacks of Tesco Lightweight ten-litre cat litter – several weeks' supply for a normal household cat.'

Paternoster ran his hands through his hair. Then he said, 'All I can think of is that Eden must have bought the stuff in Tesco after I dropped her off, and someone she met in the store drove her home.'

'Pause it again,' Grace said.

Branson hit the button, freezing the image again, and looked at Grace, then at the screen.

'He's holding eye contact,' Grace said. 'His blink rate is steady; he's not covering his mouth or throat.' He shrugged. 'None of these things is conclusive, he could just be a bloody good actor. If he had been planning to murder her for some while, he might have looked up on the internet all the signs of a liar, knowing that when the police interviewed him, they'd be looking at his body language.'

'So you're saying he's either innocent – or smarter than we're giving him credit for, boss?'

'Bearing in mind his business partner vanished overboard while they were sailing off Perth in Western Australia, do we have a repeat pattern here?'

'Want me to fly out to Perth to talk to the police there?'

'Sure, ask Cassian Pewe to sanction your ticket. Tell him you need to fly Business or maybe even First so you're fresh when you arrive.'

Branson looked at him, for a moment wondering if he was being serious, then wised up. 'Maybe you should ask him on my behalf, boss?'

Grace pointed to his neck with his forefinger. 'You know what? I prefer to keep this attached to my head.'

Branson smiled. 'So we have a potential history here of our friend, Paternoster, dispatching someone with no trace – you think?'

'I'm suggesting the mantra of all experienced financial investigators, Glenn. *Follow the money.*'

Branson nodded. 'OK, so what we know is that Niall Paternoster is struggling, with a failed business, and making a small living as a taxi journeyman, driving a mate's taxi during unsociable hours. After returning to the UK from Australia he met, charmed and married Eden, who – maybe coincidentally – has a house worth over half a million quid, plus a fair stash of cash. And now he's offed her? Am I on the right track?'

Grace nodded. 'That's how the evidence is looking.'

'Apart from his body language, boss?'

'Apart from that – which we know is only an indication,' he replied, then continued, 'We made the decision as part of our interview strategy not to ask him specific questions about what has been found at Ashdown Forest. They're still searching there and we're waiting for DNA results. He already said in interview that he didn't leave the house in the early hours of Friday morning, but we know the BMW was at the forest. The camera images don't help us as to who was driving. We can ask him questions in due course and he may not pick up about the police search activity there. You never know, he may return to that area and with any luck our people will be behind him. So let's summarize what we have so far in addition to that evidence.'

'OK,' Branson said. 'Three key issues.' He raised a finger in the air. 'First, we've established he may be lying about the cat litter and the photograph.' He added a second finger. 'The forensics against him at the house don't look good.' He raised a third. 'He has a motive, but now we have the potential sighting of Eden, his wife, on the Isle of Wight hovercraft.'

'Your priority,' Grace said, 'is that sighting. Throw everything at it.'

'We always get loads of sightings of mispers, and 99.9 per cent of the time they turn out to be wrong,' Branson said.

'I'd be happier if we'd seen Paternoster clearly lying just now, but we didn't. It would help us move forward one way or the other to either verify or dismiss that sighting PDQ.'

'Understood.'

'In the meantime, see if we can organize a surveillance team. Regardless of the possible sighting, I want Paternoster watched from the moment we release him. Killers often behave suspiciously or return to the deposition site, either out of some macabre curiosity or to make sure the site hasn't been disturbed.'

'Understood and will try.'

There were only two Surveillance Teams these days, and they

worked with both Sussex and Surrey police forces. And they were kept busy. Both detectives knew they'd be lucky to get one.

Grace stood up. 'OK, I'm going to go out to my car, for privacy, and call Cleo. I think I'm ready.'

Branson took his hand in his and crushed it. 'Good luck, mate. I'm thinking of you all.'

Grace turned away, unable to face him, not wanting him to see his tears again.

63

Wednesday 4 September

Niall Paternoster sat in the front passenger seat of the Skoda Superb taxi owned by his pal, Mark Tuckwell, as they drove out through the gates of the Brighton custody centre. It was 11.15 a.m.

'Been a bad boy, have you?' Tuckwell, a relaxed, good-natured man of thirty-five, jested.

'That's not funny – I don't know what's going on. They reckon I've offed Eden.'

'And have you?'

'Do I look like a murderer?'

Tuckwell was nonplussed. 'Did Dr Harold Shipman or Ted Bundy?'

'Thanks a lot, mate. Thought I might count on you for a bit of sympathy.'

'Not if I'm driving a fugitive from justice!'

'You are not driving a bloody fugitive.'

'So what's happened, talk me through it.' Tuckwell grinned. 'What weapon did you use?'

'I'm not in a mood for joking, really I'm not, all right? Two sleepless nights in a cell – Jesus – I'm not surprised people confess to shit they haven't done, just to get it over with. So, OK, right, Sunday we go out for a drive – Eden and me – we both like going to stately homes – National Trust places, that kind of thing. It's something to do – and something to dream about, right?'

'Dream about their heating bills and the cost of their roof repairs, you mean?'

Paternoster tutted. 'We actually have the vision to look beyond that. When we go to these places, I'm looking for ideas, inspiration, right? I want inspiration for the kind of house I'm going to buy when my new business comes good and my first million rolls in.'

'So until then, when are you going to open 507 Nevill Road to the public? Will you be serving cream teas? What attractions will you have in the grounds – a safari park?'

'Haha.'

Paternoster stared for some moments through the windscreen, appreciating his freedom; appreciating being away from the confines and tedium of his cell and from feeling, in just that brief time, almost immediately institutionalized. It was a fine day. He'd barely seen any daylight since Monday.

'You've got a nice back garden – maybe make it a dinosaur theme park?'

'Will you stop this? I'm in serious crap, Mark, OK? I need your wisdom, not your rubbish humour. Seriously. *Please?*'

Tuckwell braked as they joined the rear of a queue of traffic on the slip road. He shook his head. 'Tell you what, how long have we known each other?'

'Since Year Ten?'

'Pretty much – so – over twenty years. In all that time, all you've ever done is dream, you're always wanting something more, something better than you have.'

'What's wrong with that?'

'What's wrong is you don't know when to stop, Niall. You've got a lovely wife in Eden, but I'm guessing she's not enough; you've got a nice house – for a lot of people it would be a dream home – but you want something way bigger.' He paused. 'You know what I learned a long time ago?'

'What?'

'Success isn't about wanting what you don't have, it's wanting what you *do* have.'

'Yeah, well, obviously I'm not a success, yet. So, yeah, you're lucky, you have the perfect life – a woman you love, and a great kid. Good for you. Do you want me to tell you what's happened or are you going to carry on bloody lecturing me?'

'I'm listening.'

'So me and Eden went last Sunday to Parham House. We had a nice time there, wandering around, and a good lunch in their cafeteria. I wanted to get back to watch the Belgian Grand Prix and do a bike ride and she starts going on about needing to pick up some cat litter that I'd forgotten to buy the day before.'

'Had you?'

'Maybe, but hear me out.'

Tuckwell nodded.

'So, Eden's very specific, she wants to go to the Tesco Holmbush, because they stock the brand the stupid cat likes – I dunno – maybe it's soft on its bum or something.'

'Or it's the cheapest,' his friend suggested, subtly reminding him of his parlous finances. But the dig went over his head.

'Whatever, she promises to be only a few minutes. But I know what happens when Eden goes into a store – she's like, *Oh, I'll get some of this while I'm here*, and, *Oh, maybe we need more loo roll and we only have two bananas left and, oh, better get some more yoghurt and butter while I'm here*, and, *Oh, we're running low on tomatoes and cat food and* – and all the bloody rest, right? Cheryl's the same, right?'

'Aren't we all when we go into a store?' Tuckwell said pragmatically. 'Don't stereotype!'

'Not me, I'm in, gottit, out – *boom*! Anyhow, so Sunday afternoon, I sit in the car, she swears blind she'll be back in five minutes – and I reckon on turning that into fifteen. So twenty pass. Then twenty-five. The Grand Prix's about to finish and the store's about to close and I'm annoyed, so I go in to find her – and she's not there. Like, gone.'

'Walking back to your car?' Tuckwell suggested.

Paternoster shook his head. 'I look everywhere for her and there's no sign. I call and text her – no response. I WhatsApp her, no reply. She'd done this once before, after we'd had a row, she bumped into a friend in a store and got her to drive her home. So eventually I drive home and she's not there. Next morning, she's still not home – I call the police. They come round to the house and I can see immediately they don't believe me. The next thing, I've got some bigwig detective and his flunkey from Major Crime rocking up.' He fell silent.

'And?' Tuckwell prompted.

'I could tell from the way they looked at me and the questions they asked, they think I've done something. They treat me like I'm lying. I'm going mad with worry, but they don't seem to see that. I looked again on all her social media accounts   nothing. Next thing, early Monday evening an entire posse rocks up. I'm arrested on suspicion of murder and our house is crawling with cops. God knows what her mother said to them, especially with her track record – she loathes me, always has, but anyhow, I'm told all kinds of rubbish the next day – Eden's engagement and wedding rings and her passport have all been found, hidden. And that there's two sacks of bloody cat litter in the house.'

'Two *sacks* of cat litter?'

'Yeah, big ones.'

Tuckwell frowned.

'None of it makes any sense. I mean, I can't get my head round what's happened. People don't just vanish. What has happened to her? Did someone smack her over the head and drag her into a van or something as she walked across the car park? Or am I going crazy? I'm starting to wonder if I've got like, what do they call it – selective amnesia – or something? Seriously, I'm lying on my bunk in that cell, staring at the walls, wondering if there's some great big blank in my mind. Did I imagine dropping her at Tesco? Did I do something to her that I don't remember? Hide her rings and passport?'

'Sounds more plausible than any other scenario.'

'You're really not being much help,' Paternoster said.

'OK, another thought. Has it occurred to you Eden might have vanished to teach you a lesson?' Tuckwell suggested.

'A lesson? About what? Why?'

As they finally reached the roundabout and drove up to the A27 on the far side, Mark Tuckwell gave him a sideways glance.

'Wakey-wakey! Are you missing anything here? A certain lady?'

Paternoster blushed. 'What's that got to do with anything?'

Another glance. 'Did you climb out from under a rock, Niall?'

'Meaning what?'

'Eden's gone missing. The spouse or partner is always a prime suspect if you watch any crime show. And I read in the papers long ago that eighty per cent of all murders are committed by a spouse or immediate member of the family. The police aren't stupid – it's not going to take them long to connect you and your mistress.'

'Girlfriend.'

Tuckwell nodded. 'Is she wealthy?'

'No, but she does all right.'

They were only a few minutes away from his house now.

'Well, isn't there a motive right there? You're having an affair with a woman, neither of you have loads of money. Your wife owns the nice house you live in and has independent wealth. Suddenly she disappears. And you have got a bit of a temper on you, mate. Remember decking me when you were pissed that night at the Deep Sea Anglers?'

'You're not seriously suggesting I murdered Eden?'

'No, of course not, but where is she?'

'Jesus! Are you my friend or what? Are you hearing me? I don't bloody know.'

'So how do you think it looks to the police, Niall? You're having an affair. They can't find any evidence to back up your story that she went into the store – what do you expect them to think?'

'Some friend you are, thanks a million.'

'People don't just disappear.'

'No? Well, she has – into thin air. What game is she playing with me?'

'You had another row.'

'It wasn't a row – it was just – we were just bickering.'

'About what?'

'Cat litter.'

Mark Tuckwell grinned. 'So she'd done a runner on you because you'd argued about cat litter? If you need any, we can give you some.'

'According to the police, we have plenty. I never saw it. How could she have forgotten she'd got two sacks of the stuff?'

'Cheryl often makes me pick up stuff she's forgotten she already has. That's hardly grounds to arrest you on suspicion of murder.'

'Oh, great, finally you're actually taking my side?'

'Sure I am, I don't think you've murdered her.'

'Hallelujah!'

Tuckwell shook his head. 'No, you wouldn't murder her because you know you're too dumb to ever get away with it. You've probably got her chained up underground somewhere.'

Paternoster glared at his friend indignantly. 'I don't know why I like you.'

'Because I tell you the truth that you don't want to hear.'

They were approaching his house. As he'd been told upon his

release, Niall Paternoster saw a line of crime scene tape fluttering above the pavement in front of it and a white van, signed CRIME SCENE INVESTIGATION UNIT, parked a short way down the road. A bored-looking uniformed police officer stood on the pavement.

Tuckwell said frivolously, 'They've laid on a welcome home party for you.'

'Pull up outside,' Paternoster said. 'I'm going to find out when they'll be finished.'

Obediently, but with a cynical expression, Mark Tuckwell halted right in front of the house. Paternoster jumped out and approached the officer.

'Hi, this is my home.'

'I'm afraid you can't go in, sir,' she said.

'I know that – when are you going to be finished?'

She shook her head. 'This is a crime scene.'

A bright flash caught his eye, and he noticed for the first time two photographers, standing near, snapping him.

'Oi, get lost!' he yelled at them, then turned back to the officer. 'I know I can't go in but I need a change of clothes.'

'If you need anything from the house, sir, like wash things and clothes, give me a list and I'll ask if someone can bring them to you.'

'Yes, and where do I sleep? In a shop doorway?'

'Perhaps with relatives or friends – or in a hotel, sir.'

'Great, I'll get a suite at the Grand and charge it to Sussex Police, shall I?'

'I'm afraid I can't answer that.'

'No, of course you can't.'

'What I can tell you, sir, is we should be finished by tomorrow.'

There were more flashes. He shielded his face, but well aware it was far too late. Turning, he hurried back to the taxi and jumped in.

'Unbelievable!' he said. 'Go! Drive!'

'Anywhere in particular?'

'Just drive.'

'No problem,' Mark Tuckwell said. 'Your shout – I've kept the meter running.'

'You what?' Paternoster looked at the dash and saw, to his astonishment, that it was.

£24.30 was clocked up.

'Tell me you're joking?'

As he drove away, Tuckwell said, 'I suppose you'll be wanting to add one night's board and lodging to your bill? Full English included? Egg, sausage, bacon, black pudding and fried bread?'

'Eden doesn't approve of full Englishes. She calls them *heart attacks on a plate.*'

'You sure you're going to need to worry about her approval any more?' Tuckwell said with a strange expression, which Niall Paternoster did not like. His friend had always seen through him.

'Funny,' he said, but it came out flat.

'In case you do, Cheryl does a vegetarian option – it's very popular.'

Paternoster didn't respond.

64

Roy and Cleo sat once more in the Relatives' Room outside the ICU. An empty carrier bag was on the floor at Cleo's feet. As suggested by Imelda Bray, they'd brought from home Bruno's favourite clothes, which the counsellor had collected from them when they'd arrived.

Grace was reading through the consent forms, on the table in front of him. He paused to glance at his watch. Coming up to 1 p.m. Ordinarily, he might have been thinking about lunch, but he had no appetite. He sipped a plastic beaker of water someone had brought him, his mind churning, despite his decision. Questioning it. He held his personal phone in his hand, googling once again the words *coma*, and then *brain death*.

'You're torturing yourself, darling,' Cleo said.

She was doing exactly the same on her phone. She had it in her hand now.

'And you're not?'

She shook her head. 'I don't want this to be something that comes back repeatedly to haunt us. I don't want either of us to wake up tonight, or any other night, and say, *What if*? That's all.'

'I guess – I'm the same.'

'So.' She turned and looked at him. 'Your entire working life revolves around evidence that ultimately has to be presented in a court of law. Would it help to role-play now?'

'How do you mean?'

'Let's say you are Bruno's lawyer, fighting me, the Crown Prosecutor. You're arguing the case against donating Bruno's organs. You already know my opening argument.'

'That there is no chance, not the slightest chance, of Bruno coming back from where he is?'

'Yes.'

Grace stared at her for some moments. He tried hard to return with a cogent argument. 'People say medicine is a very inexact science,' he came up with lamely. 'There is always the possibility of a misdiagnosis.'

'From what you know, Detective Superintendent Grace, what percentage chance would you put on Bruno making a recovery? One hundred per cent? Fifty per cent? Twenty-five per cent? One per cent? Less than one per cent?'

He was silent for a long while. 'Less than one per cent,' he said finally.

'During the course of your career so far, how many suspects have you let go on the balance of a less than one per cent probability that they were innocent?'

For the first time in several hours he smiled, albeit bleakly.

At that moment the door opened and Imelda Bray, accompanied by the transplant coordinator, Charlotte Elizabeth, came in.

'How are you both feeling?' Imelda Bray asked.

Grace looked up at her. 'Pretty awful,' he said, picking up the pen that had accompanied the forms, signing and dating them. He handed them to the coordinator. 'I think I've signed everywhere you indicated.'

She checked them through briefly. 'Yes, you have, thank you.'

The counsellor said gently, 'Let's try to focus now not on your loss, but on all the good your generous decision will give. You'll need to grieve and we are here to provide you with all the help and support you will need. For now, would you like to come in and say goodbye to Bruno?'

Grace turned to Cleo for confirmation. She gave it with a single nod and a grim smile.

They both stood up.

65

A few minutes later, feeling like his shoes had lead soles, Roy walked with Cleo through into the Intensive Care Unit. They followed Bray and Elizabeth along past three occupied beds and stopped at the curtains surrounding Bruno. They were ushered in and heard the swish of fabric closing behind them.

Grace stared down at his son, who was looking tinier than ever amid all the apparatus, and felt a knot in his stomach at the sight of him now dressed in the red shirt and shorts of his beloved Bayern Munich football team strip. A large white T with four small white squares, and two smaller emblems, were on the shirt, and the emblems were repeated on the shorts.

Bruno's eyes were closed and he looked, as before, pale and peaceful. His hair was a tousled mess. Roy Grace bent down and kissed him on the forehead and Cleo did the same.

'Hey, chap,' he said. 'Cleo and I are here. Can you hear us?'

Bruno showed no reaction, and nor, from what Grace could see, did any of the digital displays. It was as if he was in a deep, peaceful sleep.

'Hey, chap!' he said again, louder. Desperate at this last minute for some sign to show that Bruno was reacting to them, that he still had brain activity, that he might yet, against all the odds, pull through.

But nothing changed.

Some minutes later Imelda Bray indicated for them to follow her back outside.

Along with Charlotte Elizabeth, they walked along the unit, past other patients in their beds, and stopped by the nursing station, well out of earshot of Bruno.

In a quiet voice, Bray said, 'We're going to leave you alone with him now. Let us know when you are ready.'

A few moments later, the two women departed.

Roy and Cleo returned to Bruno's bedside. His grandparents had already been in to say their goodbyes and had now left. They had agreed, after an initial reluctance, with the decision to donate Bruno's organs, having been persuaded they would get some small comfort knowing that their grandson would help others to live.

They sat on the two chairs beside the bed. Cleo took a jar of Bruno's hair gel from her handbag, along with a brush and comb, and set to work on arranging his hair, as best she could after his surgery, in the meticulously neat way Bruno always wore it.

Grace smiled appreciatively at her, then stared at his son's face, trying to put out of his mind, for a moment, all the technology around him and attached to him, to both monitor him and keep him – even if only technically – alive.

'Want me to leave you two alone together for a while?' Cleo whispered when she had finished.

'No, thank you for offering,' he whispered back. 'I'm glad you're here.' He turned back to Bruno. 'Hey, fella! I don't want to leave anything unsaid. I love you from the bottom of my heart and even though I didn't know you until recently, it doesn't change how strong my feelings for you are. You have taught your stepmum and me so much in such a short time. It's OK to be a bit different, a bit quirky. But now, my son, you are going to do the most significant thing in your life and we will be forever proud. You are going to give your organs to someone who needs them more than you. You will live forever in them. You will live forever in our hearts and in our minds.'

He and Cleo were sobbing now. 'Bruno, you have made us so proud and we love you. Now be at peace. Goodnight, sleep well, my love.'

There was no response. Just the constant beeps from around them, beyond the curtains.

Grace stared at Bruno for several minutes, willing his eyes to open, even though he knew it wouldn't happen. He looked around at the machines again and again, looking for some change, some signal. But nothing.

With tears running down her cheeks, Cleo stood, indicated with her finger for him to stay put, and slipped out through the curtain.

Grace took his son's motionless right hand. 'Goodbye, little chap,' he whispered, his chest heaving. 'I'm sorry we never had the chance to get to know each other more. I'm sure you're full of kindness – and life never gave you a chance to show it. But at least we can give you a different kind of chance to show it.'

He broke down crying, his head in his hands.

He was still crying when Cleo returned with Imelda Bray, Charlotte Elizabeth, a doctor and a nurse.

A male voice – the doctor – asked kindly, 'Are you sure you are ready now, Mr and Mrs Grace?'

A disembodied voice that sounded like it might have been his, said, 'I guess.'

He looked again at Bruno.

And for the very first time since he had seen his son, over in Munich, Bruno actually looked at peace.

'We'll leave you for a few more minutes,' the doctor said.

A swish of curtains.

Now it was just him and Cleo again. He took Bruno's tiny hand

and entwined his fingers in his. 'Oh God, why did this have to happen to you?'

Was it his imagination, Grace wondered, but had he felt the tiniest pressure back?

He pressed his face against Bruno's and sobbed and sobbed.

66

It was shortly after 4 p.m. when Roy Grace drove the Alfa up the bumpy cart track. Approaching the property, he had a sinking feeling when he saw two members of the local press who were obviously waiting to doorstep him for a comment. He drove past them, ignoring them, and pulled up outside their cottage behind Cleo's Audi TT. He and Cleo had barely spoken a word during the twenty-five-minute drive. Despite the knowledge that Noah and Kaitlynn were inside, their home looked empty to him.

A void.

He stared bleakly out through the windscreen at the bright afternoon and the sheep-like clouds spread across the soft round hill above them. Sights that Bruno would never see again.

As he switched off the engine, Cleo put an arm around his neck and pulled him to her. 'We must take one positive from all of this, my love,' she said.

He gave her a baleful look. 'Yes?'

'Remember what Bruno told his headmaster?'

'That he wasn't sure whether he wanted to be a chemist or a dictator?'

'Yes. Now, maybe, with the organs he donates, he has the chance to be both.'

For the first time in what felt like a long while, Grace cheered a fraction. 'Yes, at least that's something.'

'I loved him as much as if he had been our child, you do know that, don't you?'

'I do. You were amazing with him.'

His job phone rang. Glancing at it, he could see it was Glenn Branson calling.

'Take it,' she urged.

He shook his head. 'I need a seriously stiff brandy before I do anything.'

She patted her swollen belly. 'Me too – I wish. It's strange, isn't it – as one life ends, another is just beginning.'

67

Roy Grace never normally felt like a drink before 6 p.m., but today was different. He never *normally* saw his son dying. He never *normally* sanctioned the donation of his child's organs. For the first time in his life he found himself struggling to resist opening the bottle.

He returned Glenn Branson's call, forty minutes later.

'How did it all go, boss?'

'Some other time. What's your news?'

'Well – significant. The prison officer has now backtracked on her original opinion.'

'Meaning?' Grace pressed.

'Meaning the sighting of Eden Paternoster on the ferry is dubious, at best.'

'So we can dismiss it?'

'Pretty much, boss, yes. Doesn't take us any further forward.'

'But at least not backwards.' Then Grace thought for a moment. 'Still, we do know she has family connections on the Isle of Wight, so we need to find out who they are and have them interviewed. The fact that we are discounting this particular sighting doesn't necessarily mean, should she still be alive, she hasn't gone there by other means. There's a car ferry and a catamaran, and there's a small airport at Sandown – in the absence of a body, we need to establish for certain she's not there. Have one of the team speak to the local police there and see if they can help us out with that.'

'I'll put someone on it.'

'Good – OK, so we now focus back on Niall Paternoster as the prime suspect in a "no body" murder investigation?'

'I think that's the right call,' Branson said. 'I've spoken to the ACC, who sends his thoughts and prayers for Bruno's recovery.'

'Yup, well you can tell him it's a bit late for that now.'

There was a long silence. Branson finally broke it. 'Oh God, Roy – shit – boss – are you saying what I think?'

'Bruno didn't make it. There was no miracle.'

After a long silence, Branson said, 'I'm so sorry, Roy. Want to talk about it?'

'Not now, OK – just let Pewe know, will you?'

'Of course. Will you let us have the details – you know – of the funeral when you have it?'

'I will. But let's just focus back on the case, I need a distraction for now. Any luck with getting surveillance?'

'No joy for today, but Mark Taylor's team look like they'll be finished on a job sometime tomorrow or possibly Friday.'

'He's brilliant,' Grace said. 'Top man – too bad we can't get him today, but Mark's lot will pick it all up fast.'

'How about a request to the Home Secretary for phone taps on Paternoster?' Branson suggested.

'No chance – we'd only get that if we could establish there was a life at risk. I don't think I have any evidence currently to warrant any such application. What about the pollen lady?'

'Helen Middleton's starting tomorrow. She's going to look at the foot pedals in Niall Paternoster's car, plus his shoes which we've taken, and see if we can link him to the clothes we found at the deposition site. And we've arranged for the forensic archaeologist Lucy Sibun to attend. Lucy's in court tomorrow giving evidence at the big drugs trial, but she'll be at the site as soon as she can. Meanwhile, her junior colleague, Simon Davy, has made a start and will be carrying on first thing in the morning.'

Branson continued, 'In addition, boss, knowing that we still have the Paternoster car, there is a chance he may hire another vehicle, so we've put out an alert with local hire companies.'

'Nice work.'

'See, boss? You don't need to be here, just leave it all to me.'

'Yeah, thanks. That trial – that's the Kosmos Papadopoulos one, right?'

'It is, and it's not looking good for him.'

'What a shame.'

In the past year there had been two very large drug network busts in Sussex, one from a fake classic car that had come into Newhaven Port packed with several million pounds' worth of cocaine. The other had been an equally sophisticated operation, which involved drugs being dropped into the English Channel attached to floats marked by lobster pot buoys and collected by a fishing boat, concealing them at the bottom of its huge cargo of dead mackerel, sole and other fish.

This ring had been masterminded by Kosmos Papadopoulos, a nasty, violent Greek Cypriot known to the police for a long time, who always laundered his money through a string of small but legitimate cash businesses in Brighton and in several other sea-side towns in the county. But, as fortunately happened with many successful villains, Papadopoulos had grown overconfi-dent and let down his guard, trying to hire an undercover police officer to arrange a severe beating for a drug-dealing rival in a turf war. The case was high profile, making the local news most days.

There was a silence.

'But, seriously,' Branson said, 'I just want you to know how sorry I am – and Siobhan, who sends her love. If you want to chat, any time, bell me.'

'I will, thanks.'

'Don't worry about anything, it's all in hand. OK?'

Suddenly, Grace's voice stalled. He could barely utter his reply. 'Thanks. Appreciate – it.'

Ending the call, he stood up and went out into the garden, accompanied by a solemn-looking Humphrey who had clearly picked up on their sadness. He walked over to the hen house. Unhooking the door, he entered, closing it behind him to keep out the dog.

As Cleo had said, Bruno's two favourite hens, Fraulein Andrea and Fraulein Julia, lay motionless, side by side, their heads at unnatural angles.

He knelt and touched the birds. They were stiff and cold.

And so neatly laid out, juxtaposed against each other.

They hadn't been killed by a fox, which would have ripped them to shreds or just bitten off their feet or heads. Nor could they have died from being egg-bound – not in this perfect symmetrical position.

They had been deliberately killed, almost certainly by having their necks wrung.

Again, he went back to that conversation with Bruno yesterday morning – which now seemed an aeon ago.

Did you know that the ancient Egyptians, when they died and were mummified, had their favourite pets killed and mummified, to go in the tomb with them?

Knowing how much the sight of the hens had distressed Cleo, he picked both of them up, took a spade from the garden shed, then, holding them aloft, out of reach of Humphrey who kept jumping up at them, carried them out through the garden gate, shutting it on the dog. He climbed part way up the hill, stopping when he reached a large gorse bush, and put the two hens down gently on the ground.

Then, striking the spade into the hard, dry soil and pushing down on it with his foot, he began the laborious task of digging, wanting to make a hole deep enough so the unfortunate creatures would not easily be dug back up by a fox.

As he worked away, perspiring heavily from his exertions, he was thinking about both his conversation with Glenn Branson and with the hospital team, who had given him a helpful step-by-step postmortem leaflet for the loved ones of organ donors.

First up, tomorrow morning, he had to go to the Brighton Register Office to register Bruno's death and obtain the death certificate. Then he and Cleo needed to appoint a funeral director. A huge number of decisions would have to be made about Bruno's funeral, starting with what kind of coffin, what kind of service. His one certainty was that the boy should be buried in the same graveyard as his mother and as close to her as possible. Bruno's grandparents had agreed with his thinking.

But all of this was for tomorrow, not now.

He stood staring at the sky and soaking up the beautiful evening, remembering the good times with his eldest son.

He continued to dig until he felt the hole was deep enough. He knelt and laid each of the hens into it. Close by, he saw a pink wild flower. He walked over and picked it, then laid it on top of the birds, before beginning to shovel the earth back onto them.

68

Arrangements had been made for Bruno's postmortem to be carried out at Worthing mortuary, instead of Brighton, and it had taken place the previous afternoon. With the agreement of the Coroner and Christopher Goodman's solicitor, the defence proffered their own pathologist, Ashley Brown, who was also present alongside the local pathologist to avoid the need for a second postmortem. After close and careful liaison with the transplant team surgeons, the cause of death was confirmed as injuries sustained as a result of the accident. Brown informed the Coroner that he was happy for the body to be released for burial.

On Thursday, Cleo had accompanied Roy for the grim task of arranging his death certificate, and then they had made an appointment to see the funeral director today. Neither of them had gone into work, both wanting to be there to support each other.

They'd taken some comfort from the huge number of emails and social media messages of condolences that had poured through from family, friends and colleagues, including the Chief Constable, the Police and Crime Commissioner, the Headmaster of St Christopher's School and several other teachers, and one, less welcome and more mealy-mouthed, from Cassian Pewe. Grace had also been surprised to receive a couple expressing their sympathy from criminals he was known to from over the years.

A Facebook memorial page set up by the Lippert family, who

had taken care of Bruno after his mother's accident, already had messages of sympathy from a number of people Grace was not even familiar with and was headed up by a heartfelt message from Erik Lippert, who was Bruno's best friend in Germany. Grace was surprised to see a post from Cassian Pewe written in German. He wondered what that was about.

For the second time in eighteen months, Grace now found himself back in a funeral home. The last time he had been in one was to discuss the arrangements for Sandy, whom he'd decided to have buried here in England, so that Bruno would have a place to go and mourn his mother whenever he wanted.

He'd never, ever imagined he would be having to make funeral decisions about Bruno.

They'd already decided on burial, rather than cremation – Roy wanted Bruno to be laid to rest in the churchyard of All Saints, Patcham, in a plot as close to Sandy as possible.

They had also decided on the same firm that had handled Sandy's arrangements, and Grace was pleased, as they entered the curtained-off front of the establishment, to be greeted by the proprietor himself, with whom he'd had the previous dealings, Thomas Greenhaisen.

A tall man in his late fifties, with a shock of grey hair and sparkly blue eyes, the sombre-suited funeral director managed somehow to have found the right balance between being both warm, almost jolly, and reverential and respectful. He looked like he was capable of throwing off his work togs at weekends and picking up a banjo, or maybe a ukulele, and joining a band, Grace thought.

Greenhaisen greeted them both with a sincere bow, before shaking their hands, in turn, taking Cleo's first then Roy's, holding each of them for several moments as if taking possession of them, before saying, 'Mr and Mrs Grace, may I say first how terribly sad I am to be seeing you again so soon. My very deepest condolences for your terrible loss. An eleven-year-old boy.' He shook his head. 'I doubt there is anything I can say to console you at this time, but I can assure you we will do everything we can to take as much pressure off you as we can.'

Cynically and irreverently, Grace was reminded for a moment of his former boss in the police, some years back, Dick Jackson. He'd been a Detective Sergeant and Jackson had been his Inspector. The poor sod had planned to cash in his pension on his retirement and open a funeral parlour because, Dick had said, a little smugly, the two businesses you could never lose money on were food and death. People were always going to have to eat and they were always going to die. He'd joked that he was going to call the business Yours Eventually.

But Dick had dropped dead from a heart attack, swimming in Tenerife, just two months after his retirement. The grim reaper, Grace thought, had yanked the poor man's chain just a bit too hard.

It had been a timely reminder that retired police officers used to have one of the highest mortality rates of almost any profession. One moment you had your warrant card – which an old copper had described to him as 'a free pass to the greatest show on earth' – and the next, the day you handed it in, you were suddenly a civilian again. Joe Public. Joe Shmow.

A lot of officers felt lost after retirement. For thirty years, and sometimes more, they'd held a position of unique power – and respect. But then those thirty years vanished in a flash and they were having their retirement party in the upstairs room of a pub – the more generous ones sticking money behind the bar. A former colleague would give a speech, joking about their blunders, praising their achievements. Maybe show a video of the highlights – and lowlights – of their career. And that was it. Wake up in the morning with a hangover to find you were a – a what? A *was-copper*?

It came to everyone. Some had made good plans and were fine, picking up well-paid jobs fighting the virulent menace of cybercrime or going back into areas of policing as civilians. But others were left bewildered. Like pot plants that had once flowered magnificently, but now had been left in permanent shade, wondering where the sunshine had gone.

Yours eventually. The phrase had lodged in Grace's mind. Was Thomas Greenhaisen looking at him and Cleo and thinking the same – that one day they, too, would become customers of Greenhaisen & Sons? Hopefully not until it was '& Grandsons'.

Just how sad to see them was Greenhaisen really? Was the first qualification to be a funeral director that you had to be a good actor? Or was he being too cynical?

'Thank you,' Roy Grace said politely.

'Please, come through into my office. May I offer you some refreshments, tea, coffee perhaps?'

'I'd like a strong coffee with some milk, please,' Grace said.

'If you have a peppermint tea?' Cleo asked.

'Of course, no trouble.'

As they followed him through into a small office, with a large, opaque window obscuring the view, no doubt, of the hearses parked out back, he picked up the desk phone and asked a man called John to bring in the drinks. Then he ushered them to a round table at which were four comfortable-looking chairs. As Cleo sat, Grace saw a framed certificate on the wall above her, proclaiming Thomas Edward Greenhaisen to be a member of the British Institute of Embalmers.

When the funeral director was seated, with an iPad in front of him, he began by confirming Bruno's details – his full name, date of birth and home address, and the place where he had died – tapping in all the details assiduously with an immaculately manicured forefinger.

'May I ask next if Bruno had an affiliation with a particular church or religious group that he might have wished to officiate at his funeral?'

Grace thought fleetingly about how, from his limited knowledge of Sandy's activities after her disappearance, she had spent some time with the Scientologists, then a further brief time with another sect in Germany.

'No,' he said. 'But I never had the chance to discuss religion with him. That may sound odd, but he has only been with us since his mother died. I don't think he had any religious views – but my wife and I have decided we would like a Christian funeral, a lightweight one. With some rousing music – perhaps something in German?'

'Exactly, sir,' Greenhaisen said. 'And if I might suggest, in view of Bruno's age, some of his own favourite music – are there any singers or bands he particularly loved?'

'Yes, good point,' Grace said. 'We'll have a think about that.'

The funeral director nodded. 'I'm sure that would go down well, especially as there are bound to be many of his young friends attending.'

Roy and Cleo shot each other a glance. But neither commented.

'As I told you over the phone, we would like the service and committal to take place in the same church where his mother and I were married, and where she is buried, All Saints, Patcham,' Grace said.

'Well, we are very fortunate in that choice, the current vicar is quite an enlightened man – unlike some,' he said. 'If you know what I mean?'

Cleo smiled. 'He's not a Bible thumper?'

'Precisely. Now, are there any pressing questions you have?'

'I guess,' Grace said, 'because Bruno's organs have been donated, will that cause any problems or delays in his funeral?'

'Well, that will depend on the Coroner. As I understand – and please correct me if I am wrong – the driver of the car in the collision with your son has been interviewed in relation to his driving?'

'That's correct,' Grace said.

'In which case, there is the possibility of a prosecution and criminal trial.'

Roy interrupted. 'I understand the postmortem was carried out yesterday afternoon with the defence pathologist, Mr Ashley Brown, present as agreed with the Coroner. The cause of death has been ascertained and Bruno's body will be released straight away for burial.'

'That's good news then, we can fix a date. If it is any small consolation,' Greenhaisen said, 'on the subject of costs for a child of this age, we would make no charge for the basic funeral arrangements.'

'Really?' Cleo said, astonished.

'I assure you, we understand a little of the grief that parents like you must be going through. We would not make any charge for the basic funeral, which would include bringing your son into care, providing the hearse, a standard coffin, the bearers and the funeral director. Most churches also waive their fees, although I'm afraid not the gravediggers. Music is provided free of charge. It's only the extras you would be required to pay for.'

'This is very generous of you,' Roy Grace said.

'It is the very least we can do,' Greenhaisen said, almost simpering.

'But I want Bruno to have the best funeral we can give him,' Grace continued.

'And the extras would be?' Cleo asked.

'That would be the flowers, newspaper announcements and printed order-of-service sheets. The monumental masons would also charge for any headstone, and perhaps, if you so wished, for altering the inscription on your late wife's headstone to include your son. Then there are special requests, such as releasing doves, a horse-drawn hearse – or anything of that nature.'

The couple were silent for some moments. Then Grace asked, 'When you say "standard coffin", what is that, exactly?'

'A choice of any of our wood veneer finishes. Although for a young person, parents sometimes prefer to go for a paper veneer, which we do have to make a charge for. These can be painted a bright colour – a favourite colour, perhaps – or they can be printed with virtually anything: photographs, views, scenes, characters. I can give you links to a few websites that might give you ideas. If he had a favourite toy or TV show, or football team, perhaps?'

Roy turned to Cleo. 'What about the colours of Bayern Munich?'

She nodded. 'Yes,' she said distantly. 'That could be nice.'

'Another thing,' the funeral director said, 'I don't know whether you or anyone else would like to visit Bruno? If so, we would suggest our embalmer has a look at him to make sure he is at his best?'

'We've already said our goodbyes,' Grace said.

Again Cleo turned to Roy. 'What about his grandparents?'

'No, they've said their goodbyes at the hospital. We won't be seeing them until the funeral, which is probably for the best.' He had a long, difficult history with Sandy's parents, who had, for all the years Sandy had been missing, made out that they believed he had murdered her. They'd taken their suspicions to the highest level of Sussex Police, resulting in Cassian Pewe ordering a ground-penetrating radar search of the garden of his and Sandy's former house in Hove. He would never forget how this twisted, horrible couple had lied to him rather than tell him she had been alive and living in Munich in Germany.

'Once you've made your choice of coffin,' Thomas Greenhaisen said, 'you might consider whether you would like a framed photo or a favourite toy or book to go in it with him. Also, if I may suggest, youngsters are usually dressed in their own clothes. And a final thing for you both to consider is the frill colour of the coffin. It's usually cream, but we can accommodate any other colour – whatever you would like. With a small extra cost,' he added and nodded, his face the very picture of phoney sympathy, Grace thought. And remembered an expression he'd once heard: *If you can fake sincerity, the rest is easy.*

'OK, Mr Greenhaisen, thank you,' Grace said, cutting his spiel short. 'My wife and I will go away and have a think about all these options.'

'Of course, of course, decisions of this nature must never be hurried.'

'Indeed,' Grace said.

Mr Greenhaisen raised a perfect, soft hand that had clearly never actually dug a grave. 'I would just say that – very sadly in our city – there is always a waiting list for venues and officiates, so the sooner you and Mrs Grace can make your decisions, the sooner we can make the necessary bookings – subject, of course, to the Coroner.'

'I appreciate that,' Roy Grace said, irked by the man's sudden pushiness. 'But I don't think our son is in any hurry. Would you be?'

Greenhaisen floundered for a reply, his lips twitching. 'Of course – I mean – of course, please take your time, these are important decisions.'

'Yes,' Grace said. 'They are.'

He felt tears welling up. He stood, shook hands with Greenhaisen, thanked him with a faltering voice and turned away.

69

Roy and Cleo arrived home shortly after 1 p.m., to be greeted by Humphrey holding another of his collection of ragged stuffed toys in his mouth – with half the stuffing gone, like most of them. He was wagging his tail but seemed more subdued than usual. Grace knelt and hugged him. 'Brought me a gift, have you, fellow? Thank you.'

Humphrey dropped it, a small bear with both eyes missing that had once been Noah's before he'd appropriated it, then looked at him, a tad balefully. Did he sense something? Roy suddenly remembered a book Cleo had given him for his birthday last year, a volume of short stories titled *Explaining Death to the Dog*. Did this creature understand something? That Bruno wasn't coming home again?

Roy heard beeps and tings and a series of quacks and grunting sounds coming from the lounge – Noah was active in his play area, with his noise-maker toy.

Out of the corner of his eye he saw Kaitlynn approach. 'I thought you guys might be hungry,' she said gently in her Californian accent. 'I've done you a tuna salad and I found some bagels in the freezer which I thought I'd toast to go with it. There's no need to speak, I know how hard this is for you both. Just know I'm here and can help when you need.'

'Thanks,' Cleo said, 'that's really thoughtful of you.'

Roy stood up and smiled his thanks, not trusting his voice.

'I've taken Noah and Humphrey for a good walk, so you don't need to worry about Humphrey for a while,' she added.

'Just going to go up to Bruno's room,' Roy said to Cleo. 'See what I can find for some ideas for his—'

'I'll come up with you,' she said, and turned to Kaitlynn. 'Lunch in ten?'

'Sure, tell me when you're ready. You OK?'

Cleo nodded and said in a quiet voice, 'Yeah, thanks, trying to hold it together – we just feel like we're in a daze.'

They went upstairs and entered Bruno's immaculate bedroom. His trainers, football boots and shoes all neatly in a row in front of his white wardrobe. Grace looked at the two posters of Bayern Munich football team on the wall. Alongside them was a large photograph of his local hero, the German footballer Pascal Groß, who had joined Brighton and Hove Albion and was dressed in the team's blue and white strip. Below, sat a red model Porsche Turbo on a shelf beside a row of books and computer games.

'I'm pleased we can have his coffin printed in the Bayern Munich colours,' Cleo said.

Roy's reply was interrupted by his job phone ringing.

'Detective Superintendent Grace,' he answered. And heard Glenn Branson's voice at the other end.

'Boss, sorry to intrude, but you said to call if we found anything.'

'Tell me?'

'The team excavating the deposition-site area have found a bone – they think it might be human. Lucy Sibun's assistant attended and says it could be a lower arm radius, but we might not know for sure until Lucy gets here – which is not going to be until early evening. Meantime, they're emailing photographs of it to Dundee.'

Dundee University ran the UK Centre for Anatomy and

Human Identification. They could normally identify bones as being human or belonging to another animal within a few hours.

Grace thought for a moment. Glenn had the search under control and, strictly, he wasn't needed. But as the SIO, with there being a potentially significant find, he wanted to be there. And besides, not really wanting to admit this to himself, it would be a welcome, temporary distraction.

'OK,' he said. 'I'd like to see the site.'

'I'm heading there, want me to pick you up? I could be with you in forty-five minutes.'

Grace thought briefly. He didn't feel like talking to anyone at the moment and wondered about driving there on his own. But maybe it would be good to have the company of his friend. 'Sure. Where exactly is it?'

'Want me to give you the what3words location?'

'Thanks.'

'It's *boil.stunner.throwaway*,' Branson said.

Memorizing them, Grace entered them in the what3words app on his phone. The app had recently become an invaluable tool for the police. The entire world had been gridded into three-metre squares, each of which was given a three-word ident. *boil.stunner.throwaway* showed him a location in Ashdown Forest a short distance from what looked like a parking area.

Thanking him, Grace ended the call and told Cleo.

'Probably do you some good,' she said. 'Focus on something else.'

He nodded. 'It's the only way I can deal with this horrendous time. I've got to distract myself, though I know it's not how everyone would deal with it.'

And in the meanwhile, there was nothing he could do, other than mope around. Plunging back into work was the best way to take his mind off it.

Half an hour later, he heard the sound of a car pulling up

outside. He scooped some tuna salad onto the two halves of bagel that Kaitlynn had toasted, squished them together and wrapped them in several sheets of kitchen towel, then went outside.

'You want some lunch?' Grace said as his greeting.

'Thanks, boss – I'm starving!'

'Fill your boots,' Grace, who had no appetite, said sullenly, passing him the package.

The DI devoured the bagel in five bites, then started the engine and did a fast U-turn, narrowly missing the only tree on the entire driveway.

70

'Sorry about that – I remember watching Lewis Hamilton do a doughnut at the Goodwood Festival of Speed.'

Grace looked at him. 'No disrespect, he's probably a bit more talented behind the wheel than you.'

'Yeah, but he'd probably be a rubbish detective,' Branson said, restarting the stalled engine and heading off, at a subdued pace, along the bumpy cart track.

'Apparently, there used to be an entry in the *Guinness Book of Records* called "The Loneliest Tree in the World",' Grace said. 'It was in the Sahara, 250 miles from the next nearest tree, and was knocked down by a drunk Libyan truck driver.'

'Are you trying to tell me something?'

'Just saying. It's all a bit sensitive at the moment.'

'Thanks, boss, I understand.'

'It's fine,' Grace said. 'But we're not in a rush. OK? If Eden Paternoster's been dead since last Thursday, she's not going anywhere, is she?'

'Good point,' Branson said. He eased off a fraction. But the horizon was still approaching way too fast for Grace's comfort.

'Better?' the DI asked.

Grace waited until they'd survived the next corner before replying tightly, 'A little.'

Over the next twenty minutes, aware Roy wanted to avoid

talking about Bruno, Branson updated him on the latest developments on the enquiry. He was meeting the Surveillance Team leader, DS Mark Taylor, now that his team had been signed off from their previous job, to brief him – maybe Roy would like to be there for that? He said he would. Branson had already arranged for a fixed observation point at the Greyhound Stadium until the Surveillance Team were available to monitor Paternoster's activity.

Neighbours on both sides of the Paternosters' home had all been questioned by Jack Alexander's Outside Enquiry Team, and had informed the officers they'd heard the Paternosters having a violent row last Thursday night. None of them had seen Eden since. Work colleagues at the insurance company, Mutual Occidental, where Eden was employed, who had all now been interviewed, had confirmed that her failing to turn up to work on Friday – and not phoning in – had been quite out of character. She was normally scrupulously punctual and diligent.

All the close friends and relatives, whose names and details Niall Paternoster had given, had now been contacted, and all confirmed they had not heard from Eden since last Thursday at the latest. Branson added that her mother had apparently been the most vocal, saying she had always thought her son-in-law was not good enough for her daughter. She had tried to warn Eden off marrying him. And, more worryingly, on one occasion some months ago, Eden had come to stay with her overnight in a terrible state, saying Niall and she had split up, but then they'd subsequently got back together, much to her disappointment.

They had come back with positive DNA matches on the blood on the kitchen floor to both Eden and Niall. Grace knew, as all detectives, that if a kitchen knife was used in a stabbing it would almost certainly cut the assailant's hand, too, when it struck bone. That tallied, possibly with Niall Paternoster's cut finger, explaining his blood in the kitchen. There were more positive matches with Eden's blood on the stairs, the en-suite tiles and on her T-shirt found secreted in there. Results were not yet back on the items of clothing found at the grave.

Grace made a number of notes. Bit by bit, the case against Niall Paternoster was building. A 'no body' murder was acknow-ledged by all SIOs as the hardest to prove. It required compelling circumstantial evidence to convince the Crown Prosecution Service to agree to proceed – the notoriously demanding CPS solicitors were always reluctant to commit to the expense of a prosecution case and all the costs of a trial without a degree of certainty that they would win.

But Grace was feeling uncertain. His early instincts, from his meeting with Paternoster, felt right. Maybe the bone that had been found would prove it beyond any doubt. But he felt there was something still missing.

He looked down at his what3words app.

They were almost at the scene.

Grace knew this forest from his earliest childhood days, when they'd had occasional school outings here, running around and being mindful that there were adders living in the sandy brush. And dense woodland was historically a deposition site for murder victims.

Branson was braking hard and indicating. Moments later, he swung in left.

A cluster of vehicles, including the large white CSI van, in the sandy parking area confirmed they were in the right place, as did the outer cordon of crime scene tape just beyond them.

71

Friday 6 September

Few police officers would disagree over what was the most shit job in the entire force. A minority might suggest it was being on public order duty during a riot, but at least that could be mitigated by the potential for getting into a fight – a good old *roll-up*, which most young, eager officers enjoyed. One of the money-can't-buy perks of the job.

But to be delegated the duty of a crime scene guard was universally agreed to be the most numbingly boring. In the city, in daytime, the task tended to be given to PCSOs – the lower cost Police Community Support Officers. But PCSOs weren't considered as robust as fully trained coppers, and they didn't do night duty.

Togged up in their white protective oversuits, shoes, gloves, headgear and masks, Grace and Branson approached the poor sap of a PC who was the current scene guard. The officer watched them with interest, probably the only excitement and break in the monotony he'd had in the past hour or more.

Aware of the man's vigil, as Grace showed him his warrant card he asked sympathetically, 'How long do you have to go?'

Presenting the two detectives with the log to sign, the hapless young PC said, 'Midnight, sir.'

Grace smiled at him. 'Done it myself. It's not much fun, is it?'

'Not really, sir, no. But,' he added hastily, 'I don't mind. I'm

307

hoping to be a detective one day, so it's interesting to see a crime scene like this.'

'What's your name?' Grace asked him. 'I'll remember it.'

'Conall Bartlett,' he said. 'Thank you, sir.'

'You're Graham Bartlett's son, right?'

'Yes, sir.'

'Your dad was my boss once, some years back. A great copper.'

The PC smiled. 'Thank you – it was seeing how he loved the job that inspired me.'

Grace smiled. 'You're a pretty useful football ref, too, I recall?'

'Well, I don't know about *useful*, sir, but I try.'

'Good lad!' Grace signed the log and handed the clipboard to Branson, saying glibly to the PC, 'Excuse his scrawl, he's barely literate!'

'Yeah, yeah!' Branson retorted. He picked up the pen and deliberately and painfully slowly wrote his name immaculately neatly. Handing the clipboard back, he said cheekily, 'In case you can't read my colleague's, he's Detective Superintendent Smudge.'

Conall Bartlett took it, uncertain whether to smile.

The two detectives ducked under the tape, strode the short distance to the inner cordon tape, ducked under that, too, then walked along the metal track that had been laid by the police Forensics Team. Its purpose was to cause minimum disturbance to the route the killer had likely taken to the deposition site.

It led a couple of hundred yards into the woods where there were two open-sided tents, one small and square, inside which was a generator running noisily and two tables. On one table stood a kettle, mugs, a jar of coffee, a box of tea and two open packets of biscuits. On the other were laid out several sealed and tagged evidence bags, each containing an item.

The larger tent was rectangular, brightly lit by jury-rigged overhead lights, over a shallow grave. Dotted around on the ground outside the tents were numbered yellow triangles, indicating where possible evidence had been found.

James Gartrell, the highly competent CSI photographer whom Grace knew well, busy recording the area on video, paused to nod a greeting. 'Afternoon, boss.' He was also in full protective clothing.

'How are you doing, James?'

'Fine, boss, thank you. Lorna and Simon are inside the tent.' Then, obviously knowing Grace's news, asked sympathetically, 'And you, boss – I'm so sorry about—'

Grace silenced him with a grim smile and a raised hand, then approached and opened the larger tent. Inside, he saw the white-suited backs of two people examining the shallow grave. The POLSA, Sergeant Lorna Dennison-Wilkins, and the assistant forensic archaeologist, Simon Davy, stood at the edge, Lorna sipping from a steaming mug, Simon standing over the two search officers, watching them. Both turned immediately as they heard the footsteps.

'Sir,' the Sergeant said, addressing Grace. 'I heard you were coming.' Then she gave him a forlorn look. 'I'm sorry about your news.' She shot a smile at Branson by way of acknowledgement.

'Thanks, I appreciate it, Lorna,' Grace said. 'So, what do we have?' He walked over to the freshly excavated area. The two specialists – impossible to tell who without seeing their faces – were scraping the soil at the bottom with trowels, with the painstaking and back-breaking diligence of archaeologists on a dig, checking the freed, loose soil with their gloved fingers before discarding it over the top, onto a growing pile.

'Well, sir, Simon has some early thoughts which might be helpful.'

The assistant forensic archaeologist, in his early thirties, only a small part of his face visible, said, 'The soil in the grave is quite loose and there appears to be recent disturbance, which indicates to me that it was probably dug earlier and then back-filled not that long ago.'

'Planned and made ready?' Grace asked. 'Is that what you're saying?'

'Yes, sir – that's how it looks to me.'

'What have you found?'

'Well, sir, apart from the items of clothing we've retrieved so far, some of which have been sent by Sergeant Dennison-Wilkins to the lab for analysis, the grave contained traces of blood and lots of evidence of animal disturbance. And as I believe you've been told, we discovered a bone nearby just over an hour ago, it may have been dragged away by animals.'

'Human?'

'Possibly – we can't be sure at this stage. Would you like to see it, sir?'

'I'm no anatomy expert, but yes.'

Grace and Branson walked behind Lorna and Simon along more track to the smaller tent. The forensic archaeologist picked an evidence bag from the table, which contained a clean bone with a gnarled double lump at one end and a skewed knot at the other. Both ends appeared to have been chewed.

The detectives studied it carefully. 'Humans have two lower-arm bones, if I'm right?' Grace said.

Simon nodded. 'The radius is one of two forearm bones – it's the shorter of the two but thicker than the other, the ulna. It runs from the lateral side of the elbow to the thumb side of the wrist, and parallel to the ulna.'

Grace looked at it again for some moments. 'You've sent a photo of it to Dundee for verification, I understand?'

'Yes, they're pretty good about coming back quickly.'

'What's your own assessment of the bone, Simon?' he asked.

'Well, Lucy's the expert. In my view this could be human, but it might well be a roe deer tibia – this forest is home to a large number of deer.'

Grace continued studying the bone, none the wiser. 'The fact that there are no body parts present in the grave could be put down to predation.' He looked at Lorna and Simon for confirmation. Both nodded.

'A dismembered body, especially in woodlands like this, can be carried off by animals within days – even more so if the grave is on a fox or badger run. But bones picked as clean as this, in less than a week? It's possible, I guess – do you agree?'

'It is, I – we – have seen it happen, sir,' Lorna said. 'Especially underwater. And, of course, acid is always a possibility.'

Grace had worked with Lorna in the past when she had been in charge of the now disbanded Sussex Police Specialist Search Unit. He'd seen instances of human bodies on the seabed being picked clean by fish and crustaceans in a very short time. And he'd seen his share of skeletal remains in acid baths.

'But,' she continued, 'it can happen in woodland situations like this, where there's a lot of wildlife.'

'Fair point,' he said, swallowing back those memories of past bodies he'd seen, picked clean. He didn't want these memories right now. He looked down at the row of evidence bags. In one was a popsock; another contained a headband; another, a substantial kitchen knife.

He picked up the bag with the knife in his gloved hand and held it out in the daylight. There was dried blood on the blade and handle. 'This is the knife that was found in a bush nearby, Lorna?'

'Yes, it is. I've sent a picture of it back to the incident room to see if they can get a match with the set of knives in the kitchen of the house.'

'Can I see the bush?'

She led Grace and Branson a short distance from the metal

track and stopped at a yellow triangle on the ground. It was marked '7' and was right in front of a tangle of brambles, with ripe blackberries on the branches.

'It was in there.'

Grace studied the bush and then looked around. There were several more similar bushes nearby, but each of these much bigger and far denser. He frowned, looked at Branson for a moment, then back at the surrounding bushes.

'Seeing something I'm not, boss?' the DI asked.

'Something that's not making total sense,' Grace said. 'Why this bush?'

'Because it's close to the grave,' Branson suggested.

Grace fixed his gaze on him. 'OK, think about it for a moment. I always try to put myself in the killer's shoes. Let's hypothesize that Niall Paternoster murdered Eden, dismembered her body, drove the remains out here to a grave, along with the clothes she had been wearing when he killed her, and interred her in this grave. Why didn't he put the knife in with her?'

Glenn Branson frowned in thought. 'Animals? Or maybe he was in a red mist. Like all crims in the aftermath? Right? So he brings her out here in the early hours of Friday, he's all ramped up. Buries her and all the clothing, covers the grave over and then – shit! He realizes he's forgotten to bury the knife. So he discards it in the first bush he sees?'

'A simple, stupid error,' Lorna Dennison-Wilkins said. 'Seen it before many times. The killer in a panic.'

Grace shook his head. 'This doesn't fit. He wasn't in a panic. So, let's suppose he was planning to murder Eden. The trigger was the row they had last Thursday night. Maybe he deliberately created the row.'

'But isn't that a bit daft?' Branson asked. 'Wouldn't he have known the neighbours would hear?'

'Not necessarily. If he's a narcissist, bigger on ego than he is on brains as you and I both thought after talking to him, perhaps he thought that the neighbours hearing a row would lend credence to the story he's giving that she's left him – done a runner on their marriage. But without thinking through how all his movements would be picked up on ANPR cameras and GPS tracking of his phone.' Grace shrugged. 'That wouldn't be the first time a killer's been trapped that way.'

'Good point,' Branson agreed.

'So let's go down this route for now. When he brought her body – or body parts – here, it was nearly 3 a.m. Pitch dark. No one around. He had all the time in the world. He had the choice of at least six far thicker bushes within flashlight range, as we can see. So why did he choose the one so near and so sparse? And I'm not buying red mist or panic. He was clear-headed enough after killing her to remove her wedding and engagement rings and conceal them, and to hide her passport. But two things here are really bothering me.'

'Which are, boss?' Branson asked.

'We know there were a number of true crime DVDs in the house. Let's hypothesize that he learned through those that one of the best ways to dispose of a body is to dismember it and bury it in a shallow – rather than deep – grave, in woodlands. Because that gives you the best chance of predation, which we believe has happened here. The body parts conveniently carried off. So why was he dumb enough to leave items of her clothing in the grave also? Do either of you think that's consistent with his planning?'

Grace looked at them all in turn before continuing. 'Then, after all his planning, Niall Paternoster clumsily chucks the knife into the nearest bush? When there are several so dense and prickly it's much less likely a member of the public would find it. Why would he do that? I think it was more likely that the deposition site was his way to get rid of the clothing and I think animal disturbance has caused the knife to be moved, especially as it has soil on it. But I don't completely reject the possibility it could have just been chucked away by him.'

'Are you saying what I think you're saying, boss? That he wanted to be caught?' Branson asked.

Grace shook his head. 'No. I don't think so.'

'I'm confused.'

Lorna Dennison-Wilkins looked equally bemused.

'Join the club,' Grace said. 'None of this is making sense. Was it buried or was it thrown away?'

The DI looked at his watch. 'Boss, I've got to get back to HQ to meet Mark Taylor for the surveillance briefing. If we leave now, I've just got time to drop you back home.'

'I'll come to the briefing with you. We can spend some more time here. I want to take a further look round.'

'On your own?'

'No, come with me.'

Grace, followed by Branson, walked further into the woods. They became increasingly dense, all paths a tangle of nettles and brambles, with dubious-looking mushrooms and toadstools free-standing or attached to tree trunks.

Finally, Branson, looking at his watch, said, 'We really need to head back, boss, for Mark Taylor. It's after 3 p.m.'

Grace nodded.

'Any conclusions?'

'No. You?'

Branson shook his head. 'Right now I'm all out of conclusions.'

'You and me both.'

72

Kosmos Papadopoulos sat in the glassed-in dock of Court 3 at Lewes Crown Court. A tall, confident-looking man, with slicked-back hair, he wore an expensive suit, stylish cream shirt and blue silk tie, accessorized with bling rings and an even blinger watch. He could have done without the unwanted accessories on either side of him, a male and female security guard, in their shabby outfits. But at least his brief, Kiaran Murray Smith, a sharp-eyed QC in his early fifties, and his junior, Madeleine Wade, had been doing a pretty good demolition job of the prosecution, so far.

His legal team had been doing so well that Papadopoulos could scent victory in the expressions of the jurors.

And now, the neatly dressed woman in her mid-thirties, with long hair the colour of straw, who was taking the oath in the witness box, didn't look like she would say boo to a goose. Yet another in a string of so-called 'expert' witnesses called by the prosecution.

She swore on the Holy Bible to tell the truth, the whole truth and nothing but the truth. Yadda, yadda, yadda. The poor deluded woman actually sounded like she meant it. Yeah, good luck with that one, lady. When you arrive at the Pearly Gates, if you're expecting St Peter to unclip the crimson rope and let you turn left, you could be in for a spot of disappointment. But hey, that's for later.

The witness over the next hour relayed to the court her evidence. She gave this in a quiet and assured manner, concentrating on conversations of the defendant that she had witnessed. Once the prosecution counsel had finished with the witness, the defence counsel got to his feet.

Murray-Smith was straight on it, going for the jugular.

'Sharon Orman, could you please tell the court your academic and professional qualifications?'

'I left secondary school with nine GCSEs and three A levels in mathematics, computer science and biology,' she replied.

There was a short silence while he let the jury absorb this.

'And, subsequently, what further qualifications did you achieve?'

'None,' she said falteringly. 'I saw an advert for Sussex Police, looking for people to join under their diversity programme. I joined the Digital Forensics Team before moving to the Surveillance Unit.'

Murray-Smith gave her a big, confidence-boosting beam and a sarcastic tone. 'Would this have been because you fancied a career change?'

There was a brief interruption as the prosecution counsel objected. The judge allowed the defence counsel to continue.

'In your evidence, as an expert witness, Ms Orman, which was pretty damning, you claimed that you had watched, via binoculars, the defendant in conversation with another person. You read out from your notes your recording of what Mr Papadopoulos had purportedly said. I will repeat it, just for the avoidance of any misunderstanding.' He picked up a sheet of paper and read aloud from it, directing his words at the jury box.

'You told this court that, according to your interpretation, my client said, "There's a drop in the Channel, one mile north of the Palace Pier. Eight million quid's worth of crack cocaine at street value. I have two other bidders for this – do you want in? If so, give me your price by midday tomorrow."'

Murray-Smith looked up from his notes, straight at the woman. 'Is that correct?'

'It is,' she confirmed.

'Word perfect?'

No hesitation. 'Yes.'

'So, Ms Orman, as we have heard, you've had no formal qualifications or training in the art of lip-reading. Yet you claim to have observed my client in discussions over what might or might not have been a business deal. Pretty damning evidence if true, wouldn't you agree?'

'I would,' she said.

Murray-Smith went in for the kill. 'So, as I understand it, Sharon Orman, you have no qualifications and no formal training to be a member of the Surrey and Sussex Police Surveillance Unit. Is that also correct?'

'No, I have had surveillance training,' she replied.

'So, it is agreed,' the defence counsel pounced, the bit between his teeth now. 'We've asked what training you've had and you have told us. We have asked what qualifications you have to give this evidence and you've replied that you have no qualifications. So, you have come to court as a so-called "expert" witness, telling this court very damning evidence about what my client is alleged to have said. You're not qualified to give this evidence. What gives you the authority to come here and tell this court what you have? Why should any of us here in this court believe what you have said?'

Calmly, her voice more assured now, Sharon Orman said, 'Well, in childhood I lost my full hearing. I've spent the last twenty-five years of my life reading people's lips, watching their movements – just like I've been reading yours. That's the way I survive in the modern world. I think that's all the qualification I need, wouldn't you say?'

For a fleeting instant, Murray-Smith's suave features took on an appearance of a bone-china cup that had been dropped from ten storeys onto a concrete block. Instantly regaining his composure, although not his confidence, he turned to the judge. 'No further questions.'

73

At 3.45 p.m., Roy Grace and Glenn Branson met Mark Taylor, their Surveillance Team leader, as well as DC Keri Brogan, the Intelligence Development Officer, who was to be the liaison between the Major Crime Team and the Surveillance Team on Operation Lagoon.

Brogan, late thirties, had the stocky build of a hockey goal-keeper, which Grace, having met her some while back, remembered was her passion. Shoulder-length hair, set in tight curls like a judge's wig, but brown not grey, framed her face. She was dressed in casual clothes and new-looking trainers.

Detective Sergeant Taylor, who was in his mid-forties, had shaggy, collar-length hair and chiselled good looks that reminded Grace of the actor he'd last seen in *Game of Thrones*, Nikolaj Coster-Waldau. He wore a thin leather jacket over a grey T-shirt, jeans and basketball boots. Not a man to be messed with, Grace knew from his background. He had joined the police at the age of twenty-five after six years' distinguished service in the Royal Marines. On finishing his two-year probation, he'd immediately, at his request, been posted to CID, then Surveillance. Subsequently, the quietly spoken man, who did not suffer fools, had worked at all levels of Surveillance, including a three-year stint with Scotland Yard, before transferring back to Sussex Police after the birth of his first child.

Cradling a cup of coffee, looking at the two detectives

opposite him across the small table, Taylor asked in a warm, slightly gravelly voice, 'So what are your objectives? I have a briefing with my team at 4.30 p.m. and will inform them.'

Grace, out of courtesy, glanced at Branson, who nodded for him to go ahead.

'OK, Mark, this is what we've got. A husband, Niall Paternoster, aged thirty-five, we think has killed his wife, Eden, aged thirty-one.' Grace filled him in on all the details of his suspicions, before continuing. 'We know that, in his past, Niall Paternoster worked as a butcher's apprentice. This may, as we suspect, have enabled him with sufficient knowledge to have dissected his wife's body. We believe in the early hours of last Friday he may have driven to Ashdown Forest and deposited some or all of her body parts, except for her head, in a grave.'

Taylor made some notes.

Grace continued. 'He currently works as a journeyman taxi driver, mostly on lates. We suspect that he may subsequently have disposed of his wife's head off the end of the east mole of Shoreham Harbour. At this stage, other than a single bone that may be human, but more likely not, found at the deposition site, we have no hard evidence against Paternoster. Catching him returning to the deposition site would be very helpful, for starters.'

Taylor tapped some further notes into the tablet in front of him.

'In terms of a motive, we have reason to suppose that Niall Paternoster may be having an affair,' Branson added. 'Last Sunday afternoon, some while after he claimed that his wife went into Tesco Holmbush and vanished, he had a meet-up with a person unknown at this point, at Devil's Dyke. All we have is an unregistered – presumably burner – phone, which has been traced to one of a number of houses in Barrowfield Drive, Hove. We're checking who lives there.'

'Posh address,' Taylor said. 'I'd love to live in that area if I could ever afford it. So you don't know whether the owner of the phone is male or female?'

Grace and Branson both shook their heads.

'But there were four kisses,' Branson added.

Taylor pursed his lips. 'So it's likely to be a shag.'

Grace nodded affirmation. 'Intel from his phone and from the car's satnav and onboard computer show he's had regular meet-ups at this same location over the past six months – as does the triangulation plot from the burner. I'm hoping we get lucky with your surveillance and he goes there again.'

Taylor nodded. 'What actual evidence do you currently have that Niall Paternoster has murdered his wife, Eden, sir?'

'At this stage, we have no actual body to prove murder,' Grace replied. 'Our evidence is entirely circumstantial. I would like your team to put twenty-four-seven surveillance on him. I'd particularly like to see if he goes back to the deposition site, for any reason – perhaps to check if it has been disturbed. And we'd like to see if he has any further liaisons with his contact – and to monitor, if possible, any conversations between them. His financial situation may be significant – we are led to believe that he has much to gain from his wife's death. So the principal objective of this surveillance is to monitor his movements and secure evidence.'

Mark Taylor nodded. 'OK, sir, what I suggest is I put two teams of officers on it, both on twelve-hour shifts – they'll stay longer if a changeover would compromise a particular situation. All our comms will be on our secure radio channel on our phones. I'll be running five vehicles, a motorbike, a mix of sexes, some solo, some dual. A mix of cars, white and grey vans, some with fake company names. When it's dark we can also put a tracker on his car, after getting the necessary authorization. We'll also figure out a way of bugging his house.'

'That could be very helpful.'

'We also have drone operators available, with infrared cameras, if that should be necessary, sir,' Taylor said.

'And you'll start straight after your briefing?' Grace asked.

Taylor shook his head. 'We've already started, sir. I have, thanks to the cooperation of the Greyhound Stadium opposite the Paternosters' house, an observation point, with an officer already in position with a long-lens video camera. He's taken over from your guys. I've also got a vehicle at each end of Nevill Road in case he goes anywhere before the whole team's ready. I will also have one of our brightest members, Sharon Orman, who is hard of hearing – you would never know it – joining the team after giving evidence in court on a current trial – hopefully she'll be done there today and able to join the team. Her particular expertise is lip-reading from long range. She's remarkably effective, even through night-vision lenses.'

Grace thanked him.

As soon as Taylor and Brogan had left his office, Branson asked Grace if he'd like a lift back home.

He shook his head. 'Thanks, mate, but I'd like to come to the evening briefing meeting. I'd prefer to keep occupied than go home and just let it all—' He stopped, his voice choked up. Thinking about Bruno lying in the hospital bed in his Bayern Munich strip, surrounded surreally by all the technical apparatus. He gave Branson a soulful look. 'If you understand?'

'Of course.'

'I don't want to steal your thunder as Acting SIO – you can lead the meeting if you'd like?'

'No way,' Branson said in a voice that brooked no argument. 'If you're going to be there, you're the boss!'

Grace looked at his watch. It was now 4.45 p.m. 'If we could bring it forward, from 6.30 p.m. to 5.30 p.m., it would help. Then

I can get home to be with Cleo – she's pretty cut-up too, as you can imagine.'

'Of course, 5.30 p.m. it is.' Branson extended a hand and squeezed Grace's arm, looking into his eyes. 'Look, I know you're an old wise man, and I'm just a humble upstart wannabe, but I've been through grief in my time, too. I lost my close friend, who was everything to me, when she was around Bruno's age – I told you, I'm sure, she had a brain tumour. I got through it, eventually, by bawling my eyes out for days on end. I bawled and bawled until I had nothing left inside. Somehow, I got it out of my system – well, the worst of it. The sense of losing her and how unfair it was. Now, all these years on, whenever I think about her it's only good thoughts. Smiling at the fun we had together. That's my advice: don't bottle it up, sodding well let it all out. Yeah?'

Grace smiled back at him bleakly through blurred eyes.

74

As soon as Glenn Branson had left his office, closing the door behind him, Roy Grace began to cry. He had been managing to hold it together in front of his team, but moments like this, on his own, were when his sadness returned. *Should he even be here?* He called Cleo.

She sounded strained as she answered.

'OK, darling?' he asked, putting on a brave front.

There was a short pause. 'Not really, no. I can't stop thinking about him.'

'I can't, either.'

'I see all these dead bodies all day long at work. Old, middle-aged, young – and kids. But I don't know them, I don't know their families, their stories. All I know is these are people who woke up one morning – mostly, other than those who died in their sleep – with their day ahead of them. Then something happened. They said goodbye to their loved ones, went out and they never came back home. They fell off a ladder. Got crushed to death on their bike by a cement lorry. Were texting as they drove and went head-on into another car. Got into a fight outside a pub or a bar and hit their head on a kerb. Or had a stroke, a heart attack, whatever. Regardless of the plans they'd made for that evening, the following day, the weekend, whatever. Fate got to them first. And now it's got Bruno.'

'I know,' was all Grace could think of to say at this moment.

'It's not fair, Roy, is it? Bruno was just getting through all the shit from his crazy mother.' She fell silent for a moment. 'Darling, I'm sorry – I don't mean to be insensitive.'

'No, it's fine, she was nuts – or became nuts. I don't know what demons were inside her, but yes, you're right, it's not fair.'

'I've been thinking about what the funeral director said – that all Bruno's friends at school would want to attend.'

'I've been thinking the same,' he replied. 'Maybe, with a normal kid of his age, that would be true. But from what we know of how few friends he had – and how many of his fellow pupils he'd upset – we could be setting ourselves up for a fall.'

'I have a suggestion.'

'Go on?'

'Why don't we announce it's going to be a private funeral – family members only. If it then turns out that loads of his fellow pupils did want to attend, then we could have some kind of a memorial service later?'

'I like that,' he said. 'Let's talk about it when I get home. I've got a 5.30 p.m. briefing and I'll head home straight after that – should be back by 7 p.m. latest.'

'Any thoughts on what you'd like for supper?'

'I don't know, I'm just not hungry – not right now, anyway. Want me to pick up something on the way home? From that Indian place in Henfield, perhaps?'

'Sure,' she said. 'I've got the menu on the wall in the kitchen – want me to photograph it and send it over?'

'No need. A king prawn balti, something like that. Some pop-padoms – oh and maybe some cheese naan. And some pickles. Maybe a tandoori chicken starter.'

'And you're not hungry?' she said with a hint of sarcasm, her voice lightening up a little.

'And something for yourself! I'm thinking about food now, and anyhow, we can always have leftovers tomorrow if we don't feel like eating much,' he said. 'If you can call them, tell them I'll swing by around 7 p.m.?'

'I'd better tell them you'll be there at 8 p.m.'

Grace was about to correct her, then realized it was just her mocking him. But she was right. He would invariably end up staying longer here than planned.

75

Mark Taylor sat in the square, boxy room at Police HQ, briefing his night-shift team of nine surveillance officers seated in front of him. Six male and three female, all in plain clothes, some deliberately scruffy, wearing reversible jackets and with a variety of caps and beanies stuffed in their pockets, others in varying degrees of smart casual. They would be joined soon by Sharon – Wazza – Orman, and they were aware three of their colleagues were in situ outside the subject's house.

There was a nickname for everyone in this team, with many not able to recall the real names of their colleagues, due to how infrequently they were actually used. Nicknames were easier to use when communicating amongst the team.

A monitor on the wall behind him showed a view across a wide street of four nice-looking 1950s semi-detached houses. Two were rendered in white plaster; the other two, one with a red ring drawn around it, were in brick. The ringed one had a blue Fiesta parked in the drive; they had seen the subject pick it up from a local hire company. This house, like its twin, had a deeply recessed front door behind an arched porch.

On the top right of the screen was displayed the time in hours, minutes and seconds. Immediately below that were GPS coordinates. It was the start of the evening rush hour and a steady stream of cars, motorcycles, lorries, vans, buses, cyclists and pedestrians passed by in both directions.

Taylor thumbed the remote he was holding, freezing the image, then turned back to his team. 'This is Nevill Road, Hove, taken twenty minutes ago, from Gummy's van inside the Coral Greyhound Stadium car park, almost directly across the street. The van's marked all over with the Coral logo, and it's one of three parked up together, so it won't draw any attention. Gummy's going to remain in situ for the long haul.'

They all knew what this meant. Gummy – Jason Gumbert – would be concealed inside a crate in the back of the van, videoing through the rear windows, which were two-way mirrors. He would have several days' supply of food and water, would pee into containers and, if he needed to, shit into plastic bags, which he would then seal.

'I imagine as locals you're all familiar with the area – anyone not?'

All shook their heads, one managing to do that while chugging from a water bottle at the same time.

'Smithy, good to see you multitasking!' Taylor ribbed.

The wiry DC, Darrell Smith, had a naturally furtive face, with permanently half-closed eyes, giving him the deceptive appearance of dozing. Removing the bottle from his lips, he replied in a slow, pedantic voice that belied his sharp brain, 'It's a new skill I've learned – I can drink and listen at the same time.'

'And this from a bloke who six months ago couldn't suck mints and walk at the same time!' quipped 'Long Tom' Thompson, who was a shade over five foot seven.

Taylor, smiling, looked back at the display. 'The house ringed is the Paternosters'. Niall Paternoster, the subject, is about to appear.' He pressed a button in the remote, starting the recording again, and a skip truck passed. A moment later, a muscular man with tousled hair and bulging arms, wearing a T-shirt, shorts and flip-flops and carrying two seemingly weighty carrier bags, stepped into view, hurrying across the road and making for one of the brick-faced houses.

Taylor froze the image, then zoomed in close so that Paternoster and the bags he was carrying were in clear focus. Then he looked inquisitively at his team. 'Anyone tell me what you can figure out from this image?'

'That he's ugly with bad hair?' said a shaven-headed man, nicknamed Hulk.

'I'm looking for something a little more worthy of your detective brains,' Taylor said, acknowledging Hulk with a faint grin.

'The shopping bags, sir?' suggested Lucy Arndale, nicknamed Frog Girl after once spending almost two days and nights semi-submerged in reeds at the edge of a river, waiting for a drugs drop.

'Go on,' Taylor encouraged her.

The slight woman in her late twenties, with shoulder-length brown hair and thin lips, said, 'Those are Waitrose carrier bags, sir.'

'Good shout,' Taylor said. 'And your point is?'

'Waitrose has a reputation for quality, but also as being one of the most expensive grocery store chains in the UK. So, I'm immediately wondering, if Niall Paternoster is struggling for money, what's he doing shopping in Waitrose?'

Smithy shot up his hand. 'Boss, could it not simply be that this store is the closest to his home? So he went there for convenience and hang the cost?'

'I'd buy the convenience angle,' Taylor responded. 'But he could have jumped into his car and, for the minimal expense of his petrol, made big savings from buying at Tesco or Sainsbury or Lidl or Iceland. So for a man so short of money, doesn't Waitrose seem a little extravagant?'

'Perhaps he's celebrating the end of his austerity, sir,' Lucy Arndale posited. 'He thinks, in his small mind, that he's successfully murdered his wife, with nothing to connect him to her killing, and now the house and whatever cash she has are going to be his to enjoy – with his girlfriend, perhaps the lady he's suspected of meeting at the Devil's Dyke car park last Sunday evening?'

The DS nodded. But before he could reply, a string of low-level beeps came from his phone, alerting him to a radio comms. He put the phone to his ear and pressed the 'listen' button. It was Gummy, his voice urgent.

'Boss, subject's on the move. He's out of the house, getting in the Fiesta.'

Taylor immediately switched the video from playback to live feed. They all watched.

Niall Paternoster, looking spruced up now, in a pale-blue shirt and white chinos, walked round the rear of the Fiesta and zapped the door lock.

'Too bad we don't have the tracker already in place,' Taylor said.

'If he leaves the car out all night,' Smithy said, 'it'll be a doddle.'

'Unless he's going to dismantle it and lug it in through the front door, he probably will leave it out all night, Smithy – since the house doesn't have a garage,' retorted Long Tom.

Smithy looked at Thompson. His voice sounding even more pedantic than ever, he said, 'How does it go, Tommy? "When you assume, you make an ass out of you and me"? He could have a lock-up round the corner somewhere, couldn't he?'

Thompson nodded. 'Fair point.'

But all the team's focus was now on the Fiesta trying to reverse into the stream of traffic. An old red van eventually stopped to let it out. Then the Fiesta accelerated away, heading north.

It was 5.10 p.m.

76

Five days earlier: Sunday 1 September

As Niall drove Eden's BMW into the car park of the Tesco super-store, three miles to the west of their home in Brighton, he was immediately annoyed by the queue of cars in front of them. 'Look at this – shit, baby – this is going to take ages,' he said.

'Just stop the car and I'll jump out and run in while you park. Then I'll come and find you,' she replied.

'That stuff's heavy – are you sure?'

She gave him a sideways look. 'When did you last actually get any?'

'Um – I don't remember.'

'So how do you think it appears in the house? By magic? Does the Tooth Fairy bring it?'

'OK, OK, muscle woman – look, I'll pull in over there.' He swung into an empty bay, some distance from the store.

Grabbing her handbag, Eden jumped out, blew him a kiss, slammed the door and hurried off through the maze of vehicles.

When she was confident she was out of sight of his rear-view mirror, she stopped. Thank God the store was so busy and she'd had an excuse to jump out far from the entrance. From her previous reconnaissance of this place, she knew they were well beyond the range of the store's external CCTV cameras. She'd deliberately picked a Sunday because she'd hoped it would be rammed with people doing their shop for the week – and she'd been right. Checking that the parked cars around her were all empty, with no one to see her, she knelt, removed a loose-fitting long-sleeved top and lightweight, equally loose trousers from her handbag, and donned them. Next, she pulled a grey hijab from her bag, wound it around her head and low over her brow, then put her large sunglasses back on.

Keeping crouched low, she edged her way along the bays on the outer perimeter of the car park until she reached the little dark-blue Nissan Micra, which had been left for her earlier this afternoon in the agreed spot. Still crouched, she pulled the spare key out of her handbag, unlocked the driver's door and slipped in.

Briefly checking in the mirror that the hijab and glasses were masking enough of her face, she opened the glovebox and pulled out her secret phone. She sent a brief text.

Plan A is a go! See you sooner than soon XXX

She started the car, drove to the exit and then out onto the road. *Yessssss!* she thought, exhilaration surging through her. *So far so good.* The plan, starting with the row she'd engineered on Thursday night, so their neighbours would hear, was working a treat! She looked at the car clock and then at her watch: 3.23 p.m.

Amid the ridiculous number of apps Niall had accumulated on his phone, he had never noticed the one she had added a week ago, ExifTool. It enabled you to change the date on any photograph you took. So simple. She'd used it to good effect in the BMW a short time ago, while Niall was driving, then deleted the app. He would never have noticed.

By her reckoning, and her knowledge of Niall, he would wait in the car for fifteen, maybe twenty minutes, before his patience ran out and he went to look for her. He'd search Tesco, then maybe Marks & Spencer, all of which would take at least another quarter of an hour. Quite possibly longer, but she wasn't going to allow herself the luxury of any margin. From her dress rehearsal, she could do everything she needed to do and be away within twenty minutes.

As she drove east, towards the city of Brighton and Hove, for the first time in a long while she was happy, her life filled with a new purpose.

She just had to get through the next hour.

And a very good plan would be to not get stopped for speeding. The speedometer was registering 45 mph and it was a 30 mph limit. Shit! Stupid!

She lifted her foot off the accelerator and braked sharply.

And as she did so, her heart lifted up.

The nightmare was nearly at an end.

Just a few tiny obstacles to navigate, and then . . .

She allowed herself a private smile, invisible to the outside world inside her headscarf. Just as she was.

And would remain.

No more having to put up with him. No more being with someone whose eye was elsewhere. No more having to put up with his infidelities – she knew about all of them because he was so rubbish at IT.

No more living in terror about his plan to kill her.

77

Eden passed their house and drove a couple of hundred yards up the road before pulling in and parking. This was the dangerous part. None of their immediate neighbours had any outward-facing CCTV but, even so, it was a concern. She just had to hope that no one was bothering to look out of their window at this hour on a Sunday. And if they did, they would see a woman in a hijab strolling along. Not an uncommon sight.

The time was 3.40 p.m.

She had to be out of here by 4.05 p.m., for a clear margin. Although in reality she probably had until 4.30 p.m. But, no unnecessary chances. She only had this one. A few cars passed in both directions, and a cyclist, none taking any apparent notice of her. Then she froze for a moment as she heard the banshee howl of a siren. A police car, on blues and twos, shot up the road, passed her and disappeared.

Entering the front door, kneeling briefly to give the cat, Reggie, a stroke, she pulled the checklist out of the inner pocket of her bag and began working through it. She would really miss this cat, she knew. Was there a way to bring him with her? Later, she thought, all in good time, she would figure a way to get him picked up once Niall was locked away.

First was her diamond engagement ring and her wedding ring. She placed them in a bag together with her passport and hid them beneath a loose wooden floorboard in the upstairs spare room that was his home office.

Tick.

Into the utility room to check the store cupboard. Tick.

Next, she removed the clothes she had been wearing earlier that day, a T-shirt, popsocks, shorts and trainers, putting them into a plastic bag, and changed back into her loose-fitting clothes, hijab and a spare pair of shoes. Then – and she hadn't been looking forward to this bit – she went into the kitchen, clutching the bag, and pulled the large, serrated-edge kitchen knife from the block. She pressed it to the base of the index finger of her left hand, closed her eyes, took in a deep breath and, as she exhaled, drew it quickly across the skin, slicing deeply.

Stifling her cry at the sharp pain, she opened her eyes, pleased to see blood running from the cut. She let a couple of drops fall on the work surface and some on the floor, before ensuring some more spots went onto the T-shirt, her shorts, one of her socks and onto one of her trainers. Then she wiped the floor and work surface with a kitchen towel so that the blood would be invisible to Niall's naked eye. But not to the equipment of any subsequent investigating CSIs, if what she'd gleaned from all the crime shows she'd seen on television was correct. She put the towel into her handbag. She then used the cloth and bleach to wipe the skirting boards in the kitchen to make them visibly clean.

Tick.

Wrapping the blood-stained knife in cling film, she put it, also, in her handbag, then went upstairs with the bag of her clothes, letting a couple of droplets of blood fall along the way, smearing each one with her right hand onto the wooden treads, and entered their en-suite bathroom. There she squeezed her finger, letting more blood fall on the tiles, once more smearing it in, so Niall wouldn't notice.

After quickly dabbing on some antiseptic and winding a plaster round her finger, she removed the T-shirt from the bag. Then she took out the screws from a small wall-mounted grille and placed the T-shirt in the cavity. She secured the grille but deliberately left one of the small screws on the floor, ready to be found, hopefully, by police forensic experts. She glanced anxiously at her watch. Still a safe fifteen minutes to go. She put her switched-off phone in a drawer under the bed, covering it with some underwear.

Tick.

She hurried over to the window and peered down at the street. No sign of the BMW or Niall.

She looked at her checklist. All done.

A plaintiff *mlaowwwww* made her look up. Reggie was standing in the doorway.

'What is it, darling, you want your dinner? I'd love to give it to you, but I can't, because your daddy will know I've been here. He'll be home soon – he'll remember.' She knelt, scooped him up into her arms and kissed his head. 'I'm going to miss you,' she whispered.

Reggie's answer was to purr contentedly.

'You're a nice cat, you know that?'

He continued purring.

'Thanks for being the one good thing in my life these past years.' She kissed him again and set him down. He looked at her, then rolled onto his back. She knelt again and tickled his tummy briefly. Then she stood and glanced around their bedroom. She looked at the framed prints of Victorian Brighton on the wall, one of the Chain Pier and one of the Daddy Long Legs train that ran above the sea, which Niall had bought her for their first Christmas here. It would be the last time she would be in this room. And it was her last chance to take anything, but she couldn't risk that, however tempted she was to take the one piece of jewellery Niall had bought her – in happier times – that she really liked – a

Cartier tennis bracelet. Of course, he loved to tell anyone and everyone he'd bought it for her, like some sort of trophy that she had to be grateful for.

But, hell, why take the risk of him noticing? And besides, all it would do is remind her of him.

When she wanted to spend the rest of her new life forgetting him.

She adjusted the hijab in the hall mirror, pulling it as low over her forehead as she could, and put her sunglasses back on. Then, clutching her handbag and Waitrose carrier bag in one hand and keys in the other, she let herself out of the front door and strode up the pavement towards her car, without once looking back.

78

Ten minutes later, Eden was driving along the A27 with Cyndi Lauper's 'Girls Just Want to Have Fun' blasting through the car's speakers. It was one of the songs that Niall hated. Just like most of the tracks on the playlist – her Freedom Playlist – that she'd secretly put together these past few weeks. Singing aloud to the track, she was heading north-east to Lewes, and then would take the Crowborough road towards Ashdown Forest.

Finally, she slowed, approaching the turn-off into the same car park into which she had driven the BMW last Thursday night. It was after Niall had fallen deep asleep – with a little help from the sleeping pills she'd popped into the whisky she gave him after the barbecue. She was hopeful the police would find this turn-off from interrogating the BMW's computer and his phone, which she had also taken with her, leaving hers behind.

As she pulled in, onto the sandy surface, she was relieved that no other cars were here, no one to witness her. Pulling on rubber gloves and locking the car, checking around warily for any cyclists or dog walkers, she carried the plastic bag off into the woods. Who was it who said, *If you want to make God laugh, tell him your plans*?

Well, God wasn't laughing today, but she was pretty sure he was smiling.

Just as she smiled as she removed the spade – the one she'd bought at a garden centre a while back – from the thick gorse bush where she'd concealed it. Then she began to scrape out the soil of the shallow grave she had dug in the early hours of Friday morning. Next, she unwrapped the cling film from around the bloodstained kitchen knife, put the wrapping carefully into the bag and dropped the knife into the soil.

Forty minutes later, when she had finished interring the clothes she had brought and covering them sparsely with earth, ensuring some were showing on the surface, scratching the ground to make it look like it had been disturbed by an animal, she returned to her car, placed the spade and the bag – the sole contents of which was now the cellophane in which the knife had been wrapped – in the boot and climbed into the driver's seat.

Before driving off, she keyed a text and sent it.

ETA 25 mins XXXXXX

Moments after starting the engine, a reply pinged back.

Make it 24 mins, I can't wait that long XXXXXXXX

79

Moments after Gummy announced that the subject was on the move, Mark Taylor and the team members in the room with him were watching on the live feed. The Fiesta hire car, followed by the old red van that had let it out, and a further stream of cars, headed north up Nevill Road and vanished from view. One car, three back, was a dull grey Nissan Micra – call sign Alpha One. A moment later the voice of the driver, Kim Howe, came over the radio.

'Alpha Seven, I have eyeball on subject.'

With all the team listening, Taylor replied, 'Alpha One, stay with him for as long as you can.'

'Stay with him, Alpha Seven, yes, yes,' she replied.

The image on the monitor switched to a road map, with Alpha One, now an avatar, a grey car-shaped symbol, moving steadily along the road around a long curve. She was heading towards the junction with King George VI Avenue. Two further vehicle avatars, one green, one blue, were spaced out behind her.

'Subject waiting at the junction, indicating right,' Howe said.

'Alpha One, you have Alpha Four and Alpha Eight trailing you. If you end up directly behind subject, let one overtake you. Copy?'

'Alpha Seven, yes, yes.'

They watched the symbol now move north, heading uphill towards the roundabout at the top which would give four options – onto the A27 in either direction, north towards Devil's Dyke, or south-east towards the city centre.

'It's the second left, left, left,' Howe's calm voice came through. 'I'm now directly behind.'

Taylor felt a thrum of excitement. From his earlier briefing with Grace and Branson, the car park at the Devil's Dyke beauty spot was where Niall Paternoster had a previous suspected liaison. Was he headed there now?

It was a fast, narrow road to the Dyke, which demanded maximum concentration from any driver. There were fields to the north, sloping down into a deep valley, and further on, the Dyke Golf Course. There were open farmland fields to the left, down across a panoramic vista to the urban conurbations of Southwick and Shoreham, with the harbour and sea beyond. A short distance on, to the south, was another golf course, the nine-hole Brighton and Hove Golf Club.

Quite apart from being stunning scenery, this whole area, Mark Taylor well knew from his police experience, was the place that many young dating couples in Brighton and Hove, who had access to a vehicle, would sooner or later go for perhaps their first proper kiss – and likely more. It was also, occasionally and sadly, a favoured local deposition site for bodies.

Taylor watched the blue avatar right behind the red one and spoke into the mic. 'Alpha One, Alpha Four is tailing you in a blue Suzuki Vitara Jeep – let him pass. You'll then have Alpha Eight in an old Mazda MX-5 behind. Let him pass and he'll then pass subject.'

All the team watched the manoeuvres. However vigilant Niall Paternoster might be, he would have struggled to figure out he was being followed.

Three minutes later, Howe reported, 'Alpha Seven, subject has entered car park and is heading to the far end, where I can see just one other car, a white-and-black Range Rover Evoque, index

Golf November Seven Zero Charlie Papa November. We're all parking up, and I'm keeping eyes on him.' A moment later, she said, 'Subject exiting the Fiesta holding a carrier bag that looks like it contains a bottle. Someone inside the Rangey has opened the passenger door for him. Alpha Eight has parked right opposite, may have a better view.'

A different voice came on the radio. The chirpy voice of Nigel Hurst. 'Alpha Seven, Alpha Eight here, boss. Subject having an embrace with a blonde lady in the Range Rover. Now he's inside and closed the door. Possible Ugandan discussions,' he quipped, quoting the euphemism coined by the satirical newspaper *Private Eye* for illicit copulation.

Taylor radioed the Range Rover's registration number through to a controller, requesting an ident on the owner. The information came back in less than a minute.

80

Just as he was about to enter the conference room for the evening briefing, Roy Grace's phone rang. It was Mark Taylor.

'Sir,' the DS said. 'You told me in our briefing you suspected Niall Paternoster was having an affair. We currently have eyes on a Range Rover Evoque parked up at Devil's Dyke, where he appears to be having a liaison with a lady. The index of her car gives her as Rebecca Watkins of 17 Barrowfield Drive, Hove.'

'Nice area,' Grace said, memorizing the name and address. 'Quite posh. Paternoster's trading up, is he?'

'Very much so,' Taylor replied. 'A dream house – fat chance on my pay!'

Grace ignored the comment, thinking hard, visualizing Devil's Dyke. 'You should have enough vehicles to cover any of the possible routes Paternoster takes from there.'

'Yes, sir. There's only one road out of the Devil's Dyke car park. Soon after, there's one junction, with an option to go straight on or turn left, up past the Dyke Golf Club. We can cover that easily.'

'Good.'

'Something else, sir,' Taylor said. 'Subject has parked out of direct sight of the Range Rover, including its mirrors. The area's fairly quiet and we think we have a chance to put a tracker on subject's car, while he's otherwise preoccupied. I already have authority.'

'Don't take any risk of anyone being seen,' Grace cautioned.

'That is my job, sir.'

Grace felt the reproachful tone of the DS's voice like a rebuke. He should have known better, he realized, than try to give advice to a man of Taylor's calibre.

'Of course, Mark. I understand.'

'Thank you, sir.'

Grace took his place next to Glenn Branson at the table in the conference room, thinking to himself how the receiver of the text message from Sunday night was almost certainly Rebecca Watkins. As the team filed in, he rapidly familiarized himself with the notes he had prepared for the briefing. Over many years, he had imbued the importance of punctuality in all his team members. On one occasion, when a particularly arrogant young detective had sauntered in ten minutes after the decreed starting time, Grace had given him a withering look and said to the DC, whom he had never used again, 'You know what being late tells me? It says that your time is more important than mine and everyone else's gathered here.'

On the dot of 5.30 p.m. on the wall clock, with everyone present, Grace said, 'This is the seventh briefing of Operation Lagoon, the investigation into the disappearance and suspected death of Eden Paternoster.'

A phone rang. Lorna Dennison-Wilkins glanced at the mobile on her desk then raised an apologetic hand. 'I need to take this, sir.'

He nodded to her.

She answered, hurriedly stepping out of the room and closing the door behind her.

Continuing, Grace said, 'We've had confirmation from Lucy Sibun, a short while ago, that the bone found in the grave of the deposition site in Ashdown Forest isn't human, as her colleague suspected – it's the tibia of a roe.'

'Oh deer!' Norman Potting said, looking around, but there was no response. Undeterred, he quipped again, referencing an enquiry many of them had been involved with some time back. 'Stag night gone wrong, was it?'

'Not today, Norman, OK?' Grace turned as Dennison-Wilkins came back into the room, looking like she had news. 'Sir,' she said to Grace, but addressing everyone. 'That was PC Bennion-Jones, who's working with the team at the garage examining the Paternosters' BMW. He called right away because he thought it might be significant to our enquiries. They've found a magnetic GPS tracker concealed under the rear of the car.'

81

For some moments no one in the conference room spoke. The silence was briefly broken by the sound of Abba's 'Dancing Queen' bursting out of a phone and being rapidly shut off. Roy Grace looked at a red-faced Jack Alexander.

'Sorry, boss – Kaitlynn put it on my phone as a joke. Thought I'd got rid of it.'

The silence resumed, to be broken again by Grace exclaiming, 'A tracker under the Paternosters' BMW, which must have been there before we seized the vehicle? What is that about?'

'Bennion-Jones told me it was a TKSTAR – a good brand, waterproof, with a three-month battery life,' Lorna Dennison-Wilkins informed him.

'A tracker under the Paternosters' car,' Grace repeated, more calmly now. 'So who put it there? Niall Paternoster? Eden? Someone external – not the police, so far as we know – but we need to check that.' He turned to Potting. 'Norman, I'll give you the action of eliminating the police from putting it there.'

'Yes, chief.'

Grace was pensive again, then said, 'Whoever put it there wanted to see where the car was going. This was a vehicle that both husband and wife shared. Did one of them place it there and, if so, which one? And why? Or could it have been someone else altogether?'

He looked around a sea of faces deep in thought. 'Lorna, did

JBJ give you any sense of whether this is a rare or common tracker?'

'He said it was one of a number widely available, sir. This particular one costs around thirty pounds – it's sold in a lot of shops and on Amazon.'

'Do we know if it was active or dormant?' Grace asked. 'Could it have been there for years perhaps, from a previous owner of the vehicle?'

She shook her head. 'He said it's a recently upgraded version that's only been on the market for a couple of months.'

'OK, well that might help us find out where it was bought from and by who.'

Martyn Stratford called out, 'Sir.'

'Yes, Martyn?'

'I've just looked up this product,' he said, nodding at his laptop screen. 'There seem to be a very large number of retailers – including Amazon, as Lorna just mentioned.'

Grace made a note. They needed to check the Paternosters' laptops for Amazon purchase history. 'Let's hypothesize for now that it's either Niall or Eden Paternoster who has put this there. For what reason?'

Norman Potting raised his arm and caught Grace's eye. 'There's normally only one, chief. Suspected cheating.'

'So speaks the expert!' said Kevin Hall. His remark was greeted with laughter, which momentarily broke the unusually sombre mood of the team.

Potting raised his arms and took a bow by twirling his hands.

'So, taking your point, Norman,' Grace said. 'Who has suspected who here? Husband or wife? What—'

Grace's phone rang. Glancing at the display, he saw it was Mark Taylor again. 'This might be important,' Grace apologized, answering it.

It was.

'Sir,' Mark Taylor said. 'Just to give you a heads-up. The lady got out of her Range Rover to kiss lover boy goodbye. We've got some good photographs of her, I'm pinging them through to you now.'

As he spoke, Grace felt his phone vibrate, signalling an incoming email. 'Nice work, Mark.'

'Lover boy's walking back to his car. He's looking pretty happy with himself, if you get my drift, sir?'

'Like he's had a *happy ending*?'

'Well – exactly.'

It took a few moments for the photographs to finish downloading. When they had, Roy Grace was staring at a woman in her mid-to-late thirties, with short, stylish fair hair that was looking a bit ruffled. She reminded him a little of the actress Sienna Miller – she had a certain beauty, but a hard edge to her face. He handed the phone to Branson, telling him to pass it round. 'We believe this lady may be called Rebecca Watkins,' Grace said. 'Niall Paternoster's girlfriend. I'd like you all to take a look at her. Rebecca Watkins. Anyone recognize her?'

Everyone in turn studied it carefully, each of the team shaking their heads, until it got to Polly. She stared at it rigidly for several seconds. Then she looked directly at Roy Grace. 'I thought I recognized the name, sir. Now, seeing her face, I'm even more sure. I interviewed her along with a bunch of other people at Eden Paternoster's employers, Mutual Occidental Insurance. If I'm right, Rebecca Watkins is Eden Paternoster's line manager – her boss.'

'You're sure, are you, Polly?' Roy Grace asked.

She hastily looked at her notebook.

There was a short silence. Just the sound of Martyn Stratford tapping his keyboard, who then looked up. 'I can confirm that Rebecca Watkins works for Mutual Occidental.' He held up his laptop, showing a photograph of the woman, looking even more severe in a dark business suit and white ruff collar.

There was little doubt in anyone's mind it was the same person as the one in the photographs that had just been sent through to Grace's phone.

A moment later, Polly confirmed it.

82

It had happened more than once before in Roy Grace's career, when a fresh piece of evidence out of left field had turned an investigation on its head – or at least threw into question all their lines of enquiry, he well knew.

'This information, combined with the discovery of the tracker, is making me think there are two other dimensions to this case that we need to investigate,' Grace said.

He had everyone's complete attention.

'So far we've been focusing on Niall Paternoster as our prime suspect, with all the evidence pointing to him having murdered Eden. Now we have evidence that he's having an affair – and with his wife's boss – could we be looking at a conspiracy between Niall Paternoster and Rebecca Watkins to murder Eden? Or should we be looking at something completely different al-together?' He stared around at his team quizzically.

'A set-up?' suggested Luke Stanstead.

Grace nodded at him. 'That's my thinking. We have no body so far, despite all the evidence of murder and the deposition site. But is it possible that it could be there to mislead us? Along with the photograph at Parham House? All we have at that site are some items of clothing in and around a shallow grave, and a knife that in my view has maybe been put in the wrong place – a far too obvious one.'

He paused to let that sink in. 'It's possible that having murdered

Eden, dissected her and buried her remains, Niall dumped the knife in a red mist of panic or, just as likely, it was dragged from the grave by an animal. But we know he, or at least his car and his phone, then went to Shoreham Harbour. So if he was going to the harbour to drop his wife's head into the sea, wouldn't he also have disposed of the knife there?'

He let that hang in the air for a moment, looking around at this team. No one contradicted him. 'We always need to consider the alternatives in any case,' he continued. 'Let's suppose for a moment that the kitchen knife was deliberately put in that sparse bush, instead of one of the much thicker bushes close by, so we would find it?'

DC Soper raised a hand.

'Yes, Louise?'

The smartly dressed Detective Constable, her brown hair elegant as always, her discreet Hublot watch the only clue to her private wealth, held up a sheaf of papers. 'It's a good point, sir. I've been going through the forensic report on the Paternosters' BMW, as I'm sure we all have, and something's struck me – as I'm sure it must have you.'

'Which is, Louise?' Grace encouraged.

'If Niall Paternoster had murdered his wife and transported her to the deposition site in Ashdown Forest in their BMW – which all the evidence from the car's satnav and onboard computer points to – why is there no DNA evidence in the car? It's a two-door convertible – so most likely he would have put her body in the boot, or at least on the back seat, although that would have been awkward. Yet there is no DNA evidence – so far at least – of her being in either.'

Grace nodded. 'A good point, Louise.'

Norman Potting raised a hand. 'But if Niall had wrapped up all the body parts carefully, say in bin liners or plastic sheeting, there wouldn't necessarily have been any DNA in the car.'

'Yes, Norman,' he replied. 'But if he'd had the presence of mind to wrap up the body parts carefully, in my thinking that doesn't square with the seemingly careless way he'd disposed of the knife – if that is in fact what he did.'

He saw the Financial Investigator trying to attract his attention.

'Emily?'

'Sir,' Denyer said, 'as we already know, the house in Nevill Road is owned by Eden Paternoster. We found out that a year ago she paid off the mortgage, but does he know that? It looks like she used the income she had built up from her rental properties. I've now discovered two things of interest late this afternoon. The first is, just ten weeks ago, she raised a seventy per cent mortgage on the house of £420,000, from the Lothian Bank of Commerce. And secondly, possibly even more significant, six weeks ago she transferred that entire amount to a nominee account in the Cayman Islands. I am awaiting more information from the Land Registry but I doubt Niall is aware of any of this.'

Grace felt a beat of excitement at this new information. *Am I being set up here?* he began to wonder. *Have I missed something?* Niall Paternoster was having an affair with Eden's boss. Had she suspected her husband and placed the tracker under their car? Or did she hire someone to do it? Did she suspect he might be about to divorce her, so she'd moved all the assets she could overseas? And, holding down a senior job in IT in a major international company, she was clearly tech savvy.

He thought back to the chessboard, with the game in progress in the Paternosters' living room. Roy Grace's grandfather had taught him chess when he was about seven, and he'd played often with him, and also occasionally with his dad – until his father stopped playing with him because he always beat his old man too easily.

Chess was about strategy. Thinking as many moves ahead as

you could. The fact that both Niall and Eden played chess against each other indicated both were strategists. Was Eden Paternoster still alive? Who was out-thinking the other here in a game beyond the board?

83

Addressing his team, Roy Grace said, 'I want to run a parallel line of enquiry, looking at the possibility Eden Paternoster is not dead and has set this whole thing up – and if so, why?'

'Could she have done this to get her husband locked up on a murder charge, boss?' Glenn Branson said.

'On the face of it, that would seem the most likely,' Grace agreed. 'Maybe she planted the blood-spotted T-shirt, hid her rings in a place they would be found, took items of clothing to the forest? Far-fetched? Maybe, but an angry, hurt partner in a relationship is capable of going to any lengths to hit back.' He continued, 'But we should consider this might only be a smoke-screen and there's another motive behind it. I want to stress these are only hypotheses and I don't want to deflect our complete focus away from the current lines of enquiry. So I'm going to divide our resources.'

'You mean like punting each way on a horse race, chief?' Norman Potting interrupted. 'Hedging your bet?'

'That's a rather crude way of putting it, Norman, and I'm not so much a betting man these days, I prefer to follow the evidence, but point taken. I'm giving you and Velvet the action of establishing whether Eden Paternoster is still alive.' He looked at both officers.

Velvet Wilde nodded. Potting pursed his lips. 'Five to two on the husband being the killer, ten to one his wife's still alive.'

Frustrated now, Grace snapped, 'This is not a game, Norman. These are people's lives.'

Immediately he realized his nerves were frayed and he was exhausted. And he felt guilty for snapping at Norman, who was going through his own particular hell right now. Maybe he should have stayed home and not come in.

Looking suitably crestfallen, Potting said, 'Sorry, chief.'

Moving on, Grace continued, 'What if when Eden left their BMW in the Tesco car park she went round the back of the store and got into another car? One of the actions you need to start with is to check all local car hire companies and see if her name pops up. Recheck the CCTV cameras around the outside of the store and see if you can spot anything that might support this theory. Perhaps she had a disguise planned. A wig, different clothing. Maybe she had an accomplice – a lover or friend waiting in the car park?'

'What about checking all ANPR cameras around the roads out of the store, sir?' Emma-Jane Boutwood asked.

'I've been thinking about that, EJ. But that's a big ask – the exit leads onto a main road going in two different directions, and we don't even know what vehicle we're looking for. If any. If Niall Paternoster is telling the truth – and it's still a big *if* – then Eden might well have left the Tesco car park in a vehicle. If we could identify that vehicle, then yes, definitely.'

'What about a number-plate match to any vehicles on Nevill Road in the window of time before he could have got back there, boss?' Jack Alexander suggested.

Grace nodded thoughtfully. 'OK, you're suggesting, depending on where the cameras are located – if any are in either location – that we see what vehicles left Tesco and then drove along Nevill Road? It's a big task, but something we should consider if there is a camera there.'

DS Stratford interrupted them. 'Sir, there is one ANPR camera a quarter mile to the east of the store. The other is just over a mile to the west. But there are none covering any part of Nevill Road.'

'Shame,' Grace said, and looked back at Alexander. 'It was a good idea.'

DS Stratford focused back on his screen. Grace turned to the Financial Investigator. 'We need a thorough breakdown of Eden Paternoster's finances, Emily. Drill into her background, look at her maiden name, Townsend, and any other family names she might possibly have used as an alias.'

'Yes, sir, already on it, I should have an update tomorrow.'

'Excellent. Glenn, any update from your press conference?'

'Unfortunately no sightings of Eden or useful information from the public to date; it's drawn a blank, boss. Two crank calls and that's it.'

Roy Grace looked again at his team. 'One piece of evidence from Digital Forensics that's been driving our investigation towards Niall Paternoster so far is the examination of his computer. It's shown that he'd been searching for ways to commit murder and dispose of human bodies. Norman and Velvet, I need you to ask Aiden Gilbert at Digital Forensics for a log of all the times when Niall Paternoster was supposedly looking at murder and body-disposal methods. Then you need to speak to the taxi owner, Mark Tuckwell – he must have a record of the times that Paternoster was using his taxi.'

'To see if it could have been Niall Paternoster online at those times, sir?' Velvet Wilde asked in her rich Belfast accent. 'If he was out driving the taxi that would indicate maybe his wife was accessing his computer, perhaps?'

'Exactly,' Grace said. He hesitated for a moment, before continuing. 'I'm not saying this is what I believe happened but we need to eliminate that as a possibility – or not.' He looked around. 'What I am saying, at this moment, is that I don't bloody know.

Right now we have a woman who has disappeared and her husband having an affair with his wife's boss. There is evidence her husband murdered her – but we have no body. I also have grounds for suspecting Eden could have set this up.'

Chris Gee raised his arm. Grace nodded at him.

'I'm wondering if I was Niall Paternoster and innocent, how would I be reacting right now, sir? Would I be taking this calmly or protesting my innocence loudly? Which has he been doing?' the Crime Scene Manager asked.

'Good question, Chris,' Grace responded. 'From all I've seen so far, Niall Paternoster is hard to read.' He turned to Potting and Exton. 'You've been conducting the interviews – what are your views?'

Jon Exton replied, 'When we arrested him, boss, his first concern was for their cat.'

Several of the team giggled.

'Bless!' EJ Boutwood said. 'He loves animals, he's clearly innocent.'

'Hitler loved animals, too,' Potting mumbled.

'For most of the interviews we conducted he alternated between being belligerent and going "no comment",' Exton said. 'I found him hard to read.' He looked at Potting.

'Same here, chief.'

'OK,' Grace said. 'We need to talk to this Rebecca Watkins urgently. Have we found any more about her?' He looked at DS Stratford.

'Yes, I've been doing a search on her family, sir.' He leaned over his shoulder and pointed at the association chart on one of the whiteboards behind him. 'Her husband, Ned, runs a successful advertising agency based in Brighton. They've been married five years, no children.'

Grace thanked him, then looked at Polly. 'I'm very curious about this lady, I'd like to meet her myself. I think we'll pay her a visit straight after this briefing – then you and I can bring her in for a formal interview.'

'Might that not risk potential issues with her marriage, sir?' Polly asked.

'And your point is?'

'Just saying, sir.'

'Polly,' Grace retorted, 'Rebecca Watkins is Eden Paternoster's boss. Eden has gone missing. That's why we're going to talk to her. I'm not about to tell her hubby that his wife is having an affair – are you?'

'No – sir,' Polly responded assertively.

84

Half an hour after the seventh briefing of Operation Lagoon had ended, Roy Grace, accompanied by Polly Sweeney, turned the silver, unmarked Mondeo estate off Dyke Road Avenue into Barrowfield Drive, an exclusive residential enclave of smart, detached houses. The entrance road was narrow, more like a country lane than somewhere in the middle of a city. The only giveaway was the yellow lines down each side at the start of the drive.

A wide mix of houses could be seen, Edwardian, mock Tudor, ultra-modern, colonial with columned porticos and a few old-fashioned, country-cottage style. Several had expensive motors in the driveways, adding to the air of moneyed exclusivity.

'They ought to have a sign at the entrance to this estate,' Polly observed. 'No riff-raff here.'

Grace, following the car's satnav, smiled thinly as he made a left into Barrowfield Drive. 'Nor anyone on a copper's salary,' he added.

A man in his fifties, wearing orange earbuds, jogged past in the opposite direction.

'Any of these fit your idea of a dream home, sir?' Polly asked.

Grace shook his head. 'Houses too close together. They're beautiful, but if I had the kind of money to buy one of these, I'd get something in the country. Rolling acres, that kind of thing.'

'Fancy yourself as Lord Grace of Grace Towers, do you, sir?'

Grace shook his head. 'Nope. Never had any desire for that kind of money. Did you ever read the novel *Catch-22*?'

'No – is it good?'

'Brilliant, a classic. I read that its author, Joseph Heller, was at a party in New York thrown by some billionaire for a bunch of writers. Someone asked him how it made him feel that, no matter how successful he was as an author, he would never make the kind of money his host did. Know what Heller replied?'

Polly shook her head.

'He said, "I have something he will never have. And that's the knowledge that I have enough"'

Polly, smiling, checked the numbers, then said, 'Here, boss, number seventeen.'

Grace pulled up outside a fancy, mock-Georgian mansion, with a Grecian-columned porch. A Range Rover Evoque and a matt-black McLaren were parked ostentatiously in the curved driveway out front.

Grace, automatically clocking their licence plates, smiled too. It was good to be back properly on the job – it was helping him so much to escape, however fleetingly, from his grief over Bruno.

They climbed out and walked up the path to the front door. Polly glanced enviously at the McLaren. 'Wouldn't mind one of those,' she said.

'What colour?'

She wrinkled her nose. 'I'm not fussed.'

85

Entering the porch, Roy Grace pressed the doorbell – one of the modern ones, a Nest, with a built-in video. Even the chimes they could hear faintly sounded expensive. He half expected a butler to open the door.

A dog yapped. Followed by a man's voice calling out, 'Kiko! Kiko!'

Moments later the door opened a crack, then wider. A lean man in his mid-forties with an equine face, a dishevelled mop of thinning fair hair covering the front of his head, stood there. He was dressed in a T-shirt, running shorts and trainers, and clutching one of the smallest dogs Grace had ever seen – it was barely larger than a rat – to his sweaty chest. Despite his clear recent exertions, the man smelled of cologne. Staring at them without an ounce of welcome in his expression, he said flatly, 'Yes?'

'Mr Ned Watkins?' Grace asked and held up his warrant card, as did his colleague. 'Detective Superintendent Grace and Investigating Officer Sweeney of Surrey and Sussex Major Crime Team.'

'Yes, that's me.'

'We would like to speak to your wife, Rebecca. Is she home?' Grace said.

The dog, its eyes like wet marbles, was sizing them up.

'What about?' he asked.

'Is your wife home?' Grace repeated politely.

He hesitated then said, 'She is, yes.'

'We'd like to speak to her,' Grace said.

'Would you like to tell me what this is about?' Ned Watkins said insistently.

'It concerns a work colleague of hers, sir.'

'The woman who's gone missing?'

'That's correct, sir.'

He opened the door wider and stepped aside, ushering them in, still clutching the dog. Then he called out, quite stiffly, Grace noted, with no affection in his voice, 'Becky!'

From somewhere in the house a voice, equally lacking in affection, called back, 'Yes?'

'It's people from Sussex Police wanting to speak to you.' Then he closed the door and set the dog down. It glared at Grace and Polly, yapped a couple of times, then scurried off, disappearing into a doorway.

'OK!' the voice called out. 'Just on a call, be there in a sec.'

Ned Watkins looked at them both. 'I'm just back from a run. Going to take a shower – I'll leave you to it.'

'Thank you, sir, we're sorry to intrude.'

Without replying, Watkins walked down the hall and disappeared up the ornate, curved staircase at the far end.

The hall had a crisp, modern and arty feel. A polished oak floor with a black-and-white patterned runner carpet; abstract art on the grey walls; a chaise longue that looked like a giant lobster with its back hollowed out. *Weird*, Grace thought. Not something he'd want greeting him when he arrived home.

A woman appeared through the same doorway the dog had run into. She was barefoot, with razor-cut bleached blonde hair, dressed in stylish gym kit.

No mistaking her, Grace thought, glancing at Polly out of the corner of his eye. He recognized her instantly from the photographs Mark Taylor had sent through. An attractive, slim woman in her mid-thirties, she looked more like a model or an actress than someone who worked in a rather more mundane IT position in the insurance world.

She approached them, followed by the dog.

'Good evening?' she said, polite but unsmiling. Her voice had a faint accent. Normally good at regional accents, Roy Grace could not immediately place hers. A Midlands accent she was trying to suppress, perhaps.

'Mrs Rebecca Watkins?' Grace asked, again displaying his warrant card. He repeated his and Polly's credentials. 'We'd like to have a word with you – is there somewhere we can talk privately?' Then, lowering his tone, he added, 'Discreetly?'

A shadow flitted across her face. 'What do you mean by that?' She looked for a moment at Polly, a tad too closely. 'Didn't I see you at my office earlier this week?'

'Yes,' Polly said. Then, lowering her voice, 'We'd like to talk to you about your whereabouts this afternoon, Mrs Watkins.'

She jumped. It was as if she'd just stuck a finger into an electrical socket.

There was a faint hiss and whirr from upstairs – the sound of a shower running, Grace thought. 'If it's not convenient here, perhaps you could accompany us to Police HQ?'

'Here's fine,' she said stiffly. She indicated a door on their left, opened it, led them through and closed it behind her.

The detectives entered a lounge, bizarrely decorated in vivid colours. There was a life-size model tiger, a silver giraffe head on one wall and some very strange modern art on the others, as well as a white baby grand piano.

Rebecca Watkins gestured them to one of two curved blue sofas facing a glass coffee table, inside which – and Grace didn't care to look at them too much – was an assortment of preserved spiders and beetles. She then closed the door firmly, ensuring it clicked shut.

Grace looked at the piano. 'Do you play?' he asked, trying to break the ice and to get a reading from her face.

'My husband,' she said dismissively, as if it were an affliction rather than a talent. She sat down opposite them, bolt upright, crossing her legs and then her arms.

Defensive pose, Grace noted.

'Who's the entomologist?' Polly asked.

The woman threw a casual glance down at the table. 'Oh, that's my husband, too. Not my thing at all. Critters, yech!' She shuddered.

Grace wondered, curious, if she didn't like the insects why she allowed it to be a centrepiece of their living room. She didn't look like a pushover to him.

'So, officers, I must ask, do you know Bill Warner – he's a cousin of mine?'

Grace nodded. 'Yes, one of the best police officers I've ever had the privilege to work with.'

'Lovely man.'

'He is,' Grace said. Then, lowering his voice a few octaves, he said, 'Mrs Watkins, could you tell us your movements over the past four hours? As I said, if you would prefer to talk somewhere more discreetly we could go to Police HQ?'

She locked eyes with him fleetingly. 'Why would I need to talk somewhere discreet? I've nothing to hide.'

'OK,' Grace said and glanced at his watch. It was 7.02 p.m. 'If you could please tell us your movements since 3 p.m. today?'

She shrugged. 'I've been attending an IT seminar in Hastings for the past two days, which finished at lunchtime. There was no point going to the office – I work up at Croydon, as you know – so I took the afternoon off and went to Waitrose in Brighton to do my weekly shop. Then I came home, unpacked everything and began preparing our evening meal.'

Grace, focused on her eyes, asked, 'You work for the Mutual Occidental Insurance Company?'

'I do, yes. Your friend here knows this, I saw her there this week.'

'With Mrs Eden Paternoster?'

'Correct, yes.'

'Did you go anywhere else during this time, this afternoon, Mrs Watkins?'

She shook her head. 'No, like I said, I was here preparing supper.'

'And your husband would be able to confirm that?' Polly said.

Both detectives saw the hesitation in her face. 'He only came home at about 6 p.m. and then went straight out for a run.'

'What time did you go to Waitrose this afternoon?' Grace asked.

'I don't know – around 3 p.m.'

'And how long were you in the store?'

'Half an hour – maybe forty minutes.'

'Then you came back home?' he continued.

The hesitation again. 'Yes.'

'The CCTV in the Waitrose store would be able to confirm the time you arrived and left,' Grace said. 'Are you sure you came straight back home?'

'Yes, of course, I had stuff that needed to go into the freezer. What is this about?'

Grace reached into his inside pocket and pulled out a series of photographs, which he laid, facing her, on the coffee table. She was good, he thought, with sneaking admiration, she barely twitched a muscle. She just looked at them, completely dispassionately.

'You can see in the first photograph a black-and-white Range Rover Evoque, the licence plate is the same as the one parked on your driveway. Is that your vehicle, Mrs Watkins?'

'Yes.' Still defiant.

'And is that you in the other photographs?'

'Yes.'

'These were taken at approximately 5.30 p.m. today in the car park at Devil's Dyke. You say you were at home all afternoon, after returning from Waitrose, that's correct, is it?'

'Obviously not,' she said. 'I forgot about that bit.'

Grace glanced at Polly. 'We're not here to make any moral judgements, Mrs Watkins. We are investigating the disappearance of Mrs Eden Paternoster, the wife of the man in these photographs with you. We believe she may have been murdered. You and Mrs Paternoster are work colleagues – you are her line manager, if I understand correctly.'

'You do.'

'Are you aware that Niall Paternoster, her husband, is a prime suspect in our murder enquiry?'

'It's been all over the news,' she retorted. 'It was front page on the *Argus* yesterday and headlined on Radio Sussex and BBC television. But if you think Niall was responsible, you are very wrong. He's a sweet man who wouldn't harm anyone.'

There was a knock on the door. Polly immediately leaned forward and grabbed the photographs, just as it opened.

Ned Watkins peered in. He shot a 'still here?' look at the detectives, then addressed his wife coldly again. 'Off to poker – everything OK?'

'Fine,' she said. 'I'm going to my kick-boxing class shortly.'

'See you,' he said.

'See you,' she replied stiffly.

As he closed the door, the lack of affection between the two hung in the air like the vapour from dry ice.

'Mrs Watkins,' Grace asked, 'where were you last Sunday, September the first, around 5.30 p.m.?'

'I took our dog, Kiko, for a walk on the Dyke.'

'Is that all?' Grace persisted.

Outside they heard the roar of a high-powered engine starting, followed by what seemed to the officers to be several unnecessarily loud revs, as if Ned Watkins was signalling some displeasure. Then came a squeal of tyres and the *vroom* of the McLaren, they presumed, roaring off at speed.

Seemingly ignoring the sound, Rebecca Watkins gave Grace a long, hard stare. 'I'm guessing you know the answer to that. So, before I say anything else, am I a suspect – is that what this is about? Should I have my solicitor present?'

Both detectives shook their heads. 'No, you are not a suspect,' Grace answered. 'Not at this moment.'

'Meaning?' she rounded on him.

'If you were a suspect, we would have arrested you,' Grace said. 'We are aware that you appear to be in some form of relationship with Niall Paternoster, who is a person of interest to us. The purpose of coming to see you is to be able to eliminate you from our enquiries.'

'Or implicate me?'

Roy Grace stared levelly at her. 'We need to make sure you didn't help Niall Paternoster murder his wife, Eden, and dispose of her body.'

'That's absolutely ridiculous!' she replied.

'Then you have nothing to worry about. We would like you to come to the Police HQ in Lewes tomorrow morning to be interviewed as you are an important witness. What time would be convenient?'

'I'm in a meeting at work all tomorrow morning – it's the monthly appraisals of my team, we're having to do them on a Saturday.'

'Fine,' Grace said. 'What about tomorrow afternoon?'

She shook her head. 'I've meetings booked all afternoon.'

Grace stared back at her. 'Would you prefer us to arrest you on suspicion of conspiracy to murder?'

There was a long, silent stand-off. Then she said compliantly, 'Would 9 a.m. work?'

Grace glanced at Polly, who nodded. 'OK, 9 a.m. If you go to reception at the front entrance of the Police HQ in Lewes, they'll have a car park space reserved for you.'

'You don't seriously think I have anything to do with Niall's wife's disappearance, do you?'

'So long as you don't, Mrs Watkins,' Grace said, 'then you have nothing to worry about.'

'Good,' she said. 'Then I'm afraid I have to be off, I don't want to be late for my class.'

86

As the detectives drove away from the Watkinses' house, heading back to HQ, Roy Grace turned to Polly. 'Your thoughts?'

'Her husband is one angry man.'

'A right loving relationship – not,' Grace said.

'Has the husband found out about her affair?' Polly asked. 'Should we include him on our list of suspects?'

Grace, halting the car at the junction with Dyke Road Avenue, said, 'If he was going to murder anyone it would be his wife – or Niall Paternoster. He wouldn't have any reason to harm Eden – unless I'm missing something?' He turned left.

'There's a very strange dynamic going on in that relationship.'

'For sure. But there's always two sides in a marriage breakdown.'

'We've been focusing on Niall Paternoster as our prime suspect, sir,' Polly said. 'But that Rebecca Watkins, blimey O'Reilly, she is one cold fish. Hard as nails.'

Grace nodded. 'Hard enough to have murdered Eden, to get her man?'

'I was wondering that, sir. Does she look like a murderer?'

Grace smiled. Something Glenn Branson had once said, quoting a movie as he so often did, came into his mind. He was trying to remember which, then it came to him. 'Did you ever see that Hitchcock film *Strangers on a Train*, Polly?'

She frowned. 'I think I may have done.'

'There's a line in it that gives you your answer; it's something like, "I'll tell you what a murderer looks like. A murderer looks like anyone."'

She nodded. 'So true. Worth putting surveillance on Rebecca Watkins as well?'

Grace shook his head. 'Nice idea, but we don't have the resources. And, despite what we've seen of Niall Paternoster and Rebecca Watkins, I've still got doubts about Eden's disappearance. Maybe we'll know more after we interview Rebecca tomorrow. Wear plain clothing. Nothing to distract the subject.'

'I've got a shirt that DI Branson would be ashamed of,' Polly said with a smile.

'Sounds perfect.'

87

Friday 6 September

It was just past 9 p.m. when Roy Grace pulled up outside their cottage. It was dark and as he climbed out of the car, hearing the distant bleat of a sheep somewhere, he felt a small amount of weight fall from his shoulders. The air smelled sweet and he breathed in the almost intoxicating smell of freshly mown grass. Before his thoughts returned to Bruno.

Inside their house, he could hear Humphrey barking his greeting. He stood for some moments, looking up at the hill, thinking. Thinking that Bruno would never see this again. That he would never see Bruno again.

His only link with Sandy now gone.

He put the Indian takeaway into the oven to keep warm. At least, now he was on the Paternoster case, he was no longer at risk of being called out in the middle of the night to a crime scene – someone else could have that pleasure.

'Hey, darling, I'm home.'

He was really hungry, he realized, having barely eaten all day.

'I'm home!' he called out.

Silence.

As he went through into the living area, Humphrey walking along beside him, he saw Noah's baby monitor on the coffee table in front of the sofa, beside a book Cleo was part way through.

'Cleo!' he called out, then climbed the stairs and entered their bedroom. No sign of her. He slung his jacket onto the antique chaise longue in front of the bed that they'd bought at the weekly auction in Lewes, tugged off his tie and dropped that onto it, then undid the top two buttons of his shirt and walked along the corridor to Noah's room, rolling up his sleeves. He opened the door. The curtains were drawn and he saw the silhouette of his son asleep.

He crept over and looked down at the boy, curled up in his cot – which he would soon outgrow – clutching his special teddy and a small stuffed monkey close to his face.

Blowing him a silent kiss, he retreated, closing the door softly, then climbed the steep attic steps and opened the door to Bruno's room. Instantly, he felt a tug in his heart. Cleo was sitting on the end of his bed, on the red-and-white Bayern Munich bedspread, dressed in a loose smock, her hair clipped up, hands folded in her lap.

'Darling,' he said gently.

She looked up at him through red, tear-stained eyes, her face a picture of sadness.

He strode over, sat down beside her and put his arm around her, kissing her on her wet cheek.

'It's just so horrible, isn't it?' she said.

He hugged her tightly to him. 'Yes.'

He gazed around the cosy little room at the poster of Pascal Gross looking triumphant, scoring a winner for Brighton and Hove Albion. He looked at the television screen on the wall and Bruno's beloved gaming box, wires trailing, beneath it. The little dressing table with a neat row of bottles and tubes of hair gel.

He was tearful now, too. 'I still just – I just—' He fell silent for some moments. 'I knew him for such a short time. I just wish we'd had longer. I'm sure in time I could – we could—' He fell silent again.

Cleo squeezed his hand. 'You would,' she said. 'I know you would.'

They sat in silence again. Cleo finally broke it. 'I know he had his strange ways, but he was a nice person at heart, I'm sure of it.'

Grace thought suddenly about the dead hens. Neatly laid out. Remembering what Bruno had said to him in the car on Tuesday, just three days ago, when he'd been fine, alive, alert. His comment about the ancient Egyptians.

Had Bruno somehow known he was going to die that day? Had he prepped for it? Killed the two hens – his favourites?

Was he wanting them to be mummified and buried with him?

'He had the most rotten start in life,' Cleo went on, 'but he really did love the hens – and Humphrey.' She paused. 'You loved him, didn't you?'

'Yes, I did – and I know you loved him, too.'

Another long silence.

'How's the case going?' Cleo asked at last.

'It's just got a whole lot more complicated.'

'And just when you don't need that.'

'I've not yet met a considerate criminal,' Grace said. It made Cleo smile, albeit fleetingly.

'Want to tell me anything about it?' she asked.

One big difference between Cleo and his late wife, Sandy, was that Cleo was in many ways a work colleague, with whom he could share confidential things, knowing they would go no further. 'Turns out that the husband of our missing – presumed dead – woman, Eden Paternoster, is having an affair with his wife's boss. And it seems Eden may have been aware of this and might have put a tracker on their car to monitor hubby's movements. Sometime before her disappearance, she's moved all her cash into a company with nominee directors – which Emily is currently digging into. Has she faked her death to dump her husband in the deep doody? Or have her husband and his lover conspired to kill her?'

Cleo looked thoughtful. 'You once told me that motives for

murder could be put into four sets of Ls: *lust, love, loathing* and
loot. Yes?'

'Well remembered. So which do you think applies here?'

'I'm thinking what motive could Niall Paternoster have for
killing his wife? If he's having an affair with her boss, fine, he
could file for divorce – or so could Eden. But that would mean
divvying up whatever financial assets they have. If Eden was
dead, that would be much easier – except for one thing, the seven-
year rule.'

'Exactly.'

Under English law, as Grace knew only too well, a person
could only be declared legally dead if they were missing for seven
years. Until that time, all their assets were frozen.

'If money is the motive, they're playing a long game.'

'A very long one,' Grace concurred.

Cleo thought hard again. 'Lust, love, loathing and loot. So, we
rule out *loot*. Leaving you with *lust, love* or *loathing*.'

'Yup, and I'm finding it hard to see a motive for murder in any
of those three. Sure, I got the impression from interviewing
Eden's husband that their relationship wasn't great, but she was
the breadwinner. Maybe he thought by killing her, he would
inherit the house – and didn't know she'd transferred most of its
value out of his reach. That's the only motive I can come up with
so far.'

'What do you know about Eden's boss, that her husband's
having the affair with?'

'Polly and I have just been to see her at her home. She's a cold
fish – in what Polly and I agreed was clearly a toxic marriage. No
love between husband and wife. A difficult lady to read, I'd say, a
tough nut. We're interviewing her in the morning as a significant
witness.'

Cleo frowned. 'What do you think's going on?'

'Honestly? I'm really not sure. Niall Paternoster lived in

Australia for a time in his twenties, where he'd set up a sailing instruction business. He had a business partner who died – according to him washed overboard from a boat in a storm. Her body was never found, so the police had no evidence of foul play. But luckily – or conveniently – the business became all his and he sold it shortly after for a nice sum, and moved back to England.'

'His wife, Eden, is the one with the money, here, you told me?' Cleo said.

'Yes.'

'Sounds very straightforward to me,' Cleo said. 'He murdered his partner in Australia, netted some loot and came to England. Found himself a wife with some assets, then did the same again. A pattern?'

'On the face of it, yes. But there are some anomalies that don't fit. Cassian Pewe wants an update tomorrow, should be interesting.'

'When is he going to be—?' She made a cut-throat gesture.

'Any time now – the wheels of internal investigations by Professional Standards grind slowly, if thoroughly, especially when two different forces are involved. It will happen and it will be very sweet. But until then I still have to kowtow to the corrupt creep.'

'I don't know how you do it.'

Grace smiled. 'Remember when you were a small child, what it felt like going to bed on Christmas Eve? Waiting for your stocking to arrive? Waiting for Christmas Day? All that excitement? That's pretty much how I'm feeling. Or I was, until dear Bruno.'

He looked around the room, then continued. 'Mr Greenhaisen talked about including some of Bruno's favourite things in the funeral. His music, toys, his passions.'

'His Munich football team,' Cleo said, glancing down at the bedspread.

'Definitely,' Grace said. 'What else?'

'Something else that he loved,' Cleo said. 'Maybe his favourite toy, his Porsche? And a photo of his mum?'

'Sure,' he replied. 'Let's do that.' He kissed her and stood up. Stared around the room sadly. 'Life sucks sometimes, doesn't it? Let's go and eat that food.'

'Yeah, good idea. You know, I heard a quote today that I love, from the author Chuck Palahniuk, about how it's hard to forget pain, but harder to remember happiness – because we don't have scars for happiness.'

For some moments it sent Roy Grace spiralling back into memories of Sandy. The good times. The good years. No scars to show for that.

But plenty of scars since her disappearance and all that had happened subsequently. Scars, he knew, that would be with him for life.

88

There were scars that Eden Paternoster would have all her life. They were on her left arm, both above and below the elbow. She'd had severe bruises and fractures to her arm and two ribs after Niall had punched her in a drunken rage in her swollen abdomen, sending her hurtling backwards down the stairs. She had seen flashes of his frightening temper before, with him lashing out physically at his supposed friends, but it was on that night that Eden had first suspected Niall was capable of killing her.

They'd planned to have an early meal that summer evening as Eden had a horribly early start to drive to a sales conference in North London in the morning. Instead – and not unusually, in those months following the start of his business decline – the loss of a major printing contract after a disagreement and the banks threatening to foreclose his loans – Niall, railing at the injustices of the world, had arrived home from the pub. It was just after 10 p.m. and he was drunk and abusive – and hungry.

She'd been angry at him, a build-up of jealousy about the wife of a friend of theirs that she felt he was flirting with, and she'd confronted him.

Whether it was the punch to her midriff or the fall, she would never know. But it had caused her to miscarry the baby they'd been trying to have for two years. And had succeeded, finally, after several expensive and unsuccessful IVF attempts.

The emergency team who dealt with the miscarriage had

saved her life, but the price had been that she would never be able to conceive another child.

Niall, of course, full of remorse, professed his love for her, begging her forgiveness, begging her not to press charges with the police and promising her on his mother's life that he would change. And for a while he had, becoming again the attentive, loving husband, turning back into the man she had fallen in love with and married. But she could never forget nor in her heart forgive him, and she knew she could never trust him again.

But more than that, she had made the decision that one day, somehow, she would get her revenge on him. She remembered the adage that 'Revenge is a dish best served cold.' That's when she had started planning, changing her will after entering into a secret relationship with someone who was in an equally bad marriage as her own. Someone she thought really did care for her, the new love of her life. And she had begun, subtly, to move her assets out of Niall's reach.

One of her purchases with these assets was this remote country property, named Woodbury Cottage, where she had been living in the days since her disappearance. Converted some years back from a derelict shepherd's croft, it was half a mile up a farm track near Chiddingly, in a dip in the South Downs. And the love of her life was due to arrive any time! She looked at the kitchen clock: 8.05 p.m.

She opened the fridge door and checked that the bottle of Prosecco she had put in earlier was now nicely chilled. Then she popped open a tin of her beloved's favourite anchovy olives and poured them into a bowl. Having done that, she pulled on oven gloves and checked the beetroot-based vegetarian pizza in the Aga. It was about done, so she moved it to the warming oven.

A ping on her phone signalled a text. She looked at it.

Three minutes! XXXXXXXX

She texted back:

Make it sooner XX

Then, thrumming with excitement, she raced upstairs and into the bathroom. She checked her hair in the mirror, sprayed mint fresher into her mouth and dabbed perfume around her neck.
Ping!

30 seconds! XX

Eden heard the roar of an engine and the scrunch of tyres on the gravel outside.

She felt so happy, so incredibly excited as she threw herself back down the stairs and raced over to the front door.

Flinging it open, she said, 'Oh my God, I've missed you!'

'And me too!'

Their mouths met, soft, sweet, and they stood on the doorstep for many seconds, kissing hard and holding each other tight, before breaking away and staring, breathless, into each other's eyes.

Then they kissed again, for even longer, every cell in Eden's body tingling with desire. Craving this incredible person, this incredible body.

She felt fingers running through her hair, down the side of her face, then down her body.

'I love you so much, Eden!'

'I love you even more!'

They were so entwined they almost fell over as they stumbled through the door, before Eden kicked it shut behind her. 'God, I've missed you, Rebecca,' she said.

Their lips met again.

89

Friday 6 September

Half an hour later, Eden Paternoster and Rebecca Watkins lay naked, wrapped in each other's arms. Rod Stewart's 'Maggie May' was playing softly in the background.

'You're amazing,' Eden said, grinning.

'Yeah, you're a lucky lady,' Rebecca replied teasingly.

'Drink?'

'Why not?'

Eden slipped out of bed and, without bothering to put on any clothes, walked out of the room.

'Jesus, I'll never tire of looking at that body,' Rebecca called after her.

Eden wiggled her bum cheekily as she went through the door. She returned a couple of minutes later with the opened Prosecco, two glasses and the bowl of olives. They sat up in bed, with the olives balanced between them, and Eden filled their glasses. 'To our future!' she said.

'To our future!'

They clinked glasses and drank. Then Rebecca dug her hand into the bowl and ate several olives. 'I must say, I love my kick-boxing sessions.'

'Kick-boxing sessions trump poker evenings, right?' Eden said.

'Every time!' Then, eating more olives, Rebecca said, 'I'm ravenous.'

'Supper's ready downstairs.'

'You are the best lover ever! Did anyone ever tell you?'

'Only you.'

Rebecca punched her, playfully. 'Liar!'

'It's true.'

'OK, your male lovers, then?'

'The best I got from Niall was that I'm a great shag.'

Rebecca looked at her quizzically. 'Was it ever as good with him as it is with me?'

'Not remotely; not in a million, billion years.'

'And I'm meant to believe that?'

'Well, you're shagging him, too – and your assessment is?'

Rebecca wrinkled her face. 'Yech.'

'Did you – you know – shag him today? Weren't you seeing him this afternoon?'

She gave a shaking motion with her hand as her reply. 'Just a hand job.'

'Really?'

'We were up at the Dyke in the car park. And I didn't want – you know – before seeing you.' She shrugged. 'He was fine with that.'

'Well, he is a wanker, through and through.'

Both women giggled.

Eden then looked at her, serious now. 'Any news? What did he say about the police?'

'Not much, really. He's been released on police bail. He's still totally mystified about your disappearance. He just repeated what he's said before, that he thinks you've set him up. He's worried about the evidence they've thrown at him, but he's sure they won't find any proof – that they're not going to find anything. I think, actually, he's angry because he knows, in his heart, you've beaten him.'

Eden smiled and raised her glass again. 'I bloody well have.'

'You have.'

'*We* have!' Eden replied.

'I'll drink to that.' Again, they clinked glasses and drank.

'So the police haven't been in touch with you, other than questioning everyone in the office?'

Rebecca shook her head. 'Nope, not at all.'

'What's the word around the office?'

'Everyone thinks something must have happened to you. I've spread the word, as subtly as I can, that you once confided in me you were worried by Niall's mood swings. I helped the rumour mill along by letting people know he had been arrested. And I made sure to take along a copy of the *Argus*, with the headline about his arrest, and leave it in the canteen.'

Eden grinned. 'Smart.'

Rebecca drained her glass. 'What was it you said about supper?'

Eden ran a suggestive finger down Rebecca's chest, and on down, past her stomach. 'Can it wait?'

Rebecca took her hand and kissed a finger. 'Later,' she said. 'I need sustenance first. Then I'm going to have you all over again.'

They locked eyes. 'I love you,' Eden said. 'I really love you.'

'And I really love you.'

There was a brief moment of comfortable silence between them. Then Eden said, 'It's incredible, isn't it, when a plan works out?'

90

Saturday 7 September

Polly Sweeney met Rebecca Watkins in the Police HQ reception, a single-storey building by the entrance barrier which was also now the reception for the East Sussex Fire and Rescue Service HQ.

Rebecca wore a navy two-piece business suit, ice-white shoes and an even icier expression as she walked alongside her in the morning sunshine, clutching a classy handbag and studying her phone, ignoring Polly's attempts at small talk as she escorted her up the hill towards the bland, red-brick building housing the Major Crime suite.

She followed Sweeney up the stairs to the second floor into a small, modern room that smelled of fresh paint and new furniture, where she was ushered to one of the four seats at the table.

'Can I get you anything to drink, Mrs Watkins?' Polly asked politely.

'I'm hoping not to be here long enough to need anything,' she replied tersely, glancing out of the window at the view across a car park. 'I have to get to a meeting in Croydon for 11 a.m.' She switched her focus to her phone.

'We won't detain you any longer than necessary,' Polly assured her. 'I'll be back in a moment if you'd just like to make yourself comfortable.'

Rebecca looked disdainfully at the plain blue chair. 'I take it that's your poor attempt at humour?'

Ignoring the barb, Polly left the room and returned after a couple of minutes with Roy Grace. They sat down opposite her. 'Thank you for coming in to talk to us, Mrs Watkins,' Grace said.

'Did I have any choice?' she replied. There was frosty humour in her voice but not in her eyes.

'Just to repeat what I told you last night, we need to interview you to see if you can help in any way with our enquiries into the disappearance of Eden Paternoster,' Grace said calmly and politely.

'Because you think I'm having an affair with her husband?'

Grace watched her face carefully. 'Are you?'

'What does that have to do with anything?'

'Quite a lot really, Mrs Watkins. Eden Paternoster has been missing – according to her husband – since around 3.15 p.m. on Sunday September the first. On the evening of Thursday August the twenty-ninth, the Paternosters' neighbours heard them arguing loudly – not an uncommon occurrence, they have informed us. According to you and your work colleagues, Mrs Paternoster never turned up for work on Friday, despite there being an important meeting that had been pre-arranged, which she was due to attend. Is that correct?'

'It is.'

'Is that in any way characteristic of Mrs Paternoster?'

'No, not at all.'

'Since Thursday there has been no activity on any of her social media platforms, despite her posting regularly, normally – at least once, daily – on Twitter, Facebook and Instagram. Nor has there been any activity on her credit cards. You are her line manager at the Mutual Occidental Insurance Company. How concerned are you that you've not seen her since last Thursday?'

Rebecca nodded. 'Very. It's completely out of character, as I just said. Eden was – sorry – *is* – a model employee. She's hardworking, scrupulously punctual and brilliant at what she does. This makes no sense at all, it is totally out of character.'

Both detectives shot a glance at each other, clocking her momentary use of the past tense.

'Do you think there is any possibility she has deliberately disappeared?' he pressed.

'Deliberately disappeared? Why on earth should she do that? She was up for promotion.'

'I don't wish to pry too much into your private life, Mrs Watkins,' Grace said. 'But as I'm sure you can understand, our priority is to discover what has happened to Mrs Paternoster – and as you are, from what it would seem, in some form of relationship with her husband, we are hoping you may be able to help us.' He fell silent, waiting.

'Of course, I'll give you any help I can,' Rebecca Watkins said. 'But I really don't know anything.'

'So her husband, Niall, has said nothing to you about her disappearing? Nothing at all? Did he have any explanation for her not turning up to work on Friday?'

She took some moments, with Roy Grace watching her face closely all the time. 'No,' she said finally. 'He was surprised when I told him.'

Polly interjected. 'Mrs Watkins, you told us that on Sunday afternoon, at around 5.30 p.m., September the first, you took your dog for a walk up on the Dyke. Was that all you did? Did you see anyone, talk to anyone?'

She hesitated. 'Why are you bothering to ask me? You know who I saw there.'

'Niall Paternoster?' Grace asked.

'Well, it wasn't the sodding Pope,' she retorted insolently.

'Did Niall say anything about him dropping off his wife at a Tesco store to buy cat litter and then not reappearing?'

'To be honest, we didn't talk, that wasn't why we were there.'

She tilted her head and gave a sly smile. 'Prince Philip used to sail a lot, and had a friend, Uffa Fox, who skippered for him. Fox had a French girlfriend who didn't speak English. One day, legend has it, Fox told His Royal Highness that he was getting married to this lady. Prince Philip asked him how on earth he could marry someone who didn't speak a word of English, when he didn't speak a word of French. Apparently, Uffa Fox replied, "There are only three things in life worth doing, eating, drinking and making love. Conversation adds little to any of these." Wouldn't you agree?'

Grace looked at her stonily, not rising to her challenge. 'Did Niall Paternoster ever confide in you about marital issues with his wife, Eden?'

'Of course he did, but I'm not a marriage wrecker. Eden confided in me, too.'

'She wasn't happy?'

'As I just said, I'm not a marriage wrecker. I wouldn't have done what I did – am doing – if I felt they had any future in their marriage. She'd told me on a number of occasions, when I'd seen her looking upset, that she was in a marriage she wanted out of.'

'So,' Polly said, 'you stepped into the breach, a kind of support?'

'It's not like that.'

'Really?' Grace said. 'What exactly is it like?'

She looked at each of them for a brief moment, warily. 'I'm afraid I've told you all I know.'

'I don't think you have,' Grace replied calmly. 'I think you know a lot more.'

She paused. 'If I'm reading you right, you suspect that Niall and I killed – murdered – Eden?'

Grace leaned forward across the table, locking eyes with her. 'Did you?'

She stood up abruptly. 'I'm sorry, you asked me to come in to help you with your enquiries about Eden Paternoster being missing. You didn't tell me you were going to accuse me of her murder. This interview is over. I'm not prepared to talk to you any more without a lawyer present. If you want to arrest me, go ahead – otherwise I'm out of here.' She stared at both of them in turn, challenging them. 'Are you going to arrest me?'

Grace shook his head. 'No, we are not.'

'Fine, goodbye.'

Scooping up her handbag, she turned her back on them and strode out of the room.

91

As the door slammed behind Rebecca Watkins, the wake of her perfume hanging in the air, Roy Grace and Polly Sweeney looked at each other.

'Nice lady,' Polly said. 'Not.'

'Her junior work colleague confides in her about her marital difficulties, so she lends a sympathetic ear, then goes and shags the woman's husband. What does that say about her?'

Polly looked bemused. 'She's just a kind and caring person who thought it would be the best way to help her colleague through her difficulties?'

'My thoughts exactly. Very altruistic of her.' Grace looked equally bemused. 'You know what surprises me the most about human behaviour, Polly?'

She shook her head. 'What?'

'It's that the older I get, the less anything surprises me. When I first joined the force, I met so many old sweats who were such cynical bastards – as my dad was. I vowed never to become like them, that I would always keep my faith in human decency. But that gets harder with every passing year. I'm turning into my dad.'

'My dad had an expression – he used to say it often after a particularly trying day.' Polly's father had been a copper, too.

'Which was?'

'Don't make excuses for shitty people. You can't put a flower in an asshole and call it a vase.'

Grace laughed. And suddenly realized it felt like a long time since he had. 'I'll remember that one.' Then, serious again, he said, 'So, what's your assessment of Rebecca Watkins?'

'A proper ice maiden. What a bitch.'

'Well said, but personally I wouldn't be so polite.'

Polly raised her eyebrows. 'She's hiding something.'

'For sure. The question is, what? She's definitely lying to us, but her arrogance – confidence – is telling me she's not done anything illegal here – not committed any crime.'

'Such as murdering Eden?'

Grace nodded. 'My reading of her is she's defensive of Niall, which indicates she doesn't think he's committed any crime.'

'What do you think, sir?'

Grace took a moment to reply. 'Something's been bothering me from the very start. When Sandy vanished, I was frantic with worry that something bad had happened to her. In those first hours and days I was in a complete state of panic, particularly when it became evident she really had gone and wasn't just staying away overnight. I don't get any sense of panic – or even caring – from Niall.'

'You loved Sandy,' Polly said. 'Seems like a different situation with Niall.'

'And with Eden, too? If we follow the money, we have a trail going back some months of her moving assets out of her husband's reach. Why is that? To shield her assets against a divorce? Or to build up a war chest to fight any divorce proceedings? Or . . . ?' His voice tailed off.

'Or?' she prompted after some moments.

'Did she have some other plan?'

'Such as?'

'I don't know,' Grace said. 'As I've wondered all along, there might be something else going on here, all being not what it seems on the surface. I suspect our surveillance on Niall Paternoster might lead us to the answer. What I—'

His job phone rang.

Answering it, he heard a voice he recognized, DI Lawrence Thompson, Staff Officer to Cassian Pewe.

'Sir,' he said, respectfully, 'the ACC would like to see you as soon as convenient in his office.'

Grace quickly checked the calendar on his computer. 'I can be there in fifteen,' he said.

'Thank you, sir. I will inform him.'

And stick your phone up his jacksie while you're at it, Grace thought irreverently. He knew that Lawrence Thompson shared his views on Pewe. Not many employees of Sussex Police who'd ever encountered the man didn't.

92

Usually these days, the ACC didn't invite Roy Grace to sit, instead making him stand in front of his desk for their meetings. But today, with an odd, almost simpering smile, he shook his hand firmly. 'Good to see you, Roy, thanks for sparing the time to see me.'

As Cassian Pewe spoke, he ushered him to one of the two-seater corner sofas and perched himself on the other. 'Would you like some coffee?'

That was almost another first. This must be Pewe's way of showing sympathy, Grace thought.

'I'm fine, thank you, sir.'

Pewe looked closely at him, still with his faintly unintelligent expression. 'How are you bearing up?'

'OK, thank you. Being at work is helping.'

'And your lovely wife, is she coping all right?'

'Cleo's trying to be strong – she's gone into work today as well.'

A frown flitted across his face. 'I understand the PM on Bruno was carried out at Worthing, is that right?'

'Yes, to spare Cleo from having to be involved. The funeral directors are collecting his body from there.'

'Very sensible,' Pewe said. 'I'm so extremely sorry, Roy, for your loss. You have my very deepest sympathy. You will please pass my condolences to Cleo and his grandparents.'

'I will, thank you.'

'I think it was Aristotle who said, "The gods have no greater torment than for a mother to outlive her child."'

'Fortunately for Sandy, if you can call her a mother, she didn't.'

The wan smile again. 'I'm sure it applies to the father, as well.'

'It does,' Grace replied. 'And Aristotle was right.'

Pewe nodded, clasping his hands together in a gesture of sympathy. 'If there is anything I can do, if you need to take some time out as I've said before, please let me know.'

'I appreciate that, sir.'

'And when you have made the funeral arrangements, please also let me know.'

Was he intending to send a donation to the charity he and Cleo decided on – which they were still discussing – Grace wondered? God forbid he was planning to attend. All the more reason to make it a private, family one. It had been bad enough when he'd attended Sandy's, he didn't want this creep polluting their grief at Bruno's.

'We'll be putting an announcement in the *Argus*,' he replied.

Pewe nodded.

'Perhaps you could let me know, in case I miss it.'

Grace grimaced by way of a reply.

There was a moment of silence. Then Pewe's face clouded into a back-to-business expression. Evidently the ACC was still blissfully unaware of the tsunami heading his way. That thought was the only thing that cheered Grace up at this moment.

'Right,' Pewe said. 'Good. So, I need to talk to you about resourcing, Roy.'

'Resourcing?'

'As you are well aware, Operation Lagoon is currently using half the entire Major Crime Team's available manpower, as well as one of only two Surveillance Teams our finances currently stretch to, so I thought you might like to give me an update?'

'With pleasure, sir.' Grace said the word *sir* happy in the knowledge he wouldn't be saying it for much longer. Not from the moment Professional Standards acted on the information Guy Batchelor had provided. But for now, he maintained a facade of respect. 'Should we still be calling it *man*power, sir? Not a very up-to-date expression, is it?'

Pewe looked, as he so often did when confronted by anything distasteful to him, as if he could smell something nasty. 'Do you have a better term for it?'

Grace gave him a deadpan look. '*Resources?*'.

For the next five minutes he filled Pewe in on their progress to date and the major turn of events with the discovery of Rebecca Watkins's affair with Niall Paternoster. When he had finished, Pewe sat for a while, saying nothing. Finally, he nodded.

'You've established, through the surveillance, that Eden Paternoster's husband and her boss, Rebecca Watkins, are having an affair? Nice work.'

'Thank you, sir,' Grace said politely, expecting the sting was about to come.

Pewe didn't disappoint.

'Clearly, Roy, you believe in the possibility that Eden Paternoster, far from being murdered and her body dissected, may still be alive and well and in hiding?'

'It's one hypothesis.'

'Do you have others?'

'Three. The second is that she was murdered, either by her husband or by Rebecca Watkins – or by both of them – and her body subsequently dismembered, some of it buried in Ashdown Forest, some deposited in the sea off Shoreham Harbour. My third is that Niall and Eden Paternoster have conspired together to fake her disappearance.'

'For what reason?'

'Financial. I've been reading up on that couple, the Darwins, where the husband, John, faked his death to look like a canoe accident in the North Sea some years ago. He did it with the connivance of his wife for financial reasons in that case, collecting the life insurance on him. Emily Denyer is currently looking hard into the Paternosters' finances as a major part of our enquiries.'

Pewe ran a manicured finger, sporting a Wedgwood signet ring, through his golden hair. 'Would I be correct in saying that in your view, Roy, in all three of your theories, there is no life at stake at the present time? No life in danger? Eden Paternoster is either dead, or alive and well and in cahoots with her husband, or something else entirely? Would you agree with that summary?'

'On the evidence so far, yes. *Sir.*'

Pewe smiled, his upper lip rising like a theatre curtain, revealing a stage set of immaculately whitened teeth. He looked to Grace, at this moment, like a piranha in a blond wig.

'Here's my dilemma, Roy. With the greatest respect, one of our Surveillance Teams is currently engaged in an operation to try to protect a teenage girl we believe is being trafficked into the sex trade by a Brighton criminal gang. This is vital work to protect a vulnerable person.' The gleam of his teeth again, before he continued with the sucker punch.

'I have a request, from the Divisional Intelligence Unit, for surveillance to monitor a very large drugs consignment believed to be on its way from Liverpool to Brighton. If they can put this in place, they think they could scoop up some of the major players on the Brighton drugs scene. So, what should I do with my resources? Deploy my Surveillance Team to discover the outcome of a marital dispute or to potentially save the lives of many Sussex citizens by cutting off a major drugs supply chain? I don't like to raise this today of all days, but life has to go on and decisions have to be made.'

'I don't think it's as straightforward as you think, sir,' Grace said.

'You're suggesting it's not as clear-cut about the Paternosters?' Pewe retorted.

'Correct – *sir.*'

Pewe opened out his arms expansively. 'So, convince me.'

'I need more time to keep him under surveillance,' Grace said calmly. 'As I told you, something's going on that I'm not happy about. At this moment I'm still of the opinion that Niall Paternoster may have murdered his wife, with or without the help of Rebecca Watkins.'

'But you are also considering that Eden Paternoster may have set this up and disappeared of her own volition? Or conspired with her husband?'

'Yes, I am.'

Pewe picked up a globe paperweight on top of a stack of papers on his desk, then laid it back down again. 'To repeat myself, you currently have no evidence of a life at stake. You also currently have very little evidence that Mrs Paternoster has been murdered. Correct?'

'Correct.'

'So what do you need the Surveillance Team for now?'

'I need them to continue monitoring Niall Paternoster's move-ments. If he has conspired with his wife, he may lead us to her. If he has murdered her, he may lead us to her body – we know that killers frequently return to the deposition site. It's possible that the grave in Ashdown Forest could be a decoy. As I told you, I'm unhappy about the location the kitchen knife was found in.'

'You've also told me you don't think Niall Paternoster is very bright. Now you're saying he's bright enough to have created a decoy grave and left a clue, in the knife, in an obvious place? Or perhaps conspired with his wife to fake her disappearance?'

'All of these are current possibilities, *sir.*'

'There's a tracker in place beneath his rental car, placed there by the Surveillance Team?'

'Yes.'

'And you have access to the data from the tracker?'

'We do. On our computers and phones – and tablets.'

'Fine,' Pewe said. 'It seems to me that for now the Surveillance Team has served its purpose. I'll leave it with you until 6 p.m. today after which I'm going to redeploy it to the Liverpool operation. But I will instruct Mark Taylor to leave the tracker in place. You and your team will be able to monitor Paternoster's car on your computers, tablets and phones. The rest you'll have to do the old-fashioned way. Right, I think that's all. Don't forget to let me know when Bruno's funeral is.'

Grace glared back at him.

93

As Roy Grace left Pewe's office, his private phone rang. It was Cleo. He answered walking down the stairs. 'Hi, darling.'

'How's your day going?' She sounded strangely on edge.

'Not great, tell you in a moment, just hang on.' He hurried along the ground-floor corridor, past the offices of several senior officers and support staff who worked in the handsome Queen Anne building that gave the HQ its name, Malling House, and out into daylight. 'Just been properly dicked about by you-know-who again, even after everything we're going through. Such an idiot,' he said quietly, although safely out of earshot now.

'You won't be for much longer, hopefully.'

'Nope. How are you? You OK?'

'I was OK, until a boy, a year older than Bruno, was brought in – went under the rear wheels of a twenty-tonner yesterday on an electric scooter.'

'The one I read about in the *Argus*?'

'That's it. I told the team I was sorry – I just couldn't handle it. I've come home.' She began crying. After a few moments, through sobs, she said, 'I'm sorry, I shouldn't be disturbing you.'

'Of course you should. I couldn't have handled that either, certainly not at the moment. I'll be home as early as I can.'

'No,' she said, her voice on the edge of cracking. 'Stay as long as you need, keep your mind occupied – there's no point sitting at home dwelling . . . I just needed to get away.'

There was a brief silence as Roy walked on up the hill towards his office, then, sounding a little more composed, Cleo said, 'I've just spoken to the funeral director – Mr Greenhaisen. Subject to a couple of lab reports from Bruno's postmortem that she's waiting on, the Coroner is happy to release his body tomorrow. The vicar of All Saints, a lovely man, says he could fit the funeral in on Monday, September the thirtieth.'

'Thanks, that's good news.'

'He's given me a list of stuff we need to go through – we can discuss all that tonight when you get back. We'll need to decide on the music and whether anyone should do a eulogy.'

'Sure,' he said. 'I can't immediately think who.'

'Maybe you could say a few words?'

'OK, we'll discuss it later. I really do want this to be a private family affair. I've a feeling bloody Pewe is planning to come and I want to keep him out.'

'I've just had Bruno's headmaster on the phone. The school are already conducting their own investigations and it appears Bruno got out over the gates. He asked me to pass on his sincere condolences and said that he and several teachers would like to attend, and perhaps some of Bruno's schoolmates.'

I didn't know Bruno had any mates, Grace nearly said, but he held it back. 'OK, I love you.'

'Love you, too,' she said forlornly.

He ended the call just as he reached the entrance to the Major Crime suite and made his way to his office, his mind swirling with thoughts both about the impending funeral and his meeting with Pewe.

He made himself a coffee, putting the milk in the mug first and then the coffee before adding the water, something Sandy had taught him, insisting it tasted better that way – and she was right. He used the time it took for the kettle to boil to start focusing back on the investigation.

Carrying the mug through to his office, he sat at his desk, glanced through his emails, then called Glenn Branson and Jack Alexander, in turn, asking them to come to see him right away.

When both detectives were seated in front of him, he told them of the developments following his meeting with Pewe. Neither of them, nor any other members of his team, had any inkling about the ACC's impending fate.

'What planet is he on?' Branson retorted. 'So we have to take over from Surveillance ourselves?'

'Yes, as best we can.' Grace tapped his screen. 'I have the tracker on Niall Paternoster's rented Fiesta showing – currently stationary outside their home in Nevill Road. Aiden Gilbert's doing some wizardry and it should appear on all the team's laptops and phones. Glenn, I'm giving you the action of organizing a rota for this weekend of three team members to man the observation post, as discreetly as possible, to confirm when he drives away from the house. We will have his whereabouts on our screens.'

'Will do, boss.'

Grace turned to Alexander. 'Jack, I need you—'

He was interrupted by his job phone ringing again. Raising an apologetic hand to the two detectives, he answered. It was Emily Denyer.

'Sir,' she said, 'I've been going through the documents seized from the Paternosters' house by the Search Team. There's a solicitor's letter regarding a will made by Eden Paternoster. It was hidden under the paper lining of a drawer in an antique bureau which appears to be her writing desk and where she keeps all her private papers along with a life insurance document.'

'How recent was this document?'

'It's dated March seventeenth of this year.'

'What's the gist of it?'

'It's pretty simple really. I think you'll find this interesting, sir – any death benefit was to be paid out to Rebecca Watkins.'

94

Glenn Branson and Jack Alexander both sat in silence for some moments, absorbing what Roy Grace had just told them. Trying to make sense of it.

Then Grace called Aiden Gilbert, whose team was working on recovering documents from the hard drive of Eden Paternoster's laptop. He told Gilbert what he needed very urgently, and he promised to take a look immediately.

True to his word, less than five minutes later, a document labelled *New Will* as well as the life insurance policy taken out by Eden Paternoster in favour of Rebecca Watkins came through on Grace's email.

The three detectives immediately studied the documents. The will was a short and simple document, properly signed and witnessed by two people, one called Jo Cabot, Legal Executive, and the other, Miro Afonso, Assistant Solicitor. Attached to it was a covering letter, signed off by a woman called Jill Riddle, Head of Wills and Probate, Cardwell Scott LLP.

'Let me get my head around this,' Branson said finally, looking baffled. 'She's basically leaving everything she has, bar a few small bequests, to the woman who's sleeping with her husband? Or am I missing something?'

'I'd say you'd just scored what golfers might call a hole in one,' Grace replied, looking equally baffled.

'Her boss,' Alexander commented. 'The Ice Queen? Excuse me, but what the hell is going on here?'

'Oh, what a tangled web we weave,' Grace replied.

'"When first we practise to deceive,"' Alexander quoted.

Both his colleagues looked at him.

'What film's that from?' Branson asked.

Alexander shook his head. 'People think it's from *Macbeth*, but it's actually in Walter Scott's poem, "Marmion".'

'Never took you for a poet, Jack,' Branson said.

'I'm not. But I am a mine of useless information.'

'Who do people generally leave their money to in their wills?' Grace asked.

'Their other half?' Branson ventured.

'So,' Grace said, 'we've been putting all our focus on Niall Paternoster – and perhaps that's not misplaced. What about this as a hypothesis – bearing in mind we know from what Rebecca Watkins told us last night that Eden confided in her about her marriage problems.' He paused before continuing.

'A big part of these marital problems, unknown to Eden, is that Rebecca Watkins is having an affair with her husband – Niall. Only Rebecca Watkins and Niall Paternoster know this. Rebecca plays on Eden's vulnerability and builds a friendship with her. She plays the game of being the considerate, trusted, forever friend, someone who will support her out of this situation, help her build her life back and plan for the future.'

He paused to let this sink in. 'Rebecca then puts a cunning plan to Eden – leave all your money to me, fake your disappearance, setting up Niall as the possible murderer, but without sufficient evidence for him ever to go to trial. And bingo! There's no body, but as we're going to map out the rest of your life and get you to a better place, what's a seven-year wait to be declared legally dead to collect the cash?' He looked at the two detectives. 'It may sound far-fetched, but we need to consider everything. Where are we with obtaining Eden's medical records?'

'We've requested them, but they haven't arrived yet. Maybe we should go and pay the solicitor who drafted the will a visit, boss?' Branson suggested. 'I know the firm, they're local, just opposite Brighton Library.'

Grace looked at his watch: 11.34 a.m. 'They'll be closed today but we'll go Monday morning, Glenn. Maybe we can catch her between clients, or else in her lunch break.'

'Will she talk to us? You know what briefs are like. Or should we get a warrant?'

'No, that would be too heavy-handed and I think we'd struggle to get one for this – client confidentiality is sacrosanct. Let's just try our natural charm.'

Branson gave him a quizzical grin. 'Yours or mine?'

'Really? You think you have some?' Grace replied.

His colleague shook his head. He shot a glance at Alexander, who was smiling, then back at Grace. 'I honestly don't know why I like you.'

'Could it be my natural charm?'

95

The police search officers had finished at the end of last week, the crime scene tape had been removed from the front of the house and Niall Paternoster had been allowed to go back inside his home. Although, to his chagrin, on searching round, he'd discovered the police had carted away almost every scrap of paperwork, and he had no idea when his laptop would be returned.

Now, he sat in the kitchen, drinking coffee with milk that was almost on the turn and scanning through the *Argus* for any mention of the mystery of his missing wife. But, it seemed, the news had already moved on. Fatboy Slim had a whole page, publicizing a free concert he was giving on Saturday night on the seafront. The headline story was a gruesome murder, dismembered remains found in a wheelie bin. There was an article on the superstar blogger Zoella. A family were concerned about the wife's missing eighty-four-year-old father, who had dementia and hadn't been seen in four days.

Nothing about Eden or himself.

If she was alive, just where the hell was she? What game was she playing? And, more to the point, why?

Had she had an accident?

Then a wilder possibility came into his mind as he thought suddenly about the Hitchcock film *Psycho*, which they both loved and had seen several times. The irony of Janet Leigh embezzling money and disappearing, only to end up staying at the Bates

402

Motel and being murdered by Norman Bates. Could something like that have happened to her?

It was a crazy idea, but nothing else made any bloody sense. If she'd stayed away for a night, as she'd done before when they'd rowed, that was one thing. But *this many* nights? That was very different. Had she somehow discovered his affair with Rebecca? But if so, surely she would have confronted him and not simply disappeared? Or was fitting him up – as she clearly had from all the police had told him – her nasty idea of revenge?

In six hours' time he was due to head over to Mark Tuckwell's and do a long stint in the cab, first collecting a couple flying in from Tenerife to Gatwick and taking them to their home near St Leonards. Then up to Heathrow Airport to pick up a Mr and Mrs O'Connor arriving from Munich. After dropping them home, to Tunbridge Wells, he would head back to Brighton and spend the rest of the night picking up the detritus of weekend revellers blowing their latest wage packet on booze and drugs. All the time hoping none of them would throw up in the cab or do a runner.

Then tomorrow, Rebecca's hubby was off to France for a golfing holiday. They would have a whole week together. Happy days!

His phone rang, a WhatsApp call, intruding on his thoughts. Glancing at the display, he saw it was Rebecca. 'Hey, gorgeous!' he answered. 'I was just thinking about you – how much I'm looking forward to tomorrow! I've told Marky I'm not available to drive for him for the next week – told him I need to wait home until *she* turns up. Know what I'm saying?'

She sounded strange as she replied. 'I've been interviewed by the police. I think they're suspicious.'

'Of what?'

'Hello? Eden has disappeared. They've seen us together up at the Dyke. What would you be suspicious of if you were a cop?'

'Yeah, I know how it looks. But at the end of the day I haven't harmed her and nor have you – unless you're not telling me something?'

'So now you think I've killed her? Thanks a million!'

'Of course I don't, my gorgeous.' After a brief moment he added, 'I love you.'

There was a silence.

'Do you love me?' he queried.

'I don't think we should be talking like this over the phone. If they've got us under surveillance, they might have bugged our mobiles.'

'I don't think so. And anyhow, WhatsApp is encrypted. They won't be able to listen in.'

'Really? So how did they find us at the Dyke?'

'Other phone records? Are they watching us? I dunno. But I googled the authority the police need to bug anyone – there has to be a life at risk.'

'And they don't think Eden's life is at risk?'

'No, they think she's dead – that was the gist of my interviews with them after they arrested me. They think I murdered her, as I told you.'

'Even so, I think we should be careful over the phone.'

'I bloody love you,' he blurted. 'I want you.'

There was a long silence. Then she said, 'Did you not hear what I said?'

'Yeah, sorry.'

'See you tomorrow,' she said tersely, ending the call.

96

The offices of the law firm Cardwell Scott were in a red-brick building occupying a corner site diagonally opposite the piazza in front of the modern glass edifice of Brighton Library.

Roy Grace and Glenn Branson walked in through the front entrance and up to the curved reception desk, behind which sat a woman with elegant, dark hair. She gave them a polite smile.

They showed their badges. 'Detective Superintendent Grace and Detective Inspector Branson of Surrey and Sussex Major Crime Team,' Grace led. 'We would like to speak to Jill Riddle.'

She glanced at her computer screen, then looked up at them. 'Do you have an appointment, officers?'

'No,' Grace said. 'But we need to speak to her urgently on a potential murder investigation we believe Ms Riddle may be able to help us with.'

'Take a seat, gentlemen, and I'll see if she's free.' She indicated to a sofa in front of a table with a spread of newspapers and local magazines, then lifted her handset.

'How was your day, yesterday?' Branson asked, his voice sympathetic. 'And how's Cleo taking it all?'

'She's pretty cut up.' He shrugged. 'I don't know – I never thought she had much fondness for Bruno, but clearly she cared for him a lot more than I realized. But we had an OK day, thanks. Noah tried to make scones, which basically meant covering most of the kitchen – and Humphrey – in flour. He's turning into a little rascal, nicking the cheese when Kaitlynn wasn't looking.'

Branson grinned.

'Then Jack came over and we did a Sunday roast. Good to have a bit of normality. But I haven't really slept.'

The receptionist replaced her handset and looked at the detectives. 'Ms Riddle has a fifteen-minute window before her next client.' She pointed over to her right, to a lift. 'If you go to the fourth floor, her assistant will meet you.'

They entered and rode the irritatingly slow lift upwards. Finally, the doors jerked open to reveal a neatly dressed, middle-aged woman with a wavy fringe shaping her face standing on a small, sterile-feeling landing. She greeted them with an uncertain smile. 'Follow me, please, gentlemen,' she said.

They walked along a corridor, past a number of closed doors. She rapped on the last one, then opened it and ushered the detectives through. Grace led, followed by Branson, into a small, tidy office, with one wall lined with bookshelves filled with legal tomes, and a window overlooking the library.

A woman with wild grey hair, wearing a blue two-piece over a white blouse secured at the neck with a looped, bootlace-thin black bow, gave them a quizzical look. On her desk were several stacks of documents bound with ribbons, as well as a silver photograph frame showing two young men, seemingly twins, dressed in mortar boards and graduation gowns, and another of two Golden Doodles. There were more bound stacks of documents arranged on the floor next to the desk. On another wall Grace clocked a practising certificate and a large framed photograph of a women's hockey team.

She stood up. 'Gentlemen, good morning.'

Grace and Branson showed her their warrant cards. 'Jill Riddle?' Grace checked.

'Yes, what is this about?'

'I'm Detective Superintendent Grace from Surrey and Sussex Major Crime Team and this is my colleague Detective Inspector Branson. We appreciate your seeing us at such short notice,' he said. 'We're investigating the disappearance, under suspicious circumstances, of Mrs Eden Paternoster, whom we believe is a client of yours.'

She nodded. 'I've been reading about this in the *Argus*.' She indicated the two chairs in front of her desk. 'Please sit. Can I offer you any tea or coffee?'

'We're fine, thank you, and we know you've only got a few minutes, so we'll keep it brief. We believe Mrs Paternoster may have been murdered and her husband, Niall, is currently our prime suspect. Our investigating team have located a will on a computer hard drive which appears to have been drafted by you. I have a printed copy of it here.'

He removed the document from his inside pocket and handed it across the desk to her. She studied it for a few seconds, then looked back at him, her demeanour turning slightly defensive. 'Yes, we drew up this will.'

'Thank you,' Grace replied. 'We think it may be significant in our enquiries that her husband has been excluded and that the principal benefactor is her line manager at the firm where she works, Mutual Occidental Insurance. We appreciate your duty of client confidentiality, but we are in a very serious situation, in which her husband is claiming he's not seen or heard from Eden since last Sunday afternoon. But the fact is there's been very little to indicate she is still alive since the previous Thursday, August the twenty-ninth. We are extremely concerned that she may be dead. Or, maybe, she has run away and is pretending to be dead? Any information you can give us would be extremely helpful.'

She opened out her hands and a bunch of bracelets slid, jangling, down her wrist. 'What information are you looking for from me?'

'Did this will supersede a previous one?' Branson asked.

She looked at both officers. 'I shouldn't say so, but in light of the gravity of the situation, yes, it did.'

'The previous one leaving everything to her husband?' Branson pressed.

'Pretty much, yes.'

'You drafted that one, too?'

'Yes, Mrs Paternoster has been a client for a number of years. Normally any conversations would be subject to client confidentiality, but I am prepared to relax that on this occasion given that I am worried about what might have happened to Eden.'

'If you can cast your mind back to when she asked to change her will, Ms Riddle,' Grace asked, 'did she seem normal to you? Did she say anything by way of explanation? It's a pretty unusual situation where someone in a marriage changes their will to exclude their partner, isn't it?'

She smiled sardonically. 'Not as unusual as you might think. I'm afraid, doing probate, I see it all. Not much surprises me. And – I'm not saying this is the case here – but I've known people take masochistic pleasure in deliberately excluding someone who would be expecting an inheritance. They leave it to a dogs' home or some other charity. I had a client, some years ago, and now long deceased, who left an estate of over £4 million to her cat, just to stop any of her children, whom she'd fallen out with, from benefiting.'

'So, clearly,' Grace said, 'Eden Paternoster didn't want her husband to benefit. But leaving it to her boss strikes us as strange. Did she say anything to you about her reasons for that?'

He held back on revealing the information his team knew – that Rebecca Watkins was having an affair with Eden's husband – wanting to hear the solicitor's reply.

'She did, yes, she told me her reason. She told me her husband wasn't very tech savvy. She'd become suspicious that he was cheating on her, after reading texts on his phone. From what she told me it seems she confided in her boss – her line manager, Rebecca Watkins – and one thing had led to another. In a short space of time she realized she had fallen in love with this woman, and this was where her true feelings lay. She told me she felt liberated, as if she'd shaken a monkey off her back.'

Grace and Branson looked at each other in utter astonishment.

'That's why she changed her will?' Grace asked.

'There's more to it than that.' She gave both Grace and Branson a hesitant look. 'When she came to see me back in March' – she glanced down then looked up again – 'March the twentieth, she was in an agitated state.'

'For what reason?' Grace asked. 'If she gave one?'

The solicitor hesitated, as if wondering if she should say any more. Finally, she nodded. 'Yes, she did. One night, while her husband was out doing his taxi work, she'd looked at his computer. Perhaps, she told me, he didn't realize that text messages were stored on that as well as his phone. Whatever, she found a string of messages between him and some other woman. The last one said that he had a plan to "get rid of" Eden. Such a clever plan, he boasted, no one would ever be able to prove a thing.'

'Was it serious, do you think?' Grace asked.

'I asked her about this. She said there were times when he'd been violent before, where he threatened to kill her – particularly around the time his business went bust. She said his mood swings frightened her.'

Branson said, 'So he was in turmoil. Perhaps he saw her doing well in her career and resented that she was now the breadwinner? That's ugly.'

'When we interviewed him, he struck us as being pretty macho, the kind of man who might resent *the little woman* doing better than himself. A big ego?' Grace probed.

She gave a thawing smile. 'From what Eden told me, that's a pretty accurate assessment.'

'How frightened was she by these mood swings?' Grace asked.

'She was scared – very scared.'

'But she was never scared enough to go to the police?' he continued.

Jill Riddle looked at each officer in turn, then laid her palms flat on the surface of her desk. 'All too often in my experience, officers, it isn't that people in abusive relationships, both male and female, are not scared enough to go to the police,' she said. 'It's that they are too scared to go.'

97

Back outside on the pavement in the bright sunshine, the lunch-time crowds out on the streets, enjoying the last few weeks of the summer rays, Glenn Branson said, 'That's something I seriously was not expecting – that she's in – or was in – a relationship with her boss.' He pulled his shades out of his jacket pocket and put them on.

Roy Grace looked nonplussed. 'In this job, always expect the unexpected.'

'Indeed.'

'Remember that and you'll seldom be disappointed.'

Branson pursed his lips thoughtfully. 'And didn't your old mate Nick Sloan once say, "No matter what happens, at the end of each month the golden goose will shit into your bank account"?'

Grace grinned. 'I miss his humour.' Instantly, he looked serious again. 'Eden's in a relationship with her boss and her boss is in a relationship with her husband. It's all a bit *Jeremy Kyle*, don't you think?'

Branson glanced at his big, loud watch. 'Ten to one – want to grab a quick bite before we head back to the office?'

The Detective Superintendent checked his more modest watch, too. 'Are you thinking healthy or a carb fest?'

Branson looked wounded. He patted his six-pack midriff. 'Healthy.'

'But not *too* healthy, eh?' Grace suggested.

They ended up, a few minutes later, perched on stools in a sandwich bar, Branson munching on a vegan wrap and Grace a tuna one with a bag of crisps on the side. Branson drank bottled water and Grace a Diet Coke.

'Too scared to go to the police,' Grace pondered.

'Yep,' Branson said, through a mouthful of food. 'Too scared of what their partners might do when they found out. Or too scared of being on their own, on the shelf. That's what abusive bastards do, isn't it? They destroy their other half's self-esteem to the point where they believe they are such rubbish human beings that no one else would ever want them. So they stay on in the relationship, in some kind of desperation, rather than risk being alone for the rest of their lives. What's the stat? Something like the average person in an abusive relationship endures an assault thirty-nine times before going for help.'

'That's about it, very sadly.' Grace tore open the bag of crisps and passed it to Branson, who shook his head dismissively.

'I don't eat crisps – you shouldn't either, they're bad for your body.'

Grace watched his friend then dig his hand into the bag and scoop out almost half the contents, shovelling them into his mouth. He grinned and raised his eyebrows.

A woman, wearing light blue earbuds, sat down on the stool to Grace's right, placing her phone in front of her. With a sly glance, Grace could see she was listening to a talking book, *Humankind*. Taking a bite of his wrap, he chewed, thinking hard. Swallowing and lowering his voice, he said, 'Eden confides about her brutal husband to Rebecca Watkins – who is clearly in a failing relationship with her own husband. They become lovers. Then, at some point, Rebecca Watkins starts a relationship with Eden's husband. What the hell is going on here?'

'Eden Paternoster falls in love with Rebecca Watkins,' said

Branson, his voice discreetly low, barely above a murmur. 'She feels secure enough to leave Rebecca all her money. In the interim, Eden has been moving her assets into an overseas company controlled by nominee directors. Emily Denyer's working on establishing who actually owns and controls that company, and I'm betting on Eden Paternoster and Rebecca Watkins.'

'I'd bet with you. So Rebecca Watkins has pulled a flanker? Has she conspired with Niall Paternoster?'

'That wouldn't be the most outlandish scheme we've ever come across, would it, boss?'

Grace drank some of his Diet Coke. 'No. But there's a bit missing.'

'What bit?'

'The missing bit.' He took another bite of his wrap.

Branson gave him a quizzical look. 'You've gone cryptic on me.'

'It's the bit between charming Rebecca Watkins becoming passionate lover and future life partner to Eden Paternoster, and her getting up close and personal with Eden's husband. How did that happen? Why did that happen? Who is driving this? Rebecca Watkins or Niall Paternoster?'

Grace's job phone rang. He answered and heard Mark Taylor's voice.

'Sir, subject's on the move. We've been tracking him north out of Brighton and heading into Croydon. Looks like he's going to the industrial estate where Mutual Occidental Insurance are based.'

'For a spot of nooning?'

'Could well be, sir.'

'Thanks for the update.'

'I'll keep you posted. And I just wanted to say I'm very sorry, sir, that we're again being redeployed this evening back to the drugs job, Operation Cockerel. But we will still be with you until

6 p.m. We're glad to give you this extra day and we're hopeful we'll be back with you full-time later in the week.'

'I appreciate it, Mark.'

Ending the call, Branson frowned at him. '*Nooning?* What's that?'

'Sorry, I forgot you've led a sheltered life.'

'Haha.'

Grace brought him up to speed with Taylor's report, adding, 'It means having an illicit lunchtime liaison.'

'Ah.' He dug into Grace's crisps and ate most of the rest of the packet. Munching on them, he said, 'Just saving you from yourself.'

'I appreciate your altruism.'

'I'm all heart.' Then Branson frowned. 'OK, so no surprise they are meeting at lunchtimes. Rebecca has a husband expecting her home after work. To me, the big question in all of this is where does Eden Paternoster fit in?'

'Or where did she?' Grace posited darkly.

They'd finished their food and the place was getting increasingly rammed. 'Let's head back and talk outside,' Grace said, and drained his drink.

As they walked up Church Street towards the car park, Grace, who had been silent for some minutes said, 'We've had our share of *femme fatale* characters in the past, haven't we? Ashley Harper and Jodie Bentley spring to mind.'

'We sure have. Think this is what we're dealing with here?'

Entering the car park, Branson inserted the ticket into one of the pay machines, followed by his credit card. The area was deserted. 'It is interesting that Rebecca Watkins made no mention of this relationship when we interviewed her at headquarters. She appears to be cunning and resourceful.'

'She is.'

Collecting his ticket, they walked up the three flights of stone stairs to the level where they were parked. Grace waited until they were in the privacy of their car before continuing. But he was interrupted by another call from Taylor. He put it on speaker.

'An update, sir. Subject is out of his car, walking down the street, holding hands with Rebecca Watkins.'

'Sweet,' Grace commented.

'Orman is parked up close – looks like they might be heading somewhere for lunch. When we get the location, she'll go in.'

'Good work, Mark.' Ending the call, he turned back to Branson. 'So which came first, the chicken or the egg?'

His colleague frowned. 'Meaning?'

'Was Rebecca Watkins already having an affair with Eden's husband, and they hatched a scheme between them for Rebecca to seduce Eden and become her lover, get her to change her will and then kill her, making it look like she'd disappeared?'

'The flaw in that, as I see it, boss, is how would Rebecca know that Eden would be up for being seduced?'

'Fair point,' Grace said. 'Maybe it only started as a friendship and they became closer? I don't know, it's just another hypothesis. But it seems to me that we have two people in deteriorating relationships – Niall Paternoster and Rebecca Watkins. We know from Emily Denyer's investigations that Niall Paternoster is skint, apart from the small change he makes as a taxi driver.' He paused. 'With me so far?'

'I'm on your bus.'

Grace smiled and went on. 'Rebecca and Niall are lovers. Niall's wife has a considerable net worth. Somehow, whatever Eden Paternoster's proclivity, Rebecca Watkins succeeds in seducing her, and then taking it further, to the point where they are planning a future life together – at least, in Eden's mind. Rebecca convinces Eden to move all her assets out of Niall's reach and, for extra security, she gets her to change her will in her favour. Then Rebecca plots with Niall to murder Eden, making it look like she has simply disappeared. But Niall has screwed it all up, leaving a trail of evidence.'

'But they've still been smart enough to dispose of Eden's remains, leaving us with a "no body" murder investigation – perhaps aware how hard they are to prove. Remember all those crime novels and true crime DVDs in their house?'

'I reckoned we had enough evidence on her husband, until the will popped up,' Grace said. 'But, of course, it provides another motive if he knew about this more recent will.'

'Do you think we might have enough for the CPS to consider a "conspiracy to murder" charge against both Paternoster and Watkins?'

Grace shook his head. 'Not yet.'

His phone rang once more. It was Taylor again. 'Sir, subject and Rebecca Watkins have entered a pub. Orman's only two minutes away and is going there now.'

Ending the call, Grace shook his head. This was the level of professional surveillance he needed for this case. Hopefully Orman would get a line of sight on the couple and be able to lip-read their conversation. 'Pewe,' he said. 'What a bloody idiot.'

Sure, he understood that, as the overall head of Major Crime for Sussex Police, Pewe had to make decisions on deploying his limited resources. But drugs came down from Liverpool all the time – the docks were a major point of entry for them into the country. You'd bust one lot and another supply chain would take their place. But this was a potential murder, one he felt close to cracking, and the ACC had taken away his most valuable resource. At least, a small win, he'd been able to get them for today.

Branson gave him a sympathetic look. 'I don't know how he's got to where he is. His entire career, he just seems to have failed upwards. Where does he go next – Chief Constable or Commissioner of the Met?'

Jail, hopefully, Grace thought, but did not say. Other than to Cleo, he'd not breathed a word about the evidence he had against the ACC. Maybe this would be the last time Pewe would mess things up for him, he hoped. But he was getting increasingly concerned that no action, as yet, had happened against the man, and he was starting to have doubts. Had he made a big mistake, trusting the word of a disgraced former officer, no matter that they had once been friends? Had he been stupid to ignore Cleo's warning that this could all backfire on him? Professional Standards normally acted swiftly to suspend an officer if there was any whiff of suspicion – but now eight days had gone by since he had given the information to Alison Vosper. Although, of course, they would need to secure the evidence before taking any action.

Could he have made the biggest mistake of his career?

'Still with us?' Branson asked, breaking him out of his thoughts.

Grace smiled. 'At the moment, yes.'

98

Rebecca Watkins and Niall Paternoster sat, side by side, on a curved banquette in a corner booth of the rammed Green Dragon on Croydon High Street. Rebecca had in front of her a half-eaten plate of prawn salad and Niall a beef-and-mushroom pie. He raised his pint glass, which he had nearly drained, and clinked her glass of white wine. 'To the future!'

'To *our* future,' she corrected.

'To our future!'

They clinked glasses again and locked eyes. Niall's right leg pressed tightly against her left. They were so absorbed in each other that neither of them noticed the lean woman with long hair, wearing ripped jeans and a lightweight jacket, who was standing at the bar, drinking a lime and soda and picking at a sandwich, who kept glancing in their direction and then making notes in what looked like her diary.

'How's your week looking?' Rebecca asked.

'Pretty dull – so long as I'm not rearrested for my beloved wife's non-murder. Otherwise I'm free all week.' He gave her a cheeky look. 'Do you have something in mind?'

Her hand was sliding provocatively down between his legs and pressing against his crotch. 'Hmmn, maybe,' she said, nudging up closer to him. 'I have the thing I'm holding in my hand very much in my mind.'

After a quick glance around, he gave her a kiss on the cheek. 'And I have you very much in my mind.'

She squeezed him a little harder and he gasped. 'We have our annual sales conference this week, at the Grand in Eastbourne. Hubby's not coming, of course, he's away. I have to make a presentation on Thursday afternoon, then put in an appearance at the dinner – but I thought, if you're up for it, we could have ourselves a cosy rendezvous late night after I've escaped.'

'Like, your hotel room?'

She shook her head. 'Too many work people around. I'll have a think. Somewhere wild, crazy, deeply romantic.'

The erotic tingling inside him was so strong, Niall could barely speak. 'I like it.'

'I'll text you. Late night, somewhere where there won't be anyone around. I can put the rear seats of the Rangey flat. You bring a bottle of Prosecco and glasses?'

'What sort of time?'

'Whenever I can get away without being rude. Probably be near to midnight. Does that sound like a plan?'

He winced as she stroked him. 'It sounds like a very good plan.'

'The best plan you ever heard in your life?'

'Even better.'

After a discreet glance around, checking there were none of her colleagues about, she kissed him on the cheek. 'You'd better be there.'

99

There was now a fourth whiteboard behind Roy Grace in the conference room. It was labelled *Rebecca Watkins*. Two photographs of her taken through long lenses, and another of her and Niall Paternoster walking on the street, captured by the Surveillance Team, were stuck to it. Below them was a partially filled-in association chart, showing her known network of family and other contacts.

It was 5 p.m. Grace looked up from his notes at the crowded table. 'This is the twelfth briefing of Operation Lagoon, and we have some significant developments. The first is that, unfortunately, our Surveillance Team has again been temporarily redeployed, but they're leaving the tracker in place beneath Niall Paternoster's rental Fiesta.' He turned to Alexander. 'Jack, I'm giving you the action of arranging the monitoring of all movements of his vehicle until we get the Surveillance Team back.'

'I'm on it, sir, and I'm sharing with all the team.' Addressing them, Alexander said, 'You'll each be able to track any movements on your computer and phone screens.'

DC Boutwood raised her hand. 'Yes, EJ?' Grace said.

'Sir, why have they been redeployed at such a critical point?'

'I'm sure ACC Pewe would be happy to explain, EJ.' He shrugged. 'Resources – I'm afraid it is what it is, and we have to get on with it.'

'Understood, sir.'

420

'I'm glad you understand, EJ,' Norman Potting grumbled. He turned to Grace. '*Resources* – is that shorthand for being dumped on from a great height, chief?'

'I couldn't possibly comment, Norman,' Grace replied with a thin smile. 'I'll leave you to form your own conclusions, but we do get the team back later in the week.'

Potting shook his head, making a tutting sound. Ignoring him, Grace continued. 'I've called this briefing earlier than usual because I particularly wanted to have Sharon Orman here this afternoon before we lose her valuable skills. Orman, as some of you know, has developed a formidable lip-reading ability. Around 1 p.m. today she followed Niall Paternoster and Rebecca Watkins into a pub in Croydon, where she was able to observe them from a safe distance and pick up most of their conversation.' He turned towards her. 'Sharon, could you tell us what you saw after you entered the Green Dragon pub?'

'Yes, sir,' she said, then read from her notebook, 'Niall Paternoster was in a corner booth with Rebecca Watkins. They were sitting intimately close, eating lunch. He raised his glass of beer and clinked her wine glass and said, "To the future!" Rebecca corrected him, "To *our* future". Niall then repeated the toast. "To our future".'

She glanced at her notebook. 'Next, Rebecca asked, "How's your week looking?" Niall replied, "Pretty dull – so long as I'm not rearrested for my beloved wife's non-murder. Otherwise I'm free all week. Do you have something in mind?"

'Rebecca Watkins was acting in a very provocative manner, arousing him discreetly with one hand. She then told him she had her firm's annual sales conference in Eastbourne this coming week and that her husband would not be attending because he was away. She said she had to make a presentation on Thursday afternoon, then put in an appearance at dinner, but suggested they have a rendezvous afterwards. Subject suggested her hotel room, but Watkins dismissed that, saying she would have too many work people around. She suggested she would find somewhere and text him – she didn't say what time precisely but suggested it would be around midnight. She said she could put the seats in her Range Rover flat and suggested Niall bring along some Prosecco and two glasses.'

Potting grinned. 'A cosy little mobile love nest!'

'Speaks a man from experience,' Velvet Wilde retorted.

'Nice work, Sharon,' Grace said. 'Right, today's information – and revelations – about Rebecca Watkins are a significant development for our investigation. Let's review where we're at. Niall Paternoster reports his wife missing after allegedly dropping her off at Tesco Holmbush on Sunday September the first. We subsequently became suspicious of his story and he was arrested. The search of the Paternosters' home provides strong evidence he may have murdered his wife.'

He glanced down at his notes. 'Digital examination adds weight to this from analysis of his phone and computer, showing he appears to have lied about his and Eden's whereabouts on that Sunday. Further, from tracking his movements on his phone and on his car's computer, we find a shallow grave in Ashdown Forest, as well as the potential murder weapon. Niall's movements indicated he may have deposited some body parts in that grave and others off the end of the east mole of Shoreham harbour. Under questioning following his arrest, Paternoster denies everything vigorously. We release him, having insufficient evidence to charge him at this stage, but put him under surveillance while we continue our investigation.'

He took a sip of water. 'The Surveillance Team follow him to a rendezvous with Rebecca Watkins at the Devil's Dyke parking area. They appear to be lovers. This is the same destination that, according to digital comparison, Niall visited on Sunday September the first, just two hours after – according to his story – his wife had gone missing. I suspect that we will be able to tally the phone records with the check on Watkins's Range Rover Evoque's computer that she was there at the same time as she alluded to in interview.'

'Is it your intention to check the Range Rover now, sir?' DC Wilde asked.

'Not at the moment, no, Velvet. I think she's more useful to us if she doesn't know she's a primary suspect.' He looked up. 'Anyone disagree with me so far?'

No one did.

'So up until now we've had a clear motive for murder. Niall Paternoster has a girlfriend. Murder his wife to get her out of the way and clear the way forward for his relationship with Rebecca Watkins, who may herself be in a terminal marriage.' He looked up at his team again. 'So far so good?'

There were several nods.

'Then this morning, following the discovery of a letter concealed in a desk used by Eden Paternoster, DI Branson and I visited the solicitor to whom it referred, Jill Riddle, Head of Wills and Probate at the law firm of Cardwell Scott.'

'That lot!' Potting exclaimed. 'They had a toxic little runt of a Legal Aid solicitor called Donnelly – Paul Donnelly. I had a couple of run-ins with him. Then he got struck off after being found to be negligent.'

'I didn't know that, but good,' Grace replied. 'Jill Riddle confirmed she had drafted a new will, in which, basically, Eden Paternoster leaves almost her entire estate to Rebecca Watkins.' He paused to let that sink in.

The effect on his team was seismic.

Emily Denyer raised a hand. 'Boss, I've been looking into the overseas company into which Eden Paternoster transferred ownership of her Nevill Road house, along with most of her cash – Cormorant International Holdings. It's an offshore company providing overseas tax shelters, with links to Cardwell Scott.'

Grace frowned. 'Would you say, Emily, it might be more than a little coincidental that Eden Paternoster's will was drafted by the same firm that helped put her assets potentially out of her husband's reach?'

Denyer gave a wry smile. 'It just might be, boss.'

'So,' Grace said, to the whole team. 'Who is playing off who here? Eden Paternoster has moved the majority of her assets into a jurisdiction that is traditionally uncooperative with British police and tax authorities – assuming that is still the case, Emily?'

'It is. Not just the UK but pretty much the entire world, sir.'

Grace was silent for some moments, then he said, 'Emily, from your experience, is it possible that Rebecca Watkins might be able to access these overseas assets without any form of counter-signature from Eden Paternoster?'

'It would entirely depend what instructions Eden Paternoster has given, which we're not privy to. But yes, in principle, very possible.'

'Right,' Grace said. 'To hypothesize for a moment, could we have a scenario here in which Eden moves her assets overseas in the belief she and Rebecca Watkins have a future together, and in the hope that she has framed her husband sufficiently to get him convicted of her murder? A very clever ploy? Or is it Rebecca Watkins who is the clever one, in cahoots with Niall Paternoster, playing the long game?'

'By the term "long game", boss,' Denyer said, 'are you suggesting Rebecca Watkins has conned her lover, Eden, into moving her assets overseas and giving her access to them, with Eden believing she is secure in her relationship with Rebecca?'

'I am, Emily, yes.'

'But,' Denyer said, 'Eden doesn't realize she's been tricked – conned – and the woman she thinks is her future life partner,

Rebecca Watkins, is about to run for the hills with her husband and scoop up all her assets?'

'That's what it increasingly looks like, to me,' Grace said.

Glenn Branson, who had been silent for the entire meeting until now, spoke. 'How much of any of this do you think Niall Paternoster was aware of, boss? I mean, if he and Rebecca were – are – an item, and he knew Rebecca had access to all Eden's assets, why did he need to kill Eden? Couldn't he and Rebecca simply have taken off, grabbed all the offshore money and had enough to start a new life somewhere else?'

'Because she would track them down,' Grace retorted. 'If they ever wanted to live somewhere that recognizes international law, they'd never have been free of the threat of arrest.'

Branson nodded.

'But,' Grace continued, 'are we making a dangerous assumption here?'

He had everyone's attention.

'Rebecca Watkins is an interesting character. Let's look at the possibility she has another agenda altogether. What if she and Eden Paternoster have agreed – conspired – that Rebecca is going to seduce Niall and become his lover? Eden is going to fake her disappearance, leaving a trail of evidence that frames her husband for her murder. She needs to appear dead for her plan to work, to be free of him and free of the risk of arrest when she and Rebecca attempt to start a new life together. But she realizes her plan hasn't worked out quite as well as she'd hoped. The police don't have the evidence they need to charge him with murder. So she panics, perhaps?'

'Knowing the threats Niall made to kill her, boss, that she might have seen on his phone?' Branson suggested.

Grace paused to clear his throat. 'Indeed. Perhaps she's desperate now, and maybe not thinking clearly – as we know, that happens when people panic and they do irrational things.'

'Such as what? What are you thinking?'

'I don't know, I'm beyond second-guessing anything on this case. We need to be prepared for anything, which means we are going to need all our resources.' Grace thought for some moments, looking at his phone, then said, 'We need to be truly prepared for Thursday night, to see just what is going on. From what Sharon has helpfully told us of the conversation between Niall Paternoster and Rebecca Watkins in the pub, they're expecting to find a quiet spot.' He looked around at his team. 'Everyone agree?'

Everyone did.

'Are you making this a full-blown operation, boss?' Branson asked. 'Gold, Silver and Bronze?'

Grace shook his head. 'I've thought about it, but I want to make it very low key. The Surveillance Team will be behind them, and you and I, Glenn, will be out with them, tucked away but ready to move fast if anything develops.'

Grace looked at his phone again, tapping it for some moments. 'The forecast is mainly clear.' With a twinge of guilt, he asked, 'Anyone got plans for Thursday night they can't move? Defrosting the fridge or something?'

There were a few grins. Potting raised an arm. 'I've got a date, chief.'

'The future Mrs Potting?'

He shook his head. 'Nah, just meeting some old pals. I can – you know – reschedule.'

'Your altruism touches all our hearts, Norman,' Glenn Branson said.

100

'God, I love you!' Rebecca said, bursting through the front door of Eden's cottage and throwing herself into her lover's arms.

Eden kissed her on the forehead, riffling her fingers through her hair, and kissed her on her lips. Then, staring into her eyes, she said, 'I'm crazy for you.'

'I'm crazy for you, too!'

They kissed again. Then, kicking the front door shut, Eden asked excitedly, almost breathlessly, 'So? How did it go?'

'He fell for it. Hook, line and sinker.'

'For sure?'

'For sure.' Rebecca smiled. They kissed hard. As they reluctantly parted, she said, 'Trust me, he fell for it. He'll be there. You'll surprise him. One hard push. *Ooops! Plop! Bye-bye, Niall!*'

'And what if he pushes me, instead? *Ooops, plop, bye-bye, Eden?* No more Eden for real, this time?'

'It won't happen. You'll be taking him by surprise. He'll be gone in the darkness before he knows what's happening. And no one will see him fall, not at that hour. It could be several days before they find his body. I've heard that because you can't see the bottom of Beachy Head from up top, it can be some while before a body is found. Probably someone from the pub will report his car has been in the car park for several days – whatever. By then we'll be long gone, sipping margaritas on our sun-loungers. Sound good?'

'Sounds – I guess . . .' Eden said, still a little hesitant. 'Sounds a plan.'

Rebecca smiled. 'An elegant solution for the police. Niall Paternoster murders his wife, after a history of domestic violence against her. Then, wracked with remorse and scared the cops are closing in on him, he drives to Beachy Head in the middle of the night and ends it all. Constrained by their tight budgets and their need to show results, the detectives are only too happy to get this off their desks. Result. Boxes ticked. Case closed. And you and I swan off into the sunset. Guilt-free because you know what a monstrous shit he was, right?'

'Right,' Eden said, but her heart didn't sound in it. 'I'm – I'm just not sure I can do it, Bex. Murdering him was never part of our plan.'

'No, it wasn't. But the plan to get him arrested and charged hasn't worked out how we'd hoped. And, of course, my affair with him was only to get the inside track on what he was thinking and doing.'

'I don't know how you did it.'

'I hated every minute, Eden, and I don't know how you pretended to put up with him for so long. What we're doing will keep us moving forward. Just remember, he was planning to kill you. You do know that, don't you?'

Eden nodded, still fretful.

'And don't for a moment think he's not capable of it. He knows you're up to something, obviously, and he's not going to forgive you for this.'

'I know, you're right.'

'So you're just playing him at his own game. You don't have to feel guilty, you're doing what you're doing to save your life. That's why you ran away, faked everything. That's why you're going to do what you do on Thursday night, to give yourself a future. OK?'

'I suppose.'

'Good, give me a high five!'

Eden gave her a reluctant high five. As their palms met, she felt a flicker of hope.

The start of her new life?

But still a nagging doubt. 'I need a drink – a stiff one.'

'I need you first,' Rebecca said.

Eden shook her head. 'A stiff drink first – then you! Then another stiff drink. And then?' She gave a smile. 'What time do you have to leave?'

Rebecca waved a dismissive hand and gave a smile back. 'No rush at all, I have all the time in the world.'

They went through into the kitchen. 'Just think, after Thursday,' Rebecca said, slipping her arms around Eden's back, pushing her hair aside and kissing her on the neck, 'the rest of our lives together.'

Eden pulled out two cut-glass tumblers from the cupboard and poured a generous slug of Macallan into each. 'To the future,' she said, handing her lover a glass.

'To *our* future,' Rebecca corrected, downing a large amount of whisky in one gulp.

A short while later, they lay in the large bed, entwined around each other, with Elbow playing on the Sonos system. 'There's just one thing that's still worrying me about the plan,' Eden said.

Rebecca took her hand and kissed it. 'My love, don't let anything worry your pretty little head.' For emphasis, she lifted herself up a little and kissed Eden's forehead. 'Has that made your worry go away? Is it better?'

Eden grinned. 'Much.'

'So what's worrying you? Your cat – Reggie? We can figure a way to bring him to Cancun, or wherever we ultimately decide to settle.'

'Not Reggie, no, Bex. It was when the police were questioning you – I just had the sense, from what you told me, they weren't buying that Niall had murdered me. Not totally.'

'You're right. They're not buying it totally. But my sense is nor are they discounting it, they still think it's a strong possibility. That's what I mean by this bringing our plan back on track. Cops are suspicious and cynical – that's in their DNA, yes?'

'I guess,' Eden replied.

'But, as I've said, they're all under pressure to solve crimes, meet targets. When Niall's body is recovered from the bottom of the Beachy Head cliffs, it's going to be an easy tick-box exercise for them. He's claimed his wife has gone missing. The evidence points to him lying, and to him having murdered her, even if they don't have actual proof. All the stuff you did with his phone, our clever work making sure your car was in all the right places at the right times, all the evidence you planted in the house. And the master stroke of the shallow grave. It's there on a plate for the plod. If they had concerns before, this deals with them. They're going to be happy, you and I will be happy. It's a win-win!'

'Can't we do this without killing him?'

Rebecca cocked her head. 'You'd be taking a big personal risk. Think about it. You've faked your disappearance and in the process left a complex trail of evidence indicating that your husband's murdered you and disposed of your body. Do you want to risk ending up in court and getting a criminal record? That would finish your career and prevent you from ever getting a decent job again. And leave your bastard, abusive husband out there biding his time for revenge?'

Eden was silent for a long while. Finally, she said gloomily, 'What a sodding mess.'

Rebecca shook her head. 'Nope, not at all. As I said, trust me. I have a plan.'

101

When Roy Grace arrived home shortly after 6.30 p.m., Cleo was sitting on a sofa in the living area, her laptop on the coffee table in front of her, wearing headphones and nodding her head to music while reading a book.

She clearly hadn't heard Humphrey barking his greeting to his master, nor the sound of the door, and she looked up with a start as her husband entered the room. Instantly, she tapped a key on her laptop and removed the headset. 'Darling, hi! Great you're home early! I thought you'd be much later.'

He kissed her, then hesitantly said, 'Managed to escape!'

'Good!'

'What are you reading?'

'It's by Laura Whitmore.' She held the book up and he looked at the catchy cover.

'*No One Can Change Your Life Except For You*,' he read out. 'Is it good?'

She nodded. 'It is, yes, very. I bought it because I thought I might learn something for Bruno. I like the way she writes, really down to earth, no nonsense. Listen to this.' She flipped back a couple of pages and read aloud, '"We can blame the selfish or thoughtless actions of others for our circumstances, but we can't change those actions. We can change how we comprehend them or how we act."'

He nodded. 'Very true. So, how are you?'

She gave him a wan smile. 'I'm bearing up, I suppose – how about you?'

He took a deep breath. 'The same. I'm fine so long as I'm busy. The moment I stop, I start thinking about everything. How's Noah?'

'Kaitlynn said he's been bloody awful all day. She reckons he's finally entering the terrible twos.'

'So if he's started late, let's hope he finishes them early,' Roy said, peeling off his jacket, loosening his tie and fiddling with the top button of his shirt until he prised it open. 'We can only hope!'

'Chance would be a fine thing.' She grimaced. 'I've been working on the music for Bruno's funeral.'

He looked solemn. 'Thanks, that's great.'

'I've only made a start – I need your help.'

'Sure.'

'I've been going through Bruno's Spotify playlists on his laptop.'

'No password?'

'I found it on a Post-it stuck to the inside of a drawer in his bedroom.'

'I've always said you'd make a great detective.' He smiled.

She shook her head. 'No, I wouldn't – I have a life.' She gave him a strange look.

It wounded him. Even more at this moment, when he was about to break the news about his commitment for Thursday night. 'Hey! Meaning?'

'You know exactly what I mean. I would never want you to change, I know how much you love your work. I'm not saying it as a criticism, it's what you are, it's what makes you the man I married. It's what makes you the man I love.'

He sat down on the sofa and put an arm around her. 'You do an incredible job, too, being with people, comforting them at the worst moment in their lives.'

'Thanks, but I'm worried for how much longer I'll be able to do that,' she said. 'It's the thing I love most about my job. But new technology is taking that away from me. Nowadays identifying a victim is dealt with mostly by DNA or dental records, and relatives are no longer identifying their loved ones in person. I'd really miss that human contact. It's always tough. Someone leaves home and drops dead, or is killed in an accident, and I feel a real sense of achievement if I'm able to give the loved ones some crumb of comfort. I'd hate that to be taken away. You're lucky, in one way, no matter how grim – you'll always have that human contact.'

Grace mentally skipped over the times when, as a junior copper having to deliver the death message, he'd been punched in the face, had furniture thrown at him, had to try to calm someone lying on the floor screaming, clawing at the air. 'I guess.'

He bided his time; this wasn't the moment to tell her that he'd be working Thursday night. 'Can I hear what you've put together on the playlist so far?'

She leaned forward and tapped a couple of keys.

102

On what felt like the longest evening of her life, Eden was a bag of nerves. Riddled with doubts. Thinking how few killers ever actually got clean away with it. There was almost always something, one mistake or one witness or one clever, probing detective who finally got the killer to crack. And even when that didn't happen, oftentimes killers found themselves tormented by guilt.

She couldn't stop reflecting on a novel she had read, years ago, called *Thérèse Raquin*, because it reminded her so much of her current situation. Maybe stupidly, she'd downloaded it onto her Kindle a few days ago and had been reading it again during her isolation. Thérèse was married to her useless husband, Camille, but desperate to be with her lover, Laurent. They murdered her husband and life should have been wonderful from then on, except it wasn't. They were both so haunted by the knowledge of what they had done that ultimately their guilt destroyed them.

Could she live with the knowledge that she had sent Niall to his death? However much she hated him? However much he had hurt her in the past? And despite knowing he had been planning to kill her?

Would he really have gone through with "getting rid of" her? Was she being pushed by Rebecca, coerced by her into doing this? Was she being weak in not standing up to Rebecca and telling her she couldn't go through with this? And – she churned this over and over - what was going to happen when she met Niall, face to face, shocking the hell out of him?

Or would it shock him at all?

Niall knew she was almost certainly alive and he would be mad as hell with her. Crazy mad for all she'd put him through. And she'd seen him mad before. Scary. Very scary. Definitely capable of killing, like he did with their baby. Was it smart to meet him, in pitch darkness, on a remote clifftop?

As if further dampening her thoughts, a heavy shower was pelting down outside, rattling as loud as hail on the roof of the small conservatory adjoining the kitchen. It was just gone 10 p.m.

She craved a drink, but didn't dare risk it – being stopped and breathalysed would screw everything up. Although, she reasoned, as she sat at the little dining table beneath the glass roof, digging her fork into a microwaved pasta – turning it over, letting the steam escape, her stomach too knotted to consider eating even a mouthful – maybe that would be the easy way out of all of this? Just get drunk. Pass out at home. Apologize to Bex later.

Or have a couple of drinks and take her chances. That was so tempting right now. And if she got arrested for drunk-driving, fess up and see what happened. Surely it wasn't illegal to disappear? OK, she'd left a trail of evidence to implicate that bastard, but she hadn't harmed him, she hadn't made any false claims against him. Rebecca was wrong, surely – she hadn't committed any offence, had she?

More wisps of steam rose from the white slop in the carton. Tagliatelle or rigatoni or cannelloni – she'd forgotten what it had said on the label. The cheesy smell made her stomach churn.

Just a small drink? A tiny whisky to settle her? One wouldn't do any harm, would it?

She got up, poured herself a finger of Macallan and downed it in one gulp. Wincing at the burn as it went down her throat and hit her stomach, she stood tight. Then it began working its magic and she started to feel better. Not much, but a little. Dutch courage.

What the hell.

She raised her glass and toasted her weak reflection in a windowpane. 'Cheers, Eden!'

Although she wasn't actually Eden any more. According to the driving licence and passport that Rebecca had somehow obtained for her – no questions asked – well, only a few – she was now Ginevra Mary Stoneley, tenant of Woodbury Cottage, Chiddingly, East Sussex, and the not very proud owner of an inconspicuous, dark-blue, ageing Nissan Micra.

She even had a new appearance, a brand-new hairstyle and bright blonde colour, courtesy of a hairdresser friend of Rebecca who'd spent two hours at the cottage this morning.

Raising her glass again, this time she said, 'Cheers, Ginevra, you hot, sexy creature!'

Ginevra winked back at her.

Was Ginevra about to become a murderer?

She put the glass down and checked her watch. Needed to pace herself. Only 10.10 p.m. Another twenty minutes before she had to set off for her rendezvous.

She opened the cupboard door, removed the bottle and took it outside, ducking through the rain and putting it on the passenger seat of the Micra. One final nip of it when she was at her destination. Didn't warriors always get something to stir them into battle? She'd read that the Zulus fought their wars so ferociously because they were tripping on magic mushrooms. The GIs fought in Vietnam high on cannabis. How else could anyone kill a fellow human being face to face?

Then she sat back down and stared at the steadily congealing pasta. Rebecca had told her to think through to beyond tonight. To the far side. To the fortnight they had booked in a villa with its own pool in a resort in Cancun, Mexico. And to their life beyond.

For years, she could never have imagined being with anyone other than a man. Now she could never imagine being with anyone other than Rebecca.

She would do anything for this woman.

And was about to.

103

Roy Grace and Glenn Branson sat in the unmarked Ford, parked on Eastbourne's almost deserted seafront. A short distance away the streetlights ended, and a steep dark hill rose ahead, the start of the Seven Sisters chain of chalk cliffs, the most notorious of which was Beachy Head. It was just gone 10.57 p.m. and they'd been here for the past hour. Grace was both anxious and bored. Branson just seemed plain bored. The other members of the team were at HQ awaiting deployment.

Peering through the windscreen, made opaque by the pelting rain, Branson said, by way of conversation, 'You don't like heights much, do you?'

Grace shook his head. 'I get acrophobia. If I look down an unguarded drop – or even a guarded one – I feel a strange pull to jump, almost as if I'm being tempted or my brain is taunting me. You ever get that?'

The DI nodded. 'This is about as close to the edge as I like to be: a good quarter of a mile of terra firma between me and any drop. I get acrophobia standing on a kerb!'

Grace smiled distractedly.

Glenn looked at him concerned. 'You OK, mate?'

'I'm OK, I just get flashes when it hits me and I think of his accident. I just hope to God he didn't feel anything. But I'd rather be here, especially if we get a result tonight.'

Then he focused back on why they were here. Despite what he

had told his team at the briefing earlier in the week, he had been toying ever since with turning this into a full-blown operation, with Gold, Silver and Bronze commanders to cover his back if anything went wrong. But mindful of Cassian Pewe's scepticism about this entire investigation, he worried the ACC would order him to abort his whole plan, so in the end he'd stuck to his decision of keeping it low-key, not getting Pewe involved.

And hoped it wasn't all going to go badly tits-up.

Although the weather had already gone just that. Far from the forecasted clear night, at the moment there was dense cloud cover and a heavy rain shower was falling. It pattered down on the roof of the unmarked Ford as Grace sat with Branson. A strong wind was blowing, too, sending something – an empty drinks can, Grace guessed – rattling along.

Three of the vehicles of Mark Taylor's Surveillance Team, each with a crew of two, one with Sharon Orman, were parked up close by, covering the exits to the conference hotel where Rebecca Watkins was staying. The others were stationed on the main roads out of Eastbourne. Inside his jacket pocket Grace had a printout of his risk assessment for tonight. But his nerves were ragged.

A figure, head bowed against the rain, walked along the pavement with a dog on a lead, and passed by their car. Branson yawned. 'Think you need to use a better weather forecasting method,' he said with a wry smile, watching the rain. 'There's technology you can use, apps, you know? They're a lot more reliable than sticking your finger out of the window – or was it the entrails of a chicken you were studying?'

Grace gave him a withering look.

'Sorry, boss, that was tactless.'

'You could say that.' He grimaced at the reminder of the previous week. 'I looked at the forecast for around midnight, it's meant to be clear skies then.'

'Definitely, for sure it will be, somewhere in the world, just not here,' Branson retorted.

But Grace barely heard this, he was back in his thoughts, again thinking through what lay ahead tonight. The words of Sharon Orman, relaying the conversation between Niall Paternoster and Rebecca Watkins in the pub in Croydon. *Whenever I can get away without being rude. Probably be near to midnight. Does that sound like a plan?*

A lovers' rendezvous? Was that all it was going to turn out to be? He would have egg all over his face, for sure, if he'd organized an operation simply to watch a couple getting it on in the back of a car.

What, he wondered over and over, was he actually expecting to see tonight, if not that? But all his instincts were sensing this was going to turn into something more than a simple bit of canoodling lovers. Rebecca Watkins was up to something.

But what?

Where would she choose? Which remote location, ideal for lovers wanting to be away from prying eyes, and yet close enough to Eastbourne to be just a short drive away?

Both had their phones in front of them, on the road-mapping app Mark Taylor had instructed them to upload. It currently showed Niall Paternoster's rental car stationary at his home address.

In order to keep as silent as possible, and avoid any sounds from their radios, both of them wore earpieces plugged into their phones. Each of them also had night-vision binoculars.

Glenn Branson spoke suddenly, quietly, in a caring tone. 'How are you feeling, mate, you know, about the funeral?'

'Not great. I've spent the last couple of evenings going through the order of service with Cleo, listening to Bruno's playlists, trying to figure what music he would have approved of – and what would sound appropriate in church. Something I guess to do with all he had to overcome – you know – all the difficulties with his mother, then her death, then moving to a new and strange country, family, school.'

Branson was silent for a while, thinking. 'One suggestion, although it's not for me to say and it might not be entirely appropriate . . . how about Mike Doughty's "I Keep on Rising Up". It's about overcoming adversity, and he has a beautiful voice, soulful – that's one that could work.'

'I don't know it, but I'll have a listen tomorrow, thanks.'

'I'll try and think of some more.'

'So,' Grace asked, 'wedding still OK for next month?'

After a long and acrimonious divorce from his wife, Ari, and a custody fight for their two children, which Ari had mostly won before her untimely death, Glenn Branson had finally moved on and fallen in love again. Siobhan Sheldrake was a very charismatic and fun person, but as the senior crime reporter for the *Argus*, Grace could foresee some awkward pillow talk between them in the years ahead. On the other hand she had been really good with his kids and loved being a stepmother to them.

'Yeah,' Branson said. 'All set.' Then as he looked down at his phone, he murmured excitedly, watching the red dot of Niall Paternoster's car, 'Subject one is on the move!'

As Grace looked too, both suddenly heard communications in their earpieces.

'Alpha Five here, subject two, Range Rover Evoque, index Golf November Seven Zero Charlie Papa November has just left hotel.'

Grace felt a beat of excitement. That was Rebecca Watkins's car. He heard Taylor's voice.

'Alpha Five, roger that, keep eyes on it.'

'Copy that, sir, am following at distance.'

A few minutes later, Grace heard a voice. 'Subject two's turning into Beachy Head pub car park. I'm carrying on past.'

Grace looked at the red dot heading up Nevill Road. Even

driving fast in light traffic, it would take Paternoster a good half-hour to get here. They could reach the car park in less than ten minutes. He radioed Taylor. 'Grace to Alpha Seven.'

'Alpha Seven,' Taylor replied.

'We're going to check out the Beachy Head pub car park.'

'Roger that, sir, we'll put units either side but not too close.'

Grace turned to Branson. 'Fire her up. Get there quickly but quietly.'

As Branson started the engine, Grace looked down at the red dot again. And again hoped to hell this wasn't going to turn out to be a massive waste of everyone's time.

104

Glenn Branson drove fast out of Eastbourne, heading along the steep, twisting, clifftop road, with the darkness of farmland to their right as they left the town and the darkness of the English Channel, beyond the cliffs, to their left.

'Coming up on the right,' Roy Grace said.

There was a sign for the Beachy Head Chaplaincy on their right and then one for the pub. Branson slowed right down as they approached the pub's huge car park. It was almost deserted. Just the Range Rover, on one side, parked close to some kind of mobile industrial unit, and a large camper van with German plates some distance from it, almost at the far end, facing towards the cliffs. The camper van's roof extension was open, and the interior lights were on. Holidaymakers settled in for the night, Grace guessed, an idea forming.

'Don't go in, drive on by.'

As they did so, a figure emerged from the camper van, from a door on the far side to the Range Rover, and sparked up a cigarette.

There is a God, Grace thought. 'Spin her round, go into the car park, drive normally as if you're deliberately heading to the camper van, and pull up beside it, on the far side of it to the Rangey.'

Branson threw him a puzzled look and complied. As they approached the camper, they saw a man in shorts, a vest and flip-flops, sheltering beneath a small awning above the door. He looked at them warily. Grace lowered his window, smiled and said, '*Guten abend!*' He smelled the sweet aroma of the smoke.

The man smiled back and replied with something that Grace, with his very limited German, failed to catch. He climbed out of the car, holding up his warrant card but still smiling. Putting a finger to his mouth to indicate they should be quiet, Grace said, '*Polizei! Sprechen Sie Englisch?*'

'*Ja!*' the German replied. Then he added, 'I am very good to speak English.'

'We are just keeping an eye on someone.' Grace pointed at the binoculars around his neck and the man nodded. 'Is it possible we can sit in your camper for one hour, to observe?' He jerked a finger surreptitiously to the far side of the car park, in the direction of the Range Rover. Again quietly, but loud enough for the German to hear, he said, 'Criminals.'

The man's eyes lit up with excitement. He crushed out his cigarette, opened the door, and they entered. It smelled of damp clothes and grilled meat. A middle-aged woman was sitting watching a movie in German on the video screen, a bottle of wine open beside her, two glasses on the table. The man spoke to her in German briefly. She froze the film, turned and waved at the two detectives, then said something to her husband and held up the bottle.

'My wife asked if you would like a drink? A glass of wine?'

'*Nein, danke!* You are very kind. Can we go to the front seats?'

'Please, be free. You want lights in the cabin off or on?'

'Off, as they are, *danke.*'

Grace and Branson settled into the front seats, Grace with the left-hand-drive vehicle's steering wheel in front of him. They now had an unobstructed view, through the rain-blurred windscreen and side window, both of the Range Rover and of the road and clifftop ahead.

As he lowered himself in his seat to be as inconspicuous as possible, Branson murmured, 'Looks like she's still in the car.'

Grace raised his binoculars. 'She is,' he confirmed.

As soon as he was settled, Grace looked out of his side window.

Then they both stiffened as they heard the roar of a car approaching at high speed. Headlights appeared. A boy racer shot past in what looked and sounded, in the darkness, like a clapped-out Subaru with a boombox exhaust.

Then silence again.

The rain had lessened, but a strong wind buffeted the vehicle. Grace watched the red dot on his screen, all his sadness over Bruno momentarily put to one side, into a compartment, his focus now completely on the job he was here to do. And he realized that being here, right now, in the moment – the thrill of the hunt, the anticipation, feeling the buzz – this was one of the things he loved most about his work.

A call came in from another surveillance car, further along Beachy Head Road, the detective nicknamed Smudger. 'Nissan Micra, Bravo Delta Five One Sierra Mike Romeo, driving slowly, seems to be looking for something.'

'Copy that,' came Taylor's voice.

Moments later, just as the heavens opened again, headlights appeared, and then a small car turned in. Watching through his night-vision binoculars, Grace saw it was a Nissan Micra, with the licence plate Smudger had just given. He watched it drive around the car park, before coming to a halt some distance from any of the other vehicles. He immediately called the Control Room. 'I need a PNC check on a Nissan Micra, index Bravo Delta Five One Sierra Mike Romeo, please.'

The Control Room operator came back in seconds. 'No trace lost or stolen. Registered owner is Ginevra Mary Stoneley of Woodbury Cottage, Chiddingly, East Sussex. Postcode—'

He cut her short. 'Thanks, that's good enough.'

Turning to Branson, he said, 'Ginevra Mary Stoneley, that name mean anything?'

He flipped his phone face down, not wanting the light to show, and signalled to Branson to do the same. Then he picked up his binoculars. He could just make out the silhouette of the driver, through the rain, but it was hard to see the face clearly. They were wearing a baseball or golfing cap pulled down low, and sunglasses, despite the darkness.

'Ginevra Mary Stoneley? Unusual name, Ginevra. No, doesn't mean anything.' He also trained his binoculars on the Micra. They both watched through the rain that was coming down even harder now. The occupant of the car was just sitting. Biding her – or his – time – for what?

Meeting someone? Or just for the rain to stop and go for a walk? Or to jump?

Lowering the binoculars, Grace turned his phone over and glanced at the red dot of Niall Paternoster's rental Fiesta. It was very definitely moving in this direction, the app estimating a time of less than ten minutes away.

Mark Taylor confirmed over the radio that a surveillance car had it in sight.

It was 11.42 p.m.

The shower was slowly dying down. Passing through.

'Occupant's getting out!' Branson said.

Grace raised his binoculars again. The driver's door of the Micra was ajar, the interior light on, but their view of the driver's face was blocked by an umbrella. Then the figure alighted, the face still completely hidden from view by the umbrella. The door was pushed shut, then the indicators flashed – the car had been locked by remote.

'Shit, who is it? Male or female?' Grace whispered.

The person's back was to them now, walking across the car

park to the road. A calf length dark raincoat with a hood raised over the cap and jeans tucked into walking boots.

'Female, I reckon,' Branson said. 'From the way she's walking.'

Grace nodded as the subject's stride quickened across the car park towards the road. The figure, umbrella still raised, crossed over and walked a short distance up a grassy incline on the far side, towards the edge, before turning right and striding off into the night.

Both continued watching until the subject was out of sight, then they lowered their glasses and frowned at each other in the faint glow from their phones. 'What's going on there?' Branson said. 'A late constitutional along the top of the cliffs?'

Grace shrugged. 'I don't know, but it definitely does not feel right.' He turned his binoculars back on the Range Rover. The figure was still in the driving seat – Rebecca, he was sure, but he couldn't see her face clearly.

'A lovers' rendezvous – perhaps just being ultra-cautious – the partner parked up somewhere, concealed? I mean, they're hardly going to be able to do it in a Micra, are they? Not unless they're extremely small.'

'Yep, good luck with that one,' Grace murmured.

The rain suddenly became heavier again, worsening into a torrent. Grace looked at his phone. At the red dot. Six minutes away now.

A minute later the rain stopped, almost as suddenly as it had started, and there was a break in the clouds. Branson kept his binoculars glued to the Range Rover. Then he exclaimed, 'She's on the move!'

Grace raised his glasses. He saw a female figure in a knee-length belted coat and jeans, umbrella low over her head, walking across the car park towards the road. She then crossed, striding determinedly over the grass in the direction of the clifftop.

'What the hell?' Branson asked.

Both detectives kept their binoculars trained on her as she walked up the grassy slope towards the cliff edge.

'What's she doing?' Glenn said. 'Why's she going there?'

Grace looked down at the red dot, which was moving ever closer. 'I don't know, mate,' he replied.

She stopped some distance short of the edge, then stood, as if she was looking out to sea admiring the view. Except, Grace was well aware, in this darkness there was no view, other than the possibility of a few silent lights far away on the horizon, of supertankers and container vessels out in the English Channel's shipping lanes.

Suddenly they heard Smudger's voice. 'Vehicle containing subject one approaching from west.'

Grace felt a rush of excitement as bright lights appeared from their right and a Fiesta came into sight, driving slowly. A red glow inside might have been the driver, presumably Paternoster, smoking a cigarette.

A second later the car began indicating and turned into the car park. As it did so a trail of small sparks of red flared fleetingly behind it.

105

Niall Paternoster was in a sunny mood, despite the darkness and the crappy weather. And his mood improved even further as he put the window back up, barely noticing the sparks of the remains of his fag in the rear-view mirrors as he drove into the car park.

Rebecca was already here!

He glanced happily at the Range Rover and thought about what lay ahead with his lover – his very adventurous lover. He liked that about her. A lot.

Sex with Eden, more recently, had become so bloody boring. So bloody *unsexy*. But with Rebecca – wow. It was the real deal!

He was pleased to see she'd parked in a discreet spot, shielded from most of the rest of the large car park by a temporary industrial unit. Only a few other vehicles in here, he clocked, looking around, making sure her husband's car wasn't one of them, spying on her. But there was only a Nissan Micra, a camper van and an empty dark-coloured saloon parked alongside it.

Pulling up close to the Range Rover, he reached into the door pocket and pulled out a pack of mints, popping one into his mouth. He felt the tingle of arousal deep in the pit of his stomach. In daylight he'd have had to wait to get out of the car until his swelling had subsided. But hey, in the darkness it was fine. Who could see it?

His phone pinged with a text.

u have to see this, incredible! XX

Frowning, he texted back.

u need to see what I have for you! XX

A reply came back seconds later.

I mean it! Reflection of the moon on the sea – like, something magical! XXX

Where are u?

Walk straight across the road and keep going, you'll see me! I'm crazy for u! XXXX

Coming! XXXXX

106

The rain had stopped now and the moon was shining through a break in the clouds. The woman at the cliff edge, with her back to them, lowered her umbrella, still facing out to sea, her stance showing she was braced against the wind. Grace and Branson could clearly see, through their binoculars, her razored blonde hair rippling. It was Rebecca Watkins.

But wouldn't she have heard the Fiesta arriving? Caught the headlights out of the corner of her eye? Why didn't she turn to see if it was her lover, instead of continuing to stare ahead without even a glance? Staring as if she was looking for something far out to sea. A signal from a boat? No, that made no sense.

Grace swung his glasses in the direction of the Fiesta, and a few seconds later the distinctive figure of Niall Paternoster appeared on the far side of the vehicle. Grace watched as he hurried across the road and headed over the grass towards Rebecca. She still didn't turn round.

'What the hell's going on?' Branson asked.

Grace didn't reply, he was watching intently. Again thinking back to the words relayed by Sharon Orman. The rendezvous between Rebecca Watkins and Niall Paternoster. Something at the time had felt wrong about it, and it felt even more wrong now, but he couldn't say why. Something about Rebecca's body language?

Through the green glow of the night vision, Grace watched Paternoster getting closer to her. Closer. Closer.

She still wasn't moving, just staring ahead, like a statue. Rocking slightly in the wind.

Was she aware he was coming up behind her? Could Niall be about to push her over the edge? Was the sound of the wind making her unable to hear him? For a split-second Grace toyed with hitting the horn or flashing the lights to warn her and distract Paternoster. He braced himself, ready to leap out and run across. But he held himself in check, dismissing that thought. This was two lovers meeting. Their rendezvous. Their *assignation*. Meeting for sex according to the conversation Sharon Orman had lip-read in the pub.

But Grace still didn't think that was all. Something else was going on, he was more and more certain. And hoping to hell he wasn't going to be proved wrong.

107

The grass was wet and Niall Paternoster was only wearing suede loafers, his brand-new, very expensive, tasselled beige ones, and they were going to be ruined. They were already soaked through after just a few paces, making his bare feet inside them wet, too. His hair was being torn from its roots and his eyes were watering from the wind.

What was so special about a moonlit sea that was worth ruining his shoes for? If he'd known he was going to have to traipse through uncut grass, he'd have worn boots – he'd only put these on because they'd be easy to kick off. Who the hell wanted to waste valuable time undoing laces? Quick release! It was for the same reason, speed – as well as a surprise for her – and turn-on for him – that he'd gone commando tonight.

His foot squelched in something – mud, please God, not dog's mess. Yech. Why was she putting him through this? He didn't really give a monkey's about the view, he'd not come all this way to look at that. The only view he wanted was Rebecca's gorgeous face, while he held her body in his arms.

Honestly, he sighed to himself, striding on towards her, feeling excited and annoyed in almost equal measures. 'Hey!' he called out. 'Hey, gorgeous! This view had better be worth it!'

She didn't react. She just continued facing out to sea.

Was it the view that was distracting her? he wondered.

When he was just a few feet from her, about to put his arms around her, she turned sharply to face him, brandishing the umbrella like a weapon.

And he froze.

108

In the camper van, binoculars glued to his eyes, Roy Grace shouted, 'Shit! That's not Rebecca Watkins!'

'It's Eden,' Branson said. 'Jesus, what's going on?'

'We're about to find out,' Grace replied.

'Nice to see you, Niall,' Eden said. 'But not that nice.'

He opened his mouth, too astonished for a moment to speak. Before he could get a word out, Eden, holding the point of the umbrella out in front of her, said, 'Shut up a minute, just wait.'

'What the hell is this about? What bloody game are you play-ing, Eden? Do you have any idea of the shit I've been through? Do you have any fucking idea?'

'Whatever it is, it's not enough for all the crap you've put me through.'

Despite shaking with nerves, she managed a smile, managed to keep the tremble out of her voice. That gulp of whisky she'd taken before leaving the car was helping, a lot. She gave him another very sweet smile. 'Aren't you pleased to see me? You don't look very happy that I'm still alive.'

'Very funny.' He grimaced, his mind a furnace of fury. 'Don't push your luck, baby. This is just you and me. I could shove you over the edge right now, after you've set your disappearance up so cleverly. They'll find your body in a few days and mark you down as a suicide. I'd have just left you dead. Have you thought

455

about that? How it would look to anyone? You tried to frame your husband and, when that didn't work, you decided to end it all?'

'Oh yes, I've thought about it, Niall,' Eden replied, speaking verbatim from the script Rebecca had written for her. 'Which is why I'm wearing a wire, with every word you or I say being transmitted to a recording device at the Police HQ in Lewes. I saw the texts to your lover, whoever she is, where you talked about your plans to "get rid of" me.'

She saw the hesitation in his face and knew her words had struck home – enough to sow doubt about whether she was telling the truth or not. 'Still going to shove me over the edge?'

'Look, we need to talk,' he said. 'Like, those texts – they were just a joke, you know.'

'Great joke, so funny, they had me in hysterics. Can't remember when I laughed so much, Niall. Especially the bit about my will, thinking you would inherit everything when I was gone. And you and your lover had a plan. You told her you knew exactly how to kill me and dispose of my body so it would never be found. I particularly liked that bit where you told her that if the police couldn't find a body, it made a prosecution very hard. A "no body" murder, I think you called it, right?'

He stared at her in numb silence.

'So, I thought I would turn the tables. You deserve it. You killed our unborn baby and ruined my life, you evil bastard. Can a dead person commit a murder, Niall?'

'There's one flaw in that, Eden,' he said, more calmly now. 'The police don't believe you're dead.'

'Obviously not if they've wired me with a mic.' She smiled. 'Do you want to hear what your lover told me, while we were in bed together?'

'What?' Now he stared at her both confused and dumbstruck.

Rebecca had told her exactly the words to say and the moves to make. Keep taunting him, ramping it up, and up again, until he lunged at her, and as he did so to instantly hit the ground. He would trip over her and be gone, over the edge.

But she couldn't do it. She knew the words, what she had to say. The taunt about his manhood. The first time he'd ever hit her was when she had done that, and totally unintentionally then.

The script was so clear in her head now. She just had to say the words and he would lunge, he was that livid.

She also told me you couldn't satisfy her.

But the words lodged in her throat. She couldn't get them out. Instead, she stared at him, at her husband, at the man she hated so much, on the edge of a 500-foot drop, knowing just how easily he could kill her, and that he could do it without any sense of remorse. But she was unable to spit out the words that would trigger him.

'You don't have a wiretap, Eden. You and I have watched enough police documentaries to know that. Police never put a key witness in danger like this. You're lying. Bullshit. This is just you and me. No one's listening. No one's coming to save you. You're lying about the police and Rebecca. Whatever your crazy plan is, your stupid ploy, you've actually just made it very easy for me.'

She froze. Her eyes adjusting more and more to the darkness. Staring at him, at the anger in his face.

And suddenly, now, she was scared. Really scared.

'Like I said, Eden, you're a very stupid woman with your hare-brained plan to try to frame me. All you've actually done is set me up with the perfect alibi. I don't need a "no body" murder any more. You see, it's not possible to murder a dead person.'

He took a step towards her. 'Too bad you didn't work that one out, but then you never were as smart as you thought at chess.' He took another step towards her, remembering the words of the tall, burly copper who'd first come to the house to interview him. 'Our unfinished game, Eden. You thought you were beating me, but you'd made a fatal error with that one. A move you hadn't spotted. Black Queen's Knight to King's Pawn three, eh? Shall we call this my last checkmate?'

'Shit! Something's going to happen here,' Roy Grace yelled, dropping his glasses and frantically looking for the door handle. 'GO, GO, GO!'

He clambered down from the camper and, closely followed by Branson, sprinted across the car park towards the road, radioing Taylor for backup as he did.

Suddenly, all Eden's confidence had drained away. Niall was just inches away from her and the cliff edge was just two feet behind her. She stared at him, trembling in terror. There wasn't enough room between them now for her to drop to the ground, as Rebecca had instructed her. Her brain raced desperately, thinking of what to do, what to say.

Then a tornado erupted from a bush a few feet behind Niall. It slammed into him, propelling him sideways. Then forward. Then forward again.

Eden heard a thud. Another thud. A grunt.

Then, suddenly, he was gone.

Vanished.

A faint, terrible, piercing scream that faded away.

Followed by complete silence.

109

Friday 13 September

'Bex!' Eden screamed at the figure in the hoodie and baseball cap, and lunged at her in blind, shocked fury. Rebecca stepped back, then back again, parrying her flailing arms.

'Bex – what – what have you done?' she screamed again.

Her lover looked at her with an expression Eden had never seen before. It wasn't the face of the woman she knew. It was almost as if something totally alien was looking mockingly back at her. 'I've done what you were too spineless to do, Eden.' Her voice was icy and as dark as the night.

Suddenly, Rebecca lunged forward, grabbing Eden's wrist in a vice-like grip. 'Join him, why don't you? If you loved him too much to kill him, then join him, have him, have him forever, he's all yours!'

She was being propelled towards the cliff edge, Eden realized, her brain too frozen in terror to make any sense of what was happening. This wasn't Bex, this was some kind of a demon. Pulling her towards the edge.

'Bex! Stop!' Eden tried to break free of Rebecca's grip. But with one sharp tug she was propelled forward again, straight at the edge, only Rebecca gripping her wrist preventing her from falling. As Rebecca did so, she swung Eden round.

Eden screamed, convinced she was being thrown over the clifftop. But Rebecca kept her grip, swinging her in a wide arc, right to the very edge, then back round until she was now between the edge and Eden.

Eden felt the wind ripping at her. Stared back at the strange, manic expression in her lover's face. Her lover who was now a total stranger. The cliff edge was just a few feet behind Rebecca now. But she knew that with Rebecca's skills, if she tried a lunge, she could be flipped over her head in an instant.

Panic completely gripped her. She did the only move she could think of and threw herself backwards and sideways onto the ground, taking Rebecca face down with her. She lashed out with her free left hand, feeling pain in her knuckles as it struck Rebecca's face, then twisted, desperately trying to break away from the grip on her wrist. She rolled over sideways and her arm came free, but she was disorientated now, as Rebecca leaped back on top of her. Rolling. Eden didn't know which way. Towards or away from the edge? Pinning both arms to the ground now.

'BEX! What the hell are—?'

Rebecca's face was inches from her own. She felt her lover's warm breath on her face. 'You never thought it through, my lovely Eden, did you? So sweet of you to leave me everything, then join your hubby in a suicide pact. I'll always be so grateful to you.'

Suddenly, Eden felt hands gripping her hair, pulling her even closer towards Bex's face. So close she was now staring into her eyes, nose to nose, forehead to forehead.

'You really fell for it,' Rebecca said. 'But we did have some very special moments, didn't we? Too bad we won't get to have any more. In a different life, I could have been really hot for you.'

Eden suddenly felt herself being jerked sharply and agonizingly upwards by her ears. Upwards. Upwards. She flailed with her arms, hands, feet, trying to get traction on something, anything. Then, in a lightning move, Rebecca released her ears and gripped both wrists. 'This is goodbye, darling. There's nobody here to save you, nobody's been following us. It's just you and me,' she said.

A loud shout startled them both.

Eden felt the grip slacken momentarily.

'Police! Stop right now, this is the police!'

An instant later, in a whirlwind of confusion, Eden felt herself being barged over, Rebecca's grip broken, and she crashed to the ground. She was being dragged on her back by her coat through the wet grass, yelling, writhing her body, trying to lash out with her legs.

Finally, she was released. A man, tie askew, was kneeling over her. 'It's OK,' Roy Grace said, 'I'm a police officer, you're OK, I've got you.'

She stared back at him in the darkness for an instant, then all she could think of was that she was being arrested. She tried to get to her feet, but he held her down. She began struggling, shaking wildly, screaming hysterically now and lashing out like something possessed, trying to break free. 'Let me go, let me go, let me go!'

Desperately aware of another struggle going on just a few feet away, Grace did the only thing he could think of. He yelled, 'Shut the fuck up, I'm here to help you, not nick you!'

Somehow it did the trick. She calmed down instantly, staring up at him with blinking eyes.

'I'm a police officer, understand?'

She nodded.

He let go of her, in time to see Branson rolling around on the ground, entangled with Rebecca Watkins.

Glenn Branson felt like he was wrestling with a creature that had a tiger's head and the body of a vicious, writhing snake. Using all his training, he tried to pin the woman's arms to the ground, but, catching him by surprise, she shifted her hips sideways, slipping her arms free, and jammed her fingers, agonizingly and blindingly, into both of his eyes.

He'd done self-defence training back in his days as a night-club bouncer, and he realized at this moment she'd clearly had combat or martial arts training too.

He tried to log in his mind where the edge of the cliff was, and had his arms outstretched to keep her off while he regained some of his vision. But then he felt a searing pain; she'd seen the opportunity to hyperextend his straightened arm and was attempting to pop his elbow.

He flung himself sideways, breaking free, before he felt her body slam into his hip from the side, pushing him.

Pushing him where?

He couldn't stop her. Her base was low, and she'd seized her opportunity to use his own momentum as he lunged sideways. Even though she was far smaller and lighter than he was, it was nigh on impossible to drive back against her.

His training was kicking in, his brain almost going into slow motion. Thinking. But all he could see was darkness. And from the swirling updraught on his face, he knew he was just inches from the edge, from a drop into – oblivion.

Had to get away from the edge.

Had to seize the advantage. He needed to do a move she wasn't expecting and surprise her.

Suddenly, he twisted back towards her and, keeping low, sprang at her with every ounce of strength he had in his body. But he could not believe the almost superhuman strength that came back at him, as if she'd been expecting this move.

A second later she slammed him down hard on the ground, her weight driving into his ribs, and he heard a loud crack as the air left his body in an involuntary groan. Dazed by the blinding pain in his midriff, alongside the shock that he had just been slammed by someone half his size, he tried desperately to think clearly, to work out what to do. He was compromised, hurt and in real trouble.

Wind tore at his face. He was on his back, and she was on top of him, and suddenly had her hands around his neck. Crushing it, pushing her thumbs into his windpipe. He saw her grunting face right in front of his as she pushed all her body weight down on him to tighten the choke. Despite struggling badly for oxygen, he knew this was his chance.

He snapped his head forward and down, hard, and heard the loud crunch, at the same time feeling the pain as he smashed into the bridge of her nose. She yelped, loosening her grip. Seizing the instant, he pushed up and sideways, again with everything he had.

He heard a choked yelp of surprise as her weight was suddenly gone from his chest. A split-second later he felt a vice-like grip on his ankles and a terrific weight.

Pulling him sideways and down.

Shit. He was right on the edge. She'd gone over, he realized, and was hanging onto his legs. Her weight pulling him steadily over, too.

He tried to lash out with his feet, but her grip was too tight.

'Help me!' she yelled, her voice stricken with terror. 'God help me!'

Glenn's hands struggled for a purchase on the sodden grass. But they were sliding, gripping at tufts that tore away. His whole body was sliding towards the edge. Closer.

He was in agony all down his chest, and he tasted blood in his mouth. 'Roy!' he yelled in desperation, the wind whipping away his voice. Sliding further. And suddenly there was no longer any ground beneath his bum. He grabbed frantically at larger clumps of grass which instantly ripped free in his hands. Then he touched something hard, solid, with his right hand – a rock – and gripped it tightly. For a few agonizing seconds, his chest feeling like it was being ripped in half, it stopped his slide. Then, to his terror, he was losing his grip and he slid forward again, the woman's deadweight still hanging from his ankles.

He would be completely over the edge in seconds now. He could feel the bottom, way below, drawing him, reeling him in.

I'm going over, I'm going to die.

It was no good, he couldn't fight it any more.

He would go over the edge and the 500-foot sheer drop. To oblivion.

'ROY!' he screamed in his last gasp of desperation. On the very verge of plunging. 'ROYYYYY!'

Then hands clamped on his wrists, trapping his scream in his throat.

Grace's voice shouted, 'I'm here, mate, I'm here. I've got you.'

'Help me!'

Branson's body, hanging from his arms, swung backwards into the hard edge of the cliff face with a jarring crash and he screamed with pain. The woman still hanging on his ankles, the weight was stretching him out. Racking him and yanking his rib cage down as agony tore through his torso. He could feel her hands slipping. On his boots now.

Roy Grace lay on his stomach, half blinded by the wind and stinging rain, holding on to Branson's slippery wrists. But the weight was getting too much for him. His arms were being pulled out of their sockets. The massive weight was pulling him steadily forward towards the edge.

Trying desperately to think what he could do, he kicked the toes of his shoes hard into the soft soil, getting a momentary purchase before they were dragged free. Then they stopped against something hard and solid – a rock or a stone. He kicked his toes again hard into the soil, trying desperately to dig in deeper and get a better grip. His feet held, but the strain on his arms was getting too much.

I can't hold you, mate, I can't hold you, he thought, his brain racing, his arms agony. His clutch was starting to weaken.

* * *

'ROYYYYY! HELP ME!' Branson screamed again. Then, suddenly, he felt the weight drop from his ankles. It was accompanied by a faint cry. Then just the wind.

Instantly, to Grace's relief, Branson felt lighter. He was no longer sliding forward. Looking down into darkness, at the silhouette of Branson's head, smelling the fear in his perspiration, he was now having to hold just his deadweight. But, even so, his hold was still slipping. His right hand felt Branson's massive palm.

'Grip me with your fingers, interlock them!' he yelled down.

And, to his relief, felt Branson's strong fingers entwining with his own.

'Get me out of here, Roy, oh God, please don't let me fall,' he pleaded.

'I'm not letting you fall. Just keep holding on!' he gasped, trying with everything he had to lift Branson up, but he couldn't even manage a few inches.

And now the stone he had his feet jammed against was starting to move, to lift out of the ground.

Oh Jesus. Glenn, his mate – his best friend in the world – he was holding his life in his hands. Somehow, he had to save him, he couldn't let him fall to his death. Had to do something. But his strength was sapping with every second. He was weakening.

'Stay calm!' he yelled down. 'Stop wriggling, you're pulling me over.'

'Roy, I can't hold on much longer, my arms are going.'

The stone was moving more and more. Any second it would come out of the ground and—

Grace could feel the grip on his fingers slackening. Slipping. Was this how it was going to end? No way could he let him die. His mind was a chaos of thoughts. He dug his toes in again, digging, digging, digging in desperation.

'I can't hold on!' Branson called, his voice sounding weak. 'I'm going, mate.'

'You fucking hold on!' Grace yelled back.

'Tell Siobhan and the kids I love them?'

'You tell them yourself!'

'I mean it. I'm going. I'm going.'

The fingers were letting go. Grace stopped them, clenching his hands even tighter. Seconds from having to make the decision whether to go over with Glenn or release him.

He kept on gripping his hands. Somehow. His arms felt as if they would rip free of their sockets at any second. Christ, if he didn't let go he was going to fall with him.

Then a shout.

Voices behind him. And, suddenly, bright lights flashing all around.

Strong hands were gripping Grace's ankles. Pulling him backwards, as he still gripped Branson's hands, but Branson's deadweight had suddenly lessened.

'You can let go, sir!' a female voice said. It was Sharon Orman. 'Mark and the others have Glenn. I'm going to help them.'

'He's coming back up,' Taylor shouted. 'We've got him!'

'Shit, you're a heavy bastard!' Smudger grunted as they dragged Branson safely back onto the grass.

Grace struggled to his feet, hurried across, then knelt and stared down at his friend's face, Branson's eyes blinking against the bright torchlight. He was bleeding from lacerations in several places and panting hard. 'You're safe, mate.'

Branson mustered a pained smile. 'Yeah, but what about my threads? This suit – it's brand new!'

Grace looked down at him, feeling a surge of relief flooding through him. 'I think you've lost a button, mate. Get over it,' he said, his face creasing into a smile.

110

Veins of pink streaked the pre-dawn sky through the windscreen as Roy Grace finally turned into his lane, the Ford bumping along the unmade track. Every muscle, tendon and ligament in his arms and upper body ached like hell, and his heart was heavy at what lay ahead, and behind him, and the terrible tragedy that had so nearly happened out there on the clifftop.

He honestly didn't know how much longer he could have held on. Seconds at most. He shivered at the thought of what might have been.

Halting the car outside the cottage, he switched off the engine and just sat there for some moments, feeling the early morning breeze through his open window, too drained to even get out of the car.

In the distant farmyard, he faintly heard a cockerel crowing. The car clock showed 5.53 a.m.

He felt in turmoil. His dearest friend had so very nearly died. He wondered how, on top of the tragedy of Bruno, he could ever have lived with that. And he was shaking at the knowledge that he himself might not have been alive to see this dawn. To see Cleo and Noah and their unborn baby. He tried to blank that from his mind, but he couldn't.

He'd insisted that a loudly protesting Glenn Branson be ambulanced to hospital for a check-up, while he waited at the scene for the Coastguard's air-sea rescue helicopter to arrive. The crew radioed that in its searchlight they had seen the body of a man at the bottom of the cliffs. Presumably Niall Paternoster, but they wouldn't be sure until after the body was recovered later in the morning by the lifeboat. Roy then phoned the control room to make the necessary arrangements for notifying the IOPC.

Rebecca Watkins had been lucky. She'd crashed through a tree and dense shrubbery onto a ledge twenty feet below the top of the cliff. Just a short distance to the right or left and she'd have missed it, joining Niall on an unsurvivable drop onto rocks at the bottom.

She was injured, just how badly Grace wouldn't find out until sometime tomorrow. She'd sure been more fortunate than Niall – or maybe not completely so, depending on her injuries, and depending on what happened after she'd stood trial for murder. But that was for another day.

After the helicopter had winched her to safety, he'd gone back to HQ with the rest of the team for a quick debrief, where he learned that Eden had been arrested by a member of the Surveillance Team while attempting to flee, and was now detained at Brighton custody centre.

Grace then cleaned the mud as best he could from his clothes, face and hands, before driving to the hospital at Eastbourne, where he waited while Glenn was being X-rayed and checked over.

The A&E doctor reported, after a long wait, that the Detective Inspector had suffered two cracked ribs, and they were keeping him overnight for observation. It wasn't until the doctor had assured him that his friend was OK, and not in any danger, that Grace had finally left the hospital.

Utterly all in as he finally entered the front door, he was glad that Humphrey hadn't come trotting over for his usual hug and pat – he wasn't sure he had the energy even for that. It took everything he had just to take his clothes off and brush his teeth, before crawling into bed as quietly as he could so as not to wake Cleo.

But she was awake.

'How did it go?' she murmured.

'Fine,' he said. 'It was – you know – OK. Sort of – thing—'

He was sound asleep before he could finish what he was going to say.

111

'Wakey-wakey, sleepyhead!'

Roy Grace opened his eyes to see Cleo standing over him. Although the curtains were still drawn, the room was light. He blinked several times. 'Hey.'

'Any idea what time it is?'

He shook his head. He had no idea at all.

'Midday!'

Sitting up with a start, he said, 'What?' He looked at the bedside clock for confirmation: 12.07 p.m. 'Shit!'

He'd planned to be in the office by 9 a.m., although he'd told his team members from last night to come in late.

'Your buddy, Cassian Pewe, rang you a couple of hours ago. He sounded sweet as pie. Asked if you could call him back whenever it suited you.'

'Ten years would suit me,' he retorted. 'That do? Although that would be too soon.'

'So, he's still not been arrested?' She looked worried.

Grace shook his head. 'It's taking longer than I thought – they'd normally jump on something like this as an absolute priority.' He reflected for a moment. 'Maybe I shouldn't have listened to Guy Batchelor. Perhaps evidence from a jailbird doesn't cut the mustard so far as Professional Standards are concerned. In which case I'm going to be the fall guy here. And if that happens, my future in Sussex is toast. Anywhere else in England you fancy living?'

She frowned. 'Seriously?'

'If Pewe remains here and gets to find out, which he will, that I'd presented evidence against him, then I don't have a future with Sussex Police – not for as long as he's here.'

'You've always got the Met as an option.' Cleo sat on the side of the bed. 'Let's get the funeral behind us and then worry about it, shall we? We're not going to let that creep affect our lives. You said Alison Vosper would have you back in the Met like a shot. So even if you had to commute to London, we could still live here, couldn't we?'

'You're right. Let's deal with the funeral. Put everything else on hold until then.'

She kissed him on the forehead. 'Tell me about last night, what happened?'

He hesitated. 'I've got to go into work today.'

'You're not a machine, darling. Can't you take the day off? It's glorious out there. Let Glenn handle it today?'

'There's a slight problem with that.'

'Oh?'

He reflected for a moment on all he needed to do. 'OK, I'll leave it till later. Let me go for a run, then have a shower and a strong coffee, then I'll tell you over brunch. Want me to make it? Poached eggs on crushed avocado on bagels?'

She grinned. 'Take it away, *mon brave*!'

As she left the room, he reached for his phone, his arm painful, every bit of it aching. He dialled Branson's personal phone. It rang twice, three times. Was he still in hospital?

Then, to his relief, the DI answered.

'I'm still alive, boss,' he said. 'Wow, you are one strong son-of-a-bitch.'

'I'll take that as a thank you.'

'You'll get a proper thank you when I see you. Meantime, don't make me laugh, it hurts.'

'I've been there, had busted ribs. I won't make you laugh, I promise.'

'Don't even think about it.'

'I promise!' Grace grinned.

'I called in and I had an update from Norman,' Branson said. 'Niall Paternoster's dead, Rebecca Watkins has several broken bones and extensive bruising but she'll survive. I'm sure we'll finally get to the bottom of what's been going on. Trust me, I'm a detective.'

'Yeah?'

He heard a loud cry of pain. Then, 'Don't make me laugh!'

'Apologies,' Grace said.

'You might try to sound more sincere.'

'Well, you might try to sound a little more grateful that I saved your life. How about losing some weight, so you're a bit lighter next time I have to hang on to you over a cliff?'

'Is that why you called me, to cover yourself in heroic glory?'

'I should have bloody let you go!'

There was a long silence. Then Branson said, 'I love you, mate.'

'Yeah, well, I quite like you, too.'

Grace lay back against the pillows after he'd ended the call. He was now feeling fully alert. He called the Incident Room and asked to be put through to Jack Alexander.

A few moments later he heard his voice. 'Sir? How are you?'

'Apart from my arms feeling like they've been pulled out of their sockets, I'm OK.' *And all set to face a shitstorm from the IOPC*, he thought glumly. 'As a priority I want you to speak to the ANPR team in the Control Room. I need to know more about the movements of Rebecca Watkins's Range Rover, index Golf November Seven Zero Charlie Papa November, over the past two weeks. The vehicle was abandoned at the scene last night – or rather, this morning. I've a feeling that, also, if its satnav locations over the past couple of weeks are interrogated, it may provide useful information.'

'I'll be right on it, sir.'

'I also need to know the movements of a Nissan Micra, index Bravo Delta Five One Sierra Mike Romeo over this same period, please.'

'I'll get straight on that too, sir.'

'Top priority.'

'Top priority.'

'And, Jack, set up a team briefing meeting for 5 p.m. – I'll be in before then.'

'I will, sir.'

112

Roy Grace, in shorts and a T-shirt, loped up the hill, accompanied by a delighted Humphrey. The Galen myotherapist who Humphrey had been seeing had warned him and Cleo that, with potential arthritis, any long run might be painful for the dog, but Grace was only going a short way and Humphrey seemed in his element.

It was a bright day, with a clear sky, warm sun and a light breeze. He ran a little way along the top of the Downs and then back down, and as he reached the gate to their garden Humphrey gave him a look as if to say, *Is that it?*

An hour later, showered, dressed and brunched, with the papers spread out between them, Roy and Cleo lounged back on the swing sofa in the garden, while Humphrey snored at their feet and the hens pootled all around.

Finally, reluctantly, he picked up his phone and called Cassian Pewe.

The ACC answered, all charm. 'Roy, so good of you to call me back. I trust this is not inconvenient?'

Swinging the seat back with his feet, Grace replied, 'Not at all, sir.'

'Good. So, last night you were back at our favourite haunt, eh?'

Grace thought for some moments before responding. Then decided to put Pewe on the defensive. 'Good old Beachy Head, where I saved your life?'

He relished the hesitation in the man's voice.

'Exactly,' he said finally. Another hesitation. 'But, if I understand correctly, you did not obey my instructions, did you?'

'You sanctioned the surveillance, sir.'

'But you accept responsibility, correct?'

'Correct, sir.'

'*Correct*, Roy. A very good choice of words. *Correct* me if I'm wrong, but did your actions not result in the death of one person, the serious and possibly life-changing injuries to another and very nearly the loss of a member of your team?'

'All completely *correct*, sir,' Grace responded, unable to hold back the insolence in his voice. 'But are you ignoring the fact that the first duty of a police officer is to protect and save lives, not solve crime?'

'And you seriously think that's what you were doing at Beachy Head last night?'

'I do, yes, sir.'

'Well, we'll see what the IOPC have to say about that and whether they agree, which I very much doubt. I want you in my office at 9 a.m., sharp, Monday morning. I am seriously considering suspending you from your duties, pending investigation. Do I make myself clear?'

'Enjoy your weekend, sir,' Grace replied.

113

Friday 13 September

Roy Grace was surprised – although not that surprised, knowing his friend's resilience – to see Glenn Branson, his eyes red and his face lacerated, with three sticking plasters across his cheeks and forehead, entering the conference room for the 5 p.m. briefing.

But he was even more surprised to be given an enthusiastic round of applause by the entire assembled group.

Blushing and grinning, he took a seat, putting his briefing notes and Policy Book on the table and raising his arms in a gesture of thanks.

'You are all looking at a hero!' Glenn Branson said. 'He saved my life last night – even if the bugger did trash my suit in the process!'

'I'm sure we can get you a new one out of police funds,' Grace replied with a smile and a wink.

'Not when they find out it came from Gresham Blake. Proper expensive.'

'Are you going to keep whinging?' Grace asked mischievously.

'Nah, I'll get over it.'

DS Alexander raised a hand. 'Sir, we have a major update.'

'Yes?' Grace asked.

'I've just heard from the interviewing officers and Eden is, surprisingly, cooperating fully with them and telling the whole story.'

'Nice work,' Grace said, relieved that at least one of Cassian Pewe's gripes was now nixed.

Grace turned to the Crime Scene Manager. 'Chris, as Eden Paternoster is under arrest, I'd like you and Lorna to take Search and Forensics Teams to Woodbury Cottage, Chiddingly, and see what you can find.'

'Yes, sir,' Gee said.

Emma-Jane Boutwood raised a hand. 'Sir, there is one other small thing that's come up.'

'Which is, EJ?'

'The Paternosters' Burmese cat, Reggie,' she said.

There were a few smiles.

'Has that changed its name, too, EJ?' Grace asked facetiously. 'And its hairstyle?'

Several members of the team laughed.

The DC smiled. 'No, sir. But since Niall Paternoster was arrested, their next-door neighbour has been looking after it, popping in every day to feed it – she has a key. But she phoned earlier this afternoon concerned, because she's off to Cornwall on Monday to stay with her daughter and her family for the next month. So we need someone to take care of it – unless Eden is going to get police bail and return to the house, perhaps?'

'That's not going to happen,' Grace said. 'With the charges she's facing, and her behaviour to date, she's a flight risk. I think she's going to be remanded in custody.'

'In which case,' EJ asked, 'how are we going to look after the cat – another neighbour, perhaps? It's quite a docile creature. If not, we'll get it taken to a sanctuary – Raystede or somewhere like that.'

Grace knew that Cleo would jump at the chance of having a cat, she had been talking seriously about getting one only recently when she'd seen rodent droppings in their utility room – and mentioned that a bag of Humphrey's biscuits had been gnawed open. 'I might be able to help out, EJ,' he said. 'I know it's not correct procedure, but I'll speak to my wife and get back to you. I just need to ask her how she thinks our dog would get on with a cat.'

'Thank you, sir.'

114

Cleo was thrilled about the idea of fostering the cat, even if it only turned out to be for a short while. She told Roy that Humphrey seemed to get on really well with cats – he'd loved playing with both her sister's cat and her parents' two tabby cats. And maybe this one would sort out the mouse problems she was increasingly certain they had.

Over the weekend, Grace had gone into the office several times, to arrange the interview strategy for Eden Paternoster and observe the interviews with Glenn Branson. He'd also briefed Norman Potting to arrange with the Magistrates' Court a request for a warrant for further detention, which had been successful.

EJ had checked there was a cat carrier basket in the Paternosters' house, and Grace planned to pick Reggie up on the way home. As he drove into the Police HQ just before 8.30 a.m., he reckoned he might be going home in less than an hour's time if ACC Pewe carried out his threat to suspend him when they met this morning.

He parked behind the Major Crime building, then went into his office to check his email for any updates and, out of force of habit, the overnight serials – all the logged crime reports in the county.

Then at 8.50 a.m., wondering what awaited him, but surprised how relaxed he felt about what could be a career-changing meeting in ten minutes' time, he stepped back out into glorious warm sunshine. As he did so, his private phone pinged. It was a text from Cleo.

Thinking of you XXX

He texted three hearts back, then headed down the hill towards the rear entrance of Malling House, which housed the Sussex Police brass and their key support staff.

As he approached, he was puzzled by the sight of two unfamiliar vehicles, dark-coloured Audi A6s, parked up outside the building. He clocked their licence plates, but neither were familiar, and he knew from memory the indexes of pretty much all of the local unmarked cars.

He walked past them and was about to enter the door when a burly man in a grey suit came through it. He was followed by Cassian Pewe, his face chalky white, then another tall man in a blue suit bringing up the rear.

'Good morning, sir!' Grace said to Pewe breezily. 'I'm here for our—'

The ACC walked past stonily, without acknowledging him.

An instant later, the man in the grey suit opened the rear door of one of the Audis. As Pewe entered the side behind the passenger seat, the burly man pushed the ACC's head down protectively. Then he closed the door. Blue Suit opened the door on the far side, slid in behind the driver's seat and pulled the door shut.

Grey Suit then climbed into the driver's seat. The car glided away, down towards the main entrance barrier, which rose as it approached. Then it was gone.

Grace hesitated, uncertain what to do. Was this it? Clearly, Pewe had been arrested, he thought to his immense relief. Hadn't he? It certainly looked like it.

He wondered if the crew of the second Audi were searching his office.

He turned and headed back towards the Major Crime building, unsure whether to be elated or worried. Then his phone rang.

It was Alison Vosper.

'Roy? How are you?'

'Well, ma'am, I'm not entirely sure.'

'I just wanted to let you know, before you heard it from anyone else, that we are arresting ACC Pewe – the evidence you gave us checked out. He has been suspended with immediate effect.'

For a few seconds, Grace was speechless. 'Thank you for telling me, ma'am.'

'I know this may not change anything, Roy – other than perhaps doing myself no favours. But my offer to you of a job in the Met remains open.'

'I appreciate that, ma'am. I really do.'

'One day, perhaps? Call me any time, you know where to reach me.'

'I really appreciate your faith in me.'

'Until then, stay safe.'

'And you, ma'am.'

Moments after he ended the call, his phone rang again. It was Cleo. He answered and she sounded surprised.

'Sorry, darling,' she said. 'I was just going to leave a message. Have you had your meeting with Pewe?'

'No, he's otherwise engaged.'

'Meaning?'

'Meaning he's just been driven off in the back of a car, under arrest.'

'No way!'

'Yessss!'

'Oh my God! You've done it!'

'Here's hoping.'

'You have, you've done it!!!'

'With luck!'

'I was just calling to say that when you collect Reggie – or before – could you swing by Tesco Lewes and pick up some cat litter?'

'Yes, sure. Shall I get some cat food as well and some treats?'

'Treats for you or Reggie?'

'Haha!'

'Just don't vanish, eh?'

GLOSSARY

ANPR – Automatic Number Plate Recognition. Roadside or mobile cameras that automatically capture the registration number of all cars that pass. It can be used to historically track which cars went past a certain camera, and can also create a signal for cars which are stolen, have no insurance or have an alert attached to them.

CID – Criminal Investigation Department. Usually refers to the divisional detectives rather than the specialist squads.

CPS – Crown Prosecution Service.

CSI – Was SOCO. Crime Scene Investigators (Scenes of Crime Officers). They are the people who attend crime scenes to search for fingerprints, DNA samples etc.

DIGITAL FORENSICS – The unit which examines and investigates computers and other digital devices.

FLO – Family Liaison Officer.

HOLMES – Home Office Large Major Enquiry System. The national computer database used on all murders. It provides a repository of all messages, actions, decisions and statements, allowing the analysis of intelligence and the tracking and auditing of the whole enquiry. Can enable enquiries to be linked across force areas where necessary.

IOPC – Independent Office for Police Conduct.

PM – Postmortem.

POLSA – Police Search Adviser.

SIO – Senior Investigating Officer. Usually a Detective Chief Inspector who is in overall charge of the investigation of a major crime such as murder, kidnap or rape.

CHART OF POLICE RANKS

Police ranks are consistent across all disciplines and the addition of prefixes such as 'detective' (e.g. detective constable) does not affect seniority relative to others of the same rank (e.g. police constable).

| Police Constable | Police Sergeant | Inspector | Chief Inspector |

| Superintendent | Chief Superintendent | Assistant Chief Constable | Deputy Chief Constable | Chief Constable |

ACKNOWLEDGEMENTS

Writing during a pandemic has not been without its challenges, but there have been positives as well: fewer distractions and travel, and being able to spend more time with our ever-expanding menagerie.

As ever I owe thanks to so many people in so many fields, especially Sussex Police, the medical world and, for this book, the world of the car salesman! I always find it heartening that so many people are willing to take the time to share their knowledge, and even industry secrets and tricks of the trade in some cases, to help me get my novels to feel as authentic as possible.

My most heartfelt thanks start with Sussex Police. To Police and Crime Commissioner Katy Bourne OBE, Chief Constable Jo Shiner, and to so many officers and support staff actively serving under them, as well as retirees from Sussex and other forces. I've listed them in alphabetical order and beg forgiveness for any omissions.

Inspector James Biggs, PC Matt Colburn, Financial Investigator Emily Denyer, DC Jenny Dunn, PC Philip Edwards, Inspector Mark Evans, CSI James Gartrell, CSI Chris Gee, Aiden Gilbert in Digital Forensics, DCI Rich Haycock, Inspector Dan Hiles, Chief Digital and Information Officer Joseph Langford, Chief Superintendent Nick May, Sergeant Russell Philips, Chief Constable of Kent Alan Pughsley QPM, Chief Officer of the States of Jersey Police Robin Smith, James Stather in Forensic Services, PC Richard Trundle, and Police Chaplain Fr Richard Tuset. Also Beth Durham, Suzanne Heard, Jill Pedersen and Katie Perkins of Sussex Police Corporate Communications.

And retired officers: Chief Superintendent Graham Bartlett, Detective Superintendent Nick Sloan, DC Pauline Sweeney, DS Mark Taylor and Detective Superintendent Jason Tingley.

A big thank you also to Theresa Adams, Julian Blazeby, Mike Canas, Neil Chapman, Jeanie Civil, Sean Didcott, Tim Griffiths, Victoria Grogan, Anna-Lisa Hancock, Phil Homan, Haydn Kelly, Rob Kempson, Dr James Mair, Dr Adrian Noon, Ray Packham, Richard Parsons, Graham Ramsden, Judith Richards, Julia Richardson of Galen Myotherapy, Kit Robinson (role model for Noah Grace!), Alan Setterington, Helen Shenston, Lucy Sibun, Carolyn Smith, Sam Smith, Steve Soper, Orlando Trujillo, Derek Warwick and Mark Willmett.

A very special thank you also to my mentor Geoff Duffield, my amazing editor Wayne Brookes, and the team at Pan Macmillan – to name just a few: Sarah Arratoon, Jonathan Atkins, Lara Borlenghi, Emily Bromfield, Stuart Dwyer, Claire Evans, Samantha Fletcher, Anthony Forbes Watson, Elle Gibbons, Hollie Iglesias, Daniel Jenkins, Rebecca Kellaway, Neil Lang, Rebecca Lloyd, Sara Lloyd, James Long, James Luscombe, Holly Martin, Rory O'Brien, Guy Raphael, Alex Saunders, Jade Tolley, Jeremy Trevathan, Toby Watson, Charlotte Williams and Leanne Williams. And my brilliant structural editor Susan Opie.

Thanks also to everyone at my fabulous UK literary agency, Blake Friedmann: Lizzy Attree, Isobel Dixon, Sian Ellis-Martin, Julian Friedmann, Hana Murrell, James Pusey, Daisy Way and Conrad Williams. My US agent, Mitch Hoffman, at the Aaron M. Priest Literary Agency. And a big shout-out to my fabulously gifted UK PR team at Riot Communications: Caitlin Allen, Preena Gadher and Emily Souders.

While writing is a lonely job, I have an amazing support team around me. I'm blessed with two incredibly hardworking people

– my wife Lara and former Detective Chief Superintendent David Gaylor – who head up Team James. The other invaluable members of the team are: Sue Ansell, Kate Blazeby, Dani Brown, Erin Brown, Chris Diplock, Jane Diplock, Martin Diplock, Lyn Gaylor, James Hodge, Sarah Middle, Amy Robinson, Mark Tuckwell and Chris Webb.

David Gaylor not only has the patience of a saint, in answering my queries about policing and other aspects of my stories at any time of the day or night; he also has an incredibly creative mind, and contributes so much to every aspect of my novels, and now to the *Grace* TV series also. I owe him enormous thanks. I'm extremely excited about this series: the scripts by Russell Lewis, based on the novels, are brilliant and the cast, headed by John Simm as Roy Grace and Richie Campbell as Glenn Branson, are more than I could ever have wished for.

And my most special thanks of all are reserved for my beloved wife. I've always believed that, while novels are above all stories, they are also so much about how they make you feel. Lara is incredibly in tune with that, and gives me vital help with the emotions of my characters, as well as the storylines and with every aspect of our lives. She has also been of immense help with so many aspects of the Roy Grace TV series.

Something that puts a huge smile on my face is to hear from you, my readers – I owe you so much for your support. Do keep your communications coming, the whole team loves hearing from you by email, Twitter, Facebook, Instagram, YouTube – and of course by traditional snail mail. We learn from your views, and it is always helpful to know if I've made an error in my research, so I can correct it. A special thanks to the reader who informed me that brass does not rust, it corrodes. And to the one who sent me an eight-page letter explaining the difference between cement and concrete, complete with diagrams! I think I now know the difference, but I'm sure you'll correct me if I get it wrong again . . .

Above all, stay well and stay safe.

Peter James

www.organdonation.nhs.uk

contact@peterjames.com
www.peterjames.com
@peterjamesuk
peterjames.roygrace
You Tube Peter James TV
@peterjamesuk
@peterjamesukpets
@mickeymagicandfriends

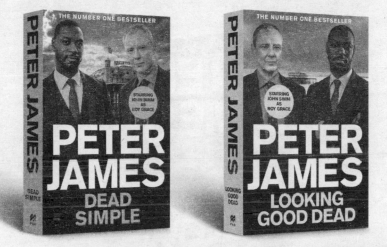

'Another stonking story from
the master of the craft'
EXPRESS

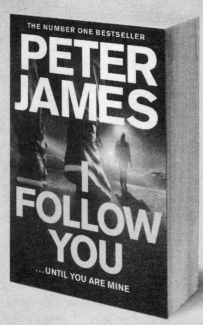

To the outside world, charming doctor Marcus Valentine has
it all: a loving wife, three kids and a great job. But there's
something missing.

Driving to work one morning, his mind elsewhere and not on
the road, he almost mows down a female jogger who is the
spitting image of his first love, the girl who got away.

Despite all his attempts to resist, his thoughts are consumed
by this woman. And when events take a tragically unexpected
turn, his obsession threatens to destroy both their worlds . . .

AVAILABLE NOW IN PAPERBACK, EBOOK
AND AUDIOBOOK

'A theatrical masterpiece'

Encore Reviews

'A thrilling evening of suspense'

Southampton Daily Echo

PETER JAMES'
LOOKING GOOD
DEAD

STARRING
EASTENDERS'
ADAM WOODYATT
AND
GAYNOR FAYE THE SYNDICATE

UK TOUR 2021 & 2022
Book now at PeterJames.com